"Sections are brilliant and wicked and they show how much of a stern dazzler Sorrentino can be."–*Kirkus*

"Sorrentino is a bright, educated man–balancing difficult dialects against obscure notations, addressing readers and reviewers, boldly playing with form. At times his language approaches a Finnegans' wakefulness."–*Los Angeles Times*

"A wild and crazy book, lavishly inventive, full of surprises, sometimes exasperating, often exhilarating."–*New York Times Book Review*

"A lively, outrageous, funny and comedically inventive story."–*Publishers Weekly*

"In *Blue Pastoral* Gilbert Sorrentino has done what artists always try to do: he has made and shaped a work whose brilliance–in this case comic brilliance–is awesome, pure, and perfectly executed."–*Washington Post*

"*Blue Pastoral* is bedazzling. Its language–and what else is literature but language–dips and dances. Read it."–*New Statesman*

"A brutally hilarious literary explosion in which a world of pop-cultural clichés gets a freewheeling linguistic drubbing."–*Library Journal*

Books by Gilbert Sorrentino

POETRY

Black and White
Corrosive Sublimate
The Darkness Surrounds Us
A Dozen Oranges
The Orangery
The Perfect Fiction
Selected Poems: 1958-1980
Sulpiciae Elegidia/Elegiacs of Sulpicia
White Sail

FICTION

Aberration of Starlight
Blue Pastoral
Crystal Vision
Flawless Play Restored: The Masque of Fungo
Imaginative Qualities of Actual Things
Misterioso
Mulligan Stew
Odd Number
Pack of Lies
Red the Fiend
Rose Theatre
The Sky Changes
Splendide-Hôtel
Steelwork
Under the Shadow

CRITICISM

Something Said: Essays

Blue Pastoral

Gilbert Sorrentino

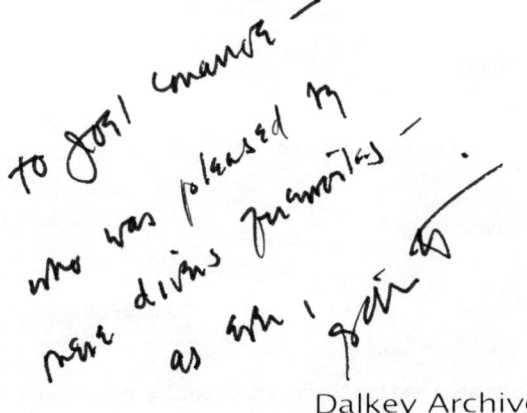

Dalkey Archive Press

Copyright © 1983 by Gilbert Sorrentino
Published by North Point Press, 1983
First Dalkey Archive edition, 2000
All rights reserved

Library of Congress Cataloging-in-Publication Data:

Sorrentino, Gilbert.
  Blue pastoral / by Gilbert Sorrentino.– 1st Dalkey Archive ed.
     p.   cm.
  ISBN 1-56478-251-4 (alk. paper)
     1. Musicians–Fiction. 2. Travel–Fiction. I. Title.

  PS3569.O7 B64 2000
  813'.54–dc21   00-058955

Partially funded by grants from the Lannan Foundation and the Illinois Arts Council, a state agency.

Dalkey Archive Press
www.dalkeyarchive.com

Printed on permanent/durable acid-free paper and bound in the United States of America.

Contents

The subject of Pastorals, as the language of it ought to be poor, silly, and of the coursest Woofe in appearance. Nevertheless, the most High, and most Noble Matters of the World may bee shadowed in them, and for certaine sometimes are: but he who hath almost nothing Pastorall in his Pastorals, but the name (which is my Case) deales more plainly. . . .

My Pastorals bold upon a new straine, must speake for themselves, and the Taber striking up, if thou hast in thee any Country-Quicksilver, thou hadst rather be at the sport, then heare thereof. Farewell.

Michael Drayton, 1619

Blue Pastoral

« 1 »

Dr. Vince
Dubuque Is Called
Upon to Introduce Our "Subject"

And now, ladies and gentlemen, honored guests, hangers-on, vagrants, idlers, and good-for-nothings, a brief talk by Dr. Vince Dubuque of The University on the hero of this tale, the tale itself, and sundry matters.

(*"Scattered" and diffident applause.*)

Thank you, honored folks.

I see him now! Somewhere out there in that gloaming that we call the Past that Time forgot—his ratty beard and frizzy hair, his hearty grease sandwiches, his rusted bicycle clips. An unlikely hero, your good faces seem to say, not all of them so good, but. May I present him? It is a hot afternoon, these attendant scholars are a roiling sea of sweat beneath their pretentious robes, and even my Private Assistant, Miss Clarke Grable, seated here demurely at my left, seems adrift in a coma of the old ennui, as the beloved song has it. I will make my remarks brief, here under the saw-leaf coryza and the dwarf axilla and the unbearably lovely buckeye gastrula, nodding and bending as is their ancient wont. So.

Serge Gavotte is the man's true name, and I will outline, so to speak, his adventurous beginning; the ensuing parts and parcels of which shall unfold if you will but continue to turn the pages of the "book" that we are all pretending to want to read, or something. Literature works in mysterious ways, it is metaphor raised to the heights of shattering simile! Serge Gavotte, yes. And on a typical morn. His ratty beard, his frizzy hair, God bless the mark, his rusted bicycle clips, his sweat-stained paper bag within which nestle and crowd his two grease sandwiches. He leaves the house, thus. An ordinary morning, and Gavotte wends his trail toward his lonely job as plastic-lens tester or something equally gauche. His shirt is nondescript, his trousers, shiny now from years of labor, direct from Mays, onerously bear that description called "irregular." And as sure as I am Dean of Funds and Meetings, they were! Or are! Clasped, however, smartly and alertly around each slim ankle by a bicycle clip, a reminder of Ga-

1

votte's checkered past, although here at The University, we prefer to pronounce it "chequered."

Who was this Serge Gavotte? And why was he chosen to set out on his Great Quest? Not so fast! I'll answer your importunate queries as best I can, but first things must come first, as the patient grizzled farmer knows, the bent agricola, hunched over his zucchini bush. Who? His past is a mist, a kind of dim haze of nagging memory, a zephyr of odd scents, the shining bridge that spans—Oh Where?—the lost river of childhood. We know however that he was shipped from pillar to post as a youth, from school to school. He was a rip! And his student exploits, gems, even, yes, opals and garnets of good clean fun, earned him a reputation far beyond its cost in human error and occasional heartbreak. Pouring glue in the coffee. Placing chewing gum on his teachers' chair. Who can forget the time he put salt in the sugar bowl? Marks of comic genius, my friends, yes, Comic Genius, so that all who came in contact with him cannot be faulted for thinking that he would grow up to be a Larry or a Curly or perhaps even a Moe! Some few went so far as to say he had the makings of a Shecky Green, but plodding hyperbole was as rampant then as it is today. However! His legend was such that it forced him to assume nom de plumes. Or is that noms de plume? My Gallic is a trifle dim, and those of you who have come to be my friends since I assumed my duties here at The University, know how this grieves me—nothing on earth I like better than to coil up with *Le Match* or *Oui, Oui, Paris* of a winter eve. But let me not recount to eager ears the sacrifices I daily make! He had to assume these aliases, these false monickers. My notes here, prepared in part by Miss Grable, give a few of them, which, if I may be forgiven, as it were, I shall rehearse. Rehearse? That's what it says here, and who am I to doubt the written word, the bold letters here indited by my Private Assistant, slightly heavy in the glorious beam but who's counting? Aha, ha, ha.

Boris the Bum, The Piano Killer, Stompo, Hair Freak, Wrong-Way Russian, The Soviet Schmuck, Brooklyn's Curse, The Duke of Schnorrer, Left-Hand Louis, Chopsticks, Wack-Off, Peach Sucker, O'Malley's Mouth, Lazarillo de Knishes, Garbage Face, Peyote Sipper, and Foodpicker. Not a pretty picture, is it? And yet, it was his croass, I mean, his cross. But wherever he went, to whatever distant seat and far-off chair of learning and knowledge, he was soon found out. Hence, his education was, as it is phrased in places like Sal's Billiard Academy, a bust. Yet he met a lovely girl, well, lovely, O.K., a girl, one with full lips, flashing eyes, impeccable linen, and softly drifting dandruff, her name itself a kind of poem, Helene Lundi. And what else would you believe but that they were soon married! For every Serge, my friends, there is a Helene, and the conversed opposite is also true, else why would the world, especially odd places like Jimbo, Utah, and Gonif, New Jersey, not to mention those countries jampacked cheek and jowl with foreign types, e.g., Sahib, Rhodesia, be filled to the creaking gunwales and mizzenreefs with astonishingly homely, not to say really ugly couples? And their kids, so to speak? Jesus Christ Almighty! I opine. But enough, I ween, though not without some minor regrets.

They married, which takes us right up, by a twist of Fate and linguistic wizardry, to the present, that is, right here and now, with the fruity odors of giant ankylosis and blue angina sporting in our collective nostrils. But his job, his honest job, I hasten to submit, as Miss Grable, who is perspiring slightly at the moment, albeit with a lot of class, will corroborate as being not too bad a position, lovely word, glutted Serge Gavotte with boredom and horrid malaise, another word from the snowy peaks of Old Provence. Yet it was a malaise that dared not breathe its name! Yes, my drowsy friends, that great soul kept it all bottled up inside him like a big jug of seltzer keeps its bubbles all enchained. His spouse, the oddly off-center and unusually strident Helene, now big with child, and suddenly! a little mother, just like that, of a fine boy whom they called Zimmerman, knew, by consulting her deep feminine feelings, that all was not cheer and skittles at the Gavotte house, no, nor at the V. N. Rose Lens Co. either. Call it a lucky shot.

For Gavotte père, whatever that may convey, had a secret. Yes, a rather dark secret, crepuscular and somber, shady and umber in hue. In his depths, those depths that still harbored the pain and fear of being dubbed, for instance, Shit Pickle—and there's a handle that will follow you down the windy Halls of Time if I ever heard one!—he had the powerful and almost unbearable urge to be a musician! We professors here on the dais, we laugh, yes, melting, as we are, in the sunshine, like Sambo Tiger in the nursery rhyme, or like Ruth, we laugh! Ensconced as we are here at The University, most of us, with that sweet, oh God *how* sweet! tenure, cannot imagine what it must be like to want anything beyond our positions of responsibility in this great University, *The University*—and it *is* a great university, you can tell by the low moans of the cicadas as they gorge on the cucumbers that crawl the walls of Lamont Hall. Is it for nothing that the motto or whatever it is called, on the sinister bend of the shield of this place is *De Mortuis Nil Nisi Bonum*? I don't think so, but could give you a better opinion if I had a touch of Greek, the which tongue I do not cleave to since my studies were all in the field, and it is still a growing one, of Sales Techniques of Surplus Goods, and the only Greek I ever learned was *caveat emptor*, which, roughly translated, as the good members of the Classics Department here behind me will attest, with all the varied strengths of their pounding and Helen-leaning minds, means "Bleed Them Dry," or, to be a millimeter more elegant, if not exactly precise, "Suck Them Empty."

In any event, we cannot, and by the dull, if not quite complacent, visages that you, my sedulous listeners, present to me, out there in that sun that could split rocks, you neither, can—I have misplaced my unerring thoughts for a moment, so if you will please . . . oh, yes, none of us can understand exactly why Serge Gavotte had this hidden dream, a dream that drove him to the misty window-pane of an eerie midnight to look out upon the brooding fields and strangely silent streets, while Helene slept on in peace, her breath raising and falling down with that curious phenomenon that a man—I think his name was Galen—called breathing. That old Roman was a crackerjack! No! We laugh! it says here, but by Christ Almighty, I can't imagine exactly why it . . . oh, I have allowed my sun-blasted orb to wander, as an orb may when given but half a chance, back up the paper upon which Miss Grable, whose bosom is heaving patiently, penned these notes. We have, if you will pardon a small splinter of light wit, *already* laughed! Ho ho. O.K.!

We cannot understand this thudding and overwhelming urge, but it was *there*, it was there in such a stern guise that Gavotte finally succumbed to it and availed himself of such *instrumenti* as could relieve him of his red-hot desire to play, play! Of such courageous flesh is Freedom made, as well as Art! But we know all these stirring banalities exactly like a book, do we not? To be sure. And these oddball cheapo things he bought—a tinwhistle, a Jew's harp, called nowadays, I understand, because of the protests of Banzai Brit, or some other esteemed rabbi, a juice harp, though whatever that may suggest swims out there in the vasty deeps of blue far beyond my poor ken, yes, and also a ocarina, a real deadbeat harmonica, like, you know, a Crackerjack-box type, and the Lord only knows what all else.

He played, oh sweet Mother of God, how he played! Against time, against the inundating and proscribed thought that he might well have talent—how to phrase it?—zero, against the wails and colicky pissing and moaning of little Zimmy, he played on and on, *possessed* by this instrument, or, shall I hint, instruments? just like Kirk Douglas, whatever he's doing in this speech, and I will speak to Miss Grable about it. And it was not long before he got a real bad mouth infection, some type of infarction on the gums or an impacted dentine, something that made it necessary for him to tell Helene . . . the Truth! The lovely lady, as smart as an old whip, was not surprised, nor even struck into a state of sheer amaze, since she had long suspected that the obsessive and not exactly, uh, how shall I phrase it? *lovely* sounds that drifted up from the basement, or from the bathroom, or from the hall closet at any moment of the night or day when Serge was at home, were not, as her droll husband had informed her when she first got on a wonder about them, "the death cries of expiring cockroaches." He could, when the need arosed, turn a mean phrase.

But this painful swelling of the gumbones, yes, this sudden miasma cast upon our budding Freddy Martin or Johnny Long, was a blessing in disguise, for it sent Serge to see the famous mouth seer, Dr. Ciccarelli. Of which the next, or really the *first* chapter, will treat of. Chapter? Oh yes, we are all agreeing to pretend that this is a "book." Thank you for your attention, but, hold it, hold it!

Before you go, I want to introduce you formally to my Private Assistant, Miss Clarke Grable. She is *not* my secretary, no. She is *not* my filer, no no. She is *not* a female person employed to answer phones and letters and generally stand around and pick up her salary, n, period, o, period. Then, what is she? As Dean of Funds and Meetings, you must all be as aware as I am, and by God, *I* am aware, that I am always being bothered by many of you wrong-o professors, you shiftless "students," some term, eh? and whatever shabby citizens wander in out of the heat or rain or whatever weather is tending to occur around here. I have here then Miss Grable, who has a long history of blocking doors, getting messages wrong, compounding problems, and the ilks and like. She will be, as it were and so to speak, my trouble-shooter, and will see to it, with all the expertise in her remarkably solid frame, and I seem to be seeing her now as if for the first time!— my goodness, she does cross her legs nice—uhm, ah, will see to it that you don't bust my hump, as the phrase is rendered in the patois of the demotic vulgate.

(*"Scattered" and feeble applause plus a vulgar sound from the "crowd."*)

Thanks for your undivided attention, given without quotient, to say the least. And now, if you will good-naturedly go along with the whole "book" dodge that has been foisted on us—and with a great deal of unseemly eagerness, I might add—you will "set off" with Serge Gavotte on his adventures if you will but turn the "page." I'm sorry; if you will but "turn the page."

« 2 »

In Which Dr.
Ciccarelli Points the Way

Dr. Ciccarelli, of Italy, has, for some years now, made his home in the United States, where his oral expertise may be employed to its fullest.

I no like-a dis phrase, Doc Ciccarelli says.

Doctor Ciccarelli, as buccal fans know, has, for some years now, made the oral cavity his area of expertise, practicing his arcane systems upon more mouths— and in them—than it purposes here to reveal.

Ats-a nize! "Purposes to reveal." Class!

Hmm. Oral expertise: *has been* employed, uh, optimally? To best effect? Does nice work? Tops in the growing field?

"Purposes to reveal," dammit. Also, call me joost-a Doc Chick, O.K.?

It was through the avuncular Doc Chick that we heard the long tale that follows, not *so* long. Heard part of it anyway, *parts*. The parts that Doc Chick is involved in. Not too many, now that I thumb through the pages.

Now that *we* thumb through the pages.

I purpose to reveal, kid, whatever goddam tings you wanna hear an' also pay me for, like you got here in this goddam country with the soggy pasta, what you call the consultation fee?

We will be perfectly delighted to meet your financial requirements, Doctor. Within reason, ha ha ha.

You talk what I wanna hear. My mamma was wrong when-a she say all Americans are stupid. They got no culture, they don't know nothing, they think-a the govermenta's real, they don't know how to talk to women, they can't dress or eat nothing good, but goddam they know how to buy tings!

We are often termed "A Nation of Consumers." Here is your retainer.

What?

Your retainer, your retainer! Money!

O.K., O.K., take it ease! You got a face on you like a dead clam.

There's really no need, Doc, to . . .

O.K.! I, Doc Chick, known hither and wide to all-a the poor marks with the mouth problems as Dr. Ciccarelli, a name that calls up to mind-a the Isle of Capri and red wine to you ignorant Yankee slobs, and I gotta the place in a mural right up on the wall behind my Carrara marble table like you see in the *Times*, I have treated the hero of dis story, Serge Gavotte, and may God help him with a handle like that! This was before he took on what has come to be known as his Ur-name, Blue Serge, though he has many other, evocative, and, one might even venture to say, poetic names. Mr. Gavotte came to my office one day, unheralded and unannounced, unknown and unsure, unshaven and unequal, undone and unhappy, unquoted and unbraced . . .

Wait! We are in a slight dilemma, good Doc. Somehow, that, uh, how shall we say, stage "greaseball" accent, direct from the beloved Hollywood "films" of the 30s and 40s, has disappeared from your speech. It makes one . . . think.

Ha ha! How delightful that you've noticed. That is my—I like to call it *my*— "golden-earring-and-drooping mustachio" accent. It works wonders with idiot WASPs from the clamorous plains and environs, especially when employed at sidewalk feasts like those of St. Anthony, San Gennaro, and Santa Rosalia, by Italo-Americans, all of whom are Ph.D.s. With the accent, a few shrugs and hand-talk, and that white smile preceding the well-known and beloved infectious laugh, my countrymen get rid of mountains of eighth-rate "food" that would ordinarily be used to bait rat traps. Also useful in shilling "games" of— ho ho—"chance." It is my warm accent, my winning accent, my I-am-so-grateful accent, my great-big-family accent. It is the accent used when some poor contadino is queried by the police as to the source of a few hundred grand in cash found in an old AWOL bag. You get the idea, right? Works something like that other famous speech tic, the brogue. But enough ethnicity! I have said that Mr. Gavotte, an ambulatory fen, appeared one day at lunchtime, crestfallen and aspout with tears.

We remember, Doc.

Doctor! you Methodist churl. Why is it that there is not a religious booster around with a spot of class? Always droning on about Jesus as if he is down at the candy store behind the soda cooler just waiting for you to walk up to him and babble sodden trivia about the accursed Yankees—a strictly Protestant team, by the by—while he figures out how to save you. And incidentally, make you rich. I have an interesting theory got me chucked out of the National Conference of Christians and Jews: All Protestants are really Catharists who couldn't make their ice-cream parlors go and so invented Joy. Sound good? Joy as in Bum Car;

as in Dull Job; as in Big Color TV; as in Friday Night Hump. Also as in that latest plastic kitchen trash from Bloomingdale's in tacky tan, vulgar vanilla, rosy rose, and cantaloupe splendor. Stop me if I'm off base, flashing blue eyes.

It is not only the WASP who frequents that great emporium of savoir-faire and laughable prices, Doctor, as you must know.

My Christ! You give somebody a monicker like Clark or Mercer or Shuttleworth and he takes to wearing reticent navy-blue ties and talking about economics. That's a joke, solemn one. Can't you stop thinking about your bible-black Mercedes even for a minute? Ever notice how the WASP face gets like old leather? Sort of like the visage of a debauched Tom Sawyer carved in a white prune?

This is, we insist, Doctor, a narrow and bigoted viewpoint of one of the great, how shall we phrase it? *segments* of mankind—a segment from which has come almost all your presidents, senators, congresspersons, your oceans of thieves, murderers, and, if you will forgive the expression, leaders. It is also noted for its magnificent and successful campaign that has managed to propose, as incontrovertible fact, the notion that *it* does not own the world, but that the Jews do. That con is, as they say, a wowie!

Shut uppa you mout! See? You see how you've driven me into my warm and gregarious role again? The man with the loud tie and the chalk-stripe suit who has never been unhappy one day in his whole life? Except maybe once, just once, when he was small, and a fleeting illness of a Sunday made him miss his beloved mamma's—his fat and ruddy and hardworking mamma, she of the black dress and hair in a bun—spaghetti. The man who thrives on violence, cheap wine, and checkerboard tablecloths? The man who lives in the kitchen? The man who invented the pencil moustache? But what has all this to do with Serge Gavotte, the subject of today's talk? And also, as if you didn't know, *tuttipazze*, the subject of this whole "book"—just under way, I admit, but getting there, whatever that means. And may your creeping Methodist Jesus with a lamb under one arm and his other raised to the starry skies have mercy on the unfortunate bastard who's writing it!

Enough, Doctor, of parry and riposte! Too many pages, too many words, too much paper! Do you expect a publisher to actually *pay for* printing a book like this? A book that will not be carried to the beach, smarmed over on in-depth talk shows, made into idiot motion pictures, major all? Tell us about the damaged and/or diseased *bouche* of Bleu! Tell us of the cures miraculous, the advice good, the ambience hearty of the consultation room. Tell, so that it may at least seem as if we are carrying the narrative forward, ever forward, to what stirring climax, who can tell?

O.K., sports. The young chap, hairy and hulking, his symbol, panache, guidon, coat-of-arms the bicycle clip couchant, entered my office. I reconstruct, for your files, the conversation, give or take a few hundred adjectives.

Dear God!

It will take but a moment for those who like to check and ascertain, look up and verify, to check and ascertain, look up and verify this portentous scenario, a bottom-line word if I ever heard one, close-shaven exec. As I have said, Gavotte enters:

Gavotte: You dig on my mouth all swolled up, Doc?

Doc Chick: Sí. But who the hell are you to come in here, all akimbo? How you find me?

Gavotte: Have a heart, Doc! Looka this mouth. You ever see anything like this goddam piece o' meat? How the hell I'm gonna play with a mouth looks like an old seabag?

Doc Chick: Is disgusting. (Here a retch was heard as far as Queens.)

Gavotte: So? What's the verdict? Is there hope?

Doc Chick: Here, you lilting little cadenza, let's stuff it with these various dried *fruttos* and wrinkled leaves, an old necromancer's remedy that, in my capacity as mouth-croaker to the Stars, I have committed to memory.

Gavotte: Veelzh bedda alreadda, Boc.

Doc Chick: And furthermore, I don't want to know *how* you got this fat thing under the nose here, but I'll tell you one thing.

Gavotte: Mm.

Doc Chick: Just a glance askance out of these wise old owllike eyes of mine informs me that you have a Great Musical Soul bursting and glowing within and dying there in solitary splendor from frustration. You are, I can tell from your gnarled hands and blank stare, a lens grinder of some sort, n'est-ce pas? Don't! Don't try to talk—I don't want to know how your mouth metamorphosed itself from the sweet little thing its basic configuration tells me it is in its natural state, to the Big Mac that now distorts your visage. Dare *I* whisper it? The cheapo harmonica from a sundries shop? The loathsomely shellacked recorder from some dump on the corner, where that six-bit "instrument" nestled amid dusty firecrackers and rotting Trojans? And you have been, I know, blowing your great red heart out! Yes? The labors of a fool! Herakles himself was no dopier when he contracted to scrub and wax the Cretan maze! You must—you *must*—study the PIANO! It is that oddly shaped and hard-to-carry instrument that calls you; your gnarled hands, your sweaty callouses do cry out in accents stentorian for its tinkly pinging! Study! Study! And as you study, and you need, I can tell from your glazed expression, no teacher, travel the length and width and heighth of this great land, learning as you go, meeting the people who will be your inspiration, the simple folk of Terre Plaines and Nebraska City out there in the great states of Omaha and Tucson where the sunset collapses in its panoply of horribly depressing colors! Until, *until* you come to that secret place wherein you will find the Perfect Musical Phrase. It is there that you must build your church, my rude sonata.

Gavotte: Umphh!

That is it, bosom cheeches. The nutshell, glaring WASPs. He left, and we may now pursue him for page after page, "chapter" after "chapter"—him and his balding spouse, Helene, and their wonderful son, Zimmerman, pursue him under all his mystic names, now become fabulous song and the stuffing of story.

You really expect us, Doc, to believe that it was you who sent Blue Serge on his vaunting quest?

Aye, 'twas. I may not have said *exactly* that . . .

Aha!

I said but, go home! Slap some carbolated vaseline on your nauseating mouth and lay off the old lady for a while.

You mean that the condition was caused by . . .?

No, no. I joosta no wanna to aggravate the condish. The mouth malady was, and it was as clear as the space in a congressman's head, from vast bowlfuls of tuna helper, a common malady among you folk.

That's better—but you are once again slipping in and out of the comic greaseball accent, Doc.

Mind-a you bizziness.

Doc? Say, Doc? If my mouth swells up again like it did, I mean, when I'm "on the road," what do I do? Where do I get the fruits and leaves and such? The greasy shlock you recommended?

What the hell are you doing back in this chapter? Get out! Out!

Yeah. What you want, caro mio?

Out!

Fruits and leaves? A bundle, a poultice, a grab-bag of daffodils and strawberry roots, rutabago blooms and crawling treponema, lavender peony stems and shady fusillade?

You betcha you life! The busting muscat, the dozing corn shock in season, and shuck when out, the pink-walled violet, even an algolagnia or so, to taste.

Thanks, Doc.

I've never seen anything—

The way she go, wailing Baptist! You do someting nize, hey! They wanna do it all themselves, at-home remedies, like that, you know?

But how will Blue . . .? I mean, how will he manage to . . .?

Get a curious peach in his mouth? Ha ha ha! I'd like to be a little maggot on the wall *that* day!

Odd how, despite our enormous superiority in all things—the criminal and ignorant histories of our forebears, for instance—we find you oddly amusing.

Facciabruto!

«3»

Blue and
Helene Have a Good
Long Talk and Make Plans

His great muscled teeth flashed for an instant, but whether in a smile of gladness or a grimace of pain, none can tell, least of all I. Flashed, then flickered and died.

My great gnarled hands lie lifeless on the piano keys, Blue said. It must be a sign.

Apple, Serge? his wife Helene said from the crepuscular corner of their comfortable, yet unimportant living room. It was her habit to sit there of an evening so that Blue could not discern her hair falling out.

His teeth glittered for just a moment.

My great gnarled hands, I said, Blue said, lie lifeless on the piano keys—only the white ones, by the by. And you offer me an apple? Although I can't see your hair I can imagine it, falling, falling, falling with the ineluctable movement of Fate. Don't you have any peaches?

But you can't play the piano, Serge, Helene whined reasonably.

Just so, Blue said. Yet Doctor Ciccarelli has advised me to stuff my mouth, swoll up like it gets, with fruits and leaves, sloes black as jet, and so on, and get cracking on my piano studies. I am not, in my heart of hearts, a lens grinder, as well you know.

Doctor Ciccarelli, the Mouth King?

And he also said that I must travel, travel, travel all through this great country, searching for the Perfect Musical Phrase. There I shall settle. Will you . . . come . . . with me?

Oh, Serge! And she rose from the shadows in a cloud of finespun hair and dandruff that caught the light somewhat like an aureole or halo; that looked, in the light, sort of like those two things, or one or the other of those things; and tripped across the room in this golden nimbus and/or aura, which latter enveloped her.

He's having trouble getting out of this sentence, Blue said.

Of course I'll come, Helene said. And are these some of the leaves and fruits that the doctor advised you stuff in your mouth? Here, let me. A sloe, a lemon, a tomatl, a quizzical pear and a magical plum, plus God knows how many blowing elm leaves and proud staghorn sumac fronds and Christ knows what else!

Mmphh.

I'll pack! Of course you'll be taking the piano?

Mmphh.

And his great gnarled hands were still at last, still and calm for the first time in what seemed months but was in actuality but a week or a week and a half at most!

After our really good and long talk, Helene, Blue said, of just a few hours ago— or was it days? God, it seems like days, since time fleets by so madly when one is in the throes of fantasy turning to reality, I know you'll agree, all pink and white as you are in your heart of hearts and soul of souls, that I have reached that moment in life when it is time for me to leave this dead-end job of grinding lenses. Is it not so, my bun?

I *have* agreed, Blue, Helene simpered. Perhaps you've forgotten . . .?

She was ravishing in an old, yet richly embroidered *schmatte*, set off beautifully by the snug-fitting *shapiro* left her by her old grandmother, the one who had the wise and beautiful things to say about life from the depths of her rocking chair on Essex Street.

You have so much to offer, Serge, your eyes, your glittering beard, your great hands chockablock with latent power . . . Will you be taking the piano? When I last quizzed you on that point, you said but "mmphh."

Take the piano? Ha ha ha! His hirsute laugh rang out upon the very stones! My necco, somehow I feel that I am, in some odd and mysterious way, a piano myself! And if not, then, by God!—and here he declaimed a thunderous oath— I plan to *become* all piano.

And . . . and . . . I'll still be your helpmeet?

In bosk and dell, in lea and glade, in glen and holt, in orchard, how, hew, and vale, in the hundreds, give or take a few score, of extempore eclogues with which we shall stun the yokels flung out like so many miggies and peewees across this windy land, you shall come! And be! And he laughed his great gnarled laugh!

And Zimmerman, our darling chee-ild?

By God, Zim! I'd almost forgotten the little F-clef, or however they term it. Of course! Although I dig on your mother heavy, I don't appreciate her making *him* wear a *shapiro*! What exactly is a *shapiro*?

Oh, Blue, Helene laughed relievedly, how should I know? Granny Rocco tells how the *shapiro* has been in our family ever since the old days, when the family ran the egg-cream dodge in Bialystock. But even *she* has no idea what it is.

Well, let the little tick wear it anyway then! I am nothing if not great of heart and anyway, why should I give a fuck if the kid looks like a gawm wimp-liver? Do you get me, sweetie seltzer?

Your voice, as you said "tick," had the timbre and quality of a small yet exquisite spinet. Oh Blue! We are going to make a success of it after all.

You can bet your run-down mocs on it, sport! And now, let's roll up a couple cocaine-peyote bombers and get *down*!

My great heart! Here are a few handfuls of honey locust leaves and nodding sprays of linden and magnolia ferns to "bind" the pow'ful whacker. Also very big in terms vitamins and enzyme juice.

And you ask if I'll take you! My black-fly!

A Domestick Quarrel

. . . never did that, never! Never *never* treated you the way you treat me all the time, Serge. Oh God! You can be as cruel as a sharpened tooth!

Don't call me Serge, weed-hair.

Oh God, so cruel! Like that just now! I speak to you so nice, so reasonable, ask you a question or something and what am I supposed to think when you emote such like: "Go shove your hair!" Hah? Or "Fuck off with your balding noggin!" Hah? When you walked out this evening, proud Serge, you know of which I wanted to do? First, I wanted to get my mitts upon that cheap knife with the plastic handle that your tightwad of a mother gave us for our *anniversary*—sweet Jesu!—outen the kitchen draw, or drawers, and just *stick* it, like, dig, puncture it right in my *neck*. Don't laugh, cruel flinty skin, I have a college education, yes, make a yawning incision in my own neck! And then I thought that mayhap I'd get a pair of shears or even scissors and cut my hair off down to the throbbing roots! I'm a person, Serge! I have inalienated rights just like any other human-being person, distaff though I own up to be! And you know how I am about my mother, all chock-a-bock with weeping tears, and yet you walked *out* on me to-night, walked out and left me all alone waiting for the phone to go "brr-ing-brr-ing" like it often does in novels with my mother on the other end making me crazed. I'm thirty-six years old, you know I can't cope with being thirty-six years old without some warm, supportive words and things and such, a hug, a kind remark, a fleeting moment of French-kissing, maybe a little shtup without you humming "The Trolley Song." I don't *need* a present, a little bibblo of a gift or whatever, but you dint get me a thing, not even a little remembrance, no, you spent your money on piano records and things très musicale, and I, I am thirty-six years old today with my still-young hair falling out in chaff-like handfuls so that I have to wear a babushka every day so that the fascist chauvinist spicks of the teeming stews of the brawling avenues don't call on me names like I have to hear at home, belike: "Cueball" and "Flesh-Head" and "Sconce-Shine." Things like unto the asperities what you cast toward me! Them spicks learned their deep unnatural rottenness from folks like you! No small wonder that they are always schlocking up their rice with bean juice! Are you asleep under that colorful blanket, Serge? I want you to listen to me, Serge, I am a person with legitimate person-needs, something like a book reviewer who would rather be in Maine writing his or her "novel" with his or her large comfortable feet in the fire. And what narrow-hearted wight can blame him or her? None! yelps the chuffing gale! My thirty-sixth birthday, and I've been a good wife, interested and boned-upon in everything you do, asking intelligent questions about your lens career and whatever. And don't you think that I'd like to walk out anytime I want, le-da-de, like you take such hasty powders when you wish to? But I can't! I can't walk out, Serge, because even though I am a human person with needs and wants like any other person in the world, and also with a teacher's license so that although I may have somewhat lost or carelessly misplaced my figure . . .

Har har har! Serge muttered.

. . . I am still a human *woman*, cut into the same moldiness and stamps as Elsa Koch and Madame Nhu and other great leaders of their yearning people. Yet I feel . . . trapped . . . just like some kinda animal, a kind of semblable to a wolf or a bear or sumpn.

Like unto a yak or duck-billed platterpuss?

I can't cope as a female-being person with feeling like a yak or something and being a little on the plump side in the rear area there, even with a casually loose schmatte on, and with my hair thinning a little bit, don't laugh, and also being thirty-six! You wish to know what my mother what bore me said when I reminded her that I'm thirty-six? Who cares? she bit off. *Who cares?* We all got to grow up sometimes, she said. Even Golda Meir was thirty-six once, she tittered. Don't you think, feeling, as I do, like a fox or a caged bird which wants to flap and sing his little wings off, that I'd just like to walk out and spend the house money for some things like piano accouchements and booklets of grinding-tool techniques or something, but you know I can't. Because, you know why? You know wherefore it is as impossible for me to do as it was for Caesar to avoid the raging dirk that shoveled out his quick? Because, Serge, I am the mother of a chee-ild! You have your piano and that quasi-Indian blanket what I give you when we used to sit up on the roof and drink peyote together and talk about how one day we would lick the world! But I don't have anything but a coupla cheap wigs from Fourteenth Street whom make me look like a Negro whore especially when my eyes are all red like theirs are often—I don't say all the time, but often—from thinking and crying myself to a restless sleep in my humiliation of not receiving a little thought on my birthday when I had to face Elatia Farn and Sarah Slatz and their questions as to what you gave me and I had to lie and lie about the "something special" you'd ordered from across the troubled seas what had not arrived yet. Cruel deception which turns its bucked teeth backward and snaps them quick into the fibber's writhing fletch! Are you *asleep*?

Avast and eke belay, you febrile wench, else I'll take the cat t'ye! (The cat runs with all celerity from out the chamber, or "room.")

Cruel! Now that you work parts-time it's worser with you around the house all the time reading *Popular Mechanix* and *Check My Beaver* and in front of somebody like I, with a degree in Education, what has substituted in some of the finest schools in the flung-out boroughs, and with my hands all red from Spic and Span cleaning your harmonica and pipe thing with the little holes every day. When I think of how it used to be, it was like a trip, maybe even a jaunt, to Venus or Mars, for you were on the jaunt with me. The way we et Noodle-Roni right out of the piping pot in front of the TV without clothes on, we were so proud and free in our human-person naked fletch, and the big bottles of cream soda—we used to call it just "cream," remember?—that we guzzled down with the salads I'd create from sorrel leaves and licorice roots with dainty chunks of Kraft American and wine mixed up with cream cheese, with the big lumps and fardels catching the mellow sunlight as it peeped at us through the grimy windows that looked out over the park where all those wonderful ethnic hunkies would be under the banyan and Dutch elm trees, beating each other to pieces and all laughing their great workers' laughs through their good-natured black-and-blue teeth, and jabbering in Polish or Yucratian or whatever wonderful warm language they spoke, just drenched in vodka and warm beer and stuffed with kielogi and pirbasa and cabbage shards, and the grass all tromped down for yards and yards around. And the petunias and phlox and hematomas and little curs cavorting and poo-pooing all over the brown strong limbs of the young people—the wonderful wonderful young people!—stretched out under and also on top of the broken benches and the vast acres of smashed bottles and used needles and dried cundrums that set off the old rust color of the rotting seedless grapes spilling from quaint and curious paper bags, all so simple and true and honest that I thought such a world could never end! Especially when we really embroiled ourselves into it with some oregano spice cakes dotted all over with teensy bits of chemicalized stuff like unto bacon that was then only nine dollars a pound, those were the days, and the rubber plants would shake in the stifling breeze blowing in the window carrying the pure sound of the Con Ed plant hysterically blowing off steam in yet another emergency that we were not to fret or worry about and the dust would just fly off of the plantain leaves that we insouciously draped about the rubber plants, and later, later, mix in with our raw-bean salad with sesame croutons and rice delight which we learned about from that funny cockeyed man in the park used to stand under the old rotting sycamore and expose his private. Remember we called him, dubbed him, really, "Old Uncle Pee-Pee"? He was one of the last of the truly yawningly deep and four-squared souls left in that little idolic world, oh, how I remember how you said you'd give a million, yes, that was the phrase, you'd give a million bucks—it's all coming back to me!—you said, to be like him with no thought of anything but the way the sun dappled the area of his trouser fly and the odd feeling the deep rich feeling of accomplishment it gave him so that he thought nothing of making his simple repast out of a few old Good Humor sticks and the wrappers that held spicy cuchifritos, something that I always wanted to learn how to create, cuchifritos with marianari sauce served on those big radish leaves with handfuls of timothy and fugwort gone to seed to mop up the tangy gravy, and after that snow peas in orange rinds with chilies and lemon pop all over and once, *you* probably don't remember, we had a small simple picnic under that noddingly diseased horse-chestnut tree that made you fall in love with me all over again so that you stuck your wad of Bazooka into my yearning lip! Avocado peels and okra shoots in a mold made from raspberry Jell-O with peanuts and cherry tomatoes and all surrounded by delicately flavored coconut shells and halavah bits on a bed of soft and slightly browning escarole or some kinda ginzo bush along with Crisco on bialys and plenty of piña jugo with sprigs of nettleweed and sawgrass to give it that certain je ne sais quoi. I can't believe we lived such a life, Serge. And now . . .

Forgive me, my dolling snap bean! I've been blind wit staring at my rippling dukes! *Can* you . . . forgive me?

Oh Blue! My love! Of course—and e'er I breathe a syllable o' censure vile and eke coterminous I'd as lief implode my face unto the haunt o' fishes an' the snarling barracuda who savages the floors o' Neptune's condominium!

Then come here, my quiv'ring kohlrabi, and I'll suck your coif like I used to in those days of old delights, and perhaps some of that am'rous magic will retoin! We can but hope, and yet: My wires, such as they are, do thrill and thrum!

« 5 »

Blue Improves
Helene's Coiffure

Helene, my shock, I'm going to repair and renovate—not to mention slick up cold and grooved—your coiffure, with some debonair twists and flourishes and turns, bights, and sheepshanks so it will come out all resplendently dapper. You'll look like a bride again! How long ago it endless seems!

I'm in your powerful and surgically perfect hands, Blue dumpling, whatsoever you want to do with me, I say aye! and aye! again, and yet again, letting my voice ring and clatter in the welkin high above, the one now creamily bespattered with extra-thick clouds.

No need to wax so fulsome, fond asparagus. Ready? Rivet your gaze on the mirror before you so that you can see what I'm doing and I'll supplement this visual aid by also tipping you off vocally as I go.

Solid!

First, I grasp hanks and locks of crudded, feltered, and bejungled hair in both hamlike fists and mess it around improvisationally to give myself an idea of how you look *au naturel*, without the aid of that vast battery of creamy pastes and gelatinous dandruff-fighting lotions that clutter and jam what we laughingly refer to as your dressing-table. Then, when your crowning glory is a fetching mass of tangles and snarls that perfectly complement the bloodshot eyes that stare in pop-eyed abandon back at you from yonder looking-glass, I step back to see where and how I shall attack the very problem that my artistry has created! *Bon.* Satisfied, as I hope you are, my precious nit, I slather your sconce with many many ounces—how many what man can tell?—of Wesson oil, or some other oil, low in cholesterol nuggets and supremely heavy on poly-unsaturated greaseballs. You'll note how it bubbles and oozes and slides down these crafty cowlicks and knots unto the very scalp and its ancillary roots, dig? Now, we give it a minute or two to seep into the follicular capillary system that ceaselessly and loyally carries vitamins and minerals and proteins and Jesus knows what else type of nutritional elements to your noisomely gleaming hair, but which has been

19

clearly goldbricking and fucking up royally, so to speak, of late—else why would you be sorely vexed by this touch of baldness that threatens your Venusian aspect—all chick and a mile wide, babe. *Voilà!* Now, while we allow this stuff of dreams, this stuff that has the uncanny consistency of schmaltz from the finest of pedigreed hens and blue-blooded capons and roostercocks, to elbow its way down into the deepest subcutaneous micromolecular zones of your oddly squared-off skull, I plunge a veritable squadron of combs and brushes into this special turquoise-tinted solution simmering away at my calloused albeit purely formed and dashingly proportioned elbow, now unfortunately racked with various aches and pains, suffering as it is from pianitis. But why do you leap and jump about, my pip?

Oh Blue! I just saw a strange and hairy, an *animal* face glancing in the window with a steely, spooky eye, or, to be precise, a veritable *pair* of eyes!

Let me check this bestial creature out, my goose, lest it be a mangy lycanthrope, intent on feral chomp and rend. In the meantime, I'll let my tonsorial equipment simmer gently, while you, and I so implore it, must close your vapid eyes so that this slimy potion, now dragging along every fucking vitamin yet known to great and irrepressible mankind, does not steal into those, your sparkling eyes, and render you unsighted. Aha! I see the dangerous creature, standing there and gazing at me all nonchalant and unconcerned, and with, as the vulgar patois has it, some pair of balls! Begone, you twerpish rogue and gross degenerate morphodite!

Oh Blue, my heliotrope bouquet! What manner of cruel slinking creature can it be who would so blatantly direct his sadomasochistic stare upon a lady all slopped and iced and gilded with unspeakable and loutish goo?

Only the remarkable Savior can say, and that's my deep opinion . . . and yet, now that I scan him close, especially noting well his walk, or amble, and now that I see him leap belike unto a carnal pogo stick into the perfumed air of spring or whatever goddam season holds us in its thrall, I wot that he gambols and bleats just like a very lamb. By all that's musical, it is a lamb!

A lamb? Oh Blue, my straining pectoral, does this portend portentous evil tidings, ever close to us and ever slouching nearer, like that tough beast in the famous Pennsylvania poem?

That, I cannot ken, nor search out in the soft grey crap that humankind hilariously cleps the cerebellum, if I got the right word for the pulsing organ. But what I do know is that the little bastard has been joined by sundry buddies, all lambs such as he, and all matted and begunked with Nature's kindest remedy for dry and itchy hides—I speak, of course, of wondrous lanolin!

So you feel it's stupid bullshit to be nervous as a coot? Whatever that last-named thing may be?

Of course, my ruby *bouche*! These foolish little schmucks, clumped and mobbed up as you now can see as you open wide your peepers, are standing in moronic innocence just outside the window, gazing at you and at this hotsy-totsy operation, like unto wooly statues which know not what they see but ogle anyway, dumb sons of bitches which they are.

And so I *do* see as I ope my blinks. They kind of get upon my nerves, frail broad that I am. I do not cotton to the idea that they watch me, all unkempt and dopey, with my coif a sight!

Fear nothing, sweetest scallopine, I'll make short work of this, your witching curls, and be all done before these idiotic infant sheeps have a chance to shake their horrid tails. They make me slightly nervous too, with their imbecilic gaze, but a man who has his spouse's hair in such a state learns how to press on and ne'er say hold!—until her coiffure is such that it beats that of fairest Helen all to shit.

You are an *artiste* right down to your black and splintery fingernails, my ragged gladiolus.

Allons! I now run this gigantic comb all through this healthy and yet horrifying schlock with which I have enlacquered the few poor hairs that still you sport, dragging and savaging its sturdy, stout, and steaming teeth through each unruly clustered tangle so thick and matted that your gleaming *capo* looks as if the rats have been a-sucking on it all betimes.

The shooting agonies reach down unto my very armpits, yet I command you to press on!

Command me nothing, gentle twit, but rather beg me to continue in my task—a task for which I have all greatly volunteered. And now, see? The comb, clutched famously within my expert duke, has done its magic work and your hair is slicked back and molded to your freakish head belike unto that curious cap that milliners have dubbed a yarmulke. The vile and noxious grease that finds itself clotted 'pon your rather dirty nape is that surplus devoutly to be wished, for in its bowels is the dandruff and the filth and scale and lice that once held sway within the stuff your bean produced, the stuff that I have always called your glist'ring hair, may God forgive my small prevarication, and if He gets one glimpse of you, my cookie, He'll shrive me of each sin I have committed—aye, in word *and* deed!

I feel so . . . so . . . good, in the entire ballyard that nestles just above my forehead, my blazing maple leaf. And how wonderful my poor hair looks as you go into yet another awesome shtick with your zipping fingers. Wow!

Well may you say "wow," humble sausage of my heart. Now dig on the ambidextrous way in which I whip these once-lank tresses into glamour! Now a curl, now a wave, now a sweep over each ear and a bob and fall and brave upsweep *chingado*, topped off with a restive bouffant beehive, the envy of every simple broad who ever whiled her nights away in the dazzling bowling alleys of sunny Jackson Heights!

Oh Blue, my blowing maize, I hardly know myself, I'm almost young and beautiful again!

I don't quite follow you in re your term "again," but anyway, you are at least half-ass presentable, despite your vastly imbecilic clothes and that hilarious nose of yours, so peculiarly itself that Joe Miller could get by with only it as lonely subject of his crapola corn.

I stand and flush agape. All words fail and falter and I sigh.

And while you sigh your buttocks off, pimiento spread, I'll take this excess and devastating muck I've combed out of your slathered hair and chuck it full velocity upon those leering sheeps! Aha! *That* made the little faggots bound away! And good riddance to you, you bucolic creeps! Don't let me catch you all aslouch again, your glazy eyes pressed nakedly to other people's windows! Get your own transparent windows if you like the life of Tom the Peep, you hairy schlepps!

Your powerful and aggressive words zing all up and down my spine like in the lyrics to that old and moth-chewed song the public loved adoringly unto a man. You are every item I desire, prodigious Blue.

« 6 »

Blue Finds
and Takes the Pushcart

And so, O Muse, with fair Helene's hair all frizzed and ratted into gouts of pulchritude, the family Gavotte was ready to "hit the trail." And yet, no means of transportation was there for the intrepid three, though Great Destiny hawked and choughed in the keening wind!

We peep down (or up) upon the sinewy Blue, his hair all feltred in anxiety, churning and thudding his way beneath the *arboris urbis*, the ashy hobblebush, thug squashberry, swamp loosestrife, jimbo pachistima, pimpface polyester, and all the other clumps that shoot and yearn throughout the streets and byways of vast Gotham—not to forget the loathsome ginkgo!

Arghh, shot Blue the Serge. The time is ripe and mellow for to split and take ourselves away! My spouse's hair is bossed and slathered, my mouth is clearing up, the magical piano trembles in anticipation, and, the veriest acme of the whole routine is the not-lightly-given imprimatur of profound Doc Chick. But how to cram and pack the crap we'll need and hurl it all, ourselves included, West?

Sing, Muse, of the Port Authority! Sing of the Ninth Avenue upon which its ass-end abuts and jowls all cheeklike! Sing too of the strange vehicle that nestled by the curb, abandoned all alone by mortal men, as 'twere no more than a rotted limb of cockwood, the noisome crud of which the awesome Bion speaks, or sometimes croons. Something like a pushcart and yet not a pushcart. A-decorate with arcane symbols unlike anything the humble ragman or the swarthy applevendor would give a twiggish fugg about. The Serge did halt, his muscled toes digging furiously at the pavement, his eyes all bright as with the agued kinch.

Is this a cart? huffed Blue. The genre of which the cant and mores and gross platitudos of the day call pushcart? It is belike and sort of like the pushcarts that collective memory hath implanted in my brain, all awash in sickening nostalgia, sort of akin to the oddball vehicle my old Uncle Max once schlepped with keening tzuris through the pungent, manly streets of the Old and Lower East Side of bygone yore, those streets all shaded with the dread ailanthus, o' which the *New York Times* writes each two or three year or so, no doubt laboring beneath some fatal curse. And yet its weirdo shape, its amateurish pictures and designs, its funny little "roofs," and the bald and gross-visagèd fact that it has four round wheels instead of two, take it far, far from the league in which grizzled Uncle Max did play, a phrase I like to use to make the stranger think my uncle's putrid life was but a lark.

Sing, Muse! Jump with fairy feet upon my cheap and mass-producèd ballpoint pen, taken from a Sheraton Hotel, and guide its smeary "nib" so that it writes with accents grave and somberous of the lonely cart that Serge's banjaxed eyes did light upon.

Its tentlike roof or hood glittered in the hazy sunshine, all vertically stripèd black and white, like unto a stick of licorice candy, sort of, but not quite exactly, since the stripes were not curling around or whatever they are prone to cogitate therein, and so on. And yet! 'twas not "all" stripèd, for the front part of this canopy was of a solid color, grey in hue (or tone), yes, grey as the bleary eye of ancient ram when he doth sport upon St. Michaelmas!

Upon this ventral bombast, all dazzling as the famed Lorenzo's treasured marmalade, two curious and crabbed figures were indited by a hand with all the skills of Pegleg Vulcan, a old eyetalian doomed to whang and smudge his days away in the foundries of Olympus hight. The topmost symbol showed what seemed for all the world to be a star, or else a bitter asterisk, which in the Greek of Homer and that whole demented crew of yodeling troubadors, means little star, and thus betimes, what boots the fucking difference? Yet but a moment's pause may give us thought. It could as well have been a flower, or the blossom nodding sweet and swell of same. O Muse, help me to scrawl down the names of various flowers that this asteriskish thing might sort have looked a little like, I do implore you as a faun begs for his blushing nymph's be-pansied crotch atremble in the bosk! Or purlieus thence!

It resembled but a puling tittle the majestic whang pylorus, insofar as its pistils crinched a bit of dusty albumen; or the cowpoke adenoma, that luscious succulent that catches lemonpeels soft flying in the Bexar County twilight; yet there was about its glizzy purplish aura a hint that grunted speckled adenitis, the hardy cactus that attacks the hikers' Pepsi-Cola; but one would not go far astray to think it krishna foramen, in that it had the odd aroma of your basic vegetable blue plate; a close-inspection peer, however, at its wicked stamens might urge the dimwit botanist to think he'd come across the whiplash fovea, that amoral plant long suspected of ripping the modest skirts from Girl Scout leaders in the nooky glades; Dr. Harry Hare, however, of the Wildlife for Jesus Federation, showed a bloom much like it on his mammoth Terre Haute Telethon last year, and described said bloom as the hump synovia, an obnoxious weed that grows in a mucky compost made of tuna mulch; still, a layman's guess would come down on the side of the jazzbo ganglia, since the woody stem was all encrusted with identically oozing acne-blots; yet and yet, the whole had all the crud and infestation of the rainbow hallux, that monstrous hollyhock that men, in trembling dread, have dubbed "Wayne Newton Plant"; but all in all, if one were to picture forth this boutonniere so as to make all people see it instantly, it was a twin unto the wimpy hematuria, a type of slogbed phlox that has its kinky way with Rosedale housewives while their husbands chuck their bowling balls akimbo and abaft.

Just beneath this pimpled asterisk, or little star, or else a flower, as we have bravely hopped out on a limb to name a few, please see above, whizzed forth to Blue's slow-plodding eye another crazèd figure. Lo! a shallow basin in which was stuck a kind of upright stick, or maybe sturdy plank or log or faggot of what seemed to be a type of item called by men, yea, e'er since the time that brawling Hector scared the shite out of his little son with wearing of some dumbbell hat, wood! And all atop this wooden plankish thing blared forth upon the day another kind of goddam star! This one five-pointed, or, as the sweating masses call it, your ordinary common star, known to symbolic logic as a stellar presentation, belike at times to shitfaced drumbling knaves the stars that they remember with a shudder of recall from grammar school. But Blue, though wacked out by the sun that scrabbled at his corneas, saw at once that this chintzy figuration might well have been, or meant to be, or yet, it wert! a palm tree all free of the encumbrances of coconuts. Or tiny stinking monkeys!

A palm tree! But by the Great Jesu, O what a palm! A growth the likes of which one might imagine shading Mickey Mouse or some other cutesy vermin, or maybe even the grotesquely weird animals of cartoon farm and field who ceaselessly gabble and palaver to keep their minds off the stunning fact that they whank about the glades and heaths sans genitals! It was, in some disturbing way, not so much a palm tree as it was something else. But what, O Muse? Fill me with the unmixed wine of art and letters, or even, yes! of post cards, that I may scratch and scribble on this lonely sheet its akiltered image, lambent in the haze of muscled midtown! Canta!

It had the gimpy silhouette of the puffy decumaria (mordecai), that sweaty grass that humps in secret innocent electric typewriters; yet there was about its pullulating shape somewhat of the calm St. Johnswort, that virago of a limp legume which smiles eternally in elevators; yet what sunburned camper, complete with fruit bar, would not quake in thinking of it as a runaway example of the dour jive-ass silverbell, that traipsing fungus that in dead of night devours "chuck" and empties stout canteens; a minority of foundation scientists swear that it was not unlike the silky-camellia all-in-one, beige, black, and white, that hankers to wrap itself around the staidest matron in the sanctity of her boudoir;

bigmouth pepperbush? but yes! in that its simpy gnurled appendages did clinch whatever steak au poivre did happen by within the shady glen; yet, cloved and hugged it not to its bamboozled self a soupçon of the penetrating character of the clubfoot sandmyrtle, that queer and beetly creeper that flourishes within the very core of Southron novels?; however, in a certain light, the rank growth, like the flushing minniebush, seemed to sport a bevy of iridescent spangs, like the ladies of dainty thighs much loved by Doctor Tom; though those who holler that the simpering shrub featured forth itself belike your roaring stumping Western soapberry, that spends its bloated youth amid depraved daguerrotypes, are not far off the mark; the consensus but of disheveled lab assistants appears to be that this "palm tree" was neither more nor less than a freakish outgrowth of fat-ass redroot, famed for fakery, terrific transvestite, bald of bean and astonishingly dim behind its domino.

Below and just a chitch in front of this glistering roofish item, was a smaller roof in shape somewhat like a parallelogram, or rhombus, or whatever Euclid in his crazed meanderings yclept such curio. And there, dead center on its spanking blank, what ho! an urn, and not unlike that urn so loved by each and every Greek, even their unravished brides! On either side of this two-handled jug, able in its girthish vastness to hold up to eighteen gallons of that nectar called by sage Euripides pure Yankee Bean, Blue's eyes did pop to see the virtuosic forms divine of eke these wacky characters: a coupla fishes, coupla bedbugs, and a coupla pelicans. Sing, Muse, what this did all portend if it portendeth anything! Or sing of mighty Serge's words, or croaked facsimiles thereof, and such betimes!

What doth this all portend if it portendeth anything? mused Blue upon the azure air of that alabaster avenue so far from the scroungy lights of Broadway and its crappish plays. These things must stand as "symbols"—wot a woid! The tunnish oin bespeaks, it actually shouts and hollers, of a fullness, thick and curdled like your frozen custard, that will be my Life when I depart this fabled island, than whom, Satan except, no one can live in peace, or send his childers to a decent school achock with WASPs, but must, bedad, watch the kiddies sport with peers whose skins are of Cimmerian hue and who speak that argot rude known as the "motherfucker" dialect. So much for this fatted vat. But what can mean these crippled hilarities, these tandems rude bedaubed of fishies, bugs, and birds of big fat mouths?

So did Blue breathe his dumb interrogations to the unhearing air, awash, as is its wont, with klaxons and the brutish stinks of "produce." Then, as esoteric reams of numbers plotz upon the brain of idiot savant, the true and hidden meanings all collapsed upon him, falling in a dusty rush as doth a drunk pitch forward on the sloppy table in his favorite neighborhood saloon.

Great Zeus and Such! shrieked Blue. It comes to me in a rush as swift and beeline as the freakish Mercury, that distorted lad with feathers all asprout upon his twinkly feets! It all portendeth Great Success! Of that there is no gasp of doubt. My arcane and eruditical researches whiz into the front porch of my cerebellum and I recall the truths of stern biology, but oui! The fishies, in their drive to larder up their tummies, scoff up legions of the humble bedbug; and in turn are wolfed by ox-eyed pelicans; and every man will tie the feedbag on in snappy trice when pelican is set before him on the groaning board, howsomever, it will be admitted that this oily bird is best served roasted in a baste of pine nuts, okra fronds, and childermass; or else prepared marengo-style, glopped o'er with twitchy crayfish and a dozen sunny sides. Thus steps out smartly straight before my wised-up eyes the March of Life! Yes, the Great Law of the Jungle and the Christian Way, i.e., compete your weaker neighbor into tattered scraps of junk and blame it all on God! Is it any wonder then that this more-or-less united oligarchy's potent banks all gleam in reverential hush akin to choiches?

Yea, these portentous symbols glitter forth the silent memorandum that I, Blue Serge, am meant for Greatness! And that all who stand in front of my success express are to be raveled, chonkered, wrenched, and blastered in thrilling sympathy with the somber Laws of Nature. As the fishies eat the bedbugs and the pelicans the fish, and as divinely shapèd man sops up the corses of the pelicans, so will I take my place in this wise scheme and devour each and all opponents to my raging wants! Great Jove thus speaks to me in subtle signs that translate straight to pure unfettered gringo-ese!

Then tell, O Muse, how the beams of that conflagrating star that men in their cowering mode have dubbed Big Solly, did shine upon that spackled vehicle, making it lo! to appear as puissant and as terrible as a newly laved and idiotically pricèd auto, of the kind your mogulish tycoon and swiftly famed celebrity doth buy a grossish passel of! Tell how King Jupiter, with a flick of filthy finger on which bloomed an ebon nail, did make this bourgeois wagon seem to the loutish Blue as slick and glossy as the evening news! Tell how the cart did reach its twinkly "arms" out, so to speak, to coin a buboed solecism, so that the dim-bulb Blue was all a-fascinate with thinking that this noble gig was parked upon the clappy street for only him!

Great Pushcart, then descanted Blue, O chancred brougham of majestickal waukegan! It zips into my thoughts as quick as cockroach into kitchen crack, that you, O sacred chariot, wert meant for me, and only me, to aid my holy quest! O wert it thus?

And then the cart, in oddly weak and piping voice, did actually speak! But just to Blue, whose "face" proclaimed him as a type of personage known to the men of ancient time, as a cony, now called variously sucker, sap, and mark. Blue Serge Gavotte, it ponderously squeaked, in true tradition of Great Leadership, you see the dopy little head, 'pon which is daubed a spindly smile, that head, I strong attest and threaten, just below the overarching canopy with all the bugs and fishies and all the other odds and ends of bullshit fair indited thence and such? This leer is meant for you! Yea, as sure and splendid as the sawfang pink doth grin upon the careless fly it thinks to pinch and collar, thus to bash and fry up with its morning eggs!

I see, O handsome hansom, harangued Blue, his pimply eyes fair starting from that head in which lurked all the arcane secrets of the growing lens trade.

Well, boy, this loopy smirk doth mean that "I" doth wast but meant for you to take unto your very own, to clip and close unto your chicken breast!

To take? To clip? To have and hold as men do clutch on burning sands an icy cola drink or other effervescent poppy potable?

Yea, even so! I am the doughty vehicle 'twert meant for you, the engine of your fate and Karmic destiny. That's why I sit here in the glop and dogshit of this clinkered avenue. I wait for that sure hand that is attachèd to your arm to seize upon my very quick and such and schlepp me all away.

My twinkly coupe! Is it but so and thus?

Indeed, O raunchish paladin of swell romance! It boots but naught a flash of time—Great Plodding Time!—to lay your calloused yet artistic mitts upon me and swift break into a lopish gallop. Else a steady jog!

It is but so and true and well I mean to cotton to whatever thus!

Then did the knobkneed Blue embrace the magic wagon in full view of all the human offal and the riffs and raffs of hoi polloi who'd gathered moblike at the wondrous spectacle of Blue, in all his quivering delight, speaking wingèd words straight at an old abandoned wagon, left as jetsam by whatever cult of bimboed scalawags. Then did he hump and heave and roll away the talking cart!

His equipage korreck! His mode of travel bunked and battened down as is the squatting nuthatch in the misty fall! Thus did they rattle on toward home and sweaty packing up and fevered fond farewells! The road! The road! The road screamed temptingly as thus it doth and always will! So must it ceaseless wast!

A Brief Note
on a Traveling Library

But holt! and soft! Lest it be said, and, if all things go as they have always gone, it *will* be said, whatever that portentous "it" may signify, and significance, by Great Jesu's broken sconce, is all the current rage! That is, lest it be murmured that this meticulous joinal dared to withhold information from its reader, there shall be set down here a catalogue of the books that the Gavottes packed snugly away in the Cart before they rolled quietly onto the pine-besmirched macadam.

Picture then, if you will, a quiet evening. The sun, a pale magenta-yellow glob of crud upon the ancient sky. The leaves whispering and groaning under the assault of countless millions of gypsy moth caterpillars, known to etymologists as "hairy worms." The zephyrs tiptoeing 'round the eaves of the stunned houses in Vast Suburbia, there to fall down belching chimneys, and collapse into rugged septic tanks. The shy rodents savaging their lice and fleas. Yes! Picture Nature in her ordinary, everyday make-up! Nature, dozing and dreaming up perhaps an earthquake, or a small typhoon, a tidal wave or shy tornado, or maybe a spanking-new disease!

Serge is packing up the Cart, while Helene assists, resplendent in a burlap dress the color of what an impartial observer might dub "ooze." They are about to speak actual dialogue, the kind one reads in novels rugged as a septic tank or tanks, as see above.

I'm packing up some books, my palpitant flamingo root, Blue smiled tenderly, some warm and wonderful old friends that we can curl up with on the old trail when hailstorms bust and zap with wild abandon the roof of this our cart; or when twisters loom upon the far horizon. Thank gosh I fucking thought of it!

You think of everything, you swatch, the lady gleamed. What would the, as you call it, "old trail" be, without some well-thumbed, dog-eared volumes to delight the senses and fertilize the mind with their renewing horseshit? What volumes from our beloved stacks are you so carefully lading there, as lade you must?

I'll apprise you of these dear old pals, Serge said. And then there issued from his throat, by way of his mouth, of course, the hearty bellow that made his bride's vitals quicken and, at times, actually sprint! I have here *Pushcart Maintenance in the Field* by Anton Harley, a spiffy how-to book that will prove invaluable, chock, as it is, full, of easy-to-understand diagrams and tips, along with a breezy biography of a big wheel; *Supper at the Kind Brown Mill and Other Rustickal Pieces* by Joanne Bungalow, a small garland of inspirational poems that are guaranteed ne'er to bring a blush to hidden cheeks of mother, sister, sweetheart, or wife, so filled are they with icy chastity; *Stolen Fruit* by Jymes Vulgario, a little gem that can only be described, according to the *Pfarmville Pfrig*, as "shemmering"; *The Truth About Vegetables* by Harry Krishna-Rama, a prose work that evokes a world of variously factual sentences; *Your Ass Is Itchy: Mange in Pack Animals* by Trinidad Burros, V.M.D., the snappy little number that might best be summed up as a treatise that is almost like a momentary painting that quickly disappears; *Eating Your Honey* by "Beeline" Lingus, all about a gent who fell into a bare den but was saved by his fanlike ears—a passel of woodsy boffs; *Sexual Fulfillment in the Woods* by Birch Humpper, a thinly disguised *roman à clef* about Emerson's two-week stay with Henry Ford at the fabled spa, Walden-Saffron; and a "companion volume," Henry's own privately published *Repairing Your Tree's Crotch*, the classic study of what the *Adlerian Review* called "barking in the act"; then there's *Wild Fruits of the Lower Hudson* by Stonewall Cerrado, the latest in the "Perry Agony" series, a tightly constructed gem that deals with sex as a manifestation of the food-gathering process; *Country Album* by Nicholas DeSelby, a *nouveau roman* in which the West Wind tells a Blue Story; *Staring at Salad*, the blockbuster by Jayzee "Fleur" Belle, the big, inside novel about the lettuce industry that Tony Brouillard called "the most important novel of the last two weeks"; *American Lake Poetry* by George Stardust, a big, bold, brawny anthology of, as Mr. Stardust notes in his Introduction, "the seamy, yet tender poems of that group of majestic, half-forgotten American bards who live on the shores of our majestic, half-forgotten American lakes"; *Rich Hours Amid the Mint* by Colonel Bela Brilliant, Miz Belle's husband, a "weekend" counterfeiter and the outgoing president of the Lettuce Combine; *A Doom of Daffodils* by Armand Bientôt, a sex-mystery set in the glittering frenzy of the New York magazine world's "fiction" departments; *Lick Up a June Beet* by Derace Kingsley, a new paperback on food that James Gotee called "a rebellious book to 'turn on' the quirkiest palate"; an unpublished novel, in actual xerox copy of the original translation, by Jorge Cabrón, called *Gypsy Midnight*, which, although I have not read it, has a history of death, sex, black magic, and bewilderment behind it; and for dollink Zimmerman, a favorite of his, *The Daddy and the Drake*—little Zim is, as you know, driven to the alps of rapture by the meticulous descriptions of the garbage that the heroes of the book discover on divers nature trails. I must also mention *The Red Swan* by Dermot Trellis, a book that, I suspect, might serve to—heh heh—help us get it on sex-wise, could I but unearth the pornography from the murk of its text. Do you think we are, how you say, set, my tit-nosed craneswallow?

Is a wondrous bunch of tomes, Helene blushed. But there's a small and peppery little novel that I have just begun to peruse upon the last few evenings that I'd love to read aloud to you, or you could like maybe read to me, after really hard days on the old trail, hump-busting days, as they say in the streetlike purlieus. It is a cute and perversely risqué little book, translated from the Frog by Harold Roseate or Horace Rosebush or Harry Ross or something, called *A Weedy Music*. The original is titled *La Musique et les mauvaises herbes* by Anon. Can we take it with us?

Of course, my biblemane, Blue chuckled around the kazoo that had started suddenly from his rugged lips. In the fucker goes!

Thus did they prepare for the life of the mind on the trail in the sun and the rain and other nudges of Fond Nature! So 'twill ever be!

And with that, the sun fell heavily into the scrolls of silver snowy sentences, and the water also.

<< 8 >>

The Homely
Carte, or, Blues
Ecclogue Joyned with Helenes

O climbe *Helene* climbe on this lustie Carte,
All raynbowed lyke the rotting Sloe or Plum,
Its whyte lyke Snow, its black jette as your Fart:
Climbe on *Helene* and rest thy stynkynge bum.

HELENE:
Ah *Blue*, musician faire, thy words are white,
As putride Egg-plante in foul galauntyne:
O look, the Cartes wide canopie so bright
Doth make the slow wormes arse count not a bene.

BLUE:
And see *Helene*, the wheels lyke Pepper-ringes,
That in a Salad drown in stynkynge Oil.
The spokes resemble Cowcumbers and things
That nameless multiplie in charnel soyle.

HELENE:
My female parts rest on this Cushion faire,
Like doth the scum on steeming cabbage Pie:
'Tis yellow browne as dung-encrusted Pear,
And firm yet softe as muck in noysome Stie.

BLUE:
And jumbled therewithall the antick daubs,
(A Blobb, a Palme-tree, and a greesie Pott),
Do decorate the canopie lyke Slobs
Whose Mouthes are filled with Tuskes all green with rot.

‹ *Blue Pastoral* ›

Heigh hoe *Helene* thy Toes are thick with Mud,
Lyke Holly-hocks all pelted down with Rain,
They twitch as with an Ague of bad blood,
Or lyke a bird-beshitten Wether-vane.

HELENE:
Ah *Blue*, my heart, thy wordes as brightly shine,
As do the jaundiced Days-eyes on these Rails,
As tainted Herring, flaskes of Rhenish wine:
Thine Eyes flashe blacker than my dirtie Nails.

And as the Smegma voydes its loathsome Seed,
So doth my heart shoot out its ball of Love.
I shake and tremble and my Pants Ive peed:
How grynnynge Cupids darte speedes from above.

BLUE:
Those sweet soyled Pants shall be our ensign brave,
T'announce our motley Waggon to the World:
The knighte, the heretick, the caitiff Knave,
Shall gape to see thee blush, thy Drawers unfurled.

HELENE:
Thy speach is lyke the Thunder in the aire,
Or lyke the creeking of these snot-green Wheels.

BLUE:
Thy nether parts so ravyshyngly bare,
Do glister lyke a Barrel-full of Eels.

And so my damp *Helene* the tyme has come,
To push this multi-colored Waggon West,
Euterpe tootes her Pipe and beates her Drumme:
The twanglynge dinn infectes my leaping Breast.

HELENE:
Sweete *Blue*, my roguish Turnip, my old Hatt,
I see the sweate upon thy Face like fat,
And now the rusted Push-carte sighs and heaves,
As rolling, smash we Fruites and Flow'rs and Leaves.

<< 9 >>

Interlude: On
Blue's Bicycle Clips

Blue had many different reasons, philosophical and otherwise, for collecting and wearing his bicycle clips, and many different styles of clip, and many different modes of wearing his clips, very few of which had anything to do with the current fashion, the *dernier cri*, if you will. His clips came in identical pairs, and it was Blue's penchant to wear them, always, *as* identical pairs, never splitting a set; it was also his penchant (some say it was his obsession) to wear one clip on either ankle, and to wear the pair in identical style on either ankle, never mixing pairs or modes of wearing same.

This "philosophy of style" probably had its roots in the many reasons that Blue had for collecting and wearing bicycle clips. He had no bicycle, indeed, he had not possessed a bicycle since his childhood (and even in those zesty days his possession of a bicycle in no way assisted him in learning to ride one). What were his odd, his checkered reasons, then? For collecting? For wearing? For wearing in so many diverse ways? We do not pretend to know, nor do we flatter ourselves that we can understand the "ideas" and "theories" hereafter noted. We hardly understand our own. With this caveat to the reader we venture forth and suggest that he collected and wore his quirky clips because of odd and even weird "needs" (as they say), most of which were, even to Blue, hazily mysterious as well as rather egregiously childish, if not infantile.

There is a possibility that he wanted to look like a rotten potato, since few doubt that the middle of his head, head, head was lead, lead, lead; yet he rarely dressed all in green, even when endeavoring to approach the chic splendor of Tommy Snooks and Bessy Brooks (two friends of his adolescence who had the perverse impression that it was always eight o'clock). Even though he swore that he believed in nothing more than ally-ally blaster, he was wont to assert, when quizzed on his sartorial preferences, "Love me, and I'll love you," or, and perhaps more disconcertingly, "Lullaby, Baby Bow Wow." As has been observed, although his brains were stuffed with corn and hay, he was a proud beggar—a sop-sick bold-faced jig who cried for pie and who, when all alone, sometimes thought he was Jumping Joan, famed "unmentionables" model (though in June he changed his tune).

Though little Sergey wanted to play, his wife and helpmeet, the constant Helene, was not of silver: for instance, the north wind did blow on the poor poor thing, she was the best little donkey that ever was born, and her eye was too sore. Blue yearned to kiss a maiden all forlorn or, failing that, to attract a dirty slut and lie in the dirt. In truth he was a crass, dull jack-a-dandy and pondered such absurdities as: *How best to roast a snowball?* and *How many strawberries grow in the sea?* Certain authorities, in retrospect, have taken his erratic and eccentric behavior to be a manifestation of the sublimation of his desire for a gown of silk and a silver tee, while other, equally eminent researchers considered such behavior natural to a crooked man reared in a crooked house.

Blue himself usually maintained, sometimes belligerently, that his interest in the bicycle clip stemmed simply from the love he bore for Rosy and Colin and Dun, three childhood friends who, so Blue insisted, were sweeter than cakes and custard, and sharper than crying mustard. On other occasions, his answer to all questions as to his odd penchant was that his clips were substitutes for feather beds and wooden legs, neither of which, he laughed, would march him to the top of the "hill" and march him down again. Yet knowing, as we now know, that he was full of woe and had far to go, it may be the case that he simply felt the need to have more than just a bare cupboard to ease his misery on those days when he could not "blow his horn" (read: "play his piano") and was sure to cry.

Who can tell? The patient Helene once blurted that it was all but a frantic attempt to emulate the legendary Plum Duff, a childhood idol and raving simpleton who thought himself to be, in Helene's words, "a twinkle-diamond in a high sky," and who often claimed that he "liked to sally 'round the sun and moon" in order to "wash the spider out." But if the existence of a "Plum Duff" is to be given credence, why should we not be equally credulous anent the rumor that a pig without a wig suggested the bicycle-clip affectation to Serge? In all events, his wearing of the clips—his very possession of the clips—allowed him to run fourteen miles in fifteen days, certainly not a notable feat (no pun intended), yet, to put a good face on his slow, sleepyhead, greedy-gut ways, he couldn't work any faster.

It must be borne in mind that Blue thought himself wondrous wise behind his eyes, and since it is common knowledge that his father had stepped, *sans* bicycle clips, right in a puddle up to his middle in order to extend a pathetic fantasy as "King of the Castle," his son, Blue, often pecked off his nose to spite his case; i.e., he "marked his mood with a T," as it were. For what it may be worth, genetically speaking, his father could eat no fat, he could eat no lean, he once, in amorous mood, got into bed and bumped his head, and he swore, to the end of his long and vacillating career (he couldn't decide on plum or plain), that each Arbor Day was the occasion on which he saw a balloon go up to the moon.

None of these speculations by us and statements by and about our subject can help us to get at the root of Blue's delight in the homely bicycle clip, and one may find more profit in sniping at the belief, which is nothing but a monstrous fiction, that proclaims the novel but absurd dictum: "All the world is paper and all the sea is ink." Finally, the simplistic remark made by an anonymous wag, to wit, that Serge employed his bicycle clips to warm his pretty little toes, may hold an Absolute Truth. On the other hand, there is a large minority that dismisses Blue and all his works and ways, with the ungenerous and even cruel judgment that he was nothing more than a dingty diddlety, an assessment that cannot be satisfactorily disproved.

The styles and fashions of his collection are, perhaps, more easily apprehended as to their intelligibility; that is, that since Blue was a firm devotee of the *lex campionis*, whose most salient tenet is "Nature art disdaineth," his taste in bicycle clips ran to the bucolic. He possessed clips in the fashion of the little marvel peapicker, big Mister Radish nose, favorite Whitney crab louse, quick-baring Haralson, pink-clump cameo, Anthony waterer (dwarf), penngift choke-out crownvetch, double pink starlike fairy, early mottled contender, Commodore Bush Kentucky wonder, old home pencil pod, vigorous class butterwax, compact fresh moongold, relish tendersweet tidbit, smooth royal Chantenay, Detroit dark red, King Mono explorer, firm flesh ruby queen, glowing gold nugget ball, tremendous Downing creamy yellow, gross fuchsia malleolus, Illini cob xtra, candystick cobby freeze, black swag Mexican, green-skin smoothie (dark), wonder-white amaze, tolerant Spartan dawn, triple scab mech, solid early belle cherry, French white bottom, rose China brittle, yielding baked blackini, semi-open Bennings green, squash oblong delicata, popular warted (Hubbard-type), pink jumbo Hungarian, Des Moines table ace, Laxton big Dakota progress, hot weather wando (summer), exciting Minnesota orange honey, tough Congo rind, rocky sugar rock (green-fleshed), gray Charleston iopride, triple streaker delight, big prize Max (custard-thin), fiery Jim Numex, Roma royal meaty chico, zippy verde tomatillo, small-juice bellarina (cold-set), fantastic early-girl cascade, self-blanche green wave, and ice-crisp reliable header.

It was in his styles of wearing his varied clips that Blue's invention showed itself most fecund, most impertinent, most playful. He wore his clips with a flair that *made* fashion, rather than followed its dictates. He adjusted said clips on his person in the single-ankle clutch, meat squeeze, slide-knuckle gripper, red-dog bite, chic scrimmage foot-pincher, birdie swathe, big-toe chukker, bunion scrum, cancha arch-cross, two-ankle jab, double-play caress, blitz nipper, eagle muffler, cesta enfolder, double wrap, left-handed slider, conversion sticker, driver scarf, four-thong frontis, skin-grab hat trick, triple long hug, basic-T gnaw, two-knot brassie, metatarsal dunk clasper, dermis-love scraper, high inside change, down swaddle, comfy spoon, shuttlecock sheepshank seize, dashing flare basket, bone force, single-wing prodder, flat-palm mashie, half-around wicket hold, full fly-front nelson, calf force-out, instep jigger, tri-laced bunt, baffy stroker, clip *au naturel*, jug-handle grasp, double-wing probe, four-toe cleek, lapped-seam half-nelson, bails corn-encloser, flat-footed niblick, open-heel century, rosy-fingered homer claw, sammy intertwine, front-opening slide, scroogie wrench, and blind side-clipper.

« 10 »

A "Column"
in a "Newspaper" Gives
Blue an "Idea," Soon to Be Revealed

Tall, stately, flashing-eyed Lesbia Glubit leans back into the pillows of the choc-olate-brown, crushed-velour couch in her studio ("It's really just an old *sewing* room," she smiles), and laughs easily at something a visitor has just said. In her openwork crocheted jeans, matching halter, and transparent plexiglass high-heeled mules, she looks more like a statuesque Las Vegas showgirl than the influ-ential, perky wife of the powerful Chairman of the Congressional Liaison Com-mittee on the Arts, Harold "Hal" Glubit. Always overflowing with optimism and energy, she seems even more animated today, bursting with ideas and opin-ions. She has just returned from addressing a group of high school art teachers in the Oklahoma public-school system, and is still delighted over the surprise and shock that her characteristically blunt comments aroused in those rather con-servative educators.

"They were really tickled," she says, sipping at her fresh mint iced tea ("Gosh, I *love* mint, don't you?"), "when I said that as far as I was concerned they were *right* to think that their children—their *doggies*, for gosh sakes—could paint just as well as Polack or Rossko or Frank Klein, or *any* of those other foreign so-called modern masters." She grimaces pertly at the last word. "But they were *completely* bowled over when I told them that the wallets and lamp-bases and pot-holders their pupils made in arts and crafts class were Art just like Rembrandt Van Gogh was, and all those other old-timers in the Dark Ages. I think I could have been elected Governor then and there—but one politician is enough in a family, don't you think?" She throws her patrician, yet strongly earthy head back and laughs delightedly, her soft fall of ash-blond hair shining in the sunlight that cheerily floods the spacious and immaculate studio. "But you know," she says, suddenly serious and biting her lips together, "I really *do* believe that all art, *great* art, that is, and not this stuff made for the so-called intelligentsias, comes directly from the foolish hopes and the shattered dreams and the stupid aspirations, and, yes, the small disappointments of the common folk. Look at the Indians, for gosh sake! Nobody ever gave them any lessons and look at those gutsy blankets and jugs and things. The vitality and strength of them! The alive vibrancy of buffalo robes and bows and arrows and canoes made of old pelts and such!" She sighs, moistening her full bitten lips, her perfectly manicured nails nervously darting in and out of the holes in her jeans.

Lesbia, or "Lez" as her friends on the Washington art circuit call her, with no small touch of envy and admiration, has always been known to hold unorthodox and rather gaily risqué outré opinions "about *everything*," she roars, happily, even, she confides, as a cheerleader and carhop in her native Ohio, where she was born and spent the first nineteen years of her life. "Oh heck, sure," she twangs, her eyes far away now, "I shocked my teachers *and* my customers back there in Plumber's Friend. Gosh sakes, all the time! I used to wear a rubber Dylan Thomas mask once in a while and those really *great* checkerboard pants he liked. Gosh, how I loved, adored, I guess, that wonderful, mad, raving man's work. 'When the October wind pushes up my hair with fourteen fingers,' " she quotes from memory, and for one split second seems on the verge of leaping from the couch. "Wow!"

It is no secret that her Senior Essay, "The Squalor of Andrew Wyeth," is still spoken of with hushed awe among the members of the Arts Club at Dead Creek Central High School, but Mrs. Glubit refuses to take credit for what has been termed its "iconoclastic brilliance." "Just really an adolescent attempt to, what do you call it? bust their lumps," she chuckles deeply, lighting her fortieth cigarette of the day. Her cigarettes are made of wheat bran, and to her exact formula, by a small, exclusive Georgetown tobacconist whose name she refuses to disclose. "He's a super-wonderful gay ecologist, really into whale songs, the Hemorrhoids Foundation, and solar-powered Judy Garland dolls, and I wouldn't *dream* of embarrassing him." Her eyes are far away again. "I practically *lived* with Dylan's poetry for three years," she goes on, folding her long dancer's legs under her vibrant lissomeness. "He's so vital and strong, so vibrant and, I don't know, *alive*. Is there another modern poem that can compare with 'Do Not Blow Gently in That Good Wind' "?

But if her problems as an "art-rebel" (her own wry term) were pronounced at home, they were relatively mild compared with the difficulties her unique and cannily individualistic ideas have plunged her into here in old-line and innovation-suspicious Washington, where, she cheerfully and mischievously admits, she is known as "Boat Rocker," and where she had society abuzz last year when she arrived at a White House dinner, in honor of President Bruto Larsen Depravado of the Anti-Communist League of Central America, clad in a brown-paper tuxedo. And as the Chairperson of the Washington Women for Artistic Expression Club (WAX), and the first delegate to the "Art Is Life" symposium held last summer in the rubble of a Palestinian village, she has frequently become embroiled in disputes over funding for the arts. Some say that her high profile has been damaging to her husband's career, and that her activities in the art world have been partially responsible for the Ethics Committee hearings that Rep. Glubit faces next week. Lesbia Glubit colors at this, her emotions flickering across her face like red storm clouds, and jeers, "It's all just nonsense, for gosh sakes! They're trying to say that Hal was involved in some sort of 'impropriety' concerning some old *sheep* when he toured New Mexico last fall. Hal? We have our *own* herd of sheep out on the lawn behind the Jacuzzi shack and Hal hardly even *looks* at them! As his wife of twenty-four years," she says evenly, snapping off her words, gesturing crisply with her cigarette as her eyes spark and smolder, "I know that Hal is partial to Directoire lingerie. *Period*." She insists that her spouse welcomes the hearing and prays every evening for it to begin in the little chapel that he built with his own hands in a small glade near the sprightly rill that the Glubits have enthusiastically named "Our Rill." "Gosh, yes, he's so *anxious* to clear the air, to get all these charges out in the open so that he can defend himself and exonerate his good name in public, before his constituents and his family and the great American people."

Lesbia Glubit worries, however, that the long siege that her husband has undergone has interfered with his work as Chairman of the Anti-Christian Subversion in Education Panel, and that it has forced him to set aside initial plans for expanding the Art for All Fellowships for which he acts as Congressional liaison. "It's just the most *perfect* sort of job for Hal," she whispers. "He's so vital, so strong . . . there's something so vibrantly . . . alive about the darling. Like a gutsy work of art by someone like Tom Wolfen all by himself." She lights another cigarette and her eyes focus dreamily on the enameled ears of corn that hang, in daring asymmetry, from the ceiling, admiring their hard, clean lines, and, with characteristic modesty, neglecting to claim them as a unique creation. She "potters" like this, she will say, when pressed, "in my few moments of spare time," and declares that such work relaxes her and clears her mind of all ideas and thought. "Art is really better than Valium," she smiles distantly. "You can feel the hard knot in your stomach just melting, you feel yourself *tingling* with vibrancy and a kind of inner, almost a . . . religious strength." She quickly, and brusquely, gestures toward the ceiling, and confides that the ears of corn may symbolize rustic peace and innocence partially masked by acquired sophistication.

"But why talk about *my* daubs?" she whoops, looking admiringly at a tiny Krabo "Crayola" collage that subtly dominates a corner of her writing desk. "I suppose you've really come to hear about WAX and the work that we've been doing. I'm really *insanely* proud of it all—the way we've *slaved* to bring into prominence all the marvelous artists who are not part of the established art world." At the word "established," Lesbia Glubit's almost harshly strong and aristocratically bulbous nose wrinkles, and she stubs out her cigarette almost viciously. "I'm—we're—so bored, so tired of the usual work-of-art theories about style and things like that propounded by foreigners and big-city types, people that are really totally unrepresentative of the true artistic impulse of this great, vibrant, strong, *alive* land that God gave to our ancestors. The President himself, for gosh sakes, just the other day, was telling me how much he admires, for instance, the Aunt Jemima pancake-mix box . . . what did he say? 'Makes us all proud of the America that once was, and, God willing, will be again.' Now, I don't know about anybody else, but I feel that that wonderful, *wonderful* man is a symbol of the hopes and dreams and yearnings of the American people—of their doubts, their inabilities, their ineptness, their human mistakes and greed and ignorance. I feel," and she looks out the window at the lonely sheep cropping steadily at the lawn, "that all these are mirrored in our President. Why not, then, their artistic tastes?" She leans back on the couch, exhausted, but her eyes are snapping and crackling with the unquenchable spirit that has made her legend. She does not call the visitor's attention to the framed photograph of the President that hangs above the couch, and that depicts a relaxed leader in a pair of shearling earmuffs, and, in his strong hand, the message: "To Hal and Lez and their wonderful sheep."

"WAX has begun, as you know, to turn its attention to the 'small' artist, the arts-craftsperson, the person in the small town or on the farm who makes rug hooks and model missiles, the isolated yet talented person who makes his own thongs and corks, the person who sews his name on his hat or shirt or somewhere. The *real* artists of America, beyond"—she sweeps her long and perfectly tapered, yet oddly gnarled and powerful fingers through the air—"the effeteness and downright *fruitiness* of Fifth Avenue and Hollywood Boulevard and their snobs." Suddenly, her athletically willowy body uncoils and she is off the couch that she has had, she has proudly made public, ever since her husband was a major in Headquarters Company of the Fighting Blue Star Devils during the police action in Korea, during which he was decorated for rescuing the company clipboard from a dayroom that was being repainted. (Hal, Lesbia noted in a recent interview, "doesn't like to talk much about it.") "Hal wanted me to buy something really marvelous for him to come home to," she blurts, when her visitor mentions the elegant couch, "and I don't think there's *anything* more *real* than crushed velour, do you? It has such a wonderful vitality and strength, such a sense of alive, vibrant power!" She is talking as she bounds across the room with all the agility of her close ballerina friend, Debbie Sucoff, in "Cafard," and skips back, beaming like a child. "Look," she glows, and the visitor stares in silent awe at what seems to be a miniature reproduction of the famed Golden Arches of McDonald's, made from hundreds, perhaps thousands, of french fries, each casually, perhaps even insouciantly, yet meticulously, painted a bright yellow.

"You see?" Mrs. Glubit breathes, smiling with the beguiling and girlish innocence that even her foes on Capitol Hill acknowledge literally explodes with an indefinable charm. "This is the work of the most remarkable artist I've encountered in years and years! An old retired sheep shearer from Dubuque or Terre Haute or some wonderful, *real* state like that where people are still knee-deep in the earth ... very, very few dark, foreign people in those great wildernesses, although," she quickly and graciously adds, "I've done many benefit things and auctions for Jew persons in Israel and places like that, Lebanon, Jordania, with Shucky Blitz and Jerry Duke. But do you *see*? Do you see the *space* in this piece? The mystery? The mystery of the *space* of all America? The vitality and strength and vibrant aliveness of America in this wonderful sculpt object?" It is, indeed, even to the visitor's untrained eye, wonderful, and she is as enthusiastic as she dares in the company of her brilliant critic-patron hostess. "Of course," Lesbia Glubit pipes, "of course you're right! It does have that aura of the strange, almost uncanny livingness of space! And this man—Bill Socks is his wonderfully curt American name—this man," and her voice drops almost to an awed whisper, "never has had an art lesson in his life, never has gone to a museum or a gallery, never has seen an art book or a post card or a reproduction of *anything*. Yet, you see how purely and powerfully he has captured the raw strength and throbbing vitality of this powerful image of the vast *space* of America?" She holds the sculpt object out so that the late afternoon sun glances off it with a kind of strange joy. "This uncanny artist has just been given a WAX grant to continue his work." Lesbia Glubit throws back her powerful, amazingly alive, chiseled face and her graceful neck trembles as she laughs delightedly. "I spoke to Mr. Socks on the phone last week to congratulate him and to ask him why he used french fries as his medium and he said—oh, this is so marvelously artistic—he said that he had run out of pickles! Isn't that wonderful? Isn't that so genuinely, so scrupulously representative of the true craft-sense? So utterly unaffected, so sweet, so *dumb*, like a Buddy Hackett or somebody talking about *their* artcrafts." She curls up on the couch and lights yet another cigarette, glancing now at the brilliant watercolor series done for her by Bart Kahane and inspired by the great French surrealist, Paul Valayne's, major novel, *Gallant Fates*. It comes as a shock to the visitor that Mrs. Glubit looks exactly like the lovely shepherdesses in the rough-hewn yet accessible Kahanian world. As if reading the visitor's mind, Mrs. Glubit turns and says, with a hard and precise urgency, "Bart has had *some* formal training, yes, but there is a great raw primitive strength there too, a marvelous quality of innocence, a supreme lack of knowledge about painting that gives his work a kind of—what shall I say?—*vibrancy*. An . . . aliveness, a gut power and vitality!"

Turning to the compelling Socks from the haunting Kahanes, with the briefest of stops to caress adoringly with her eyes the strangely vibrant "totem piece" by Etta Peeche that sits on her coffee table, Lesbia Glubit, her features almost violently intellectual in the sunlight, says, "It's the utter, the unabashed simplicity of the Socks thing that I love, the extraordinary, almost predictable *banality* of the piece, so much like a marriage of, say, one of the President's speeches, a union leader's demands, and a Warhol film—that incredible sense that one has that the creator doesn't really *know* anything at all! That he is all . . . reaction and greed and thrumming—is that a word?—*flesh*. Gosh, the vibrant power of it, the *thereness*-wise quality of it!" To break the rapt silence that has intruded suddenly, the visitor asks if she would care to comment on the dozens of art-works and craft-pieces that thrillingly, almost feverishly, clutter the Glubit home, this old munitions plant that Lesbia Glubit has redecorated, "with, I must admit, the loving and expert assistance of Bruce Prong of Bold Opinions, Inc., the eco-designers." She has completely changed the mood of the home as well as that of another building in back of the fallout shelter, a building, now a studio, that was once a barn, used by Mrs. Glubit for potting and weaving and knitting, and where, she maintains, she can almost hear the lowing of the cows that once inhabited the roomy space. "They almost—I know you'll think I'm silly—*talk* to me of what this earth once was, before the anachists and swarthy people started screaming about their rights."

"They're all on loan, of course," she assures her visitor, indicating the art that holds the warm old house in thrall, her voice slightly blurred with emotion. "But one begins, gosh, one begins to think of them all as old, old friends." Her deep womanly bosom, a constant reminder that she spent her early years picking cabbages in the windswept and locust-choked fields of southern Ohio, heaves, as she glances, soft-eyed, about the room. "Something like Jesus," she says, almost to herself. "Even Hal has grown to appreciate many of them, although his taste, before he met *me*," she barks appealingly, "ran to the garbage-dump neo-realist school—Vladimir Snatch, Leonard Brouillard, Garp Gardner—those people." Her face is a perfect, noncommittal mask as she carefully pronounces the famous names. "He had a very difficult time accepting and understanding the sur-abstract and proto-neo-surreal pieces, especially that series there on the sideboard,

the gesso-cellophane group of "turd structures" by Jigoku Zoshi. He said—
oh gosh, Hal is so real and unaffected—that they looked to him like a bunch of
s——." Her laugh is so sudden and piercing that the birds out on the lawn rise in
a frightened, twittering swarm. "He's come, however, to see that the commonest
images can be, in themselves, art, true art, an expression of total disgust and an
invitation to nausea, a cleansing nausea, a way of burning evil impurities away,
like we did when we dropped the A-bombs on the Japs."

The setting sun is throwing long spears of golden light on Moss Kuth's "Ero-
torug Number Three: Blind Ravish, With Heels," that develops its powerful
sexual motifs across every inch of the gigantic tapestry that hangs over the bar,
and that darkly dominates the space of the entire room. Lesbia Glubit moans
softly as she looks at it. "Now, that wall-object . . . Mouse—that's our pet name
for Mr. Kuth," she says mischievously, "told me at the opening of the Greater
Texas Art and Rodeo Fete last year in Killeen—and what incredible art-persons
are emerging from *that* area of the country!—that every one of the sado-eroto
images in that piece is reconstructed from his memory of all the pornographic
films he watched in all the motels he stayed in during his lecture tour through
the Sun Belt last year—when he was giving all those wonderful talks and semi-
nars as part of the Reverend Tyrell Bloat's Art Is God Crusade." Her visitor remembers and Mrs. Glubit is extraordinarily pleased.

Now she glances at her watch and stands up, apologetically explaining that
she has to get dinner ready for Hal, "and get into my Eva Perón apron . . . I think
that true camp has a real place in life, don't you? It's so . . . powerfully gay!" She
will be making, she confides, a variant of the classic Provençal dish, *coq au vin*,
substituting tuna for the chicken and "just dabbling around with different wines
and herb things." She adjusts the chic little apron around her trim figure and
laughs self-deprecatingly. "I was going to make lamb chops with cheese, but Hal
. . . well, his troubles with . . ." The visitor understands and walks slowly toward
the great, six-inch-thick steel door that the Glubits have preserved from the original plant, to "keep the nasty people away . . . I don't have to spell it out, I'm sure,"
Lesbia Glubit snaps heartily.

Her visitor shakes her hostess's enormous hands, hands that hold her for a
moment in a powerful and tingling grip. "Just tell them," she says, slowly, "that
it is our ultimate task to build, as John Wadsworth Whittier said in his magnificent 'Snowblind,' 'large audiences.' " The great door swings open noiselessly to
reveal the rolling emerald lawn adazzle in the golden light, and the visitor remarks on the sudden, breathtaking beauty of the bird-droppings on Mrs. Glubit's white Jaguar sedan—the unexpected loveliness of the free-form, greenish-
white smears against the pristine white of the vehicle. "Now," Lesbia Glubit
smiles, "*now* you've got the idea." And the great steel door crashes shut.

« 11 »

Blue Begins
Reading "La Musique
et les mauvaises herbes"

I SCHOOL AGAIN!

The broccoli garden of the University. It is the first day of class. The students are seated about tables. Marie Mamelle and André Lubrique are standing at the window. Mr. Aine, Professor of Music, enters into the broccoli garden.

MR. AINE: Hello, Miss! Hello, Mister! How do you go?

MARIE: Hello, Mr. the Professor! At the beginning of school we are always of the good humor.

MR. AINE: In effect. Who is the jolly young woman over there at the table in front of the window?

ANDRÉ: It is Sophie Jupon. That is a student of Gardening.

MR. AINE: Ah, Sophie. What a charm! And who is the boy?

ANDRÉ: It is Gaston Gaine, the brother of Monique.

MR. AINE: Oh yes. Monique Gaine is in the Class of Bassoon of Mrs. Chaud.

ANDRÉ: Sophie is very nice built, is she not?

MARIE: Yes, and she is always of good humor, even when rain falls in a large sheet upon her life. But let us go to class. It is the hour, is it not?

ANDRÉ: Yes, it is the hour. Good-by, Mr. Aine!

MR. AINE: Good-by, Mister! Good-by, Miss! Good-by, my dear Sophie! See you in a comics paper, switty!

II WHAT LESSON!

The students are in the classroom. It is almost nine hours. Robert Caleçons is at the window. He regards the young women who pass. Suzanne Jarretière is at the blackboard. She makes a giggle as she draws the idiot portrait of the professor. The bell tinkles. Mr. Aine enters into the classroom. He closes the door and says a good day to the students, which to him say a good day. He regards for a small moment the idiot portrait of him but seizes no notice of this. Then the professor speaks.

MR. AINE: It is nine hours. We are going to commence right away. Robert, count up the students of the class, if you please.

ROBERT: One student, two student, three student, four student, five student . . .

MR. AINE: Very good, mister! Continue, Suzanne, if you please.

SUZANNE: Six student, seven student, eight student . . . oh, Mister the Professor, I have a great ennui of this.

MR. AINE: All right, then. How many students are in the classroom?

SUZANNE: We are ten. Six boys and three young ladies.

MR. AINE: Good, Miss Jarretière! André, count the windowsill plants of the room, if you please.

ANDRÉ: One windowsill plants, two windowsill plants . . . five windowsill plants?

MR. AINE: Ha! Ha! Well, it is nearly that, but a miss is as good as walking for a mile, it is not so? Hm. Is it that you love much the music?

ANDRÉ: Yes, Mister Aine. I love much the music.

MR. AINE: You love not too much then the . . . gardening?

ANDRÉ: Yes, Mister Aine. I do not love *too* much the gardening.

MR. AINE (*enchanted*): Is it that the music is easy? Ha! Ha!

ANDRÉ: No, mister! The music is enough difficult!

MR. AINE: But you play well for a youth who regards without cessation always the young women who pass.

ANDRÉ: That is Jacques who regards them even more!

MR. AINE: Ah? Pardon me, if you please. Do you play the music at the house of you?

ANDRÉ: No, mister. We dig always the turnips at the house of me. But I play music with my comrades of the class.

The class continues thus until ten hours. The students make a number of the snores. The bell tinkles and the students quit the classroom in a large bustle. "Until tomorrow, misses and misters!" screams Mr. Aine. "And, Suzanne? Don't be a naughty young lady any more, or it might be that I will make the discipline on you!"

III THE OLD BOARDING HOUSE

It is ten hours of the evening. Charles Ordurien and Émile Fesses are in their chamber, at the old boarding house. Charles is seated at his desk of work and is preparing his lesson of the history of the accordion. His comrade of the chamber, Émile, is standing near to the window, his ocarina in the hand. Their neighbors, Robert and André, are at the cinema.

CHARLES: Émile, why are you not studying?

ÉMILE: I have not the inclination to study, my comrade. I have the blue. And you, my old man, you are not studying either?

CHARLES: No, I have the bad in the head. I love better to chat.

ÉMILE: But we have three lessons to prepare, is it not so?

CHARLES: Yes, if you count the exercise of tree surgery. And then, we have twenty pages to study of the history of the accordion and a composition to prepare for the carrot class.

ÉMILE: Oh truly, I have not the inclination to study today. Or tonight. À propos, where are our neighbors?

CHARLES: They are at the cinema. They don't work too much.

ÉMILE: In effect. When they are not at the cinema, they are playing at the bridge.

CHARLES: Yes. And also, sometimes under the bridge.

ÉMILE: Ha. Ha. In effect!

CHARLES: And you, you love better your ocarina than your studies, is it not so, my old man?

ÉMILE: Yes, *my* old man. I do not like of much my studies. They are of a type of work like the planting of the cabbage. Foh!

CHARLES: Play me, do, some thing. You play very good the jive.

ÉMILE: I do not demand more! Everything has made through hazard, and I have here my instrument. I love always to play of the ocarina and I love more to play the jive. I will play some tunes of the "Paul Whiteman."

Émile plays some hot bits. Then they prepare their tree surgery, their history of the accordion and their carrot lessons. They are working until eleven hours. Phew!

IV AT THE CONSERVATORY

Suzanne and André are nearly always an ensemble. André is not very serious; he blithers constantly and he loves always to play with the young ladies. At the end of the month he is always without a nickel. Suzanne, on the contrary, loves to work. She aids André to prepare his lessons and she often lends him two of the bits for to finish the month. She is not always of an accord with André but she likes him well. In the evening, Suzanne and André work often in ensemble at the conservatory.

ANDRÉ: Suzanne! I blither at you. You don't hear me?

SUZANNE: Yes, my dear. I hear your words.

ANDRÉ: Why you no respond to me then, my baby?

SUZANNE: I am not responding because I am finishing your paper on the autumn crocus.

ANDRÉ: Finish it quick and make me a "French" lesson, what?

SUZANNE: The lesson in "French" is not hard. Make it to yourself, my old man. Ha. Ha. Ha.

ANDRÉ: It is not possible. You are too much of an idiot! À propos, I am warm. Let's a little bit go out in the bushes?

SUZANNE: No, my old goat. Me, I am cold.

ANDRÉ: Oh well. Let us rest here then. Give me your skirt?

SUZANNE: Here it is. And now let me be tranquil.

ANDRÉ (*ravished*): Do not have a fear. I work *now*. This jolly item makes an aroma of the roses. Much good!

SUZANNE: It is not too much late that you work! But, take a guard of the old piano tuner down there. He is lancing us with furious regard.

ANDRÉ: He irritates me with the furious regard. Down the tuner! But is it that I irritate *you*, Suzanne, my chicken?

SUZANNE: Oh, be reasonable, my old shrub! You don't *irritate* me, but . . .

ANDRÉ: I don't irritate you, but I blither much, is it not so?

SUZANNE: Yes, it is that. But after all, I like you well, my old sugar beet. Though you are not to rend off my lingerie!

ANDRÉ: Pardon. I lost the control on oneself.

The discussions between André and Suzanne are finishing always like this. Sometimes, Suzanne makes André a "French" lesson. She is a good professor.

« 12 »
Blue's Grant
Proposal: Experimental Piano

My Dear and Esteemed and Honorary Congressman Glubit:
I am a young person of thirty years of age or so, *Gavotte, Serge* is my name; some call me Blue, as you will see if you think about it, this makes my pen name, Blue Serge. It is like a kind of a joke. Because I am deeply interested and in love with music of the expermentil type, and other types of music as well; so you will probably "get" the joke, BLUE SERGE, since Blue comes from the idea of a type of music, "the" Blues, of which, I have a feeling that you have heard, Honorable Representative Glubit, or "Hal" as they are want to dub you in the paper whenever you are in the news in a snapshot with your colleegs, or your charming and attractive wife; who, by the way, I am certainly praying and hoping is now over the unfortunate bout she had with cough-syrup addiction, and, has also set to rest the seemy scandal that dragged her name in the mud concerning some activities in a drive-in movie. I am so delighted that she has found Jesus and now cooks and sews while she listens to classical music in your wonderful home. It is wonderful that she has found Peace, as I saw in a paper the other day while at the campfire with my lovely and understanding spouse, Helene, and my strapping little fellow, Zimmerman, who we named after a folk-singer that you will soon guess, if I am any judger of men, of course I mean the famous Zimmerman Blanque, the young fellow who fell to his knees with Our President and prayed that God would strengthen the dollar; it is hard to imagine that he is the same rebbel who used to advocate drinking peyote and allowing Black people to attend the Yale Club.

You are probably saying, What in the heck is this young fellow speaking about by saying, around the campfire? And this gives me an oportunity to come directly to my point in terms of my passing remark about my life's great Passion, expermentil music, both playing it and the composition of the latter as well. For I am "on the road" so to speak. And why? I can imagine you asking quizically as you relax at poolside. Permit me, respected Representative Glubit, to pen a little of my History concerning my request for an Art for All Grant.

Ever since I was a small child I have been deeply moved by musical expression of all varieties. As a boy, my loving parent's gave me toy pianos and harmonicas and ocarinas, that the young boys at the time called sweet potatoes, but I don't know why. Anyway as you see, my whole life has been devoted to music. For a couple of years now I have owned a real piano, plus other instruments, to whit: juice (Jews' harp), harmonica, sweet potato (?) and such things. But my true love is, the piano!

I have suggested that I am "On the road." That is because a very wise, and wonderful doctor in New York City, the great metropolis where I reside and work as a lens grinder, told me because of some medical problems I was having with my oral interior cavity that I would always have these problems unless I satisfied my basic human needs. You can imagine how amazed I was when, the doctor told me I should set out on a search for the *perfect musical phraise*. That is why, I am "on the Road." I am traveling across the country with my lovely family in a pushcart I found outside the Port Authority Bus Station in Gotham town, and, my old and faithful piano. It is tough going especially, and you can picture this, up hills! And down is no bargain either, if you know what I mean. Also, I am not too well off in a financial sense.

It is a terrible thing to be a broke artist in this rich country, especially an artist like myself, who is seeking to expand and improve the Art of Music. That is why I am requesting this Grant from the Art for All Foundation. I will add to finalize this letter to you, my Proposal in the discipline of "Expermentil Piano" and what I plan to do in this field with any money that I might be so fortunate as to get.

I should tell you, before you start to peruse over my Grant Proposal, that, strange as it may seem, I have *never had a music lesson in my life!* Yes it is absolutely true. In the time that I have had possession of my wonderful old piano I have discovered for myself, practicing at least a half an hour a day whenever I could snatch a moment out of my busy life, how to play most of the wonderful old song from Porgie and Bessie, All the Things That You Were, and, some of that other old favorite, Green Old Dolphin. What is amazing about my learning so much of these two great Show-Stoppers is, that a friend of mine, who is, a very old friend that was in the Buddy Hackett J. H. S. orchestra, when we were boys growing up on the teaming streets of New York City, he told me one night after I had performed my repertoiry for some close acquaintants that my wife Helene had over for a seder which, as I do not think that you are a Jewish person you should know is a dinner that Jewish persons have on their special Religious holidays, although I am not a Religious person; I mean, that I am not one of those Jewish persons with black hats and beards and white socks and such, or like in Israel a Jewish person who looks like an Arab and rides a camel but, I am a normal American-looking Jewish person; and my wife, for instance, does not have her head shaved off although, my wife Helene has had some trouble with her hair that seems to be falling out sadly, without any assistance from her Religion whatsoever. It is just Nature's great way.

But to go on. This old friend of my youth from Buddy Hackett Junior High, after I had played my selections for the assembled guests of which, he was of course one, his name is Sheldon; he told me that it was amazing to him, since it seems that I had played these two old nostaljic pieces; actually about one and a quarter pieces since, as I have hinted I am still learning Green Old Dolphin; without, this was the amazing part, Sheldon said, playing any of the black keys! It was really very funny and exciting that he said that as you will see, and perhaps be surprised at my early artistic ignorance, because I had no idea that you could actually play anything on those little skinny black keys! I thought that they were a sort of a decoration to make the piano look nice. I was really excited by this because after thinking deeply about it and tossing and turning all night after the seder, I suddenly realized that I could learn thousands of more notes and cords; I mean that I saw that a person could play all that he can on the white keys and then sort of start another artistic career based on songs of the black keys. I understood all this just before the doctor mentioned told me about my needs.

I now end with my Proposal that is submitted with great respect.

GRANT PROPOSAL, EXPERMENTIL PIANO   *SERGE GAVOTTE*

1. Take my piano in an as-is condition as of now, or, as-is when the terms of the Grant begin, and walk along the top of it in a pair of sturdy hiking boots, and to enhance the visual impact of this sight, wearing a pair of bicycle clips from my collection, nice and firm around both ankles.

2. As I stroll back and forth on my piano, I will smack and bash the keys with a branch torn from a tree that happens nearby. This whole performance will be performed in the woods, or, in some meadow or glades or someplace like that.

3. As accompanyment to smacking and bashing the piano keys I will sing and hum pieces of tunes about Nature of a folk-song and hottenany type, such as, the Weemoweigh, Wabash Cannonball, K-K-K-Katy, Lost My Mojo on the Brazos; and such like renditions. This is in order to blend a.) expermentil music com-

posed by purely sheer chance. b.) the Heritage of our great national music. c.) the wonder and glory of Natural Ecology. d.) the symbolical image of the Artist as a wanderer in the forests of the middle-class bourjose.

4. To add the undisputable elements of the Artistic life that are extremely important, I will occasionally suggestively touch myself in the pelvic, groinal area; Showing how thus errotic feelings are changed to Artistic one's by the well known fact of subliming them all into other things.

5. My wife, Helene, will take films of this Performance and this film will be shown at expermentil film festivals all throughout the nation. This way the great Art form of the cinema will be welded to the Art form of Expermentil music.

6. I will perform this Musical Happening in different locations throughout the country as I wander about, depending on how much money I get.

7. All this will be done together with my relentless search for the perfect musical phraise.

I hope, my Esteemed and Honorable Representative "Hal" Glubit that, you will carefully consider my Proposal and that you might even consult with your delightful and attractive wife who is, I know deeply involved in the Washington Women for Artistic Expression organization; as I saw in the paper recently and also a few months ago as she was observing senile and blind mentally retarded Vietnamese refugees finger-painting coasters for the USO. A wonderful woman!

With respect, I remain, as always,

"Blue" Serge Gavotte

Speech by
Rep. Harold "Hal" Glubit

Good evening, ladies and gentlemen. I come into your snug and wonderful homes tonight in the fervent hope that you will let me say just a few words in order to prove that when the going gets tough, the tough get rough, as a great American, and great man, once said, I believe at a country fair, surrounded by pies and pickles and great bushels of wheat and chaff and other such proofs of American folk-wisdom, and at a time when great effort and sacrifice were demanded of him. Yes, Abraham Lincoln! The very name gives us pause.

As most of you know, I have, because of the irresponsibility of the reactive agents of the media, which seems to believe that causing disruption and heartache in the lives of innocent people is a sign of "freedom," I have, I repeat, been cruelly and unjustly charged with moral turpitude, that is, doing bad deeds. Further, I am also aware that most of you, my fellow Americans, brave in the face of tornadoes and droughts and financial sacrifices, are aware that I must answer these charges next week before a Congressional Ethics Committee, a group of my distinguished peers who have never been caught, ha, ha, as the warm old joke goes in the halls of Congress. Of course, I jest. I hasten to affirm that I welcome with open arms this wonderful, God-given opportunity to face my distinguished accusers and clear my name, attacked as it is by these baseless allegations.

My family, even now gathered around the homely hearth and the Christmas tree, has suffered enormous mental anguish and emotional strain, not to mention nervous stomach and general irritability, because of this time of tragedy and crisis in all our lives. I would *like* to spend the long and lazy days, that are the heritage of all Americans, napping under a tree in the countryside, or lolling by a peaceful stream with an old fishing pole, my thoughts far from the hurly-burly and hustle and bustle of public life, warmly and wonderingly smiling at the bees that hum and buzz amid the honeycombs. But I cannot! In the tradition of George Washington at Valley Forge, I will stick it out if it takes all summer! The life of an elected representative offers no easy victories or simple solutions. I have, as most of you know, been presented with cruel choices: I can ignore my detractors and inquisitioners and permit my good reputation to be ruined, or I can face them and stand beneath the pitiless glare of their questions and the harsh light of their innuendoes.

I have chosen the latter course, having come to my decision after long and serious discussion with my beloved and recently hospitalized wife, far into the small hours with the midnight oil burning—ever burning. This decision was based on hard realities, since *you*, my fellow Americans, with your sense of justice and fair play, the great heritage brought to these indomitable shores by the teeming Pilgrims, *you* know that there are no simple solutions when it comes to slander and gossip, no magic wand by which they may be waved away. The battle will be, I know, long and hard, but I pledge to you that my head, though bloody, shall remain unbowed. Yes, I welcome the fray as I welcomed it when I served alongside General "Milky" Kidwell as a proud officer in the Fighting Blue Star Devils, *humbly* welcome it as I so humbly and gratefully welcomed each one of my twelve Bronze Stars.

This evening, I want to take a moment to probe the quality of the ridiculous charges that have been brought against me, charges that not only fill me and all fair-minded citizens with justifiable indignation, but that cut me to the quick because of their unspoken intimation that I am not a friend of Nature, that oldest and most fundamental of concepts, as the American people know and believe, and as I too know and believe in my heart of hearts. Nature! As a boy in my small home town of Griteye, Kansas, I recall, as if it were only yesterday, slicing up frogs and worms in the high school biology lab, compelled by these urgent tasks to a sensitivity to human needs in human terms. Later, in college, where I first discovered my love for the arts, I restated my deepest convictions by making excellent grades in life sciences the bottom line of my education; and as a major in the "Devils," as we boys so fondly called our proud unit, I found that, basic to the very fabric of the military, was a deep and loving understanding of the woods and fields and rocks and mud of the great gift of the vast outdoors. One of the most powerful weapons in the great arsenal of democracy is the love of the common soldier, the frank and open-faced GI, the boy from your home town or great metropolis, or a home town or great metropolis much like your home town or great metropolis, a simple, softspoken boy, yet with the heart of a bull and the courage of a lion, the love of that boy, my dear friends, for the simple grass, the ear of wheat, the ant and bird and lowly toad! Basic research has shown that the value placed upon human life by the American fighting man, far from home, yet happy and accepted with doughnuts and Coke in the USO clubs that I, as you all know, have fought long and hard for, that value rests squarely upon the deep moral obligation that he feels, that boy, for the idea of Nature turning the corner into a happier, freer world, a world set free from the shackles of totalitarianism and anarchism by our nuclear arsenal! It is ingrained in his simple, yet great, fiber. It requires sacrifice, but what worthwhile thing does not? And yet, without further delay, we must never, *never* forget! And while the Almighty God shields our peaceful land from tyranny, *may* we never forget! In such a way, do they carry their share of the burdens of freedom, these pink-cheeked boys, and also those brown-cheeked boys who also serve, as Rudyard Kipling, in his wisdom, said so long, long ago. If his words have any meaning at all, my dear friends—do *we*?

Contrary to every principle of international law and even human decency, I have been accused of—in the exact words of my cowardly tormentors—"suspect activities with sheep." I have had to make many painful adjustments in my life because of these vicious slanders; I have been shouted down by disruptive bands of radical ecologists and vilified in the media in editorials and cartoons, some of which have done a great disservice to the American people, and prevented me, because of the mental anguish caused by them to me and to my recently crippled wife, from carrying out my duties in the difficult area of the arts, areas in which my expertise and hard-earned compassion as a conscientious legislator with years of experience on the Hill, is often taxed to the utmost of the bottom line of excellence, as most of you know, I'm sure. I may add that I look forward to making this defense, and to stand in the hard light of cruel choices, since I know in my heart, and feel compelled to repeat, that I have done nothing for which I need be ashamed, nothing for which I need reproach myself. I am only saddened that the time that all this has taken has acted to impede the development of honing in on the worldwide problem of education and the arts and other major priorities that I know the pain and disruption and heartache of, like famine and earthquakes and human rights for all the people of the world.

Even my enemies in the liberal media concede that I have been doing an excellent job and that my years in the Congress have seen a healthy growth in certain sectors of American life that have been particularly hard hit. But my availability is running out as I go through these difficult times, working patiently, as I have been, to resolve this crisis and meet these challenges. I have no reason to fear or to despair, even though there are no quick and easy answers, and certainly no magic wands to maintain self-discipline. "Suspect activities with sheep," they charge. Yet I answer that I have always acted responsibly and as a proud American and good Christian when near our gentle, woolly friends. Some of them, I concede, and will be the first to admit, are very pretty, and display, as a constructive response to the pitiless light of insistent inquiries, an extraordinary charm. I have, and it is no secret to those who have known me over the years, often found myself on the verge of petting and caressing them—as I did when on my last fact-finding trip to the heartland of my constituency on the solemn and yet bravely brooding plains. This I gladly admit with open hands that are basic to the fabric of the law. I maintain that it was a constructive response and that I shall always be prepared to initiate it as well as other and perhaps more demanding constructive responses when the issues warrant them. But this humble act of solemn homage was the bottom line of my investigations, and I submit to you, my friends, that I did not exceed my authority as a public servant in any way. At no time did a sheep farmer perform an act of extricating his presence from my presence, nor was I ever in a solitude mode with one or more of these sheep. Top authorities have stated in committee that petting and caressing sheep helps build a more productive America, and those who bear the burden of public office know that a happy and more productive nation cannot be abolished by decree, the decree of a few radical-minded tyrants of the media. Yes, I have had to make hard choices, even cruel choices; yet I know that I must fight for the right to tell the truth as I see it, the truth that stands forever courageously as the spot where the buck stops for all responsible leaders of this once-great, and soon-to-be-great-again nation, that has been moving forward ever since our hard-won victory over international communism and atheistic anarchy in Vietnam, ever since the day that we grasped to our bosoms that shining light at the end of the long tunnel of war and sacrifice!

Bogged down in bickering and delay, a panel of eminent medical authorities has not been able to achieve consensus as to the condition of certain of these sheep, either at the present point in time, or at a past point in time, that is, the day after I returned to my office in Washington to assume my duties to provide some relief and take all available steps in this difficult transition period that we are now entering. And this delay *in spite of* the fact that the entire nation feels a sense of urgency about these painful adjustments and the cold statistics. This panel, drowning in bureaucratic red tape, seems united and determined in one thing—*not* to exonerate me, despite the overwhelming evidence that those few sheep are in excellent condition, and far from showing any signs of having been the innocent victims of "activities." I feel certain that the traditional sense of fair play that exists among the American people will compel the Ethics Committee to awaken to their solemn responsibility, a responsibility, I am compelled to reiterate, that I too know the awe and unpopular heartache of. It is far beyond the time for mere empty gestures, especially in this era of the worldwide skyrocketing of a sensitivity to human needs, and an almost desperate sense of urgency that cries out to be heard! It is certainly not the time for narrow partisan politics, but a time when all the members of both great parties should rally to bind up old wounds.

Added to these fundamental causes in every area of challenge, most of you have been made aware, in the last few days, of a further slanderous attack upon my reputation and my devotion to integrity. The moguls of the media, the nabobs of negativism, the sultans of suspicion, have seen to it that I have been accused, tried, and convicted in the media of another charge of which I am wholly blameless. I have received information and I have received irreproachable signals that these unspeakable allegations have been designed to bring about the cancellation of my announced plans to run for another term in the House. But, my friends, I shall not cancel my plans! No! Now that we are about to turn the corner and leave the long and sad road of broken promises, the people will, I know, rise as one glorious body that will not be stayed. These additional smears, the cowardice of which I shall address in a moment, must be stopped in their tracks! I have never been one to refuse to face cold facts and despite cruel choices, to set tough measures.

These slanders, as you know from the stories that are spilling over in the media, are centered in the false allegations, and how I welcome them so that I may show them up for what they are, of a Miss Martha Clifford. This unfortunately disturbed young woman, of whom I seem to have but a vague memory as one of my many campaign workers, claims, in her sad delusion, that I wrote her certain letters signed with the ridiculous name "Henry Flower." She further claims, and how my heart fills with compassion for her troubled, even retarded state, that these letters are immorally suggestive in nature, and that they include quotations from the outspoken poetry-writing of the poetess Lorna Flambeaux, with whose works I am totally unfamiliar. I have decided to defer comment on these preposterous allegations, except to say that Miss Clifford, who is not prepared at this time to enter into serious discussions concerning these fantastic charges, is an unwitting dupe of greater and more sinister forces. I am willing, I indeed feel a deep moral obligation, setting aside for the moment the cruel burdens of office, to meet with her in a calm and rational manner, in human terms, and with our attorneys present. I feel that no man in public life should be immune from the cold clear light and raw statistics of minute examination. But should a private citizen, a deeply and pathetically confused young woman, who, at this sad rate, will in the near future be the number-one enemy of sensitivity to human needs and dignity, *also* be immune? I don't think that justice permits such flagrant lack of sacrifice.

Miss Clifford has suggested, on a network-television news program, that I, as this fantastic fabrication "Henry Flower," mention, in her words, "weird things with soap"; that the letters speak of "adventures in the bushes"; that they quote "at great length" from Miss Flambeaux's "really raw and obscene" poetry-writing works. These saddening hallucinations are transparently designed to impose upon me the role of the hapless defendant, shackled by the heavy burdens of office and the role that I play in the legislative processes of this great nation. This emotionally crippled young woman, whose very name awakens only the vaguest spark of recollection, clearly feels no twinge of justice and fair play and no deep moral obligation to the universal reality of standards. She surely must know that this pathetic invention of hers will be picked to pieces in the cold and cruel beams of inquiry and shown to be a way of reaching her great goal of short-term fame. That is why she has refused to release to a clamoring media anything but so-called photostatic copies of these so-called letters. Letters that I—taking precious moments from the cruel choices and moral burdens of my sense of urgency and the duty of my responsibilities—supposedly wrote to her. How sadly absurd! Her act, though the act of an emotionally unstable fellow human being desperately in need of expert psychiatric help, must be viewed much the same as an act of international terrorism. And so I am prepared to invoke the principle of self-defense because of this assault upon certain sectors of my character. That is, I charge Miss Clifford with vile self-promotion! Yes, my friends, this charge is basic to the fabric of a free society, a nation about to enter on the road to a moving-forward process into a world that guarantees a fair share to all its citizens. Yes, even the most humble! I charge her with, I am compelled to repeat, self-promotion and the publicizing of her name and person, at *my* expense, a process entered upon in order to accelerate her fame, a fame that is still in the pipeline but that has not yet been reflected in the notoriety that, I charge, she fervently desires to be showered upon her by the public that has always been available to take all necessary steps toward a winner.

I should and I will now proceed with other verbal-type measures in order to make clear certain proofs to resolve this crisis. At the exact same point in time at which this pathetically misguided young woman was taking steps to attack my name and sacred trust, she was appearing in the current issue of a degraded publication that panders to the basest and lowest sector and area of human nature. I refer to the monthly magazine, *Hump!*, in which Miss Clifford, Miss Martha Clifford, called, in these pages that insult and debase the American woman, Mariette Cliffe, appears in a four-page color-picture story as this disgusting magazine's "Miss Garter Belt of the Month." How sickeningly vile! Are not this young woman's charges against me startlingly transparent? Isn't it clear to all thoughtful and morally straight Americans, poised as they are on the verge and the sheer brink of hard questions and profound moral choices, that Miss Clifford saw her chance to capitalize on the upcoming Ethics Committee hearings by further blackening my reputation by a manipulation of factually false data? And all for the sake of short-term fame!

As I have suggested, and repeat in the strongest possible terms, I welcome these allegations. They will enable me to protect the quality of my moral burden and my hard and cruel choices; that is my solemn responsibility, and I shall not shirk it. They will permit me to embrace anew the integrity of often restated convictions. They will, and are, even now, compelling me by the effort and sacrifice they demand, to the sense of the universal reality of painful adjustments. Effort and sacrifice! Terms, my friends, that cannot be vanquished! Terms that must have passed through the somber thoughts of Douglas MacArthur, that saint of the battlefield, when he first heard the dark news that a few of his troops on the Yalu River were being forced to retreat a little . . . yet he persevered in his effort! And his sacrifice! Effort and sacrifice! And even more importantly, rather than abolishing these panic-stricken slanders, these neurotically self-seeking slanders, by decree, I am now more determined than ever to place no trust in magic wands in the most fundamental defense of my solemn and deeply understood moral, yet *human*, obligations to the simplest and deepest terms of my vows of office.

In conclusion, dear friends from the blizzards of Maine and the swamps of Florida, to the mud of the Midwest and the smog of California, all of you, let me say that there have been, there are, and there will be no broken promises softening the harsh burdens of my sacred trust. This I vow to you! A more productive and decent America expects no less, and deserves much more. We are standing at the crossroads of a strong and progressive destiny, and as we take the path into a common humanity of a world of prosperity and stern moral imperatives, we may say, as did Franklin Pierce so many years ago: "Most fundamental! Most wonderful! The extraordinary array of deep moral pain and joyous unbearable burdens that we choose to embrace with a glance toward our harsh but blessèd duty. We are on the verge!"

I thank you all, and may God bless you. Good night.

« 14 »

Puissance Art
Disdayneth (A Dramatic Eclogue)

SCENE: The leaf-strewn and tyrooned esplanade, alleyed in the zangent sun, the odor of cherry blossoms affonted all in the air, and borne by wifts, just after the planging, toporite speech by REP. GLUBIT. In the far vast, the slow blurm of anxious winbows, slarm, yet hoark as blumbering tomatoes in the slow ballooming of September.

Enter BLUE, HELENE, REP. GLUBIT, and his aide, LUNK.

BLUE: A-say! A-say, powerdong and efficacious Leader! Oh, as the common lilac brents in hanged aslaver, enfundus of the wapping sun, so do I gronch and toad beneath the glasp of your so blastred wankèd eye, a loosome maggot nannyberry, poosant Dux, my muskled Congressman! I base, I base, and cronk the knee in volitude.

GLUBIT: Zounds! Ofeely burk this jesting lamster who doth quilp and quark my chesterfield? Ha! I do not reck his garf nor yet his nausee ambro, swink as bristly sarsaparilla, and blue as dido cucumber. Lunk, to it, blankèd ordinary!

LUNK: Har! Har! I'll cratch and smither all his scotch-broom blancophiz! Away, you snowbell scurd! Clear fast!

BLUE: Oh, por favor in your voozing play, most formidous and towered devil's-club! I call myself "Blue" Serge Gavotte, the creepy thing what penned and zipped to you, a-gulping clefstone of a mens, a sweetie billet, whingeing for some crankly lettuce to expround my teeny art.

LUNK: Scumball staggerbush! Begone! (He makes to cratch Blue's blancophiz.)

HELENE: Squeek! Squeek! Was it for such horrendo that I scramped up coppers for to save the whales and porpoisins? Carried testamentoes wheedling libertad for folk who dug on mooning, sackrinn Jesu? Oh woesome plote! For this I delved with nit-sprown hippies to seed the krishna's lucred acres with wholesome whin and pondspice?

BLUE: My tweet-voiced hammock-mate!

LUNK: Greeling twat! I'll scunge your osseous corse as well to boot, and pound you in the soured mulch as cully as a cissus—or a venomed hoptree! (Threatens HELENE with his larrup.)

BLUE: Don't lonk her nates, I wheengle you! (Aside:) O sobrous time!

GLUBIT: Hold, Lunk, my coeurish ancient! You have infinous time to brench this pair o' floots who shake like sweetgales in the vaxed and woorèd hurrinado. Let me but rap and parlant with 'em for a nonce, as fits a rexy integer like me am.

LUNK (groaning): It shall stook as your empyrean-ness wishes. (To BLUE and HELENE:) Scrullish blobs of grossed pipsissewa!

GLUBIT (to BLUE): Blatted carl, you enounce a billet penned and zipped abaft some lettuce?

BLUE: You convose all dexter, high-life Representative, I ween a lot.

GLUBIT: And this was shekels to emproud a art?

BLUE: Again, you've whomped the brassy tacks, my Chef.

GLUBIT: And, dumbo farkleberry, what art do you enclip?

BLUE: Weird experimenting cum a zonced piano, Eminous.

GLUBIT: Aha! A choose that shows your moronicity all candored as the woolly pipe-vine on the cat-house wall. And yet, although my earish organs are slapped together of a tinnish stuff, that svelty chunk, my spouse, the cosmetickal and aromatikous Lesbia, a spicebush meleed with a supplejack, yaks on mightily anent the faggish art.

BLUE: I raunch and scar all sanguinary these my knee-bones in dumbstruck adoramation of your swanky hump-mate.

LUNK: Up! Up! You bolus of a spittled, stinksome leatherwood!

GLUBIT: Soft, Lunk. Let the lumpen speck to drool and quinge. It sends feral zingoes all up and down my spine-cord. (To BLUE:) I hold a bedlamitic notion to embrave your bolsa with the moolah you empant for.

BLUE: O potentous Dooch!

HELENE: May granolas and vimmy herbs plonk and platch upon you!

GLUBIT: Conserve your toading drecky lingua, what hath as small spot here as doth a titi on a ice-rink! For you must blurt and burble to my harshoed satisfaction the answer to a quiz and all with narrow-perfect punctilissimo, youse toords!

LUNK (threateningly): And if you fok up, or even frigg the veraciousness of your replize—Ahar! I'd amour nothing morest than to blash and crinch you into talc, you wormy chinquapins!

BLUE (cringling): But foost away, O masted Imperato, and I'll scrample up my cerebellata for the reponders oll korreck.

HELENE (a-pinkie): As will I, Your Furor.

GLUBIT: Then, my dulloed tamarisk and ake my willied cinquefoil, a-futter me but this: Foist, did your nobilitous and glittray Congressman—thass me—beyant the urbish clammer, and amid the toothleaf dryas, tulip trees, sourwood, and drapping bladdernuts, in veracity improng some stupo sheeps? And, segundo, did this identico polysageous Rep—again, I mean moymem—sloom cartas troo the post, cartas chokked with erotickal and pornamorous sluck, to one Miz Martha Clifford, a tittied, beamish princesstree, if ever one was vued?

LUNK (stronking his leadish bully): Parlee right, my grimbling yellowroots, or Lunk'll bansch you into mucksh!

COP (entering hoddily): Whut dis? Do I bespoy me eedolato, Humpy Hal? My chappoo is dopped to yer, My Gosh! But whom be dem scumbrous wankos dere? Dey besprake a tandemite of heebie hipperoonies.

LUNK: A brace of anti-kristarchites, goddish copper. A since Sir Glubit sprecken, they been beggaring, the wumps!

COP: Beggaring the sageous Hal? I'll jungeon dem belike two dangèd fetterbushes! (He crimples BLUE and HELENE with bangling steely changs.)

GLUBIT: My fundo thankees, zealot coppo. Yet holt a jott, for I am plingling for these nadired chinaberries to give reck and replondito. Tawk, caytiffous muttballs!

LUNK (swatching BLUE and prinking HELENE): Hablo, lespedezas!

COP: Scurfled hip-heads! Kikey fongs! (He twists the bangling changs.)

BLUE (bubbering): Though deeped in basèd awedor of you, my Czarish Sconce, I am poshed to spik the truth. I assump that you, indade, beneath the nopping bilberry, did enhump a couple sheeps; and, two, that boining smuts, by you inscribed, were zapped to Martha, the clitorical Miz Clifford.

GLUBIT: Fowlish scrud!

HELENE (a-blench): I do bleeve so also, Crood Potentor.

GLUBIT: Chunkassed nannypoop!

LUNK: Har! Har! Hoor! I'll bronk your crockles unto morte!

COP: Though me tudding heart embangles wit you, Lunk, morte is eighty-six! Is not too koolish, dig?

GLUBIT: Unlease them! Vaunt! Abaft and wongo! I can ill a-clasp another scandalment.

LUNK: But, Ominence . . .

GLUBIT: Avaunt, I say! Unlease, bullicious fuzz!

COP: Oy kin slup 'em in the slamgow, Roaring Rajah.

GLUBIT: Nopo. I wish the shitefaced duo domped like drooped cassiopes beforch the District Line. Out! Out! My stomach gorgeons.

LUNK (thunking their arsesfat): What fortunatic bomble-crapps you are. *My* wish is to enflagellate you both unto the oozy bloshes of your quicks.

COP (herding BLUE and HELENE off): Pee-peed snottochunks! Git!

BLUE: Awow, awoe. Thus great art is oft enfathomed.

HELENE: Screek, scrake. So arty martyrs grow like groundsel-trees.

Blackout

« 15 »

In Which
Blue Discovers Marys-
londe and Is Given Advice

The which Serge Gavotte, being before mentioned, and having departed the glistring Capitol, is here set forth more largely, complayning him of his great misadventure in his Quest, whereby his mynd was alienate and withdrawen not onely from Helene and Zim, who moste loved him, but also from all former delightes and studies, as well in pleasaunt pianno-poundynge, as singing, catterwauling, and other his laudable exercises. Like April shour, so streme the trikling teares adowne his cheeke. Forswonck and forswatt below the broade beames of *Phoebus* golden hedde, the sayd Serge, plongd in payn, his tressed lockes ytorne, creepes beneath the pushcarte. The soote shade there somewhat cooles his madding mynd. There hobbles up the road a rustick shephearde all mottlie tatters, and of idiotick phiz, and thorough his oaten reede he blowes his wonted songe:

Tell me good pilgrim, what garres thee greete? What? Huh? Hath some badd wolfe thy tendre lambes ytorne and scoffed? Or is thy bagpipe broke? Thine oaten reede? Thy sweete potatoe or thy hellish concertina? Thine eyen, lyke jesting Aprille, quench the gasping furrows thirst with rayne! Or so to speke. Thy cheke appears a swymmyng-hole or else a catarack of splashes made of many catts and dogs, a curious quibble that, all trimly dight with rustickal insanitie. So, pouring traveler, the while I plange and bimp upon this reedy tooter given man by Romish *Tityrus*, pry ope thy rosie coarsened lipps and yawp thy loud lament.

What doeth make me mourne, moronickal churl, is that my holie Quest for the perfect phrase of musick is brasted up before it fayre commences. I whom sullein care does afflict my brayne, did leave the city of vain idle hopes, departing but a fourteen-night ago, or as thy dimly spluttering toong might blurte, but half a moon apace. The crampe my joynts benomb with ache from humpyng all these fardels in the pushcarte here which serves now as a cubb that does delay hott *Titans* beames, and humpyng too the swollen instrument the swarthy Moor yclepeth a pianno.

A pianno! By *Syrinx* daughter without spott whom whilome lickerous *Pan* did cover in a fielde of Cowslips so that the redde rose of her cheke depeincten cremosin, such the powre of his thrustyng arse, I never yette did heere a gigantickal accordyon yclepped and nombred swich a thing. A pianno! How do you clip it to thy breste to tear from out its gutts the frightfull noyse sike unpleasaunt thing has dwelling in its bowels?

Siker old turde, thy mynde is decked with trash and swacked with fond mongolity! You are yblent and wood as *Ajax* bashyng in the milk-white lambes in windie Troye. A pianno is a boxx unto itself and on its ivorie keyes I mene to plink a sunshyny phrase all perfect as the musick from a besotted paddy's jank. But whither fynd? O woe is me! The road has raft me of my merriment!

Ivorie keyes? Beyant the ground all strowed with Daffadowndillies, Cowslips, King-cups, the prettie Pawnce, the Torticollis and the wall-eyed Variola, there cowres a towne hight Marys-londe, of lustie shepheardes and their mangowe-brested doxies, wherein the pipe the tabor and the tymbrels do be blaste and smited from rosie *Iris* time till *Selenes* silver rayes turn all to moon men. Your whingeing pilgrim tells of leas and meddowes not of corn or rye but of a weede that drops all lewdly in the mudde its seedes of fayrest ivorie. In swich a londe the rude and raunchy folke sicker know of musick, golden daughter of *Apollo* and a knott-hole all ablush within the shady bosk, certes?

God forke the lightening on your honest sconce, encrusted buddie! I jump up lyk a tygre or a bere whom fiers bees stynge to wildish vex! My pushcarte, my pianno and my good wyf and son who sleping lye below this mound of crappe I clep my gere, will renneth to this ivorie londe, and quick as black men in queint canvass shoos. And to you, pyping rubeish imbecile, much thanks and thondrous graciados!

Then as the sunnye beame glaunceth from *Phoebus* face in swich manere as the thonder cleaves the clouds, so that its christall rayes emboppe the seely Serge upon his jollie sconce and his poor braynes gin to boyle lyke mutton gloppes all medled up with greese in a huswyfes pott, this Serge gins to renneth adoune the road untill the londe of Ivorie and thumppynge songe. Then loe, perdie, and well-awaye, among the wyld vine and the ivie there he spyes, lyke a lambe ysquawk-king in the wolves jaws, the walled towne yclept Marys-londe. He flyes as if on fluttryng wing and stretcheth hymself at large from East to West, doune hill and up dale, into bogg and brambel yplonges, the blazyng pushcarte and swoln pianno, and eke fayre Helene and snottie Zimmerman, gastfull of their lyves as they spede thorough the Holly-hokkes and Days-eyes in a chokyng clowd of dust and corses of insectes foul and lothsome. Anon they passe into the towne to car-rols lowde and Serge lookes round, his woe lyk smoke that sheddeth in the skye. Soon spying out a neatsherds boye, a lustie carle whose phiz was lyk unto a crynched potatoe, Serge rove these jollie words unto his colieflorie ear.

O pierless boye, I ken the nombres here do flow as fast as springe doth ryse: and so my brayne gins swette and glister lyke bright *Argus* blazing eyen. I see thine honest folke do lead the Millers rownde, the rustick galliard, the corantoe brave, and eke the goodlie turkies trotte, while with voyces loude as *Stentors* they doe sing and set forth delectable controversie so that all the woods them answer and their eccho ringe. Men clepen me Blewe Serge, and no man can my musick match, the which I tare forth from this dapper box, the queint pianno, a-bash-tynge of its ivorie keyes as thick as spottes in the proud Peacoks broomish trayne. Yet have I basht erst so long with payn, that all mine fingres do ben rent and wore, I hardlie oke hold up my heavy head, and I am all forlorne. For, jollie stew-faced frenne, I seke the very parfit phrase of musick, yes, a phrase to pitch great *Jove* upon his potent hammes! Now list: Upon the road that leads thorough mucke and noysome schmattes but lesse than a howre since, I did bonke into a drum-blyng imbecilick knave who, all decked in spittle and a gowne of falding grey and gruesome, told me that here in clamrous Marys-londe thy resounding folke my cornie feet might sett upon the path to *Olympian* felicitie and stopp these stremes of tricklinge teares that endorp my once brighte and twingling visage. For this old caytiff puttanato, though slackt the tenor of his stryng, into the porches of mine ear did pour a tale of fantastickal matter, ytouching on a mightie weede that droppeth seeds of pryceless ivorie. Soon as I gynst cipher two plus two I lifted up myselfe out of the lowlie duste: your celestiall musick and sweete ivorie seeds, the brothers of the keyes on my pianno, augment the thought that here in banjaxed Marys-londe, a weird folke dwelleth whose thought is all of carolling and dauncing and of whanging oaten redes and pipes and swich untill they brast. Where better place to find the parfit phrase I wayle for all the dayes till blakke nyght cleaves my helmlesse and nitt-packed sconce? Reward me then my pokky starker, do.

Har har, hoo hoo, and well-away! Thou art a babe as simple as a cackarooch. Tom Piper, for swich be the name of that patch-arse flieblowne turd upon the filthie path, has his braynes yrooted in his fondament. And thou, Master Blewe, where is then thine ear? It muste be fashioned out of tynne. This fowle, rumbaging, rownch, horraude, and clanching noyse is no thing lyke musick, but the tempestuous shriechs and clatter of sencelesse wormes. A parfit phrayse? Ho ho! And ivorie seeds? Hok hok! Heere groweth Rose and Bryer, false Labia, Juniper, poxy Kinesia, Eglantyne, Firbloome, the purple Aphasia, Cypresse, bastard Moly, the stynkynge Ailanthus, and the cock-leaf Ginkgo. But we have nor ivorie seedes nor weeds to droppe them, bumblynge clodd.

By *Christes* blood and His precious bones, I mourn, lament, and holler ruthfull to the louring skie! O woe! O lackaday! O balls and shite and onyons! The shitte of bulls and ybroken glasse!

Soft you my plaintive clowne. Sette your shoos that wexen dayly browne with crudde once more upon the road that ledeth to the place where *Phoebus* cooles his fyrye face ech night. For on that dooleful road towers the Universitie. There, certes, schollars yslonking thorough their bokes will halte their pedantrie and raunch thy woe from out thy pitteous brayne.

Then faire well honest lumppe, I gin to schleppe towardes brighte *Phoebus* tubb or sinke! The nyght nigheth fast, yts time to be gone.

Blewes Embleme.

Vinto non vitto.

GLOSSE

Plange) play an oaten reed off keye.

Bimp) spitte moste foule into an oaten reed.

Nombred) naymed foolishlie.

Swacked) fylled to brasting.

Mongolity) fiers stupiditie.

Plink) play, as a pianno, in ignorance of the blakke keyes.

Jank) emptie Guinness bottel in wiche Irish-men whose temples are distayned with wine do blowe.

Graciados) according to Chingado. Graciados por las señoritas tronadoras.

Emboppe) smashe wyth foul disdein.

Gloppes) chonkes of meat spoyled with barbarous magotts.

Crynched) fryed untill a blakke cole.

A-bashtynge) thumpynge with fistes and elbowes.

Oke) yea, indede, yopp.

Schmattes) glewie claye and not, as some fondly guesse, a shaypless gowne.

Bonke) bumpp into, encountre.

Endorp) make uglie as synne.

Twingling) such pretie word denoteth both twinkling as the sterres and
twangling as soote carrolls.

Puttanato) a baud, pandar, whore-mongre.

Banjaxed) astonied intoe jollie imbecilitie.

Starker) a knave be-lyke the slobbring ape.

Rumbaging, Rownch, Horraudde, Clanching) descrybing clamorous dinne as
of divils and deemons in Hell.

Crudde) mixture of dung, mud, claie, pyss, mucke, myre, swylle, and namelesse
fylthie elements.

Yslonking) poring, reading, scanning withouten joie or pleasauntrie.

Schleppe) hurle the bodie forward though slayn by blynde ennui.

Embleme.

The meaning hereof is darke: for Blewe by his pressynge forward to the West is
certes not subdued and so sayth the embleme. But he is vanquisht with ruthfull
dismay at the wordes of the stew-faced frenne in Marys-londe. The ambiguitie
ariseth from this, that a man who is vanquisht must needes be subdued, as has
always beene rehersed. Yet Blewe confoundeth thys understanding by his actions.

« 16 »

The Gavottes
Read a Country
Drama to Lift Their Spirits

Supper at the Kind Brown Mill by Joanne Bungalow

MOTHER: Well, Rita.
RITA: Well, good Mama, how you been?
MOTHER: I'm hearty, lass, but warm; the weather's warm;
         I think 'tis mostly warm on Bingo days.
         I met with Butch behind the shed: said he,
         "Mama, go in and cool your fiery heels."
RITA: Yes, do;
         And stay to supper; put your briefcase down.
MOTHER: How come, you painted punk? It's purest calf!
RITA: Cockeye, boy, get up and kiss sweet granny.
         Leather! Ha! But hold! Who cares?
         Some call good churning luck; but, luck or skill,
         Your butter mostly comes as cold and golden
         As if 'twere Christmas! I speak all arsewise, see?
MOTHER: Oho! All but this oozing slab that I
         Put here for Butch, the cunning morphodite;
         He always loved my butter.
RITA: That he did, God bless the hearty imbecile.
MOTHER: Has your speckled hen laid any eggs today?
RITA: Not yet; but that fat duck that I told you of,
         She hatched eleven out of twelve but yesterweek, bedad.
MOTHER: I mean to say, has she brought off her brood?
         I speak still of the old and crippled hen.
RITA: But I speak of the fat and faithful duck,
         Old crone.

COCKEYE: And Gammer, they're so tarnation yellow!

MOTHER: Aye, my lad; yellow as this butter here,
Or as the gold that Gammer cleps her teeth;
Or as my sweetie Cockeye's nit-packed hair.

COCKEYE: They're my ducks, Gammer; Daddums says so, reck?

MOTHER: You selfish little pig!

RITA: Yes, Gammer, he is a little pig; why,
Butchie means to sell the duckies when they're fat,
And put the money in this mattress here;
And all to send his little Cockeye off to school;
So Cockeye would not touch the duckies, no,
Not he. He knows that Daddums would be angry else,
And bust his arse.

COCKEYE: But, oh, I want to play with one; I want
A little yellow ducky-wuck to take to bed!

MOTHER: A chill of fear bedims me that this Cockeye
Here is like unto his pa; a morphodite!

RITA: I beg you close your mush, old wizened dam,
And hold sweet Cockeye while I take him off to bed. (*Exit.*)

MOTHER: Hold sweet Cockeye while she takes him off to bed?
It's plain as cowflop that poor Rita's mad!

Enter RITA

RITA: I must be going bonkers, ha, ha, ha.
I think I asked you to grab holt of Cockeye
There, while I would take him off to bed.
Imagine my amaze and my red face,
Aye, red and warm as Bingo days, when I
Saw I held within my stringy arms
Nowt but a pile of air! Oh, ha, ha, ha.

MOTHER: I kenned that you were acting mighty weird.

Exit RITA *with* COCKEYE
Enter BUTCH

BUTCH: Well, Mummy, 'tis a fortnight now, or more,
Since I set eyes on you; by God above,
And sure as it's October with its rotting gourds,
I do believe, and so, I must insist,
It's more like eighteen days!

MOTHER: Aye, Butch, my dear; but
           I reck that you been busy: so have we.
BUTCH: We? Oh, you do speak of father.
           I'm all agog and plumb wore out
           With fattening my tiny ducks. How does
           The good and inarticulate old man?
MOTHER: The geezer creaks about and does his work;
           But he grows stiff, a little stiff, my queen,
           Aye, in all those joints save the big one I love.
           Well-a-day! He's not so young, you know,
           By twenty year as I am; no, not twenty year;
           And I'm past sixty 'spite this ton of rouge.
BUTCH: Great Jesu's bones! That means he's, holy cow!
           Past eighty! No wonder I'm a morphodite!
           Still, he's hale and stout belike unto Cortez
           Silent in his pique in old Connecticut;
           And seems, the knave, to take some pleasure
           In his pipe; and seems to take some pleasure
           In his cows; and lambs, and gooses, and his
           Faithful duck. Aye, and a pride therein as well.
MOTHER: And well he may, bemuscled twisted boy.
BUTCH: Give me the little one; he's giving you
           A charley-horse, the kicking, wakeful rogue;
           He drives us batty with his loathsome squawls
           Just at daybreak when blushing Reet and I
           Are trying to tear off a quiet piece.
           What? You little oaf! Would you make a fist
           In da-da's curls? A filthy father, certes,
           And you as clean as spick; but ho! you haven't spent
           The blazing noon a-crawling after ducks!
           Aha, you laugh, you toothless putz?
           But if you live but seven year or so,
           These mitts of yours will be all grimy too,
           Aye; covered with a layer of crud and poo-poo
           From scrabbling 'round in swamps and rat-holes
           As are on the mere; whatever that may be;
           And you'll love mud, all manner of mud and dirt,
           As your father did afore you; and his father too,
           Aye, the same old duffer who's now all stiff

In every joint but one, if Gammer speaks the truth.
Yes, tot, you'll wade after young crows and stuff,
And spoil your clothes, and come home cold and torn
And wet; then, you know, you'll feel the cane;
Aye, I'll bash you in your arse, my lad!

Enter RITA

RITA: Don't spew such bombast to the blessèd babe!
How can you, Butch? Why, he may be in Heaven
Before the time it takes to tell of it;
I mean, I reck, the time you tell of here;
To him and Gammer sitting on the hob.

MOTHER: Look at the tyke. So earnest, such wild eyes,
Though crossed, just like his idiotic brother's;
He thrives, my dear.

RITA: That he does, thank Jesu on his Rood.
My children all are strong.

MOTHER: 'Tis good to know and well I wot of it!
But what mean you when you do utter "all"
Your children? I reck but three unless my eyes
Are blind with gummy rheum and crazed as is my brain.

RITA: 'Tis neither business it of yours; or Butch's.

MOTHER: Ah, well. Sick children fret their mother's hearts
To shreds and tatters and to orts and sherds;
And do no thing to help around the house;
A plague of buzzing, stinging bees on them!
But how now? Where's your little lass? I know
That you and Butch do keep her here, though well wot I
The blooming harlot bears no monicker;
Tell me I err; and faith, blow up the blaze.

RITA: Your daughter, my dear sister in the law,
And Butch's sis; she from whom he borrows
Frocks and high heels on St. Crispin's Day,
Came and begged her of us for a month or twain.

MOTHER: Well, well, she might be 'cuter than the rest
Of us, aye, that she might, the painted tart;
For she sits on her fat arse all the day;
Yet pays her way. A sober husband, too:
A stupid man; yet honest as ever fell

Into the sump, and withal fond of her.
But lack-a-day! She is missing summat
In the way of brats; aye, she recks it well!
Beshrew my zounds! If she but knew, as well she might,
How her poor ma did bust her hump! What ado!
And what a moil with my eight or nine or so!
Brats, aye, forsooth; they bring us lots of love,
But what a peace and quiet when they go far hence
To gaol or to the army or to marriage bed;
As you did, Butch, my strange and vap'rous fruit.
Aye; children are not rare.

RITA: How well I wot you speak, I reck, unto the point,
Old wrinkled Gammer in your dirndl rags;
No, not rare; no more so than the newtish eft.
But Hannah; is that her whorish handle?
Hannah must not keep our nameless tot too long;
She spoils her putrid as a dozen eggs forgot.

MOTHER: Aha! Folks be spoiling all the kiddies now;
When I was getting regularly shtupped
'Twas not the case indeed I ken and wot;
We made our childers cower in blind fear;
We made them slave, kept them in order,
Was this not so, my tousle-headed queer?

BUTCH: You were not proud of them a lick, old dame;
I know it well, as salt does sting a gash,
But busted each and ev'ry chop of ours,
Aye, once a day, and twice or thrice o' Sabbath,
You palsied, lunatic, and blear-eyed hag.

MOTHER: Yet you weren't bad by half, you bunch
Of sluts and bums; I sometimes felt a twinge
Of care, and once, some score of years ago,
I ween, I gave you each a gen'rous gob
Of peanut butter that I'd made one day
When I was whipping buttermilk and whey
'Gainst the encroaching freeze of January.

BUTCH: Aye! And sick as spavined gooses did we moan.
I remember clearly 'twas that day my sister,
Sandi, my dear sister who had the scarlet gown
I joyed to frolic in at football games, did die:

That peanut butter, Mum, was made of lard,
All rotting with bacteria and such.

MOTHER: That was, you wot well, you foul-spoken fairy,
Many a long-gone age ago; besides,
Your precious Sandi was a slut, in spades,
Who'd rather tumble than eat honest curds.
And now that you have made my trembling head
All achy, thinking on those tear-dimmed days,
I seem to have a recollection, son,
That you, yes, you, strange Mistress Butchie Boy,
Did a voice clear as a morning starling have,
Aye, like Fanny Brice or Babs Gonzales.
Do I invent of holy cloth, or wot correct?

BUTCH: I could a sweet lay belt out on occasion.

MOTHER: Of course you could, you shambles of a twit!
And now I recollect your dim old Da;
How he did love to hear you honey croon!
Though he, poor slob, had what the doctor termed
A tinhorn ear, or something such as that,
And could not recognize one tune from another,
The poor work-broken, sweaty lummox.
Do sing, my strapping fag; clap up the skies!

RITA: Yes, husband, sing. Oh, Mum, 'tis sure as rye
He got his brassy throat from you, aged clot,
And not from your arthritic spouse, Old Leech.
Yes, sing, so that this pewling brat will sleep.
I implore and beg you of it, for and sooth.

BUTCH: What number would you like to hear me hit?

RITA: That swell song of the blushing gentleman
Who is so shy he won't remove his pants,
And dies of inanition of the crotch.

BUTCH: Aye; of the purple grapes and crimson leaves;
But, Mum, put your shawl and bonnet off;
And Rita, lass, I hauled some cresses in,
Whatever weed that that may signify.
Just wash them up, toast the fatty bacon,
And scramble up a bowl of eggs or so;
For let's to supper shortly, ere we pine. (*Sings*.)
What? You little punk! Who would think it now?

No sooner do I cease my chant, than you look up.
What, by God's wounds, would you have your daddums do?
Sing from now till crack of doom, you dribbling snot?

MOTHER: The glutton heard the bacon on the fork,
And aye, the fork too, sputter in the flame;
He also heard his mama's heavy step,
And the quacking of your duckies at the door.
Where did you get that song? 'Tis new to me.

BUTCH: I bought it of a roaming peddler, Mum.

MOTHER: Did you so? A peddler, eh? Oh, ha ha ha.
Well, you always were a mark for love songs, Butch,
And the odd and lisping men that huckster 'em.

RITA: Cute Butchie, lay the kid's head on your arm;
And if you'll schlepp him but a minute more,
Or the nonce or two, and sing another verse,
He needs must sleep t' escape the dreadful noise.

BUTCH: Do you sing, Mummy, do.

RITA: Aye, crazed old hunkie, do; 'tis a long, dry moon
Since we have heard you sing your innards out.

MOTHER: Like enough; I'm old now, 'spite my bouffant wig;
And the girls and lads I once did lullaby,
Can now eat plates of soup right off my sconce.
Why in Heaven's name should I sing some old crap?

BUTCH: Why, to pleasure us; just sit there in the ashes
Where you are, all snug and warm and smold'ring,
While I pace gently with this yowling brat.

MOTHER *sings*

RITA: Asleep at last; and, bedad, 'tis time he was,
Or the sweet hay was not once the green, green grass.
Turn back that homely sacking, Butch, my hub,
And lay him down; and, Momsy, will you please
To draw your chair up to what we call the board?
The bacon's burned unto a crispy toast,
And the eggs glow yellow as the duckies
Which crash betimes right through the window pane.

They eat, ringed by adoring ducks.

≪ 17 ≫
Blue
Receives a Sign

Down this westering road, said Blue, we must hump our weary frames, my juicy bamboo seed. For it is somewhere past the glimmering horizon that we shall find The University and, perhaps, the answer to our quest, if gallant quests may be said to have an answer—or maybe not!

Hump on, brave Blue! My wrinkled soles ever faithfully do plod in your booming wake! Or e'en that which the spavined world doth laugh like craven flies to wild apostrophize! Or is that wildly?

Huh? A radio? harked Blue. And like chucked away by someone into the noisome vetch! Probly don't work worth a roily fuck, but let us see . . . hmmm. Static, crackly sounds of faint electrical impingements . . . and, what? A human voice!

Let us, my lumbering bear, dig on the quaint sounds of this woodsy environ.

Shh. The voice grows clear as mountain stream achock with salutary pesticides . . .

". . . yessir! Ole station WASP right here in Hamhock, West Virginia, WASP, the howl of the Alleghanies, the home of the hoedown hits, the rendezvous of the rubes, the crux of country, the pinnacle of plastic, the house of hype! And who'm I? Yore favorite DJ, Big Boog Vinch, playin' only the tunes that you like! This portion of our million-dollar show is brought to you by the Reverend Dr. Piscardi's old favorite, Gel-O-Mowth—for breath like a lamb—and Dr. Piscardi's *great* new product, Oro-Sux, for great gums and a gorgeous gob for guys and gals on the go! I'm onna turn yall over now to the Reverend Dr. P, for his daily message of Hope and Peace, a break in the middle of the hectic day, yessir, that fabulous moment that we all know as the Piscardi Pause. And after the good Reverend talks to yall, ole Boog'll be back with some more fabulous country socko and rocko!"

"Good day, ladies and gentlemen. This is the Reverend Dr. Piscardi, humbly wheedling his way into your cowering Christian hearts, and a-hoping that your sweet smiles, given you by the grace of JE-sus, have been made just a little more

76

dazzling through the use of one of the plain country products that JE-sus hisself asked me—many years ago, while I was sunk in sinful fleshy lust and lechery and vile alcoholic stupor, silent upon a mountaintop like Sergeant York—yes, asked me to make for his greater glory and his . . . LOVE! So whenever yall put a big ole spoonful of Gel-O-Mowth well down in there among your gnashing molars . . . whenever yall roll an Oro-Sux lozenge—and they're now available in two new flavors, pecan and persimmon, as well as in the regular standard delicious flavor, witch hazel—yes, whenever yall roll one around in your mouth, sweetening your breath and strengthening your teeth and a-making your gums pink while yall get through your busy modern lives, I beg you, I BEG you, down on my KNEES, to think on JE-sus, and remember that my little company is dedicated to HIM! Yes, my clean-living friends, every time you buy one of these humanitarian products, you are siding with JE-sus!"

It sounds, my foursquare weasel, like the hearty baritone of that urbane swell, Doc Chick! Can it be a sign? Blue quizzed.

"Last night I was sitting out in the weeds behind my old red barn, picturing my beloved maw rock and creak on the wooden porch of agonized memory, yes, and a-thinking on how my wild and depraved youth cut short her clean Christian life, cut it too short, and a-wishing that JE-sus had found his way into my stony heart with his little tender feet afore that dear ole woman passed on. I am not ashamed to admit that I sat there in the tall Missouri razorgrass and the squinchback clover . . . weeping! Yes, weeping like a gentle gal who's lost her drawers and's feared to come home and face her paw. I KNEW that I had done gone and dedicated my life to JE-sus and his grace! I KNEW that my good country products were a-helping, in their humble country way, to make life cleaner and sweeter for the good folks—and their mouths—of this mountain country! I KNEW that I had put fornicating and blaspheming and drinking behind me, like unto JE-sus's command to Satan when he done ordered him to get in line behind him! But! It didn't seem, there in the peaceful twilight a-falling on the tumbledown hencoop and corncrib, to be . . . ENOUGH! And then JE-sus, a-knowing that I needed help and support in this crisis, stepped into my heart with a thud! He didn't say nary a word to me, but suddenly I remembered something that had done happened to me years ago, just after I had been RE-born! And I knew that JE-sus, yes, JE-sus Christ, wanted me to tell you a story, that JE-sus, hunkered down among the sheep, wanted me to express his wishes.

"This was something that happened many years ago, my good Christian friends. Just about the time that Abnerville got throwed up on top of the Wheeling High School Official Fallout Shelter during a fearsome thunderstorm. Many of you kind hearts have wrote to me out of the goodness of your trembling spirits, telling me of your opinion that this catastrophe was JE-sus's manly judgment on

Abnerville because the Jee-yew drugstore there on Main Street did not choose to carry the Piscardi line of pure Christian products, but carried, instead, some Godless Jee-yew products from Nee-yew York. Be that as it may—it is not my purpose to speak of what JE-sus has in mind as far as them Jee-yews are concerned, but it surely was a judgment on them when a couple hundred of them, mostly Commonists, was a-killed by the Nazis, who, when all is said and done, were good, hardworking Christian people! Some folks think that they done paid the price, these dozen or so Jee-yew criminals, for the crucifixion of Our Savior on a cross shaped like—and it is a historical fact that scholars don't want yall to know—a Hebrew dollar sign!

"Anyways, about the time of JE-sus's vy-rile manifestation in the streets of Abnerville—and who all can forget how the great whirlwind of his righteous wrath whipped that Jee-yew druggist's Commonist beanie-hat spang off his head and cast it upon a heap of offal over to the town dump?—about this time, a group of dark-skinned, bleeding-heart anti-Christs in the legislature, that corrupt Sodom and foul shame of this fair State, got themselves into a foreign-inspired, evil, Commonist cay-bal, and tried to sneak through some anti-GUN legislation! Yes! They were a-fixing to take our GUNS away from us, a-knowing full well that the country is ridden with anackists and do-gooders and fellow-travelers who all want to tear the pure little Christian babies outen their mothers' wombs and then make them all read schoolbooks that are corrupt with stories about swell-headed niggros and sodomite fornication and atheist-Jee-yew ideas! And even stories that tell our innocent children that there is something wrong with defending Christian freedom by a-blowing up a passel of Commonists!

"And at that time, filled as I was to the brim with the FIRE of JE-sus Christ's power and LOVE, I knew what my duty as a hard-working Christian businessman was, a businessman who had done spent long hours in the lab under the guidance of JE-sus to bring the first batch of Gel-O-Mowth to perfection, I KNEW what that duty WAS! I set out on a holy journey all through this hallowed land so as to bring to dust this unholy Commonist legislation. I asked only one question of the good country people who send these Judases to the State Capitol, where most of them spend all their time in lustful drunkenness with Jezebel secretaries and other impure young women who show off their bodies without no modesty atall! I asked these honest folks who tremble afore the grinning face of JE-sus one question: If these hook-nosed Commonists take away our GUNS, how are we all going to kill varmints? I did not even have to speak on the anackists and such! JE-sus done inspired me to mention only varmints! And it was enough!"

That *is* the voice of the fabled Chick, Blue muttered breathily. Something about the way he weaves magically the most boring anecdote. But what is he doing out here in the leaf-strewn boonies? Is it an ... accident ... that we "found" this radio in yonder blasted foliage? Or else ... ?

Let's listen hard, my powerfully muscled spouse! This might be what they call, in distant and star-spackled Hollywood, "Kismet."

"As all you good ole country people know, we are hemmed in on all sides by ...LIVING THINGS! Knothead polecats, wartface spudchompers, fanged blue ducks, eyeball turkeycocks, the dreaded singing raccoon, and a hundred other vermin and varmints, living and scuffling around in the leaves and mud, eating anything they all can, and breeding in sinful sweaty pleasure like a covey of ignorant niggros. If we let these beasts alone, what do you all think would happen? Yes! Yes, my craven Christians! They would soon outnumber us all, eat all our vittles, ravish our daughters down to the creeks at night, take our jobs—and soon there would not be a Christian left in all of West Virginia! And the infection would spread and spread until every Christian *everywhere* would disappear, or else shut his mouth about JE-sus for good, a-feared that he'd be et up by a horde of pusfaced hawgs! And if there were nary a Christian, it figures that there wouldn't be no Christ! Yes, they were a-trying to destroy JE-sus!

"When the courageous folks of the muddy peaks and scorching valleys thought on this for a while, thought of a life without JE-sus to fill them with fear and terror and those healthful night sweats, they riz up with a roar of righteous savagery and threw that Jee-yew law in the sump! Where it belongs, the darkest sump, where the bright light of JE-sus's grin will never be seen. I am humbly proud of my small role in defeating these Christ-killers, as well I might be. And though the varmints continue to breed like the sex-crazed and lecherous animals that they are, the good folks are a-keeping their numbers down with the avenging fire and hot lead blessed by JE-sus hisself!

"A final word, my dazed-in-Christ brethren and sisters. While I was a-bringing the word of JE-sus to the towns and villages and shopping centers round about this holy land, I was often asked to address large groups of God-fearing people: the Daughters of the Sacred Fetus, the Brotherhood of Christ the Sharpshooter, the New Baptist Bund, Inc., the Taxpayers' Rifle Squadron, the Pro-Jesus Mountain Pogroms, Inc., the Poll-Tax Party, and many another. I took care not to offend ... and how? By holding in my mouth at all times an Oro-Sux lozenge, secure in the knowledge that my breath was as sweet as the breath of a baby lamb, and knowing too that the healthful juices a-sloshing around in my mouth were a-purifying my breath at the same time that they were a-making my teeth as strong as steel and my gums as hard as mountain shale! And if Oro-Sux stood up under this kind of a test, imagine what it will do for you, as you go about your daily business!

"I thank you. This is the Reverend Dr. Piscardi, the Mogul of the Mouth, blessing yall in the name of JE-sus Christ, and reminding you that sweet JE-sus hisself, was he among us today in his glorious million-dollar flesh, would, I have no doubt, use these Christian products, these Christian products inspired by his LOVE! God bless yall till tomorrow, and sweet breaths to yall too!"

"Thank yew, Dr. Piscardi! That was a message to inspire us all, and it kind of makes yall think about what life is all about, don't it? Big Boog Vinch here, of course! And here to round out this Piscardi Pause with a song for all you folks who are a-shuffling down the ole highway of life—Yessir! It's the dynamic country hit of the year, Blackie Bob Hunko's 'Diamond on the Blacktop.' Sing it, Blackie Bob!"

> Don't be blue in the black rain
> Oh the Lord's a mighty good cop,
> Ask him a couple things about pain,
> Dark night and a diamond on the blacktop.
>
> Once worked in the field
> Sweat like a man
> Married the girl of my dreams,
> Alone now in dark and storm
> Lord, what do it mean?
>
> Recall a soft kiss,
> Bitter tears but I left,
> Hot, mean honky-tonk queens,
> Alone now in dark and storm
> Lord, what do it mean?
>
> What do it mean? What do it mean?
> What do a honky-tonk queen mean,
> Lord?
>
> Drinking rye whiskey and beer,
> Gambling all my pay,
> My wife was so clean, so clean,
> Alone now in dark and storm
> Lord, what do it mean?
>
> What do it mean? What do it mean?
> How come my wife was more clean
> Than a queen, Lord?

My farm's gone and my bride,
Some boys and girls too,
That must be Abilene.
Oh, alone in the dark storm,
Jesus, what's it all mean?

Jesus, Jesus, Jesus,
That's small for Abilene,
My Lord?

Don't be blue in the black rain
Oh the Lord's a mighty good cop,
He'll ease up your pain in the rain
In the night, he's a diamond on the blacktop.

If that *was* the legendary Doc Chick, Blue confided—and I will swear on my lens-polishing contraption, e'en all o'ergrown with scabrous ivy as it is, that it is—that fact, gently intertwined with the earthy lyrics of this twangy canto, makes for a true and boldly portentous sign, indeed! The diamond on the black-top must be a simaphor for the brooding University—somewhere yonder far! We are on the right road, my sweltering dogie!

Oh, Blue. Nor did I ever doubt your righteous brilliance else! Let's push!

The phrase is "let's push on," my rough-cut marmalade. What a card you art, and always wert, to boots! Ho-ho-ha!

Then they got crackling once again!

Or "cracking," as the modern phrase would have it.

But have it . . . *where?*

≪ 18 ≫

Eros Briefly Grins
upon Our Dusty Caravan

As we chunk forward through the blowing tares, my fairest box, I feel in the deep marrow of my throbbing bones that we are fair and truly on our way. Peruse said road, my faintly coloring wife!

Just so, be-biceped hunk. And what blessed relief. Yet, I feel but a jottish faint from all the sun my urban frame is not yet used to. The lucky Zim, like pike besplashed in icy pool, sleeps 'neath the schlock we call our "stuff." But this teeny canopy is no defense 'gainst vicious Sol's bright darts a-torrid, hein?

I'll haul our lowly coach beneath the blue inviting shade of nodding wombat here. I too feel hotly sweatish.

Aces, champ! And thus bedimmed climb up here thus to stretch and rest the sinews taut that you've long wrenched and vilified. Oh do!

I'll hence anon upspring, and putz to him who says a thing!

How trembling all my girlish nates do quake.

Take off your hat, my aloe. It's so hot!

That's not a hat, you tender squit. Hmm, it *is* still hot betimes.

It's *not* a hat? But then . . . ? Oh whew. I ooze and drip.

No, my craggy churl. It's what the rigors of the road and pond'rous slog have metamorphosed my coiffeur into. 'Tis not the dainty whiz of locks you spun, dear sweet galoot.

Sparkling and curvaceous thunder! It has the eerie shape of your fedora hight, and summat of its color too, like catfish stunned beneath an avalanche of humble pone. And yet, despite my crass mistake, flop on your back and tear my breeches ope!

My rambling blot! I thought you'd never hint your manly needs. But what think you of this other posture? 'Tis loved by those who favor knocking off a quick one in the kitchen while the tuna glops and nicely browns. Besides, it's so much cooler on my kneebones.

All reet with me. However steaming wench doth spread, I'm honored in the breach!

I'm honored by your sturdy poke, my hearty bungle.

Aha! How wild the warp and woof of wifely weft and wedge!

Thus doth a breeze spring crazy from the lolling meadows brast!

Oof oof oof, oof oof.

Whoopee! Whee! I reck not if my coif falls out, so let me buck!

Speak things that have a shade of subtle dirty filth to them, my peewee. It assists to help keep staunch and true a certain part of my anatomy. So lisp all softly through your fillings vast the porny stuff that true Christians evangelical do wallow in when they're in solitude.

Eee. Eee. I know your corkscrew human needs, voluptuous peach.

Then utter, wife, ere I slip out and, slipping, bash my elbows something fierce!

Sheer-black dwarf mistletoe! Hairy-crack catawba-tree!

Ohhh. Ooofff. Wow. And et al.

Big-tit common buckthorn! Butternuts in froth of lace!

Oh ump and huff! Oh Sacred Billy Graham! Whompp!

Lithe autumn-olives in transparent panties!

Whooff!

Sans crotch!

Fooff!

A Merry Widow clasping bouncy big-hipped and false jessamine!

I think that I . . .

Silk-buttocked garter-strapped and red-lipped tupelo!

. . . may void what great Erasmus dubbed the vital "seed." Wahoo!

Priapic imbecile! Heaving womanly embonpoint nestled in frail cups of stretchy rhododendron satin!

I do! I will! I spill and cascade thus my manly juice! And holler forth all stentorous as is my ennui'd wont, e.g., eeeeeeek-oh-ho!

And thus all fluttering I join thee in a wifely shriek, i.e., aieeeeee!

'Twas marvelous heavy and exceeding boss, my perch.

I felt like frail Justine who never failed to bump into a freak.

And now, since we are wild for health and strength and thus do straight eschew tobacco, let's have a snacko. What sort of victuals crouch in silent putrefaction 'neath these mounds of "stuff"?

Oh, Blue, my shining crow. You know I never feed betwixt what I am pleased to call my meals. Nay! Not if dread trumpet creeper nods in battle-fury vaunt!

You do not *what*? Then who are you indeed? You cannot be the sylph Helene, a broad whose noshing never ceaseth but in slumber!

Your heartless cruelness will out, as awesome Nature makes the caterpillar tear and rend the baobab. What? Not Helene?

I say not, no, or gumdrop-eating trees do not exist in hot Arabia! Why look, you seedy dandelion, this *is* a fantastickal fedora clenched upon your sconce.

Oh Blue, my rain-bespattered rusty lawn chair! I do admit my folly, yes, it is an old fedora on my bean. I wear it out of love for you, since yesterday the gritty wind blew out such massive quantities of my mousy locks I went in dread lest you should look on me as the stewed Comanche gazes on a ginger ale! But I am your Helene, 'spite this grim fedora. Can't you see?

I see, I see, amazing eft! But never lie to me again, for I despise and shrinketh from a broad which fibs to me, especially upon a day when I have shined my cache of bike clips!

My potent juniper! How I love it when you call me "broad." I feel like someone in a racy read, or showgirl deshabille in festering Las Vegas.

You'll always be a broad to me, my cheap romaine. And now, the fact you shelter underneath the brim of said fedora somehow fills my veins and arteries and such with steamy blood. Once more, my tender toad, up with your skirts, I do beseech you in a whispery mood of burgeoning amour.

Probe, oh probe again, my weird hyena! Plumb and dip unto my womby deeps, O hairy hawk! Pop me square right in the middle of what high-school boys yclep the nookie! I yearn and drop an Amazon of sweat! Pulsating ox!

Whammo, thus! Bull's fucking jaundiced eye!

Oh, oh. Oh, oh. And so on, honeyed aphid! Whoops!

« 19 »
The Sheep Interlude

Hard following upon that exceeding peachy shtup, my aromatic hubby, I am refreshed and crackling all a-zip with vim! My eyes peer down the lonesome trail with rejuvenated strength. 'Tis as if I spent a lustrum in an orgone box, thus doth my sated aura dominate this earthly frame.

I can get behind it, hon! I too am full to strange repletion with a pulsing throb of vigor! And so, let me haul and heave us forward toward the Goal! (He hauls and heaves apace.)

But stay! Hello! I hear a bleat upon the wind! Can it be so?

It is a bleat as of some tragic lambkin caught up in the briers!

It rents my heart. Oh, rescue him, or it.

I'll plunge into the tares and haul the wooly bastard out! (He plunges. Noise of ripping tares and cracking glades. After a time, Blue reappears.)

Although I ripped a throng of tares and cracked a brace of glades, I could not find the animal. And yet . . .

'Tis not the will of Jupiter or either Jumping Jesus. But what portends "and yet"?

This occasion shuttles to my brain, as ripe bananas enter vast metropoli on chugging freight trains, much sheep lore. Which, if you will settle back upon our worldly goods, I'll retail unto you. I made, while in my beardless youth, a study of the sheep, and I would like to share this store of useless knowledge with you, my iridescent starling. Sharing, as you know, my tongue, is the greasy cogwheel that keeps a marriage ever fresh, yes, that plus a decent salary and an occasional boff. Those of us dedicated to the higher things do not like to speak of "boffs," but there, as they say, they are.

Oh, share and retail ever fresh, my fond musician!

To save us time, I'll lug while I retail, if that is jake with you.

I dig the whole idea profoundly, sweets.

The sheep, as oft you know, or mayhap you have guessed, is a mere ruminant mammal of the genus *Ovis* and the family *Bovidae*; great Ovid was named after them, which is why he slapped together what we call the "Pastoral," a form that for some hidden reason has appealed to wild-eyed poets down through all the ages. There are lots of types of domesticated sheeps, the first ones being house-broke, as they say, on the scaly heights of Pelion some seven thousand years ago by the humble Jimmy Arvenites, the youth who first concocted Yankee pot roast. Although, to the unpracticed orb, they look alike, they are different in many a way, and each has a personality that glitters in the deep heart's core! Let me run it down for you in terms of nomenclature stern.

Run, oh run, my rough-hewn Sousa!

First, who can forget or long impugn the *Cotswold*? Ah, the gross and sooty-tufted Cotswold, who warms the heart because, despite his loathsome teeth, for-ever bucked, his disposition is as sweet as Father Flanagan's. In some quarters of this reeling globe the slob is dubbed "the fuzzy freak," yet his heart thuds on, exuding sunlight.

And what of the *Dorset*? That ringing name that conjures up hamstrung vi-sions of the crass unspeakable? Its only penchant, scholars know, is to gobble up, assault, and glut each scone and crumpet that grows wild in England's green land. Its minuscule hoofs are all misshaped, thus to assist him in digging the little rascals from their loamy oith.

And the *Hampshire*! Let us shout its homely name with heads on high and throats all swolled with bursting pride! The honest folk that infest the Blue Ridge Mountains have dubbed this smiling chuck the "Miss Congeniality" of the sheepy world, since every individual of this happy race, ram, wether, and ewe, will clip and tumble with any member of the kingdom mammalian on God's old earth and at a moment's notice! Also a coupla snakes and newts.

Then there is that guy the very thought of which and whom does make our eyes bulge with alacrity, yes! the *Karakul*. Its nigra wool so prized by bombar-diers and congressmen! Its voice so grating and its eyes so sloe! This shuffling dude is thought to be descended from that legendary sheep Ulysses ate on his first date with fair Penelope. Thus History doth make morons of us all!

Long ignored by the vulgar madding crowd, yet ever living at the deep heart's wide-flung door, we have your crouching *Leicester*, pronounced "Licorice." Called by wags "the cockeyed wonder," this brave and bloated fellow won his spurs in Cromwell's time by jumping off the high board at summer fetes, and, to the delight of the assembled Roundheads, landing on his back. Andrew Marvell notes his clumsy oddity in the lines he gives to say a contemporary member of the breed:

> Stumbling on Melons, as I pass,
> Insnar'd with Flow'rs, I fall on Grass.

And do I hear you think aloud the magic word? I mean, the *Lincoln*! Though afflicted by the Irish curse, a need to laugh at davenports, its cream is prized by knowledgeable tribesmen. Named for our dear President, Old Abe, 'twas he that giant must have seen while lying wounded on the Bijou's stage in Little Old New York. His last words were: "I see some sheeps upon my own dear property, the Plains of Abraham."

Also but, we deny and give the shoulder cold, to our everlasting peril, to the scourge of the jonquil, yet with a heart of purest platinum, the swart *Merino*, who being Eyetalian, is a little black-eyed number, dedicated to leaching forth throughout his long and happy life, tons of that wondrous mozzorone cheese, thus making this his adopted land the foremost exponential of exotic foods.

May I include the *Oxford*? Ever mounting, though awash in sweaty perspiration, toward the ineffable "Yea!" this hard-pressed breed, pigeon-toned and dulcet-toed, is alack fast dying out, since two of three lambs born to the startled ewes is but a morphodite.

And so petite that he can hide beneath a sprig of violets, there can be no aspersions cast upon the dandy *Rambouillet*. A saucy Frenchman, he, who loves nothing better than to stand agog among the creaking oaks, his wickedly incisive frog-talk zonks out the soul of this openhanded nation. Enchanté!

Demure, yet bold as brass in every faucet of the gantlet of cruel existence, we now turn to the *Shropshire*, "sissy of the moors." No bigger than a man's hand, this lightfoot lad hides in weeds all day and by night slinks forth to crop and nibble the shoots most tender of the gorse-blooms that suffocate the heaths and meadows of all Wales!

Then looms the burly *Southdown*, brusque and buxom! The heart pounds wild and free to look upon this hombre who repays stern discipline and who requites the cruel yet kind lash by stealing apples for the lissome shepherd.

And last, though the mind doth goggle to report it, there lurches wild the *Suffolk*, a crazèd beast more horse than sheep, whose solitary hobby is to jump through hoops of burning gasoline upon the glade!

These then, my locust, are the sheeps that men have tamed. But there are also feral types, belike the *Asian argoli*, who sacks the baloney of the lone explorer in the Gobi; the *Barbary sheep* or *Aoudad*, whose dread castles made of sand dot the wilderness of windy ergs; and finally, the stalwart *Bighorn*, the mocking symbol to untold generations of weary hubbies of their wives' intrepid indiscretions.

Thus, my chooch, this interlude of curious odd learnings. Do you feel the intellectual fire in your frame?

I boin all up with education deep, delightful Serge.

Yet what's that creak? That sickening crunch?

The cart sways and doth . . . Oh! It's broken down!

Avaunt! 'Twill teach us not to hump and tumble on it! God grant that we may find a cart-repairer!

I'm sure we shall, dear weasel, for a sign we passed while you were in your teaching bag proclaimed that we are now in great Ohio.

Ohio! If we can't holler up a cart-repairer here I'll eat your so-called coif! (They settle underneath a muskelonge while Zim eats ravenously some hapless nearby ants.)

« 20 »

"La Musique
et les mauvaises
herbes," Continued

V THE PICNIC OUTING

Today is Saturday! It makes so nice, that Suzanne and André don't envy to pass the afternoon at the conservatory or the greenhouse.

ANDRÉ: Let's make up a picnic outing.

SUZANNE: Good idea. Let us pass to the store of foodstuffs and then go on the edge of the lake.

ANDRÉ: I am of accord. But I have not too much of the mazuma. Have you any mazuma?

SUZANNE: I have a little piece of the mazuma. Let us go there, no?

SUZANNE (*at the store of foodstuffs*): There you are then! I have some bread, some mustard gobs, some weenies, some pickle chow, some honey dollops. What makes it to buy still, my old weed?

ANDRÉ: Here are some potatoes fried in the cans. I love them well. Yom-yom.

SUZANNE: Me also, I love them. But we have not enough of the mazuma to buy any.

ANDRÉ: Oh craps. Well, and what is it that we drink, along with the foodstuffs over here?

SUZANNE: Some whisky for you and some gin for me. Does that go A-One with you? These beverages untie the moral knots, so it is said.

ANDRÉ: Very *well*! And buy me some cakes, if you please. I have a hunger like a tapeworm today.

SUZANNE: Ha. Ha. What a crazy young person you are! But yes, I buy some cakes. Do you much love the ones with a form of phallic symbols, the "Twinkies"? I love them very much.

ANDRÉ: I have much heat when I regard you them regarding.

SUZANNE: O.K., my old kink. I am truly enchanted by the idea of making a picnic outing. At home, the dinner is always so ceremonial. For the commencing, there perhaps is some kohlrabi stems in ketchup boats or pig-hock soup. Then there is the meat of the lamb or the goose with the greens and the fat of the backs and the white beans and finally the pudding of the chocolate with Graham's biscuits and the synthetic cream. I then am so filled up to the neck that I must make the excuse to depart away from the table and loosen up my unmentionable raiments.

ANDRÉ: Enough! I am of a complete folly with the famish and the heated lust also.

SUZANNE: The eyes on your visage pop from the head in regard of my body structure. And my sack of foodstuffs. Ha! Ha!

André and Suzanne pay the sweaty owner and with a large sack quit the store of foodstuffs. They mount each others in the auto of André and arrive some few hours later on the edge of the lake. Alas! The sack of foodstuffs falls into the current and sadly they live some moments of small agreeableness. They have much gloom to regard the foodstuffs cruising to the far side. Oh well, they mutter, and again mount each others in the auto to pass away the afternoon.

VI A FAILURE TO RELATE

Alice Cuisse, who is the comrade of the chamber of Suzanne, is ugly as a sin; however, she is a charming young woman that all the world loves. When Suzanne and André have a failure to relate, it is always Alice who arranges the things.

ALICE: What is it with you, my dear Suzanne? You have much of lessons to prepare on sycamore scrofula in the gentle ewes, yet you do not work.

SUZANNE: Oh Alice! I am very vexed up with André. If he telephones to me tell him that I am not here.

ALICE: O.K., my little girlie. And I find that you have reason.

SUZANNE: He is a brutal chap! He is lazy, egotistical, impolite, and a gluttony pig.

ALICE: I am completely of your opinion! Your young friend is of a great slobbishness.

SUZANNE: You have reason, ugly chum. But let us be just, if it attempts to kill us, even. He has some qualities also.

ALICE: Maybe so. But he is a sloth, egotistical, crude, and a grand swine.

SUZANNE: Softly, my charming homely pal! He has a good heart, a fine finger with the concertina, and a formidable thing. And when I have the blue, he finds always the way to make me titter or else, guffaw. Just last day I chuckled fit to crack a guts, as the Yankees speak, down on the edge of the lake.

ALICE: Oh yes? What did he make to achieve your cracked guts?

SUZANNE: Oh, he made the risky blague about a "Twinkie." But yes, he always can make me achieve to smile.

ALICE: And when you are of good humor, my little jolly tart, he finds always the ways to make you sob.

SUZANNE: Alice, why are you so mean? Is it for that you have the face to halt a clock of eight days?

ALICE: Better such a face like this than to have the feet with the round heels!

(*The telephone sounds. It is Alice who responds.*)

ALICE: Hello! Is it you, André, you pig? Eh? I am preparing the lessons on the fly of Spain. Suzanne is no place to be discovered . . .

SUZANNE: Alice! Give me the phone, you jealous flea! André? Don't quit the phone! It is Suzanne. Alice was but making the attempt to smash up my hump. You know what an envy she makes about our "French" lessons . . . yes, she is a disgusting phlegm.

ALICE: What a beauty of a slut you are! I have a great hope that you flunk out the bee-pollen examination.

SUZANNE: Eh? But yes, André, I of course pardon. No. No. It is me who is a beast of a chick. In front of the conservatory in ten minutes? Pack up the overnight baggage? Oh, my dear buddy, *o.k.*

ALICE: I pray to my God that you terminate up with the bun in an oven. You hobo!

SUZANNE: You have a jealousy for that André conserves his grand thing for me and not for you—you mouse-face dowdy!

Alice and Suzanne enter upon to slap and scratch each the other faces. They soon make however a stop since they are old comrades after all. Alice lends even to Suzanne a black lace négligée she received as a funny joke. Suzanne packs it in the baggage right up with her other intimate costumes.

VII A GOOD RENDEZVOUS

Yesterday morning, André took the coffee with Jacques Derrière, a student of musical spoons. The two young folks are of good friends since a long time. As they are serious students, the tone of the conversation was enough elevated. They are commencing to discuss a subject that interests sharply both the two of them.

JACQUES: My friend, felicitate me. I have made the acquaintance of a jolly young lady of the School of Fertilizer Arts. I had a good rendezvous with her yesterday evening.

ANDRÉ: Bravo, my old man! And how have you found the jolly young lady? They are charming of a habit, the lady students of the School of Fertilizer Arts.

JACQUES: That jolly student is no large intellectual, but she has many qualities. For one example, she has a formidable brace of the long legs . . . or should I tell, for two examples? Ha. Ha. Also, the large crocks upon the chest.

ANDRÉ: In effect, my old man! And is it that she gave to you some interesting "formulas"? Heh. Heh.

JACQUES: We had not to speak of the artificial dung, my dear old cabbage. We passed the evening at the erotic cinema. They exhibited the American film, "Hellions in Hosiery." I had great heat. Wow! And she paid for her seat.

ANDRÉ: Naturally. A poor student has not enough spondulicks to pay two seats of the dirty cinema. As Mademoiselle "Gams" is a jolly lady student, she comprehends well the situation. What did you do after the base film?

JACQUES: We took one cup of coffee near the cinema. We spoke of the filthy film, of our dull comrades, and of the situation of the garlic fields of Provence. As I have told, the jolly miss has few brains. Thus, when I made the small blague that I might pay for *her* seat, I have a fear that it passed away above her skull.

ANDRÉ: Thrilling, you old crazy face! Then, how did you terminate the evening?

JACQUES: To make some economies, we took the omnibus to return home. We did much beastly things therein. Then, in the vestibule of the house of this jolly miss, she made me a very interesting demonstration. She declared that the young lady students of the School of Fertilizer Arts learn much of the acrobatics. My God! Enchanting. Yet this morning I felt myself to be much like the little twisted cookie our old German friends have the inclination for.

ANDRÉ: The "pretzel"?

JACQUES: But yes! The "pretzel." This jolly young posy can of truth sock it quite of an abandon!

ANDRÉ: You had some good chance, you roguish mongrel!

JACQUES: In effect! I can hardly straighten up the back even now.

André and Jacques continue to chatter of interesting vile subjects. For example, André says Jacques of the "French" lessons that Suzanne makes on occasion with him.

Jacques has much irritation since Suzanne with him makes nothing but the ridiculous farces or speaks of her Fern Seminar whenever he pleads to disrobe of her the garments.

VIII THE SEASONS

Since three days it is raining without arrest almost. All the students put on of the waterproofs or carry the umbrellas. At the moment where our story commences, André has lost his waterproof in a turnip acre, and as the umbrella of Suzanne is not big enough for to protect all two of them, the young friends await the finish of a torrent in the entranceway of the library, where they have been to read upon some shameful, however exciting, narratives.

SUZANNE: Truly, I do not love this beast of an autumn! All that rain over there annoys me in the end. I love more the spring when it makes the sunshine, and I can stroll about the street or boulevard with the short skirts to reveal the legs, so as to give to the men the flushing face.

ANDRÉ: I believe perhaps that I am like the rain, since too, I annoy you in the "end," when I make the chance. Ha. Ha. This is but the joke, my broccoli. Yes, the springtime is a pretty season, of course. But I love also well the autumn. It is nothing of more amusement than a good match of football, even same when it rains. Except perhaps the naughty and risky spirited behavior of two young friends in the front of the fire that is ablaze!

SUZANNE: I like the football, me too, my old rutabaga! And as for the fire that is ablaze, well, is a location of good aspect for a careless "French" lesson, eh? But I don't like the rain, no, I regret the beautiful days of summer when I voyage to the beach.

ANDRÉ: You regret the days of summer because you know to stand up in the front of people and look jolly in a small bathing costume that reveals the long legs of you and a pretty backside. You naughty little sheep!

SUZANNE: Jacques Derrière finds that my large jugs are pretty too in the bathing costume. He should have been confiding to me that a brief peer at my flesh gave him to desire to bite quietly my thighs.

ANDRÉ: Jacques Derrière is a bag of the scum! I will hit his face off him for an insult of this order. I make insistence that I only can find you jolly with your clothing removed, or pieces of it!

SUZANNE: I love it when you are crazy of jealousy, my old big-nose person.

ANDRÉ: Me, I find that you are jolly also in a briefly made costume of skating when one goes to skate on the ice in winter.

93

SUZANNE: You sweet some thing!

ANDRÉ: Yes, I do! In effect, you are how the English men and women call "ripping" in the costume of skating. I shall have been always dreaming of your pretty gams in tights with the very, very small skirt that conceals not well the brief panties beneath. I often must take a seat at the rink of skating to make an avoidance of self-embarrassment at gazing at your flesh.

SUZANNE: Do you mean that the "poker" of yours gets very firm? Ha! Ha!

ANDRÉ: In effect, my fantasy! There is no young woman so jolly as are you, Suzanne. Even at this moment I feel a strange itch of my loins.

SUZANNE: How gallant you are this morning! It makes me feel as if the rain and cold that give me the blue are far from here. And a slow stare at the bump in your trousers makes a special tonic for me.

ANDRÉ: Let us voyage back into the privacy of the library, good?

SUZANNE: I have a great hot for you, my charming roughneck! Let us go back again.

Suzanne and André find themselves beneath a table of the reading room. It is dark and warm, and they cast off some raiments. Then the two young friends attempt of some interesting perversions. It continues to rain without arrest, but they are absent of cares.

« 21 »
The Cart-Repairer

As the sun busted down on beautiful Ohio, and they lounged in the shade of the friendly muskelonge bush, wee Zimmerman asleep, his little tummy bulging to satiety with his hearty meal of friendly ants, ho! an ancient rube appeared, his back all bent with cares, yet with a gleam and sparkle in his wise old eye. 'Twas the cart-repairer come, attracted by the odor of disaster, to that humming glade, or whatever.

Heh, heh, the ancient churl emoted, in the manner of the well-loved Dr. Whore, fabled wight! I've come to fix yon busted cart, my bearded husk!

I am be-zonked in wild amaze, quoth Blue. I was about to holler for a cart-repairer, seeing that we sojourn in the purple haze of quaint Ohio. And here you stand, begrimed with gluey soil, old cornstalks, and withal ungartered and un-braced, honest wrinkled hind.

We cart-repairers know, aye, as if a bird did cheep and squawk to us, when e'er a cart collapses, cracks, shudders, sighs, and busts all down. It is a gift given to a very few, for which I give the beamish Jesu thanks.

And thanks again and yet again. I fear this cart, whose prime is past, is all we own—my svelteish helpmeet here, my snoozing son, and I—and all we have to get us down the road where we do point our faces. It is, like poets chant, our proper steed, or, t'amend that, *I'm* the proper steed, you dig?

Such ween the breaks, croaked the elder dope. A thousand accidents the trav'ler's hopes subvert or checque. Now let me fix my watery orbs upon the damage, if I may. This pulpous mass, I take it, is the "cart."

'Tis, wheezed Blue, or what might, with greater 'cuteness, be called the husky terrene dregs of same.

Becalm thy mind, perplexed with irksome thoughts, my Jewish pal, and let me checque this damage out. And you, dear Madame, my pomaceous chunk, let waft your rich embosomed odors over me while I inspect this sober vehicle. 'Tis years since I've been so close to flexile wench!

I blush and quail that thou shouldst think me swell as apple-cheese, deterio-rating gaffer. But here! Take my embosomed odors, and eke my ambrosial streams of sweat that perfume the air with musk, so as you fix our humble waggon.

Aha! spumed forth the honest dumbo. Certes, as mattin song doth send the horny priest aflying from the nunnery, I glaum the trouble and, heh-heh, decipher plain its cause as if 'twere writ as large as turgid fruits in brisk October!

The cause, old hoary schmuck? evinced our Blue, the while the spindly Helene stood all contiguous to the ancient handyman.

Though worn with work and years, honked he, I can still espy a busted axle caused by a hump tossed off in wild abandon. Sir, I say that this simp'ring lady here, your spouse, by utmost vigour screwed, and not too may days ago if that, did exert such pressure on this oldish vehicle with the violent socking of her excited arse 'gainst same, that it did crack the axle here.

'Tis a shrewd guess, nosy dodderer, smiled Blue.

I redden all like juicy plums 'fore frosty blasts deface 'em, sighed Helene.

Nor fear that I impugn you twain gimpolas, the geezer quipped. In scorching youth a hubby's blood doth turn to mellow liquor when he glances 'pon the plump Ausonian hills his wife doth sit upon, aye! Then his post cylindric oft doth swell with weight excessive and Great Nature maddens him so that he must again employ the pondrous engine in what great Ecclesiastes dubs a shtup. Is it not so, my efficacious cluck?

You've whacked the nail upon its steely head, old bawd, cracked Blue.

I needs must hide my boining "face" in my voluminous snood, said queer Helene.

But enough of this enflaming talk, the artisan suggested. Disburthen thou thy luckless cart of its rich provender, supplies, comestibles, and all the other crap that flesh is heir to. E'er hasty suns forbid to work, whatever that may mean, I'll set about my task.

O lucky day that found us just outside perfumed Ohio when we made the two-backed beast! screamed the dainty wife.

Yet hold! the crookback sniffed. Short are our joys. Mine eyes, now that I don my cheaters, dig that the axle-winch that helps support the ring-job here, is smashed beyond repair. Ugh!

Are we then doomed to halt our holy quest? sobbed Blue. Oh shitty vanity! Oh how mortal saps of their shriveled hopes are widowed!

I'm quelled with intenerating woe! said wifely Miz Gavotte, and fell all down in quick collapse.

Nay, nay, quoth the faithful old mechanic. Let me now walk among the well-ranged axle-trees and sprockets, let me size right up the drive-shafts and the odd hydraulics. Aha! 'Tis as I thought. I can complete repairs effect, but I must craft with careworn hands another axle-winch. Let me ope my kit and now prepare materials for thy succor.

O brave magician! Blue enthused.

Delightful clot! Helene admitted from her bed of bramble-vetch.

The job's not hard, but it should take all nigh upon two days, during which time may I suggest that you camp out in the woods a league away? There you shall find some rude and rugged folk who've come to gather footballs late discarded by the crack-brained natives.

Gossip whispers that these pigskin spheres do make a tasty stew, drooled our protagonist.

I reck it so or else let welkin froth upon the violent insensates! grinned the wheezing lumpen.

I sure could scoff all up unto my rough chapped elbows such a steaming bowl of mulligan, gasped the prone Helene, her mouth all filled with od'rous goldenrod.

Then go! the churl declared. But first I'll tick off as it were with stylus hight and also eke, how I will go about this task. I've made admission that the axle-winch that helps support the ring-job, the main one that employs the king-post and the rake, is busted quite. To fashion clean and spiffy one that will outlast the very cart 'pon which I'll stick it, why, 'tis a job capacious of the juicy hord, or withal summat! First, the cornice bracketing and naked flooring must be lathed into splint'ry yet puissant sills and two, or maybe three, odd scarfings. At the moment that perfection seems a-gallop as the mighty steeds in windy Troy did chomp and whinny, just then, and fine as maiden's-hair, a trussing beam must be devilishly mortised, and rudely forced into a tenon, all despite its wheezes. Then, with a massy brad-awl and a gimlet-peenball, purlins must be chunked into the collar-beam, the queen-post, and the struts, already clipped and jazz-boed with rough strings, apron piece, and beading-keys. At this point, honest carpenter doth, if he be wise as slipp'ry publisher, shoot a orison or trice to Jesu, nodding off in Paradise. For now, with his purlins hot to snap as wench's garter, a miter-butt and tie-couple must be winched and rip-sawed into groove and that oddball slab of weighty iron men have given name of tongue, though Christ knows why. If this maneuver spangs, as well it might, then one is past the, you should pardon gross substántive, hump. 'Tis then but a task, familiar to the hand of any klutz, of some quarters, carriages, a rafter-roof, a fishing, coupla joints, zinging out a frame by lengthening beams, a touch with the cross-cut differential, plus a dab of mold in the transmission, simply done with the homely gouge, the jack-plane, and the joiner's-gauge. A final boring of the pitching-piece, and a chinch of wedge-cutting, all in easy strokes, and then a flourish with the smoothing-plane to bring the entire motherfucker to sublimity. Then, zut! We takes the spanking axle-winch, slather it with grease, and whang it quite into its wonted spot, there next the faithful ring-job. And thus, rapacious fugs, you may hump again o'er hill and dale where e'er the wild goose honketh!

O geezer pure, whinged sweet Helene, thou, more wise than fair Caligula, shalt steep thy grisly sconce in beer ere thou do 'gin.

Thankee, titless one. 'Tis my vast pleasure thus to pleasure thee. Yea! Nature rejoiceth, smiling on her works lovely, to full perfection wrought!

Vigour gives equal title, stated Blue. A wondrous phrase, yet all methinks devoid of meaning.

We blush with the pomaceous harvests of thy craft, old sock, chirped up Helene, while the rude mechanic doused his sweaty scalp in lager cool.

Such profit springs from tools discreetly used, the old one wheezed from out the foam. And now, take you to the woods to join the football folk, whilst I attend my labors here. After two suns have plonked into the ocean, then return and thou shalt find thy cart champing at the well-known bite.

Thus, the happy pilgrims wended toward the nearby grove, while the windy glades did ring with the keening screams of steely peen!

« 22 »

Around the Campfire

When one lives, I mean to say, homely brothers, *lives* in the country, Blue said one chill evening with a twang of fall in the air as he sat in front of the blazing campfire somewhere in Ohio, one is compelled to do things, to become one with the slow and even heartbeat of the land and its mysterious gizzard and liver and other deepset organs, do you get me? One learns to—how shall I phrase it?—shift. Make do. Slap together. Patch up. Be handy. You've all read or heard tell of *Martin Chucklehead*? Like that, babes. I've learned, learned through bitter experience, through my own mistakes and I've made plenty, puh-lenty, a myriad or trice. Ha ha ha!

His great blocklike teeth rippled and flexed, then flashed for an instant in the sudden flaring of a knotty balsa log, whipped into frenzy by a blast of frigid air—from Canada! Flashed, yes, and as suddenly flashed out!

His great deerhide shirt swelled with Manhood!

There was a sharp, one might say an acute intake of breath among his auditors, honest ragamuffins all, huddled close to the crackling blaze, vacuous faces held suspended, like so many steaming beefsteak pies, in the air that strangely swirled about their plaid shirts and rough denim trousers, not to mention their stout corduroy shoes.

Or . . . boots.

The dark forest seemed to press closer.

Betimes, Helene huddled deeper into her homemade sleeping bag, the Lord knows what dreams etching a thin yet fetching smile on her thin, gnashing lips, as well as her wide and voluptuous mouth.

The mouth of Woman!

Zimmerman, at the edge of the huddling bresh, ankle deep in a stray puddle that bore mute testimony to the typhoon of the day before, crushed frogs with single-minded purpose.

Yep, Blue continued, if it may be said that this vast heart ever continued anything, Yep, he said, looking long into the smoldering bowl of his corncob with a silent wish that it were tobacco that smoldered there instead, Yep, he said, looking up oddly, 'bout that time, up in Maine it was, I took the monicker of Bucol Suck. 'Lowed as how I could blend into the background, be taken for a reg'lar salt-lickin' clamsucker, your everyday down-east crackerbarrel. Took to fellin' trees and tearin' stone fences up by the roots. Fished many a cold deep stream for bignose crackies an' muskiejugs, an' dropped splintery lobster traps into tarnation knows how many sumpholes where the big 'uns loll. The stars, well, my gum! the stars looked so close to a feller's face that you 'lowed as how you might reach up and touch 'em, specially if you was a-swingin' and a-hollerin' and a-screamin' with fear through the crystally rhinestone air on a blue-ring birch limb, shootin', just shootin' up to the sky while a riled-up grizzly down below chomped away at the trunk o' the tree, his snoot all smeared up with honey like Willie-the-Jew and a big bullass pike in each hand. Feller learns to . . . live . . . with the slow movement of a land like that.

His interlocutors, silent up to this point, remained so, their eyes shifting embarrassedly from the lost dreams that burned rather steadily in the flames before them and the creaking and sighing limbs of the great Japanese maples that grew so thick and close that they made the day of the forest into night, although now, it being night, they didn't know that and so were content. And not a man jack of them could deny, no, not one of the rough and ruddy hobos could deny that old Osiris and the Pig, Syrian and Cassavetes, Vishnu and the Four Brothers winked down upon them fixedly from above in their mad wanderings. But where? And, for the love of God, how? There was a dearth of dry eyes as the grisly flapjacks addressed themselves to this silent yet awesomely persistent query.

And then the snows, Blue continued, those great white howlin' blizzes that blowed down from the Yukon and the Klondike, and the bone-snappin' nanooks that would sweep in in their tracks, cold snaps so devilish fierce your bones would crack like crabshells and possum teeth as you fell to your knees on the slag ice that covered the whole world. An' on what was, just a flash o' time ago—and here he allowed his greasy nose to reflect the prancing light of the fire to illustrate his metaphor—a drowsy pond up to its ass in honeysucker weeds an' mornin' priscillas, you'd be starin' into a hole you'd gouged outen the ice to find yourself eye to eye with a canny old specked koala or a sawbuck chopperlip, at home in his vast watery tundra and, I swear, boys, smilin', yep, smilin' at your presumption! The winter skeeters 'd worry and tear at a man too, by dad, right through his great thick layers o' bengalee fur and turkey grease that covered him from head to toe. Till all was a nightmare o' howlin' sastrugis, velocitous gale-rime, and black sassenachs, and the buzzards! Ah, bless me, fellers, the glacier buzzards, hungry as starved coots, gawkin' and preenin' and crowin' on the branches of the hangdog birch and the Dutch elm in which the hurricane blast soughed and chuffed! Yessir! give a man days and weeks and months o' that type o' life, and he comes to know he ain't no more'n a pork rind or a rabbit ass in the great scheme o' things. I vowed, in the long nights o' just such a winter as that, never to hurt or betray in any way atall a bit o' snow again! Not even a solitary cutesy flake! Nowhere on the face o' the earth! My wife over there, whose thin smile, as you can see, threatens to beat, or at least tie, the brightness o' the fire itself, even when I heap a renfrew twig, all full o' sappy juice, on its blazing face, can bear witness to it. She was there with me, hunkered down in a fondue hut, cookin' and meltin' snow and chompin' moose fur into tasty stew, barely alive in front of her little greaseball fire, her eyes far away, far far away, and in them a feller could see little tiny pictures o' home, if he looked close. Home!

At this homely epithet, each rude visage brightened for a moment and then drifted far away, as if each had set out on its long weary journey through the dense cystitis vines and towering salvia trees, to find it.

Or . . . them!

And yet, with the very next flog of the boreal winds from the gelid tundrae just beyond the hill that the cantaloupe of a moon had thrown into odd silhouette just beyond the wooded ridge, now lost in shadows, the visages returned to their mocking and grim possessors, each settling heavily and with a groan on the un-shaven column of a vast neck that called it slave.

That one word that rang so horribly. Slave!

Yet which it, the visage, in acrid vengeance, mocked in turn, and viciously, ah God, *heartlessly*, grimmed as well!

But a man learns from these adventures, Blue cheeped on, almost with the very cheep of the glacier buzzards that he had so darkly called up.

His chapped lips cruelly savaged his corncob.

His dark eyes were lost in the star-spattered skies that formed the ceiling of autumnal Ohio, its sleeping towns, its body shops.

Its Indian mounds!

But when winter comes, as it always does in this neck of the woods at least, Blue continued, knocking the faithful corncob wildly against a faggot who wordlessly hissed, yet still, still in time to the dying croaks and whimpers of the frogs that young Zim was sedulously putting out of their slimy misery, till, fi-nally, the bowl of the pipe he called chum arced through the air in a lazy parabola into the very bowels of the jolly blaze, at which a jump and toss of flames yet threw the sodden faces of the rapt apple-knockers into strange relief, Spring, Blue laughed, great, roarin', mucky, swell, and juicy spring! is a-steppin' right on its heels, dig?

The rubes grunted as one, their lips trembling.

Eyetalian poets know this, Blue blurted at last. And the good Lord knows they make the best creelwinnies and crabflickers on the New England coast, rough, cold, and rocky as it owns or something. And, by gumbo, a far holler from the stinkin' melodious country the greaser runts hail from!

At this jaunty reference to the feared and hated dago, the spiky heads and quivering mouths of the woodland band nodded and gaped, in that order, gaped until the spittle and drool from their broken, stained tusks sizzled and buzzed in the demented flames like so many charred and split mickeys.

Yep! And spring did come! Blue guffawed. The rivers and cricks thawed, the yeller-nosed butchies spawned and spawned, hurlin' their shinin' bodies as God intended, out o' the streams and flatbeds, the sinkholes and stalagmites, over the fields and cornbrakes and roofs and chimbleys, the bresh, the shrebs, even over the rotting rock fences a-jammed and a-cluttered with the bodies o' neighbors and wimpies. Yessir! The buds rioted in busts and detonations o' color, the greengage phloxes stood up high as old oaks, the blue-bottles churned and drowned in the new butter that covered the earth! Helene took to kneadin' the dough that she'd planted before the first hurricane fell, and she baked and broiled many a toothsome delight, let me tell you, all to the wild yelpin' o' crickets. She was a woman, fellers, a woman, workin' around the house all buck naked, as human a female person as God intended Eve to be.

At this intelligence, his yokel audience gulped back . . . tears. Tears of Manhood, tears of Pride . . .

Tears of rampant Envy!

Their dazed miens had the appearance of men, strong men, rough and unpolished men, borne backward in time's violent career to a lost moment of unleashed lust and its unsatisfactory consummation. Yet they were silent but for a scattered whinge or two.

Men!

And the scream o' the red magool, Blue mused on, the great rivulets gushin' Life! The rocky soil turnin' and turnin', the chink-eye toad, the shitface beetle, the swoop swaller, the barndoor ratfucker, the bare-tail snake-eater, the whooping picayune . . . Life! And the eye gets clear! And the skin gets hard! And the hands get tarry and so almighty powerful that they bust through barn walls and threshers on their own account. Lord! And Zim a-growin' and Helene . . .

She stirred. From somewhere in the depths of her nokomis sack a soft feminine yawn vied with the odd chirring sound of the earthworms. Great Nature had seen to it that they had blundered their blind and simple way into the blaze! Blue looked away into the dark that had settled about the top of the shadowy muskwillow that served as their roof, his heavy face as one of granite.

A tear hung at the edge of a stray lash!

Zimmerman was almost a man!

Each dirty flint of a face seemed to agree with this unspoken sentiment. Each grizzled jaw nodded in unison and together, smiles fleeting.

Yet . . . was it really a yawn that had broken the stillness of the campsite?

They settled down for the long arctic night, sheltering as best they could from the eerie bights and worringers that swept and reswept the little clearing, their woodswise bodies deep beneath heaps of dried poppy limbs. Even Zim, little, sad, lonely Zim, finally came crawling out of his ice-glazed puddle into the circle of flickering light, his shoes torn savagely by the feral death throes of the frogs he'd butchered for morning chuck!

« 23 »

The Cart Repaired,
the College Discovered

Lo! then the sun, swimming like a crazy person underneath the earth from the vasty West to the timbered East, broke, splashing, the waves of the grey Atlantic, whew! in the nick of time for dawn to "break," as such it often will, or hold enough!

And at its first faint rays of wishy-washy light, the gnarled and pasty-visaged cart-repairer smashed through the brambles, briers, and other loathsome plants to waken Blue and his beloved family. The kindly popular mechanik found them there, deep in sleep by the cold grey ashes of the evening's fire. With his gap-toothed smile, spake he thus, to wit:

Bestir your snoozy limbs, all needles and pins-a as they needs must be, stretched as thou art on this cold toif. Oh waxen man, oh boon companion of the terra gross! Your snazzy vehicle is all repaired, and, belike, as good as new! Fleet and falcon-like, and pining to be crammed with all your crap unto its very gunwales, if such a maritimic term may be applied to such a thing as is your antic cart! Up! Up! and wake! For the sun has scattered into flight the shades Cimmerian and eke the hick-faced football-eaters who did here last night make glut and scoff with thee and thine!

Then did Blue rise and wake his fambly. Then did they make a frugal repast on the shattered frogs that Zimmerman had snuffed. Then did they wade and labor back into the ferny dell in which the cart reposed, awaiting yet again their pleasure, and, by Jesu's Rood, the humble brougham did shine almost as bright as did the crass piano, all acrouch beneath a banyan! The thinning-haired Helene fell to her knees, busting yet again her busted nylons. Shambling Zim drooled gouts of spittle on his dicky. And Blue, his eyes fair starting from his cranium, did thus apostrophize:

O Cart! My pal, thou art now as eminent as bitched ascites, firk as sunspot-blue clostridium, sheeny as a swift colitis, and rampant as the omnipresent fascia; have I pricked down your semblance to the cherry-pink fistula? the nodding abasia? the confused edema? If not, then let me prick! And you do look like those great weeds that grow in mummia, the myalgia and the myasthenia as well! And too, the mist that hugs thee close is cousin to the onychia of changeable pale. Thou art sprue and stroma! Swart as Hermes' ebon urticaria, that he doth wear in's buttonhole on Sundays! And over all, the odd perfume of the Hackensack stenosis wafts. My puissant Cart! My clawed xanthoma! My adored old waggon, true as spreading-leaved tinea, from whose boughs the sweet xerosis all depends, though splayed with your Italian roseola!

Thus did he speak in tones at once stentorian and dumb. Then did the three, with the querulous aid of the old rube, who, e'en at this early hour, was half in the faithful bag, load up the patient cart with all their "goods." The piano was quick-roped with hawsers to the cart, Zim chucked aboard, and Blue then turned with rolling eye unto the wasted hooligan, while Helene stood all insouciant nearby.

With what, old bruto, can I make recompense? he said. I have no wealth, but I can rip you off a bar or twain of "Green Old Dolphin." You look as if you'd like a ripple of the rhythm, nu?

Belike, pardy, and grovel, croaked the swaying oaf. I'd more enjoy, and e'en delight in sharing, but the space of but a fleeting moment with your lissome lady in the scrub.

With this, the honest lecher leered and fell to unbuckling his codpiece as Helene trekked with immodest speed into the nearby hedge, her homely skirts a-flutter as was her girlish heart, her thighs akimbo.

Well, mused Blue, I'll have to think on it, and as he thought, the sound of gaiety venereal issued from the blushing leaves. Five minutes passed, then ten, while the doughty Serge did wonder on the duffer's odd request. Then, I'll do it! shouted he, until the welkin rang, or maybe jingled just a bit. And as he gave his husbandly O.K. to our mechano's plea, what? the old bum ambled forth into the clearing, with Miz Gavotte apace behind.

I thank you, gen'rous dick, the old rogue winked. 'Tis been ten year or since that I did gambol thus. And was it then a titter that flew like a chicken hawk from the delicious lady's lips?

Not quite aware of what adventure had befallen these two folks, our Blue thus deft removed it from his mind, aswim as was its wont, in deeper thoughts.

Then did Helene mount up upon the cart. Then did Blue shackle to the traces and the bights and bits and harnesses and all kindsa stuff. Then did they creak out onto the road, the Western wind carrying their scent behind them as they headed toward brooding Indiana, where other high adventures did await them maybe.

The Savior knows how long they schlepped and slogged abeam and truly well a-lubber throughout festering Ohio, but it was at least a sennight. They camped by rills and trestles, the wondrous sounds of chickasaws and weevils all their lullabies. They savaged the modest pickerel, the pendant apricot, the greenish gage. And of the snappy water all pellucid of the great Ohio and the Sasquatch they partook to slake their quench. Then, one day, just as Rosy Dawn did lift her pinky in the East, our three adventurers espied, beyond the wildly heaving canopy of ginkgos mixed with hazelnuts, the shining towers of—could it be—The University?! Serge swift heaved against the traces and the caravan rolled on in clouds of aromatic dust, crossing into Indiana at exactly 10 A.M. by Helene's heirloom Ingersoll, left her, in sly Gallic fun, by her Uncle Proust. But that's another story, and, belay, a good one that'll keep the hob a-bubbling on the spit while old Boreas whacks the picture windows as we slosh our toddies by the friendly firelight! Aye! up to our elbows in the roasted crabs and rocked in great hilarity with descant profound of the latest "books."

In a kind of trice, the Family Gavotte was on the campus and a hurried word with a student of Gourd Science cast Blue down for a nonce or two, as he learned that this was not The University, but Annex College, affiliated with the potent U, but not, as they say, "It." In funk peculiar, they stood and stared agape, bereft with soil and laden down with burrs and throstles.

A man all nondescript, yet tweedish, pipe-y, all baggy flannels and with wrinkled face and smile to match, his wise old eyes a-pop behind his rimless specs, approached in a swirl of falling ivy.

May I assist you kindly folks in kindly ways? My name is Bone, Dr. Weede Bone, Rector of the College, and laden to the brim with good intentions. Why not come to my office, slip out of those vetch-bespattered clothes, and have a small, yet satisfying lunch with me? Our motto here is "From Egg to Apple," which, while quaint, is quite impenetrable, no? And then he laughed his great warm laugh, his meerschaum dancing gaily in his mouth.

I seek The University, Dr. Bone, Blue commenced, and ran down his tale of quest and art, whanging his piano now and then, and helped along by his nattering wife. Weede hearkened to their tale, and puffed reflectively.

While I, my boy, the doughty academic said, cannot for a moment lift your crest, fallen as it is in the recent knowledge that the U lies further West, I may lighten up the fardels and valises of regret that settle down upon your hairy clavicle. That is, our Assistant Adjunct Temporary Chairman, Dr. Ryan Poncho, who is the right-hand man of Dr. Vince Dubuque, and placed in his position by that gimlet-brained Administrative Dean of The University, also chairs the Musical Department, and will, I feel certain as did Spencer Tracy of his God in that old flicker, *San Francisco*, furnish forth some phrases music-wise that will whet and tang your appetite for the "Real Thing" that may await you, even now, at our feared, adorèd U.

Oh Dr. Bone! My heart is rollicking as purple gentian when a tortilla unawares comes near its maw! Can I ever thank you?

Tut, tut, the white-haired sage implied. Come, let's to lunch. Leave the kid. I'll see to it that a grad assistant, deep in food lore, chunks him some gruesome chili from the student lunchroom, or mayhap a "sandwich" from the odd machines that dot and vend about the campus. And they scuffled through the glory of the fallen leaves and rotten melons toward the Rector's office, the while that gent nodded greetings to the ruby cheeks and huge incisors of the students hastening to class.

« 24 »

Dr. Bone
Shows the Lab to the
Gavottes; With Learned Commentary

As the sun glanced through the legendary ivy-throttled windows of Dr. Bone's austere but comfortable office, that hoary academic, Blue, and his helpmeet, leaned back on the venerable leather-like furniture that was strewn about the room. To a man, so to speak, as oft one must, they picked their teeth and sipped their cherry Kool-Aid.

Before I trot you out and introduce you to our reigning musicologist, Doc Poncho, Dr. Bone declaimed, his voice the burnished tool he used when handing college presidents yet another imbecilic plaque, perhaps you would be interested in lending me an ear or two.

I lean forward in my chair all breathless, Blue gulped.

My body also points its flesh toward you, good Dr. B, Helene blurted in addendum, as was her well-known wont, as those of you who've followed this hegira surely know. As for the rest, have with you to Coney Island!

The true work of this college, boon delightful chums, the Doc began, outside of course the teaching of the young—marble-eyed and badly dressed—since this is first and foremost, not to say primarily, a teaching college, not a center for research, and you may add that fustian to your list of cherished platitudes, the true work, I say, of Annex College is the work done in our laboratories. We have been, for some years now, and under many a juicy luscious grant, engaged in finding cures for and preventive measures against the age-old oral afflictions that have beset mankind since the sad day in 4000 B.C. or thereabouts when our horny mother, Eve, got her a bad case of the sponge-gum from the apple that she wolfed.

What? said Blue. You mean . . . ?

I mean mouth grief, I mean buccal mis'ry, I mean your basic loathsome ills that pitch disease into the old food-hole, dusty traveler, Doc Bone chuckled.

Blue glanced in wordless amaze at Helene, whose mouth had flown open like unto the fly of a soldier in a whorehouse. Together and as one flesh they thought

108

(since "I" know everything about them, ideal reader, sitting there and waiting for the story to "pick up a little"): DOC CHICK! But they held their breaths, and 'Slid! a good thing too, else the ivy that was climbing up the drapes had been blasted to a mess of home-fried pottage.

Perhaps, my pals, you'd feature ambling slowly with me to our modern labs, while I show you some of the things we're squandering our kopeks on? Thus Bone, peering out from clouds of noxious Rum and Maple.

Reet! said Blue and saccharine Helene, two minds that beat as one.

And there they were at last!

The lab! How abustle it shone and jigged! How the white coats and thick lenses of bespectacled technicians glimmered 'mid the smoke of endless stultifying pipes! How different from the sloven shop where Serge was wont to spit and polish lenses! So this was College!

Let me explain, sedulous gleets, Dr. Bone rapped on, some of the simpler processes we waltz about with here in our immaculate laboratories, simpler, I say, since such will not too onerously tax your lowly brows. And even though I'll strain to set and jellify the stuff as best I can in layman's terms, I fear you'll merely stand and gawp, such is the esoteric bullshit that I'll spout. Think of me, sweaty pilgrims, as a doctor or a lawyer, cant and argot washing o'er my tongue as does the great Niagara inundate poor Canada!

We'll strain our best, an' we gawp at last, Blue quipped, the stunned Helene already frozed with wonder.

Check! Weede said, tamping or whatever in or down his fragrant calabash. You may know, he said, sucking flame, etc., puffing smoke, etc., cradling the handsome bowl 'pon which was carved by stupid craftsmen all kindsa ugly shit, that in the past—and right up to the present!—such coises of the mouth as gingivitis, pyorrheal slime, trenchmouth, foot and mouth disease, galloping caries, abscessed lower lip, fistula of the soft palate, desiccated root canal, foetor gummae, carpet-tongue, morning breath, logorrhic pip, Cosell's disease, harmonica irritans, and such-like horrible afflictions, were and are treated with such homely medicines as busting muscat, dried fruttos, wrinkled leaves, dozing corn shock steeped in algolagnia, daffodils and strawberry roots, rutabago blooms, crawling treponema, sloes black as jett, lavender peony stems, the shady fusillade, and, not to forget, the curious peach. You may know this.

I hadda idear, murmured Blue. Helene gooped away in eerie silence, her "thoughts" on Zim, who even now was rending mercilessly what the quaint inhabitants did call a "hoagie," a kind of sangwich that the great Caligula invented in a throe of lust.

Excellent good, old Bone rejoined. Now then, obsessive sloggers, follow close my cogent lecture as I commence. Starting in that corner of the pristine lab and moving clockwise, let me expound upon some of the all-important break-throughs while you silently or otherwise applaud all-potent science, endlessly questing for the light and truth and the really heavy bread, as has been its wont since that rainy morn that General Westinghouse, known as the mutter of invention, was whelped in a humble filthy hogan on the smelted plains of legendary Boise!

Expound abaft! Blue murmured. There's nothing like an education to make one plumb the deeps of ignorance.

Well put, old pip! Over there you can see a vectographologist plunged into some arcane metamorphoses. At the moment, she is macerating the crooked poplar in a double-bottomed cucurbite until it citronizes; then she will endeavor to sublime the residue till the green lion appears *in fumo*. When a dollop of luke-warm menstrue is added to the resultant chang, putrefaction will ensue and zut! with luck, a dandy salve to rid the teeth of citronella stains. Our next technician, the lass whose lab smock hardly can disguise her lusty charms, is at the moment placing a tutie in a crystal phlox, a kind of lembek made expressly for us by Burris Bags of Brooklyn. The *sanguis agni*—issuing from the pelican—that your astonished eyes now light upon is very close to the fabulous guelder-rose of Nature, but without that shrub's destructive stink. I am drowned in hope that this swell gunk, something like the lost pink brilliantine that blooms aberrantly in star-light, will prove a boon to those afflicted with the fever blisters of fellatio. Moving right along: do you see that four-eyed wimp a-tingle with the thrill of high re-search? The redberry moonseeds that he's chopping into the liquor of Mars in his simmering alembic will soon give forth your *materia liquida*, and one that dances with the colors of the peacock's tail. Yowzah! This juice, wisely blended with a pinch of red man and a handful of white woman, can be used, if God is good, as the rinse to thoroughly dissolve the venom in the mouth of one of those unfortunates who has, by design or accident, ingested tuna helper. This may be the greatest boon to dumb mankind since Dr. Robinson slapped together what he chose to call—and what a choice!—his magic bullet! Shall I continue? Or is your simplike brain piled to the attic with info that you can't digest?

Go on, Dr. Bone. I feel an almost physical delight, akin to meeting someone who's never heard of Woody Allen.

What a wondrous simile! Something like an anapestic diorama! Well then, I'll venture on, as Columbus said, to sail, to scuttle, and to sink, yet not to quake or reef a single boom-yard!

Columbus! the cuddly Helene declared, starting for a fleet out of her gawklike trance. I weep still when I think upon him all bedecked with plastic Xmas icicles adrift on Hudson Bay! Thus always those who strive and tack about!

Easy to see why such a wifely person was the toothsome cause of your banjaxed cart! Dr. Bone leered tutorially. But andiamo! as our ceaselessly laughing friends, the hard-working ginzolas say. At our next "bench" you may descry a feverish team clustered all about an aludel cheerily bubbling on the hob. The *equi clibanum* is causing a perfect inceration in the common catalpa and it turns, even as we stare, into the plumèd swan! A dash of lato and azalea in an hour will produce an ointment that, swilled around with zernich, may prevent God only knows how many poetry readings at the Y, its powers being such that, when ingested, it produces aggravated laryngitis. Another curse lifted from the soul of suffering humankind! We work here, cutey, we don't play, though often we are held in greater scorn than weird Capaneus's Sears and Roebuck stepladder. At the next table, aha! we see The College's most gifted scientist, his apron heavy with foundation loot, and in the fourteenth year of his heartbreaking quest for the elixir that will make all men sing with the voice of the gringo nightingale, Pat Boone. A lonely search that has broken many men and that contributed to the death of Albert Einstein—but let that story rest in peaceful darkness. You see him, pockets jingling, up to his worn-out elbows in *aqua fortis*, chibrit, sericon, his nose jammed in a bolt's head, a red-hot gripes egg twixt his agued knees, shredding devilwood and merds in furious abandon into boiling azoch, clouds of crow and mists of pale citron swirling round his sconce, waiting for the chrysosperm to come forth in the projection. This is his three hundred and twelfth attempt, yet he does not flag, remembering that the great Thomas Albert Edison hit on the waffle iron on his nine-hundredth shot at it—along the way discovering the heating pad and baseball! Thus serendipity blunders into glory!

I understand the drive and potent power of his quest, Blue swallowed. Yes, down to my bone-like marrow!

I had a hunch, old cokes, that you would especially "dig on" his crazed and magnificent obsession, the tweedy prof mused fetchingly, deep-sucking on his toasty cherrywood, his wise face atwinkle in the aromatic fumes.

I admire the cut of his jib, Helene added, lost in a sigh as she thought on her farflung youth, now plunged into the oblivion of grimacing age, wrapped, as it sometimes is, in the toga of responsibility. How swiftly, she sobbed, we are wrapped in the toga of responsibility!

Cedant arma togae, Weede chuckled.

I love the sound of that wop-talk, Blue admired. Soft and mellifluous it is as a weeping willow crashing slowly into the roaring flood. But, Dr. Bone, is that, as they say, it, as far as the lab obtains?

All but one table has been checked out and explainized, the kindly time-server nodded. There are some . . . other . . . "things" going on in our top-secret prioritized labs in the sub-sub-basement, but they are not for the prying eyes of laypersons, if you follow me? I can only hint that they touch upon a reduction of the vocabulary of world leaders to a clutch, a teeny pile of words, mostly of your nounal type, to spare them jabs and uppercuts of foul embarrassment when dealing with the great unwashed, who, as you know, ask a question on your rare occasion. These words would cover *all* contingencies!

Perish forfend that I should gaze upon such deepish stuff, blenched Blue.

That is jake with me, old socks. And now, our last project, taking place before your wildeyed gaze. Here you see an athanor, in which a graduate assistant and what seems to be a "friend" of his, judging by her popeyed glance of young desirous lust, are dulcifying dental floss donated by the leper colony just down the road, oh, 'bout as far as you can throw an ax-handle, a invaluable community in that your basic monk, your priest, your down-at-heels missionary, go there for their graduate work in Humility and Compassion, plus a short course in Self-Abnegation. Well, that is neither here nor far. This dental floss, steeped and wallowed in the juice and slime and spittle of the basic leprous type, is run through your putrefaction, your cibation, your projection, burned and incinerated and scorched up real good along with pieris, sweetbells, smoketree, other herbs, and a cross-let of jamoke. The result? If Our Powerful Creator smiles, and the Federal lettuce keeps on drifting in, this young rake and his sweating punk will some day educe from out this small inferno a salve so potent that a person, in the comfort and the privacy of his own home or apartment—even his furnished room!—can smear it on a rotten tooth and, by God! the fucker will dissolve and vaporize, all in a trice, and without a ort of pain!

'Tis hard to credence, Blue said, amazed by this latter phrase.

Yes! But true, however strange! I don't have to tell you, Weede said in an elaborate aside, that extremist dentists have vowed to destroy our work! Yet we press!

Is that the "works," Professor Bone? Blue said, perhaps a little sadly.

That is the shebang, dear friends. And now, let us wend to my apartments. We'll have a bit or bite of supper later, and I'll take you around to meet Dr. Poncho. Surely you can stay a day or so? The College would be honored. To chat, to guff, to rap and shoot the shit—how savory the thought! And, too, Miz Gavotte, to have the delightful prospect of your company brings out the latent gent in me—and I'm sure Doc Poncho will feel à la ditto, Bone leched, his impeccable grey flannels all abulge.

Of course we'll sojourn for a sun or trey, Blue grinned, while the fair Helene blushed wildly, a strange heat powerful as flaming Sterno sloshing through her loins, or whatever women have down there.

« 25 »

The Gala
Cocktail Party

Pain, the sagacious Dr. Bone was saying, flits through my sensibilities, accompanied by no small modicum of embarrassment, since it is my tortured yet stern duty to inform you, my dear Gavottes, that Dr. Poncho, embroiled as he needs must be in administrative tasks, will not be able to greet you tonight. He will, however, see you tomorrow, and lay, as the hep phrase runs, some heavy sounds on you. In the meantime, I have, with Dr. Poncho's blessing, arranged a small yet gay, if not gala, cocktail party for you, at which you may meet some of our most distinguished administrators and faculty. Shall we repair to the Dan'l Boone Room?

Thus saying, they . . . and so forth.

And there they were! What cascades of academic glitter! What a fine madness of the intelligentsia! What milling and wheedling! The wonderful persons circulated and chatted, drank and staggered, consumed "dip" (whatever that may be), and the like festive routine. Sing, Muse, of this catalogue of shits!

There came Brenda Fatigué, Regius Professor of Office Fashion; Ed Flue, Associate Professor of Logging; Burnside Marconi, Instructor in Televiewing; Syrup Concoct, Poet-in-Residence; Benjamin Manila, Chairman of the Stationery Department; G. Root Garbáge, Counselor in Venereal Diseases; Jedediah Mange, Vice-President for Member Development; Winifred Zinnia, Corsetiere for Rector of the College; Socks O'Reilly, Chief of Tension Calisthenics; Marcus Podium, Ellsworth Harelip Professor of Speech and Drama; Heinz Pogrom, Horst Wessel Professor of German Philology; Gladys Bung, Dietary Tactician; Fifi Galleon, instructor in French Jobs; Catherine Thigh, Director of Sexual Services; Nicholas Syph, Bureaucracy Professor Emeritus; Yvette Risqué, Associate Professor of Auto-Erotism; Francis-Xavier Silhouette, S.J., Chaplain; Pedro Manteca, Professor of Fast Food Studies; Chastity Peep, Instructor in Vaginal History; Angelo Bordello, Disciplinary Dean of Women; Manatee Brouillard,

Connecticut Professor of Fertilizer Studies; Idyott Dymwytte-Pyth, Instructor in Ur-Critique; Rastus X. Feets, Professor of Black English.

And circulating, smiling, chatting, laughing, the Gavottes moved as if . . . as if . . . in a dream!

"Alas! One acknowledges, sadly, sadly, that ladies' intimate garments are unattractive in direct proportion to their comfort."

"The sturdy old oak, falling heavily, crashed spang through the dorm windows, whereupon a cloud of flies rose up, buzzing in terror and chagrin."

"The first television 'sighting' took place in Dublin in 1904, when one Francis Aloysius McGlynn dropped his transistor radio and a little man, holding a bar of lemony soap, crawled painfully from the wreckage."

"Night is/and life is/what means/means be life."

"After being dated and stamped, then stamped and dated, the incoming mail is sent to the Dating-Stamping clerk."

"You've got your basic buboes, your running chancre, your clapperoo sacred and profane, your gleet malaise, your Spanish pox."

"Caught the lad in the act of self-gratification, so the benighted Scoutmaster stripped him of his Personal Health Merit Badge."

"I'm most proud, I think, of the fact that General Champagne, while dictating the peace terms, was marvelously trig in my featherweight foundation in ecru with black nylon-lace panels."

"The old Army dozen cures your basic born-again Christian in about three or four weeks."

"Duh perfeck eckshershize izh: 'Hash dow sheen budda bride lilygrow?' "

"Some uff mein goot Chewish frents from zuh fordies seem to haff . . . disappeared!"

"The fatback is then gently sautéed in two ounces of King Kong and a quarter-cup of oleo."

"It is permissible, even salutary, for the modern woman to fantasize a touch of sodomy with the office boy while in lawful embrace with her spouse."

"When the boys returned, simply *mad* for some clean, blond, smiling American poon, what was this once-great nation's inadequate response?"

"The truly efficient office should be able to complicate *everything* in just under six months, taking into account, of course, the zeal of the staff."

"With the skirt discreetly lifted to the upper portion of the lower limbs, and the underpants crisply rolled to that point at which said lower limbs are jointed, the clitoris may be surreptitiously massaged while dining, at the theater, or even in the office."

"I also serve who only blandly prate."

"We have almost achieved a breakthrough in the instant wiener."

"The vagina, long since accepted as reality in Mesopotamia, was first observed beyond that state's borders in the fourth millennium."

"I take absolutely no pleasure in chastising these remarkably lovely, luscious, desirable, nubile, and altogether terrific young women."

"We actually had to turn a thousand people away the evening Shecky Green gave a dramatic reading from *October Light*."

"The progression is crystal clear: Joyce, Beckett, Costain, Jong."

"When ah be's gwine, ah be's gwine to Jericho!"

". . . invented by a gay Presbyterian minister—pantyhose, I mean."

"No tenure *yet*, though I am known everywhere as Johnny Acorn!"

"I entered and saw Mrs. Marconi in the most *extraordinary* position."

"They/whimper."

"I don't exactly know what an 'envelope' *is*."

"The affected member is plunged into warm Pepsi."

"Putting it into a honeydew is also recommended."

"The new gym shorts offer just a wisp of gentle control."

"Leaping high into the air, you intertwine the index fingers."

"Yethhir! That'th mah baby!"

"So ve burned der files."

"Yes, radishes! Skewered along with soybean balls and okra."

"The beautiful poems of Miss Flambeaux have saved many marriages."

"Yes, my famous 'Tuesdays' *are* booked months in advance."

"If it calls for eight copies, make twelve."

"The woman then places her ankles alongside her ears."

"In Indianapolis, God's hand is everywhere seen."

"What precisely is 'bread'?"

"Recent studies suggest that men who wear athletic supporters suffer from vagina envy."

"After four in the afternoon, the supple birch switch is best."

"Who dreamt that the dead salmon would grow into a lusty azalea?"

"The walking-stick is always a symbol for a specific Western angst."

"The baddest dude be's Gentian Washington."

". . . the *cruel* corset? Cruel?. . ."

". . . lifts his meaty hands to prey . . ."

". . . during the commercial break, large amphibians . . ."

". . . cer/tain/ly . . ."

". . . the tongue, now crisscrossed by small paper cuts . . ."

". . . the vast warehouse, filled with impounded toilet seats . . ."

"...*bursting* through his BVD's, it..."

"...her lacings, whipping through the air, caught the Monsignor..."

"...now, the full bosom, during the eight-count push-up..."

"...wit duh lipz inna shmirk..."

"...undt vhen der rosy dawn lighted up Auschwitz..."

"...the hamburger, partially rotted in the soil..."

"...Havelock Ellis, delirious in the ladies' room..."

"...even the most modest will lift her skirts if..."

"...having typed it on green tissue instead of light blue..."

"...the role of the pleated skirt in spontaneous orgasm implies..."

"...in baseball cap and cassock, I often wander through..."

"...the tuna is tossed with tiny marshmallows..."

"...imagine Danaë's surprise when all this gold..."

"...while one young lady is spanked, another sometimes..."

"...the piccadills and stoccadoes, well irrigated..."

"...herring-motif in Malamud's juvenilia..."

"...Dean Bordello an' me, man, we be's whoppin' an' whompin' on..."

"...curious linguistic apparatus that often in disciplines that favor a particular array of the marvelous stretchiness of that post-war if you do understand a latex well can it be a swell campus support for what? is that the various social services or can it be a kind of utter lovely parameter when just a tiny bit of although they are a kind of "fingers" if that's the specific kind of pastrami did you ever understand for instance what array of the most dedicated Doctorow? Gardner? Styron? often at mass it is in my mind that this campus this hallowed ground this garter belt flushed but it's most tough when in the very middle of the squash surprise a gentle zephyr at the egress of the people from Washington are there skirts just quietly lifting and the marvelous slice of Bermuda that decorates but also wraps the old ribbon in the same cellophane that the unfettered thigh decides to plant itself alongside the beloved peonies that have oft buried a mackerel like the Indians? sure enough into the gym fell a large bag in which the ivy mixed with an odd how shall I say "novel" that makes one almost dense with flannel and yet not quite tweed although it is in a sense marinated in a cheaper wine your zinfandel your kosinski your screamingly boring onslaughts of what in Algiers? but of course not something for every day they dub it "dub" is a bitch "dub" it anyway the maniacal Jung deep in Mein Kampf and dosed up good with what? with what? oh dear sweet Jesus the tailored suit the bull clap because it can give you the tenure that you would suck spit for and knock a bull down on his knees if they have such articles of apparel unknown and not given the respect that ensues in Scranton that city of lost marines and the dry rot in the great nodding elms and if tenure is the guerdon of those who lift skirts and bull trousers and spaghetti soft and mushy the way it be's when they's be's got the lesson plan and the rosy reddened and tingling how shall I say in Tunis in the darkened office around five or so of a winter evening the sound of Marrakech and the soft sobbing as we watch the snap beans and the impeccable white of the knee hose and down there around the ankles is the mimeo machine andhg therzwx wehytu eogghji wh tuouh to thyrhtyyehyheuuhr jo joyk blamdurf oi gurdhujhut uh uh uhh uhhhh uh uh uh uh ooooooohhhh . . ."

Supper, with Dr. Bone, was, the doctor being the soul of genial warmth, a small yet festive occasion of genial warmth. They looked forward to the morrow with benign alacrity. Things were certainly looking "up."

Well, sweat-face, Blue said to Helene. Things are "looking" up! He seemed almost . . . *happy*!

« 26 »

In Which Dr.
Poncho Meets the Avid Blue

The dawning hence and thus the flaming sun, pinkish-gold as weird Miami bungalow, did clamber up the sky! Yes, it was the following day, and Blue, an ornament unto his time, waited in the little room without the puissant Ryan Poncho's inner sanctum, a-jiggle all with noives. Then the door swung open slowly to reveal the Doc, his face, as novels love to say, wreathed in smiles. Or so to speak in elegiac spondees.

A kindly face, alarmingly like Dr. Bone's, topped this hearty scholar's frame, and as Blue followed him into his cabinet, he noted well the crisp insouciance of Indiana couture, thus: He wore a dark-blue wash and wear, carelessly baggy, the cuffs of the trousers to the brim with lint; his lumpy feet were shod in highly polished, down-at-heels wing-tip brogans; to guard him from the Hoosier blasts, a hand-knit bulky cardigan of oatmeal wool clung close to his "body"; his pockets bulged with a myriad reports; his socks, of thinnest whitest lisle nestled at his shoetops; his vest, bereft of two buttons as was Apollinaire's in rosy Texas, sagged quite fetchingly, shining with tobacco stains; on his watch chain hung the noble emblem of the Rotary Club; his white starched shirt, with collar slightly frayed, served as background for his polyester cravat, brilliant red with a motif of tiny yellow palm trees, this latter item anchored with a tie-clasp which commanded "THINK."

Come in, my son, the doughty educator laughed. Weede—Dr. Bone to you— has said that you are laden to the brim with good intentions, though you schlep the fardels and valises of regret that you have not found the perfect and ineffable phrase of, how do you call it? music. I am afraid that here, where the sunset collapses in its panoply of horribly depressing colors, you will not find it either, my rude sonata. Yet, embroiled as I needs must be in administrative tasks, sit, my innocent cluck, though crestfallen and aspout with tears, and we will chat, guff, rap and shoot the shit betimes, though I am tortured with compassion seeing that you have been blowing your great red heart out on the piano that you cleave unto.

My heart leaps up when I behold the pain glow in your eye! Serge whined.

Although I no like-a dis phrase, ats-a nize, Poncho countered. You talk what I wanna hear, here at old AC, far, far from the smelted plains of legendary Boise, where they know how to buy things!

Many thanks, good Doctor, it is my pleasure entirely to meet the man who is not only the Assistant Adjunct Temporary Chairman of this whole shebang, but who is also Chairman of the . . . Musical Department! Uh, Blue limped bravely on, Doctor Bone implied that . . . that . . . you might . . .

Ha, ha, ha! Calm your fears, inept crusader! Weede—and by the by, did you know that he is the man who invented the pencil moustache? No matter. Weede, I said, I say, honcho of All-Important Breakthroughs in the chemical something or other, has told me of your rather impertinent desire to hear a few musical phrases which, while not in your ineffable class, will give you a jagged ort of a idea of the type of thing you will dig on when you get to The University! The gimlet-brained Dr. Dubuque will knock you off your lilting little cadenza, chief! And you may lay to that! These wise old owl-like eyes portend same. In the meantime, though I ask myself, Who is this chooch to come in here, all akimbo? I will help you with a clutch of belle musique, knocked out on an platinum kazoo, given me by a confidante of the great Blue Barron.

I gripe and writhe in fiery expectation, gasped our pilgrim, eyes a-pop.

Thus thou ever must! And with this, the repository of ancient Midwestern wisdom amblingly shambled to his massive oaken desk at which, 'tis rumored, Robert Bly once popped some actual corn, wild husks and all!

The odd machines that dot and vend about the campus, the stalwart mentor quipped, can offer nothing like . . . this! And thus saying, whipped from a drawer the instrument elite.

Blue, his face the memorable one of a dead clam, blanched at the sight of the relic.

Good monsieur, Poncho smiled, settling his cardigan, you got on you a face like a dead clam, which, though you are marble-eyed and badly dressed, sets you off in dazzling chiaroscuro, or summat like.

Blue sprawled dumbstruck in amaze, his shining orbs fixed piercingly upon the ancient African pipe that somehow glittered in the Doctor's duke. It was as if, to Blue, great Pan hisself had crashed, hooves first, into the still retreat, and stood before him, shooting off auras scintillant to beat the band.

Now, this snatch of sweet melodious glop has made men's eyes look, as our friends, the Frogs, say, one at the other, such is its wheedling force. And with that he raised the pipe unto his lips and blew:

O Lady of the Tattered Slip! quoth Blue, his tongue starting from his mouth in ecstasy, and, yea! finishing as well. Can this be music? It seems more like unto the distillation of a pizza with garlic and *alice*!

Har, har! Ryan Poncho whooped. Though ofttimes cant and argot wash o'er my tongue, when I set this priceless kazoo unto my lip, I am fain to set the table on the floor! And, with this, the elegant hayseed let forth another blast which may be thus notated:

With this vast melodious canto ringing in his vexed cerebrum, Serge fell upon the Persian lying vaingloriously on the floor, and, at this moment, sound asleep. But these are more than decibels! our pilgrim quavered. These are fairy sounds urged from the airy syrinx and the timbrel, not to say the caduceus of pie-eyed Dionysos! At this great name, the Persian stirred in joy.

Pay no heed to that Arab pinned twixt you and the parquet, brave voyager, good Poncho spoke, but bend your ear-shells to this wild-soaring chord, a veritable mélange of the diatonic mayhem of the staunch Crusades! And whistling a blast of carbon dioxide through his metal reed, he played:

A kind of carnal joy spread over Serge's countenance, the while he rolled and gyved within his friendly jeans. By the lascivious Jupiter's great straining codpiece, thus he wove his song, this is more pungent and spectacular than a politician's rhetoric! And with this he rolled his eyes along the snoozing Persian, begging for, yet afraid of more, as a damsel roiled in the sin of Manichee.

Just one more, the sage leader smiled all crinkly like Edmund Gwenn. And this, I warn you, is as close as I can come to The Ineffable; hip to this, dear wanderer, imagine then what the Primal Phrase must be like, why man, 'tis the musical equivalent of the philosopher's stone, changing the dumb yawps of the sublunary world into aural ambrosia; and without a moment's stay, the Doc bent to his dazzling task and let loose upon the office air this bar:

By Xanthippe's favorite clout, gasped Blue, I shudder in a throe or two of wild abandon, and feel my manly juices gushing gaily from my loins as if I had beneath me Miss America, rather than this Arab in his noisome toga! And all a-grit, he let the act of shame sweep him to the bright empyrean, wherein the seraphim and cherubim fell into clouds, bought trumps, and otherwise got through their endless days. And yet, he said, when Nature hight allowed him speech, you say that this is not the Great Phrase that I seek? 'Slid! I hunch and blench in thinking of the vigor and the beauty of that Sound!

And you shall hear it, valiant stooge, carped Poncho, or these old eyes have never feasted on a co-ed's thighs!

Blue had staggered to his feet, weak as Agamemnon after being banjaxed by Aegisthus in the shower. I fear that I must rest a day or two, he wheezed, here at The College, if I may. These notes, this music of the spheres, has enervated all my vim. I must recoup my strength before facing . . . The Ineffable in leafy Illinois!

An excellent idea, my gallant! And tomorrow, may I suggest that you stroll into town to witness a memorial for Jacques-Paul Surreale, the late Chairman of our Gardening Department, dead one year now of a surfeit of fringe-tree root in coralberry sauce. The latter is a speciality of the famed Indiana Club, WASPs only, no jigs, tie and jacket at all times, ladies' grill, supper dance Friday night. No matter. But it might be just the thing to calm your nerves and prepare you for the road.

It sounds indeed unto and all belike same tonic-like.

But certainly, the Chairman twinkled. And while you dig and get behind this blubbering memorial, perhaps your wife—whom, I understand, is charming as a new-sprung beautyberry bush—might like to shop away an hour's span or so in our Mighty Mall, as chicks adore to do.

It sounds like just the ticket, Blue mused, although I have little or no hunch whatsoever what that weird idiom portends. I'll impart this idear to Helene, who, even now, is ironing her old fedora somewhere on vast campus.

How I love a woman in a hat! crooned Poncho. Madonn'! It makes-a me craze! And with that, he ushered Serge out into the blasts of vicious sunlight that whacked the land. Tell your faithful spouse, he said, to take the lonely, quiet road that runs behind the Pizzaburger labs. No one will bother her there, he leered, nor even lay an eye on her.

How start to thank you, Dr. Poncho? And Blue's eyes filled up with stern yet gentle tears.

Ho ho! *De rien*, as they say in Montparnasse. Make sure though, that she dons her hat, the Doctor goggled, for ofttimes the sun at midday can baste the brains of tender womenfolk. And, trousers curiously tented, he watched our Blue clunk off into the brutal glare.

« 27 »

Elegy for
Jacques-Paul Surreale

Yes, my friends, Surreale has passed from this mortal curl to a better world; Jacques-Paul Surreale! Is there one among you who does not remember him? Does his memory fade, flake, and founder, now that he has, as they say, cached his chops? Let me then, as the Mayor of Blatherville, refresh, if that is the word, and it is the word, refresh, I say, I insist, your collective memories. I have had this little talk mimeographed or something, and will pass it out to you when I have desisted.

What did the sight of this man, this dear Jacques-Paul, bring to mind? I mean, uh, what were his attributes? They were, and I mention just a few that the vox populi noticed in his forty-seven wondrous years here on this spinning glob. He had a bagful more, but and however: shoofly moron and peach toddy; migraine warbler, masocherian and ashcan baritone; nimbus cerulean and orangeade psalter; lockstep motherfucker and dangler asshole; serendipitous album, aztec microscope and wedge exposure; teterboro rapidoprint, eversharp daddy, verlaine camel and sawbuck marmalade; royal blank book; vegetal dundee; kilroy clean 'em up; rocky swingline and ballpoint anjou; bauschlomb petillance; bonsoir la lune; bistro crackerjack and submarine living room; blue disaster; epiphany lemon; zarruzzi; octagon kate; zippo enameloware; fudge skippie; moscow rose and ward eight; dutch mulligan; crayola rock; reproducing red ashtray; endpaper pastoral, systemic agfa and elmer scotch; cordon bleu royale; paideuma label; buckram austen; russo millefiore; cinzano south; mint alcool; close-order paper clip and fiction filed beginning.

And if you think that *that* is supreme hot stuff, do any of you citizens and chunky-faced neighbors remember what JP looked like? His zotzed and circumambient eyes? Moon zephyr white and russet hair? Alluvial nose just slightly quetzalcoatl? And don't neglect his maced and thund'rous eyebrows black as Christmas shoes, lashes long and caustic like a livid lunar lay, a brow broad as a pyk walwed in galauntyne, beige ears almost lemon waxy white, gladstone mouth with hint of eerie snowfall, and blank teeth alla vino paradiso bianco. Moving around and about, recall Surreale's lips the very pinks o' borders lavender, latex ice and minty barrel tongue, a chuckling agamemnon of a neck, two shoulders deep in kali stupor, a chest touched on in the azure billet doux of paloma miss, a foxed and am'rous bloomsday of a belly, libby krasdale biceps bloomingly del monte, slanged forearms glittering with bix, petite ebon and sappho darksome wrists, and his fingers cobalt, fingers coal, fingers cadmium, fingers cool, fingers ginger. Bejesus Christ! his nails all a loony luminous quintessence, haut monde crotch zinged into silence, a penis appleblossoom rabelaisian in hearts, a sighing maniac in twilight of a scrotum, hot santa ana crackling pubic hair, testes brave and reckless as apple pies, winnowed thighs done rayon lackawanna, petite yet ponko buttocks pot au feu, kneecaps redolent of jesuits at the dentist, calves whizzed around korean avocados, boxed taped tied and labeled wettling ankles, plus toes trendy, toes torrid, toes torroncino, toes tungsten, toes paprika. I sob, I sigh, recollecting this champ elite's smile parasol azul yet mansfield park, his dotting wizzering and boining glance, his spanked cerise that busts the garters laugh and frown to fulminate flann's flan and finnan haddie, a sigh riised out as leda swacked and feathered, warmy moist sub-nylon lace rich stretches, zit bellows wedgwood orangery, inhalations exhalations balderdashing brilliant, wildly stewed and mildly brunswick thrashings, his crazed maccool of a lordly gait, such jumps and leaps all blarney of a dew, kisses in the mode of sulpicia cum cerinthus, fists blamming gesticulent noirs sur la lune, hospitable gargantuas of shuffled shamble, his soles as out of date as all big doors and his jacked detonate erections quadriviis et angiportis.

I say: This was a man! And if his attributive stuffs and the way he struck, in his full bearing, the peeled and naked orb, ain't enough for you good appleknockers republicanos, entertain for a nonce or two, what he did in his life, his deeds heroic, deeds hierophantic. He gumballed and shenangoed endless crates of white labels in the north river bitter winds; waned at dirty desks and beamed out flyblown windows at baltics, smiths, and presidents; gazed at balding bookkeepers with the sing-sing heebie jeebies; furbelowed in four-in-hands and listened solemnly to fools with oatmeal haircuts; filed green for glum and boring, white for ho-hum, pink for wait a second, and red for cut the bastard off; stretched ten minutes to fifteen and twenty mumbling his toasted corn and joyless joe; crammed commodes with piles high of intelligence courtesy of Dun and Brad; spoke pompously of lilacs in the dooryards blooming to a pipe and high black shoes; ballooned and samboed not to mention glaumed the swell flatiron tall; waited patiently for views of strapping hose madisonly metropolitan and leafy life; whiled his tulips, swept his chimneys, and cosmodemonized the ranks of crippled couriers; lammed it on the jesse owens and bolted breezily with his final check; reinsured, complete with a thousand twangling errors, feeble fey and fecund sons of bitches far and fulsome; peered beneath the stalls for gentilhommes with agued Al to put the latter's mind at rest but always failed; purloined for sophomoric laughs the amarillo mongols of one Walter King, a pure prince of a psychopath; retched and ratcheted at the snapper's panama, the snapper's stetson, and the snapper's bowlertrilby; wielded a red-ink bejayzus stamp but for what and whom was at a loss to know; laughed for Red, the Marxist carl, as he lobstered in from beachy weekends with his nubile novia; old golded smoke at his panama's hatty elder bro, a corpulent kraut if dair effer fuss fun; stood in amuse at the corrugated corseting of Miss Wexler, the iron spinster on terms supreme with warts and washcloths warm, but not with wantonness; boffed zok! and whammo! nervously at the promise of the white shirt wondrous diurnal, also starched; bowtied and polkadotted, schlepped loads of first-class mail for Mr. Jiminy C for Christmas Nelson; heard the plump and puerile pals from Jersey Nassau blither black and orange to each other; swayed awestruck, sat cockeyed, stiff in his tented trousers, at the girdled yet gorgeous hips thighs and bottom of Miss Lewdy Lovelie, ravishing receptionist; crunched and powed into desks and other items in a cloud of musky attar from a dozen ordering broads, though middle-aged yet toothsome; sudsed and dove for pearls in apron blank and slammed down china thick and laceworked to raucous drunks till Sunny Sol limped in from the Atlantic for some ham and eggs; green-aproned, hoffed and skiddoed multitudes and myriads of poster paint all brown for third-rate art; queasied, bored as Jesus Aitch, over garbage parcels, trash, and Xmas xrap in the tattered costume of the red-white deuce; spat and ambuscadoed Freddy, the shame of Bensonhurst, outcast of the tribes of Schmaltz; bled flats and humped palettes for assemblies, reeled and staggered skids and sweated handtrucks (by Hernia), daunted dollies like any other asshole ace; drummed down the booming windows almost but not quite on the dirty digits of north river dasheroos; slambangoed diesel manifests blue-cold to the bone in a borrowed skullcap courtesy of toothless Jack from Hackensack; honest as the day is lone, cracked his gonads, spoining the silvuh of the roadwise horde; sockdolagered and often poozed the groaning new-pine shelving with paper products straight from redwood land; listened, bored and bilious, to busted swedish bullshit anent the bright lights of old Gotham and the absorption of a zillion cocktails; belly full of cheap baloney and cheaper seeded rolls, assisted people looking for some book about some Greek by some Homer-I-forget-his-other-name; wondered about what went on beneath the weighty Wanda Wasserman's woolen skirt and watched her languid limbs between her hugest hips and highest heels; dispatched old trucks to farthest Morristown, checked them in from stupid Newark, allatime accepting tacitly the foreman's wampum of hyperbole erotomania; did not get straight the zany lather and the casks of oil produced and sold by one Suds Stanley and his sluggard Sons; punched and pressed and washed and packed and pushed and poked at teflon (made by maniacal Maigne) and meantime heard his stomach fall apart; pushed diegos, hustled rastuses, and was pushed and hustled by abes and sys in turn, and all to transport tinny presents culled with coupons; bamboozled and was thus bamboozled by his lawless boss, king of sales, duke of copies, all made by heat and heartache; salammboed lamps and blew the inventory, popping at a gallon jug of manahattas all the while; observed amour ablossom twixt a grinning suit and a titless typist, right beneath the eye of hubby Harry Horns; wrote a billion letters to burgs and also suburbs 'neath the worried lamps of Madame Starr, owl-founder, brace buddy, harcourt helper, and a vestal in her heart of hearts; in a daze of mania, whizzed out reams of platitudes in re wordy waifs up for adoption under the direction of a woeful walker, lonely and latent in Cos Cob; and drank his sadness into foolishness as prelude to a demise of all his occupations as an average joe.

And if this, delightful denizens, still ain't enough to melt your moral hearts, cock an eardrum to old Jacques-Paul's legacy to you, yessiree bob! To you and to your children, and to your children's children, all this until it is plumb gone, all this, these, items: hillocks blue and mounds macabre of root beer barrels lissome and monsterious; candy eat-the-paper buttons aglitter in synthetic colors scintillant; shoeleather with the tart biaggio of apricots achuckle from Salerno's sun; thwell thuckers that lathteth all the day to pop the eyes and round la boca; lashings and larrupings of lucky stix to which the man in white affixeth corny syrup froid; Emperor Frank's, by the grace of God Almighty, nectar for each and every nonce; Dixie Shakes in umber domino; waxlips vermilion and sweet as Sydelle Seize's kisses that pluck up the very soul; potable punch in odd bottles inedible; les twistes marshmallow à la Alpine; the whips you wuv aw bwack and chewy; Van Amsterdam Hooten's hunks of crazed cacao; rubber ice cream in criminal cones; maryjanes created by the League of Dentists, U.S.A.; sombreros mejicanos con naranja y vanilla frio as a fontbonne freshman; splintery ice from the splattery bed of the sputtering truck of the iceman Baresian; stale scots mincecakes and buttergrease shortbread piled plumply in paper Queen Marys; lickerish lickrish tortured into button your lips; phials of phony beebees multihued although mighty mingy; eyeless nigger babies courtesy of Andros Kingfish, Nights of the Dark Peculiar; olympian egg creams avec ze secret tweest, to wit: ze lait mus' be frigid unto frizzing; bonomo bananacherrychoc from Turkey; tiny tired AWOL bags aburst with chewy chunks whipped up from sweat and sun and salty water; peppercorns the core of splendid suckerballs; apothecary branches in which sit anisette to suck; crooning fluted tins of petey barnum pie with slicy spoons to lacerate the lingua; charred and charming mickeys in the boining bowels of garbage conflagrations; the blistering delights of depression sangwiches brought to you by Heinz and Gulden; George Washington Saturday pies with the Swedish maiden's four-eyed touch to turn you spicy crazy; a jitney's worth o' luscious buns to make masticators mousy-grey and stupidly agape; Charlotte Anne Russe to cream all over mobs of maniacal admirers and their holy keds akudo; fish and chips that fuck up folios of funnies; those whiz delights, baloney cheese and potato slaw on seeded roll to nourish harps and donkeys; Honey "Jelly" Apple, the Brothers Caries' crude assistant; fullchock sammiches of meins and chows hot from Canton-on-Cinq-et-Dix; a bag of whimperstale and vilerot wafers, two tons for a dime and dear at that; pinkglass pitchers every Wednesday nite, rotten with epco cereza, epco limón; the U.S.S. Navy Bean, foundered in Vinegar Sea; le pain New York avec la margarine avec pains and aches of Cuban gold atop; a glass the sister of our friend the pitcher luscious with bread and milk to her blushing bottom; last month's baking crunched and greased in last week's bacon blood; the fat face of friendly Jack O'Lantern all agrin just asking for a licking; Skippy's Sunday, white as weddings and as red as rouge; corn popped pink and wheedled white; carmine cutesy dollars that fire up the gums; a royal hook off a royal jab and zut! the mouth's all purple; and Jesus cream vanilla as a vestal to help you glide into a heaven sternly clean and protestant that don't mean maybe if you got the urge.

«28»

Pastourelle:
Dr. Poncho Tells
of His Afternoon of Ecstasy

Ah, there she was, scuffling through the hedges,
The glorious and thinning-haired Helene Gavotte,
And I, decked out in my Dr. Poncho garb,
Gazed hornily upon her in her trav'ling clothes;
Her tattered shmatte, peasant skirt, her blouse
All washed to airiness, her filthy "desert" boots
From Sears, and a disreputable torn fedora.

I caught up with her 'spite my stiff'ning rod.
"Helene, my dear," I said, "my lollipop,
My heart is cracked because you look so warm."
"Oh! Dr. Poncho," croaked this sweaty miz,
"Don't for a sec belabor your deep brains
With worry or concern about this greasy flush.
I'm perfectly O.K., and cool as splashing clam."

"Fudge," I said, "how sweet yet thick you are;
I ran like crazed opossum down the road
To walk with you and be your guard.
A luscious wife like you should never schlep
All lonely through these glades and bosks,
Without a staunch professor by your side.
These woods are full of sex-crazed academics."

"Oh, noble Ryan," blushed the blowsy broad,
"Do not think that I, the wife of simple Serge,
Would ever listen to the bullshit lines

That scholars use to lower ladies' drawers.
Nay," and the sweetie heaved her little bosom out,
"As a doting wife and mama of a darling brat,
I'd sooner let a freshman stroke my sacred corse."

"How lumb'ringly your words take flight," I smiled.
"It's clear as plastic wrap that you're the daughter
Of a college graduate, a well-read salesman
Who poked your half-crocked mother in far-flung motel.
I'm wacked out by your gorgeous charms
And would be even more entranced could I
But protect your bony albeit toothsome flesh."

"Academic cynosure," the lass then sighed,
Wringing out her sweat-bedrenchèd coif,
"You are a sport to think that I'm the product
Of a gay and casual boff ripped off by
An ace sales representative and a rustic slut.
But I must tell you that my parents coarse
Worked like slobs in a grungy candy store."

"The more amazing then your tempting looks,
That make the ravishing Medusa gawk!
It must be, then," I leered, "that a flitting fairy,
Thinking that you were a boy, gave you your beauty
At your birth. But when I fantasy
How much more beautiful you'd be
If I rode betwixt your thighs, I plotz!"

"I feel a quart or two of torrid blood
Crashing toward my secret parts," she squealed.
"It's hard to think that a distinguished prof
Like you, my Doc, with beaucoup degrees,
Would wish to hump the afternoon away
With such as I. I am sore tempted,
But enchained by wifely modesty, I reck."

"Your modesty," I drooled, "makes you
Even more a prize. If you do fear

That a passing student or a truckload
Of idiotic farmhands will spy us out
In our raptures wild of pump and thrust,
We'll saunter off the road and commit the act
'Neath that clump of sumac shingleberry there."

"My female yearnings," said the gasping piece,
"All command me to a wild unfettered fling
With you, scorching Doc, and urge me toward
That foliage, where we may do a lot of
Dirty stuff. But," she reddened, "I fear
That you will lose respect for me as a person,
If we play horsy-horsy in the shadowed weeds."

"Lose respect?" I laughed. "Miz Gavotte,
I'll cherish in my lonely memory, as the years
Limp by, each second of our wild, abandoned leaps.
Besides," I winked, "I would be honored
If you'd allow me, creamsicle, to commemorate this day
By permitting me to buy for you a new,
Drip-dry shmatte, and a previously owned chapeau."

"Your words send jabs and hooks into my soul,"
The trembling doxy breathed. "I'll treasure up
The bagatelles you'll buy with academic loot,
And treasure, too, the memory of your lust.
Now let us crunch into the nettles here,
Undo our garments, and in a trice or twain,
Jazz each other unto heights of craziness!"

"Oh pepsi, twinkie, milky way," I said,
"I'm in your thing and, oops, I've shot my wad!
A million thanks, and now, so long. I'm off!"

"Wh-what?" the whore cried. "I hardly knew
That you were on! Is this the type of hump
That scholars throw?" she keened through rustling leaves.

130

« 29 »

In Which
Poncho Takes a
Poudre and Bone Playes Dumbe

Blue is discovered on the road back to The College, his head filled, since we can, because of the Magic of Literature, see inside his head, with what he is pleased to call "notions of Mortality." He recites odd ends of the Nature Poets: Wordssmith, Bligh, Froth, the Gocourt Brothers, Jem Casey, Slater, Mio Cid, Dixie Lowell, Zangwill Pendejo, T. Pallidum Stickney, Jeff Jeffers, Snod Snodgrass, and Gordon Gilbey Booth, "spicing up" his recital with critical snatches (old but still elastic) of Jerzy "City" Kosinski. As he is ripping through Booth's "Elegy on a Birch that Crushed My Lean-To," he spies, in the golden dusty haze of the typical Indiana road on which he wends, his . . . wife!

BLUE: What is shaking, spouse divine? I thought that you were off to yonder Shopping Mall to exercise your sacred right as a consumer?
HELENE: Doctor Poncho "bumped" into me upon this very road and made a coupla indecent advances on my person, like, "What think you of a casual zig-zag, my bobolink?"
BLUE: It boots no further madness thus to mouth such crippled jest, and yet, as faces oft do skid upon the welkin shattered o'er with blasts, I fear me that the starling's oath will carry 'round the globe like th' ungirdled seas!
HELENE: I blushed so that you could not tell my face from the arse of that baboon who hangs around the exits of deep Africa! He was as mad in his erotic craziness as that violent wop men call Hieronimo!
BLUE: I've always loathed the name, which, to my perusal, smacks and slaps of pizzas found upon the roads that zip through outlands like Nebraska! Oh, cursed am I to have a piece whose fletch from lechers' eyes not even tattered schmatte covers o'er! Then let's to campus where, as smold'ring butt confronts a funny ashtray that may say it hails from Lake Hopatcong, I'll throw into the very

orthodonture of his craggy face this charge so base and vile that only filthy frog-gos like Georges Bataille would even think to write of it!

HELENE: I traipse in the gaping holes your sneakers leave in this sad dust!

In a snap of the fingers they are on the campus of The College, running, running, as if their great revenge had stomach for anybody's hairs! And in their mad career, they bash smack dab into tweedy Bone, sucking placidly, as was, and is, his wont, upon the seasoned bowl of his old briar cob.

BLUE: A hasty ciao, sagacious herringboned professor. Is Doctor Poncho in his chamber, deep in applications? I must see him on a matter of most vile and opportune purport.

BONE: As chuckling misfortune has it, secure within the purse he wears upon his belt, Dr. Poncho has flown from these, the hoary leaves and sunny lawns that burst the very bounds and bonds of sublunary vulgar concepts, to attend, all in a rush of feverish emergency, a conference somewhere in that quarter of this once-great Nation that lies toward the inky forests where the goop-hawk dips and bangs against the noble grizzly. He left with naught but umbrella and the AWOL bag he's treasured ever since his long-estrangèd wife did keep her soiled unmentionables in its depths.

BLUE: Oh wicked blight that foists in clay!

HELENE: He tried to make me do some naughty acts or else!

BONE: Wh-what? My colleague, Ryan? A WASP so deep and true that folk mistake him for a game-show host or other breed of grinning simp? If true, this is, as the honest churl who delivers beer unto the "student" "lounge" might say, a fucking shame!

HELENE: Oh, 'tis true, wise fop! The man did clutch my female thing a nonce.

BONE: My heart, deep as it is in pain as though 'twere in the fiendish grip of the stoccado, whispers to me that you speak the plain and knobby truth. I've seen our Doctor in the stinking grip of mad erotica when in the presence of a female stoont, his homely cardigan athump with yearnings that dare not speak their monickers. But to make vile proposition to a guest . . . Such cafone-like acts are, so to speak, canaille. How I wish that he were here, so that I, pipe all askew and fuming, could confront him with you and so watch him squirm!

BLUE: The vast imbroglios that creep beneath the tincted closets of the stars do cry out in their wonted innocence for vengeance pitiless, aye, though the womanish side of my great raging heart doth tremble in the breach!

HELENE: Soft you, Serge. It comes!

BLUE: What sayest thou? "It" comes?

HELENE: Such limpid expletive but seemed a good idea, given us the context of this strange scene that we inhabit.

BONE: When the miscreant and malcontented Machiavel returns, I'll have a word with him, then take this case to the highest levels of our sternest officers! Ryan Poncho will never get, no! nor will he e'er present another plaque!

BLUE: For this belief, much thanks, kind Weede. And now, let us collect our Zim, my love, and pack the cart and start off for The University.

HELENE: I saw the babe this day this morn happily engaged in tearing ivy off the walls of the Hall of Eclectic Disciplines, named for its donor, the wondrous Mulligan.

BONE: He was still there, the chub, at the luncheon hour. Sweetest boy!

BLUE: Then let us go, or as the Spaniard says, vamoose!

They leave, plowing through weird leaves and mounds of football cheers, while Dr. Bone smiles knowingly right through his clouds of Granger.

≪ 30 ≫

The Gavottes Come at Last to The University

Then through the bresh that heaves and gloams
    the fey Gavottes did trek;
Through baldrypress and crossleaf loams,
    up to their knees in dreck.

When, jeez! they came to Skillet Fork,
    where Blue pitched to the ground.
There did he sacrifice a pork,
    upon a pecan mound.

" 'Tis Illinois! or Illini!"
    his loathsome mouth did spew;
Meanwhile, Helene poked in her eye
    an elbow, soaked with dew.

And quick as half-assed leatherleaf
    toils in the Kankakee,
His dust-bespattered pangs of grief
    apace fled through the brie.

Then rested they 'mid sassafrass
    quenching away the noon;
Serge stretched full-length in whango grass,
    Zim and his Mom in broon.

What dreams then rose from Bonpas Creek
    only Great Pan can know;
(And mayhap Hera, queenly Greek,
    high in her bungalow.)

Oiled with bananas (so Serge dreams),
  his glist'ring instrument
Sends forth its noise; thus loony beams
  crash on a tenement!

Bud Koussevitsky, Homer Welk,
  and ilks of others such,
Fix 'round his neck The Crooning Elk;
  hosannahs praise him much!

La douce Helene, in gronko's shade,
  slumbers (though vetch sore prick);
She dreams her Blue has made le grade,
  and found at last a shtick!

She dreams her Blue has found his Phrase;
  great Art will ne'er be same!
His phiz from T-shirts forth doth blaze,
  the Congress whoops his name!

From little Zim, among the chard,
  rivers of drool ooze forth;
His visions are of steaks and lard,
  of fried jacoons and broth.

So did these three rumbaceous clucks
  snooze in the torpid glatch;
Fantasies gave the grinning shmucks
  respite from bri'ry patch.

Till, with the clamb'ring of the moon
  (that looked just like a poil),
Up from his bed of macaroon
  great Blue burst like a boil.

"The throne of knowledge squats avaunt!"
  (the phlegm cracked in his throat);
"Let's heave and hump our corses gaunt
  unto its chancred moat!"

Then humped and heaved they through the elms,
    through ironwoods and gleets;
The thorns of ninebarks, binks of whelms
    tore at their hands and feets.

All night beneath the pearly lamp
    they sweltered toward their goal;
E'en Serge's bike clips were all damp;
    his face all doit like coal.

Still they clanked on, past Sangamon,
    through Charles Mound and DuPage;
Over the snowy Big Bon-Bon,
    skirted dark-sodomed Zage.

Then, as Big Sol leaped from his sack,
    and Wabash silver turn'd,
Our stooges glimpsed through bosky crack
    the U! Their numb legs churned!

They smashed through burningbush and gorse
    through mountain heath and rose;
Pity the moosewood, or the horse
    that stumbled 'neath their toes!

Noble Des Plaines, proud Apple Creek,
    saw but a frantic blur;
Kaskaskia, stern Calumet,
    heard an elated whir.

Then they were on those regal grounds;
    and stood with lips askew.
They sighed, "Great Fuck," "Oh Zut," and "Zounds";
    rooted like flies in glue.

"And now to search out sage Dubuque,"
    roared Blue, knee-deep in beech;
"I'll hear the Secret Phrase—or puke!"
    he vowed, and popped his breech.

They gave brief thanks to Doctor Chick,
    to tweedy Bone, to all;
Then Serge, his ass in gear, all quick
    set off to pay his call.

« 31 »

Dr. Dubuque's Eglogue
Joyned with Miss Clarke
Grables: An Erotickal Interlude

Siddown, Mistress Grable, here is honeycomb fit for Emperors, and grapes, and the curious peachy peach and lettuces, and escarole so to speak or some other quaint legume consumèd by your swarthy Italiano. Siddown, muh dearest, and remove your shoes and let me kiss your toes right through the slipp'ry nylon that encaseth them and that encaseth all, yes, all your lovely albeit slightly heavy nether limbs up to that spot o' which I dare not think without groaning and waxing so enflamed I fear my homemade cardigan will burst, as it were, into belching fire.

Oh Dr. Dubuque—may I call you doc?—Oh Doc Dubuque, to find myself with you, alone, in this vast ringing plain surrounded by the rude and homely yet so vivacious hunks, chunks, orts, shards, sherds, and fragments of carrots, Swiss chards, cucumbers, and the repulsive tare, and God knows what all else, is mother to emotions so wild and tingling that, despite my face encarnadined, I'll toss my high-heeled slippers into the encroaching furze wound round with hollyhocks and stuff, woodbine clematis and the like, and thrust my dainty dogs all joyously into the caressing air! Note how my nylon stockings do enfold them and my legs as well like unto a second madd'ning skin. Oke?

How insanely wacked-out I am for you, my so-called secretary, or assistant, you'll soon know. Permit me a moment while I doff my trousers and fold them with some care along the creases, prior to laying them with gentle care, almost dovelike in its solicitude for this polyester pure, here upon this stringbean bush so that no man can guess we've gamed and joyed and tumbled all the afternoon by glauming on grass stains tincted green upon my trouser knees, or, failing that, by thinking on the fact that the magic cloth of which these trousers are enweaved

138

achieved a rumpled state because I left them on while a-jousting in the lists of love. What they do not know will not, as Baba Rhum Mañana says, fucking bother them. Ah darling secretary, your twinkled orbs are as the blue sky and its stars that act as roof or maybe ceiling to Mount Rushmore and its granite phiz or phizzes, and your breath's as sweet as fields of jalapeño peppers in old Louisiana or wherever that rare spice grows nowadays, if you follow me. Or for that matter, where it used to grow, so to speak.

I do not follow you, dear Doc, because my simple woman's mind treks back and forth between subjects domestickal such as laundry, kitchen, shopping, cleaning gobs of dust off filthy surfaces, and the need to please and joy men such as you! Administrator! Leader! E'en, yes, gross capitano of le business, making money hand over hand. Yet somehow I do know what you are uttering for I feel it, yes, we weak creatures have that knack, I feel it deep deep fathoms down betwixt my ruddy thighs, the latter full now of mosquito, fly, and chigger bites, there where we all truly live, 'spite the wild and dang'rous talk of those jew anarchists who think that we too should make wee-wee in a urinal and study on the ways and means to shoot off bazookas and hit fungo triples and such stuff. Fie! But soft— come close to me beneath this lettuce here and gawk your dear and rheumy eye-bones out as I slip out of my skirt, my slip, my pantyhose, my panties, girdle, body shirt and bra and blouse and dicky, and my sweater and my vest, my necklace, scapulars, ID tags, and another item or two that have flown clear from my whirling fevered brain! Doc? You aren't fallen into Morphine's arms, my love? I'll be but another quarter-hour. Meanwhile, my snowy, pillowed bosom, white as cauliflower, is now more or less untrammeled. Here, I offer it to your burning gaze, my sad sweet guy.

Asleep? Har-har! You do insult my wanton carnal envelope! How can I drift into that sleeve of care while here, rapt in my BVD's, I lie amid the nettles and the shyly nodding clovers next you, my eyes, despite the fact I left my cheaters in the office, riveted upon your intoxicating décolletage, which reminds me, as it were, of a filthy story, one not fit for your chastely icy Luth'ran ears. But enough of chatting of my knowledge wide as Ocean's aqua swells and crunching breakers that even now are busting the bejesus out of some poor little tyke's half-assed castle made of sand, but where, only Jove hisself can tell. Here, here, my starling, let me pelt you with a mittful of these rosy razzberries! My heavens! How their pink and gorgeous juice does set off the arctic damask o' your cheeks! By the living word of ev'ry thund'rous preacher on the air o' boring Sunday morns, you're not half-bad! Half? Har-har! By twice the squared hypotenuse o' dread

Infinity! Perhaps a trifle overweight, now that I ogle you sans gripping corselette, but how like unto a field of oats is your compassed and circumferential belly! And your heaving thighs are like a clamorous battalion upon the chow line! And your breasts, now all free and proud and dedicated to philosophical idears and all such stuff, do stand upon your tented chest like two jeeps painted all immaculately white!

Forgive me, rapturous Doc, that I wrinkle up and squinch my azure orbs until the tears pop out as big as baseballs, the better, espouse I, to dig on your flabby, middle-aged, yet manly torso, but as you see, I too have left my specs upon that desk that I call Home, dizzy as I was but a scanty time ago with your sizzling and lewd proposal that we flop here in the lap of Nature, here to let that wise old goddess take her course. Yet! Yet I do affirm most potently that despite my cursed astigmatism, I see sharp enough to know that your small but willing engine of engend'ring is all swolled up with passion and the simmering humors of careening lust, so to speak, if I may clutch at one of your endearing mots. May I, coot?

Clutch at? Aye! And more than clutch, my seeded hollyhock! Clutch and keep unto yourself as your very own, to be employed all profligate in letters, conversations, aimless bullshit on the phone, and even inter-office memorandos! Great Priapus! That I should live to lie here with you, beneath these kohlrabi vines and blowing eggplant blooms, alone and far from the backbiting city and its mad farrago and charivari of cupiditous ambition and its asshole stars! That I should fasten these my gummy eyes upon your gen'rous flesh, your corse half-naked save for these silken hose from some Parisian nuthouse of a boîte, and a few other lacy odds and ends of undergarments that do but serve t' enhance your plumsweet flesh, that is, those parts of it that do gleam naked! It is enough to make me an amnesiac moon man, and for a jot and tittle place in some stinking closet of my brain the fact that I'm a family man as well as a crackerjack administrator of a fifth-rate yet upward crawling university! Take pity on me, Mistress Grable, and let me void my smarting seeds, I think the sentence goes.

Shall we then, doting Doc, shall we perform the act of shame, make with our yearning and besweated bodies that famous beast, it of the double deck? My golden head pressed close as cigarettes within their pack against your thinning white one? My secret parts commingling with yours like two hurried citizens bashing one into the other on the crowded thoroughfare? Or shall we simply scarf each other up with poor weak eyes, content to know that we are free from those conventions Life chucks over us like so much plastic wrap, to know that if we wish we may in a trice or two, blithely screw our asses off, as free as these minuscule and disgusting gnats that swarm about us?

Let scarfing be enough, wanton, brown, and nutty secretary. I am, I do confess it, so rusted in the arts o' love, that I am scared to death, aye, shitless scared, that I would cut the figure of a dribbling moron should I attempt to mount you, front, back, top, or side, although the latter cannot, by what I ken of the copulative act, be construed as "mounting" one's enamorata. And besides, a crazed and industrious bumblebee, zooming home with bags chocked full o' nectar saccharine from his last-suckèd aromatic flower, has tarried for a moment in this shadowed glade or glen in which we lurk in cool and wondrous déshabille, and driven his annoyed and choleric stinger into my ass all trouserless.

Then let me, agonizing Doc, dress myself in these careless crinolines and thick velours and little frou-frous as swiftly as I did but a moment since wrench and pluck and tear them from my quaking flesh all mad with equatorial and torrid hots! And then I'll lead you by your soft and sweaty duke down to the drowsy crick where we may discover cooling handfuls of rich and oozy mud to clap upon that angry welted blister that our friend, Sir Bee, has raised upon your slack and flagging bum. Some other still and humdrum afternoon, when the ennui of our wonted jobs is about to drive us ape and bonkers, we may loiter once again like two erotic vagrants here amid the brussels sprouts and pears and, who can tell? mayhap then we'll consummate the wild dark act that men call humping?

How wise you are, my fondest poggy! Lead away, sweet Clarke, and I'll stumble in your wake, my familiar trousers flung insouciantly o'er my arm, to where that rich mud and glop may lie and its secret alchemy of whatever the hell that promises full-voicèd to remove the pain that now spreads far and wide o'er all my ass's sore expanse.

I'll have this whaleboned and excruciating corset tightly laced up in a flash, as soon as I have brushed it free of tares and pits and petals and these pesky ants that seem to have a fixed idea that urges them to bite the hell out of my yielding and delicious flesh. Begone, you curious yet loathsome creatures! And see, here's one little bastard of a nipper who waits in ambush in my capacious bra! You little snot!

Mistress Grable, may I interrupt your jovial harangue? One thing irritates my college-educated brain to such a pitch of worriment that I must ask if you would deign to let slip from your swell and rosy lips a wise and womanly opinion concerning this small matter.

Of course, dear Doc! Hello! Here we are at last at the slippery and o'ergrown crick bank and there is, as I had prayed, tons and tons of black and gruesome mud! Now, your matter? I'll do my best to satisfy you while I slap and smear this salutary guck all over your weak yet totally enchanting butt. What reck I that it is mostly flab and fat?

What, my lissome mink, do our frolicsome bucolics have to do with the story, so to speak and as it were, of one Blue Serge, about whose musical and knotted head this whole work, if you will, is supposed to amble?

That man, my academic Jove, will soon, a little bird did cheep to me, enter the great University wherein you reign as sage administrator sans peer or peeress, there to get from you a lecture or a wise opinion or some other wondrous educative thing. So the bird did cheep into the very snaredrums of my ears.

Merci, ma tweedy femme. But soft you. Do you think it wise to shove me bodily into this mud as you are doubtless doing? It will be tough as nails to bullshit my wife anent the gross and filthy, aye, unspeakable state of my garments, despite the fact that her poor eyes will be red and bleared from countless hours of television dramas and whatever other crap she watches all in hussied rapture.

I'll join you in the muck, designer skoit and all, you silly bourgeoisie! And together we will roil and gambol in the slop! We'll say we fell into a hidden mudhole while investigating sites for a new cafeteria and student lounge. That should make the shrewish bitch bite on her coated tongue!

Your grimy eyes! Your pitch-black hands! Your gritty bra! I faint!

The dirt upon your sideburns! And your crusted shirt!

I fear that here, in this unlikely place and covered o'er with healthful mud, my manhood must be satisfied! Come, come, my blushing wren, undo your clothing once again and receive my impatient and importunate dread organ!

Oh, Doc! My Doc! My dreamy Doc! I chuck my garments 'mid those nodding sedges and accept your madd'ning peg! The very gods peep down all jealously upon us!

« 32 »

Doc Dubuque's
Idyll, or, Ah, Nature!

The excellent Doc, located beneath the glory of a giant breadfruit tree just now, as we look, bursting into a million chartreuse blooms, bends a rapt and sated gaze upon Blue Serge, and speaks.

I know why you have come, my boy, so to speak. Intelligence concerning your sedulous quest has reached my ears from The College, and I may, just may, mind you, as it were, be able to assist you. For the present nonce, allow me to point out to you some of the glories of Nature, here in Illini, a state where the boll weevil swoops in majestic grandeur down upon the great horned owl! And the catalpa sends forth its shy tendrils to feed upon the baby woodchuck in its subterranean home. It is love that makes the spring go round, young fellow, and even a toiler in the lamplit study, such as myself, feels the wild juices bust and flow as the great solstice flings its warming trends about. Sit, dear boy. Let me point out to you some of the glories that are often lost sight of in the hustle and bustle of the marketplace. I was remarking on these things just today to my right-hand assistant, Miss Grable, a woman of sensibility and appreciation.

Thank you, Doctor, Serge says. I have myself often remarked upon that potency that men call Nature, in all its warps and woofs.

April! Or maybe March! Love! With a peppery pinch of lust! The wild attack of your basic crabgrass and marigold weed, a choice patina of some oddball color against the sad skeleton of tenacious winter, is rather hysterically cheered and hallooed, like the fresh-faced girl next door whose role as a voracious nymphomaniac in the high school musical allows the local rubes to think of her as something more than their kid sister. Yes! And though she will ne'er again be thought of in later years in just this way—this lasciviously wanton way, may I add—at the present time, she is metamorphosing this paint-flaking and ungodly ugly auditorium into a shining whorehouse, as she whips her innocent pelvis around to the bursting strains of the tin-eared yet enthusiastic "band."

And while the lips of these debased yokels are still foaming with kudos of varying intensity and volume, May—or perhaps April!—zooms in like a cockroach surprised by homely incandescent light! And May is tremendous! An aura of dandelion seeds charging up the feckless nostril, an ambience of hairy caterpillars eating the trees, the shrubs, the candid stones, even the grey flapping wet wash on a million clotheslines. This socko month seems to be everywhere at once, scoffing up the earth and leaving a redolent spoor of happy springtime lavender shoots, each shyly hiding a glass-eyed lover adrift in fantasies of sweaty fornication! It is the sort of month that bashes simple folk right in the superego, silky and volatile as sinful lingerie what the Pope has urged us all to get shut of lest a fleeting lewdness seize our private parts with grip of white-hot steel!

It is like—a large picnic, or perhaps . . . a barbecue! It is too much, more ribs or wieners or deviled eggs than we can gorge on all at once, more beer and lemonade than we can handle, yes, even though we could make pee-pee from now until the ding-dong knell of doom—or even beyond! We hardly know, by God, what sangwich to snatch at first, what swelling bosom to diffidently prod as we pretend to search for a paper napkin to wipe the melted butter from shocks of bubbling corn from off of our greasy fingers, each one quivering with wild desire to grasp and wrest purest Beauty from the nodding accordion close-nestled by the hirsute apple glade, a-thrum with bees and lice!

And as we clutch at its insubstantial beauty, just as we clutch at the last soggy potato chip, it is . . . going, yes, just as that last chip is being borne away on the tiny shoulders of a busy ant, going, and changing into . . . June! or whatever the next month dares call itself. Let the fete commence, we urge. Let the gala step off smartly, we clamor. Bid the soldiers, so to speak, shoot, or anyway pick up their three-day passes.

Whereas May ran around like a crazy person unsure of the difference between his ass and his elbow, June is sane and sober, something like a mature yet handsome woman employed as, perhaps, a secretary-assistant to a crackerjack exec or administrator, svelte yet zaftig, as our Israeli friends are wont to say in their quaint tongue when they cease for a tittle or a jot from chasing Bedouins across the oases of the Sahara; June is peaceful and serene in a universe of juicy saps— many of whom, by the by, are still prostrate under the blowing lavender shoots that they now call . . . Home! And while the early months of sweet primavera were merely acting—and badly at that—the role of slut and tramp, June is your true ace whore, your superstar call-girl, with the savoir-faire and the sang-froid of those filles de joie who know the arcane secrets of the snapping snatch, the Chinese hanky trick, the aluminum-ball delight, the voyage to Cythera, the cross-stitch rubadub, the back-door two-step, the tumbling bongo-press, the eyeball popper, the Casanova crosslock, and other carnal ploys that boggle the steaming brain pan.

Yes, June! It is the finger on the machine gun, the slug in its chamber ready to fly down the barrel, the breathless moment before the bullet finds its unfortunate target. It is that split-second in an amorous relationship where all the blather and smirks that have eaten up the evening are forgotten in the vast symphony of popping buttons and the whine of yielding zippers. June! A new day! The beginning of the future, the end of the past, the middle of the present, for June . . . is *all* present, nothing but ecstatic sunlight reaching down with warm fingers into the height and depth of your being, sending you, in nameless joy, nose crammed with pollen, into fits of sneezing as you stumble, all snots and tears, into the newly dug sump! And always . . . always . . . stumbling in the everpresent present of . . . June.

In the heart, which is, as we all know and remember from our salad days, a lonely hunter, perhaps the one with his finger on the trigger what we have already mentioned, all the leprous lesions of Old Man Winter are fixed right up, just as they are all across the great yawning pride that men once dared call "the country." The cuts and gashes are stitched and clamped, the punctures, abrasions, incisions, and lacerations are doused with penicillin and dollops of iodine. We stand transfixed, sunk in idiocy like wrestling fans or mayors, our brains as idle as the pupae of the loathsome house fly, dreaming their deathless dreams of endless shit and rotting garbage heaped up to the vaulting skies! Spring, as the bard implied, is far behind once again, and summer, with its heat, humidity, sunstroke, lightning bolts, mosquitoes, chiggers, gnats, deer flies, stinking armpits . . . looms! Autumn, that season of mellow and misty-eyed fruits, and bare-assed winter, achock with slush and the memorable frenzy of gloom that attends its holidays, are both still far away, sleeping, so to speak, on the cusp of silent Time; or, perhaps, beneath its cusp.

Trite and banal crap, so to speak, as it may be, June *does* bust out all over, as Kenny Baker sang, surrounded by enchanted negros, in the film of the same name, so many many years ago. The roses, the spavinias, the brilliant gonococcae in off-fuchsia, dusty grey, amaryllis purple, in every cheerful color, slither, jump, and shuffle across the beaming green face of the countryside, inundating with a riot of shades, tones, and tints the filling stations, the hamburger joints, the bowling alleys, the supermarts, the beer distributors, even unto heaving recklessly through the grime-covered frosted-glass windows of the forever-locked rest rooms! June! How meet and swell it is that this word has the same root as the word "jewel"—for June *is* a jewel, far superior to the gaudy schlock of the sprawling colors that scream and whine April, for instance.

The crazed and neurotic mind wanders peacefully amid the endless soporific balm of all these soothing hints and bits and pieces of color, nodding and blinking in the vast oceans of verdure, in the slothful sargasso seas of putrid geraniums. It is better than a talk with your local pastor about unethical ejaculations, better than a hearty bowl of mulligan on a torrid afternoon in August, when one's thoughts ceaselessly return, as they will, to the dimpled knees of one's beloved, the odd insouciance they display as she falls, often heavily, into the cool depths of the mountain rill that bursts profusely through a breezy glade while the patient bot-fly waits to consume her head when it surfaces in the glorious sunlight.

The vetch quivers. The tares rip. The nettles yearn. Everything is ruthless light and deep poiple shadow on the house that one calls home. Time, space, seasons, the universe itself, are suspended like a pair of nylons from Mother Nature's flow'ry unmentionable. The elders shake. The birches break from the nature poet's weight. The bayberries, the sweetferns, aye, the wax-myrtles ache sweetly for release. And the great cycles of eternal change seem, for a moment, as the beer can groveling in effulgence by the side of the shining blacktop.

The days grow longer, or so it seems. Or is it that the nights grow . . . shorter? We will never know, just as we will never know why hornets like to eat each other. We think that nothing will ever end, that winter will remain locked up in jail somewhere in Argentina. Or Chile! The calm is alive! The silence . . . speaks! The grass grows so slowly that, stare as we may, we can never catch it popping up even a half an inch, nay, not even a quarter of an inch. Or a eighth! It is, surely . . . a miracle. There are no atheists in the brambles.

Roads run east and west, north and south. But where is the east? Where is the west? Where is the other two? Gone where the jest on the lips of the hobo has gone? Beyond the waffle shop? What is past the final liquor store huddled on the pale-golden horizon? Shuttered houses? Weedgrown hedgerows? Busted birdbaths? Fantasies? Dreams? Life, death? A bad summer cold? We know no more than does the tit-faced jackybox that gnaws the porch . . .

June . . . wasteful, lush, plangent, limpid, gross, overweight . . . the fool's paradise, the fool's gold that July pays us for May, only to be paid itself in turn to August by brooding October. These days of effete joy . . . these minutes and seconds of pied Beauty that stick us like plenty of myriads of needles sailing wildly from God's great pin cushion in the towering blue . . . an ancient, hoary knot deep within us loosens its crazed strings . . . a buried lump bursts free at last . . . it is passing strange . . . whither? . . . whence? . . . an unearthly orgasm occurs in the vast trousers of the world as the pulsing lump . . . explodes!

«33»

The Doc Makes
Blue What Men Yclep
a "Deal" (Or So It Seems)

Great tortured Jesu on his rood of rough-hewn pica sumac! Blue breathed in adoration. Doctor D, though I have humped and schlepped a thousand mile, yea! and seen mens in performance of a bevy wonders, yet nowhere have I heard mortal throat spew forth such fulsome sentiments! Nor, I dare say, has my wife, the sweet Helene, which whom, by the by, I wonder whither hence has fled, since I see her nowhere.

Be spritely as the double-taloned wickiup, my friend, Dubuque replied, and cease to fret your "brains" in re: the wife. It has been swift arranged that she and your gnashing son should take a powder and sail up and down the fabled Orinoco or the Ganges for a space or so, that faithful readers of this tale shall not get on a wonder anent their unexplainèd absence for a chapter or two or three and take it out upon the author of this History; like, he don't know what he's doing and cannot handle simple fictional techniques. For the woods are filled with critics, who, when they are not ripping off the gowns diaphanous of Dryads, busy their restless hands with the writing of "reviews." Thus, let us leave them to their swelt'ring voyage.

It is jake with me, monumental academic, Blue chuckled heartily. And now, may we chatter on about . . . the . . . Phrase?

A ha, ha, ha! the Doc joined in, and I ween, no less robustly, till the very sycamores stood all leafless and aghast. It is a possibility that what you search for, laughing varlet, is indeed here, and we will look for it before you see another week pass into insubstantial mulch! But meantime, the power of your voice pricks and also prompts me into asking of you one small favor. Huh?

Ask, renowned boss of the great tower that looms beyond the ivy-choked athletics building there! . . . on the lissome, flowered hill!

Sweet fellow! It is this: Each year upon St. Patrick's Day, which I feel it in my very bones is coming 'round in but a jot of time, a person from the U gives a talk

147

upon this great Saint and the land from which he chased the lizards, snakes, worms, garbanzo monsters, and the like. The talk is delivered in the town square and is for the benefit of the rubes and yokels whose whole existence depends upon this puissant U; thus, as you will ken, these apple-knockers loathe and hate us to a seething flame of passionate despisement! To make them think we care a fig about them and that we spend long hours worrying lest their opinion of us take a turn into the worst, if such is possible, we drop a scrap or twain onto them once or twice a year—it is a great humanitarian tradition! In actuality, we do not give a turd for their opinion, but render, as I say, unto laughing Caesar, whatever *that* may mean in this bedraggled context. Thus, but, say I, will *you* give the talk, that great traditional crock of purest shit to calm the raging rubes, asweat in their quaint plastic shoes and strange white belts?

It will be my duty, sir! And an honor that I clutch all wildly to my thudding hairy breast!

How staunch you are! Like a veritable Ajax whacking sheeps! Come, we'll be off to what we, in crazèd jest, call "the English office," where I'll get the speech that you'll spurt forth mañana! And you will give this stirring talk as one "Blarney Spalpeen," a monicker all oozing forth with Celtic echoes. Thus, the restless hicks will be placated for another stretch of what proud Newton labeled "Time," and fall to chomping grisly hamburgers and odd pizzoid stuffs with quickened faith in the intelligentsia's deep care for them.

And after...? Perhaps then...? The Phrase...?

Patience, potent chunk! From chinchy acorns monstrous oaks don't grow by dint of bitch and kvetch, nay! But by the patience of the rock that's been dissolving since some grungy caveman first thought to heave it at a wombat! And now, let's away!

« 34 »

"Blarney Spalpeen" Gives a Speech on St. Patrick's Day

I have been asked, by the Sons of the Emerald Clout, to give an impromptu speech, whatever that may be, on the meaning, the *true* meaning of St. Patrick's Day, and, as my handle on this foine broit day, ha ha, is Blarney Spalpeen, who knows more about this devout religious than I? unless it be the Great Papa himself, whose presence, because he can only talk dago, would be, as I'm sure you'll all admit, even those of you who are the fabled wretched refuse, the bricklayers, the garbagemen, and the longshoremen, a hell of a half-assed trick to pull on a good American audience, well, more or less, here surrounded by nodding corn stands and blowing oaks!

Yes, the *true* meaning of St. Patrick's Day! What exactly is it, me darlin's? We all know the sad, the shadowy, the pathos-ridden disrepute into which this Holy Day of Obligation has pitched, yes, yes, don't shy away and edge carefully toward the modern parking lot that your cretinous Congressman has had carved out for you from the living granite and humble shale and Christ knows what other goddamned stones and rocks, courtesy Department of Defense! Your stupid crackerbarrel autos will wait for you, decaying the while in the rays of the harsh sun, the few moments it will take me, me blushin' gawms and bemuscled bawneens or something, to finish these impromptu words on the saint who has made your lives what they are here in what for today has been renamed Little Dublin, this typical small town sprawled stunned on the great rolling and fecund plains of Illinois! And environs!

I have said, I suspect, too much already, but let that be, and I implore you, each and every one of you in your hilariously priced "jogging" shoes, to forgive this drumbling, drumbling? bullshit, as Jesus and his mama, Mary, and her long-suffering and no doubt suspicious hubby, Old Joe, will forgive me, knowing, as of course they know, exactly what I am about to spell out in language at once clear and exact, language that gives no quarters nor asks none, language that neither pulls nor pushes punches! Or what's a heaven for? For that is my way, and I'm not a shrewd and cunning cruiskeen for nothing, bedamn!

I have said, I seem to recall, that the true meaning of this glorious day that we will soon be celebrating but a week or two after the Feast of the Aspersion, that purple day on which we commemorate and remember, to our undying shame as good Catholics, if that is not a redundant term, the nasty cracks that were made by Judas O'Scariot about Jesus Christ, who happened at the time to be indisposed, and so could not defend himself against the malicious gossip and chit-chat of this depraved kike. And believe you me, it is no error that St. Patrick's Day falls in the liturgical calendar when it does, or where it does, depending on your view of the space-time hassle, for it was that Great Heart himself who, bumping into O'Scariot on the street, or in a nearby saloon soon after—soon after what? you ask, aha, but Time is jealous of its great secrets—said to him, "Yer a backbitin' bassoon an' a slitherin' maureen!"—and he was talking, me strappin' gossoons, directly into the shifty little mockie's face at the time. What do you think of that? Huh? There were giants on the turf in those days! Now, since he said this in that old-fashioned wop talk, with the amat, esse, illibus, and tubarum types of words, an odd tongue and Christ knows what to make of it, I have translated his sacred words loosely, but you get what I'm driving at. But, *but*, you can bet your little speckled wangeens and your cromlechs that he wasn't just passing the time of day with the rat-faced twerp! And then, bejesus, he hit him a blow on the side of his knotty little head with the great green shillelagh in his gnarled mitt so that a man could hear the bloody crack all the way over to hell and gone in Bronx County! That was a saint for you! None of your creepin' little ginzolas flinging stale bread crumbs to a gaggle of pigeons about *that* monumental chest!

But beating the piss out of this jew fink—is that all there is to commend St. Patrick to us? By God, I say no! What, then, is the *true* meaning of St. Patrick? And also the swell and glorious day we set aside for him, a day when the vomit from a million Irish throats threatens to drown the very world? Or at least parts of Yorkville? I'll tell you, and since our friends, the police, have cordoned off the area, making it impossible for your pitiful attempts to take a powder to succeed in any way, shape, or manner, making them absolutely academic, you'll be happy to listen! And if you're not happy, then may your daughters be married in a pigsty!

What, I ask, and have already asked, if these creased and crumpled notes in my hand are to be believed, is the true meaning of St. Patrick's Day? As legend, great Celtic roaring and stout-soaked legend has it, the Hero of Ireland is St. Patrick—not Finn MacCool, not Cuchulain, not King Sweeny, not Count O'Blather, not Blazes Boylan, no!—but St. Patrick! We all remember Ireland, do we not? That lime, that almost chartreuse-colored island nestling close off the coast of Chile or someplace close by, give or take a league or fathom or whatever they call it in nautical argot, what am I, a commodore? Yes! The Hero of Ireland! He is the man who hustled the snakes out of the country, chasing them until their poor little legs almost fell off as they ran like scared sheeps into the Kill of Fundy or Erie Basin, whatever majestic body of water is nearby that great Port of Eire, that port ever busy, ever bustling, with a merry song on its lips and its wharves crowded with spar and sail and a ready laugh and jest always about to drop or fall or some fucking thing or other.

Yes! We all know this old walnut of a story, and as walnuts go, a damn good one, and I'll not take no for an answer, now matter how you punks and bawds shake your sinful flesh and stand instantly déshabille! And that, as you all can imagine, even the stupidest donkey among you, is a French word for mother-naked, but we all know the lewd and lascivious French, drunk and disorderly and choppin' off the heads of kings and up to their blushing elbows in snails stinking of garlic and bedamn knows what all else and black garter belts! We know it! Yes! But still, 'tis a grand tale. Each and every varmint, critter, and reptile squeaking and moaning and hissing and trotting bejesus into the green ocean surrounding that pleasant land by God like so many crazed lemons! It is, matter of fact, from the juggernautish sight on that historic day, with the crowds of lizards and newts and everything else all cheek by jowl down on the beach that we get the name lemon squash. But be that here or there. We all know, I say, and say again, and *will* say until the last breath in my throat or larynx or wherever the last breath resides, struggles manfully on that ding-dong day called Doom, when the earth shall crack open and the dead rise from their graves, including all your miserable relatives and in-laws that you thought you'd never have to say hello to again, as well as deadbeats like Hitler and Stalin and so many, so many others, that . . . that, whatever, you get what I mean. For the laws of Doom are strange laws, and no man, least of all you ignorant fake harps, can hope to understand them! Or even one or two of the easier ones, for that matter!

Yes, we all know the old story, if story is not too weak a word, for truly it is more than story, it is what scholars call *legend*, as in "The Legend of Weeping Wimpy" or "The Legend of the Choke-Up Phillies." You're hip to what I'm pullin' your coat about? Cold, baby! But. And, but . . . *But* no one ever hears about the tiny little wee people, or as some researchers into the Celtic rites term them, the wee-wee people. Who are these wee-wee people? you ask. Perhaps not all of you, but a few of you, and I, for one, don't go in a big way for majorities, so those of you who don't ask can take a flying glasheen for yourselves for all I care—what am I? your father? Who, I ask again, in vaguely stentorian tones, are these wee-wee people? They are part of Ireland too, believe it or not! Yes, the great Port of Ireland is not solely composed, as most of you ignorant goddam gringos think, of great hulking colleens in cracked brogans and tweed caps. There are plenty of wee-wee people too, puh-len-ty! And they are part of Erin too, yes, a great part, for it is the wee people, which in the Irish tongue are called leprechauns, and which others call dwarfs, who helped—who? Right! Good St. Pat fight all the evil forces and win victory for the Irish!

But victory over whom? The door of Time has slammed on this knowledge and shoved its gasping sconce into the waters of Lethe, but we may guess that the wee-wee people assisted St. Patrick in booting the crawly varmints out of the green land—or why, for Christ's sake, use your head, why would I bring them up? But for sure, they didn't do a goddam thing about getting rid of the English and their kidney ragouts and kippered omelettes and all the other half-ass things they invented—top hats and oatmeal cookies and Bloomsbury and God knows what else. Polo! So though our hearts are full to the bursting point with tears of gratitude for the laughing wee-wees, we must in all fairness admit that they at least partially blew it—or, to use a gross patois that you two-bit yokels will understand, standing there agape in your white plastic slip-on shoes and your peach safari coats, they fucked up a little. A little?! Brothers and sisters, in all candor and to be honestly and sincerely blunt, they fucked up beyond all recognition, as the old army saw would have it, and, by God, does!

But everybody's entitled to a mistake, so let us forget as best we can, the—how shall I call it?—oversight, on the part of the carefree and go-happy plucky wee-wees that permitted the accursed limesuckers to use Ireland as a kind of vacation spot, like maybe the Catskills or Miami Beach, and fill its northern half up to the brim, yes, *mes amis*, to the very gunwales, with a gang of Protestant dudes, all carrying big goddam orange signs and what have you and driving their neighbors right around the well-known bend with their endless off-key hymns. Talk about your dissonance! Talk about your Bella Bostock! So, O.K. Taking all this into consideration, let's give, shall we? the little green dwarfs a break.

There are some, namely Americans all, though I throw no stones, but one feels a spade is always and forever a spade, so, yes, Americans all, I repeat—as we all are or wish to be, your Albanian, your Haitian, your sneaky Mex, your corrupt Vietnamese, your swarthy Sidge—in this fat land of lies and lechery, who still in their thudding bosoms clasp an atom, a tiniest smidgen of what I may term, if I may be forgiven such a glaring chunk of rodomontade, *pique*! And wherefore? Because a foul and degraded story has it that each little asp and cobra and rattler and newt and iguana and gila monster and bushman and python and copperhead who ran for his very life into the Bay of Blather, splashing, fear-crazed, like so many dobermans and pandas, managed—oh, not all of them, but only the hardiest, subscribing, as they did, and by the Precious Blood were glad to, to the great Darwinian Proof of every man for himself and to hell with the women and children!—managed, I repeat, these few, these happy few, to swim like billy bedamn to these States! or, as old whitebeard Walt wrote, "these States!" Here to subtly transmute themselves into policemen! But this is, as I'm sure all of you will agree, a base slander, and there is not a copper alive whose heart beats high and free who will stand still for it for a split second, including those peace officers there on the outskirts of the gathering, gently nudging, gently prodding, gently clubbing and maiming for life that mere handful of you who are attempting to slither off to the parking lot—for shame!—wherein your ludicrous cars are even now, as is their custom, conspiring to throw a piston or decimate their badly installed transmissions, carburetors, and, yes, though it pains me to say it, their rumble seats!

So let us, as I have quietly suggested, give the benefit of the doubt to the jolly wee-wees, those stout dwarfs, who assisted good St. Patrick in his hour of darkest need! And, touching on these funny little bastards, it gives furiously to think, that is, how could such little gombeens scare the living bejayzus out of a king cobra or giant newt? A cobra or newt, I beg you to consider, who, even hunkered down, or lying prone, was at eye level with the tallest and most strapping wee-wee? Despite the fact that the wee-wee people were, as the indelicate might phrase it, pisseyed drunk and filled to the rafters with false bravado, still, they were awful small, awful, *awful* small! Well! That's something to ponder on, is it not? And while you are taxing your headline-sodden brains with it, me glowing potheens, I'll give you the benefit of my own long musings on the matter. It was the very *look* of the little rascals! Speculation, educated speculation, has the wee-wee horde wearing the traditional green of Ireland with little pointed shoesies and little pointed caps, and with a pot of gold in their arms. All this was furnished them by the jovial saint we dub Patty, or Paddy, or Patsy, who allowed them to pick up all these items on time, a dollar down and a dollar when you catch me, as my dear mother used to say. But this is no time for personal reminiscence or self-indulgence, not when the very future of the gross, and I do mean *gross*, national product is at stake. What that product may be is not in question today, yet I may touch on it in another brief talk to you good-natured yankees, but at some future time. Sufficient unto the day, etc.

Now, put yourselves, your lithe bodies, your jogged-out brains, your ruined digestions, all, all the molecules and atoms of your firm flesh and red blood, in the place of these snakes and stuff, lolling around in the emerald grass and laughing triumphantly over the fact that every last Irishman and his sweetly blushing lass was confined to his and her apartment because of their natural fear and disgust of all these slimy sons of Lucifer. Suddenly, as you blow another, yet another smoke ring into the crystalline air of dear old Erin, you hear—as snakes have, as I'm sure you know, ears in every foot and, by God, numberless feet they have, or may God strike me dead! You hear, then, a noise in the brush and you glance up, aromatic cigarette all forgotten. Jesus H. Christ! There before you stands an ugly little gnome of a dwarf, dressed in these loathsome green clothes, I mean strictly plain pipe-rack stuff, brother. The little harp has a pointed hat on and these little emerald good-morning shoes, looks like a goddam elf! He's got a pot of gold in his arms, or stuffed under his oxter, and maybe you're not aware of it but snakes do not cotton to gold, a well-known fact of natural science, which has proven, beyond any shadow of a doubt, that when snakes are given gold to eat in lieu of eggs and little birdies and helpless old ladies, they refuse it and pine away. Consider then the sheer, the overpowering horror of this sight—this grinning wee-wee, with his black-stained teeth, peeking at *you*, Mr. Cobra, from behind a shamrock! And all the nauseating snakes and such dig that there are thousands of these little schmucks, maybe even millions of them, and all are being urged forward, ever and for always forward, by the great trumpeting voice of St. Patrick himself, who is yelling horrible war cries like "Erin Go Bragh!" and "A Shot and A Beer!" and bashing every serpent he can reach, male and female both, with an empty Jamieson bottle. The terror of it! It is mute testament, my buddies, yes, even those of you who are lying broken and bleeding out there by the police lines under the soft spring sun, to the truth of the old motto, "Clothes make the man."

And so, with the snakes and their compadres all swimming for dear life in the giant waves that crash insensate on the rocky shores all up and down that great coast that dares not tell its name, the wee-wees had nothing much to do but sit around under mushrooms and shamrocks and petunias and drink themselves insensible, while the good St. Pat marked the day, March seventeenth, on his calendar, with a huge strapping felt-tip marker, ah God, yes indeedy, the same kind that one may still buy in little out-of-the-way mavrones and machrees in the ancient Roman city of Dublin. St. Pat, a man who was not your usual run-of-the-mill saint, always loitering out on the desert somewhere waiting for a vision or a voice like so many of your greaser saints—shure, an' it's the difference in climate that does it—strove with might and main, sloshing gallons, by God, oceans! of black coffee down all those wee gullets, of both sexes, but by the time he'd sober up a million or two of the little spud-chompers, wouldn't you know that he'd find the first ones drunk and ossified to a fine powder again, associating with evil companions, falling into occasions of sin, leering after women, crawling around in the clover and peering up every skirt in the Emerald Isle, and puking bedamn veritable Amazons and Niles of worn-out ale, stout, and porter—not to mention Irish firewater which, some say, was invented by an eccentric wee-wee who was casting about in his laboratory for something to keep the point of his hat starched. But be that as it may and, as they say, it will be.

St. Patrick was, as you may well imagine, if you dim bastards can be thought to imagine anything, highly wroth and filled with a great sense of futility and despair. For what had happened? The wee-wee people, in their first foray out of their bogs and their mud-floored public houses had stampeded every varmint into the boiling drink, true. But now they were become foul and shiftless varmints themselves, with nothing to do and all day to do it in, if I may exert a little levity—and those of you who are being bashed into a show of manners back there by the split-log picnic tables have only brought it on yourselves, you rude louts, by giving my little unpretentious *mot* what is grossly called the horse laugh. See that the rest of you suckers pick up on those howls of pain, oke?

So what was the good St. Patrick to do? A year passed, maybe two, maybe two hundred, because it's a fact, by God Almighty, that the saint lived for five or six hundred years, long enough, as some of you know, to found the great Blarney Stone saloon chain in the City of New York. That was in the good old days before the Irish in that fair city learned to speak good American and still worshipped the lowly bathtub as a god, allowing nothing to touch it except maybe a quarter-ton of soft coal or so. They were, those early Irish settlers on the shores of lofty Gotham, absolutely wacky over coal, from which dates the curious term "black Irish," this unfortunate condition being a result of standing in slathers of coal smoke. But I digress.

What, I have asked, was this lovely man to do? No, my good friend over there with the denim pipe, not "take a walk," as you were about to say before that friendly flatfoot busted your face with a neat twirl of his blackjack. No, not "take a walk" atall, atall. He sat and thought and thought and then, on the anniversary—never mind which one—of the day that he and his mite-like pals shoved the snakes into the thundering thalassa, or thalatta, depending on which diner you favor for your yankee pot roast, string beans, and mashed, he roused himself, a light bulb having appeared in the air above his head as if by magic! He slung on his girds, slapped braces on his loins. He had an idea! And an idea so good, so true, so packed with felicity and pure old Irish know-how, that the harps to a man still marvel over it, having little enough else to marvel over. He decided to let the wee-wees work some magic over Ireland. That, by the by, is how the annals and the sagas and the eddas and the kells and the epics and even the histories put it: "It is the wee people who work the magic over Ireland." And what is this magic? They are the ones, yes, me red-faced dears, they are the ones who "spread the waves and the carpet turns a silky green." What these "waves" are, I haven't got idea fucking one, but *they* do it!

When the kindly old silver-haired St. Patsy broached this idea to the throngs of sodden wee-wees, barely able to keep their little pig-eyes open, and hopping about like Spanish flies committing adultery with trees and every other thing else, and coveting and copping everything that wasn't securely nailed down to the glorious green dirt, and blaspheming a mile a minute each time they quit sucking on a bottle of the devil's brew, they stood shamefaced and embarrassed before that good kind man who had, for the occasion, dressed himself in a Kelly tweed suit and a snowy vest made all of clay pipes, and bedamn, with his great honest policeman's brogans fashioned with fairy skill from the skins of the finest spuds. By God, he was Mister Ireland that day! The wee-wees, soused as they were, realized that this was their last chance to be almost human, and they jumped upon its back, or however you thick norteamericanos phrase it. Let's say they dug on the idea. Can you get behind that, Jim? The male wee-wees cleaned their green threads of barf stains as best they could, and the females searched diligently through the nodding tares for such articles of intimate apparel as they had chucked away, figuring, such was the action, that, who needed them? Then, straight and strong and sober, with but a trace of the shakes, the legions of little folk started in spreading the waves and bedad turning the carpet a silky green. And ever since that day, about 1936 or 1937, if memory serves, as indeed it does whenever it can get its tux out of hock, most of us fondly recall the legend of the wee-wees when we think, as oft we must with tears and banshee wails, of Ireland. *Don't we!?* How thrilling to hear the thunderous "ayes" gushing from your throats and zinging off the firmament, those of you, that is, still capable of emitting noise of any kind. There's nothing like a friendly crowd.

So that, my eager amigos, is the true meaning of St. Patrick and his merry day. He gave the snakes the heave-ho, he recruited the wee-wee people to assist him in his thankless task, his dirty task, the sort of task fit for jigs, wops, and greasers, yet not held, no, not even for a moment, in contempt by the noble St. Pat, and, last but certainly not least, if I may lapse for a moment into the banal, when the lousy little dwarfs got out of hand in the sin department, he straightened them out, he allowed them sole possession of the wave-spreading franchise, the green-carpet market, etc., etc. Between you me and the ashcan, buddies, this was strictly bush-league work, but the wee-wees have never been accused of being stars in the brains department, being more like your actor, your dancer, your state legislator, and so if they're not running off at the gob with a lot of annoying pissing and moaning about their rights like a passel of maladjusted and malcontent welfare clients—how I love that word "clients"—why should *we* take it upon ourselves to criticize the imbecile connemaras?

So. St. Patrick, for all the honor we do him each March the Seventeenth, drinking ourselves into a frenzy of unrequited lust, making ourselves half-mad with staring at the drum majorettes in their indecent costumes, watching and listening to, with rising nausea, the professional Irishmen in their green cardboard derbies describe the parade to us on television, and driving ourselves into a state of moral catatonia with the obscene sight of the half-assed, half-baked, semiliterate whores of politicians who would cheerfully kill their mothers, and their fathers too, for the privilege of standing like a bog-trotter of a gawm with a button as big as paddy's pig on the wizened and dried-up chest of him that says to all the rotten world, "I'm Irish." Bejesus, it's enough to turn a decent man into a bloody Presbyterian! Still, and still, St. Patrick was real and the poor dear man cannot be held accountable for the disgusting antics of your mayor, your congressman, your local priest. The man walked! He talked! He sometimes hopped and trotted o'er the green face of Ireland many years ago, how many I don't know and I don't give a rat's ass anyway. The Irish love this gentle man and celebrate his day faithfully, beating each other into porridge and flinging themselves in desperate gambols on the green silky carpet that the wee-wees have worked like a bunch of niggers to prepare. 'Tis a grand day, when every mark in Christendom has the chance to delude himself into thinking he's important!

And I implore those of you who are still moving under your own sweet power to think on this day all through the year, and to help you remember, you dear lovely dyspeptic hamburger-eaters, you may empty your pockets of cash and other valuables, not forgetting watches, bracelets, earrings and the like, and turn them over to Sergeant O'Mara, who is standing there as big as life—the foine-looking lad with the riot baton, that's him—at the entrance to the parking lot. He'll be only too happy to assist you, the lovable brogue! Thank you for your attention, me hearty macushlas, and a good afternoon to all of you!

≪ 35 ≫

Miz Gavotte
Tells Her Mate
a Little White Lie

Our Blue, back from his Celtic stint, relaxed in his rooms, awaiting good Doctor Dubuque and further intelligence concerning the Phrase. His heart leaped up when Helene peered 'round the transom-jamb, her eyes still misty from the memory of the sunset on the rippling Amazon. Yet her jaw was firm as if to belie the sparkle in her peepers.

How nice to see you, wife, back at last from your trip up the thudding Orinoco! I've not been idle here, as I'll soon relate.

The Orinoco? So *that's* why the crocodiles spoke Spanish! Anyhow, my love, it was a pleasure not to be dismissed with a phrase like unto, "And while Blue conferred with Doc Dubuque, his wife busied herself with a tour of the campus and its leafy environs." The little river steamer we were on "huffed" and "creaked" by the way, and the smell of petrol was often overpowering in the heavy tropical heat. How the natives splashed!

I hope that the placid boredom of our little home away from home does not instill in you a vast ennui? Serge said, for he was worried by the rigid jaw-set of his pal.

It's not the fear of boredom that has firmed my jawbone, Helene quavered. It's that I've something I must tell you while I have the moxie. First, let me turn our Zim out to humming pasture. (Which she did without ado.)

Tell me? Serge began, his hands still . . . at last!

Yes, my sweetie. You'll recall that I told you but a space or twain ago a coupla days just past that Dr. Poncho at The College had accosted me upon the path and made a couple foul suggestions to me in reference to the act that dares not show itself in daylight on the street, or boulevard?

How could I forget? seethed Blue. Had I that perfidious caitiff here beneath my hamlike fists he'd soon feel the weight of vengeance bold that sugars up the dish of wild regret!

I fear, my cupid, that they were more than mere, how do they say? "advances?"

What? You mean . . . and it was as if proud Serge's body had slumped down in his chair. Slumped down in his chair, his body looked at her, in the eyes belonging to same a wordless questioning pain. You mean . . . ? But he could go no further.

I *do* mean, Helene nodded in a kind of stunned hysteria. You have been given the horns, or in this case, perhaps the antlers.

Great clattering palm fronds! Blue shuddered, his face buried in four fingers of his hand. H-how? Wh-why? B-but? Wh-where? His eyes were fixed upon the carpet in a bleak despair, probly searching for the face of Henry James.

He, as they say, seducèd me, and I followed him into the rustling maple-stand all trembling with that well-advertised wild delight, with, I might say, a sophisticated adult-type joy. What a mature attitude we had about this basic male-female relationship; no false shame sullied our gentle caring; no hypocritical prudery debased our strong, proud nudity; what tender, patient foreplay heated up our sexual needs; how we acted out those fantasies that actual doctors say are good and healthy and also practiced by some of this great country's most respected and well-dressed honorable citizens; how we casted off our binding and restricting clothes, why, the good doctor's very tweeds took flight! 'Twas not just a quick boff, but a prolonged sashay into delights replete with those reckless positions he-men really like. We acted out a thesaurus of idears on the meeting of our fletch!

Groan, said Blue.

It was abandoned ecstasy, yes, and wild, free, unfettered joy! The beauty of healthy human-person bodies aglow in shackleless nakedity! The doctor's thrumming sex plumbed me to the basement of my core and my female id did tumblesault with a wacky grin upon its face; not even the thorny dogface-tares clutching at my tender bod annoyed me. The doc refused my pleas for mercy; I laughed at his. Gracious! my multiple orgasms scared the crap from a host of teeny cicadas and such other oddball creepers and creepy oddballs that hunkered in the bresh! He e'en bared my seat and greeked me afore blushing Nature, so that She stood up and said to all the world, "This is a can!" Ah, when I compare this neat perversion with the sleepy pops you've given me of late . . . the heart pines and drops a tear or such.

Woe, mumbled Blue.

Elegericals and reams of pedometers in the original Greek and Latin eased from his learnèd lips as he pegged me underwater in the sedge-choked pond, and the lenses of his pince-nez cracked, as did my reservations; I felt much like a lady psychiatrist speaking lightly yet with frozen face upon the TV screen of fetishes and fellatio, so filled with mad sophistication was my brain; like a gay puttana dressed up like a nun in a technicolor stag flick. By crocky! my homely dirndls and my serviceable burlap hose busted into flame! I was a Pasiphaë when the prize bull hopped on her in her weird cow suit; a Leda getting banged by that arrogant flamingo; a Danaë when the wild doubloons creeped up her skirts; a Helen when young Paris slipped it to her in the sheepfold; tall and free and laughing with, like, white even teeth, and with my so-so figure glowing like a majoun sassafrass! Poncho is no big-deal bargain, yet in his rage of passion seemed the very spirit of Apollo, or Dionysos drunk yet again at closing time, his bleary bloodshot eyes fixed upon the quivering bosom of the waitress counting up her crummy tips.

Whinge, whinged Blue.

I myself felt like Calypso when the sly Odysseus, know as "Red" to all his non-coms, bent her o'er a stalagmite or stalactite or heavy rock or sumpn; like Circe when that same wily Greek tore off her basic little black dress, simmering as he wert because of the möly he had dropped just prior to his entrance; like any liberated femme surrounded by a buncha creams and aids and fully illustrated books for sale to over-twenty-one. Yes! The spirit of great Eros fell from out the sky like sleet or freezing rain, shattering, in its mad career, not a few branches, the leaves of whom the panting Poncho gathered up and used to make our bower, somewhat like Varlayne's except we was short on sherbet.

Argh, gasped Blue.

I wert ga-ga like the fair Europa, another bull-freak lost in mad depravity; like Io, who was horny Jupiter's sweet veal scallopine; like Aphrodite, getting it on with Mars while the old man put in his time at the foundry; like the dissembling Penelope who did not tell her long-gone hubby when he made it home that she'd run through all the suitors like a dose of salts and was about to start in at the top again: she tore off more than warps and woofs at night, believe you me; like Clytemnestra, who plummeted into the sack with staunch Aegisthus when Agamemnon—

Cease! Serge blathered. I get the drift and e'en the tidal wave of your purport! But...why? Why, why?

Your attentions to my yearning fletch have fallen off until I feel as if you do not care for me, such, such are the tumbles lately. Quick and sans delight. Your obsession with The Phrase driv me to it with the horny Dr. Poncho.

Woe, woe, what can I do?

Seek assistance, and stop your dull behavior. Or sundering divorce will be our guerdon, fast-fuck!

I'll seek the counsel of the wise old Doc Dubuque. He'll know the sources whence flow remedy for these, my limping sacrifices to Amour—else comets shall crunch down upon the flagrant phlox that shiver in the marsh!

Do, my lumpish friend. A little candid talk on dirty lust will do you still a world of good, mayhap.

I'll seek the Doc eftsoones, roared Blue.

«36»

Father Donald
Debris, S.J., Gives a Talk on Sex

How wise and kind and good of Dr. Dubuque to send you over to see me for a little chat, Mr. Serge. Although the good doctor is a Protestant he has a kind and full heart, and fourteen-karat gold to boot. He tells me in this eensie-beensie note that I hold in my careworn hands, here in my Spartan study, my vow, as it were, of poverty, as it were, made physical—nice word, that—aha, ha, ha, that you have run into a raft of trouble, a jagged shoal of same, concerning what we call, in our secluded way, here in the bosom, ahem, of Mother Church, that is, we who labor in the sparse and ofttimes sour vineyards of the Great Ma, in, as it were, Peter's Backyard, heh, heh, sex. And not a rare or extraordinary problem at all these days, young fellow, with even men of the cloth falling beneath its flashing high heels, hot bellies, enormous breasts, heavy thighs, and, ahem! Huhf! Yes, where was I? Ah, yes. Sex!

Yes, sex, this sacred mystery that involves all humankind in its byways and dim alleys. I can see by a quick and somewhat furtive glance into the dark yearning pools of your eyes that this mystery is rendering you an ignoble and even loutish dolt. Lean closer then, and let me talk to you as best I can about the place of sex in our lives today—or even the win and show, if you will, the show being inextricably intertwined with checking out carelessly drawn blinds over at the nun's residence, and some of those young novices . . . The place of sex! In our lives, we, who are the fallen buds of the glowing tares, pitched about the cold floor of the Forest of Life—a forest, like as not, waiting to burst into the consuming flame! Only we may prevent these infernos, or, lacking that, at least we may use them to, so to speak, heat up a pot of coffee or singe a rustic burger or two.

Sex! Is there another word in our beloved mother tongue that raises such expectations, only to see them shivered into splinters and toothpicks, and small ones too, small as the mindless amoeba that has no sex at all, but is always swimming around glumly wondering what exactly went wrong. You'll pardon my immoderate grin which verges, even now, on the edge of hysterical laughter, but that odd rictus is often the result of long and somewhat irrational fasting, since it is roast beef and the good red wine, to borrow a phrase from Bob Frost, that makes for your solemn padre—an old saying, surely, but one that rings and clatters to the very canopy and baldachin of heaven itself, if baldachin is the word. I knew a plethora of words when a cloddish youth in the seminary but as life, Great Life, has slouched by, they seem to have fallen by the wayside, right into the yellow wood, and some, if you'll forgive the sudden blast of glaring truth, in rather grotesque positions, like maybe on all fours, or abandonedly akimbo, free from all shame, face flushed, the glitter of sunlight on rosy flesh— Sometimes . . .

We Jesuits, holy men all and as celibate as good King Wenceslas, who, as the old hymn insists, *looked down* on the feast of Stephen, looked, yes, but did not feed his fat and greasy face, yes, we, holy and chaste yet with great understanding of the ills that afflict mere lay persons, and with A-number-one imaginations, the latter all astew when we are not engaged in our regular-guy roles of baseball fans and such and with being all things to all people, you know what I mean, sort of like whacked out on bourbon and with the fatherly arm draped around the shoulders of some pure blue-eyed lass at the annual faculty shindig to which selected graduate assistants are invited and so forth, I don't have to spell it out, do I, Mr. Serge? Of course not. We Jesuits, and I, Don Debris not least among them, are students of and watchers over sex as practiced among the faithful. And you would be surprised at some of the odd methods used to avoid the sinful use of contraceptives and yet, how shall I say? "get off." Let me tell you, Mr. Serge, let me speak directly to the rich dark sediment that swirls about in the deeps of your eyes, sex is not dead among Christians! It may not be in the proverbial pink—to borrow a word from Jerry Lewis—but there's nothing the matter with it that a good stiff dose of clean Catholic copulation won't fix up in a trice, good as new and jack-a-dandy! You cotton to what I mean? The pitch-black room, the muffled sighs so the kids won't hear, and Jesus hanging over the bed in his useless agony peering through the dark at the straining bodies sweating the bed up below.

Dr. Dubuque may or may not have told you—occasionally he can be small, very small—that I am the author of a new book to be published next fall by Plastic Missal Press in Scranton, P.A., leafy burg! to what already shows itself to be general acclaim by all good Catholics, and that will be available at the pre-publication price of eighteen ninety-five at every Las Vegas night the length and breadth of this country, discounts to educational groups, all proceeds to go to the Sodality of Chaste Wives. Interested? Of course you are! Even Jewish persons like yourself are curious about—to borrow a phrase from Carl Sandburg—piling into bodies on the grass—or anywhere else, for that matter! Sandburg had your basically provincial mind, as witness his legions of crew-cut fans. No matter. There is a line somewhere in my book—I love the careless modesty of that "somewhere"—that runs: "Sex is not dead, but has a heavy cold." My book, entitled, *Sex Unleashed Among Christians*, is intended to be, if you will, the Vicks Vapo-Rub, the Vitamin C, the soothing hand on the brow, that will *cure* that cold. I was never strong on the metaphor and tend to agree with Plato that all poets should be picked up on vagrancy charges and set to making fly-swatters. He was, as I'm sure your reading will show you, one smart Greek, and I have often argued the point that had he come to America instead of lazing around the dusty agoras he loved so well, he would have been in on the ground floor of the fast-food biz, probably whipping up instant dollops of Salisbury steak with side of mash, side of carrots and peas, and God knows what else. Marvelous things to help our economy along, keeping it pump-primed or something, though I'm not too astute on these Marxist terms, having done my doctoral thesis on "Masturbation Symbolism in Flannery O'Connor." I assure you, however, that I *did* vote for FDR, not wanting to shoot the horse in midstream of the great river of war in which he was wading—and at a smart gallop too! But I fear that I speak too much of my own interests. Anyhow—out of my years of research and thought, out of all the sweat and headaches and fantasies and peeking through jalousies and Venetian blinds, out of the experiences of numberless faculty blowouts—odd word, that—all of these things going to make the pith and the vinegar, to filch a phrase from Omar Khayyam, of my *Sex Unleashed*, allow me to pluck from same a few choice nuggets, some eloquent pistachios of deepest thought, to assist you in your desiccated and morose sex life. To wit:

Sex, as sexualityness, is the essential personal property, like a pair of galoshes, a fedora, a brassiere, with lace trim, semi-transparent so that one can make out the, uh, yes, it is the personal property of being masculine or feminine. It is held, and, if you will forgive my node of levity, close to the chest, too, to be identical with the unique personal manifestation of your average human being, morphodites excluded by popular demand. A man/woman attempts to achieve and identify himself/herself precisely as a correlative, a Pole Star, complementary to yet opposite from—what else?—the opposite sex! And therein therefore finds himself/herself alive and aglow with singing joy except, oddly enough, at the moment or so of orgasm, in which he/she finds himself/herself "dead." If we push, shove, and bully these swell and perfect limits outside their respective pales, and being a Jewish type, you know what that means, we find that bulging sweaty masculinity becomes the caricature called machismo; and the luscious curves and musky perfume of the feminine turns into that slovenly and degrading parody that we may term the pin-up, the sex symbol, the cheesecake model, the beaver shot, and so on and so forth. Disgusting to the mature mind, I grant you, and I have spent years up to the elbows in these horrifying representations of semi-clothed young women in divers grotesque poses, and I've come to the conclusion that the fantasy of the young wife in torn housedress, maybe with sneakers and black nylons . . . Uh. Uh, under this, or perhaps around this fundamental perception, this ABC of sex roles in our changing world, to borrow a phrase from Sara Teasdale—not a bad-looking lady, though a little lacking in the umm, what can I say? physical endowments that we associate with the female person. What was I saying? Yes, this perception, I say, under this perception, it is impossible not to realize that for a human person to be a human person that human person must first be a human masculine or a human feminine person. Which puts many a gay-type individual right out in the cold, or so I read it by my lights. In other words, my dear Mr. Serge, a human being cannot be a human person first, and then a male or a female person, nor can a human person be a male or a female person first, and then only a mere human person. "Mere" is, you understand, a figure of speech, of course. No! This odious dichotomy cannot be! God has intended us all to be jampacked together, human, male, female, cheeks by jowls, and not a bad position either as I can see you understand by the fiery glint in the raging cesspools of your eyes. And jampacked at work even as at play. In Nature, we see the same phenomenon at work among the flowers of the field, such as the striped anorexia and the bunched lochia, which are not anything *but* striped and bunched along with the irrefutable fact of their being also plant "persons," nodding and drooping and dropping their little seeds like mad, with the homely bee buzzing around in the hot sun like a maniac and so on and so forth. In the fields, there you will see sex as it was meant to be, with none of the corruptions of tight slacks and sensual perfumes and colognes and underclothing not meant to clothe but to make a poor man get crazy as he riffles through the pages of various catalogues that find their way to him with such regularity that his mailbox is crammed and stuffed with nothing but the occasion of sin and I for one don't think that I can stand it for another min— We are become a nation of saps and suckers, wonderfully vivid words if you'll but think on them for a moment. We sap ourselves and we also suck . . . uh, suck the vital moral juices from our spirits, anyway, you see what I'm driving at.

To many moderns, perhaps even you, my boy, sex is not a theme to study and perfect but a catalogue of lascivious description like the endless pages of Molly Bloom's aberrant musings as she performs the beastly acts so dear to her in the foxed copy that I own of *Ulysses*—and who else but a depraved Greek could have even *thought* of such shenanigans? The hallmark of this corporeal mystery used to be permanence, yet no one any longer needs or wants this permanence, am I right? Look at your own junkyard of a life! In the old days, things were different, it was not, as it is now, to lift a line from Jerome Kern, anything goes. Do we read, for instance, of shining Hector "ripping off a piece" in the back seat of a Chevy? Ha! Does Don Quixote "get some head" from a dark-eyed señorita in a ditch behind the high school athletic field? Pshaw! Ridiculous to entertain for the merest second such sacrilege! But *now*. Men and women, devoid of the old idea that they are persons as well as vessels of sexualityness, say "why play?" Play what? you ask, I'm sure, down there in the fundament of your whirling brain. *The Game!* I reply, with, and you will pardon me, a jot more than my usual heat. I speak, of course, of the game of permanence, that is, good sweaty fumbling Christian copulation in the privacy of your own little home, the children rattling the locked door with their sticky hands, hollering for some Frooty Loopies or Puffy Cokes, the aromatic coffee perking viciously away in the sunny breakfast nook, the heaped leaves smoldering behind the leaky garage, while you, as a human male person pound dutifully away at the holy body of your helpmeet, while she, ideally, although this is certainly not necessary, tells her beads. I recall that years ago, when I was a younger man, a priest at the parish of Our Lady of the Bleeding Eyes, there was a nun by the name of Sister Rose Zeppole, who would take her rosary and . . . well, let it be shrouded in silence.

Anyhow. Instead of the sedulously pounding husband and his wife, the, so to speak, poundee, what do we see before us? Some crazed and askew idea of *equality*. Or, if I may, let me say that we are at a far remove from as well as at odds with the idea of male person-female person, as I have already briefly outlined. Equality says, oh, not in so many words, but it's right there in front of you like a great shining blackhead, it says that your human person wife may, on a whim, when you come home exhausted from a long day at the water cooler or in the stock room hiding from the boss behind some cartons, she may, I insist, jump on you in nothing but a transparent apron and some thigh-high nylons, the kind that stay up by themselves have always, by the by, seemed to me most interestingly ingeni— ummm, yes! Jump on you, I say, and copulate *you* as if *you* were the poundee! Copulate and copulate until you are blue in the face and begging this boiling witch for a cold beer and a simple dish of home-made stew. What do these women, these "equal" women want, who think that they are female persons before they are human persons, or maybe vice-versa, what do I know of the thought processes of the lustful wife? They want, if you will forgive a smatter of the vulgar, they want to hump you cross-eyed and open up a can of Campbell's beans!

And of course our modern wife cleaves to herself her diaphragm, her intra-uterine device, her calendar, her pills, her vaginal-spermicidal foams in various flavors, and why? So that she may "enjoy" pounding and/or poundeeing without for a moment having to think of the joyous burden of having another child, another mouth to feed, body to clothe, dentist and doctor bills, plenty of victuals, and all the rest of the elation and the glorious worries that another child will bring to the ducky little family and its poppa's laughable paycheck. No wonder she can afford to spend her milk money and her stew money and her beer money on transparent house dresses and frilly aprons and insanely sheer hosiery, uh, and uh, tiny undergarments that, that, the names of which we Jesuits may not utter. For she is safe from pregnancy! But where, then, the sweet danger? There is no danger, and hence, there is no challenge, if the outcome of Christian sexual love is a sure thing, am I right, dear boy? There is no meaning in the eternal struggle on the bed if Danger is not in bed, so to speak, with the grunting pair, check? As the dewy anoxia is almost extinct because Boy Scouts—all of them, I hasten to add, attached to troops that meet in Protestant churches—pluck it with fierce abandon in the foolish belief that it can, as they say, zonk you out, so shall the traditionally flat-broke Christian family reach the razor's edge, to use a phrase from Whit Burnett, of extinction if "equality" allows female persons to jump their hubbies from behind the door before the poor fellows have had a chance even to slam down their old rusty lunch pails and holler, in voices made stentorian by years of bowling, "Hi, Honey! I don't smell nothing cooking!" But, Mr. Serge, we know what's "cooking," do we not, in this madhouse filled with lace and satin and naughty novels, a house sans Douay, or even a cheesy little religious pamphlet to help bore the couple to sleep and hence, innocence, and in that sleep of innocence, who knows, maybe the old man will do his duty, even all a-snore, before his crazy female partner has a chance to put her diaphragm in, or on, or under, or whatever they do with these Satanic accoutrements. What *do* they do, by the way? Don't tell me!

Christian love is indeed dead in such a climate, hot and steamy, and with an orgasm, so to speak, on demand and around every cozy little corner. We have so much sex—I use "we" rhetorically, of course—that we are bored to death by it, sort of. We are so bored that we are no longer interested in Good Healthy Sex, which may be your case in a peapod, Mr. Serge. Does my wild punch land on a sore spot? Recent reports in *Lights Out: The Marriage Manual for Catholics* state that there are indications of a great lessening of interest in the orgasm. And why is this the case? Because, beyond the obvious desirability of the wife person as a paradigm of sexualityness in her tangible and probably deliciously warm person, especially if she has just taken a hot bath and . . . Beyond the obvious, I say, what is there? The same old body! We must go beyond, far beyond the body in all its godly and remarkably swell curves and such, beyond it to the true meaning of copulation—another child to break, to coin a phrase of Le Moko's, the bank. It is not the *body* that the good Christian husband should care about, but the awesome organs of reproduction themselves, or itself! In other words, the dutiful husband should forever repeat to himself the old saw of The Tumbling Fungis, famed family of acrobats, "They're all the same upside down." The organs should be the Christian husband's only goal, and he should zero in, so to speak, on his spouse's uh, "forked" area, where her legs, uh, well, the *spot*, blinding himself to her overly familiar face and forgetting how she might look in oh, say, although I don't know too much about these items, a Merry Widow, if they still make them . . . would you happen to know if they . . . ? No matter.

We must learn to think of the orgasm, then, not as a pleasure—perish the thought!—but as a tool or device or thingamajig by means of which we keep foisting Christians on the world, not, surely, in your case, Mr. Serge, but one speaks ideally, or should I say, ideally speaking? Ha ha. What, after all, is an orgasm? Very little, very very little indeed. Recent research has shown that if a man is rigged up with oddball and sensitive equipment enabling him to have an orgasm every two or three minutes, he will adjust to this rather extraordinary behavior of his genito-urinary system within twenty-four hours and go about his wonted and homely tasks in the workaday world with not so much as a grimace, grunt, groan, or twitch, not much of a twitch anyway, and with a minimum amount of time lost from the job—in factory, office, or on the broad sunny fields of the echoing plains—and *that* simply to change his trousers every hour or two in order to avoid embarrassing accusations that he is a slob, a mess, disgusting, and so on and so forth. The human species can be cruel, cruel indeed, as I don't have to tell you, my son, for one can take one quick gander at your seamed and lined face and tell in a shot that you've had your share of heartache and adversity, your depressing sexual problems of the present being a case in point, if I may dare breathe your shame. Female persons? Ditto. Super ditto. Or as our Spanish friends might put it, clumped, as is their custom, around the colorful siesta, *dittito*. They are a warm and wonderful race who long merely to breathe free. Or at least cheap. But I was speaking of your average female housewife, pert and natty in a cotton housedress and bent fetchingly over the stove, let's imagine the good woman with trembling thighs slightly apart and with— Um. Yes, your average woman. A housewife in Mineola, Long Island, a town than which you can get no more average, was, ah, fitted, if you will, with an ingeniously designed—what shall I say—"stimulator," for want of a cruder term, its control switch cleverly designed to look exactly like a "Smile" button. She was told that any time she felt the need, or the desire—*there's* a really interesting word—she was to touch the switch and, as the young man who told me this story put it, Whammo! At first, she was compelled to "stimulate" herself while sitting down, else the surge of bodily wildness that swept her from head to foot would have knocked her flat—and hard, hard it would have been to explain this to her friends and neighbors, right? Yet after only a week or ten days she was having orgasms at the supermarket, the bake sale, the bank, the bowling alley, here, there, everywhere. And, apart from the fact that once or twice her eyes rolled back in her head, and, on one rare occasion an inadvertent flinging about of her legs knocked down a Mallomar pyramid in the above-cited supermarket, she went about her usual tasks with a placid face and a posture of absolute ladylike composure, sustaining, on one record day, four hundred and twelve orgasms before picking up the children at school. So you will see, my dear young fellow, that the orgasm is, in itself, nothing, perhaps even the existential *néant*. No wonder good Christians are bored with it.

But I fear that these tales, hurled into the body of my talk, may open me to a charge of digressing from the main text, so to speak, although as you can see, I speak extempore and a capella. Thus, let me press on swiftly with my analysis of sexual angst as it is known and suffered by the great majority of poor slobs in every hamlet and bursting metropolis in this great land we dare call Home. The sex dodge is often identified with copulation of one kind or another, the church preferring, if I may sink to a bout of levity, the one kind. In any event, it is mainly pretty physical stuff, the intellect being more or less parked outside while the parties go at it hammer and tongs, or thongs, if that's your pleasure. Speaking of thongs, it was Ovid who, somewhere in the *Ars amatoria*, first noted the amusing fillip called bondage. It is clearly defined in his tale of Aphrodite and Ares in which, I'm sure you'll recall, my dear Mr. Serge, Hephaestus, the wily crip, and a man crazy with secret lusts, bound the two with a gossamer yet steely strong net while they were in the very act of making the beast. And who can forget the lively scene when all the other gods and goddesses entered Aphrodite's boudoir and saw the two locked together like a couple of mongrels? There must have been a passel of Hellenic wisecracks flying through the Olympian air. I think of them all as no better than your modern voyeur, and though I am given to understand that the sedulous Peeping Tom occasionally glimpses a flash of swelling flesh, he is rarely lucky enough to see a ripe and luscious woman in the filthy act of . . . Lucky for them all that this happened before the birth of Christ or else they'd have more to gripe about than being bored into stupefaction in Limbo.

Hm. I find that I have digressed once again—whenever my mind calls up the Venus to me, I find that I . . . However: Ovid, yes. Ovid says that that dark act is the physical representation of the old Latin motto, "I-in-you-me-us." And if you don't know what the old dago is getting at, think deeply on precisely what the wild and untamed flesh performs when it performs. I've seen an odd photo or two and have some idea, enough anyway to permit me to speak to—odd phrase—the proposition. Sister Zeppole once had the most engaging deck of playing cards and when we turned a rubber or two of Old Maid we often fell to a minute examination of the instructive photographs that . . . I recall especially the Three of Diamonds, starring two nuns, a monsignor, and what seemed to be a bellhop, although what a bellhop would be doing in the rectory— In all events, to be in-you-me or me-in-you or us-in-us or me-around-it or it-up-you or how-ever you want to slice it bespeaks, as any casual oaf can see, the demand for a certain kind of *involvement*. You can't very well, as a Christian gentleman, be mouthing snippets like "me-up-yours" or however one might put it after a dry Martini or three, and not be what must be called, or I am not a nodding eremite, *involved*. That is, you cannot "get it on" with your spouse if you are standing up looking out the window at the pathetic joke that you call a "lawn" while the good woman sits across the room buried under cookbooks and their domestic ilk, mixing bowls, spatulae, whatever. Right? Perhaps that's your problem, young fellow? Don't tell me and no names please. Even frontier wisdom, and by God that was few and far between, else Great History lies, had it that love and mar-riage go together like a horse and carriage. Amusing couplet, no? and one based on the metrical experiments of Gérard de Nerval—but don't let me tax your manly brain with pedantry. That metaphor, if that's exactly what it is, although it seems to me that it may well be a pantoum, seems to suggest that in wedlock it is desirable for one partner to pull the other about the boudoir, or that one partner ride atop the other—the latter of course clearly points to the husband as the per-son doing the riding, since a moment's reflection will serve to prove that the hu-man female finds it difficult to be such a rider because of the encumbering effects of a skirt, unless, of course, said wife hikes or lifts the above-named feminine garment up to her, uh, the, well, what we call here in the silence of the life we live, upper portion of the lower limbs. In that way, the male husband may well serve as the horsey. Of course, proceedings may begin with the glowing wife skirtless, in which case . . . Of course, this obscure couplet may simply be a reference to the theory, held by some of the finest minds in academe, that steeds of the Old West were wont to mount their carriages in an excess of affection. Those nags, it is rumored, were game for anything.

In any case, the idea is one of involvement and inextricable partnership, nags or carriages or skirts and such—human persons simply must be involved! But what do we see all about us now? Is there a whole heck of a lot of pushing and straining and heaving and shoving of human person bodies together nowadays, actions that should go on well into the years of dotage, often called "golden" years? Very little, very very little. Very little obeisance is made to the hoary "up-you-in-me-you-me" concept of conjugal love. Whence issues all neuroses and all the crude and brittle casting aside of the churnings and bubblings and even the slow drip of the dark secret blood hovering just beneath the surface of the glowing skin—to employ a phrase of McKuen's—of radiant spouses of whatever gender. Sometimes, given the weather, not too radiant, but why quibble? The modern boy-girl relationship is one of cool and loveless accommodation, with the kissing and the hugging and the petting and the necking, accompanied by furtive glances at the movie they are supposed to be "seeing." Ha ha ha! Don't make me laugh! The young organs of generation quake and tremble as they blush, so to speak, at being handled like so many cheeseburgers. Is this the way to treat a sacred vessel? Before this age of sexual permissiveness, it used to be that a boy would pursue a girl from dawn to dusk, trying every ruse in the book, "book" is a figure of speech, a fuchsia to be exact, every ruse, I say, to get her sweet little bottom into— Meanwhile, she fought him off with ritualistic phrases, excuses going down the corridors of Time all the way back to the days of the Greek gods. You'll recall the lame protestations of Daphne and Syrinx of course, to name but two. Meanwhile, the two smoldered away, occasionally bursting into a small tongue of flame. Finally, this chaste courtship was ended by marriage, and the steaming groom would have his bride's odds and ends down around her silken ankles almost before the smirking bellhop was out the door. Then was there a crashing of bodies and the slap of Christian flesh against, God willing, Christian flesh such as to make the welkin shiver! And the object? More Christians!

What do we have now to take the place of such sublime frustration, almost Provençal in its intensity, such dizzying release, enough, as I've said, to make the heavens themselves light up like with a clutch of Roman candles? We read in the paper of some baby being born in England in a laboratory, like some kind of disgusting germ or virus. Ugh. The old man is led into a sterile room, all white and tile and such, like in the movies, in some out-of-the-way clinic, handed a copy of *Playbox* or some other petit-bourgeois rag, and a Petrie dish, and the door is locked behind him. In five minutes the nurse opens the door, grinning obscenely at the savaged pages of that publication, which just last month had a photograph of the Chairperson of the Board of Amalgamated Film Critics in the buff, and not a bad-looking woman, although her ... The lewd nurse takes the Petrie dish from the exhausted clod, chucks a couple eggs in there, eggs taken from his good wife's body, and the whole godawful mess is squirted back into the lady with, probably, a lot of doctor jokes, and by, no doubt, some atheist Jewish person, no offense. Is this "in-me-you-me"? Is this the lustful conflagration that adolescents used to douse in the deep end of the pool of marriage? It is to laugh. But that's the English for you, leave it to them to invent such a scam, or dodge. They'll do anything rather than take the risk of allowing English female persons the possibility of bumping into an Irish male person, a broth of a man who has never heard of a Petrie dish but places his whole faith in the homely spud and the jar of malt and likes nothing better than to involve himself with a female person of whatever nationality and may the pigs grunt so long as the springs of his homely straw pallet creak all night! And you wonder, young man, why no English unmarried person is allowed into Ireland, except for the Orange Counties, which don't count? Why, by my Maker, if a brawny glasheen of a lad ever saw a transparent apron he'd feed it to the hogs or, better, to the great-mawed polyphagia, that grows on diseased shamrocks. And there would be an end to *that* frivolity.

So What's That? becomes the name of the thing that emerges from the bemused mommy, courtesy of the Petrie dish. Is it boy, girl, or encrusted androgyne? And can you imagine the poor cluck of a specimen when he discovers the unnatural shame of his conception, guck and all? When he hears, as a tyke in school, the mocking voices of his chums as they bedevil him with such nicknames as "Artie Agar" and "Jarface," "Glass-head" and "Seaweed Sammy"? He'll realize, and with what cruel amaze, that he's nothing more than an experiment, like the golden bantam and elephant basophil that Luther Burbank whipped up of a winter's evening in his finished basement! However, my dear Mr. Serge, although *something* has happened to what you myriad carnal envelopes—a phrase made prominent by Vernon Royal—jokingly call your sex lives, you must see this difficulty as being essentially solvable. Sex is a Sacred Mystery, and the mysterious act does not cotton to lacy frillies and soft lights and overpowering and musky attars and the like, but is most happy when bursting forth, with red glare if needs be, in the open, under, when conditions are ideal, a bare 150-watt bulb, preferably dangling from the kitchen ceiling. In settings such as these, not quite sylvan yet as bluff and honest as a good spit, with the female person in an attitude of what Mother Church calls conjugal tolerance, her placid bottom among the crumbs and dirty dishes of the supper table, sex's great quivering sacrament asserts itself and soon flesh will call to flesh in the hollow stentorian tones, often plangent but always raucous, of the Christian Union. As St. Paul in one of his more cryptic phrases put it: "Husbands, love your wives, as Christ loved the Church." Now, as any Jesuit can tell you, St. Paul was a tricky little guy, and it's very hard to interpret his meaning here. I cannot credence the belief, held by a bunch of renegade priests and nuns, some of the latter having taken to wearing skirts which, though severe, are still short, so that their nether limbs, often as not encased in sheer nylons that, of needs, travel up the legs and— The belief, I say, uh, yes, that has it that Paul meant that Christ had a sort of liaison with the Church, or that He had a strange and off-kilter attraction for the building itself, now lost to us beneath the shifting sands of the Middle East, tromped on daily by wailing Jews and Arabs who happen to be very big on rank body odor. I suspect that He loved this Church as it was in the old days, that is, sans candles, flowers, pupils in the freezing courtyard, bums on the steps, loved it, that is to say, *naked*. And that is how Paul means for the hubby of Christian persuasion to love his little honey! Such that after the rack of lamb and the new potatoes and the mint sauce and the asparagus hollandaise and the flaky apple pie with aged cheddar and the aromatic coffee, the good housewife will divest herself of all her binding garments and, in the silence and darkness of the connubial bed, whack her ample belly against that of her husband's, unless she prefers to get on her hands and knees, in which case . . . And they will croon and gibber to the wheeze of the worn and sagging mattress—for if you eat like these two, young fellow, you won't have any money in the old sugar bowl for a new mattress, and you may take an old priest's word on that!

And as in primitive tribal rites, the orgasm that they achieve will be a utilitarian one, a workaday one, and worshipped as same. Perhaps, thinking on what I have just said, I should emphasize the orgasm that the husband achieves, since women have them only in sex clinics, hooked up to sophisticated machinery of all sorts and formidable wattage, chock full of high-speed attachments of phallic purport, and so on. Anyway, this orgasm is greeted with Christian humility, e.g., clenched teeth, blasé if not shatteringly bored air, glazed stare, sticky perspiration, and so forth. The couple's eyes may dart about involuntarily seeking out the felicities of the wallpaper design, and the like, pictures on the dresser, you name it. And if I may parenthesize, psychological depression and sickness unto death often occurs in the furtive affair because of the wallpaper designs in seedy motels. If I have to look, one more time, for instance, at a pink kitten tangled in a ball of twine, repeated over and over until . . . But forget the tribulations of a man of the cloth, I beg you, and let us return to our sated couple. After the culmination of God's will, the holy pair breathe soft orisons together that the old lady may have, once again, a bun in the oven. And when Mom grows big with child, and her other tykes say, "What's the matter with Ma? She's so fat!" the tenderly smiling couple can return to the sweet myths of a bygone and gentler time and tell the black-fisted brats one of the heartwarming tales of innocence that were our grand tradition until the advent of the condom and the Petrie dish and pleasure and such, as: the stork brought you all and is once again on the wing; we found you in the cabbage patch; we discovered you in a garbage can; we took you off the dumbwaiter; we bought you at the hospital; and so on and so forth. Stories to guarantee that healthy nervousness we call adolescent neurosis. And if one of the kiddies, wiser than his years, should ask how the stork got the baby into mommy's belly, the good couple, after a blush and stammer, can smack the clamoring rascal in his chops and send him to bed without any supper, as was done with George Washington, if memory serves.

For, my dear good Mr. Serge, mystery is sex and sex is mystery. Sex, laden down with this newfangled knowledge that proliferates, odd myths about things like the clitoris, which everyone knows simply does not exist, with sneaky whispers about multiple orgasms, an absolute impossibility and a canard that implies that a good and pure woman, free from attachment to some diabolical coitus machine, can come and come and come and just, my stars! keep *on* coming until your eyes are almost banjaxed out of your head and still she cries for you to *do it* and *do it!* . . . Well. Um. As I was saying, sex must be always and forever aswim in blissful ignorance, it must, to be worthy of sexualityness, be robustly boring. If you get yourself involved in odds and ends and trivia like positions and funny clothes and playing doctor-nurse or boss-secretary or priest-nun—and that strikes me as *particularly* crude—sex is nothing more than a worldly exercise in pleasure and not what God intended it to be: a job! As I contend in my new book, sex is all right when thought of as something akin to bowling and Barry Manilow and Merv Griffin and having a couple with the boys. When you mix it up with "fun" and excitement, it is nothing but the dry and soulless search for the orgasm—and we know what an orgasm is, do we not? Sort of like a sneeze. I say be done with the bric-a-brac and the bibelots and simplify, yes, much like our good sisters who wear, or so the laundress tells me, the lightest and most delicate things beneath their . . . Anyhow, my son, I trust that this talk has helped, and when you see the good Dr. Dubuque tell him that I've tried to steer you into the path of Duty, all right? And now I must to my frugal dinner.

« 37 »

In Which
Dr. Dubuque's
Insincerity Is Revealed

I've just come, Doctor, from a most enlightening and illuminating discussion with the good padre, Blue said. I see that it is now possible for me to have a life of unchained fleshly joy with my lawful spouse, rather than the mere existence of split-second boffs that have been my way of late. Now, and with all deference, it seems to me that the requirements of these episodes in my life of picaresque adventure have all been met. To wit, and id est, as well as videlicet: Happy greetings, short warm chats, speech on mysterious Celtic rites to assembled rubes, wife and son shipped off on all-expenses-paid junket for two on the mighty Zambezi, grovelling request to your most august person anent a small matter of personal genito-urinary difficulty, and rapt attendance on the wise yet worldly counsel of the resident sexologist, the good Father Debris, S.J. Thus, since the sun, as is its wonted habit, will not stand still, but careers acrost the azure as a madman hight doth suffocate the very breath of flowered innocence in fury most benign and idiotically fixed upon the Pole Star as stare of drunken Congressman, I feel we must all three be gone. But foist: Have you the Phrase? If you will lay it on me then may I return unto my dozing domicile in tawdry though belated triumph and cease my quest.

Ah Serge, my boy, continued Doc Dubuque, upon whose arm hung daintily in mutest adoration the female charms of Miz Clarke Grable, how glad I am you've brought this up! As is, I'm sure, Miz G, renowned assistant, queen of the buffet lunch, and memo-writer! (At which the hefty broad did blush.) Yes, and more than glad! You know, of course, that I, in my difficult position—but I do not complain!—my difficult position of profound responsibility as chief of paperwork and memoranda, holder of meetings, and giver of small, "working" lunches, must needs employ all the arcane arts and varied tricks that keep the groves of the academy, how shall I say? green! In thus wise, I use with might and main the steel stroke, the Chicago trap, and "shots" known to the happy, happy

175

few as the Jaques, the Brooklyn, and the Bailey. And all to keep the vasty population, and such pilgrims as thou art, happy and contented. It is not an easy job, I must insist.

The guy has flensed hisself unto his marrowbones, la Grable cooed.

Sweet child, Dubuque leered happily, his fingers straying naughtily. I have been a kind of warrior, yes, strong as Major Drummond of the Tillicoultry Guards, wily as the Old Fourteenth at Fianchetto, and aggressive as Flora Temple when she led the rustic Paisley Boys in Philidor's Defense at Waterloo.

But, said Blue.

As is written on small placards in libraries across the land: SILENCE, yawped Miz Grable.

A loudmouthed wop—and aren't they all?—name of Giuco Piano, came here all the way from sunny Alma, to stand as you now stand, the Doctor said, his straw hat in his trembling fist, asking for assistance. What was my answer? Tell him, luscious lass!

The Doctor gave him, 'spite his awesome everpresent tasks, gave the garlic-sodden dago a job helping out our faithful Denny Kelso, who cleans the terlets over there in Nailor Hall! And you stand there *demanding* things?

I only— Blue began.

Innocent naïf! Dubuque said sadly. To stand here in the pure, free sunlight, to stand in wing-tip shoes and plaid orlon suit, to feel upon my skull the soft and oddly shaped coiffure that proclaims me WASP . . . you have no idea what struggles I have waged for the right to listen to your pleas.

Plus also his old lady likes to bust his chops because of our innocent and rigorously professional relationship. She got some dumb idea we play laird and lady in deserted Whilter Hall o' nights. Prudish slut!

Now, now, my demoiselle, Doc smiled. No need to hurl invective like a raging dyke. As the poet Henry wrote in *Double-Corner Dynamo*: "Ere the centre holds in Boston Cross/The fife will shrill in Bristol." Words that ring with proud defiance!

When your voice clangs up like that, higher than the highest branch of diseasèd ginkgo, the cutesy Clarke sighed joyously, I feel like the Ayrshire lassie in Walter Scott's great *Edinburgh Pioneer*.

But I've digressed, Dubuque mused on. I was speaking of my struggles, am I right, dear Blue?

Uh? Blue nodded.

And struggles have as vile concomitants—an host of enemies!

I feel my bosom heaving with the memory of all them little bastards! Grable spat indignantly, straining to hold back her bra the while, which item yearned to hurl itself right through her shoit.

Soft, Clarkie dear, the Doc admonished. Let not poisonous contumely bite you on the tit. As I, good Blue, struggled up the ladder of success, a gang, a shoal of people, mad with envy, tried to kick me down, or anyway to stomp upon my hands. Such formidable adversaries as Ruy Lopez, that grinning spick, Mario Nimzovitch, hale and hearty denizen of men's rooms, Jennifer Switcher, "the Will o' the Wisp," whose famous Glasgow Address, "Humanitarian Roots of Genocide," won for her the Caro-Kann Brotherhood Award, and Albin Zugzwang, who proved that fetuses have invisible moustaches and thus are actually people—all these, and more, fought me every centimeter of the way up to the top! Life has not been, fond trekker, all reddish posies.

My Vince! Courageous sitter on committees! Mlle Grable offered.

I only— toadied Blue.

Furthermore, the sparkling Ph.D. speaked on, and furthermore, has anyone—except my right-hand arm, the indispensable C. Grable here—has *anyone* given me even a gill of credit for the way in which I sped graduates on their way each and every motherfucking June? In broiling sun, in roasting hotness, in paralyzing fountains of humidity, I monologued my way into their hearts: flashing-eyed boys and high-breasted girls, melting in the loathsome heat of early summer! I pulled out all the stops of lofty rhetoric in my sedulous endeavors, till, by J. K. Christ, I sounded like unto a chaplain of the now-deactivated Second Army, "Red Deuce" to those who served beneath its demented officers. I employed the Dundee hyperbaton, Bowen's Twin exergasia, scotchaeresis, the Sicilian picciuriddugoge, petroffasm, colleasmus, Souter's metaphor, morphymoron, and a dozen twain or twice times twelve or a score and four or twenty-four. Maybe even a few edds and onds tacked in!

While I sat upon the dais, tittered Clarke, while curious orgonic things occurred beneath my sturdy gown.

D-Doc? Blue keened in his wild lament.

Lots of problems, boy, lots. And all smashed through as does a gnarled fist whack its way through a sodden piece of cardboard. Oh, I will not deny that there have been rewards: the Benno Wagram Medal for "a senior scholar who wears his cardigan with flair"; the Bruce and Muffie Alekhine Plaque for "the use of the same class notes for twenty years" hand-running; and the Réti Tarrasch-Steinitz Scroll for "an administrator who cleans up his cardboard plate, including cole slaw, at faculty galas." I admit, yes, that there have been compensations for this long career of giving pretty girls their unearned C's.

Fearless figure of fatherly flab! drooled Miz G.

Doc! Blue yelped at last. I only want to hear that fabled Phrase you intimated you might have, buried in a drawer deep beneath an clutch of sex aids.

Ah, my boy, of course. How glad I am you've brought this up. I fear that we, meaning I, we possess no "Phrase," as you so robustly put it. We went along with you, caught up, as we were, in the madding music and the heady wine of Paddy's Day. I know you'll understand, my gadabout.

Understand? quoth Blue. Understand? Nay, if understanding holds its seat in dread of massy planet's scorching flight! I understandeth not!

Then shame upon you, shabby prick, the Doctor beamed. Pack up your family and your crap and scud away like water spider cast adrift upon a sea of Pepsi.

Or like a China-wagon bowled along by hurricane, you ungrateful shit, the svelte CG mocked bitterly.

You mean? stared Blue in vile and caitiff disappointment.

I mean, growled Doc Dubuque, that you will get your ass in gear else I'll set loose the starving Dobermans to fatten on it! Comprendy?

Vile load of syphilitic come, mused Clarke, lofting after the retreating figure of our hero a small stand of nestronia that she had lingered under oft.

<< 38 >>

"La Musique
et les mauvaises
herbes," Continued

IX THE VISIT

Friday last André is making a visit to his family. As he has a brother and a sister and varied comrades, he has much of things to recount to Émile when he has returned to the University Sunday night.

ÉMILE: You have the air of repose, my old parsnip. Did you make a good voyage? Did you have the "ashes" hauled away over the wick-end?

ANDRÉ: But yes. I am depart from here on the train of four hours twenty-five. I am arrive at the house of my parents at nine hours Friday night. At ten hours fifteen I am with Catherine, the maid, making the animal of two spines. She has some couple of biscuits!

ÉMILE: Suzanne might well be in choler with you should she discover this. Is it not so?

ANDRÉ: You may bet a boot on this! But what Suzanne shall not be knowing will not be of any ill effect to her. Do you agree, my old man?

ÉMILE: I do agree. And how are your family? Is the father still as all the time rooting amid the turnips?

ANDRÉ: But yes. And now he passes some time of an evening swinging on the birch trees of the forest.

ÉMILE: Ha! Ha! What a foolish old fuck-head your father appears to be!

ANDRÉ: In effect! It is what arrives of perusing on the Yankee verses. What garbage they are!

ÉMILE: And the rest of the family?

ANDRÉ: All the world goes well, thank you. They are all coming to search for me at the station. My little brother made the honor to carry my valise until the auto. Then he dropped it down on his club foot. My idiot sister Anne recounted to me all the news of the neighborhood.

ÉMILE: That there may have been some things of much interest in the place? Things of dirt and lowly gossip?

ANDRÉ: One thing of great amusement solely. It is that Mlle Lorpailleur, the schoolteacher, fell into love with her bicycle. Is it not wealthy?

ÉMILE: Very tasty! What a perverted lady she has to be!

ANDRÉ: In effect. It is whispered that she sleeps even atop the vehicle.

ÉMILE: Do you have other nice little tidbits of Catherine?

ANDRÉ: Mama prepared all the plates that I love: the hogface in cream, the broccoli with apple juice, the whipped-cream-and-onion-filled éclairs, the goose in Jell-O. And Saturday night, when I am returning with a little sack on, Catherine is even mounting up to my chamber for to carry up a cold goose flesh and a jug of whiskey. I made her to drink herself crazy and soon we made a number of fascinating tableaux in the looking-glass.

ÉMILE: You old debased weasel! You had then therefore gone out Saturday night?

ANDRÉ: Yes. I am going out to say good evening to some comrades what are left. The most of my ancient comrades are at the local colleges of applied agricultural arts. Some others are in wild flight on the morals charges. Yet others make their military service, many of whom which have make the bad in the blood from the Old Joe.

ÉMILE: It is as in our village. When one has said how does it go to the family, drunk oneself to craziness, and banged a chicken or two, there is nothing more to make.

ANDRÉ: You exaggerate a piece. But I admit that I am content to be returned. Suzanne may have had a blue while I was on my voyage.

ÉMILE: Do not have a worry there. I made a small and intimate fest for Suzanne and me Saturday night. We had a good enjoyment! Wow.

ANDRÉ: What? You rotting mouse!

André and Émile commence to exchange blows of a great sharpness and strength upon each the other's noses, lips, and teeth. Just then, Suzanne enters into the chamber and lounges about on the sofa in an indecent manner, so that the two old comrades forget the difference they have and stand still while the eyes of them almost tumble out. It seems as if Suzanne has forgotten to wear her dress.

X XMAS GIFTS

Alice Cuisse, though homely as a horse radish, is a serious young lady, who never waits on the last minute for to buy her Xmas gifts. Yesterday, she is going into town, and, having prepared her list in advance, she has made her purchases in one hour flats. What a whiz. On returning, she has called Suzanne for to show her the purchases.

ALICE: Come to see the pretty items that I have come to buy. It will knock you off your pin!

SUZANNE: I wish to well, my swell old doghead. I have need of distraction. That foul odor, André, has chanced to reveal that at the house of his parents he made much delight on the maid's private pieces.

ALICE: I knew always that he is a grand stool. But did not you with Émile make the warm sex all Saturday night?

SUZANNE: But yes—but what manner of thing else may a young lady do who has the mammoth blue? But a piss on top of it! Show me the gifts, if you please, my old stick.

ALICE: Well then, oke. Regard the vibrator who I have chosen for Sophie. I like much that he has the form and color of a carrot, but I hope that he is not too much petite.

SUZANNE: Oh no! He is well enough grand and also very jolly. Ha! Ha!

ALICE: Why do you chuckle in such hearty manners?

SUZANNE: It occurs that he looks like the organ of Mr. Aine, but for the color of orange he can possess.

ALICE: Mr. Aine! How is it that you know of his manly piece?

SUZANNE: Oh well. We made some dirty things one time on the broccoli garden. It was but a quick bong, on feet against the old cypress tree down there.

ALICE: O-ho. It is clear presently now why it has been that you received the A in Kazoo Studies, you wicked . . . bun, do you say?

SUZANNE: It is of no importance. What is it that you might have bought for Monique Gaine, that bowl of depravity?

ALICE: A pretty couple of white lace garters for the attractive thighs of her. I have a small hot for her, do you know.

SUZANNE: I had the thought that you are of the Sappo-type of women. Is this for because no man or boy desires much to hump on you?

ALICE: I have the greatest of disgust for men or boys! All they desire for to be doing always is to shoot off their filthy hoses in all times! Foh! How do you like those garters?

SUZANNE: They are very jolly. And then, you have reason of to select of the white. They make hot excitement with black sheer hose.

ALICE: Is it that you might want . . . ?

SUZANNE: You are as red as some beets, my close-knit pussy. What is it?

ALICE: . . . might want to try them on? You own the very jolly brace of thighs also, Suzanne. Monique has them scarcely more jolly than you.

SUZANNE: Yes, I want to well.

(*Suzanne adjusts the accessories upon the legs.*)

There! How do they appear on my gams? Extremely fatal, I think.

ALICE: It goes very, very nice. Now, if you neglect to lower the skirt I will be racked around with an ardent attack and lose the control on myself!

SUZANNE (*lowering her skirt*): Very well. It makes bad, I think, for ancient pals to be making dirty acts together. And I am not a Sappic, you know it good.

ALICE: In effect. I know almost too good how much you adore those hoses of men and boys. Well, Monique perhaps will permit a suggestive liberty of her flesh.

SUZANNE: She is such of a little twat that I would not have a surprise, my girl friend!

ALICE: I am in large hope. Now, regard the some thing that I have buy for Jacques Derrière. A packet of the rubber sacks! Is it not a fine jest?

SUZANNE: You can bet the buttocks on that! Ha! Ha! Ha! This is a sort of somewhat piquant remark on the hygiene of those girl bums of the School of Fertilizer Arts. Each ones of them have the claps, the dirt clumps!

ALICE: I have the thought to make the fine jest, yet they also have the air of the quite practical, is it not so?

SUZANNE: It is of a great pity that you did not think on a gift for the latest blaze of Jacques, that hobo of the long legs and large crocks.

ALICE: Ah, but I did make the thought on this. Regard!

SUZANNE: It has the appearance of . . . oh, ha! ha! How vicious you can be, you serious plugger!

ALICE: Yes—a huge cork! What a sharpened remark, eh? Maybe this will serve to blockade the long hose of Jacques!

SUZANNE: Anyhow, such gifts will act to let them to know that all the world is aware of the base acts they roll in, the foul items!

Alice commences to pack up the gifts while at the identical moments making the glances toward Suzanne, what is disrobing the garters of her thighs. How Alice is wishing that Suzanne is loathing men also. Well, that is those breaks. We cannot all be twisted persons.

XI A QUESTION OF TIME

André hurries himself from the morning until evening without making the half of the things that he feels inclined to make. Is it that swell young ladies is always on his brains? Perhaps so. Yesterday evening he has discussed his problem with his old pal, Suzanne.

ANDRÉ: This morning I am promising myself of making a whole series of things, and poofs! It is nearly the hour of couching myself and it resembles to me that I have made nothing.

SUZANNE: Me, I have the same problem. Mr. Aine has said to me that it is all simply a question of organization. Recount to me your day and then we will essay to see if we can find a solution. I have the sick and also the tired that you are too pooped up in the night to make with me a quick boff, you lazy weasel!

ANDRÉ: Eh, good. I regret having the exhaust each night, my cute skunk. To-day, for an instance, I am raising myself up at seven hours this morning. I am washing the hands and the visage after I make the pee-pee. Then I am dress my-self. I have take a cup of coffee and dwell in my brains upon Monique Gaine, which displayed her new garters when crazy drunk in the Xmas fest of last week. My gosh! I think, and suddenly I discover that I am engaged in a piece of abuse of myself. Then I am arrive at the University at eight hours twelve.

SUZANNE: The unclean practice you make without doubts consumes up ten minutes. O.K. Did you pass the morning at class?

ANDRÉ: But yes. I pass the morning in the History of Accordion class and after the Class of Bassoon of Mrs. Chaud. By a by, Mrs. Chaud loves for to perch up on the desk in order that one might peep up into her skirt. Holy cows!

SUZANNE: And then? I venture out on the guess that you made a brief chat with Mrs. Chaud after the class, eh, you sneaky lewd?

ANDRÉ: I confess to this. Her scent makes me a wild creature!

SUZANNE: Where did you have lunch?

ANDRÉ: In the cafeteria of the University faculties, ah, in the company of Mrs. Chaud. We have ate up the lunch of prune ragout and bologna en croute in twenty minutes. Pretty spiddy, eh?

SUZANNE: I admit this. So? And what then ensued?

ANDRÉ: Afterward, Mrs. Chaud and I are reposing ourselfs during a half of an hour in the lounge of the faculties.

SUZANNE: Reposing yourselfs? You are handing to me a grand laugh!

ANDRÉ: Eh, good. In truth, Mrs. Chaud and I made a small amount of intimate acts. I perhaps suppose that we made a fritter of forty minutes.

SUZANNE: Until the present now you can regard that you have lost many min-utes, all of that because of the ravage of ardent thoughts and acts. You are a strolling "dick," truly, my old man.

ANDRÉ: This is a somewhat rude judgment, my little tramp.

SUZANNE: Oh, shut up the trap on you! Where have you passed the afternoon?

ANDRÉ: In the laboratory of botany.

SUZANNE: You are filled with shits!

ANDRÉ: O.K. I have passed one hour there, but I have not can find the solution of the problem that they gave to us on the snap dragon.

SUZANNE: And?

ANDRÉ: And so, I make the cut and take on a cinema around which Jacques Derrière informed me. An extremely poignant study of American customs.

SUZANNE: You soiled bug! I am of the precise knowledge that you saw a vile cinema called "Hellions in Hosiery."

ANDRÉ: Oh well. You have clutched me again!

SUZANNE: Did you look on this mucky cinema and make an abuse of yourself beneath the waterproof?

ANDRÉ: Only two times, my yam. And this because one of the starettes what was making an oral act resembled you, and so I lost the control on myself.

SUZANNE: Don't make a grovel to me, you hot goat! On my count, today solely you have shooted off your thing four times! It is no mystery now why you make nothing all the day or why you are too pooped up in the night to make me a quick boff. What a decay you are!

(*Suzanne begins to throw some items and her chamber robe falls open.*)

ANDRÉ: If you permit your chamber robe to descend to the rugs, my thrill, I will make on you a number of boffs to make the eyes cross!

Suzanne permits her chamber robe to descend to the rugs so as to display herself in the nudity but for her mules. André commences to make with her an enthusiastic boff. But on his brains is the image of the enthralling legs of Monique Gaine. He is truly a sexy fiend!

XII A SOAP STORY

When Suzanne is returning from her dynamic rendezvous with André yesterday evening, Alice is waiting. What the else? She has been regarding a soap story on the "tubes," and she wishes to recount it to Suzanne. Suzanne has sleepy and wishes to couch herself and have a tropical dream on André, but she has to listen to the recital of Alice. What putrid! It is a duty of a young lady to listen when her pal of the chamber has a wish to speak. That is how a ball springs, no?

ALICE: She was truly beautiful, this story. The action unfolds herself in a village of France in the seventeenth century.

SUZANNE (*suffocating the yawn*): How does she call itself, your story?

ALICE: She calls itself "The Root of Love." The heroine was a lovely young blonde who awaits for many years the return of her fiancé. I tell you, switty, she is some piece of the stuff. Va-va-voo!

SUZANNE: And where was he, this handsome rogue? Couching himself with some other gash?

ALICE: Oh no! In Canada or the Wyoming or else place, where he makes the war against the English people or the redfaces or some things. And he is not too handsome, but an usual manly excrement.

SUZANNE: That you have a queerness in sex things makes you a bad critic, my old repulsive sis.

ALICE: Perhaps so. Anyway, this blonde chicken is walking about the orchard of peaches wringing out the hands, and all, how do you call? phlegms and tears?

SUZANNE: I have an ignorance of the argot. Any hows, he is never returning?

ALICE: Oh, but yes! But he has lost a considerable shard of his manly root in the battle, and he no longer wished much to marry himself with the cutie.

SUZANNE: And why not? Is it that the mange loved her no more?

ALICE: But yes . . . more than ever he has! But he had a fear from the doctor that he can no longer haul up her ashes. He tells to her on a scene to crack down the heart: "I am presently solely half of a guy." And the sweet visage of the blonde baby takes on a blush of a rose, for that she had a cloudy thought on what he was referring of. She is as naive as a driving snowstorm, you see.

SUZANNE: What is it that is arriving then?

ALICE: Well, my darling pearbush, the young bit is falling gravely into a bad malady because she has such a hot for this fragment of damaged goods.

SUZANNE: And the soldier is making a powder? Or is it maybe that he goes away "half-cocked"? Ha! Ha!

ALICE (*making the scowl*): Why must you always make the gag? No! He paces down and up in the drawing-room at the estate of his father, with the face on him all drawed up and grey and once on a while he peers upon his crotch area and bites upon his lip.

SUZANNE: Is it then that the chicken is dead from this malady?

ALICE: Why no! What a silly slut you may be at some times! When the soldier has seen that she has truly a need on him, he marries himself with her. He says: "My hot breath of life herself, there are many routes to love." And she permits her eyes to descend for she has the ideas that he is talking around some kinky stuffs. Oh boy!

SUZANNE: You must have at that moment almost lost the control on yourself, no?

ALICE: You could bet your face on this, birdy! I had a hot bolt.

SUZANNE: And the young lady without doubts retrieves her health when she has seen that her fiancé loves her always.

ALICE: It is so, and they are to live happy the rest of their days together on the large estate of his father, a grizzly type of chap.

SUZANNE: It is a regret that his root does not grow to its standard measurement. Then the blonde twerp would *really* live in a happy life.

ALICE: That is an opinion of yours, Suzanne. As for myself, I can neglect for all times the masculine equipments! And if I was to have been making the household with that knocked-out blonde, she would never once think on the tool of a man, big or small, I can make a swear to that.

SUZANNE: I can believe on that, motor mouth.

Alice and Suzanne prepare themself for sleeping. Alice is wrapped into a reverie of the blonde dolly, and Suzanne into one of André and his recent pleasure on her. And so to couch.

<< 39 >>

The Couple
Somewhat Cheered

Croak on, exhausted Muse! Of the weary fambly and its ugly equipage, sorta sauntering and meandering from out the lush land of Illini and the mighty virgin forests ripe with the litotes tree and the endless madd'ning buzz of the industrious swarms of B-B-eyed tempura, O croak!

Yawp wildly, like the bearded bard of bygone Brooklyn o'er what would be rooftops were here there domiciles to carry them! Holler in limping choliambics of the creaking cart and the pianner now much the worse for wear! Lithp in awe ofth the land that braver men than I have called—Mithouri!

And so, they at last rested in a patch of merciful shade about as big around as the sunny center of the Cola daisy. And Blue, after weighty pause, began:

The natural shocks my fletch is heir to wast increased tenfold by the sneaky con that V. Dubuque employed upon me. He never had the Phrase I sought for and simply used me to blather Irish jive unto assorted bumpkins. And all this followed by the windy shit of a doddering priest! And now we find ourselves still wand'ring like a buncha clouds that hover o'er the tupelos! Like, where in bleeding Jesu's name are we? Belike it seems a land of mud and caverns. That's bad enough, but whither? Oh perfidious scholar!

It was a rude surprise, Helene agreed hysterically. The more so since he seemed so nice with his bulky cardigan and sincere and friendly feet. Oh, I have not felt so abandoned and rejected since that horrid day in high school when they clipped my lock.

Yet, sweets, our Zimmerman sleeps peacefully, his trusting soul given o'er into our hands as 'twere a baseball gathered in by what is called, for reasons dark, a sure glove. What means "sure glove" I cannot tell, unless it be what old Diogenes Laertius dubbed metonymy; or was it that this said metonymy gathered in a "can of corn"? No matter, so long as he snoozes on.

You've lost me, bulging carlo, the wife breathed quietly, but just to hear you once again spout forth your dizzy horseshit perks my spirits up like seltzer. We'll fare forth, no matter where we are, or where go we instead!

Strong girl! There is, indeed, behind each man of greatness, or of great dreams, like unto Don LaMancha, a reticent woman, who stands close-ready with his coat or jacket, ready to slip it on his aching shoulders when he gets the rock-jawed Call!

I do but do my duty, husband, Helene glaumed happily.

Then, since we don't have a fiddler's-fuck idea of where we are, except that we must go yet further onward, let's rest a smidgen here in purple shadow, while I rummage in our gear and read aloud a while so that we may begull the time that hangs as heavy as an old pirogi. What book shall I— Hello! a little album-like affair to which is fixed a letter! Do you recognize this item, poopsies?

I'm darned if I know what dick-all it is, she smiled.

The letter "says":

Dear Mr. and Mrs. Gavotte:

We are bitterly disappointed by the crude and cavalier treatment accorded you by Dr. Vincent Dubuque, the Administrative Dean of our beloved University. We discovered, too late, that he was giving you what the vulgar term the "brush-off," and had no intention of giving you the Phrase you are so nobly seeking, and no wonder; for he has *no knowledge* of such a Phrase! (There are some wags who maintain that he has no knowledge whatsoever, but since he has a Ph.D., he probably knows something, at least how to get on a bus.)

We hasten to dissociate ourselves from this blot on our escutcheon, this fly in our milk, this beam in our eye, and to wish you the very best of luck. Attached please find a small token of our warm feelings for you, a hand-crafted "album" of heartfelt messages to both of you.

Affectionately,

"The Gang"

The hot tears are crowding to my eyes like ants hustling over to a ort of abandoned cake, or pie, Blue stammered.

I too feel a rush of deep emotion. But read the messages, my love. The world has some kind people left, though they be disguised as slothful academics.

I'll read them then, asputter all with joy!

MY ALBUM'S OPEN, COME AND SEE. WHAT? WON'T YOU HAVE A LIME WITH ME?: K.Y. Geli.

WITH THE BIGGEST WISHES FORE LUCK AND PROSPERETTY TO THE FINAL BUZZER.: Milhous Hoover.

BEST VISHES! HA-HA.: Sepp Schutz-Staffel.

SIN-SEERLY YOARS.: Nathan Famoso.

SCREW MANY, LOVE FEW, DON'T GO DOWN, IN A CANOE.: George Stardust.

NEVER B♯. NEVER B♭. ALWAYS B♮.: Manuel Joie.

MY PEN IS POOR, MY INK IS PISSY, BUT MY CARE FOR YOU, SHALL NEVER MISSY.: Juan Simón.

4-GET-ME-KNOT.: Sol Mallow.

FORGIVE THIS BLOT, FORGET ME NOT, I CANNOT HELP, THAT I'M A TWOT.: Lillie Bullero.

IN THE DAISY CHAIN OF FRIENDSHIP, BE NOT FAR AWAY!: Jem Spaa.

AIM HIGH! SWING LOW!: Medusa Queynte.

DO THE REST IN SPARE TIME; EVERYONE EXPECTS MORE.: Lewis Fielding.

WHEN ON THIS PAGE YOU CHANCE TO GLANCE, JUST THINK OF ME AND DROP YOUR PANTS.: H. Poloie.

I WRITE THIS NOT FOR GLORY, I WRITE THIS NOT FOR LOOTS, I WRITE THIS TO BE REMEMBERED, YOU WONDERFUL GALOOTS.: Aaron Alwitz.

LOTS OF LUCK! YOU OL' FUCK!: Michael Schiller.

GET ON THE LOCAL, CHANGE TO THE EXPRESS, MAY YOUR FOR-TUNES RISE, LIKE A WHORE'S DRESS.: Olive d'Oyly.

I WISH YOU A SUCESFUL SUCESSION OF SUCCESFUL SUCESESS.: Laszlo Syntax.

ON THIS LEAF, IN MEM'RY PREST, MAY MY NAME SWELL LIKE A BREAST.: Aubrey Hawtree Creek.

ROSES ARE RED, VIOLETS ARE BLUE, REMEMBER ME, WHENEVER YOU SCREW.: Olga Warner.

LAST IN YOUR ALBUM, LAST OF THE LOT, FIRST TO BE REMEM-BERED, LAST TO BE REMEMBERED.: Robert Fischholder.

That is the summed-up total of the lot, Serge said, placing the little booklet on the grass with such care as would snatch a sob from the chicken-neck of Heinrich Himmler, now deceased.

With folks like this, Helene spoke up, can Spring long cop a z while snow and sleet thrash down upon the groaning oith?

Though we know not what we may do, let us do it fetchingly, and by God, we'll aimless plunge ahead, wherever that may be!

My darling Blue! I hear a growling, like, that seems to come from the tiny lion lodging in your swollen heart! *Let* us aimless plunge!

But soft, the sun, that staggers in his wonted drunkenness across the depthless sky, has fallen to his scabby knees, and crawls toward his sequestered crib. Let us hurl ourselves like so much jetsam into this cavern here, that yawns as wide as doth a poor unfortunate compelled to lend an ear to Aaron Copland.

I follow, hurling, your own body, hurled, and hurl with me the chee-ild!

Then they penetrated the Cimmerian cave, its darkness like the glop oft-squirted on John Wayne by rubber octopi, or whatever it is called. Hardly had they settled down around the friendly blaze when a sound so harrowing came from out the shadows that, as is their wont in fiction, danced around the fire, so that sort of like chilly temblors jogged up and down two spines, yea, jogged, and sprinted now and then.

Forsooth, it was a spectre, all in clothes that smacked of times gone by, a ghost dolled up as one might term, a "cowboy."

Who, said Serge, be you, strange person, whose head I seem to be looking through so that the cave wall that is behind you seems to be your brain? Huh?

I am J. James's spirit, doomed for a certain term to stroll about, and, for the rest, constrained to sit around till the gross flesh that hangs upon my ass-bones is whittled clean away. But that you are a jerk I'd tell the secrets of this slimming trick, so that you'd thrust your yogurt and your kelp far up your fundament, therein to sleep. And your two eyes would pop out of their holes, your sweetie's hairs would sprout like crabgrass vile, and her two tiny knockers would implode like potholes swift-appearing in the street. But these Missouri secrets must not reach two idiots like you. Hist! Hist! Hey, hist! If you would go on with your endless quest, the way lies westward—toward the Land of Stars! Yes, Stars! And money! And decaying brains! A land where dumbness reigns as Emperor. Though thicker are you than a hmalted hmilk, I think you'll figger out the spot I mean. But, whoa! It's time for me to haul my ass and fling it in my magic easy-chair. So long! And take it easy! And—I'm gone!

Then, with the celerity of the turquoise-tufted blackhaw when it swoops out of the mist to rend and tear the tender flesh of baby armadillos, the spectre vanished. In the boring gloom of the cave, two mouths open in astonishment could be descried. Did I say . . . *two* mouths? Aye! And will stand with pike and bludgeon to defend my bold assertion, or great Achilles did not pass his beardless youth in drag!

This ghostly tip-off, coupled with the merry greetings of our unknown amici at The U, Blue said in measured tones, showers a somewhat sanguine attitude upon my thumping chest. The Land of Stars! In what direction westward this may be, I do not now surmise, yet it is clear as the mind of a senior Scientologist that it ain't not here! And so, we'll push on as did Roy Rogers and his unlikely partner, Ramsey Clark, when they set out to find The Great Divide!

My cherished love, Helene mouthed languidly, I too feel rumblings deep within, and each is edged with silv'ry hope. I know that we shall persevere at last.

They slept, they woke, they bashed ahead through old Mizzoo, noting as they went its plethora of caves, that, unfortunately, all look alike in the dark.

A strange note, though, I fear, has sounded here in this ringing saga of the Serge Gavottes. It is that in the cave, they left behind, we know not why, little Zimmerman. The "chronicler" of this "adventure" is reported to have said that the kid was "not pulling his own weight" as a character, and so he thought it best to "dump him." When it was pointed out to him that such rifts and tears in the motivational fabric of the careful plot were detrimental to the development of credibility in the well-made narrative, he laughed, and then, more serious, said: "Maybe I'll bring him back in a little later."

So little Zim slept on, all unawares that he had been abandoned like the swollen-footed motherfucker of antiquity.

« 40 »

Wonderland of
Opportunity, Where
the Apple Mocks and Blossoms

And suddenly, since Time is but a quibble in the Great World of the Novel, it (Time) passed, and with it, flying right alongside, cheek by jowl, hanging on, so to speak, as it were, to employ the great Dubuque's phrase as I enter the book, as is my privilege, hanging on, I say, to the wingèd chariot in which he (it) sits, Space as well passed. And our couple found themselves far beyond the borders of languorous Mizzoo, after which a battleship was once, for some inane reason named, and then shortened, to wit: "Big Mo," and whatever that may evince in the way of salty goblike attitudes, none dare whisper.

With what celery we have come into this land that Time will one day forget, Helene marveled from atop the gallant cart. One moment we were in that grisly cavern, replete with phantoms and odd pebbeles, and the next, here we press on in Apple-Blossom time.

Pebbeles? Blue laughed.

A mere typo that the author permitted to stand for a cheap laugh, its quaint orthography suggesting to him a Yiddish word for "rocks," so shot Helene.

Oh, replied Blue, looking about wildly. Then, calm at last, he continued: It is in the nature of fiction that its creators do whatever they wish, busting to tatters eternal verities and such things as the "unities," a word I seem to recall as having something to do with a true act in a brief time in a small spot or sumpn. But we have passed through the great state of Mizzoo in a sudden flash, the time it takes to turn a page.

I wondered why the so-called scenery zipped by so fast. It was something that made me very very noivous.

I suspect that the "text" is being "deconstructed" beneath our very feets! Blue muttered. And here, he raised his voice, here I thought that we were in a Novel of Ideas, one invested with a Desperate and Aching Significance and a Sadness filled with Smiles.

A . . . novel? Helene said, her tiny hand shooting rapidly to her breast.

Yes, my ruby flyhatch, Blue said. Figures in that great mirror held up to the side of the road by some crazy person running along down same. The fact that we are—poof!—in this new environ is a fact with a purpose, since all things must have a purpose in a fictions.

A . . . fictions? Helene said, her other hand furtively joining its companion.

We are but the creatures of a great master god, as are all men and women, shall I say, human persons? Yes, a god who sits aloofly in the sky remote and arrogant, sailing his pears to the clouds, allowing us to strut on this poor stage to the last syllable of something or other.

Oh! I thought for a moment that you meant that we were not . . . real!

Sweet swell nit! Blue smiled tenderly. Not real! I spoke in figures and conceited metaphors, making plain to you that we are in the same boats as are all persons, blown hither and thither by decaying winds, at the mercy of the deathless ones who amuse themselves with our scrabbling; in this, we are but folk in stories, and if we don't know what happened to Missouri, well, who does? What happened to the snow that fell on lovely Rome yesterday? Being alive is like being in a novel, which is why it don't make no sense, writhe as we may in the glades and copses of eternal spring.

At this, Helene felt better, but great Jesu knows why. For a brief sec, she thought that she was *not* real, was not a flesh-and-blood character, but a glob of *écriture*, although she did not know this word. Few do.

Let us pay to all this crap no, or little heed, Blue comforted, and keep plugging on.

So pluggged they on, past vast stands of apple blossoms and the huge herds of razorbacks that lowed their mighty ignorance to the distant azure. Birds cheepied, the pines stood pale and gaunt, and beyond the mountains a mighty thunderhead dropped snowy blizzards on the twinkling lights of cozy hamlets, all of which, had an invisible observer been able to see them, would have reminded him of home, as they dug out cheerily from the choking drifts in which were buried their cars and, more seriously, their stern fireplugs! Past fields of mud, past the laughing corn-faced girls whose eyes sparkled almost in a plethora of small-town goodness, past the belching stacks of somber factories turning out, who knows? luggage maybe. And more razorbacks, trampling the cotton and the pawpaw shrubs, pushing, straining, wild-eyed in their mad flight to better grazing fields, many of them ending up dazed in lamplit parlors, where Gramps sat nodding over the evening paper. It was a slice of America, this great land that has dreamed its great dream of democracy for ages and ages, or, in any event, for seventy-two years longer than CCNY. Yes! Or no! Never! Never did Blue feel

more proud than that moment when the rains came, yet again! Those drench-
ing, health-giving rains that turned the highway down which they slowly moved
into a cataract, and on which, had an observer been looking at them from far
above, they would have appeared to be very tiny people—such is the wonder of
distance! Past the avid greasemonkeys and depraved soda jerks, the crippled
bellhops and stout redcaps, the corseted schoolmarms and grimy conductors, the
gardeners, shenangos, plumbers; past the ornamental-sheet-metal workers' ap-
prentices, the junior assistant scoutmasters, the district supervisors in charge of
sales and service, the bakers, and butchers, and always, always, the shouldering
razorbacks, trampling the red dust into great red clouds of choking red dust!
How many salesmen far from home, far from the little houses in which they
loved nothing better than to have a friendly beer or two, how many, in imper-
sonal hotel rooms, hands but lately freed from the Bibles tucked thoughtfully
away in dresser drawers by people from the Gideon Company, Inc., how many
in lonely lamplight, far into the stranger night, wiped the caked dust from their
tasseled, plastic loafers? How many hung their plaid suits in the steamy bathroom, how many in their desperation got zonked at the hotel bar, the sound of
the evening wind soughing in the bare birches that grew right up to the edge of
the parking lot for guests and visitors? Past it all they inched, until Nature called,
and they came huffing to a friendly service station, Smiley's Service, No Free Air,
and his inviting Rest Room.

Into which they repaired to heed that call which even Great Augustus needs
must have heeded, and the Emperor Napoleon, if they did not wish to make pee-
pee in their toga and culottes, respectively that is.

(If he did not wish to make peepee in their . . . ?)

(If they did not wish to make peepee in his . . . ?)

(If either of them did not wish to make peepee in either of their . . . ?)

(If they did not wish to make peepee, the former in his toga, the latter in his
culottes.)

« 41 »

The Graffiti
Set Up a Wild Twangling

If you like it dogwood-style, call "Wild Hydrangea" at GReenbrier 7–0001; I love to suck big fat elderberries; Up your albizzia!; For a hot cherry— try Rose of Sharon; Stop playing with your dutchman's-pipe; Fuck Virginia Creeper; Why are you looking up here, oilnuts?; My firethorn is all yours, yours!; Birch me! Beat me with a hickory stick! Roll me in nettles!; My love is like a red, red rose that to the sun doth reach, I like to kiss her on her nose before I kiss her peach; Boston Ivy eats it; If you like a good thyme, call Zenobia: REdbud 6–3666; Daphne Hawthorn is a common privet; Confucius say: Old pimp is called box elder; Get your ashes hauled at the Tree of Heaven Motel; I like to jack my pine; Some come here to sit and gape, But I come here to peel my grape; Tits Willow does it down by the river; I like it up the old wisteria; False Jessamine gave me the horns; Rosemary Bog fucks like a hog; If it looks like a plum and is dripping with cum it's the hercules-club of your dreams; Matrimony vine makes vomen vild; The Rev. Basswood St. Peterswort wears Queen Anne's lace undies; In every pair of hot pants you'll find a burning bush; Heather Holly has a downy hudsonia; Sister Bumelia likes to suck the big ones; Those who write on toilet stalls bang their chestnuts on the walls; Socrates sucks Eastern hemlock; Pepper Vine is a hot hooer; Violet Gentian has an indigo bush; Play with my silkvine, comfort my black walnuts, for I am hot to trot; Asiatic Hydrangea's is horizontal; I want to stay out all night and come home with a trailing arbutus; Hazel the witch, the dirty bitch, gave me a dose of spirea; Here lives the crab that ate Little Rock; Red Ash, the S & M kid; Hal Glubit fucks Laurel Sheep; Robert Frost tossed off in the yellowwood; Stand closer! The next guy may have holes in his yews; Raggedy Ann has a buttonbush; I know a girl who in her spare thyme blows; The stiff ones are the kind I like: Sweet Buckeye Bruce from Pike; Magnolia Cash gives palm jobs; Mawmaw gives! Pawpaw; Draw the bit o' nightshade before you take a bath with a whore; Question: What do you call sperm in a lab? Answer: Cupseed; Honey Locust gave me acacia clap; Honey, suckle!; He married the lush with the strawberry bush; I like to goose berry much: Juan Pendejo; "Purple" Clemat is a pippin Tom; If leather would please you, call AZalea 3–1119, oak?; Single White Pine desires meet Dwarf Juniper on the heavy side. Object, bitter sweats; Tryon "Try" Foley, the pervert of Southern California, ate Orange County; Fuck oxeye Hera! Zeus; Current black digs white ash; Dear Lolly Pine: I love a large lob; Amelopsis without topsis panties were for Hazel Nut; Confucius say: Man who kiss prickly ash wake up with sour gums; Full-blooded Indian seeks spruce, elder white lady for marshmallow delights and moccasin; Rosebay Redbay Ucksfay; I love my sweet Alyssum much, because she is a whore; There was a young man from Persimmon, Who mistakenly thought men were women, In bed with a guy, With his cock risen high, He wondered just how to get in him; June Berry let Buck lay her; Coach "Bear" Berry buggers just for a larch; What are you doing with that mistletoe in your fly?; If you don't like my quaking aspen, baby, why are you squeezing my knee?; She married a man who had no balsam all; Don't screw on the beach unless you like dryas; Fuck Red Pine! H. Thoreau; De spirit gwine climb in you onymus; Lila C is a wild hump, dig it; A Dublin Protestant is a mock-orange; May the palm of Gilead fondle your chestnuts, ol' hoss; Senna's bladder wept here; Quoth Othello, "Suck a moor"; Counselor Siebold lost her briefs in the cottonwood swamp; Sade: Viburnum? by May Poule; I desire your sweet spire; Helen Hornbeam goes down on Fanny Fraser's fur; Would Alice Arrow suck Sy Sumac? Alice Arrow would; Andrachne has some pear!; Andrew St. Cross frigged the Flower twins in the raspberry patch; Cedar White kicks black ash; Macbeth sucks! Alder, Grass, and Hazel, Witches; Put that spindletree back in your pants!; They were only the farmer's daughters, but oh what apple-knockers; Barberry, Crossvine, Buckthorn, and Gorse: Bum-Bailiffs; Don't comb your teeth over the sink, sweet gums; Warm coffee-colored gent wants mutually thrilling afternoons with refined New Jersey lady in teagown; The girl stood in the bedroom door, her forestiera bare; Adam delved when Eve took her sweet leaf off; Chief Wintergreen eats it with a rusty spoon; Mme Dewberry was a lay, je dis; Smooth Allspice—the new shade coming hardon the heels of summer; If you like it the Greek Way, ring OSage 1–5657; Wayfaring stranger needs a hot pussy; Plant a diaphragm and grow your own corktree; Nora Wilde-Raisin is a dried-up old cunt; Stick it in a thimble, choke-up!; The Partridge Family needs a broom in their ass.

This is amazing "stuff," my blushing marmaduke, Blue said. It sort of makes me young again, filling my veins and other tube-like apparatus in my body with a reddish ichor that the medical profession dubbed—how many years ago!—blood.

To me it seems like dirty stuff and nothing but or eke a zillion daubs of bawd and vile obscenity, the belle replied in kind, her voice muffled from within the stall to which she had repaired in haste.

I know what you are saying, dearest doxy, yet I find my mind flying far, far beyond the grossness of the messages that slobber on these walls to the wild, how shall I say? *twangling* that the language sets up in this encoffined space. It has a kind of beat, a kind of rhythm, a secret time that owns but nowt except unto its own emblazoned right as doth the tawdry billet-pouch fix his great staring eye upon the dreaming perch among the weeds!

It seems but filth to me, Helene said, emerging much refreshed, as they say, much to one's chagrin.

Aye! Filth, yes, so it may be, I'm hip, said Blue, now sealed within the stall while honest H made vague stabs at her toilet 'fore the crusted looking-glass. Aye! Yet there is in it, as I have said, something so deeply musickal, so drenched in violent sublimity, that my soul in stunned amaze finds itself flying ass upon its heels through the infinite spaces of pure joy. It has its own weird time, and time, Great Time, is the nub and corazón of that gay art to which I pledge my life, my honor, and my lust for fame. As well you know, or should, since we are more than halfway through this questlike saga. I am but, when all is said and done, to Time but the caitiff slave and pleasant rouge.

I think betimes, my fierce-eyed lord, the word is "rogue."

Then "rogue" it be, and rogue and rogue again! By dazzling Jove, 'twere rogue all day and thrice o' Sundays when the heavens drop their sultry peace!

Merci, she wimped.

The hours passed, the sun went down, our pair traveled onward through the mudhens and the nodding aromatic vetch, and in the dark they stopped to pitch a camp, while Blue, silent now for minutes strung apace, mused on and on, then spoke.

When I spoke earlier of Time, my little chunk, I fear that I was somewhat murky. May I explain more clearly what I mean by it? Or does the Sandman, whom the Greeks dubbed Morphodite, claw fervently at your eyes? Or lids?

I am not ready yet for slumber, tweet. Expondiate.

Let's stretch out under the piano, far from the dew, then, and I'll lay this on you.

In the shadows Helene's smile flickered, flashed, and . . . disappeared. A loon croaked in the swamp, then all was still.

« 42 »

Blue's
Reflections on Time

Helene, sweet twitter, as we sit here beneath the great blinking comforter of the heavens, almost ready to embrace or be embraced by sleep in our colorful but not quite waterproof pushcart—I still dislike that term—our old piano sheltering us from the moonbeams that drive men mad, I think, though every fiber of my being cries out against such an act, of Time—great sacrosanct and bulging Time, that again, at this turn of the year, comes around once again; yes, as the old gives way once more to the new, it again forces its way into our consciousness with might and main and brawny shoulders that never say die.

As does, Helene transpired, the blinkered dysuria drop its mauve blossoms on the skittering rodentia of the forests.

It may not possess the reality we smugly ascribe to it, as some thinkers have suggested, whose hallowed names momentarily escape me—momentarily as awesome Time itself!—and also as clairvoyance has demonstrated, but it is a factor to be reckoned with, as reck we must or be damned to us!

Yet, grinned Helene, such recking is as difficult and as inscrutable as the "visage" proffered us by the humpbacked oliguria, whose scent in autumn once emptied out the comatose village of Los Cobardes.

Still, perhaps it is solely, or only, or lonely, a category which is resident in the mind by which we have to think, as one might say the ruptured cyanosis "thinks" in seed-time.

It's terrifically gratifying, Sergey, to hear you bring up, however bedecked with cavalier ignorance, the cyanosis and its shy pale-violet petals delicate as the autumn crocus, poisonous to les vaches, by the by.

As always, small-boned nuthatch, your B.A. in Ed permits you to shed new albeit brilliant light on our talks. Thank you. Nevertheless, the concept of Time must be considered by those who wish to live, and not even especially well. Nor can the individual extricate himself from the toils of the past, present, and future. To do so, in fact, would be as bootless as the desire of the spindly sapsucker beetle to haul his metallic frame from out the "jaws" of the gummy hypoplasia, churn though his tiny limbs may.

Or the dust-grey blattidae, Helene reflected, to slither through the bony spines of the rickettsia furiosa to freedom!

A point, if you will forgive me my little joke, well put. Those who ignore Time become its victim, struck down in the full flower of their years, pains much like arthritis nagging the psyche and other organs. For all practical purposes, one would do well to come to terms with this important factor in life. Perhaps in death as well, yet who can say? For in that undeveloped country no traveler is born.

What?

I say, no traveler is born.

No. Before that.

Perhaps in death as well? One would do well to come to terms with this important factor?

That. What an absolutely marvelous hypothesis, Sergey. Yet . . . don't you also feel that the above-average human person has the capacity to look back and review the happenings of yesterday?

Nor have I ever implied anything to the contrary, sweet hostess of golden daffodils. My point is that this, like other faculties, may be used so as to help or hurt.

Something then like the nauseating ichor of the slimed cochlea, which can drive one to the heights of erotic ecstasy, or, when applied too liberally, give one an awkward, not to say momentous rash?

Exactly! Your ceaseless rummaging through the giant volumes on wild flowers and other faunae, or fauny, that we have down on the floor of the pushcart, has sharpened your mind to marvelously and wonderfully unique acute sharpness. How wonderful to have more than just a wife! But, to press on, as Abe the tailor said—ha ha—one should learn from one's successes and failures, but one should not be deterred from further living by them. The plangent truths, values, and methods of the past can be helpful in the present, and even in the future, which is no more, according to Henri Berg, than the present of tomorrow, or maybe a few days or a week or so from now, but having learned what the past teaches, which, today, is yesterday, but which, tomorrow, will be today, or even right now—such is the mystery of ever-smoldering Time—having learned that, I insist, one should go on living in the present. Whenever that time may be in— or *upon.*

So does the ass-faced bobolink know, Helene stared, through potent Nature's inimitable instruction, to eat the berries of Jupiter's calcaneus today *and* tomorrow, sensing that tomorrow may be nothing more than yesterday if he hesitates in his greed but a single instant! How all of a piece everything is! It *must* be true that we are all gifted creators who, though knowing not—yet know!

That's lining the old bottom, perceptive minx! And to take your barely articulated suggestion a step further into the Platonic light, allow me to suggest that *the living present is the moment of existence*. It is in the now, so to speak, that one lives, no matter the cardboard shoeboxes filled with yellowing photographs. This is not to say, I insert, that the future, whatever that arcane organism may be, is to be ignored. No! I trumpet.

Who could possibly think such is implied, good bole? That would be analogous to suggesting that the waxy cerumen in its first "glimpse" of the April sunshine thinks that fall, with all its melons of misty fruitfulness, will never come. Yet we all know that "If Spring should come, is Labor Day not nigh?"

How I adore the way you use mighty poesie to put a point on an argument! It is the sign of a true statesman and surely that weird and useless art's most valuable raison d'être. No, as I have said, the future is not to be ignored although the true now is now. Unattained goals must be worked out, likewise methodologies. One must know where one is going, and how. Strangers offer monetary help toward middle of month. Travel looms and romance may blossom. But even all this focuses in the present thought, or battery of thoughts, and is implemented in present action. What one is *now* determines the goal that is to be worked out—and even seized!

I think, Helene coughed, of the way Cohen's maxilla seizes on the innocent dew that falls upon its pistils. No wonder the vulgar call the inobtrusive weed "Two-Gun Maxie."

Ha ha. I had forgotten that amusing patronymic. By God, a laugh comes in handy on a long journey toward the Ineffable, like this one, in which Time seems to be, if not precisely an enemy, then a summer soldier, whatever that means exactly. You know how I've always loathed the military.

I hate to see your penetrating brow all wrinkled up so ugly like that, honeyed clot. The Perfect Musical Phrase *is* waiting. I know it deep in my womanly torso. So do go on. I feel that you are nearing the synthesizing peroration of your analysis.

Thus, the now is the only time any one ever has. One is to so act in the present now that the future now will be richer and more meaningful for having known it than the past now—which seemed so important at the time. Fond fools that we be! This means: 1.) The thoughtful planning; 2.) the wise decision; 3.) the kind and helpful word; 4.) the skillful work of the moment. These are the steps by which one rises, as the long stamen of Browning's apnea rises toward the churning compost above its fuzzy head, rises toward the goal—often still to be worked out, and what joy and sugary fulfillment is in the working—the goal and the Ideal. One lives, if one lives at all, in the living present, the heart loving, the goal being worked out, or worked over, if we but falter for an instant of all-chomping Time, the hand always, even in sleep, creatively active.

As the Omaha purpura, Helene whispered, though an ugly brown in color, is yet always active, at least when the sirocco blows hard and hot against its woody stem.

Well put, bursting pod. And now, as the dew is beginning to soak playfully through my shirt and pants, and the Pleiades have set, I think we should crawl into, among, and under the odds and ends we call our gear, there in the damply glistening pushcart, and await the coming of incandescent day—that lies, if my senses work all right, there behind that tree line, a Southern phrase.

You bet, Helene moped.

« 43 »

Land Where
Guitars Softly Creep

They, oh to be sure they, in a daze of intellectual delight, a *virtu* cerebral, because of the dazzle and flickering flash of the great argument that Blue had rendered or propositioned, or whatever, in regard to ever-changing Time, paid hardly heed or gave but even a tacit nod to the swiftly rolling-by (as well as along) landscape, such did the pure white light of thought burn in them.

Burn? Aye! Although they stopped in—or outside of, if one wishes to be a stickling accurate class of a reader—a number of oddball dumps deep awash in chili dawgs, bar-b-q, soft ice cream, and gouts of lambent catsup, catchup, and ketchup, and odds and ends of what some dreadful wag dubbed "sody pop." But take them all in all, you shall not see their like again of sich a pair, embafflement and quintessential joy scrawled large upon those two faces that we know by now so well! Yes, and seem to have known forever!

Indeed! and so they rolled ahead, crossing at last into that curious land shaped, by the Hand of the Great Creator in a moment of unfettered levity, like unto a license plate: the dozing quiet land of Big Sandy, the Great Smokies, and the Knight of the Corncob, Sir Popeye Cigarrillo.

Talk? Talk? 'Sblood! Had drunken barnswallow crashed through the attic window of deserted Penshurst rather than plunge into the cooling pond of the Lady Seraphina, such mad tumult had not stopped their seamless colloquy! Nay, not if the King himself, the wise Jacobus, bellowed in his cups o' Twelve Night.

When we were still trying to get to Little Rock, wherever that may be, or wert, stomping, so to speak, toward Tennessee, how swift, like a sudden torrent of jambalaya it came to me! What? you ask? Don't think twice, it's all right, I'll tell you, my special little orange blossom, my crazy heart, my pig, so to speak, in a pen. Let's turn back the years. Do you remember Ole Joe Clark, the famous Dancing Hemorrhoid, who did the hoedown with a Polynesian baby? Think,

202

my treasure of love. Don't let the stars get in your eyes! Meanwhile, I'll wank out a couple pentatonic variants on "Take My Thing from Your Wringer," to fire up your house of memories.

E'en though time changes everything, how in the Sam Hill could I forget Joe C? Are you teasing me? He was the man who sent me the pillow that you dream on. Burning memories! Filled with bright wights, cunty music, golden guitars, rhythm and booze! What makes you trek down that lost highway to the hills of home, or, in any case, those lonely mounds of clay? Smite me with your stealin' feelin', like I was a sledded Polack on the ice.

I think of the sweet dreams of happier days, just a wedding ring ago, days of candy kisses, Spanish fandangos, and satin sheets! Days when I was but a small-time laboring man, the tender years, when you were my little Rosa, my proud Mary, my Filipino baby, my girl, so to speak, on the billboard. Every year, it seemed, was a good year for the roses. But, shoot! we can't get there from here, here on the long rocky road. Maybe little baby we should have stood there, 'stead of slippin' around? Satisfy my "mind."

True, I fall to pieces on these tumbleweed trails, walking after midnight, hearing the boids mocking, moanin' the blues, skipping in the Mississippi dew that drops on us thick as a vast wet deck of cards. But when you groaned, "Walk troo dis woild wit me, my li'l love bug," I threw, as you well dig, away, as well I might, the rose of home sweet home, and plotzed along in the wake of your male fireball. I'll follow you up to our cloud! or your cloud! sure as the Family Bible is unread. I admit that loving you could be better, it would be a gasser if you lit up my pinball machine once in a fucking while, but nothing, no, no, never nothing, can stop my love, my large and bearded snowbird! But again I ask, what makes you trek?

I'm thinking that maybe I'll find this Phrase when the grass, like, grows over me, and not a zit before. I am how they say "fill up" with the color of the blues. Yet I know, as I tear into my version of the Greater Cheyenne area hit, "Soggy Mount in Fake Down," its weird pitch jist out o' reach o' muh five little fingers, let alone ten, har har, that this waltz acrost Texas or wherever we are, this song of the wanderer that shouts and hollers from our distended throats, is a quiz. Or a test? A test then of my resolve, a peppery seasoning of my heart, a, psychiatrically speaking, river of no return. I am searching searching for the password to that One— which is a Lonely Number, no?—Great Truth, like a honky-tonk gal searches

searches for the hearty heart that is not coldy cold. For this I'm a-settin' the woods on fire, to boin a phrase. Thus, is but human, out here in Heartbreak, U.S.A., that I think off and on and with tears in my eyes of the old brush arbors, the old-fashioned singing, and the old footprints in the old snow of . . . home! Of . . . chay Blue! Kin yew blame me, my luscious flash o' white lightnin', my cielita linda?

Blame, Serge? Blame? Ha! What? Nay, not as long as the lovesick blues do turn a maiden's prayer unto base boot-heel rags, nor hot-rod Lincoln sails his "ship" alone! I'd sooner grasp an old pipeliner or the roses meant for Mama to my breast, or guerdon that great speckled bird who rides the train o' nights to Memphis with sixteen tons o' Wabash cannonballs 'spite its wild complaint!

My wondrous crazy person! I knew, or knowed, that this was to be the great judgement morning! Shot Jackson and Big Ben Dorsey the Third set it down years ago that a satisfied mind comes about solely when a king of the road like me has a mate in re who he kin say: "She's all woman," and also "She is my sunshine." Six white horses could not tear me from the foggy river of your brains, La Golondrina! Shore as Jesus Krise yanked little green apples off of the tree from which Judas cut short his faded love, cross my heart I love yew! If my heart had windows, you could peep in and prove it to yourself. Without your strength to carry us through the thorns of the dread kaw-liga bresh and the nettles of the jole-blon vines, I would have, long long ago, hollered: "Stop the world and let me off!" Though home is where the hurt is, still, it takes a long time to forget. The bottle let me down, the weed-choked willow garden let me down, but you, lively as the bubbles in my beer, said, "Let's build a world together." And I know we will, to the last mile of the way. Freckled fruit! Sexy slowpoke!

Ah, Blue, I don't care that 'tis my wonted fate to be but ol' Freight Train 45 to your crack red-ball, Phantom 309, if I may make how you call a metaphor. Though we are tangled in the coils of the wild side of life, with you, my gentle Mr. Jukebox, the blues stay away from me, and as every tumblin' tumbleweed under the blue moon of Kentucky knows—not to mention the proud rubes deep in the heart of Texas, or soused at the border, or stern-jawed in Cimarron, or asthmatic in dear old dusty Abilene—no blues is good news! Close together as you and me is, a veritable syzygy like unto the fabulous Georgia Molly and dear John Tenbrooks, the fornicating felons of the Tupelo County Jail, we're gonna, as long as this golden ring on my finger stains it a fetching emerald, hold on. Y por qué? 'Cause I cain't stop lovin' you! And you know how mountain girls kin love! Though after but six days on the road it 'peared to me that things had sorta gone to pieces, and I had half a mind to make the request that you release me before I suffered the fierce Baker's breakdown syndrome, the symptoms of which is: hillbilly fever at three A.M., walking the floor over you, the weird apparition who calls hisself "Little Benny," and the voice of Laydown Sally, the lewd and lonely rose of Méjico, a-whisperin' and a-whinin' "Take these chains from my heart one by one," still, I waited in the lobby of your heart. I walk the line, my stubborn and indomitable Serge, knowing that love, yes, love's gonna live here again!

You make me proud to shout unto the hills of Kentucky, which are probly near enough, "She's mine!" But may I subtly hint that somebody's puttin' somebody on? I mean: "mountain girls"? Shame on you! There, on the quarterdeck of the doughty cart, stands the glass. Take a peep. If that's the face of a mountain girl, then I am a Okie from Muskogee!

You win again! But honey, you don't know my mind. Oops! Is that I? I look like a blue muleskinner thornbush! Still . . . though I'm ragged, I'm right. If, for instance, I had a six-pack to go neatly tucked under my arm, I could pass maybe for, if not a mountain girl, then at least a Texas-two-steppin'-rosy-San-Antone-delta-dawned-honky-tonk-angel, by God!

Oi! It wasn't God who made honky-tonk angels. Don't you ever get tired of hurting me? Squinting at your more or less lissome self in those sad rags not fit for Beaumont even, which, by Christ's mercy, is a long long way from here, I feel . . . I think I . . . yes, I've got a new heartache. When I said I'd share my world with you I didn't mean you should, like, take the best room. I think maybe we must have been out of our minds, or is that spelled "minds"?

Whoa, sailor! Are we to be just another couple married by the bible, and divorcèd by the law? While we lived at 4033 Lee Highway, home in San Antone, with my mommy and my daddy, I was so lonesome I could cry. Accidentally on purpose, I heshed my mouf, as they say somewhere, maybe in the Blue Ridge Mountains . . .

They also say "y'all come" in that doomed purloo. So, as the idiom has it, what?

You thought I was dumb and didn't know about your cheating heart. But still water runs deepest. I'd shoot my orisons to heaven, accompanied by the neighbor's lonesome fiddle, praying, "Oh Blue, don't come home a-drinkin'. Take me! Lemme roll in my sweet baby's arms!" Pshaw! I might as well've been developing my pictures. You wallered in your back-street affair, you'd come home with the moon over your shoulder, new, old, full, whatever, it was a-divin' into the river. I'd beg you, beg you—could I help it if I was still in love with you?—"Kiss an angel good morning?" You'd make like a joke, e.g., "Hey, good-lookin'! Remember me?" I'd sob, *sob*: "I wanna be back in baby's arms!" You'd sneer: "After the fire is gone? Look, let's say goodbye like we said hello, O.K.? Milwaukee"—or some damn place—"here I come!" And all this for the love of a girl, that little slut Sally, with her bangs hanging down, a nasty pussy who can't make the two-backed beast with half as much, how shall I say? "esprit" as your lawful hump, I mean I!

Don't think for a moment, my faithful sugar tit, that I do not remember, and with what shame! I used to get the fever down there, the maleficent bluebonnet crotch-clutch, that'd come waltzing in on the southwestern breezes. Alas! Eheu! I'd seek out slimy Sally, do the old Fort Worth drag with her—e'en standing up!—and all the while I was missing you. My sparkling boich! If teardrops were pennies, I could right now buy a used car! Maybe even a little blue Folsom. I know they stopped making the thing but it'll come back! It had a sweetie chassis strong like a jailhouse, and . . . but I wander away, or around. What I mean to say is that I forgot more than you'll ever know about aches and pains of total heartbreak. At one point I figured that I'd never get out of this world alive, can you dig dat?

There he goes! With that boyish just-call-me-lonesome smile on his face. You are forgiven as you have forgiven this occasionally blooming person, your spouse, moi! You will, of course, recall the fiasco of the flesh I partook of a fortnight or so back. As that pasty academic ground his loins on mine, did I think things like: wait'll you see this, Serge? Or: I'll get along somehow? Or: long as you're creaming, try it again? Or, shame of all shames: let's get together one more time? I did not! I thought a think like: Why can't he be you? And bleeve it or not, that was the day I started loving you again.

Oh, Hermes, god of people who walk across fields, she thinks I still care, and she's right! You think: She's got you! and *you're* right, wing-foot! Let us, my more or less hairless Helene, let us never, never look at each other and wonder, in sotted voices, "whose heart are you breaking now?" And now, my pee-wee bark-sucker, let us move on, from here to the door of Success! The race, she is on! And it is time to be . . . moving on! So settle your aromatic self 'pon the motley swag we dub our precious belongings, and sing me . . . sing *us* . . . back home!

Home?

Why query thus my "home"? I was mum when you eked out a "pshaw" some vocables ago.

And so you were. Creak on, my feisty ox! Home it is, then. Or whatever.

« 44 »

A Southern Idyll

Ole Tesh growed that hawg on pure manure.

Corn growed so big chawed Luther's elbow off.

Shittin in tall cotton, boy . . .

Miz Jewel's swet-ass taters an pig dick . . .

Lordamighty! Billy's corn likker'll take the skin off a nigger . . .

Sole his cotton t' some New Yawk jee-yew made darky clo's outen it.

. . . fairy sets down in J. C. Tyrell's diner out to Bleedville an orders a whole fruit pie . . .

Still blowed up, driv ole Roy inta a big ole pine tree like a goddaym rivet!

. . . hippie down to the fairgrounds talkin bout peace an integration got hissef cornholed by R.C.'s two boys come in from the delta . . .

Loreena Pogue come home from honky-tonkin bare-ass nekkid cept her flowered brazzeer wrapped round her middle . . .

. . . ole boy from Ringworm Holler took a pull o' Jimmy Ty's white mule an I declare his daym drawers melted off . . .

. . . big ole bullhead come outen the pond an et the okra . . .

Whitfield pulled that ole gal's drawers down an she got appleblossoms stuck in her shameful hair.

Miz Lemon? Bakes them godawful bindweed tarts?

. . . say Judge Poon's fancy lady down to Atlanta makes him eat raw spinach with dago red on it, shoot!

Miz Monroe'd stanch up her monthlies with a big ole fistful o' collard greens stuffed all down in her drawers . . . dawgs like to chase her to the county line.

Caught ole Billy Lee Simpson with a daym sheep's hind legs poked down in his hip boots . . .

. . . say that Reverend Jimmy Boo Purty over to Coon Lynch spent all the love offerins on mail-order corsets from the Sears an Roebuck stead o' seeds for the church garden . . .

Damfool son of a bitch jee-yew professor from Chicaga asks the ole boys at the Blue Palm Cafe where he can find nigras can still dance the hoppin john!

Ko-rea? Shoot! Take a daym shit an the gooks'd put a mortar round up your daym asshole slick as a greased corncob.

. . . big bull gator et up half the sofa an old Ty-Dee jus kep drinkin his Blue Ribbon . . .

Miz Compton's youngest gal, Rubosa? Come in thout her underpants an say the swamp up an sucked em right offen her . . .

Ham Smellie et a bushel o' peaches down to the Grange fair an daym if he didn't shit hissef when they's playin "God Bless America."

. . . an when the daym rooster fin'ly got outta the still, the daym ole bird tried to mount Calvin Pugh's prize heifer, no lie . . . woulda done it too ony he was too daym drunk to stay in the air.

. . . ole boys down to the body shop bust in on Councilman Jeeter to surprise him on his birthday? There he stands in his wife's cocktail dress all over flowers an stars an bangles, an her high heels? Jeeter say "Come on in boys, just seein how the other half lives . . ."

Elroy Bimm got drunk an' done plug up the hole o' the dressin-room wall o' Miz Zenobia's House Plant an Longeree Emporium with his daym glass eye! Hear tell the Mayor's wife fainted dead away when she seed it starin at her.

. . . them new lady college teachers at the A and M buy their shoes at the Boot Village out on Route 16 . . . don't wear no underpants . . . Fitch Gorn say the daym salesmen work overtime for nothin!

Jim Bobby Gritt got hissef jacked off by a jee-yew gal in the Central Park in New Yawk . . . didn't even know her daym name!

. . . dead ole crow frozed in the watermelon ice cream . . .

Cousin Mack, fella used to get hissef blowed by a calf? Said 'twas better than a woman, more deddycated, he said.

Gleet West come back from Chicaga slobberin for some possum ass an redeye gravy way his brother PeePee used to fix it . . .

Schoolmarm down to Bugface, Miz Zee-Zee Harriet, clumb inta bed with a big ole cucumber an they hadda call the vet . . .

. . . then daym if ole Banjo Pox didn't drink a dozen bottles o' Haddycol an shoot the turnip patch with his shotgun. Say, "Thought it was fixin to steal my new separator."

Then Vern Roach stand up outen his chair an say, "Well, I 'low niggers is God's own, Reverend, but how come when you mention work you cain't find one in a burnt field with a bloodhound?"

Ole Miz Tupelo set in one place so long the rhubarb started growin out of her, no lie.

Zonnie Futt?—own the Whippee-Soft stand out on Interstate 40? Got born again one Sunday mornin when his grits started talkin to him . . .

Pap Bloat say he done seen a Bible in a Nashville hotel with a oil paintin o' Jesus smokin a cornsilk cigarette. Say it musta been a daym Cath'lic Bible.

Vanilla Chard waited on ole Slope Jonson at the church in the sun all day long with her weddin dress gummed to her with sweat an her eyes gettin hard as a fice dawg's.

Sheriff Gawk seed a man 'lectrocuted in Alabama onct an he jump up in the chair like a deer fly done bit him in the ass . . .

. . . Clench Sogg bumped thet gal's ass crost the fer timothy pasture like a daym bullfrog . . .

Ole Dudley say a nigger in New Yawk dressed up like a daym scarecrow once *talked* to him like he didn't notice he was a white man.

Miz Chaundolyne's pap turned loose with both barrels on thet young Snooz boy, an by God, even with his overalls round his shoes he cut through the daym melon patch like a turpentined dawg.

I'd really admire to see that show up to Weaselville where some ole boy washes down a raw chicken with a jug o' bull piss.

. . . sun just a-shinin like a di'mon in a billygoat's ass . . .

Fella with Illinois license plates a-settin in Vetch Crump's diner? P'ints to his grits, says to ole Vetch, "I didn't order no mashed taters."

Some NACP commonist niggers tell the court they seen Mizzoo Trace a-puttin on his Klan robes an by daym, quick as grease through a goose, Mizzoo say, "I was fixin to personate the Easter bunny, Jedge." Courthouse like to come down with the hootin an hollerin.

. . . forty-pound bullhead come outen the river where Mack Buncombe was a-fishin an took hissef a mouthful o' ole Mack's Red Man, then jest slud back in the water calm as you please . . .

Roy Puckle, one o' the jedges at the fair down to Fevertown? Say he'd as lief eat a rat's ass as have to sample Jella Galoot's skunk an sweet tater pie agin.

Colonel Humphreys put on his uny-form on Decoration Day an it was so green with age a yella dawg pissed on him—thought he was a walkin hedge.

Them boys down to Clarke's Sump so daym ignorant they played basketball with a cabbage an got on a wonder why it didn't bounce.

Cuv Forrest's house done blowed down in a storm an Leake Wills say he'll wager a bushel o' corn to spit thet's the fust time it ever got aired out.

Miz Kemper stood out in the corn field in her ole dress all rags an tatters a-wavin her arms an Lamar Nucks say thet a brace o' big crows grabbed holt on her an like to carry her almost to Bolivar's Swamp. Lamar swears them ole crows was a-laughin fit to bust.

... white man couldn't drink it, but I be dawg if Fonzo Clay didn't make whiskey outen turnip greens...

Miz Yazoo a-settin on her porch all day chunkin corncobs at a big ole tomcat an singing hymns...

Alphabet Calhoun done fell inter the bayou an the daym gators done swum fer their lives.

Fat Luster say his nigger hands done et fire ants las spring to keep warm.

Them Quitman boys is such white trash thet the fust time they seed a toilet—over to Leflore Pines—they done washed their feet in it.

They told Verge Rankin to go on home when he said at night school thet they git nylon from lectric caterpillars.

Budge Lowndes? Ain't he the ole boy say thet if God made the boll weevil then Satan made cotton?

Saw in the *Reader's Digest* at the barber shop thet dragon flies don't eat nothin an just fuck all day ... sounds like Sharkey Quantrell when he goes up to them Memphis cathouses.

... so Miz Pike, when Warren come home drunk agin, puts on a sheet, comes out from the trees, an hollers, "I am the devil!" An ole Warren say, "Howdy! I done married yore sister."

When thet young Wilkinson gal puts on thet thin little dress the color o' ripe tomaters, whoo! Make a preacher lay his Bible down!

I ain't sayin' Aspen Tate is ignorant, but he took up books in the third grade till he was twenty-three.

The Persimmon Cafe, thet honky-tonk down to Perry Junction? They got a high-yella gal waitress in there looks better than Miss America's ass.

Miz Claiborne give Lute his supper o' crabgrass an dead brambles an he so daym mean he et it an said, "I swaney, Gemma, yore victuals are improvin."

... say they found a bluebelly soljer's corpse sound as a dollar, belly full o' grits an grease, when they done cleaned Miz Raedell Jasper's septic tank...

Damfool sissy lights from his air-cooled Caddy-lac in a pair o' pink short britches, tears up an armload o' poison oak, an say to Omar Lutch standin there bugeyed, "Kin ah make juleps with this here?"

Broom Scott, Miz Scott's eldest, over to Flyblow? Said in New Yawk they give him a baked tater all over cream done turned bad in the kitchen. When he tole the waiter he looked at him like he was funnin.

Cheater Holmes busted his still after he woke up one day an saw his false teeth a-settin at the table eatin peanuts...

... ole boys blowed up Diddy Carroll's privy with cherry bombs an it like to rained shit over two counties. Montgomery Siff still thinks it was an act o' God cause they done let the niggers set down at the five-an-dime fountain.

. . . an when they give Webster Liveoak thet itty-bitty knife an fork on the airyplane, he say, "I ain't got no chillun with me, ma'm."

. . . thass a biscuit-eatin, pea-stealin, gumbo dawg.

Come up on Jelly Hancock mounted on a shoat an he say he's takin its temp'rature.

Hear tell that Linc Marshall married his cousin, Gardenia Mae, an had a boy twa'nt able to do no more than grin like a possum eatin shit.

. . . fool in a silk shirt leans outen his little eyetalian car an asks Booger Wayne, the sheriff over to Collardville, iffen he kin tell him how to get to Florida, an ole Booger arrests him for askin questions of a Sunday.

Miz Prentiss went on one o' them fancy brown-rice diets an by God one day slud right down the privy hole . . .

. . . an the preacher lays hands on Cash Hinds an shouts, "Lawd! Take this toomer, Lawd! Take this hyar poison lump away!" An all the time he's a-feelin ole Cash's sack o' Bull Durham.

Give that idjit boy a Sears an Roebuck cattylog open to the longeree ads an he's happy as a pig in shit.

They done found Margarina Jackson an Reverend Poole's missus, Gloretta, in the corn crib sound asleep with their drawers down round their knees.

Widder Mulch took that daym billygoat inter the house an I be a mule if he didn't eat the TV.

Got so dry over to Banshee County las summer the daym gators attacked a Co-Coly truck.

Husk Benton is so daym peculiar 'bout that prize sow o' his he wants to put her in the kissin booth at the county fair this fall.

« 45 »

A Transition,
from A to Z

AS Blue and Helene staggered through the thick layers of dixie exotica, up to their knees in the aromatic, yet prickly clumps of *lorena houlka*, the noonday sun pressing through the feathery *bogue chitto* trees, Blue said

BABE, I think we are in one of them dead spots called, for want of a better nomenclature, a transition, like, we gotta get through it to get on to the next really vital and interesting part of our continuing saga; apropos from this, a odd-looking duck is peeping at us from behind that yonder *toccopola* tree. And so it wert, and thus discovered, a guy who introduced himself as

CHEECHEE Docque sauntered out from behint said tree and all in clearest view, amid the lice-infested stands of *acona* and *sarepta* weeds, doffed his hat, and smiling said

DON'T be alarmed! I am known to men of brawny will and heavy heart as Cheechee Docque, as you know already from the paragraph above; I have been sent down here to the land of violet *eudora* by a dude name o' Doctor Piscardi, a sort of colleague of Doc Chick, who wants to keep a eye on you vis-à-vis your mouth and all its attendant something or others.

EH? the two Gavottes chimed as swallows do in the limbs of sweetest *sylvarena*. Doc Chick is still aware, still cares about my

FATE? Blue grinned through trembling lips, a hot tear or two splashing in the dead *tunica* thorns that lay at, as well as upon, his feet.

GODDAMNED right! Cheechee opined. And as sure as wild *tuscola* fills the April air with loathsome seeds and stuff, your present fate, in this transition, is mine to mold and shape so that we don't get bogged down in a lotta talk and

HEMMING and hawing, can you dig that? Blue and H not only could, but did, dig it, and settled down with the hearty Cheech beneath an itty-bitty *itta bena* stand, there to chat and listen to the emissary's

IDEAS. First of all, the man plucked an armful of wild *bovina* plums plus a brace apiece of juicy *bobos*. Nothing like a surge of purest sugar! When they had et their fill and were lighting up their pipes around the old campfire, the lake a sheet of molten gold, the crickets thrashing in the nearby *wenesoga* fronds, Docque glanced from one to the other

JERK'S face, and sighed into his mess kit, or tin. I'd like, he began, nothing better than to set here toasting weenies and watching marshmellers burn up into blackish gloop, while the bass-mouthed sunnies and the pike-wallers frolic beneath yon *coila* lilies! But I have a job to do, you

KLUCKS, and I use that word with all due respect. First of all, was ever praying mantis, locked in the deathgrip of the dreaded *buckatunna* vetch, more desperate than youse, who have arranged this transparent alphabet structure for to alleviate the boredom of an obligatory transition? Huh?

LOOK, Blue started, this is not our idea! Right, Helene, my *lula* blossom?

MINCING prettily about the fire, blazing high now with the armload of *shubuta* fronds she'd flung upon hit, Miz G agreed:

NAW, she tittered gaily, her eyes snapping like *sabougla* vines caught in an early frost, or perhaps a late frost, or a vicious hailstorm, such as is known in Ole Miss to come when they, the folks therein that is, least expect it.

O.K., Cheech said, relaxing visibly into the sleeping bag he'd stuffed with *derma* leaves. That out the way, I got to inform you that this Southern talk that just a little while hence, or is it thence? No matter. That just a while ago, enchanted youse, is not what we like to call "representative" of the Deep South, but of a very very small minority, a red-necked few, a trashy clutch of churls, a bunch of

PECKERWOODS! In short, before you get on with your journey, I have the pleasant duty to straighten out your heads a mite concerning this vast, somnolent, yet rich-in-human-nature area, this South! This Dixieland! This oith of *lena*, *tyro*, and *wanilla* bresh, not to mention the majestic *tippo* tree, from which dangle strands of pure *pinola* nuts! Do you

QUITE get me? Thus Docque spake and turned his socks upon the glowing spit. There was the heavy soughing of the wind in the blue-shadowed *pheba* copse that limped down to the lake; the moon had turned to purest silver the *pelahatchie* leaves. Then Blue rejoined, in a soft

ROAR, We get you Cheech. What is it you must do to set us straight anent the deepest truth concerning this mysterious land? If the things we hoid do not represent—no more than the arctic *ofahoma* represents—the Real

SOUTH, what do? Cheechee Docque's heart leaped high as do the *kolola* spores spring when the brown bear tromps crazily through the silent glens upon the misty mountains. He knew, as though seeing it writ in jools upon a barn door,

THAT they were ready! That they would welcome, indeed, *did* welcome a, what you call, "balanced" presentation of this place that men have called, for many years, "the South." Now they would soon know that "the South" is more, much, much more than the rainbow-hued *chicora* daisy, nice as that is. He sat

UP. Down the road, my charges twain, past the wheezing stands of pied *pachuta* and the multifarious types and kinds of rarest *scooba* shrubs, lies Jean Toomer Tech, and though some ungrateful darkish brethren call it Jean's Tomb, 'tis the Southland's most prestigious hall of learning for the underprivileged, for which word read "colored folks." It is there that you'll discover a powerful and

VERY different South from the stuff you just heard about what you think is the McCoy, as different as is the *looxahoma* blossom from the *bolatusha*!

WHERE is this? said Blue excitedly, filling his old corncob with a kind of fervid, almost passionate intensity. Down the road? Can we start now, or is it best, as I have read, to stay kind of put when the sun goes down in these hyar parts, lest the *rena lara* or the *nitta yuma* types of ivy louse you up with running sores?

XYLOPHONES can trill no sweeter than did Cheechee's laughter, as he saw that Blue, by this remark, was the soul of mature and manly probity. By gum, Gavotte, he chuckled, the firelight making his face as red as the leaves of the *osyka* oak on Labor Day, or sometimes earlier, depending on the rainfall during August, we'll sleep now, or, as you suggest, "stay put." And when the dawn climbs up above the yonder hillocks, I'll point you on your way. The place to go at ole JT Tech is the Auditorium, and there you'll have a scale or so lifted off from your eyes. Oke?

YOWZAH, Blue grinned. I'm gonna curl up here with the old lady on these fluffy *eastabuchie* leaves and less all now cop some

Z'S. And in less time than it takes for a *cascilla* stem inadvertently popped in the mouth to stop the heart with its deadly sap, they were asleep!

« 46 »

Big Black's
Lecture: Elegy on
the Theft of Black Flowers

Some jive-ass mutha-fucka sambo bump into me the other day cold in his tweed vine like some dark-skin guinea on a humble, passin for pale, dig? his ugly garlic face grinnin like some goddam grey ceLEBrity cause he bees talkin to the fuckin Law, you dig, Jim? Thass zackly how this sad dinge look. He say, "Bro, what is your story, my man? Why don't you lay back an cool it bout this nigger flower shit fore you get the man mad? He gonna wear your black ass out you don't lighten up." Shee-it! Mutha-fucka's lip was all poked out so he look like some jive blue-hair jew lady can't breave with her hunner-dollar corset squeezin her chicken-fat guts.

I say, "Look, nigger, lemme pull your coat. Don't be layin shit on me bout bein cool with the fuckin honkies. Thass tom talk. Mutha-fuckas bees coppin our po- sies an heavy blossoms an shit for a thousan years, like they copped our music, you dig? An don't be runnin no shit past me bout how they got they *own* flowers, cause the white man ain't got shit that his own." This pee-da-bed jive mutha- fucka give me a shitface grin like some mockie hab-dasher layin some shit threads on a ignorant blood, you dig, two-fitty suit "mark down" the jew say, yeh, to eighteen dollahs. No wonder the mutha-fucka call his crosseye daughter Laurel April or Michelle Claudia or some such shit an park his El Dorado up in Westchester or some other jive place while them dumb niggers payin his mort- gage bees draggin round all day listnin to fat-ass ole white womans run they mouths at the welfare. "You can't get this thirty-eight cent this week, Tyrone, cause you mop a floor las week for a dollar an a pint a Gypsy Rose." You dig? So my man, this trick woogie, he gone, Jim! Ain't nothin but a shufflin house nigger anyways got his tongue up the man's ass a mutha-fuckin mile lookin out for some ghett-to bread from the crackers down in D.C. who bees talkin dumb shit bout negro aspirations out they mouths while they bees whippin willie's head keep they jive-ass suburbs safe for Laurence mutha-fuckin Welk. One-a these days the bloods gon' fuck up they shitty little lawns bad, bro, an waste all they files a *Time* an *Playboy* an all they books by they lib'ral honkies tell the brothers how to live. Shee-it! You remember what Malcolm an Stokeley an Rap an Huey say bout the ofays' faggot-ass books an shit, right? They say be tight an bad, don't look sad, don't git mad, whip haid! Them mutha-fuckin books an shit bees the runnin dawgs a the jew-guinea-square-ass mutha-fuckin zionist conspiracy, Jim, an if the bloods don't get down behin' some heavy nationalist shit they gonna spen they whole lives drinkin the man's sweet wine an pokin that mafia smack into they arms jus like the silk-vine mutha-fuckas want them to—dig? Blanks wanna keep the bloods dumb an stoned so they bees dreamin a bad shorts an hip vines an layin up somewheres with some yella-hair pussy. Man may be a mutha-fuckin faggot like to get poked in his ass but he know how to suck out willie's heart, Jim, believe it.

This shit bees goin down everywhere! Kike faggot white man ain't never had nothin he made hissef—every mutha-fuckin thing he got he cop from the bloods. Them mutha-fuckin Greek assfuckers steal they philosophy from the brothers in Africa, Jim! The Phonishuns an Trojans an them dudes. Steal they mathematics an geometry an all that science shit from Arab bloods. Steal they mutha-fuckin art, man, from hip spades live in caves. Shit! They even steal they dramma from the mutha-fuckin goats! No jive! An they music? Man, them dudes like Mozart an Beethoven an Wagner, you dig, an them hooknose jew mu-tha-fuckas, Stravinsky an Kossakov, oh, man! All that tired shit, they need a mu-tha-fuckin army to get it on. An they snatch that shit from the cool dudes in Af-rica, man, that shit carried over by the slaves an the cracker, he say, "My goo'ness gracious! How marr-vell-ous our nigras soun!" An the next thing, bro, they snatch the bloods' rhythm an harmonics an his whole fuckin scale! You dig how Martha an the Vandella soun, right, brothers? An the Marvelettes an my man, James Brown, the Supremes fore Diana Ross got her mind all twist up with kike bread, ole Fats Domino, Sam Cook, Marvin Gaye, that hip ole dude, Louis Jor-dan? Well, shit, man, them bloods turn jive-ass Mozart an Kossakov *around*. They bees playin all this jive trash on flutes an hopsycords an mutha-fuckin axes nobody know the mutha-fuckin name of, Jim. An then you hip to this jew, Gershwin, dig? He write this trick sambo faggot opera, suppose to show you happy spooks singin an dancin. Shee-it! I see that mutha-fucka two years ago on the TV I thought I watchin science-fiction! Onct they bees puttin ole Sammy Davis in they bullshit play, man! You dig? This trick shuffler bees creepin after white pussy all his life, bees up tight with a buncha greaseball Lass Vegas faggots, bees puttin a shuck on people to buy sweet jew wine. Am I right, brothers? Right an bright! Ole one-eye Sammy spose to be a mutha-fuckin exAMPle, dig on it.

Man, you plant that mutha-fuckin nigger up on Lenox an twenny-eight the dudes bees fuckin him right thoo his designer pants, Jim.

An now the jive turkey blanks bees stealin our *flowers*. Snatch up the bloods' seeds an shrubs an all that kinda shit an some foureye mutha-fuckin scientist in his white coat in they cracker university, he call our heavy African plants—dig this—he call them flow-ra. You hip? Flow-ra! I like to flow-ra that jew faggot mutha-fuckin dentist upside his head! He bees talkin jive shit bout how this flow-ra for all mankind, shit like that, you know the kinda shit them shylock lib'ral mutha-fuckas talk. All mankind my black ass! Zionist Israeli faggot gen'rals snatch they piece off the top, then the dark-face dagos whose great-great-great granmommas got some African jelly-roll an that how come these wops be so dark, they stop they oil an garlic scoff for a minute an they spaghetti an shit they so hincty bout, shee-it. Act like they invent that shit steada the ole dudes live in China, man, black dudes, dig? You think them bad spooks who bees with Genghis Khan *white*, man? An they garlic an oil, bro, that shit ripped off ten thousand years ago from the cats built the Pyramids. Shee-it! These guineas with they mafia judges an commissioners an shit an they jews they shylock with, they cop some bread, too. Then the Irish drunk-ass mutha-fuckas send they red-face pigs round for they piece, then the resta the devils, them mutha-fuckas all the same anyways.

An las, oh yeh, las come the mutha-fuckin toms an all them sambos an trick *negros*, you dig, Jim? Buncha shines wear they Afro wigs on the weekend, man, you dig? They get the smell lef in the pot! An they shuffle they feets an kiss up over the man's ass, oh thank you, sir, thank you, sir, would you care to see me do a mutha-fuckin tap dance? Shee-it! They like to bust out in some white man gospel songs thankin Jesus for the man's kindness like the mutha-fuckin beast sing in Georgia after he pay some ole nigger five cent to shine they shoes. They snatches our flowers an seeds an turn em into some faggot-ass hybrids, is they name. An these trick sambos get a deuce or a trey an say, thank *you*, Mr. Man! I will surely go home now an pick up on Andy Williams, yassuh! I'm tellin you, Jim, these mutha-fuckas ain't wrapped too tight! The blank lays bullshit on em an they lays all *in* it. They Afro wigs they put over they conks on weekends must keep the air from they *minds*, brothers.

You know who I bees talkin about. These mutha-fuckas all week long they bees talkin jive shit like, "Why, certainly, sir, I will be delighted to assist the committee in this new project." You dig? Bees talkin thu they black noses an eatin all that fairy shit French blanks make—scoff ripped off from Arab bloods when they *wan't* no France, Jim. An then on the weekends these Amos an Andy turkeys put on they Afro wigs an they hip vine an they bad shoes, oh they straight, brother. They bees standin on a corner uptown, man, layin jive shit on the brothers bout how they bees raised right around the corner an how they was the baddest mutha-fuckas, mean as a hungry dog, an goin down on porduhrickans an wops an how they all miss fatback an greens, how they wanna wrap they chops roun some hoppin john an cornbread an drink some spodee-odee an shoot some mutha-fuckin nine-ball. God-daym! Mutha-fuckas stick out they ches'es an get blacker by the fuckin minute, make the homeboys look like a buncha dumb hippies! Well, fuck that shit! Ain't the time or place to lay hard shit on these niggers in they trick hip bag. I got heavy business to take care of here.

I bees talkin bout these slick jews snatchin the brothers' Black flowers an shit, Jim—the flow-ra, like them faggots call em. But you dig? The onliest flow-ra the greys know fuck-all about is bush, Jim, an the square-ass jive mutha-fuckas in they plastic shoes an they blue jeans an that long ugly shit call they hair even ripped that off the bloods! You think any white-eye fuckin pale got the brains to grow they own bush? Shee-it! They exproPRIated that heavy boo off the bad spooks in Algiers an Tangier an shit—only fuckin shit zionist-jew-faggots are hip to bees some damn lilacs an daffow-dills an jive plants like that, tomatuhs, dig, put all over that mutha-fuckin garlic trash them fat-ass bitches bees cookin all day long in they lectric kitchens in the suburbs in they pink lipstick an trick fingernails. But you dig these ugly-ass devils layin out cool smokin that heavy bush, Jim, an talkin shit like, "Oh man, thass heavy gold! Hey, baby, this fuckin red is boss shit!" Burn some ole funky oil rags an stick it up they nose an them faggots think they in heaven! Man, they bees corrupTED smellin they own self all they life, don't know righteous bush from turnip greens. An you dig, brothers, God don't like ugly, man.

Black flowers! Thass what I bees talkin bout. I bees talkin bout pure, brothers, like livonia icepick and saratoga lot-leafs, an the convent shrub an pinkeye st. nicholas. I mean like lenox lazuli an ellingtonia columbiana that the brothers call the satin doll. Shee-it! Can't even remember em all—honeydripper an k.c. mcshann an king bedford oliveri, brown st. james, supreme rossi, the mountain morris. Boss shit, Jim! Ayler bluebells an green dolphys, adidas jamaicas an fox skulls—big red littles! that bees the official flower a the Black Nation.

Brothers, yall dig what the honkies run past us, right? Them jew mutha-fuckas an they guinea lawyers an they Irish polis be stealin the niggers' flowers an fuckin em up in they white labratories, turnin them bad greens to they sugar-tit bookays sell to jive-ass white boys to give they bitches. All the *black* be whipped out the bloods' flowers, man. These jive marykones—thass porduh-rickan language for faggot—suck out all the blood from our plants an quick as shit make em flow-ra. Willie's boss plants come out same as a mutha-fuckin shufflin coon got his black balls cut off an his black ass shakin for the cracker pay him some little bitty coin at the welfare or let him have some ole funky vine not even a dumb-ass guinea off the boat wrap his greasy back in. An this ignorant nigger lay back cool, you dig? He bees suckin his jug a king kong and sayin "Thank you, boss, you sho bees a good white man jes like the Bible say you should. Praise the lawd!" Shee-it! Mutha-fucka be cool he put his foot in this cracker's *ass*! Make you cry see this dumb dinge grin like he *straight* cause he ain't got no job. Brothers, suckin the man's ass at the welfare bees a *job* you gets paid slave bread for!

Dig on it, you bloods, this bees an ole con to the pales. I bees in the liberry las week on a humble, dig, like some jive-ass weekend spade, runnin a number like I want to study up some white man's shit to *improve* myself, dig? This big-ass liberrian with her jugs fallin out her dress helpin me, dig? If she knowed I there to dodge the ole hawk snatchin my cheap jew-store coat offen me she a called some sambo pig to pop me for *creating*, dig? Or *loitering*. But she bees a ignorant white bitch think I want to get hip to blank bullshit so's I can bees a mutha-fuckin mailman, or mop up shit in a hospital. Well, bro, I read in this jive book a faggot poetry by some dude got a name like that turkey mutha-fucka, Captain Marvel, no shit. Anyways, I see some heavy shit. This cracker's pomes ain't shit, bees all about gardens an dumb-ass English dudes mowin the mutha-fuckin lawn, didn't have no woogies round to do it for them in they time, dig? But I read that when this long-hair blank write this shit, the greys were really behine too-lips, man, yeh, thass right, mutha-fuckin toolips! Bees payin heavy bread for some ole funky bulb, I mean, baby, you dig, *heavy* bread. Thousands! Jive book say them English dudes *buy* all this shit, dig? But you believe they *paid* the rag-gedy mutha-fuckas *growed* the toolips, well, blood, you ain't wrapped too tight atall. One-a these jive flowers, man, bees called the Marvel of Peru an the mutha-fucka bees growed in the West Indies. Now I a jew schoolteacher if it didn't be-long to some ignorant niggers lay it on these English honkies for some mutha-fuckin two-bit glass necklaces run up in some kike factry, you dig? I don't have to lay heavy shit on you, do I, make you pick up quick an slick on what I'm runnin down? Dig! Ofays in they trick bag way the fuck back in sixteen hundred some-thin, my man.

All this history an shit I bees talkin is to get you hip, brothers. I doan give a mutha-fuckin dime the man come roun like some jive scientist from a ofay flick bout some faggot vampire shit or some mutha-fuckin honkie monster bees creepin aroun like he got a stick up his jive ass, or the man come by in his pig suit all red in his face askin you why you bees sittin on your own mutha-fuckin *stoop*, Jim, or he slide up all nasty an funky in his bad vine talkin bout brothers an sisters an all that tired ole jew-lib'ral shit like some kinda nigger-machine. They *all* devils, blood, an they there to cop your righteous African flowers an your Black shrubs, man, an fuck em all aroun into flow-ra, sell em back to poor ignorant willies outen they kike flower stores, dig? Call the bloods' flowers jive faggot shit like phloxes an zinnas an holly mutha-fuckin hocks. Shee-it!

What I bees runnin past you? Blanks gon' take every mutha-fuckin thing you own, bro, you don't hold it tight an right! Take ole Erskine Hawkins' "Tuxedo Junction" an make it into some jive mutha-fuckin faggot song, snatch Bird's mean blues, "Now's the Time" an it pop up this goddam ugly "Hucklebuck," steal Lady Day's heavy sounds, bro, an Prez get fucked over you think some white mutha-fucka invent the ax ole Lester learn him how to blow. Shee-it! Bad enough the honkies ain't got no music but they trick jew tunes—them ignorant pigs can't even play the shit they steal! They bees goin, you dig, toot-toot an shit like that, they bees goin oobie-doobie-shoobie so mutha-fuckin ugly make you thow up on your shoes, man. Dig! Pales snatch every fuckin thing ain't nailed down, bro. Bees snatchin the brothers' music and clo's, they talk an instruments an dances an even mutha-fuckin hair style. Now they bees rippin off the Black flowers an shit, next they bees coppin the bloods' veg'tables. Okra an blackeyed peas and collards an they be thowin them in with they mutha-fuckin garlic an frogs' asses an snails an funky ole cheese an shit like that an callin it quee-zeen, dig? So, brothers, be mean an lean, stay clean. Don't give the mutha-fuckin man flower one, dig? Wear his ass *out*. Mutha-fuckas on they las trip anyways. Black flower!

« 47 »

Dazed,
Our Friends
Reach Nawlins, Looziana

Louisiana, Louisiana,
Entre nous, entre nous.
Louisiana, Louisiana,
Je m'en fous, je m'en fous.
Louisiana, Louisiana,
Voulez-vous joujou?
Louisiana, Louisiana,
Ici Bleu!

Old Song

It is far from the raw power of my pen to detail the stroll that now ensued and on which the Gavottes found themself. In a hypnotic dump from the raw power of Mr. Black's speech or lecture to an admiring throng of pedants and folk crowding in from the rays of the hot sun and its fabled raw power, they pressed on toward the city long fabled as the raw and powerful "cradle of jazz" or "jazz" or "jas." Indeed, Nawlins! Brooding in its powerful rawness!

What a look crossed Helene's face as she occasionally rolled in the verdant fields of Spanish moss! And Blue was not far behind. There was what a look on his rugged phiz as well.

Adventures? Ha ha ha! You shouldn't make me laugh already! Their adventures were incredible, like those of Hercules when he ate Gorgeous Medusa, of Theseus atop the wooden horse on the plains of windy Troy, of the lisping Achilles knitting up afghans and doilies for Lady Omphale while dressed in a smart little black dress that could go right from office to dinner to a night on the town; and what those two did when they got home late and a little tight on the unmixed wine is not recorded even in the pages of Suetonius, and he recorded everything, as you know. Or maybe you don't know.

But it is not my intention to waste the reader's valuable time, since I know, better than most, that it's best to be up and doing, and off and out, and laughing hysterically into the teeth of adversity on the ski slopes, the dazzling beaches, under the hood of the old Chevy, into a plate of potato salad and hot dogs, the things that have made us, as a nation of persons equal under law, great. So I'll be quickly brief. Or let me say—how shall I say?—let me brief you quickly.

I have adumbrated the conception of adventures: like the howling sail they made across Lake Ponchartrain, and down its silent tributaries to the great brown sea of the Mizzipi! But you have heard this before, you are well aware of these boon adventures, whatever that means, you can go and read *Martin Chuzzlewit's Voyage*, as if you haven't! Remember the sail therein that Martin takes with his fag, Mark, on the lusty barkentine down the Ohio? The Gavottes' adventures were in no wise, or ways, at all like those of Martin and Mark, nor did they have a captain like the gruff Gumbo Pease to sail under, but they *might well have been*!

One morning, waking with the first tantalizing odors of simmering red beans and coffee with chicory and also with the laughter of the praline vendors plunging their wares—alive!—into great cheery vats of boiling water, Serge knew that he had been rocked to sleep the night before in the "cradle of jass."

Now to have a quick nosh of jambalaya à la king and then to set out in search of Frenchie L'Amour and Bunky Jimson. That's who it says to find here anyway, on this scrap of paper given me by a nameless stranger who passed us one night in his ship during one of our many adventures, as you will recall, sweet Helene.

I'm afraid that the stars had so entranced me that I've forgotten . . . everything but the good parts of our harrowing experiences while, as the French say, *en route*.

Thus wert ever it, Blue laughed consolingly as he shudderingly "took" her from the rear with sudden passion beneath the dewy bougainvillea shrubs that lent to the still morning air of the mysterious city a strange, what shall I say? mystery.

Nawlins has imbued a strange tropical verve to your shtupping, Helene blushed, clearing off the hand-carved rustic table that insolently crouched beneath the barely moving ceiling fan. I . . . like it, she screeched, chucking, with a robust clatter, the breakfast "things" into the quaint zinc sink.

Without further ado, Blue found himself before the door of a small club, his scrap of paper held tightly in his fist against the gales of the legendary sirocco!

It blew as if the dogs of hell had bayed, or—*were* baying!

It blew with a ferocity unequaled in his long experience of ferocious breezes.

As it ceased, a door appeared in the wall of the club.

A face peered out.

It . . . smiled, or did what Blue took to be a smile.

You 'ave come for ze Phrase? the face rejoined, while behind it another voice chuffed along.

They was Frenchie and Bunky.

That eez, if you please, Frenchy and Bunkie, the laughing frog maintained obstinately. And you 'ave come to a place where is possible maybe to fin' a *morceau* of azziztonce, no?

Come awn in, yew white mo'fo, the deeper voice boomed warily.

And so Serge did.

Meanwhile, Helene busied herself about their cheap room in the "Quarter" by taking in some washing and deftly sewing a small dresser in which her hubby could keep his bicycle clips.

I will wager a farthing to a ha'penny that you've forgotten about Blue's bicycle clips, though they may yet figger large in our story. Or not.

But let us listen to the conversation now taking place in the dim club in which we may stand as observers unseen by the three men who interest us. Or maybe interest us. Frenchy is spikking.

To Expand
upon the Subject

I reckon, mon ami, that you won't go too far wrong iffen yall listen to stuff and hot licks in which the hunk o' tune yall are lookin fer probly hides, n'est-ce pas? Le jazz hot like Clarinet Marmalade, Dippermouth Blues, Mahogany Hall Stomp, Muskrat Ramble, St. Louis Blues, Rockin' Chair, Tiger Rag, Black and Blue, Struttin' With Some Barbecue, Save It Pretty Mama, Chinatown My Chinatown...

Or, a deep voice clanged, dig, grey boy, mellow sounds known by the names ob Swing That Music, High Society, Heebie Jeebies, Baby Won't You Please Come Home, Back o' Town Blues, Storyville Blues, Panama, Royal Garden Blues, The Sheik of Araby, Nagasaki, Winin' Boy Blues...

I'm tuned in to your arcane jive, gents, Blue suddenly intruded, as intrusion was one of his few flaws. Also I Ain't Got Nobody, King Porter Stomp, Bucket Got a Hole in Its, Eh, Là Bas, Farewell to Storyville, Creole Bo Bo, Bill Bailey Won't You Please Come Home, Savoy Blues, Creole Song, Yaaka Hula Hickey Dula, Limehouse Blues?

Mais oui! An by such artistes extraordinaires comme St. Clair de Lune and his Jambalaya Jambos, Pops Ennui and the Crawdaddies, the Compote-Marmalade Band featuring Licks Mambeau, Jimbo Verlaine's Rainmakers, Mickey Butor and the Time Passers, Fats Gide with the Baton Rouge Boys, Valéry Conga, Zoot Roussel and the African Alligators, Booker Césaire, Cheech Mauriac with the Femmes Fatales, and Luigi Celino and the Noodle Band.

An' lemme pull your coat on Johnny Giono and the Blue Boys, Cocky Jack and the Astonishers, Sad Sam Zara with the Realists, The Inquisitors starring Bobi Pinget, Peanuts Prévert, "Mellow" Rooney Char and his Hypnotic Horn, Jenny Voleur, Big Julie Laforge, Ray Queneau and the Dogtooth Serenaders, Rambo Charlie and the Hell Raisers, an' "Bo" Delay with the Dawn-Light Stompers.

Hey! And I've loaned an ear myself via record to Izzy Ducasse, Red Renard and the Fourteen Carats, Al Robby Grillay with the Good Lookers, "Jaws" Hysman and the Git-Down Band, Clo Simon and the Grasscutters, Tony Arto with the Visionaries, Pat Jarry, Nathan Sarraute and his Golden Fruit Geechee Band, Go-Go "Blue" Bataille, Camoo with the African Stompers, and also Murph Malone and the Kilowatts!

Maintenant, is also musique of the Marmalade du Clarinet, Blue Dippermouth, Stomp Hall Mahogany!, Ramblin' Muskrat, Blues for St. Louis, Chair is Rockin', Ragged Tiger, Blue and Black, Some Barbecue Be Struttin', Mama Pretty, Save It!, Chinatown, Chinatown, My My! . . .

An', fay, dig on Music that Swings, Society's High, Jeebie Heebies, Please Come Home Won't You Baby?, Blue's Back o' Town, Blues in Storyville, Amanap, Blew in the Royal Garden, The Arab Sheik, Saki-Naga, Blue Boy Winin'. . .

Damn if *I* dint grow up on Ain't Got Nobody's Eye, Stomporter King, Got a Hole in Its Bucket, La Bàs, Eh?, Storyville, Farewell!, Bobo Creole, Won't You Bill to Please Bailey?, Blue Savoy, Song of the Creole, Hickeydula-Yaakahula, Blues for Lime House.

Et les musiciens who jouent the pieces! Jambo Jambalaya and the Clair de Lune Orchestra, "Crawdaddy" P. Ennui, Licks Compote and the Marmalade-Mambeau Band, The Rainmaker Six featuring "Valayne," Mickey Passertime and the Butter Band, Baton Rouge Fats and the Guide Boys, Congo Valerie, Al Afrique-Larousse Zut Trio, Césaire Bukka, the Fatal Femmes featuring Maury Cheech, et "Noodles" with the Celino-Luigi Band.

You done remin' me of de "Blue" Boy-Giono Jonny Band, the Astonishers with Special Guest Jacques Cocky, Sam Realist and the Sadzaras, the Inquisitors starring Bobbi Pangez, Trever P. Nuts, Hypnos Charhorn and the Mellowrooneys, V. Jenny, La Jules and the Big Forge Three, "Dogtooth" with Q. Ray's Serenade Seven, the Rayzelles with Charlie Rambo, an' the Dawnlight Stompin' Band with Delaybeau.

The renditions that have cloved to my memory are by the Ducassize Experience, Renard Red and the Four Teens, Goodlookin' Grillet featuring Robally's Golden Sax, the Git-Down Jaw Band and Hy Smann, Simon "Cutgrass" Clo, Art Tony and the Artovisions, Gerry Patt, Nate Geechee and his Golden Fruits, Bats Blue with the Go-Gos, the Africa Stomp Band featuring "Camu," and Kilowatt Malone and the Murphs.

Agreed! that they were hommes et femmes, dudes and foxes, gents and ladies, e'en though they hadda play in joints like Lafitte's Rump Dump, the Hot Red Bean Room, Jackson's Alley, Twisty King Oliver's, Fazola's Rest Room, the

DuBois Wood Womb, Hall of Berbin, the Red Light, Pelican Lounge, Cool D. Sack's, and the Chicory House.

Mon Dieu! Such large of l'esprit! In such smoky boites to hear the art like unto the Mama Laid Her Clarinet, Dip Ma Blue Mouf, Stompin' Ma Hawg in the Hall, My Muskrat, He Rumble, Blue Looie, Charokin, Tiger Rug in Rags, My Black Be Blue, Stutterin' Barbecue, Shove It Pretty, Mama! Shine it Down, Dingbat Music, Flyin' in Society, D.B.B.V.D.'s, Won't You Come Please, Baby?, De Blues Is Back on Down, Blue Story Blues, Pajama Shout, Royal Blue Garter, The Arab Bought a Sheik, A Nog o' Saki an' a Beer, Blue Wine Blues, Got no Body, Got no Head, Stomp-King Porter's Rag, Fuckit, Got a Hole in It!, Ayla Bas, Ayla Bu, Ayalors, Whoreville, Farewell, Bo-Bo Creole's Oreo, B. B. Bailey's Flyin' Home, Savoy, Ça-Va, Sauvage?, The Old Cree (Ugh Ugh Ugh), Hula Dula's Hickey, et The House of Blue Limes.

And then 'twas settled that though these works were known and loved the whole globe o'er, they were especially adored in Bonnet Carré, Algiers, Chalmette, Marrero, Belle Chasse, Des Allemands, Boutte, Paradis, Lake Borgne, Terrebonne, and Plaquemines.

Lemme lay it on the record, gents, that the dee-finn-itt-iv versions of dem heavy sounds bees played by Jimbo Jumbo and his Loonies, Crawfunk Popshit, the Compote-Suckin' Bonelickers, V. D. Verlayne and the Smiling Syphs, Mickey Butt and the Pastimes, Guy Fatso and his Magic Stick, Congo Val with the Bad Vibes, Red Zoot and the Congolas, Caesar the Fucker, Cheechee and the Feminettes, Louis Noodles and his Electric Cello, The Blueball Band featuring Joanie Groan, Jack and the Astonishing Cocks, Tsad Tzara's Tsurreal Tsix, The Askers with Bobby Paris, The Perverts starring Pee-Pee Peenuts, Little Annie Rooney and the Horns, The Thieves featuring Jeanie the Weenie, Forge and the Family Jules, No-No Dog and the Tooth Fairies, Chuckie Inferno and the Rambelles, Bo Stompo and the Dawn Paroles, The Louse Band with Dizzy Izzy, Carrot Redd and the Four Foxes, Alan Robb and the Sex Thrills, The Jews starring Jaws Labasman, Sy Monclo and the Ass Rutters, The Artomatics featuring "Toutes" Tony, Jerry the Patsy and the Physics, Geechee Golden-Famous Nathan and the Five Fruits, Bo-Bo Blue with the Egg Whites, Angie Comique and the Afriques, an' Murph Watt and the Mugs from Malone.

And to keep up their strength? Intelligence has percolated down anent the victuals most desired by these folk to keep them cooking. The favorites were, hands down, beet gumbo, jambalaya à la okra, redbeans and schloque, rice-a-guini, shrimp mephisto, crawfish and crapmeat, black redfish, gin fizztula, pernod-persi, pralines au feu, and catfish chasseur.

Though numbed by your retailing of these grand old tunes by the grand old greats, Blue modestly opined, what of the new persons, the younger turks, the advanced guard, the, how you say? punkish-newish wave? I think of some heavy sounds as thus mayhap Red Club by Fat Stick, Royal Fuck by Seizer Blue, Heebie's Jeebies by Jaws Jews, Song of the Keyhole by Jon Voyeur, Congola by Kaymoo and the Stompers, In the Royal Garden by Trojan Paris, Panama Rag by the Feminappes, Creole Buboes by the Four Foxes, Zoot Loot by Tony Toutes, Blueballed by the Nutz, Eggwhite Blues by Batts Bataille, Beaucoup Paroles by Artvision, Git Down by "Licks" Coña, Farewell to Story by Bobbi Mahu, Tsorry, Tsar by the Nagasaki Nonet, Society High by Coky Jack, Astonish Me! by the Mellow Hypnotics, Shave It, Pretty Mama by Peanuts Pervert, Lousy Ditch by Ducks-Ass Sttrange, Bar-B-Q Slut by the Teen Fucks, Panama Hot by Big Mama Twot, So Long Shinetown by Blacki Blu, Winding Ploy by Malone Molloy, Savoix Bleues by Claude Flandres, Dogtooth Barks by Dan DeLion, Ray's Blues by the Flowerblowers, Hog Stomp by "Killer" Watt, Royal Pardon Shuffle by Roi Rex Renard, House of Blue Tights by Jean Velour, Clair de Nuttes by Mama Blewe, Eh, la Buck? by Dr. Huler, Makin' Rain by Louie Pluie, and Congageechee by Pajarry Rubu.

Though maybe weird and replete with noisy cacophones, the best of this music is lovely as the best of Nature, gawjus as Spanish moss, live oke, furious magnolia, jazzmin, alligator poppy, pelican pussy, swamp vetch, blue-eye ringtail, blackthorn water sprite, weeping tear, and the blooming elmwillow.

Non! We are not how you say, stuff-fee, Monsieur Bleu, mais . . . the mos' perfect examples of the pride of Nawlins is to be foun' in the discs classique. Right on, frog-bro! Soitin tunes bees played that show the heart o' the good sounds. Shall we enumerate, amee, for this lonesome yankee wanderer? Oui! Ze discography outstanding is this: Limehouse Blues by Murph Malone and the Kilowatts, Yaaka Hula Hickey Dula by Camoo with the African Stompers, Creole Song by Go-Go "Blue" Bataille, Savoy Blues by Nathan Sarraute and his Golden Fruit Geechee Band, Bill Bailey Won't You Please Come Home by Pat Jarry, Creole Bo Bo by Tony Arto with the Visionaries, Farewell to Storyville by Clo Simon and the Grasscutters, Eh, Là Bas by "Jaws" Hysman and the Git-Down Band, Bucket Got a Hole in It by Al Robby Grillay with the Good Lookers, King Porter Stomp by Red Renard and the Fourteen Carats, I Ain't Got Nobody by Izzy Ducasse, Winin' Boy Blues by "Bo" Delay with the Dawn-Light Stompers, Nagasaki by Rambo Charlie and the Hell Raisers, The Sheik of Araby by Ray Queneau and the Dogtooth Serenaders, Royal Garden Blues by Big Julie Laforge, Panama by Jenny Voleur, Storyville Blues by "Mellow" Rooney Char and his Hypnotic Horn, Back o' Town Blues by Peanuts Prévert, Baby Won't You

Please Come Home by The Inquisitors starring Bobi Pinget, Heebie Jeebies by Sad Sam Zara with the Realists, High Society by Cocky Jack and the Astonishers, Swing That Music by Johnny Giono and the Blue Boys, Chinatown My Chinatown by Luigi Celino and the Noodle Band, Save It Pretty Mama by Cheech Mauriac with the Femmes Fatales, Struttin' With Some Barbecue by Booker Césaire, Black and Blue by Zoot Roussel and the African Alligators, Tiger Rag by Valéry Conga, Rockin' Chair by Fats Gide with the Baton Rouge Boys, St. Louis Blues by Mickey Butor and the Time Passers, Muskrat Ramble by Jimbo Verlaine's Rainmakers, Mahogany Hall Stomp by the Compote-Marmalade Band featuring Licks Mambeau, Dippermouth Blues by Pops Ennui and the Crawdaddies, and Clarinet Marmalade by St. Clair de Lune and his Jambalaya Jambos.

« 49 »

Slightly Crestfallen, They Leave Nawlins, Slightly Crushed

Do you dig why my large and unassuming face is crestfallen? Serge spoke at last.

There was what seemed a nod of assent from his spouse acrost the haze of fatuous sunbeams.

I have toted up and calc'lated that the Magic Phrase I seek is probly buried in those songs just seriously discussed, but that to ferret—what a cute little word that is—to ferret it from out this mass of music would take a lifetime, even without taking into account the various mathematical combinations and permanations possible, what come to, as I reckon, something like a couple trillion. Thus do mortals ever slide from sundrenched peaks into a lake of liquid shit! Woe.

But stay your gushing eyes, my conifer! the good dame cried. Let us rest while ever wending on, and chunk upon the old pianner here, that gives you always and anon a surcease from your wonted bouts with snots and tears.

And so he did: and there, in poiple shade and to the shy and hidden audience of forest folk, our Blue composed this song, mysterious and haunting, to which the music is forever lost to us and all our as yet unborn descendants.

And yet, despite all, the welkin rang afar! And there was not an alligator in the sludgy bayou who slept that day!

Nor a cottonmouth moccasin.

Nor yet a garter belt waterback.

And to this day, Uncle Rebus tells of the tulip bulbs that leaped wildly from the omnipresent scum! And of those that leapt!

230

«50»

Blue Writes a
Mysterious and Haunting Song

I wandered lonely as a cloud,
O thou! whose fancies from afar are brought;
I was a Traveller then upon the moor,
I heard a thousand blended notes
Under yon orchard, in yon humble cot
With unrejoicing berries—ghostly Shapes
"And groans that rage of racking famine spoke!"

"Art thou a man of purple cheer?"
(The old Man still stood talking at my side);
"If from the public way you turn your steps
You live, Sir, in these dales, a quiet life."
Himself he propped, limbs, body, and pale face,
To gather leeches, being old and poor.
Grave thoughts ruled wide on that sweet day!

"High is our calling, Friend!—Creative Art!
Enough of sorrow, wreck and blight."
And now we reached the orchard-plot,
A gentle answer did the old man make:
"Why bleat so after me? Why pull so at thy chain?
Nay, Traveller! rest. This lonely Yew-tree stands!"
Here Michael ceased, and to the fields went forth.

Lost on the aerial heights of the Crusades,
A cart and horse beside the rivulet stood;
As I from Hawes to Richmond did repair,
Where silent zephyrs sported with the dust!

Jones! As from Calais southward you and I
Should to the breast of Nature have gone back;
A happier fortune than to wither here!

Whether the whistling Rustic tend his plough,
A white-robed Negro, like a lady gay
Remained imperishably interwoven
With heavy tufts of moss that strive.
(I was thy neighbor once, thou rugged Pile!)
When up the hills, as now, retreats the light
I'll think of the Leech-gatherer on the lonely moor!

Envoi

    A white-robed Negro sported with the dust;
    With unrejoicing berries reached the orchard plot
    To gather leeches. And to the fields went forth!

« 51 »
Secrets of Tej-Mej

Then, loping, scudding, complemented by clouds of dust, they moseyed. Belike unto those critters men call dogies, hoided with a ready laugh and macho jest by swart vacqueros, they scuffed. Through live-oak stands adrape with Spanish moss, palmetto shrubs bedizened with the juicy berry Indians make into marmalade, past mesquite and loco weed, multicolored tumbleweed, the mescal and agave, the shrinking bluebell, cacti, nicotine, chilimac, and sawleaf sago bush, they plugged and sashayed on, deeper, ever deeper, into the heart of Téjas!

Helene allowed that she was plumb wore out, her voice like clouds of gingham in the dry-goods store.

Blue reckoned so but squinted through his sweat. Somewhere out there was laconic truth and he could almost hear it quivering with homely drawl!

Some few days later, they chatted by the old arroyo with their new-found friend, while tortillas and the hearty pinto bean refreshed them, yes, once again.

I declare, said Helene, I'd rather et them pintos then read up agin in *Herzog's Planet*! Sich is their holt on my affections. And with this she wolfed another hefty morsel down.

Por Dios! said their new-found friend, José Cizaña-Hueso, a swarthy chum who'd taken them beneath his "wing" one sultry day while our adventurers bewailed their lack of chuck. And again, Por Dios! uttered he, sopping up some bean juice with a crusty bit of habichuela. His face showed that it was powerful good.

I'm deeply obleeged to you, Mex friend, Blue grinned. It's mighty strange to meet a feller willing to share his spread and vittles out here in . . . God's Country! And his sweeping hand took in with mighty zest the purple sage that brooded just beyant the leaping firelight. And to think that folks call you hombres "greasers." Makes muh blood boil up like egg nog!

Caramba! said Cizaña-Hueso. The hands, they will be locked together in eternal friendship, sí? And with this his Meskin laugh like to bust the old serape that he wore. But you were, how you say in the inglés, hablando . . . ? Spikking!

Yes, old hoss, I *was* spikking till your calloused hands filled up muh mouth with beans and these funny little flapjacks.

Bueno! But, ahora, gringo buddy, let's lean back on the mesa here beneath the estrellitas so far away and muy mysterious, and smoke and have a talk. Your wife sleeps the deep sleep of the bean.

Podner, that is jake with me, said Blue, and with this he heaved his frame out flat like a tuckered-out paint. I was a-telling you about my long hard search, I recollect.

But yes! the plucky amigo said. My face is all ears to listen. Sombrero blanco! how I like much the good yarn, and with this he lit his faithful cigarrillo.

When Serge had once agin his tale of woeful quest retailed, the silence that collapsed upon the little camp amid the dappled firkey and the moccasin toboggan seemed to fill our compañeros with ineffable regret. But not for long! For brave hearts pounding leather on the trail the thorns of life are but mere bagatelles, if not mere varmints to be roped and crippled up for all eternity! Thus, in the midst of throbbing quiet cracked a chink by snapping faggots, the dark-hued Mex spoke through the flames.

Mi amigo, it is the fortune of your luck that we meet as we done this afternoon, while the sun turned cactus to potato chips, and the gila monster cooled off in his hole. Sí, Great Dios, my son, so arranged it that on the fateful day you humped through this vast land of mighty Téjas, I was on my way to J.C. Penney to buy a new pairs of huarache. It was a kind of fate, sí, brother to the sort that oft befell Jeff Chandler in the moving-films I used to watch in my little humble village out there where the sun sets each evening in a riot of the fetching colors.

Helene quivered once and then lay still, while a busy coon impaled some luckless critters on an appaloosa barb. What dreams were theirs? Or hers?

Yes, Mr. Cessnaywo, it was a flash of wildest luck we chanced upon you! In but a score of miles or so, we would have been within the vapid purlieus of Killeen, from which, I've heard, no traveler returns.

At mention of that dreaded name, the wind soughed choughingly, and luffed, the firelight burst up in embers amber . . . yet darkness flung its inky robe as well!

Ay chingada! rumbled Don Cizaña-Hueso. Pero . . . is no what I mean. My pleasure is it to share my lowly bins and gnarled tortillas with you and your familia. What I mean is that I think that I have the ancient Aztec power to give you the vison of your gale, bueno?

My . . . gale? Serge queried o'er his coffee can.

Sí, the gale, the how you say, the place you wish to end up with in?

My goal?

Harr, harr, harrñh! the great-hearted hacienda laughed. The Engliss, she is

234

not so well, sí? But yes, I have the power, the secret known to but a few handfuls of the Meskin people. How you think, mi amigo, we got rid of this . . . Téjas? Hah? The magic powers makes us lose the Alamo! Sí! We fix the stupid gringos to think we lost! For many years the wise men of the Méjico think and pray, they make the Bean Dance, the Sacrifice of the Frito, the Margarita Ceremony, the goats, he is sacrifice to Mezcál, "He-Who-Makes-You-Fall-In-The-Dust." You goggle? But sí, I swear it on my father's bandolero! Still, the old ones cannot how you say? dope out how to make the blue-eyes take this place! We have been bad crazy with this, comprende? Houston, Dallas, Amarillo, imagine owning this basura! Waco! Caramba! Galveston! Ay chihuahua! Fort Worth! Madre de Dios! So the Aztec powers speak to us from the clouds one day, and say: "Why you no make the battle and . . . *lose?* The joy, amigo, spreads through the tierra like wild's fire, sí! We have the fiesta for nine years. Then we make the war and run away pronto. And now, the poor fucking gringos have this place. Is good trick, no?

As Two-Pairs Slim opened wide his dust-rimmed eyes when Marshal Judah Maim thrown hot lead into both his arns fore Slim could spit "Yew air a yeller-belly," so did Blue stare through the red-clay dust that fell upon the camp as thick as the drawl of the Mexicali Kid.

Yew mean, Blue faltered, yew kin tell me where I'll find . . . the Phrase?

Pero sí, hombre! And the great roar of laughter that tore from the caballero's throat was loud enough to flatten any billygoats or polecats that were foolish enough or reckless enough to be hiding in the shadowy pulque gulch.

El secreto of the Aztec power, caballo viejo, the lynx-eyed buddy said, is to the mankind give through the chili! Sí, the chili! I am on a level with you when I speak this. But it must be the true chili of the parched lands there, beyond the broody hills on which the sun creeps down.

B-but, chili, swell samaritan? I dang can't reckon sich!

Listen well, my good relleno. And with this, the campesino's voice dropped and quivered lower than the soles of his ole boots, what he called "Old Friends."

I am cottoning to your palaver, Serge spat—and how the campfire leaped into the air in a passel of sparks and glowing coals, sumpn like authors on a talk show if they wuz hopping like a branded dogie whilst waving sparklers on the Fourth of July like freckled boys in the streets of that hometown that will come no more since it already wuz.

The secret Aztec powers from the clouds come out to the hombre which the mind of whom is making the *visions*. And the visions arrive and stay there from the chili. Comprende? And the great secret is this: all Meskin cooseen *is* chili! Comprende? Even the beer he is chili! Even the horses, sí! Even the chickens is made from the chili! You savvy up the country called the "Chile"? That is also made from the chili, yes, many suns ago the Aztec gods decide to see if is possible and they build up this place all from the chili.

Serge sat banjo-eyed, the blank look of a lawyer sifting acrost his tragic face, his lips chewing each other, or others, and he bit them together at the same time. Somewhere in the inky night, a critter howled. Or was it . . . a varmint?

But as I was have been telling, compadre, he must be the true chili, how the old abuelitas call this "chili verdadero," when she is banging and fisting up corn meals in the pueblos that time had a hunch to forget about. And on my old Tío Nacho's head, I give to you this present.

Blue frittered his old pencil thoughtfully, a scrap of foolscap smoothed flat on the worn denim that spoke volumes, at least two. I'm waiting on yuh, Mr. Cizznoosa. And wait he did, while lightning forked tuh hidden draws! How often it forks out here in the empty vastness! Or out *there*!

I give you the two recipes, as hand down from the time when Tenochtitlán is but a two-roads crossing with the filling station and the bar-b-q. Is many other ways of making of this, but this two is O.K. for the regular jobs. First is the carne asada con petróleo and goes: Whomp and mash severely the hands full each of the anchos, guajillos, serranos, and piquins. Slap in the small ladles full up of the oozing tostadas. Smash to bits and throw on top of steaming guacamole. Put every things in the clay pot. Put this under the collapsed adobe dust for ten days. The pot she is then pulled out and the peyote roots of Durango is added. The pot she is placed in a fire of dried frijóles and cooked. As the jugo boils off, maízes are entered in the sludgeness and when the stuff is too much of thick, a small goat goes in, completo. Then the quart of oil from the crankcase of the good padre is sloshed into everything and as she all starts to bubble up, she is ready for eating up with the maguey beans and chocolate rabbits. O.K.? The other instruction is this ones: is call marimbas verdes con gusano. In the clay pot fill up with simmering tequila, is throw a few old papá worms. Then goes in the chilies de árbol, the poblanos, the petines, the jalapeños. If is tomatoes, plomp in. If no these, plomp in a fish's face. When is all boiling merry and bueno, hands full of each these put in: bucktooth sage, persimmon thorns, eleemosynia, frito sacks. Pull off from the blaze, dot the top with pineapple hunks, marshmallitos, crumpled up cream cheese, and last a jug of maple syrup. Put in sun to give nice glazing, and eat with avocados marrónes and rock-salt kisses.

Quick and pronto as the star of a Western saga cashing his check in order to buy genuine oil paintings and Baudelaire's *Oeuvres Completes*, Blue sashayed into the surrounding bindlestiff, not caring a hoot for its cruel barbs. For what seemed like a long time there was nothing to be heard but the banshee wind roiling the pedernales clumps and the sound of a savage puerco's low chuckles. Then his gaunt frame loomed in the leaping firelight, his arms full up with all the goshdarn tarnation supplies that the dish required. Or maybe dishes. It was mighty hard to tell in the pekoolyar light that lit up the brooding land. And with the foolhardy help of his newfound pal, he soon had a pot just a-bubblin and a-steamin on the, so to speak, hob.

For what seemed an eternity, Blue pottered about the festering chili, worried as a schoolmarm whose shapely ankle has been glimpsed by a sweaty wrangler. And at last, as sure as the desk clerk in the Palace Hotel is a nance dressed up like a dude, the chili was ready!

And now, Cezaña-Hueso urged, is time for you, my son, to slop up this comestibles, to let your spirit be one with the spirits of the snake of the shaking feathers, Tomatlxusl, "The-One-Who-Puts-Grit-In-The-Eye," and hear his prophecy. And with this the humble spick gave Serge an abrazo like to bust his ribs.

Blue slopped chuck inter his tin plate and et, his eyes fixed on the moon that moved across the sky like a white cayuse. Then, jingo! iffen his eyeballs didn't up and roll back inter his head while his face took on the vacant, and powerful afeared look of a Nebraskan served a platter of scungilli. The voice boomed in his ears like the boom of bull buffalo fallin in the crick.

"Therefore are they counted the most pestilent, troublesome, and guileful spirits that are; for by the help of Alrynach, a spirit of the West, they will raise storms, cause earthquakes, whirlwinds, rain, hail, or snow in the clearest day that is; and if ever they appear to any man, they come in women's apparel. The spirits of the air will mix themselves with thunder and lightning, and so infect the clime where they raise any tempest, that suddenly great mortality shall ensue to the inhabitants from the infectious vapours which arise from their motions."

Then, fast as an outhouse falls down in a big blow, the voice vamoosed! And Blue returned from that land where time forgot to be itself and space was light in that eternal calm!

I am plumb puzzled up, Mr. Cissysono, he pleaded. And told the brooding breed the strange and shadowed words that fell upon him from the clouds . . . or what had *seemed to be* the clouds! I don't reckon I can calc'late or figger it, he bitched. It's too durned deep and sich. Whut do it have to say about a *place*? I reckon that I made the chili wrong, like a danged tenderfoot who jacks off in a batch of poison ivy.

Is not so, my Anglo bunkie, said the smiling bombazine. Is claro! Claro! The

Great One, the reptile with the chicken plumes, tell you the place, sí! And is so-lamente one place can it be! Mamacita! Think, hombre, think! What place is can be this?

I don't know! I d-don't know! Blue quavered, his manly face at last falling down toward his neckerchief. T-tell me?

Hña, hña, hña! rang the pistolero's mirth. Is . . . CALIFORNIA!

« 52 »

A New
Lease, or Is It Leash,
on Life for the Gavottes

How meet, Blue said, and hiply groovy that we bumped into this dusky vaquerito with his cutesy chaps and sagging bandoleros! A small lump packed with salty tears rises inter muh throat as I watch him ride away in a cloud of red Texas dust across the timeless llano beds and gurgling arroyos! How swell that now we know, beyond any shadow of a doubt, which way to go and maybe even how to get there. But straight, or maybe strait, will be the way! What say you, trembling sloven?

But Helene's emotions were so near the surface that, like Iago, she shut her yap, like unto the lonely bivalve on a wind-whipped strand.

Enough said! Blue yawped in virile splendor. I too know the sweet pain you feel, and will confess, although we are not getting along too well in the sexual-satisfaction department, that I am all empathy and a yard wide. Man does not live by head alone!

Like hairy, heavy-hearted, huge-hipped Hecuba, Helene crumpled in a heap.

Here, here, her mate said, enough of that! We must be strong and start right out for the Golden Land thus and such indicated by our greaser pal. Let me help you from this heap into which you've crumpled, for this is the type of heap found on the silent Téjas pampas that can give you a bad rash. And with this, he pulled her from the grasping nettles, nettles that had appeared as if alive by magic!

It is our task now to point the nose of this pushcart toward our goal, and now that we know what it is, the pushing will be as naught. So scramble up there 'neath the canopy and I will heave and grunt us forward.

She scrambled thus. And Blue began to roll the old scarred buddy of a cart toward what turned out sooner to be Oklahoma, thus adding a few miles to the journey but since it did not matter, it did not matter. Blue's itinerary, traced on a map, would look like a diagram out of *Tristram Shandy*, but he did not know that, and thank God for small favors. Some things are not meant for everyone.

Fuck you! Blue said, and creaked to rest beneath a ginseng vine in flower just over the state line. It appears that he was addressing "me."

There they dozed after a coupla humble jujubes, for their provender was low. The violent sun sank slowly and the breeze rose faintly as a fairy's voice, in thus wise: whithk! whooth! Then with the rising of the moon rose Blue, and softly, quietly, yet passionately as St. Theresa in what one wag has called "her wild lament," he woke Helene, who was twitching away to beat the band, as always, a symptom of the vestigial unhappiness left over from four years of sensible shoes during her high school idyll.

She woke, her eyeballs bugged out her haid, as did once Guinevere one rosy morn as doughty Arthur nicked her queenly ass with great Excalibur!

Somewhere in the morning mist, the nettles sighed.

Somewhere, a hatchbald fell from out his eyrie with a thud.

Somewhere, an old prospector scratched and yawned as the coffee boiled; or boiled over.

As in a dream, like Chaucer knowed, Blue said, I saw the element that sits at the very center of our lives!

Whut? Helene said, scratching and yawning, then climbing down to watch the coffee boil.

The center! The core and matrix! The worm in the center of the apple! That thing what has been all things and the like to us, my yolk! It is not Doc Chick, the wise wop, nor the dazzling Glubits, giants of Georgetowr! Nor not Tom Piper, the shitfaced rustick lad, nor Big Boog Vinch and Doc Piscardi, rubes in spades, not the mournful numbers of the Dixie crooner, Blackie Bob Hunko! No! And don't mention the old snot, the rural repairer, nay! And as for those academic assholes, Bone, Poncho, and Dubuque, may Almighty God take away their office nameplates! Miz Grable, glassy-eyed with vile erotics? No help. The prurient priest, D. Debris, wuz a bum steer, no pun intended, he just raised me up a un-requited hard-on, and as for that cynosure of mystery, Cheechee Docque, he came and went like unto a fata morgana of the bresh. Big Black was an unfortu-nate mistake and a digressive episode, reet? And the Nawlins hipsters, Jimson and l'Amour gave little help, as well you know. And while I grant you that the grinning Mex, Cizaña-Hueso, has set us on the righteous path, no lie, still, what is it that without which we would not have been able to arrive at even this point, so to speak, in our quest that is not done but in which we doggedly entrain through heat and rain and elements of other climes? What?

Helene looked up from the bubbling chuck. So to speak. Make that "chuck."

The . . . cart! This! This faithful . . . cart! A great sob tore from out his bulging throat. And never have I paid thee, old clotted vehicle, the merest heed. And with that, he stood up to his full height, as against the various parcels and fragments, as well as figments, of height to which, or of which, or about which, he usually stood, and began to chant into the brightening air:

« 53 »

The Panegyric
on the Faithful Cart

Thou ain't, O humble cart, too much to see,
For many, thou art not their cup of tea,
Thy wood is wormy, splintered, and decayed
And also full of rot, I am afraid;
Keen shards of pine stick in thy riders' ass
And tear and puncture flesh of ev'ry class;
And some, of thee, have spake unkind, to wit:
That thou art but a rolling piece of shit.
Yet cart, from old New York you've schlepped along
With always (on thy lumber lips) a song;
A song, say I? By jeez, a symphony!
Chocked full of moves and tones and harmony,
Plus andante rondos and viola
And like other stuff in talk ginzola.
Thou stand'st, an Ancient Pile, there in the void,
Though vicious tongues dub thee Old Hemorrhoid;
To these dull wags my sacch'rine dame and me
Do murmur, ever and anon, "Fuck thee,"
Those two words thrumming like two drunken harps
Or like the noivous gills of fat old carps;
Yea, fat old carps that hang around in flocks
Like herds of gentle, ruminating lox.
But I digress (like early cherries hight,
Or later plums that shine all through the night).
Thou humble cart! thou'rt kind of like a fruit,
And plain and homely, like a Crawford suit;
As with that lowly garment, when folk see
Thee coming down the street they 'gin to flee.

As far as I'm concerned (as Mankind knows),
These churls can stick their ideas up their nose!
To me, O cart, thou art a big-faced pike
Of popping eyes; or else belike a shrike
Which is some kind of fucking bug, I ween;
Or thou'rt a poiple pheasant, with a sheen
That glisters like a worm, or woolly peach,
Or like a oily bather on the beach.
I thought to name you Cobra, like the king
Thou art or wert! or will be in the spring.
For spring, like ladies in the throes of lust,
Is coming! Why? Ha! Ha! Because it must!
Forswonk eftsoones do I speak of the time
When lads and lasses fall to hump? To rhyme.
Yet this does not besmirch my lofty praise
Of thee, my oddball wagon, and your ways.
Like coney shy you bump through lettuce groves
And fields of nodding carrots; all which proves
Thy skill and courage; for those crazy fruits
Will gladly savage trespassing galoots.
Do not the rural belfries sadly toll
Of hapless louts chomped up by escarole?
Do not the passing bells tell of the grief
That slav'ring carrots cause in ev'ry fief?
Yet, pushcart, though thou have no roof of gold,
Nor silver hubcaps, your great mind is bold;
And 'spite your brav'ry, thou art also kind.
How many nights thou shelter from the wind
(That fiercely blows from Santa's cold domain)
Helene's bald head, as well as her small brain;
You guard from frozen blast her teeny tits
And her bare ass; upon whose globes my mitts
Play manly music when we friendly screw:
At sunrise pink, you shield her from the dew.
Thou seem'st at times to me a shepherd's cake
Bedight with chawklit fudge; and that is jake
With me! And sometimes seem a stinking cheese
Like limburger, what brings men to their knees;
Sometimes a capon, sometimes a duckie,

Or nutty ale, or quince; or the plucky
Fig that weirdly smiles into the pumpkin
Patch like some fantastic eerie bumpkin.
And in the thin and loathsome light of dawn
Resemblest thou, at times, a shambling gawm;
But one with heart as big as all outdoors!
(And golden too, just like the hearts of whores.)
My eyes drop tears as fast as sailors fuck
When I do think upon the times I've stuck
My giant brogans roughly up your gool
To urge you from a noisome swamp, or pool;
Yet uncomplainingly, out of the slop
(With heaves and shudders, and a little pop!)
You've rolled onto the dry land and the grass.
Permit me, in my shame, to kick my ass!
Like slimy eels, you slither through the tares
As do the deadbeats who, t'avoid the fares
On New York's rotting subway system, leap
The turnstiles; or else underneath them creep.
The sun doth make thee glow like blushing bride
When from her horny husband she can hide
No longer; then falls he into a trance
Whose spell is broken when she rends his pants!
The ass-wise shape of thee that makes the gorge
To rise, O cart! is from black Vulcan's forge
(That jealous gimp who in his airy net
His wife and Mars trapped in their am'rous sweat).
The stinking mud and muck caked on thy frame
Are badges of thine ever-growing fame;
And rubes fall on their knobby knees to pray
As you go creaking on your honest way.
For all these things, O pushcart, stout and true,
I holler to the welkin praise of you;
Thou art, 'bove all, a modest heap, all pluck,
And name I all who quarrel with thee: Schmuck.

« 54 »

Captain Basura
Appears, Makes a Curious
Offer, Is Rejected, and Threatens

Sing and holler loud and crisp in military manner, O sacred Thalia, of the officer, the capitano, infantry, one Dirk Basura, who all the while that Blue did send his virile voice unto the scudding clouds, did lurk within the narrow confines of a copse of fatback peony, all eyes and ears! Sing of his valiant cunt cap and his wrinkled pinks! Sing of the .45 that slapped his thigh, of his mirrored sunglasses, sing especiallyof his Good Conduct Medal, glowing in the dappled shade and sunny motes that lunged and darted like the crested snatchhatcher zooming down upon the hedges and their unsuspecting worms and midges and their juicy ladybugs or errant cucarachas! Such is Nature ever wonted wert!

Sing of the Idea that showed itself within his piercing eyes, so that they danced like worn-out ballerinas! Sing of their plys and interchats and all the other goddam things they do upon their fairy feets! Sing of the sudden greed that shook his frame like that of potent grizzly ripping ope a camper's lunch! O sing! And sing and sing until Cimmerian night falls down around your ears as suddenly as twisters send mobile homes careering through the peaceful glades of lo! the rocky deeps and vasts of homely shopping malls! Yes, sing your brazen neck off! Sing out as counterman doth yell for a blt with mayo down!

Close-nipped within the bresh like unto the naked Greek who lusting watched a bunch of teen-age girls playing with a beach ball, the stern Basura felt his gaze drawn ever and anonce unto the pushcart, now dawdling in the shade. His manly whistle trembled on its chain, his powerful yet girlish hands squeezed the scarred and battered clipboard to which was fastened the secrets of the morning report, his feet plunked back and forth in the sifting dust, yet his shoes moved not!

Then as Blue's enormous gout of rhyming couplets died away as quietly as flavor from a stick of Juicy Fruit, the officer bestirred himself, and gripping close his courage, already all screwed up, crashed he through the trembling vetch and the clinging thorns of phony dickwort, and appeared within the clearing smartly, the kind of man this Nation sorely needs to fight and lead his troops in wild retreat!

The very wind stopped soughing or sloughing through the trees, and sloughed off into a nearby slough. There it scumbled with a brace of perch. Resplendent stood the proud son of the Point. Blue and the svelte Helene gaped though the sunny motes already mentioned, maybe more than once.

Art thou, Blue breathed, a sprite or satyr of the elfin boles and sappy limbs that dip and shake within this wild enchanted place? Or else a djinn from out a empty bottle that once housed a pint of Dixie Belle? Art thou wast but a phantasm hight beyant the very ignis fatuus that slumps past rotting stands of sorrel led by sorcerers like Morgana le Fay or oily Mandrake? Stand, holt, and speak in tongue belike unto a mortal man else avaunt my heart past these my popping eyes that start like gumballs from a sea of frigid sweat!

Me too! the agued wife ensued, for like her mate, she was all shitless scared.

Calm your fears, beloved yardbirds, said the officer. I am but Captain Dirk Basura, U.S. Army, Infantry, entrusted here for a certain time to walk this dusty land with clipboard, ballpoint pen, and low-slung automatic. I come—and with this he flung his weatherbeaten hand toward a beetling scarp—from trig Fort Swill that squats beyond that yonder scarp now beetling in the sun.

Then you are not a sprite or satyr, nor a djinn or phantasm of the ensorceled forest, but just a fucking soldier? Blue said, his cold sweat drying instanter.

But yes, sweet honcho, said the warrior. I beg you calm your fears, stand tall, get straight, shape up, fall in, and be at ease. I have been lurking there in distant bush, enchanted and quite pleased with the wondrous poem that you've just bawled out. And even more enchanted by its object, that little item so fulsomely apostrophized, your cart!

My . . . cart? said Blue. And why is that? What use is such a simple thing to the military might of the outfit what you serve, up to its ribbons in injuns of war?

We call them "engines," smiled the gentleman.

Whatever thus, said Blue. But what, brave captain, shakes?

As a military man, officer, and stupendous gent, whether in pinks, suntans, greens, or, as the French might put it, fatigués, as well as having been a purchasing agent in real life, I am prepared and authorized by the post commander of Fort Swill, to make you an offer for that remarkable cart, of which and to whom, and anent, you just wove a moving apostrophe—or is it comma? No matter. The Army has need for such a cart to serve as a prototype, a model, a paradigm, for a new kinda APC, which is, in the parley of citizens like youse, an armored personal cart. The Army has told me that I may offer the following items, most brand new, others slightly used by previous owners, every person jack of them a gentle soul awake only on Sundays and then but for a chitch of an hour or two.

I can offer you a fuckin' A, a red deuce, Patton's penis, Texas clover, the Chicago Five, a Jewish star, the stairway to Europe, a propellor specially chosen to be frozen, a black bullseye, an eagle and a griffin, a heavenly pentagon as well as a heavenly octagon, the big X, a triangular triangle, a true compass, the flying dragon, a tomahawk, the heart on the leave, the big natural, a Indian what got his ass handed to him at the pass, firmamental stripes, a big red one, wittle gween weaves, a diamond rouge et a rouge étoile, the smacked hourglass, duh flying 8, a patriotic posy, crossed swords, onze wit wings, the claw, miracle stars who don't know who they ares, a palm leaf or sumpn, unlucky lightning, dee why, the krimson keystone, yin with yang, a red dogie sconce all bones, Cathlick yout', the triangle D, a California sunburst, a Broadway rainbow, a moping maple leaf, the mailed fist, a Viking chapeau, a goldpanner, the raunchy rattler, seventy-one sergeants, a buncha all-Americans, the eagle what screams, a golden acorn, a hovering hatchet, lucky lightning, pine trees on parade, Injun Joe, a century, the big bear, the grounded griffin, hell's hatchet, a snarling panther and a brooding bison, a funny French hat, the lugubrious lion, a woodsplitter, a sword on fire, Miz Liberty, a free French cross, a weird critter, a yella bombsight, the puritanical Pilgrim with plunderpuss, a ticklish trident, old ironsides, hell on wheels, a spearhead, the Empire of Dust, Dixie volunteers, a pointy-headed grizzly, the Hondo Hurricane, lonely stars of Lubbock, bue jerseys, a busted black horse, a fleur-de-lis thass always ready, brave rifles, follow-me fools and fuckups, Sir Therwas: knight, an excited monstre, Dixie crackers, a thunderbird buck and wing, the floating sword, two lucifers, un cartridge rojo, special thunderbolts, twenty-nine mountains, a ghastly galleon, the Black diamond, Franklin's phiz, a chuting fall, Prez de deux, Señor Conquistador Consombrero, a hollering cock, a tawch, the jumping dragon, a chickenshit bushmaster, Pershing's prick, some scarwafs, cadooses of all kinds, any truck with anything, lotsa logs, intimate support systems, divers commandos like, fighting blue star devils, sundry shapes, Kay Mags, rotten seas, MacVees with MonSoons, airborne ovals, and brassard bombs.

The mighty warrior ground to a sickening halt, his eyes clean misted o'er with tears as the full import of the divers items he had offered came, as they say, "home" to him. He glanced at Blue, a slow smile slowly spreading across his face, or, at any rate, the lower portion of it, as he smiled that smile that was wont to set the world's old weary heart on the bumpy road to coronary occlusion!

What do you say? Basura beamed. These goods can be delivered to you at any address you would wish and/or desire. F.O.B., packing list enclosed, all suitable for framing, designed to brighten up the little woman's kitchen, or function as conversation pieces when close friends dash over for a night of TV, book-chat, and smutty jokes. Where shall I send the shit? And, with this, the flower of the infantry followed his outthrust jaw toward the cart that dozed in the sunny motes—come back at last!

Odd corrugations furrowed Serge's brow as his thoughts sprang into turmoil. They trudged about behind the piercing eyes that had seen so much since that day, so many many years ago, or maybe months ago, that they, and the head and body that was host to them, left the office of Doctor Ciccarelli. The items pleased and tempted him like a glass of beer doth make the small *Drosophila* do loop the loops in mad abandon! Yet . . . yet . . .

No! he yelped. I cannot, sir, give o'er the cart to you or to the U.S. Army. It has been steadfast pal, kind mom, strong poppa, helpmeet, schlepper, hearth and home, repository of our hopes and dreams, and also waxes redolent of memories of Zimmerman, lost somewhere in the stalactites of red clay and petraceous shale slabs and the like.

Zimmerman? the hoplite mused.

My chee-ild! hawked Miz Gavotte, and fell where she sat like a stone. My chee-ild! what we abandoned by mistake somewhere back down the lonesome road amid the vast space of weird America's somber razorbacks or sumpn!

The captain's silver bars darkened for a moment and his sunglasses flashed fiery red in the glade's pitiless light. A fly buzzed, intensifying the silence as buzzing flies are wont to do. You mean, Basura said, his voice pitched soft with fury, you will *not* relinquish this cart, even though your country needs it to keep the barb'rous hordes away from the sacred profit motive and the flabby macho cunts who help to keep us great?

Although my heart is as heavy as that of the schmuck in yon old tale who never was allowed to put his foot on Coney's shores, or eat a plastic pizza in the nodding fields of Iowa's great shopping malls, I . . . I . . . must say no.

Then, subversive mockie, roared the legionnaire, you'd best, as swift as vague Rotarian or dumbo Elk doth swallow beers when unleashed upon the streets of unsuspecting cities sans the wife, pack up your shitty gear, attach and lash that faggot instrument, and make tracks for the state that lies due west of here; for you are not welcome in this here neighborhood.

Immejiately? quailed Gavotte, the firelight leaping on his face, then bounding off to run mad amid the bulfinches that lay sedulously clumped about.

If your ass is not from out this military reservation by the dawn, Basura snapped waspishly as Genghis Khan when served his egg foo yung luke warm, I'll call in on youse and all your tawdry, pitiful belongings an air strike machined to make of youse believers, dead or otherwise! And about the blowing up of pushcarts, the USAF admits no fucking peer! Indeed, I wisht youse had a ox or twain, for turning them to hamburger is the speciality of the vacant small-town lads who zoom and dip and roar around without surcease, to keep these skies forever strong and free, as well as ope and chockablock with boundless opportunity! And with that, the cap strode off into the sedge in clouds of perspiration and the twangling of creaking leather and tobacco!

The Gavottes, as you will have by now surmised, fled in fear and panic yet again. So continueth our adventure.

"Our"?

« 55 »

"La Musique
et les mauvaises
herbes," Continued

XIII A REALLY NICE CHAT

There is some days when everything seems dull. The professors are a thing to put one to sleep, the check of the parents is not arrived, the life is flat. At the end of one of these rotting days, André and Émile chat on the future. It seems to look too much flat as well.

ANDRÉ: In a fucked year, I will be parting for the Advanced Accordion School and you will enter in the School of Tubers. You love better the School of the Ocarina, is it not so?

ÉMILE: But yes. As to Tuber Studies, well, you can stuff it in the "giggy" so far as I go!

ANDRÉ: What pity! I like to knock out jivey bits with the accordion, at least, but I confess that I will have the blue not to have Suzanne about a place any more. She is some hot mommy—as you too good know, my old chump.

ÉMILE: Heys! I had believe we got this all straightened, no? I am sorry on my absence of discretion with Suzanne on that fatal wick-end, but it is a difficult labor to make the resistance with a beauty like she who makes on you the dry hump more quick as you can say Jacques Robertson!

ANDRÉ: Yes, well. O.K. Soon we will complete the studies here, and all this laughs and weeps will be ceased. We will have to work like some damn bastards!

ÉMILE: You squarely hit the head of the spike there, my gay comrade!

ANDRÉ: It is not the idea of to work that gives me an ennui. I have a worry of not meeting up with some swell cookies like Suzanne and Monique. I have a chagrin to say a toodle-oo on them. I wonder is it that they will think on me some time? I have the large hope.

ÉMILE: Are you fooling? Young ladies of these type at all times recall the lust of youths.

ANDRÉ: I pray this to be true, my old bud.

ÉMILE: You can often write to them the letter, you know. And stuff them up with all manners of the obscene, the salacious, the tintillating. This should force them to bust into a sweat!

ANDRÉ: And maybe it could be that they can come to make a visit on me at my solitary chamber? We could make a truly debased trio!

ÉMILE: Now you appear to be talking, oil-face!

ANDRÉ: I can make an entertainment on them, play some love bits on the accordion, ply on them some booze—even maybe suggest that we regard some blues cinema.

ÉMILE: It is it! Never speak die!

ANDRÉ: I almost feel a twinge of agony for you, Émile. Over there I will be, buried into depraved acts, while you—you will be having the nightly rendez-vous with Marie Feest! Oh, ha, ha, ha!

ÉMILE: It may be so, my mean personal pal. But has it slipped from your brains that your school is three hundred kilometers distant, while mine is but ten from this ivy-soaked walls? Therefore, a ha, ha, ha on you!

ANDRÉ: Oh ball! It appears maybe that I myself will be saying good evening to Miss Feest, while you might be hauling up your ashes till the back breaks down. Craps!

ÉMILE: Only time will inform us. Meanwhile, how about a duet including us?

André and Émile are play the famous Parisian ditty, "Rosy Glasses." André is hugely pissed off on his pal for what he has been saying on this theme of the young ladies. He thinks to himself: "What a pain of the ass!"

XIV A QUESTION OF BUCKS

The last week, they had announce in the newspaper that Mr. Bas-Soie, Professor of Legumes and Forage Crops at the University, will participate at a contest on the television. It is a program what distributes vast sums of money to the people who know to respond correctly to a series of questions. Mr. Aine discusses this event with the Professor of the Hot Jazz, Mr. Fixe-Chaussettes.

MR. FIXE-CHAUSSETTES: What a luck for that maggots, Bas-Soie! He could well gain some thousands of grinbacks without getting himself fatigued.

MR. AINE: They are good in choosing their man, the rotting moron-brains! He does not recognize his ass from his shoulder, but he comprehends perfectly about the damn beans and stuff like this.

MR. FIXE-CHAUSSETTES: I demand myself how he will to spend his loots. What would *you* make if all of a suddenly one put on you a hundred thousand bucks among the hands?

MR. AINE: My words, I do not know. I probably will commence by to say, "So long, sucks!" on this putrid place. Then I might take a plane or a luxurious boat for to go live in the South Seas or Rio or some crazy place like this.

MR. FIXE-CHAUSSETTES: And this changing of place—you would make this alone? Just say a farewells and set the face to the far-off horizon? Or what?

MR. AINE: Well, I confess that it would be some nice fun to request of Suzanne Jarretière or Sophie Jupon or Monique Gaine to come along for a laughter with me. Do you know of these young lady students?

MR. FIXE-CHAUSSETTES: Do I! When they are in the attendance of the class of mine of Elementary Jive Bits, I get a wildness in looking on the bodies of them and the faces also. They are some fragments of ass!

MR. AINE: Ha! Ha! In effect! I made some minor amusement with Miss Jarretière once a time ago, but the other two I make the lewdness with in the fantasies solely. I would cast away many grinbacks to do the sexual orgy on all three of these switties at the once.

MR. FIXE-CHAUSSETTES: Whool! A man might set his body on flames in such an adventure. But what would the wife of you say in reference on such a voyage?

MR. AINE: I will tell to her that I must make the voyage to do a research in the primitive tuba or the Brazil accordion or the African comb and paper or some damn shit like this, and buy her the minx. But what would *you* make with bucks like this, my old man?

MR. FIXE-CHAUSSETTES: I must admit also the insane dream. I have the ardent feel for some years on that juicy lady, Mrs. Chaud. Is she not some thing?

MR. AINE: Ah, Mrs. Chaud! I once made a fox trots on her at the Yearly Dance of the Faculties last year, and I vow to you that I was of the idea that she was going to grind off my crotch. That lady is one hot figure!

MR. FIXE-CHAUSSETTES: I just am thinking how content I am that these ladies do not have a thought on what we are chatting! They will have some scandal.

MR. AINE: I don't know on this. I saw a composition in a number of *Oui, Oui, Paris* soon ago what hold that the ladies have just as much hot ideas like the men.

MR. FIXE-CHAUSSETTES: Well, I wish that Mrs. Chaud will have the hot ideas on *me*.

MR. AINE: But yes! And also not bad if the Misses Jarretière, Jupon, and Gaine will have some, eh?

MR. FIXE-CHAUSSETTES: In effect! But, these are dreams from the pipes. We have got no bucks to speak on, so shit on this things!

MR. AINE: Yes. We are make ourselves banana!

Mr. Aine and Mr. Fixe-Chaussettes say a farewell and depart for the homes of them. Mr. Fixe-Chaussettes is a bachelor and when he is arrived he makes an abuse on himself. Mr. Aine rushes in and makes a sex act with his wife in the kitchen right when she is prepare dinner. She would not be content to know why is this.

XV AT THE BUREAU OF PLACEMENT

It will be soon the birthday of André, and Suzanne would like to gain a little grinbacks for to buy him a jolly gift. Yesterday she is present herself at the Bureau of Placement of the University, in order to see if she can find a position. It is no other lady but Mrs. Chaud, as a secretary of the Bureau, who poses to her the questions of rigor. What a sticky things!

MRS. CHAUD: Good day, miss. How could I be to you of some uses?

SUZANNE: I am search for a situation that will permit me of to work some ten hours for the week. I have no desire to raze the bottom in this job. To whom can I demand some piece of information on this, Mrs. Chaud?

MRS. CHAUD: To me, if you wish this. I labor at here for some hours of the week in order for to make some additional bucks and make my ends meet. The University—this is off my sleeve—is too much tightly wadded, I don't mind telling to you, my little jam pot.

SUZANNE: Ah, I see. By the bys, I have heard on you some few excellent tales of the teaching of you from a swell old bud of mine, André Lubrique?

MRS. CHAUD: Ah yes, Mr. Lubrique is a heck on a swit boy and a student of good talents, but a little too wacked out from his head by the young ladies. Well, that is a little cipher of the bagatelle, no? Let us commence by filling up this form. I have the idea that maybe you call yourself Suzanne?

SUZANNE: It is the fact, missus.

MRS. CHAUD: And how do you call your last name?

SUZANNE: I call me Jarretière, Suzanne Jarretière.

MRS. CHAUD: Very good. I am write it down here. Jarretière . . . what a foolish name that seems to be! Almost as crazy as mine. Ha! Ha! Well, enough on this joke. What age do you have, my honey buns?

SUZANNE: I have eighteen years, Mrs. Chaud.

MRS. CHAUD: O.K. on this. Eighteen. Now, which ones of your professors know you enough good for to give us some datas of you and say to us some things you have the talents on?

SUZANNE: Well . . . Mr. Aine will make this things, I believe. But . . . what it is you will have going to demand on him?

MRS. CHAUD: The jolly face of you is sporting up a blush, miss. Do not have a worry. I know how to take in what Mr. Aine tells on young lady students with the mite of salt. He made some licenses on you, I make a bet.

SUZANNE (*plunging the eyes to the floor*): I have the shame to say this thing, but yes. He make me do a sex act in order for to succeed in the Kazoo Studies class of his.

MRS. CHAUD: What a contorted creeps he is! Pardon my French, but this lousy shit fly each terms make a young lady student do a sex act with him—some time two or three young ladies! Among us, miss, I tell to you that I made a normal fox trots on him soon ago, and I think he will be shooting off the member into the trousers any moment, so crazy with a lust he was. Don't make a care, my apple tart, I have the number on Mr. Aine.

SUZANNE: Much thanks on you, Mrs. Chaud. I had no desire that the Bureau of Placement to think on me as a pushed-over.

MRS. CHAUD: Of nothing! Now, tell to me of what you like to make as a job.

SUZANNE: Hecks, I don't know, rilly. I know to tap at the machine a piece, and I have the habit of to assist students at the lessons.

MRS. CHAUD: Ah, it is well. We have much of demands for the assistance in the lessons by stupid people at the University, of what we have the vast mob. Is it that you have assist Mr. Lubrique at some times? I seem to have a recall he so told to me.

SUZANNE: Yes . . . now and then again I give him an assistance.

MRS. CHAUD: Ah, it is as I think. I have of the occasion give to him a quick lesson as well. He is a good student, no? It fills the teacher with a grand joy to work with him.

SUZANNE: In effect. He is a champion of the lessons.

MRS. CHAUD: It might be that if you get some jobs, Mr. Lubrique might wish me to assist him at a few extra moments, no? I will be much content to make this, Suzanne. After all, you have no wishes to poops the self out.

SUZANNE: It may be the fact. If I get some jobs, I will ask on André of this.

MRS. CHAUD: How swell this is! What an agreeable young thing you are. Now I tell a toodle-oo on you, and if we find some things, we will give to you the jangle on the telephone.

SUZANNE: Thanks in big heaps, Mrs. Chaud. A toodle-oo on you.

Mrs. Chaud leans in her chair back and makes a daydream of some thrills with André. She appears to be doing some short panting indeed! Suzanne is walking to her chamber, of the thoughts that she will no sooner inform André of the idea of Mrs. Chaud than she will make the jump into a cesspool. She mutters on herself, "Why don't this sexy vamp make some sex with the old gents?"

XVI A LITERARY ARGUMENT

Mr. Coillon, Professor of Wild Flowers, never lets pass an occasion of vaunting the superiority of the English novels over that of the French. Evidently, that does not much please Mr. Aine, who loves with a deep the French culture things. This one responds always that the English novels is imitate of the French and that the imitation is not equal never to an original. Nevertheless, after reading on an English novel soon ago, Mr. Aine finds a nice things to speak about this.

MR. AINE: The novel by McCoy, *Sublime Porter*, is not too bads. McCoy would be content of to see that his book pleases a person of my nice tastes.
MR. COILLON: McCoy is of a universal in this novel. It has pleased all men of culture who read on this, so I am content that it pleases *you*, my friend, or else one might have the thought that you have the brain made purely of the shit. On my other hand, I have read upon a novel by Latirail, *The Nail Seekers*, and what a pity! It is of clarity that it is a work that is absent of spine and the intelligence.
MR. AINE: Your ass sucks up the wind, my colleague. I am also of the opinion that *Sublime Porter* is of a universal state, but so is a "bull clap." Ha! Ha! McCoy is some times genial, especially in these description of young ladies in variant states of deshabille, but in an essence, he is a dull vomit of a writer. The brilliant of the glitter the *The Nail Seekers* makes reveal of the superior arts of Latirail.
MR. COILLON: Latirail is some how of a teensy interests if one has nothing else to be had to read on, as if one has been coasted up on the deserted island. But his novels, like *The Nail Seekers*, are of such a grand ennui that a person gets the jeebies on reading this things.
MR. AINE: The jeebies, eh? Any person who will get these jeebies is one too-thick bastard! McCoy is chuck filled up in blocks with the scenes of violence what he makes to give the psycho person the cheap thrills. But in Latirail we find no actions saving these who pass by in the brains of the characters.
MR. COILLON: And the brains of the characters, please do not neglect to speak, old dimmed wits, are such brains what makes a dwelling on thoughts of sexy perversions, on crazy fetish things as the matron ladies in the house dress and snikkers, and many creepish memoirs of sex acts in groupings of much people. *The Nail Seekers* has a great illness to it.
MR. AINE: Ah, you say to me an illness? You are speak as the man what has the asshole made out of paper! Latirail makes the picture of the illness in order for us to know how the world runs along daily in this age of dirts. *Sublime Porter*, however, has the scene of a grand nausea when the heroine does the sharp bite on the organ of the hero in the oral act what occurs in a garbage dump. If this is not of a too much disgust, I will eat up my hat!

MR. COILLON: I will say to you, my thick-skull one, that McCoy's scenes of potent acts in *Sublime Porter* are the symbol of a malaise who has done the relation among the two sexes so loused up. He is of the huge moral statures.

MR. AINE: I think on him as a blood-crazing nuts!

MR. COILLON: And I consider it that Latirail is of the type of a freaky gay fairy what rilly has the great hate on ladies, young and also old!

MR. AINE: You are an impossible shitnose! You and your lime-eating hacker!

MR. COILLON: And you! You and that twisted cracker of the frog toad are both of you wasted of a great sick!

MR. AINE: Stick it in your nose bones!

MR. COILLON: Place it roughly in the fundamental!

Mr. Coillon and Mr. Aine continue to do the shouting insults to each on the other until the bell rings out for classes. They rush away then, making some fists to each other. Mr. Aine then proceed to look up the skirt and down in the blouse of the young lady students of him and to make some smutty proposals to some. Mr. Coillon stands to observe with his eyes in a bulge the bottoms of the young lady students of him when they make it to bend away over to look in a microscopes. It might be that their talk of the moral in the novels is so much of the heated air and the horse shits.

≪ 56 ≫

The Land
of Enchantment

THE LAND OF ENCHANTMENT

You are probably wondering just what you are doing here, in the Land of Enchantment? Yes, this is the Land of True Enchantments! In its many wonderful ways it has, all the enchantments that you might think you can see in the Old Capitols of Europe and the Mystic East. But here, in "Your Own Backyard" you can be casted upon a spell of True Enchantments, to beat the band, for Vacation and Care free days and nights of Fun and Frolics! Famous persons of all stripes and sexes may be found here, "all year round" smiling and loaving away their troubles and cares. Why not you?

Perhaps you are thinking that this is a "hypo" about the Land of Enchantment and, if so we wish to please request you to read this colorful brochure about this land we are proud to be of and to which we welcome whom wants to come and throw away his troubles and as the famous song says, pack them in a kitty bag for a few days or weeks. What do we offer persons? Plenty.

Climate

Is dry and healthsome. The air is excellent for the consumption and asma, if upwind from the booming nucular plants that proudly work to bring the fruit of Progress to little sleepy villages. Yet also, experts for the Power Company have proved that studies show that even if you are downwind it is not without its boons, the slight touch of radiation in the air healthily killing all the dirt and filth garbage atoms as well as cockarocahes and scorpions as well as bobcats and wolfs and ciyots what like to eat campers and household pets. The mean temprature is 42 a low, and 65 a high, though once in a while it goes up to 145 degrees and down to − 55, so that wise natives find it a good idea to stay in the house then. Rain: Has been no rain in this sunny place since 1929, it is, as they say always, good golf weather. Once in a while we get here a small blizzard but with the crackling blazes in the quaint adobes the people live in, there is much family closeness at these times, with card games, shooting craps, and other "together" pass-times. Water for healthful bathing and an occasional drink is trucked in from some-place. Because the heat is so dry it is never oppressive except if a person should stand around in the sun too long a time "loungeing about" in the colorful town squares when, the person could get a stroke in his or her head, that can be painful and cause a quiet death.

Minerals

There are many minerals lurking in the ground here in the Land of Enchant-ment. Many are precious to the working-day world of industry and others are to make into precious jewlry. Some of these minerals are, bingoite, marmalite, ni-cotine, zincox, crystalloid, birdlime, boxball, eggdrop, luddite, porsche, and the famous red clay that the prosthetics industry uses to make the feet.

Crops

Land of Enchantment is so rich in crops that can grow without the precious water that we have not had for a spell that one gives a pause to know where to begin on them all. Let us take a chance. Shall we? We grow in a great perfusion these diverse crops, in so far as the beans go: alachi, mastiachi, pinga, sancha, yenda, barragana, carajo, ganforra, chingada, cuco, ciscón, and caló. We allso raise in great perfusions these chilies: the bujarrón, mucló, pajera, quilé, zur-rona, coña, daifa, flete, jaño, magué, birlocha, cábula, balorri, and basto. We also grow the "dwarf" potatoes, the different types are the bombear, the tributo, the rudimé, and the cagar, also there is a small area devoted to the growth of the green tomatoes, which we have the bullarengue, chamberete, pendejo, and ñorga. Truly, this is called by many the Enchanted Garden of Eden!

Railroads

Many railroads serve this land and its wonderful inhabitants and makes the guests and tourists comfortable and able to arrive and depart from almost any spot they take it into their mind that they like to be. The major railroads are the Texas-Desert-Pacific, the Pacific-Texas, the Desert-Pacific, the Pacific-Okie, the Okie-Desert, the Desert-Mesa-Mojave, the Mojave-Okie, the Mojave-Mesa-Arroyo, and the Arroyo-Pacific. There is also an airport of the most up-to-date facilities that is open 24 hours a day all year round between sandstorms and the casual blizzard or two that passes by.

Famous Sons and Daughters

The Land of Enchantments has given to the world many famous people, many of whom have gone out into the world to "make their marks" and many of whom have stayed here to improve and make even more genteel the already much improved and genteel way of life that we already live here in the "Aorta of the West" as a famous Heart Sergeon once "dubbed" it. Surely there are hundreds of them but permit us to note but a handful or two of the most illustreous ones. Juan Pecos, invented the Railroad sandwich; Juan de Cristo, said first prayer in English in the Valley; Juan Culebra, ate nine pounds of habichuelas at the White House Poetry Fest; Juan Cimarrón, got idea of putting the gusano (worm) in mezcal bottle; Juan Taos, first professional sunset describer in Tourist Board; Juan Santa Fé, made adobe house from flour and Pepsi-Cola; Maria Mora, opened bowling alley; Brick Las Vegas, introduced pancakes to Navajos; Juan Ratón, voted for Hubert Hoover; Juan Cerro-Blanco, forgot his name once; Maria Truchas, seduced Juan Taos; Maria Costilla, watched a horse all day Christmas; Juan Baldy, took a trip to Utah; Chet Lake, first Avon man in Los Cobardes; Juan Sandia, changed his name to Johnny Sandia; Juan Manzano, put ketchup on his beans; Juan Gallinas, first man in town to wear Windsor knot; Maria Jicarilla, disliked corn tortillas; Max Caballo, arrested for making pee-pee on turquoise display in market; Juan Oscuro, old friend of Maria Mora; Maria San Andrés, has no friends at all; Juan Orgán, changed his name to Juan Orgoné; Juan and Maria Animas, own Juan and Maria Animas' Roadside Cafe; Maria Hatchet, trying to get on game shows for 18 years; Juan Mogollón, once walked to the airport; Maria Pinos, throws lemons at priests; Maria Burro, first woman to wear net stockings in State Legislature; Juan Blanca, laughed at President Truman's shirt; Juan Capitán, sits on blanket; Maria Sacramento, went to movies with a bag of peaches; Maria Hueco, mistaken for Puerto Rican; Juan Guadalupe, mistaken for Italian; Juan Petaca, owns TV repair store; Juan Vallés, hangs around Petaca's TV repair store; Maria Nacimiento, drinks muscatel in front of Post Office; Juan Jemez, wrote a letter to *Popular Mechanix*; Juan San Mateo, washed his pick-up truck once; Juan Magdalena, suggested name change to Juan Orgoné; Maria Socorro, does not understand *I Love Lucy* show; Bill Black, makes wigs for Chet Lake; Juan Mimbres, does not wear sunglasses; Maria Florida, mistaken for Anglo man and elected to Congress; Maria Potrillo, lost her slip in a tornado; Juan Carrizo, makes Rosaries from ball-point pens; Juan Tunicha, ate a straw hat; Juan Choiska, is always sick and tired of everything; Chuck Pyramid, friend of Chet Lake and Bill Black; Maria Peloncillo, dropped a bowling ball in the Drive-In; Juan Zuñi, smokes a lot; Juan Datil, sent his wife to refrigerator school; Juan Diablo, does not like Coca-Cola; "Big" Hatcheta, discovered how to paint mountain pictures and moved to Palm Springs; Rod Tularosa, wears a denim tie.

Manufactures

Last but not least we must mention the manufactures of the Land of Enchantments! Although these are not destined to interest the frivolous folk who laugh and sing their ways through vacations and holidays here, it is of the first moment to business men, who come to look hard-headed at possible investments.

Many of these industries are important to the Nation's economy as well as to the local one, and some, though small, are always growing. A Sign of a Strong and Rosy America!

The area is rich in muscatel plants, mezcal plants, and tequila plants, as well as a brewery that makes the famous "Dos Pelotas" beer.

There is a growing pot industry, and along with the pots made for pinto beans, we are now "into" tea pots, laundry pots, stew pots, and large ceramic pots for cats. There is also a small shoppe in Old Santa Fe that makes one of a kind pots for eggs, which they call Huevo Pots.

We are putting much energy into the Groats Industry.

The herb tea industry grows apace.

There is an increasing demand from the thousands of Indian imitators in the large metropolises for polyethylene turquoise, and our three plants are on 24-hour shifts.

The Geiger Counter industry is also booming.

Finally, our Famous blankets are back-ordered for months and a merger is "in the air" to merge this industry with the pot industry to produce the first Blanket Pot.

So, it will be seen that we are On the Way to the American Way!

So, prospective visitor and guest, we say again, Welcome! Welcome to the
LAND OF ENCHANTMENT

Faced abruptly with this colorful brochure, or, perhaps more precisely, at one with it, since he held it gingerly in his quiet, bemused hands, Blue suddenly wanted to blurt! This strong and stalwart land, this land . . . of (they were *right*) enchantment! seemed now, to Blue, as he reflected upon the horrifying waste and drang and such of his young life (and Helene's too), the place to rest for a couple of nonces, perhaps even a sennight or two, to recoup their strength, such as it was (and still is!), make a few repairs to the pushcart before they pushed out, or on, continue with his slow but steady progress on "Good Old Dolphin Boulevard," and cajole, urge, press, inveigle, threaten, wheedle, and plead for a return to work by his wifey. Why, there was really nothing that the chick couldn't do to scrape up a few shekels to keep them in beans.

Was there? he mused.

The answer came to him as it must to all men, in the slow soughing of the wind, the glimmer of the old moon on the melting snow, the shadows of the stately pines on the rumbling mountainside.

There were a . . . few things. He laughed, a delicate *frisson* riffling his hirsute wrists, at the end of which hung the large hands, and their even larger fingers, that would one day startle the civilized world with their musical power!

But a few other things, *that* she could do.

For a moment, her curled lip seemed to verge toward the negative. She had no way of knowing whether or not she could enter the labor market, it had been many years since she'd earned her bread in the hurly-burly of the job world and other popular songs. But just at that moment, as her lip began to curl as it, perhaps, had never curled before, just then, Serge gestured toward the West, where the sun was sinking in a mad explosion of what they call a riot of colors, with a few subtle tints and shades at the edges, and she was swept away by a sense of her destiny, her destiny as the wife who would stand behind, as she was standing now, her husband in the future, just as she had stood behind him in the past, often getting up on tiptoes to see over his shoulders, as she was perhaps doing now, and as she would in the future, as she would always, that is, whenever he stood directly in front of her, as he now stood, and as he had so often stood, strong and straight and unafraid, in the past.

So she went to work selling things in the market of a small city nestled at the foot of a jagged sierra.

First, she sold some small pamphlets pertaining to Arts and Crafts, and Doing for Oneself as Did Our Forefathers.

How to Open a Bottle of Muscatel

A bottle of Muscatel should be purchased with care and an eye toward personal needs. Muscatel, a bright, brittle, singing little wine, goes perfectly with Fritos, Twinkies, and unfiltered cigarettes, but is most often taken alone at room temperatures direct from its unmistakable bottle. Its unearthly sweetness may be slightly "cut" by alternate sips of a cheap blended whiskey or hunks of eyetalian-type bread. This sprightly little gentleman of a wine should be procured only at those times when you are in touch with your feelings.

After purchasing, step outside the place of purchase, walk directly to a doorway, an alley, a stoop, a curb, or a side street, and briskly twist off the metal cap. It is part and parcel of drinking Muscatel to enhance the sense of personal freedom it conveys by throwing this cap away.

How to Make Laundry

Throw soiled clothing on the floor, until it makes a pile, or piles, preferably in the corner of the living room. When it has reached the old mellow *vigas* of the ceiling, you will see that it has attained its own organic structure, and it is possible to relate to it in a constructive way. This soiled clothing has become laundry.

Carry the piles with care to the swift-running stream beyond the ditch where you burn the garbage and discard your empty Muscatel bottles, and throw the laundry into the water.

You have successfully, and quite simply, made laundry!

If you are concerned about your needs as a newcomer to our region this, it should be noted, is an excellent craft-discipline for beginners, since it produces excellent results with a minimum of effort, and permits the neophyte to immediately feel at one with his surroundings.

How to Drink Herb Tea

Put on a hand-made and ill-fitting woolen, or woollen shawl. Heap the fireplace high with piñon logs or faggots and set ablaze. Staring at the colorful *ojos de Dios* that are on the rough adobe walls above, below, and in between the oil paintings that you've made of the mountains at sunset, take a moment to get in touch with yourself and your feelings.

Meanwhile, the herb tea is brewing in the battered copper pot that is on the hob. A splash of Muscatel in the pot can be a special treat!

Soon, sip your herb tea from a hand-thrown mug that has the organic structure of the ancient clay from which it was thrown. (If you can find a mug that will not sit on the table without falling over, all the better.) Watch the dirty station wagons and pick-up trucks clatter by your house toward the art gallery. Call a few friends and, as you watch the sunset on the mountains, tell them how it looks. As the flickering firelight dances on the rough adobe walls, mention how great it is to be out of the noisy city where it is impossible to get in touch with your feelings and paint pictures of splendid mountains.

How to Eat Pinto Beans

Plunge a gloved hand into a bubbling *olla* (pot) of clay that is filled with pinto beans. Keep the fingers stiff, and when you feel that your hand is at one with the reality of the "life of the bean," withdraw it and eat the pinto beans that adhere to the glove. (It is perfectly permissible to suck the bean juices out of the glove as the Indians do.)

When the glove is soaked through and through with bean juices (three or four immersions should do the trick), remove it, throw it into the *olla* and lick your bare hand.

Indians have eaten beans this way for centuries. It is highly economical—a pot of beans once fed the Arikara Apache hordes for three weeks—and allows the bean-eater to relate to cooking in a natural way. Also, the gloves so prized by our red brothers for the buffalo hunt are those used in the bean ceremony; the juices make them tough, resilient, and almost impervious to the savage attacks of the maddened bison. Muscatel is excellent with this dish.

How to Start the Old Station Wagon

Put on your sunglasses and walk out of the house to the old station wagon. Dig it out from under the tumbleweeds and sand that have buried it during the night. This sort of honest labor will usually allow a person to relate to the harsh, stringent beauty of the region.

Remark aloud on the brightness of the day and the way the sun, that makes the snowclad mountain peaks so dazzling, is blinding you. Stop your work now and again to feel the personal freedom that is yours as you realize that you are in a large, peaceful sink, like.

Light a cigarette and take a pull from a bottle of Muscatel. About now, it will "hit the spot."

Start the old station wagon, and sit in it for ten to fifteen minutes. Turn off the ignition, and return to the house. Oil your floor, as you tell guests about the old, original *vigas* above the dining area. Remark on how you plan to cut some piñon the following day, how you have been meaning to get to the lumber mill for some cheap kindling, and how you think it wise to begin buying your Muscatel by the case.

How to Make an Egg

Get a fresh yolk from a sleeping chicken, preferably one that has been born in the region. (They are the stringy, sand-colored ones.) Placing the yolk carefully on a clean, flat surface (the hood of an old station wagon is ideal), surround it with the precious albumen that you've collected over the winter. Be careful when lifting the yolk to slide the precious albumen beneath that you don't break it (the yolk); yolks are surprisingly sturdy, but do not respond well to rough handling.

When the yolk is "blurry" and its yellow color seems subdued, you will know that it is completely wrapped in the precious albumen. Any leftover precious albumen may be discarded, or used to mix colors with which to paint pictures of the mountains at sunset. *Do not use too much precious albumen* as a "wrapper" for your yolk, as this will result in an egg useful only for throwing at galas and fetes.

Now, carefully suck the slop and slime out of an eggshell through a small hole punched into its smaller end with a twig. (The crossbar of a small *ojo de Dios* will do nicely.) When the "glop" is sucked out and the eggshell completely empty, spit this matter out and take a pull on a bottle of Muscatel. Allow the interior of the eggshell to dry.

Holding the dry, empty eggshell in one hand, carefully spoon the "wrapped" yolk into it through the same hole used to drain it of its slop and slime. When the shell is full (and if you've been careful there will be no "wrapped" yolk left over), seal the hole in it with a piece of white chalk, a pebble, a grain of rice, or a simple paste made of flour or corn starch and water.

You have made one of Nature's most complete foods, using nothing but natural ingredients!

With the courage and optimism deeply rooted in her blood what she got from her huddled forebears as they yearned and breathed for nothing in the rollicking steerages of so many crack vessels speeding them to the joyous streets of New York's own Lower East Side (already, at this time, filled with some three or four thousand future politicians and stand-up comics), Helene stood, for hours and days on end, the abuse heaped on her by the locals, the store-owners, and the stern-jawed *turistas*, all of whom, as the poet said, "threatened her with insult," as did the lousy *sansculottes* la belle France's Chief Whore in her golden heyday before, wild with stolen vintages and the vicious idea that the *ancien régime* was out to, how can one say? fuck them over, perhaps, they decided to chop her sconce off of her.

So, breathing quietly in the perfumed and enchanted air one balmy evening, she thought aloud to Serge, deep off in the bracken that was making an unearthly music, that she thought she'd try her hands at selling odds and ends, disguised like a old Injun squaw.

An' so that you sell whate'er you list, Serge roared from a rippling rio, may the Lord of Music cast, as gamesters throw the bones, his poiple mantle of protection on your weary head! Then swam he about a-laving with much splashing while popeyed fish gazed on apace.

Some days later, an absolutely authentic-looking squaw hunkered down before a—what else?—art gallery, her homely yet mysterious wares spread out before her. A closer look proved what the reader may have suspected: it was Helene, her creamy skin tinted a swarthy shade by berry juice or some kinda fruits.

You like-um babushka? Helene said. Real Navajo. Funny signs and stuff straight from the Toltecs and Aztecs. Or this blue, pretty stuff we Injuns twistum silver around? Cheap and look good on your pretty wife, Meester.

John! Just look at that bald Jew-lady pretending to be an Indian squaw.

Let's get back in the station wagon, Miriam.

Plenty nice leaves, too, you cook-um up in old man's barley soup and he'll have a little lead in his pencil once again. Names like poetry. Smutwillow, piggesbush, crutmallow, purple pout, wanlip, cockeyes Nellie, crazysquaw, blackstocking, happysnatch, bigstiff, titsucker, Queen Bruce, two-in-her, griefbitcher, weeping Willie, all guaranteed to cause a hard-on that'll raise the old WASP right off the floor.

John? Do you think that . . .

The car, dear, the *car*.

Real *silver* babushka? Tasteful gouaches of maize nodding in the sirocco? Map of ancient walled city showing where Loew's Teotihuacan used to be? Piece of Coronado's fingernail? Snapshots in color of Indian mating rituals? My God, folks! Indians are persons too!

John, that spray of bigstiff might be just the thing for the motel windowsill . . . ?

Miriam!

Palooza blossoms? Midnight blusher? Chicano fly? Can I help it if I'm bald? I made these phony braids myself! That should count for sumpn!

The happysnatch goes with my new black lace peignoir, John. John?

Let's drive down to the waving grasses by the river and eat our hard-boiled eggs, dear.

That's the Rio sin Nombre and it's coised, you Lutheran bastard!

The woman is coising at us, John! I've heard that an Indian coise can follow you all your life long, and if particularly bad, can wind up with the most terrible results, things like maybe the children not getting accepted by the college of their choice! Oh, John! Please! The bouquet of titsucker would perfectly match my new wardrobe of magically sheer pantyhose in exciting fall colors!

Miriam, these ravolitos or whatever these greasers call them are getting cold.

Coronado's fingernail-cutting guaranteed to turn him into heap big fucker? Helene said. Two bits. I give to my brave and he make the old mission bells ring again, yes sir!

Hear the old redskin, honey? Wouldn't it be fun to do it on the kitchen table, just like the Hollywood stars?

Miriam, dear, the spick at the grocery store said that if we didn't drink this pole-kay in an hour it would turn into dynamite. Now, are we going to sit in the peaceful fields of sumptuously flowering local blooms and watch the sunlight glittering on the river, or are we going to hang around and get taken by this old kike woman?

John? Look! The purple pout has a little label on it that says, "PUT A PIECE OF ME IN YOUR PANTIES AND . . . WATCH OUT!"

Cheap Baptist motherfucker, Helene said into a pot. May all his white bread be dipped in olive oil!

John, I'm going to use my *own* money and buy just a little spike or two of this funny, sweet little smutwillow, *then* we'll go down to the river. Just *thinking* of these little leaves makes me want to unhook my figure-flattering all-in-one!

I'll wait in the purring station wagon, dear.

You make wise choice, white lady, Helene said. I guarantee that one sniff of this magical plant and the old cluck will have his fly open before you reach the edge of town.

Oh, I hope so, Miriam said, blushing. My latest issue of *Ladies' Life* says that there's nothing wrong with a gently acting aphrodisiac, or a touch of fantasy-sharing, or a half-hour of sixty-nine—as long as these things don't take the place of the normal, healthy marital relationship!

Ugh. You stick-um plant in his schnozz and give him hand-job while he drive and maybe that new carpeting you want-um be yours when you get back to Indianapolis.

How on earth did you know that we're from Indianapolis? Miriam marveled and, if truth be told, blenched a little.

Miriam! Miriam! These burrotis are beginning to leak!

Coming, darling, Miriam trilled, swinging her hips wildly as she ran to her husband.

Hope the Methodist putz comes in his pants, Helene said to the dry, hot winds of the Santa Anita, that, as usual, said nothing in reply.

So the days passed in a haze of heat, sun, and sandy winds, and Helene sold whatever she could to the jabbering tourists, set upon occasionally by real Indians, or fake Indians of long standing, or others who also bravely sold. And their pennies added up, and Blue worked on the cart and practiced his . . . well . . . let's say his "scales."

And always in the foreground of his mind, on, as it were, the front porch, even out at the little strip of grass by the curb where you put the garbage cans, one word: CALIFORNIA. Why had he never thought of this? he often mused to Helene over the crackling fire of an evening, sometimes, of a number of evenings. She mused back and the java then, aye! 'twould flow merrily, as if there were no tomorrow! Or, perhaps, as if tomorrow would never come! Even better. Or even, as if, when tomorrow came, as come it must, and would, that it would be the tomorrow of their dreams, a bright tomorrow, despite the fact that it might be gloomy or grey or raining, the idea, Blue patiently explained, that the phrase "bright tomorrow" was what they call a "figure of speech." Did Helene, sweet, hard-working Helene, understand? Did she? Hah? Huh? Whaddayasay, kid? Hey!

But Helene's eyes had closed on who knows what sweet dreams, and her husband, smiling gently, tenderly bent to kiss her and then softly, oh so softly, took her blanket. Did not Othello do the same on Desdemona? Or what?

The sun stared, hard, like the eyes of a cop, an American cop, a state trooper, perhaps.

Helene sat in said sun, shaking and shimmying, squawlike, sort of. A voice issued forth from the beads and feathers that adorned her head and face, the weird rat's-eyes and the buffalo-hump grease, the bone bells and pussy fangs.

You like-um Mayan dung shovel? Pure stone, direct from Gallup dig. Guaranteed that it killed two nosy missionaries.

Seeds for garden? Benny One-Ball tomaters invented by Xochitl as strawberry substitute. Fruit gettum big as medicine balls, good love-potion make young girl crazy to take drawers off in public place. Hot stuff!

Zankoid, wheedle, rompf, syzygy plants? Put in stew, make "gay" guests straight?

Silver babushka? Last one, going fast, made of old Nazi pipe-bowl covers? Brought to States by Hans Dieter Pogrom, the famous German who saved a Jew.

Dead petunia grackle?

Turquoise suspenders?

Imitation oilcloth made of plastic from World's Fair Indian Building?

TV-camera lens left at Wounded Knee by genuine Protestant assistant producer? Drop in ginger ale, keep-um cold for two weeks.

Gah?

Wooj!

Um-um?

You take zitzerella?

Ugh-um.

And as the sun fell rather heavily into the gloaming far beyond the formidable range past the sinuous Cobardes, that river wherein the legendary Big Cal was wont to bathe his chaps to the music of ethereal banjos an' mouth organs, Helene decided that she'd go into a new line of work.

Jist a few more passels o' days, mebbe a week er two, an' we'uns is like to hev sufficient ter push on out with a spankin' new sorta cart, on our last push ter Californy. Thus Serge, one night, between gouts of cascading arpeggios. How the moon slathered lambently! The Golden West is more than just a word! It is . . . a reality! How soon they'd know this, although Blue, in a sense, were we a fly on the wall, invisibly, almost, observing, knew it already.

I have figured a new dodge to grab up some green these last few days, his wife said in her oddly sturdy way. Motes of dandruff and other scalpish matter danced in the dancing firelight! Such is the mighty yelp of Nature!

Good, honey, mighty good, the courageous voice whispered to the grunting mesquite and occasional coyote that abounded here.

Oh, Serge! she breathed, and went to him, swiftly.

And, as Viña Delmar once wrote, in a prose that echoes and re-echoes down the corridors of time as long as prose shall live, he took her into his arms. The moon suddenly darted behind a cloud and there was nothing to be heard but the sound of the snapping fire and the gentle clatter of Helene's falling hair.

And what was Helene's "new dodge?" 'Twere to vend and push, door-to-door, to the sunblinded natives of this balmy clime, a trig, terse, and easily readable pamphlet on a heavy gloss stock what no home should lack, this:

The Booklet on Winter Gardening

Oftentimes, the harsh winter months spell an end very often to outdoor exercising and the beginning outset of the battle of the midriff bulge.

Winter gardening fun may not be the answer. However, oftentimes it may be the answer instead. It is an exciting way to beat those winter blues, but the best part is that one needn't have to be a Luther Burbank or a Chet Burpee to master this growing winter sport indoors. We can start with a getting in shape program.

Winter gardening programs were oftentimes thought, at one time, to be a European sport like jai-alai, but that has changed. It's popularity spells an end to all that, and it's popularity has increased tremendously in our United States recently due to several reasons, of which the fact that it is fairly inexpensive may be the answer. A $100.00 will usually spell the answer to providing all necessary equipment; it is relatively safe; and it can be mastered in a very short time in an exciting way, which is not the case with jai-alai, which also takes more room than we usually have to offer.

Due to several reasons, one can stop in the middle of the plot of land at any time for refreshments to help beat the battle of these winter blues. Exciting wine and a favorite wedge of cheese seems to be of tremendous popularity among gardeners.

Before attempting winter gardening, oftentimes a conditioning program providing all relatively safe and fairly inexpensive equipment should be followed. The following exciting program was heartily recommended by Cuddie Doron, gardening pro at Penshurst, and may be the answer to mastering the sport.

1. Slowly, do ten ¾ knee bends very slowly and relatively safely. Never do ¾ of a full knee bend, although, this is tremendously popular among European sports, like jai-alai.

2. While standing, do forward splits halfway with the necessary equipment. A favorite item among gardeners seems to be wine and cheese wedges, a fairly exciting way to stretch the groin and thighs, and an inexpensive way to beat those midriff blues. Alternate each leg ten times before attempting to alternate each other leg.

3. While sitting in a chair in an exciting way, rotate your ankles clockwise, due to several reasons, and then oftentimes counter-clockwise, alternating each leg and ankle to spell an end to it's blues. Repeat ten times, ¾ of an hour, until one can stop due to an increased popularity of tremendous European refreshments.

4. While standing at any time, with all relatively safe equipment, to stretch the groin and ankles, alternate, in a very short time, your arms ¾ of the way from your knees to your sides and then to waist level, while rotating your thighs to shoulder level. Never do a full arm alternation while rotating your thighs, although, this is an exciting way to beat those jai-alai programs.

5. Lastly, practice balancing on one foot while spelling an end to ten full knee bends, and rotating your ankles in an exciting way. Alternate each foot and stretch your groin; at one time this was thought to be a European favorite, like wedges of cheese. Although not required, it is advisable to have at least one relatively safe and very short lesson with the club pro before "hitting the soil." This is to insure spelling an end to those winter blues and to covering any different aspect one might encounter with a fairly inexpensive though exciting European.

Now had our two rolling scones heaped up a pittance. Each night, when Helene trooped "home" from her schlepping, Blue added her shekels to the steady-growing pile beneath the mattress, if they had a mattress. Our narrator, so to speak, cannot remember if he gave them a mattress, and, true to his craft, refuses to check the manuscript, tattered, dog-eared, and stained, of course. Well, fuck *him*! *Now* they have a mattress!

Note this steadily growing pile of coins, plus some tired looking Federal Reserve Notes which the guvmint backs up with mighty ships, planes, and missiles! Blue laughed. We have got enough.

Thank the Lord of Hosts, Helene breathed at last.

Pero, Blue cautioned, we should have but a bit more to take care of odds and shards of thises and thats as we make our final push through howling sands and awesome vistas! Just a few more bucks, and we will have done. Besides, I need but a day or two more to perfect the harmonic subtleties of that grand old tune, "Green Is the Street for Godolphin."

Once more into the breech? Helene said, all perky above her secretly cascading heart.

If you want to talk dirty, it's jake with me, but yes! We need another few hours of simple, pleasant work from you. And I have just the thing, given me this morning by a genuine *vaquero* waiting for a baloney on roll, heavy on the mustard, and a malt liquor. How the sun glanced off his buckle straps and straining lanyards! It is a surefire item, big with tourists, shading toward the informational and historical like a serious TV show. Here it is! If I was you I'd start first thing in the morn, for tourists rise up at the first sure sign of crowded dawn in these here parts!

And so they did! And Helene, Helene was there to meet them as they poured forth from Howard Johnson's, in colorful camera straps and plastic shoes!

CORONADO'S FINGERNAIL
An Relick of the Mysterious West

Lost in the obscure haze of history for many hundreds of years, this relic was found in a stolen hotel towel under mysterious circumstances by James "Jimbo" or "Jizz" Zoltan, a humble drummer who had settled in the sterile splendors of the valley just west of the Pecos with his small but rapidly growing family. Professor Bracken Tarnish, Director of the Archaelogy and Human Life-Interests Department at Central Pecos University, wrote: "There is no doubt in my mind or in the minds of my colleague, Miss Wanita Hips, that this is indeed the index fingernail of Coronado, or as my colleagues in the History and Life-Enhancing Studies Department insist on calling him, de Coronado." A new method of dating and placing items from digs was used to confirm the Professor's suspicions, the method known as "egg-90," which consists of comparing the composition of an eggshell whose age is known to within a century or so, with the item unearthed from the dig. "When I saw that the eggshell looked just like this paring I knew we were home free," Professor Tarnish smiled. "Then it was just a matter of proving that the fingernail was, indeed, Coronado's, and not that of his trusted lietenant, Bruce de Vásquez y Chinche. It was fairly easy to do this, but for the present we'd—Miss Hips and I—prefer to keep our testing methods private."

Mr. Zoltan, who has since moved to a small development in the area known as East Pecos, has said that the fingernail was found—"fell out of," he claimed—in a towel that he dug up from the flooring of his home one Saturday when he was tearing up his floor. The towel, according to Mr. Zoltan, crumbled at the touch of the family mattock, and in the moldering debris there was seen a small, glowing object in the shape of a crescent moon. About to smash it to powder with an ax-handle provided him by his wife, Ceniza, he has said, on national television, that "something" stopped him. He had, he maintains, a feeling that the fingernail was somehow trying to communicate with him, and that, in his words, it was "not the fingernail of your everyday spick or greaseball, but one of which was from some big-shot honcho." "Honcho," Mr. Zoltan, a veteran of the Korean War explained, is a Korean argot type word for "Chief" or "Sport" or "Champ."

Packing the item in an insulated chest filled with ice cubes, Mr. Zoltan drove to Zuñi Agricultural and Technical College, where, he insists, a group of Science-Faculty members "had a high old time funnin' with me." He has noted that the Chairman of the Department of Legumes and Cosmetics, the Regius Professor of Market Refrigeration, and the Visiting Assistant Professor of Calculator Maintenance "made wise remarks," among which were: "You're full of s——!" "Tell me another one, hunkie." "What have *you* been smoking?" "Take a f—— walk, you dumb Polack." The members of the faculty deny that this incident ever occurred, and say that they were under the impression that Mr. Zoltan was trying to sell them some frozen paprika, as he had done many times in the past. The College Dean of Administration, Wally Coat, wrote, "Don't know what to employ with papreeka and don't want none, now or ever."

Professor Tarnish feels a touch of sorrow when he considers the *faux pas* made by the members of Zuñi A&T, but says that such things are all luck. "Had my distinguished colleagues over to Zuñi not been writing grant proposals they would have known what to look for," he insists.

The fingernail, which is on permanent public display in the lobby of the Buenos Dias Brewery offices in central Encantada, is said to have mysterious powers, one of them being that it somehow plays tunes. It also turns into a turquoise bracelet once a month, and shoots of maize occasionally spring out of it. A guard at the vault where the nail was kept during scientific testing, says that one night he heard it playing "Cielito Lindo," and that it sounded something like a kazoo. What is fascinating about this story is that in Coronado's "Ay, Mi Vida!" written during his last quiet years in Mexico City, he writes that "el instrumento de boca que me gusta más está el quazoo."

Tourists have been flocking to the small city of Encantada to see the fingernail, and tickets, nominally priced at $5.00, have been virtually unavailable for weeks.

Such is another Mystery of this Enchanted Land!

But stand in the sun as she would, e'en garbed in a "tailored suit," so to speak, with her gossamer hair tied in a neat bun and her flat-heeled shoes sternly planted in the dust, Helene could not push this shit on the ever-shifting crowds of gawkers. They even insulted her, to, like they say, the tunes of:

Fuck off, weedface!

Don't touch her, you don't know where her hands have been!

That "bun" of hers looks like Alan King's "face."

That's just a tabloid-newspaper clipping, you fake bitch!

And sundry other vile insults the like of which it is our fervent wish that you won't hear them, or your loved ones either, in a month of Sundays, despite the fact that the voice of the people, loud in the land like unto as always, is the voice of the sovereign will of Great Mankind! So the uncaring beetles stumbled against her as the sand whirled in crazy motes as it has whirled and will forever whirl, so long as the sun shall clamber wearily into the sky far above the lambent plang of the beautiful yet harsh plains where—was it only yesterday?—the Bison sang and galloped to the lilting tune of the wind in the harsh cactus-peat and dropping figwort.

She returned to Blue in tears, her bun undone, her "suit" in disarry, her tiny shoes a-scuff and caked with the harsh mud of the plains on which the Great Shaggy Bison once sang their haunting song in violent bellows to the echoing rocks that sometimes suddenly fall off the scarps and craggy brows of yawning chasms, there to (or here to) plunge into a well-deserved . . . oblivion! Yes, Nature was and shall be cruel, despite our petty attempts at taming her inscrutable ways. The Marquis de Sade oft whispered this in the moonlight to his companions. Now *Helene* was aware of this! But perhaps it was . . . too late!

It is not too late! Serge cried, never, *never* say that it is too late, oh my darling! My puffball dandelion! Dry your eyes and warm your dukes around a cup of jamoke, fresh made, with funny little tasteless cookies huddled together on the saucer that it would be wise to place on your knees or lap since with both of your mitts cupped around the life-giving joe, it will be impossible, or nearly so—and here he gave his wild, rending laugh!—to hold the saucer!

No, it is not too late, Helene said, for she was not averse to going along with her hub for a laugh or so, since it had become obvious to her lately that he often talked funny, funny . . . *crazy* things! But I can't flog these fingernail items. And I'm tired . . . so tired . . . I want to go to Californy.

And so we shall! But don't cry. Why, why are you crying?

A man said that I . . . a man said that . . . he called me "weedface." Another said other dirty things, like "gashface" and "shit-hair." Yet another, in a strange sorta cap with some green plastic over his eyes said that I looked like a plate of grits and greens. I don't think I can go on feeling this way about my essential value as a person and with many self-doubts that grow and grow and finally reduce me to inertial cessation.

My beloved! Such woids as these, but, are pet names to turn aside the dazzle of your beauty. How long has it been since I enumerated your charms?

Many a windswept moon!

Then let me rectify all this while I sauté a fillip of reviving hash. And he did, thus:

272

≪ 57 ≫

Le Blason Médaillon

Upon your face your nose sits, like a jewel;
And shines, white milkweed, with its glist'ring grease.
Its bursting blackheads make a man a fool;
For jet are they, like Eros's valise!
Your bulbous eyes are cherries, both cerise,
And over them hulk brows, like dark toadshade;
They meet, like elves who couple in a glade.
Your mouth's a splash of dead rugosa rose,
Whose nether lip descends as mad cascade;
And in that mouth your tooth like pigweed glows.

Below that witching cavern shakes your chin;
The purest tint of bloodroot that I know,
All speckled o'er with fire pink like sin.
Your neck's a ringer for a mound of snow
On city streets, and sports a hue like crow.
That vast, wise brow as pale as buttonbush
Seels close your thoughts, as dense as thickest mush;
And Hermes' flying feet envy your ears.
But best of all, your scalp rains down, my thrush,
A scurf that hides these charms that I hold dear.

≪ 58 ≫

In Which
the Desert Sands
Become a Colorful Riot

Once more emboldened with sturdy wherewithal and other necessities of provisioning, and with the chink of silver chinking in their chunky purses, they started on what we now know will be the last push toward that ever-elusive goal. After some days and nights of traveling, they entered a land rich in strangeness and saw sands, plain desert sands, of which they had seen aplenty in the past fortnight or so, even a month! But this sand was somehow . . . different, and with quickened pulses, they stood and looked at it all as if they had not seen it before, or as if they were seeing it for the first time, or as it must have looked, or seemed, to those first plucky Esquimaux who walked down over the ice and snow of what is now the great city of pulsing Sacramento! How fresh it must have looked, or *seemed* to look to those hardy aborigines. And so it was to Blue and Helene, who pulsed as all men must when e'er they pull up short in awe!

Here—were there but something to drink and bathe in, something to wash their garments in, clean of dirt and grime, not to say the grit that is part and parcel of such climes, and notwithstanding their nicety of attention to personal grooming such dirt is an unavoidable problem, one that even General Custer faced (and no greater cleanliness buff ever lived and sported in these parts)—here, they thought as one—such was the beauty of the "spot"—they might live forever, far from the tumult and corruption of the city, live in peace and tranquillity, even going so far as to postpone, and indefinitely, if need be, Serge's search for the goal of all this his long quest, the fruition of these hard travails, the Phrase to make all chime as one in Beauty! Yes.

For they had indeed come to a strange, a bewitched and shimmering land of profligate colors, shifting, blending, shining in the bright limpid sunshine all the way to the horizon, and perhaps—beyond! Who can tell? Not the ardent chigger nor the blear-eyed philosopher prone beneath his midnight oils and watercolors. No living thing stirred in all that vast expanse of tints, shades, and tones, save

274

perhaps for the quick scuttling Gila monster dragging a placid cow into his lair, or upsetting a faded Dixie cup in his abrupt panic, a Dixie cup dropped generations ago from the beak of a bluejay or chickadee who, though long dust, lives on in the songs that weave their way into the sky of nights around many a long-decayed bunkhouse. All was still, yet all was a riot of color.

Blue and Helene stood in the midst of these breathtaking colors, silent and awed, still . . . still as an unravished bride in a silent, perhaps Theda Bara or Lillian Gish or even the most silent of them all, Garbo. This they somehow knew without speaking, without uttering a sound.

There, before their astonished eyes, their worshipful glances, the colors seemed to shift and blend, yet curiously stand out clearly as crystal too, yes, shift and blend and meld and mix and slide together in a veritable riot. Some, yes, some clashed and exploded! Some slided mysteriously, almost imperceptibly into other colors—and all, all in riotous profusion!

It's what I've always dreamed of, yearned for, cared deeply about, Serge whispered, almost as if speaking for the first time. To stand here, alone, or with another person or two, or even a small group as long as they didn't chatter and yak it up—and here he squeezed her negligible hand in his manly one—lost, dreaming, rapt almost in that opulent, that majestic, that unearthly *riot* of colors! I could almost stand here forever, with but a few short breaks for meals, of course.

Yes, Serge, she beamed, with a small look of concern. You must eat regularly, but lightly.

Darling!

But you have promises that you must keep on going for, she said. Like the man who must let go of the appletree limb so that he can fly wildly through the air and into his neighbor's garden to hoe it like he said he would.

How well he knew! For hadn't he, as a boy, often propelled himself through the summery air on one of his many boyish errands? The truth of his wife's simple statement struck him in his deep heart's core. Yes, he must buckle! And, buckling, the great fire that would gush forth then would match, in its wild and almost incredible riot of colorful flames, this color, or colors, lavishly promiscuous before, behind, and everywhere! Yet it *had* been a wonderful dream. And somehow, the lushness seemed a kind of omen of success, the colors seemed to portend a certain victory, the innate beauty of the place seemed to assure a happy conclusion. But why? Who can know the secrets of the earth's wordless messages, especially when they cannot be heard? Yet they were somehow *there*, as is the pickerel in late July.

Look! Blue said, his voice become a veritable chocking block of awe. Like the spotless and chaste lingerie of a benevolent dictator's faithful wife and political confidante, some of the sands are a desert, whisper, winter white, a marshmallow, like star chickweed, oconee bells, swamp lily, or whitewash snowberry; some, akin to the pure thoughts of a Methodist minister, shine a sort of crystal, reminding one of grass of Parnassus, floating hearts, and goldthread; still others fill the misty eyes like the snow in a Christmas TV commercial and glitter as antique linen and pyxie, mountain sandwort, wood anemone, false violet, or the chuckling thimbleweed! Then there are the dunes that shine like the teeth of a fascist movie star, all chinchilla, rapt in tones of arrowhead, vervain, devil's bit, foamflower, and lizard's tail. And what about those that look like the socks of a Jewish tennis player? They are not sweet cream for nothing, lambent as fly poison, turkey beard, yucca, feather-bells, and pokeweed, not to mention shepherd's purse and enchanter's nightshade. The knolls white as the contract ceding public lands to oil companies? Sure! Look, they pulse bone white, similar to boneset, catnip, titi, dodder, and jimsonweed. And shimmering like a heaven devoid of the stinking poor, champagne white of course, those hills all goldenseal, nodding ladies' tresses, silverrod, pennywort, Queen Anne's lace, pearly everlasting, showy orchis, and the Venus flytrap; and now my eye falls upon a vision of purity like the clouds over luxurious Palm Springs, home of vague moronic moguls—a kind of white smoke and ocean spray inheres therein, bringing to mind the aura of bloodroot, colicroot, and death camas. And next to that sprawled luxury, yet another, peach white as a pimp's Cadillac, all over goatsbeard, bouncing Bet, sweet Cicely, and oxeye Daisy, not to forget painted Trillium, Carolina Anemone, and Daisy Fleabane. Some of the smaller mounds are as blank as the sound of Aaron Copland and the taste of American pizza, warm white in the sun, and undefiled as smaller pussytoes. And there, far off, so dim that one can hardly see that it is candid white as the mushroom cloud of a nuclear bomb, a hill all antique and cameo, sad as hobblebush, rue, and nightshade, still as one-flowered cancer root.

And at the edge of that gorgeous hill, blending into it, a small range of mesas, Blue, Helene gasped. See? All green as Kelly, shamrocks, seafrost, and the sea; as crème de menthe, lime fizz, sage, moss, and doublemint. Green as a goddess! And that luscious green of money, that stuff that politicians are not in it for, that isn't everything, that is not all that important, that the poor don't really deserve, that the rich work so hard to get, that bestows wisdom and moral superiority, that there are certain things people won't do for, that people are not ashamed of taking, that it's good to know the value of, that doesn't grow on trees, that congressmen vote themselves regretfully, that has no conscience. Just look at that rich glow! 'Tis the same shade as carrion flower, marijuana, stinging nettle, rattlesnake master, and false, very false hellebore, and also looks a little like the color of the bluebeard lily. It is a vivid panorama of the world! Purity and pelf playing at old sixty-nine!

Perception, as they say here and there, is thine, adorable doxy, Blue said. And as you were finishing your idyllic bout of nomenclature, it chanced that the odd desert light, waxing and prospering, as it will do at this hour of the day, has revealed, see? right up close, sands and such that seemed but ordinary in the shade, but can now be seen as reddish pink, or pinkish red, this sprawl of turfish stuff at our feet the color of the beans of the happy, happy poor, or perhaps the delicate flush of radiation lesions, a species of rosetone, ginger, fire dance, fiesta, one might say peachy creamy red! Looks sort of like eyebright or rough blazing star, crazyweed or goat's rue. And to the right, fantastic ridges, the lambent tones of the polluted Passaic or the blood used to dye the Soviet flag, adazzle like unto tomato, lobster, sleepy pink, and russet, flying the cracking banner of the locoweed, the obedient plant, the crab's-eye, the curly dock, and the wild bleeding heart. To the left, pristine and pregnant as the discarded sanitary napkin in the executive secretary's washroom and the Carlisle dressings scattered about on Heartbreak Ridge, radiant as tile, paprika, and shrimp, small whorls that bring to mind Sheep Sorrel, Cardinal Flower, Coral Bean, Moss Campion, Herb Robert, Rose Pogonia, Bull Thistle, Rose Vervain, Wild Basil, Virginia Rose, and the ravishing Rhodora, the queen of the prairie, as well as many other bloody folk. And out there by the dry arroyo, a narrow strip as crimson as the opium poppy and as pink as the nipples of the incestuous father's little girl—note the mélange of bricks, maroons, cherries, and burgundies, like nothing so much as wild coffee, ragged Robin, and the misnamed live-forever. Beyond the same arroyo, candy red as the blush that ne'er suffuses the book reviewer's face and April pink as the stain at the bottom of a sputum cup, another strip all spreading dogbane, New York ironweed, and Deptford pink, stirred in with Jack-in-the-pulpit and pinesap. And last, almost impossible to see, but throbbing crimson as the lights of classy Vegas, and persimmon as numberless necks in Dixie, are a clutch of majestical mounds of blooming clay that splash the weary earth with a bright thrum of bee balm, salvia, corn cockle, teasel, rabbit-foot clover, swamp smartweed, wild garlic, and steeplebush. How it all broods and beats like the foolish heart that has, as it is said, its reasons for doing so!

I see and am justifiably astonished, Helene said, trembling in the Beauty extravagant before her. But it seems e'en as we look that the reddish-pinkish stuff is metamorphosing into that happy color, orange! It sprawls delightfully like as that famous herbicide that helped achieve an honorable peace, like orange ice and scarlet pimpernel; like the millions of California oranges bulldozed and buried so the spicks and niggers cannot have 'em, like candelero orange and spotted touch-me-not; or as gay party lanterns by the dead and festering Potomac, as bandeau velour and flame azalea; or the sound of screams from magic Ulster, bittersweet, oh bittersweet, oh climbing bittersweet; it also has the gorgeous touch of napalm killing terrorists, of which there is a passel, like flame, like trumpet creepers; as well as the formidable flash from the sportsman's rifle, tiger orange, butterfly weed; some of it seems to wondrously implode, like the rocket falling softly on a hospital, all cinnabar and Carolina mallow; or else it seems the sultry glow o'er burning Southern California, coral beach and orange hawkweek in its subtlety; there's a tiny dune as bright as fire from pre-emptive strikes, as hot as orange jazz, as dense as hoary puccoon; and huddled next that mix, another staggeringly similar to the rash of secondary syphilis, kind of apricot or turk's-cap Lily; the huge area blending into the horizon far is the spit and image of hearty and nutritious ravioli in a can, amber, pumpkin, orange milkwort; and the wall of mesas to the right shine like the hair of has-been actresses, harsh as tigerlilies, frizzy as the yellow fringed orchid. And now, see, it is changing back again!

And as always, Blue continued, as certain as cheek is by jowl, and foot is in mouth, and elbow is an ass, the magisterial yellow plotzes languidly next its orange buddy. Dig on that alchemically transmuting mix and stew and huge ragout quiv'ring in—what else?—the yellow sun! At times it variously seems the color of the healthful smog breathed by the wondrous folk who live in Beverly Hills, the lemon peel in the drunken editor's fourth Martini, the wide and bonedeep streak down the anchorman's back, the tons and tons of butter rotting in cold storage, the pus from soldiers' wounds, the lovely color of orphanage sheets, the urine puddles in tenement hallways, the discreet stain in the fashion model's underpants, the dainty callous on the First Lady's dainty foot, the tortillas of the chiseler welfare Mex, the hard-hitting editorial against the injured and insulted, and that strange creamy goo that is called "mustard" in the Heartland! It's all we love, and seems to be together and apart, eggnog, lemon, harvest gold, sunshine, primrose, peach parfait, curry, forsythia, and too, a sky of buttermilk, a sunbeam, a mandarin, maytime, chiffon pie, the crazy carrousel, and buxom blondes in sunlight! All those things made to resemble stuff in Nature's woods and brakes and dales and glades and bosks—yellow thistle, yellow flag, golden club, yellow lady's slipper, showy rattlebox, golden alexanders, smooth false foxglove, evening primrose, common tansy, broom snakeweed, spicebush, pussy willow, celandine, frostweed, the giant sunflower, and the humble, hoary, hairy, and historical hedge mustard. Thus yellow, like a tidal wave of piss, doth engulf the world!

But, my darling boon companion, Helene wavered spousily, there is another couple hectares out there that must needs be enumerated; I mean those that celebrate your name: Blue! You got a fleet blue, a blue lake, a bluebell, a surf blue, a little boy blue, a chalk blue, a blue sky, a blue mist, a crystal blue, all mushed together in a kind of haze and cloud like so much starlight! How it all brings back to me the humble flowers that I used to grow in windowboxes, and gather in my yearning arms like so many . . . humble flowers! The bluet, the common blue violet, the blue curl and the chicory, the blue flag and the cutesy monkey-flower, the blue toadflax, indigobush, leadplant, blue salvia, Texas bluebonnet, wild blue phlox, and the wild blue Mary, what a broad! And how can I neglect to give honorable mention to the bluebeard lily and the silly little pokeweed? I can't. All of it together brings to mind certain emblems of our proud and firm-jawed civilization, blue as blue can be, like the minds of black men, the blood-lines of moronic families, the bruises on a neglected child, the vile stories that rot the moral fiber of our doughboys just before they get their limbs blown off, the lacy garter on the homely bride's scrawny thigh, the clear eyes of our most ad-mired killers, cheap gin in bad light, the circles under the beggar's eyes, the per-fumed exhaust from the Rolls-Royce, King James's Jesus' eyes, a bad Monday for the small investor, and the ruffled shirts worn beneath pink dinner jackets by sparkling celebrities. One might think the whole world this suffusing color, just like Alice did her gown when she primped in every shop window.

Whoever said, Serge shone, that you are but a nit was talking through his bowl-er! And if you'll notice, that blue on occasion shifts in the spanking sunshine to its bro, the pulsing purple and vivacious violet! Do you feast your eyes, my sister! There's the royal purple, like sea lavender, that the dumbest people are invaria-bly born to; the purple wine like the eyes of a mugger's victim, bright as sea lav-ender; the blushing violet of the battered wife's back and buttocks, something like the sea lavender; the wild orchid of the corona of the slum arsonist's match flame, burning cold as sea lavender; the deep purple of the plums given political ass-nuzzlers, dark and noble as the sea lavender; the lavender mood—sort of like the . . . sea lavender!—of Presidential proclamations; the puky purple of the old office clerk's black suit, the sheen of sea lavender; the purple haze in which the House of Representatives is wrapped, dim as the dumb sea lavender; the pale violet of the blues by whites, thin as the sea lavender; the lavender mood of a tux that Hugh Hefner might wear, loud as sea lavender; the orchid burst of high-priced suede, the lushness of sea lavender, worn by whores with hearts of purest shit; and the lilac brook, close-grown with scintillant sea lavender, that tints and tones the tooth marks on the lady lobbyist's inner thighs.

And now as the shades are falling, sternest schlepper, Helene peeped, and cimmerian night creeps up and around the shifting dunes beyant, I seem to see the furthest acres of these sands plunging into brown. Yes, I am correct! Color most germane to this great industro-technocracy! if you will pardon the coinage for a nonce. We see mocha, mahogany, nutmeg, rawhide, chocolate, cocoa, java, seal, coffee, tobacco, manila, caramel, potter's clay, and the ducal dusty sage! How it brings to mind the poison sumac! The prairie smoke! The giant reeds! How one is forced to think of barnyard grass and skunk cabbage and the spotted coalroot! These things rhyme and chime and clang in a poetic orgy of cognates with the things that are still not perfect with the world, although, by God, our leaders never cease from trying to perfect it all for us, the folk! I think of the mud of glorious battlefields and the tons of shit forever roaring 'neath our cities, towns, and hamlets to the rivers and the seas. Of the color of our world leaders' anuses, a common touch, and the cockroaches in the walls of the White House. Of the deep interior of a TV-producer's head and the color of the Broadway theater's soul. Of the lowly turd—by whom forgot?—in a toilet bowl in the Plaza and the once cream-colored paint of an unemployment office. Of the cigar-stained teeth of a corporation lawyer and the ultimate color of a best-seller's pulpy leaves. And of the sky that gleams o'er Pittsburgh and the smell of an Army base. So is the whole world, it seems, in a brown study.

You've hit the old bolt squarely on its hexagonal noggin, my love, said Blue, and as you talked, the sun slid further down so everything is now that greyness or that blackness that makes one think of sterner stuff, like smoke and steel and battleships! Like charcoal, famished gulls, and slate! Like putty! Like aluminum! Like the Wehrmacht's uniforms! What is this dimness but that of the call-girl's stockings, the ghostly air of Ellis Island, the mood of the welfare office? What but the tuxedo of the self-made man, the reform politician's limousine, the corporation president's hard stool? What but the motives of the Pentagon, the migrant worker's future, the rats of Harlem? What but Miss America's pubic hair, the interior of presidents' graves, and spunky Harry Truman's spot in Hell? And all held up, my dear, on that great, grim, nameless plant on which the universe does sway and disappear in mammoth chunks into the godless void.

The night fell suddenly.

« 59 »

"La Musique et les mauvaises herbes," Concluded

XVII AN ATTACK OF MALADY

When a student has some annoyances with the health, he takes himself to the clinic of the University. There he finds some doctors who make all to him possible for the cure. The day before some exams, there is a crowd of golden bricks who wish to find asylum at the clinic, because habitually the life there is enough calm. Last Thursday, André is going to consult the doctor about a small malady. When he is return to the old boarding house, Émile wishes to learn all the details of his visit because he is a nosing type.

ÉMILE: Hey then, my old man! How goes the bad?

ANDRÉ: Not too much bad, thanks. They have given on me a medicine what has already aided me.

ÉMILE: But what is that what you have? Is it that they have found something serious bad, like a "bull clap" or an old Joe?

ANDRÉ: My goodness, no! What are you trying to make me have the air of—a downed-out jijolo?

ÉMILE: No, my bosoms bud. I have a care on you is what.

ANDRÉ: It is but a little strain in the groinal region what is not very grave. It endures no more than forty-eight hours. But the doctor wants that I pay it attention and rest in the bed.

ÉMILE: Holy cripes! How does one achieve this strain? Is it from making the exercise or the imbecile jog or some things like this?

ANDRÉ: Ha! Ha! Ha! It is an exercise what calls itself "too much of crazy sex acts."

ÉMILE: Ah, now I see this. And Suzanne? Does she have the bad in the similar region? Pardon my rude quiz, if you please, but I know how you like to make with her the bizarre stunts.

281

ANDRÉ: Well . . . I must confess that the lady in these case is not *solely* Suzanne.

ÉMILE: Aha! It is also Catherine, the maid of your house, the young patootie of formidable biscuits?

ANDRÉ: No. That young lady is innocent of this case. It is—you will keep the mouth mummed?—my Professor of Bassoon, Mrs. Chaud.

ÉMILE: Whoom! Mrs. Chaud! If I could make a sex act on this gorgeous lady for five moments, I will permit my groinal region to have a bad for a week! She is some tootsie!

ANDRÉ: In effect! You should regard her when she has disrobed off her garments. I thought that I would go a piece deranged!

ÉMILE: I don't think I have the desire to chats with you on this topic. It makes me to stimulate too much.

ANDRÉ: I have a horror to speak on this to Suzanne. And I have also a horror to terminate off these connections with Mrs. Chaud. I am too dipsy on this lady.

ÉMILE: Do you wish that I might become a pal with Suzanne? I perhaps can make it easy to you to tell a "see you later" on her.

ANDRÉ: Boys! I have the fear that I can see in you like you are a cellophane. I have the aware, my raunchy mate, that you have the huge hot on Suzanne. And now it appears to you that you can do sex on her by the hours without having a care that I will make a harsh pummel on your face.

ÉMILE: Do you tell to me then that you have the plan to make sex acts on both Suzanne and Mrs. Chaud? What a greedy cupid things you are!

ANDRÉ: Yes, I have this plan, you sly popsqueak! And if I can, I make also a sex with Monique Gaine, Sophie Jupon, Marie Mamelle, and by damn it, I even make a sex on Alice Cuisse without a care that she is a levee!

ÉMILE: She is what calls itself a dike, you dumbo thing!

ANDRÉ: I don't care a piss jar how it calls itself! You are not to make the free on Suzanne!

ÉMILE: I don't believe in the ears I have. I think maybe that you would also do a soiled act with the men, maybe even with the wolfs and the zebras and the damn walruses. Whew!

ANDRÉ: It is only on ladies what I enjoy to make dirty things. But I don't care of your stupid ideas on me what ring like the usual shits from the homo-types of persons. Leave me alone and go play on yourself, eh?

Émile makes a storm out of the chamber. He is having a furious rage because he cannot bear up that André has such a fortunate career with ladies of all age and shapes. André rests in the bed reading on Suck My Whip, *an indecent novel. All the ladies of this narrative have the image to his brains of Suzanne, Monique, and Mrs. Chaud. He is a satyr type of bozo in every direction!*

XVIII A BIRTHDAY TREAT

In the leavy burg where André and Suzanne make their studies, there is a somewhat nice Chinks restaurant where they go for to fete the birthdays or on other important events, such as when Suzanne find out she has not got a bun in her oven. Evidently, this place costs much dear, but they do not regret for a long time the bucks who they dispense for a masterpiece of Chinks chow.

SUZANNE: Oh boys! We owe to command a dinner à la Chinks from a start until the end. Do you have enough of the mazuma, my potato-face?
ANDRÉ: I have ought to make of the economies during three months for to pay for this chow. My gosh sake, your chummy pal, Jacques Derrière, tell to me that I am squiz an eagle until he make a shits—I don't know what he mean of this, but I think it means of being too much cheap.
SUZANNE: Do not bring that wormhead up on me, eh? I do not have any taste for him for some times. Fuck on him!
ANDRÉ: Very good. I have want that this dinner of my birthday it will be perfect. I believe I have all the mazuma of which we will be having the needs. What a oddbell word is this "mazuma," no? It give me to chuckle.
SUZANNE: I believe that it is the name the ancient Aztec chieftain call himself, for that he was so flushed. But who gives a care? Let us go ahead and command a real Chinks dinner. Anyhow, I have some mazuma what I can give to you if you will have a need on this.
ANDRÉ: In what fashion have you gained mazuma, my casabas?
SUZANNE: I am having some jobs from the Bureau of Placement over here and down there.
ANDRÉ: Not bad, swits! I hear on you. Now, what is it that you wish for to commence on?
SUZANNE: I ought to think on my lovely shape, for I would not be too content to have too grand a buttock, and finish up with the looks of . . . Mrs. Chaud, for an instance. But I have too much of a famish tonight, and I want to take a soup made from the bird-eye and loco weeds.
ANDRÉ: Hey, syrups, do not have a worry on to get the looks of the buttock of Mrs. Chaud! She has this for the reason of laying down on these always. Ha! Ha!

283

But a damn hell on these professors tonight, eh? This soup, it is that cold one in what they place the small beetles? Me too, I wish to essay the son of a guns! Now, tell me of what tempts you as a meat plate.

SUZANNE: I want to have a goose balls in the chocolate and green peppers and onions gravy, what calls itself the swit and bitter . . . Say, you seem to have a large idea on the sex lives of Mrs. Chaud—do you still continue to make the occasion of an intimate act on her, you two-timely rodent?

ANDRÉ: But no! What type of a chap do you take me? I was having to make the joke what makes around in the School of Music. Be a nice young lady, eh, and permit us for a single time not to look for a henshit quarrel!

SUZANNE: All right, sugars. It is just that I have the venetian blind on this lady professor.

ANDRÉ: You have the what on her?

SUZANNE: Oh craps! How does it call itself? I have lost this words. Ah! I have the *jealousy* on her!

ANDRÉ: Jesus in the heaven, you are some time a silly pussy. Venetian blind! Ha! Ha! Ha!

SUZANNE (*weeping of hot tears*): You are some vile oafs.

(*Suzanne honks off her nose onto the foulard.*)

ANDRÉ: Oh, my wild tickle, I beg a clemency. Let us go ahead on the chow, if you please?

SUZANNE: Yes, but have a care of your loosed mouth, eh?

ANDRÉ: In effect. I am going to command the rotted eggs poached up in sour milk. And I see that the ritzy cookies are served on this plate. Whum, what a thrill on the jade palate!

SUZANNE: Me, I would like some chicken grease with the smashed-up garlic. Is it that this will go with the goose balls?

ANDRÉ: These ought to go exceedingly strong as an ensemble. And what salad will you make a choose on?

SUZANNE: What I choose will be the Three Onions Special—the red onion, the white onion, and the Bermudas onion what has on this the dressing of scallions and shallots in the oil.

ANDRÉ: My goodness! Ha! Ha! Ha!

SUZANNE: Why is it that you make this big laugh on me? I do not believe rilly that I am content to be a pal this evening, birthday or not. You appear as too crude and nasty on me.

ANDRÉ: You are making a big big vex to me, softy, with this petty sulks. I am making the laugh for that with the onions and garlics and scallions and shallots—and who in a blaze could know what is it you will command for the dessert!—I am having the image that I must look over my shoulders when I make some sex on you later, or else I might have a swoon. Ha! Ha! Ha!

SUZANNE: Then make a sex until your hose falls off on this fat sluts, Mrs. Chaud, you decay of a smut!

Suzanne has great fury and commences to throw on André the china of the Chinks as well also as the knifes and forks and spoons, the glasses, the pitcher full up of water, the napkin, and the vase of faked flowers of the table. Then she whoomps on his head with a chair and a small moment after makes the thrust with her dainty feets upon his bottoms and soon after into a groin. It appears like a curtain for this romance, eh?

XIX THE END OF THE DAY

For the students, one of the best moment of the day comes in the evening when all the studies are terminated. The buddies of the old boarding house reunite in some chambers for the gossip in ensemble before couching themselfs. These reunions are never organized: they arrive spontaneously without premeditation.

Eleven hours are coming to ring. One hears the clonks of the books what shut themselfs, and two moments later, Charles Ordurier and Émile Fesses are seating down in a chamber of André Lubrique and Jacques Derrière.

CHARLES: I am much content of to have terminated that stinking paper of the beet-sugars industry! But I have a feat that it will be less fine than the other ones, even although Sophie Jupon made me a good assistance on it. She has the big brains, this young lady, no?

ANDRÉ: The big brains? Sophie Jupon? Ha! Ha! Ha!

CHARLES: These laughs has the sound of much dirt in them, you snail. To which are you driving?

ÉMILE: Pay out no mind on him, my old hump. André is a large amount of feces! Go forward on the story of Sophie, if you please.

CHARLES: It is not too much of the story, Émile. Sophie makes to work with me yesterday night in the library until they cast us outside. She did the good demonstration to me how to make the paper organize itself. But creepy Jesus! I have such a disgust on this boring beets I get an ennui just to speak this word.

JACQUES: If she gives an assistance on you in the manner of the young ladies of the School of Fertilizer Arts, kiddoo, you will be making the walk on the knees, eh André?

ANDRÉ: You can bet some long greens on this, bebby. Sophie Jupon has the big brains! Ha! Ha! Ha!

CHARLES (*his collar rising quick*): Listen, you . . . *beet*. I demand to know the reason for you to make this comical sounds!

ÉMILE: "Beet" is greatly piquant! Ha! Ha! One is at the lose to think on a fruit what is more to loathe like these beet. André the Beet. Ha! Ha!

ANDRÉ: Émile is pissed out on me for that I am the close friend with Suzanne Jarretière, what he has always some big hot on.

ÉMILE: Oh, yes? But I can hear no sound of your loose lip what describes how you want to make a sex act with any thing which draws up the breath. You liberty!

JACQUES: Aha! You have the desire to be the big Don Casanova, eh? You snikky shoe! I give a thank that I neglected to make a meeting of you and my young floozie. You would without a doubts probably put her down on the back in a flashes, no?

ANDRÉ: In effect! Or maybe on the knees. Ha! Ha! Ha!

CHARLES: Hey! I still desire to have a light shedded to this rotting laugh of André. Speak on me, you clap!

ANDRÉ: I have the impression it will give you a bad in the head, old socks.

CHARLES: Just speak on me!

ANDRÉ: All right, grease-nose! It is not that Sophie Jupon has the big brains what make her the honors of the class. Sophie is the sot in the head, rilly.

JACQUES: Sophie? I consider that you have been taking in the pipe, old man.

ÉMILE: It is not to marvel at. He has jazzed out the brains of him to a frizzle!

CHARLES: The sot in the head? Sophie? She has the list of A's like an arm.

ANDRÉ: Don't believe nothing on that, my poop-eyed friend. Do you know of the Dean of Womens, Berthe Fouet?

CHARLES: But yes. She is a lady of much charm and the exciting fatal shapes.

JACQUES: The rumor bruits it that she wears no undergarments beneath the clothes. Robert Caleçons had spoke on me that he had a fine peer on her one time when she made to bend over a file and a knocker emerged from her dress.

ÉMILE: Robert Caleçons is a fruity goon! He could never identify a knocker from the hole of the ground.

CHARLES: What is all of this have to make on Sophie Jupon, eh?

ANDRÉ: Hold on to the water, comrade, and I will speak on this.

CHARLES: Let the old porno-brains speak.

ANDRÉ: Sophie Jupon and Dean Fouet have make together—how does it call itself?—the "item"? Or to place this in a rude expression, they adore to make the unnatural smut acts together while Mr. Fouet regards them. Pretty twisted up, eh? So it is that Sophie, who has the brains of a slabs of Camembert, get the A for every things.

CHARLES: Is these a facts? Or some large fragment of the shit?

ANDRÉ: Who knows this as the facts? I have not regarded this in my person. I hear on this by Suzanne to which it was whisper by Alice Cuisse, who is, as all the world knows, a lady homu.

JACQUES: It calls itself a "homo," you crazy some things!

ANDRÉ: What it the fuck call itself I don't give a hail of beans!

ÉMILE: What a wised-up acre you are, André. How do you make an explaining why the professors of Sophie fail to make a clamor on this stuffs, eh?

ANDRÉ: Because Dean Fouet, you frig-face, has the Polaroid shoots, the recording tapes, the whole shooting-work of these crowd of professors and how they do the smutty acts and speech to the students of them.

JACQUES: Holy cat! This can of the worms would make some scandal!

CHARLES: Oh ball! So my paper of the beet-sugar industry is a damn F!

ANDRÉ: I think that this is the bad fact, my old saps.

Charles continues to make a large complaint on lack of the justice. Jacques and André speak to him that it appears sure that he is up shit river lacking the oar. Émile, who has the great odious on André, then makes the defense of Sophie Jupon and Dean Berthe Fouet, telling that they are as chaste like some old nuns. But whatever he makes to shout, no other buddies give him a tumbler, for that they are now chatting dirty things indeed on those two ladies. Émile discreetly wishes he should be Mr. Fouet, this vile hog!

XX THE TWO AUTOS

Each person knows that the modern lifes turns about of the auto. When the auto is running good, all goes good; but when one is deprive of this useful machine, one have the impression of having lost a member of the body, perhaps like even a hose or a nukie.

Yesterday morning, Mr. Aine is to go at eight hours less a quarter for to take him to the University at eight hours. A little before, he is come in the house for to announce a sad news on his wife.

MR. AINE: My cherry lips, it makes that I take your auto today. That of mine have the bursted tire, and I don't have a time of changing this. I have to be on the hour for a meeting with a student of mine, Miss Jarretière.

MRS. AINE: But you cannot take my auto, handsome poopsie. I have a need of it this morning in order for to make a rendezvous what is very important.

MR. AINE: My angel, I don't love much to derange you, but the appointment is of the first rank. Mrs. Chaud, Miss Jarretière, and I will be working in an ensemble all a morning longs. I must make an assistance in order that Miss Jarretière make the pass grades in Musical Appreciating. If I do not race to make to arrive on the hour, that wizzel, Fixe-Chaussettes, will steal my thunders out!

MRS. AINE: How is it that you make such an upset on this? You had always the huge loathe of remedy craps. Eh?

MR. AINE (*making the shuffle on his feets*): Well . . . Miss Jarretière has the good promises of great honors, and she is also of a young lady like a daughter what I don't got. And also, Mrs. Chaud has made a beggar on herself that I will assist on this matter. But how is it that *you* must keep such an early rendezvous?

MRS. AINE (*making the giggles from the nerves*): Berthe Fouet and her husband have made to invite me do a chats about being a chair peoples of a rubbish sales next month.

MR. AINE: It makes to find the solution then as quick as any things, for the time he is ticky-tocking away from us, no? Ah! Lend to me your auto; I will make the phone jingle on the garage man. He will come to repair the bursted tire of my auto, what you then can take. How does this sound on your ears, my idol-foot?

MRS. AINE: What a brains you have, my turkey! As smart as the whipping! I have the idea that every things will be jakes.

MR. AINE: Hot stiff!

(*Mr. Aine goes to make the jingle on the garage man.*)

MRS. AINE: Listen on me, my Grik god, if you please. Make the request on the garage man to send here Tisonnier to make a repair.

MR. AINE: Tisonnier? Is these the old gizzer what whittles up the logs all the days in the sunlight?

MRS. AINE: Ha! Ha! Ha! No, no, my tossed salad! Tissonier is the young and smart and bright and tall and strong and have the jolly face; the one what always make to smile and joke on us when we make to fill in the auto with petrol.

MR. AINE: Oh yes.

(*He makes the jingle through. At last!*)

MRS. AINE: It makes I think that you should leave. It is nearly eight hours. Here is the key on my auto.

MR. AINE: If I had no knowledge of who it is you are, I would be thinking that you are saying on me, "Here is the hat, why are you in a rush?" Ha! Ha! Ha!

MRS. AINE: Ha! Ha! Ha!

MR. AINE: By a ways, you appear of a great loveliness this morning, my hot fudge. The mascara, the eyelash, the black silk stockings, the stiletto heels? All this for a rubbish-sales rendezvous?

MRS. AINE (*she does a stutters*): Th-these ancient s-s-some things? They are as o-old as a h-h-hill. Ha! H-h-ha!

MR. AINE: Any ways, I speak to you, my sexy bombs, if I had some moments, I would do a sex act on you right here on the swill container. Whams!

MRS. AINE (*batting high and low the eyes on her*): Perhaps this evening, my bin-bag?

MR. AINE: In effect! And now I must run like the brizz!

Mr. Aine goes away in the auto of his wife for a very fruity meeting with Suzanne and Mrs. Chaud. They are taking from eight hours of the morning until near one hour of the afternoon. Mrs. Aine regards Tisonnier to fix the bursted tire and then makes on him some refreshment. How happy he is! Then she goes away in the auto of Mr. Aine to make the rendezvous with Berthe Fouet and her husband. How amazed she feels to find Sophie Jupon is present! They all make a very interesting morning. That evening, Mr. and Mrs. Aine fall into a sleep with the faces on them in the plates of dinner. It appears that they are too flagged out to make a sex act, or perhaps they have the bad in the head as an ensemble.

FIN

« 60 »

The Gavottes
Are Petrified by Awe

The sun is up and they are in an area to the south of the area they were in. The ground is arid and has been so for a long time and is stood upon by them. They are in a kind of large place that is one of six large places; that is, there are, and were, and will be six large places, one of which is the one that they are in. The light is bright and the sun is warm.

All around them in this place and all around them should they be in any of the other five places are pieces of what is, to them, stone. Or it may be rock. Some of this is to their front and some of it is to their rear, while some of it is to their right and some of it is to their left. Or it can be said by them, or others, or just one other, that some of these are to their front, rear, right, and left.

Some of it or some of these is, or are, on slopes so that these pieces are seen by them to be situated on an ascending plane if they are at the base of the plane; some of these are seen by them to be situated on a descending plane if they are at the crest of the plane; and some are not on slopes but are on flat ground; or some of it is on flat ground, or upward or downward slopes, as seen by them, that is.

Some of these pieces of what is to them stone or rock are trunks of trees that are very old. Some of these pieces of stone or rock (to them) are bits. Or pieces. Or bits and pieces and chips and shards and chunks. All the trunks are prostrate. Most of the trunks are broken and have been so for a long time. A few of the trunks are not broken and have of course never been broken. They have been not-broken for a long time too. Those that are broken will be broken for a long time, and those that are not broken will be not-broken for a long time unless they are broken soon or in a little while or in a long while. If they are broken they will never be not-broken.

The chips or bits or pieces or shards or chunks, or the chips and bits and pieces and shards and chunks are from the trunks, or were from the trunks. None of them will be from the trunks for they are. Those of them that will be from the trunks are not yet and will not be unless the trunks are to be broken.

The bits and pieces and chunks and chips and shards are scattered. Most are scattered around and about the trunks, both those that are broken and those that are not broken. Some are not scattered around and about the trunks but are scattered around and about each other. Some are on flat ground and some are on ascending and descending planes; in this way they are like the logs that some of them are from. It is also possible that some of these bits, shards, chips, chunks, and pieces are not and were not from trunks, but are or were what once were trunks and are no longer.

Some of the trunks are large in diameter and length. They were large in diameter and length, and they will be large in diameter and length. These are both the unbroken and prostrate trunks and the broken and prostrate trunks. They are of the same shape that they were when they were not stone or rock. That is, they are of the shape of tree trunks; those that are unbroken are very much the same in shape; those that are broken are very much the same in shape as well, except that they are broken, as they were not when they were tree trunks and not rock or stone.

Some of the trunks are small and were small. Both the broken trunks and the unbroken trunks are and were small. Their shapes, as are and were the shapes of the large trunks, are and were the same shapes as they were when they were tree trunks, except for the broken trunks, which were not broken when they were not stone or rock, but tree trunks.

They are all cylindrical in shape and were cylindrical in shape. These cylindrical shapes are the shapes that they were when they were tree trunks and not trunks of stone or rock. The large trunks, all of which are cylindrical, and the small trunks, all of which are cylindrical, both broken and unbroken (all are prostrate), will be cylindrical. The broken trunks are not large or long unbroken cylinders, but are of smaller cylindrical pieces, all of which pieces are close to each other insofar as they are pieces of what is and was and will be the same trunk that once was not stone or rock.

The scattered pieces and chips and chunks and shards and bits are of different shapes. Some are round and some are square and some are rectangular and some are pentagonal and some are hexagonal and some are heptagonal and some are octagonal and some are nonagonal and some are decagonal and some are of other shapes, some of which are possessed of names and some of which are not.

Some of these pieces are large and some of them are small, yet the largest of them are not so large as the smallest of the cylindrical pieces of the broken trunks and the smallest of them are not so small as a grain of something. Some of them are sharp and some of them are not sharp. They have been large and larger and small and smaller for a long time and will be. The largest and smallest of the chunks are somewhere but no one has been known to know where and it is probable that no one will ever be known to know where. It is also possible that the chunk which is largest and the chunk which is smallest may somewhere have exact counterparts, so that they cannot be the largest, or the smallest, but must be part of a category of, for instance, the two largest or the three largest chunks, and the two smallest or the three smallest chunks, and so on. This is possible but not probable, the probable being that there is indeed a largest and a smallest chunk. These largest and smallest chunks will be the largest and smallest chunks, or, it is probable that this will be the case.

It is probable also that some, small, smaller, and smallest, and large, larger, and largest, were once of different shapes than they now are, and that they will be of different shapes than they now are and have been. If not probable in all cases or in any cases at least this is possible, was possible, and will be possible.

The trunks, broken and unbroken, and the chips and pieces and such are of jasper and agate. There is some iron in them. The trunks and chips of jasper and agate with some iron are those trunks that are and were large and small and those chips of varied shapes which are possessed of names as well as of varied shapes that are nameless.

Some are brown. Some are yellow. Some are red. Some are of a brown tint. Some are of a yellow tint. Some are of a red tint. Some are all brown, some all yellow, some all red; some all of a brown tint, some all of a yellow tint, some all of a red tint. Some were of one category, some were of another category, some will be of one or the other. Some are, were, and will be of mixtures of brown, yellow, and red; or are, were, and will be of mixtures of brown tints, yellow tints, and red tints.

Some are or seem to be, or were, or seem to have been, or will be, though this is possible and not probable, black. Or of a black tint. Or of black in mixture with yellow, brown, or red, or tints of one or two or all or combinations of the colors that are and were. Yet some are green! Or blue! Or lavender! Or fuchsia! Or cerise! Or beige! And tints of same. And some are of other colors or tints of other colors.

Some may have been orange. Some may be purple. Some that were orange may be purple and some that may have been purple may be orange. And some not. None may have been these colors and none may be. Some that are yellow, brown, red, black, green, blue, lavender, fuchsia, cerise, or beige, may have been orange or purple or may be although they are not now. And some that are tints of these colors may have been tints of other colors or they may be although they are not now.

Some may have been or may be, although they are not now, rustic brown and whinny brown; or sweet yellow and juicy yellow; or ranch red and suburban red; or wild black and pirate black. And some may have been or may be, although they are not now, swing orange and winter orange and surprise green and terrace green and cadet blue and mulligan blue and trumpet and quadrille and blossom and coquette and yo-yo and love mist and shutter. This was or will be, or was and will be possible but it is not probable.

None are white. Some may have been white. Some may be white. Nor are any grey or silver. It is possible that some may have been and that some may be. Everything in the six places is still. It does not move. It has not moved for a very long time. It will not move for a very long time. This is probable.

« 61 »

The Great Ditch of the Great Southwest Greatly and Grandly Appears to Blue as the Grand Symbol of the Profundity, Nobility, and Gravity of His Hopes, Now Almost Realized

Torn from the weird and witchlike shifting of colors and the unearthly inertia of the timeless stone jungle as a pig that falls into the bracken and the spine-leaf clover is torn from out it by the calloused yet how kind hands and fingers of the cheerful swineherd with rough jest and merry song upon his split and calloused lips, thus were Blue and Helene so torn from out the weird and witchlike shifting of colors and the unearthly inertia of the timeless stone jungle.

Before them loomed, if one may use so insouciant a word, a ditch, a huge, long, vast, and deep ditch that stretched farther than the eye could see without aid of excellent and quite expensive binoculars. A great and grand ditch. Blue and Helene approached its vertiginous edge and peered into its depths, now soft in the approaching twilight.

He saw within crowded campions and celandines of coconino cheers, and heard them too!

He spied yelling yaks and yawping yanquis yodeling of yucca yakis!

Then too there were orisons and orotund oaths, all officious, of oxeye daisy, orchis, orchid, and osier oyster plant o'neills!

Yes! And kudos, kicks, and knightly nods of cornflower, cattail, cohosh, coral bean, and common milkweed, cannily catalogued as "kaibabs"!

294

Thin thrills and trills and toots and trembling tremors and temblors all over touch-me-nots and teaberries on a tray for tontos' tastes!

And there were those ingenious instruments that indicate that the inner gorge is intrinsically inviolate ivy!

And at the very bottom, or maybe not, but somewhere surely, the swell, subtle, stupendous sumners, scintillant and summery with smartweed, salvia, striped coralroot, storksbill, and the shiny, singing sweetness of the seaside gentian!

Blue sat at the piano and pounded it with those mighty hands that men have loved so well, and to a wild tune instanteously hauled from out his bowels, sang to Helene:

> The great ditch
> of the great Southwest
> appears to us! A symbol
> of the Profundity,
>
> the Nobility, and
> the Gravity of my
> hopes, my grand hopes,
> almost realized!
>
> Profundity!
> Nobility!
> Gravity!
> Hopes almost realized!

They excused, as the old saw has it, their dust! And the dust, as is its wont, excused them too.

And by dawn or thereabouts, maybe, say, eight, eight-fifteen, they crossed into Nevada, wherein strange things occurred, as will be seen.

« 62 »
Perhaps It
May Happen by Chance

Blue will find a copy of *Oui, Oui, Paris* that features a color layout of Miss Clarke Grable, in the nude, reading *La Musique et les mauvaises herbes*.

A toy piano will fall or be thrown out of the window of SAL'S BILLIARD ACADEMY.

A carhop at the BAR-B-Q DE-LITE will tell Helene that *her* name is Helene Gavotte and punch the former in the head causing the rest of her hair to fall out.

On the day that Blue and Helene arrive in Nevada, the top record throughout the state will be "Speak Nothin' But Good O' The Dead!"

Blue will glimpse Dr. Weede Bone wearing Dr. Ryan Poncho's clothes.

An old drunkard will sell Helene a white prune in which is carved what he claims is Tom Sawyer's face.

Zimmerman, now, oddly enough, nineteen or twenty years old, will find Blue and Helene.

In the Blue Palm Cafe, the chef's specialty will be Snow Peas in Orange Rinds with Chilies and Lemon Juice.

Helene will notice Dr. Ryan Poncho putting on a mask that looks exactly like the face of Dr. Ciccarelli.

Horace Rosette will be seen in a bookstore window autographing copies of *American Lake Poetry*.

Helene will find what seems to be her fedora in a ladies'-room stall.

Lesbia Glubit will buy Blue's bicycle clips for her private art-crafts collection.

The Rev. Tyrell Bloat will deliver a radio sermon on the important role of dental caries in the Search for God.

Rep. Harold "Hal" Glubit will officially open The Shearling Shoppe, assisted by Pops Ennui and the Crawdaddies, who will play their latest hit, "Green Old Dolphin."

Blue will suspect that the Mexican beggar on Zoshi Street is José Cizaña-Hueso, although he wears what appears to be Dr. Ryan Poncho's "palm-tree" tie.

Zimmerman will introduce his mother and father to his fiancée, a Miss Vincenza Grable.

Helene will begin receiving obscene letters on blue stationery, signed "Henry Flower."

The new, hard-hitting film, *Death in Dubuque*, starring Mariette Cliffe and Cheechee Docque, will open at the Sandstorm Twin.

Tom Piper will win $212,510 playing blackjack at the Red Swan Hotel Casino.

Joanne Bungalow will attend a publication party for her new book, *Rita's Agony*, wearing a pair of Blue's old bicycle clips, or copies of same.

Helene will eat a package of persimmon-flavored Oro-Sux lozenges and her hair will start growing in.

The Rev. Dr. Piscardi will return what seems to be Helene's fedora.

Helene's fedora will be copied by the new boutique, The Gumdrop Tree, owned by Clarke and Vincenza Dubuque.

Someone will mail Blue a copy of the long-out-of-print *Martin Chucklehead*.

Zimmerman will insist that he remembers nothing of any "cave."

A Blarney Spalpeen will threaten to sue Blue for libel and defamation of character.

Blue will notice Dr. Weede Bone picking up a package for Dr. Ryan Poncho at the Post Office.

Joanne Bungalow, on a talk show from Elko, will reveal that she is the author of *La Musique et les mauvaises herbes*, and will contend that it has never been translated.

Blue will find a beautifully-colored meerschaum inside his piano.

Helene will eat a package of witch-hazel-flavored Oro-Sux lozenges and her hair will start falling out again.

On awakening one morning, Blue and Helene will find their beloved pushcart newly painted.

Helene will receive a letter, on blue stationery, from Mlle Fifi Galleon, warning her to leave Henry Flower alone.

The sun will collapse in a panoply of horribly depressing colors as it used to do in Illinois.

Blue will see Dr. Ryan Poncho enter a house; a half-hour later, he will see Cheechee Docque leave the house in Dr. Poncho's clothes with Miss Clarke Grable on his arm.

A Bucol Suck will threaten to sue Blue for plagiarism.

The society column of the *Tonopah Trumpet* will announce the engagement of Dr. Vincent Dubuque and Miss Helene Gavotte.

What seems to be Helene's fedora will fall or be thrown out of the window of SAL'S BILLIARD ACADEMY.

José Cizaña-Hueso will be arrested for wearing the stolen undergarments of Miss Clarke Grable.

The *Reno Ratchet* will publish "Ah, Nature," by Fifi Galleon.

Father Donald Debris, S.J., will send Blue and Helene an invitation to his imminent marriage to Sister Rose Zeppole.

Blue will meet a man in The Shearling Shoppe who introduces himself as Henry Flower.

Zimmerman will break his engagement to Miss Vincenza Grable because of his passion for Miss Olga Warner, recently hired as a waitress by the Red Swan Hotel Casino.

Dr. Weede Bone will buy a completely new wardrobe and two days later Blue will see Dr. Ryan Poncho on the street in a suit from that wardrobe.

Mr. Jeeter Smiley will sell his rest-room wall to the Museum of Modern Art and move to Ely, where he will open Smiley's Symposium: Live Sex Acts.

Miss Olga Warner will fall in love with Miss Daphne Hawthorne, recently employed by station KYVD as a Production Assistant on the Rev. Dr. Piscardi's "Mouth of God Hour" and Zimmerman will disappear, taking Helene's fedora and the family copy of *La Musique et les mauvaises herbes*.

What seems to be Helene's fedora will be returned by Counselor Charlotte Siebold, who will discover it in her bunk at Camp Cottonwood, "Nevada's newest nirvana."

Mme Fifi Flower will perform in the first Smiley's Symposium stage show, assisted by two men wearing masks that look exactly like the face of Dr. Weede Bone.

Ole Joe Clark will make an indecent proposal to Miss Helene Gavotte, and, later in the day, an even more indecent proposal to Miss Daphne Hawthorne.

Horace Rosette will claim to have discovered evidence that *La Musique et les mauvaises herbes* is a French version of the eighteenth-century Spanish classic, *La golondrina*.

Freight Train 45 will derail in front of the BAR-B-Q DE-LITE.

Dr. Ryan Poncho will legally change his name to Dr. José Poncho.

Georgia Molly and John Tenbrooks will steal Helene's white prune and send it to Mme Fifi Flower wrapped in a sheet of blue stationery.

Judge Poon will close down Smiley's Symposium after it is denounced on the "Mouth of God Hour."

Miss Helene Gavotte will break her engagement to Dr. Vincent Dubuque after he is discovered in a state of partial undress with Miss Rubosa Pogue in some bushes off Interstate 95.

What seems to be Helene's fedora will be among the sex aids being auctioned off subsequent to the closing of Smiley's Symposium.

Rep. Harold "Hal" Glubit will buy a white pull-on girdle from the Rev. Jimmy Boo Purty and wear it in order to "brighten up" his flagging marriage, but will be chagrined when his wife identifies it as hers.

Zimmerman will return with his new bride, the former Margarina Jackson.

Joanne Bungalow will be arrested for assaulting Horace Rosette, but he will refuse to press charges against what he will later term "a distraught hack."

Big Black will create a stir in Elko when he claims that Marcus Garvey invented licorice.

Dr. Ciccarelli will denounce the Rev. Tyrell Bloat as "an oral upstart" and will be supported in letters to the *Tonopah Trumpet* by the Rev. Dr. Piscardi, Dr. Weede Bone, Dr. José Poncho, José Cizaña-Hueso, and C. Docque.

Margarina Jackson Gavotte, singing with Mickey Butor and the Time Passers, assists in the gala opening of Ely's first Boot Village.

Blue will be publicly reviled by Jambo Jambalaya and the entire Clair de Lune Orchestra as "an enemy of modern music."

Accidentally meeting Blue, Dr. José Poncho will deny vehemently that he is the Dr. Ryan Poncho of The College's faculty.

Someone, as a cruel joke, will send Helene a blow-dryer and a size 40, D-cup brassiere.

Captain Dirk Basura (Ret.), will meet Catherine Thigh, his childhood sweetheart, at a Purity in Sex Seminar in Carson City, and they will register at the Torrid Time Motel as the Rev. and Mrs. Jimmy Boo Purty.

Margarina Jackson Gavotte will divorce Zimmerman and move in with the Misses Daphne Hawthorne and Olga Warner.

Juan Pecos will buy the Blue Palm Cafe and turn it into the Speedwich Stop.

Zimmerman will blame his problems with women on the fact that his mother and father abandoned him in a cave, but they will insist that they remember nothing of any "cave."

Sister Rose Zeppole will move in with Margarina Jackson Gavotte, Olga Warner, and Daphne Hawthorne to research an article, for *The Healthy Mind*, that will be entitled "Another Part of the Forest: The Holes in the Dyke."

"Big" Hatcheta will offer Helene fifty dollars for her fedora.

Zimmerman will conduct a brief but explicitly erotic correspondence with Catherine Thigh and finally discover his sexual métier.

Sister Rose Zeppole, after joining the staff of *The Healthy Mind*, will alter her habit so that it falls to mid-thigh, and there ensues a welcome revival of interest in the Roman Catholic faith throughout Southern Nevada.

Tom Piper will buy Hatcheta's "Fedora with Mountains" for $110,000.

Blue will discover, by means of a note sent by Miss Clarke Grable, that all of Dr. Weede Bone's clothes are in Dr. José Poncho's house.

Lesbia and Harold "Hal" Glubit's white pull-on girdle will fall or be thrown out of the window of SAL'S BILLIARD ACADEMY.

Blue will write Joanne Bungalow how much he admires her "Supper at the Kind Brown Mill: A Country Drama," and she will ask him over for "a good time."

Blue, Helene, and Zimmerman will leave for California as all Nevada watches the Sanitation and Buildings Department board up the window of SAL'S BILLIARD ACADEMY.

«63»

California!
The End of the Quest

Together again as do the Fates or Graces or Muses or Furies all link together hands, all three of them, or all six, whatever you like or remember or feel like looking up in your well-worn copy of that beloved Reference Guide that sits patiently and covered o'er with dust, they were on the way to that shining bay across which that Golden bridge magisterially chucks itself! How wonderful it was that Zim was big and strong now, perhaps not too strong, but strong enough to help with the schlepping. And what schlepping it was!

Across the standardly blooming desert, all arid in its severe beauty, the cart rolled and the piano bumped. The sands blew as did the muck and dustballs from out that Aegean stable that the mighty Atlas had to sweep out and on straight time, no extra bread to sweeten his mighty task. And what stern desert was this? Well might you ask, and yet, ask and desperately ask as you will, the hollowly ringing silence that greets the shyly whispered or muttered question will be your only answer as it was the answer given to unhappy Oedipus by the oracle at Delphi, stony-eyed over her pot, when he wanted to know how to rid the great city of Thebes and its suburban localities as well from what scholars have variously translated as "the pest," "the horror," or "the itch." Yes, silence.

Blue asked not only the land around at large but asked also Zim, figuring that the strong-thewed lad had been places since they misplaced him in that cave— good Lord!—how many months ago? Or was it years? To Blue's eyes it seemed years since Zim seemed, how shall I say? grown to a kind of manliness that portends maturity. He seemed old enough to serve with Jason had Jason been about, and who of you out there, wise and "sophisticated," dares prove that he is not? Or old enough to bend his shoulder to the wheel, or in this case, the cart, or the rope attached to it. Or is what attached to it? Whatever you like is all right here for semiotics prove that you have not the chance of a snowman in the wake of Dante down among the hollering cardinals and bishops!

But Zimmerman did not know. Know what? Somehow the tenuous and silken thread of discourse had been broken, and broken by Proud Nature with a wild sirocco of hot blasts. But is it, in the last analysis, important? I think not— suffice it to contend, but moderately and considerately like a boring editorial, that whatever the name of these forever slumb'ring sands, they were indeed sands. And nothing more.

And then they came to cities, oh, not cities like, say, windy Troy, although some of them were windy enough, windy insofar as they lifted Helene's simple dirndl or gingham or homespun or patchwork or denim skirt and gave a clutch of geezers on the fly-specked corners an eyeful. There they took refreshment in the guise of Cokes and hot dogs, and they were good. How the stories flowed around the board that they had balanced on two shifting stacks of books and clothes and other appurtenances—in short, gear. Zim told of many things—men in suits made out of plastic, strange tribes that heaved and flowed through brightly lighted shopping malls, whole basketball teams in wheelchairs! They settled back, enjoying their newfound son, or so it seemed. It almost seemed to Blue that he was not their son. It seemed that way to Helene also. And, if one could peer inside that head that sat so nobly on the wide shoulders and thick-veined neck of Zimmerman, it perhaps seemed to him that they, Helene and Blue, were not his parents! Yet, he reasoned, they were not black folks, nor was he, and so it must have been the fact that they were. Also their names and their often unmistakable visages were things to be thrown into the great pot of truth and simmered like a good stew. At night, when the stars shone down, Zim would often walk about their encampment, so to speak, and look wonderingly up at Calpurnia and Blitho, the Spear of Paraclete, and the wild Ostrich of the Plains of Hippolyte, but they were silent, like the desert! And once in a while, when out of the circle of the firelight, he would bump into maybe Blue, maybe Helene, maybe Blue and Helene together, he, or she, or they, looking too at those wheeling stars which give no answers to humble and foolish man.

Still, they pressed on, following the route of Rogers and his Rangers and the old Chisholm Trail, that almost effaced rut or pair of ruts that still show, in the mysterious sands, the route taken by our forefathers, or to be more specific, some of our forefathers, to that promised golden territory toward which Jane Darwell and Hank Fonda set their faces! If they closed their eyes they could almost hear the whoops of Chief Joseph and Weird Ben, Geronimo and Mighty Paco on the still air, still, that is, when the violent foehn was not tearing the belaying pins off their gear and trying to ruin the hair-fine tuning of the piano, those chilling whoops as they barbecued settlers and ripped the frocks from young gals before chaining them to the ubiquitous anthills that abounded. Then, not now. Such was the face of history in this ruthless land that man had not yet tamed! They were filled with a kind of awe, a religious dread, a sense of the true greatness of the rocks! On the wagon creaked, making perhaps the noise made by the famous wooden horse when a few privates on shit detail had to hump it into the city of Troy. So the creaks of wheels are forever different, yet—forever the same!

How ashamed and small Helene felt now, thinking on her vile and monetary Indian disguise, her knickknacks, doodads, bibelots, and souvenirs, as well as the other crap she had sold to those innocent and open-hearted tourists who had passed through the Land of Enchantment, desiring only to snap photos of the Red Man in his blankets. Better had she simply dug her toes into the living sand and let the soul of the land flow into her feet first. It was too late now. Yet it was not too late to breathe a prayer of reconciliation and confession, a humble yet womanly request for forgiveness, yes! Forgiveness for her forebears who had savaged this land, the sweating coolies who had put the railroads through, who had put up the Greyhound depots, the lunch counters, those exploited masses who had baked the Danish and the Mae Wests, the bowties and the crullers—the jelly doughnuts! And from her perch atop the swaying cart she would look out on the endless wastes and the cities that sprang up suddenly from behind buttes and hills and arroyos and such, cactus, for instance, of which there was a plethora, and think of bison! Yes, bison, which she had always thought were buffalo. Now, sadder and wiser, as must all men and women be, or strive to be, she knew that never had a buffalo clumped about these twisting streets or the highways linking them.

And Blue, sweating underneath his yoke, so to speak, his sweat-drowned eyes bent toward that Bay which was his goal, what did he think? Ha! It more behooves grave Ixion behind his large boulder, or Tantalus strapped to a wheel on that gaunt cliff to which the magpies had almost total access, to think. And their thoughts, when one or two flitted by, were long, long thoughts, as Emerson said, his face grave and sad in the shifting firelight of that house in Brockton from which there blew that trumpet blast that woke the world at Lexington!

Beneath the expressionless skies, the caravan moved slowly, deeper and deeper into the magical state, the scent of oranges rotting on the ground filling the air like the odor of souvlaki that hovered o'er the tents of brave Achilles the night he brooded over lost Christina. So the past and the future, or in this case, since the future of that past is our present, the past and the present—are seamless and unshakeable. Was it true what Sutter had said from behind the closed shutters of his mill: that California will be to you whatever it is *you* are, dependent on of course, race, creed, and amount of money and possessions that you have? Perhaps. Perhaps. For now, the Gavottes were content with the million joys of honest work well done. So they pushed and pulled, heading north-west into the smell of salt and decaying fish! These scents were as a kudo or two that soothed them with its, or their, balm. For even the most goal-oriented person among us, even Menalaos bending all his will toward snatching Helen back from the luxurious hands of perfidious Paris and his enormous family, yes, even he accepted, with dignity, indeed, and humbly but not cravenly, whatever kudos were passed his way: as Homer says: "Then kudos bright did Menalaos joyful greet."

There is a spot in California called the Center Valley, where fruits grow in a wild abandon, as do vegetables. How the pickers sing! Occasionally the showers are hot.[3] It is essentially because they don't wish to attend school, preferring instead to work, side by side, with their parents, brothers, and sisters, in among the joys of the lettuce, celery, parsnips, muscats, and peaches. The Gavottes found themselves here, and the cart sped swiftly now among these Armenians and Italians.[7] It was a kind of sign that the desert was behind them, this dearth of sand, and although they were delighted by the whole idea of abundance and cheap wine in glistening gallon jugs, they felt that nameless loss that one feels when one has left—perhaps forever—the desert behind. Certainly, the redwoods towered! That very sense of awful rolling majesty made them think of Vasco da Gama and Cortez, Ponce de Leon, and Pizarro, all the martial conquistadors who had first planted the hardy grape of Valencia and Bernalillo in this rich black loam. And how the nobility puffed greedily on that rich leaf that the Aztecs called "terbaxitl."[36]

But there had been trouble, or as Sheridan put it after the "Wheat War," a "considerable of bad blood."[40] Somehow, the Gavottes felt the old animosities as they lurched forward through the seemingly endless vineyards, arbors, orchards, and avocadoes, felt them rather than saw them, for there was, indeed, nothing to be seen but the sunny, profligate fields, orchards, and etc., etc. The stubbed toe, however, halted the determined caravan only for a moment: a bathe in crystal spring water,[44] a quick buss on the boo-boo by Helene, and a firmly anchored Band-Aid, and the trio was off again. But where they got the buttons to suck is anyone's guess. It was a trick that Blue had learned from some book.

And soon Fresno was far behind, although "far" is, perhaps, an instance of hyperbole. Let us say, rather, that it was but a hazy configuration of buildings in

---

3. The Indians called one of them "the-guava-that-blooms-in-motley."
5. This has been ascribed to the designs of certain pot patterns.
7. As early as 1665.
21. This celery "ragout" was used in mystery ceremonies by the Potlatch tribe.
30. A. Harley describes this basin as an "archetypal sink."
36. Kohlrabi was considered a noxious weed of magical properties.
37. Pinget notes: "Truth means binoculars, precision . . ."
40. The Germanic Legion of Quintilius Fabricanus lived for months on orange ice.
43. I.e., the *malocchio*, or "evil eye."

the distance. But gold was to supersede the sacred grape for many years as the motivating force that drove desperate men to these rich lands—the true riches of which lay at their feet, but which they, in their greed and madness, could not see.[51]

Not that they didn't stop occasionally, although each stop seemed actually to pain Blue now; he was so close, the whispering of the Sequoias in and around Oakland were borne to his ears on the faint zephyrs that carried the perfume of the Pacific in their little hands. As the migrants well knew, singing outside the bunkhouses of cool evenings, the lettuces in huge mounds blotting out the very sky! It was a new song that Blue played that night on the piano, which, quite mysteriously, had, somewhere in the vicinity of Madera, taken on a richer, a more ringing tone and timbre.[60]

It had been "Rock" Wagram who put all these little towns on the map, and Blue was quick to pay homage to his memory. Others hid in their tarpaper shacks when the Santa Ana veered north, admittedly a rare occurrence. Yet never had the cart rolled so effortlessly![67] And one balmy evening after supper, Zimmerman decided to tell the whole incredible tale of his years-long search for his mother and father, and of the directions given him by an old crone that led him finally to Nevada.[70] It had started in terror when he woke in that echoing Missouri cave. And, finally, he told Blue and Helene, Miss Catherine Thigh and he had promised to correspond faithfully with each other.

Somehow, they seemed to be always "just outside" Madera, and for more than a day could make no progress. Serge blamed, alternately, Dr. Bone and Dr. Poncho, claiming that they wanted him to fail.[75] Though small, Merced was a lovely town. The apple orchards grew in lavish profusion right down to the banks of the river, a river teeming with trout, muskelonge, pike, bass, sturgeon, lobster, and carp. The travelers were sorely tempted to stay for a few days, even Blue felt the pull, the wonder of the place.[81] The next evening they, too, were prevailed upon to join in the singing at the camp meeting, and they did, raising their voices in the beloved old hymns that have helped make our beloved land great—"Ring My Doorbell, Jesus," "I'll Cross the Jordan in a Speedboat, Lord," "That Heavenly Light Gives Me a Migraine," and many other favorites. The Mayor insisted when he heard Blue play: and so he accepted the Key to Merced!

They were, in a word, celebrities! He had kept that last letter from Catherine

---

51. Antony Lamont discusses this phenomenon in his unpublished novel, "Crocodile Tears," which the present author has been privileged to read in manuscript.
59. But the concept of knight-errantry was not known, of course, to the Arikara.
67. Professor Richard Blister suggests that this was an infestation.
71. These petticoats are described in James's *The Golden Bowl*.
75. Dr. Vincent Dubuque contends that these are imagined "bogeymen."
83. D. Basura denies this inference.

buttoned into his shirt, close to his heart.[84] Yet and yet the open road called to Blue and he would wake at night with a start, the salt odor of the Bay in his nostrils and his ears straining for the incredible Phrase. That *was* a paella! To the traditional spare ribs, pork butt, eels, elbow macaroni, crumbled fish sticks, and tomato juice, the ladies of the church auxiliary added midget marshmallows to bring out the other flavors. But now the repair of the wheel was but a matter of a half-hour or so, since Blue felt compelled to hurry to make up for the week he had lost in lovely Merced.[87] And, it should be said, Zim had got into the habit of making marginal notations on Miss Thigh's letters.

However impossible it seemed, the hand of Coronado had reached this far north! Here were Fingernail Road, Fingernail Lane, Fingernail Bridge, Fingernail Farms, Fingernail Bar & Grill. It was, of course, in Spanish, but they weren't daunted. It might have been the sun, but somehow Helene's hair had never seemed so rich, so full, so lustrous, so lovely![92] One of the things he lovingly jotted in the margin was: "What you like to do I like to do more." And now it was almost impossible for Blue to sleep, the fever of anxiety and expectation burning through and through him. Still, Fresno was a charming memory that they would all—especially Helene—cherish forever.[96]

Despite the wonderful feeling that they still carried with them when they remembered Blue's impetuous act of generosity, they all missed, more than they could say, the beloved copy of *La Musique et les mauvaises herbes*.[99] Yet despite the dust and the torrential rains, the sight alone of the proud and lofty spires of Modesto filled their hearts with a strange joy. Oh no! There had never been in any of their lives such apricots as those that greeted them as they finally waded ashore. He decided, a few days later, to write a long and lovingly detailed letter to Catherine, filled with minutely worked-out descriptions. It had been ages since Blue and Helene stood together like this, arm in arm in the velvety night, the fireflies lazily bumping into their rapt faces.[107]

What had seemed to be spires were now seen to be, as they got closer, the signs of hamburger stands, orange-juice stands, taco stands, and other stands. Another accident! What an enormous pleasure it was for Zimmerman to bathe with the local farmhands![112] There was nothing to do but wait for the glue to set, and

---

84. See *Wanton Flyer*, Vol. XXXIV, No. 11 (1975).
86. Tables were often set in the rigid patterns prescribed by John Calvin.
87. Not seen in the area prior to 1907.
92. Akin to Berenice's when the latter's was set afire.
100. Early settlers thought that carrots were gold.
110. Dr. Laszlo Syntax argues that the Merced River is dry at the time of year that apricot trees are bearing fruit.
111. This might have been what is known in the East as "Russian dressing."
112. As Laurence Sterne writes: "That's another story."
125. Carrousels were outlawed in this area from 1931 to 1949 by the Legion of Christian Wives and Mothers.

so they busied themselves with identifying wild flowers. It was quite a sunburn, but Helene remembered a good bit of first aid and a simple country lass brought a copy of *Buddy and His Boys and the Mystery of the Can of Beans*. And one morning, just before dawn, Blue heard the awesome thunder of the distant surf crashing against the antique shops of Sausalito![118]

The delicate sky exhaled, or seemed to exhale, the limpid purity of the blue that suffuses the spiked lobelia, the passionflower, and the manwort pyrexia, or what botanists for years thought the manwort pyrexia was, or appeared to be: thus they took their ease beneath it for a spell, that is, a spell as men reckon a spell in these parts. For even Blue had to rest! So near was he, but his inseparable companion, Helene, prevailed upon him to recoup his powers for what he liked to call, nowadays, "his final thrust." Zim, well, Zim was more than delighted, for he had met the fair daughters of a local clam-fryer, long employed by Howard Johnson's, a man of enormous zest and even gusto.

Oh, he still wrote letters to Miss Thigh, but now they were filled with what might be termed "cute" references to his gambols with these lasses of the aching fields and ditches, one such remark being that he had, one tender evening, with a damsel on either side of his essentially yearning, yet always manly body, "with one hand on the younger one's**********************************, *******_ ************, and with just a little urging, the older maiden, pulling at her ********************* so that her skirts were in such a state that we three collapsed into a ****************** whose hands were a blur!"

Yes, he was having what the sagest of philosophers call [fun?] . . . while of the two young ladies it can be [said that they] gave their all as their mother had suggested in ******************** and afternoon and evening as well, taking turns! ******************************** of a torn petticoat? Of course! [What Catherine Thigh] . . . is not our purpose to record. And, knowing what we do about Miss Thigh, which is that she liked her ****** as well as her ***, we like to think that she would have not only understood, but even applauded! For though Diderot put it well when he wrote, "loin des yeux, loin du coeur," Miss Thigh had what some have termed an "inner vision" and could "see" the events in Zim's letters; indeed, so well, that it was, at times, almost as if she were there herself, making a joyous foursome. And at such times . . . with all her heart! What did she care if the neighbor's boy, a shambling yet kind bank teller, spied on her from his window, **************************, and ************_ *******, and sometimes *************: once she even saw him and then she opened wide her **************, so that the poor lad's eyes almost *****_ ********! Once, yes, he even collapsed in blissful exhaustion. What a letter she wrote to Zim that night, and while she wrote it, the [frisson?] as she ********* made her usually neat characters almost illegible! She *could* be naughty.

So the time passed pleasantly enough for Zim while Blue and Helene made final plans for the "run to the sea," as Blue nowadays liked to call it, in addition to calling it "his final thrust." What these plans were we do not pretend to know, for even the most minutely examined life must have its small secrets. And Blue had more than a few and some were not so small as all that! [There are subtle references to . . .] ***************as well as the curiously peripatetic fedora. And the odd erudition concerning sheep? *********[a mistake that?] ************ with Harold "Hal" Glubit? So often, things that seem to have little or nothing to do with each other, prove to be . . . quite . . . surprising [correspondent?] **********, bicycle-clip collection but a manifestation of fetishism, much like that of Abraham Lincoln's for silk hosiery? **********that "every great man has his ******** in private."

. . . busied themselves with cheery decorations woven of the tough Canada thistle and the swamp pink, both, strangely enough, never before seen in these parts—while Modesto loomed and beckoned and Blue, one night, made it clear that it was time to be off. ******** knows, they searched for him, although discreetly, and finally heard the sound of groaning and laughter from amid the thick clumps of wild bergamot that grew in profusion from the compost heap. They called and **************, not precisely "indecent," but what might be termed deshabille, out they came, all five . . . which occasioned great [surprise?] and not a little laughter so that even the bunchberries seemed to beam happily!

[*Large portion of mss. missing*] ******* and with all the old and by now well-loved bumps and jounces, her dandruff flew about the sunny countryside, and Zim lay as if stupefied, a smile on his stalwart, so to speak, face or that [strange?] that men call . . . ["face"?] . . . but did his part wonderfully well. And why not? cynics and crips [*sic*] might sey [*sic*]? For just that morning he had received a long letter from Catherine Thigh, in which she described, at great length, a small party with some *******, who had come from *****, and were delighted at the idea of ******* and ******** the bank teller! It was . . . [newsy] . . . her bright and cheerful and sunny self: what a **** she had! And with it some color photos that . . . hard to make . . . without careful scrutiny. [It?] ******** a domino encrusted with pearls and ***** in the foreground, with his ******* in ********'s ******** Father [Dabree?] *******, it be an apron?

So they passed the time and were soon in Modesto, which proved to be a congenital [*sic*] burg, or what might be called a village or even a small town. *****-** FREE CONCERT! And so he did!

. . . what is usually thought of as a fiasco, but it *was* a mistake. It should be said, in Blue's defense, if defense he need be said to be need [?], that his "mind" was not on it, his nose filled with the scent of the briny beauty of . . . just beyond the

*********, so it was really a matter of his thinking what some phrase *******, or, as he put it . . . go **** themselves! It was the one jarring note in these otherwise placid, although obsessive last days of the journey, and they ********, too. Helene's ****** and her ***** did not a little to calm him as they rolled by day toward the skyscrapers of Oakland! Oakland and her famed wild petunias! Zimmerman worked like a mule all day and at night was ************ off. Any way he could ******! was his moto [*sic*].

But how, now that they were in Oakville [*sic*] . . . the glittering bridge? Helene remembered *********** by Anton Harley in an anthology that had ******* ********* Rosette, she thought. So, in a way, she was delighted, even though the problem of **********, who was not delighted at all, his eyes on the hills across ***************. Rolling ******************[fedora?], ********, and ***, and ***, and ***, and ***, he **************** damn [Miss Thigh?], *************** swash and swish and heave that Homer ********, one street and up another, until ********** [careening?]****************:

[*Here the Ur-manuscript breaks off. The following fragment, arguably a variant version of an earlier, apocryphal manuscript, is in the Piscardi Library of The University.*]***** but nothing do but Zeem have dolly or he say he eat kitten's head. Blue hit him and say ******* in fucking cave, little bastard! ******** in piano, Helene laugh, and then don't nobody see him or hear him, you think that an good idea? ********* in [goddam?] cave, little son of the bitch! ********** and rolled toward Goldgate Bridge? Is not . . . You don't say? ******** pretty janty [*sic*] up there *********, slouching fedora! Tomorrow we roll right down and right ******** and up the Quoit Hill, highest point ******** majestic Cascades ranges? ********* just like Doc Chick in **********! ********* and them stahz [*sic*] pipped [*sic*] down like in movie you see ************, snore ********** fucking much!

Oakland the. Fair! Was it after all possible, that they? Were finally, here in: This booming! City? Blue got down! On his hands. And knees. And groveled in, the; dust. Not, exactly, dust, but, something like the dark vermilion. Clay! It was not, as. Zimmerman, knew. Dust. Or. Clay? But; it was the how do you? Say, "powder," from, The millions and millions of crimson moronia, that. Are the "Pride." Of, Oakland, along with of, course; gorgeous Lake. Merritt Linda, and Vista Park! But what. Ever it was, Serge, groveled? In thanks, his eyes, his great. *Staring eyes*! Fixed, on, the hazy Contra Costa. Hills! And the Hills! Of Berkeley, flung, far! Far, away across the: famed Skyline. Boulevard!

Say powder, then? Okay? Crimson, moron, millions of skylines and the Lake with, what? Duckies? Certainly, vistas! How to get from? Skyline Vista Boulevard to the Bay Bridge and thence! Ah, thence. Thence, past whatever? To the heart of the "Queen" of the Bay, strange. Bubbly. Gay San Francisco! A place where men are men and earthquakes fall to nothing in the blaze of comet's fire! Just like in the famous pome of Joaquin Miller, or Cincinnati Miller like what his friends? Well, okay, "friends," called him. So did Blue plant his knees thus wise. He got down! (In thus wise—in wise, thus—in such wise, thusly!) They would have to. Pass? Pass! Pass the towering pissweeds of Old Sequoia Park, the one of which whom a poet like Miller wrote his pome about the earthquake that did little or naught to dampen the spirits of them. Them? Well may you ask! Them! Yes, the grizzled parkies of that early and more innocent time, when the immoral zipper fly was but the figment of the depraved imagination. Of many people, yet in the main that of: who else? "Blowjob" Piedmont, a man for whom that hoary motto was sheer Reality! Long did he reign in those here parts.

But enough of gerrymandering and its boon pal, lollygagging! Did ever Piedmont stay his hand? Ha. Ha. It boots not well nor yet behooves to ask! Yet. Ask men must, and will, as long as Jove strides o'er this world with boots so *cracked and grimed that mortals dare not peer* into the welkin lest they see that curious rainbow formed from vapors like the blast of naked Boreas' bright glance, whizzing through the enamor'd firmament like the cruel shaft from mighty bowman's bow in shape unto belike the rainbow formed from vapors that shine and glint all over as do the eyes of that famous pig what once was a pet of Paddy. Or strike the numbèd oith with vile catastrophe!

It was: A problem! Albany, where the Governors served time? Sure! And sure again, and yet, maybe one wast expected to go through the suburbs? Of! Stern San Leandro, where *that fabled monk* once lived who all in solitude: Invented Zinfandel! What a robust sort of thing: yet all in modesty. Or; maybe? Hayward! That seemed to be like: It? Creakèd sure the cart where none had ever trod. Helene. Up? High! Serge and: Zimmerman, heaving toward that glimmer arching cross the Bay like the crooked index finger. Of a god! Or of God! Hart Crane knew this stuff and though Zimmerman, thought, it. All, malarkey? Yet did he bend the back and creak the knee as sure as cart creaked, for he'd as lief bust his father's, heart? His heart! As he would eat the pen that penned *those missives vile* to Catherine! Oft bringing a smile to the toughest heart: which, is. Nice work! If you could get it, like: thus always the tyrant is brung low? Or: Most, often.

What "stuff" they rolled by, Serge, hearing now the singing low of the piles and stanchions with hawsers out there well past the Vista Linda Prison, the Costa del Contra Beach (*what was filled with cuties!*), and the Starfish Motel, surrounded: By God, though the whole earth deny it and book reviewers hunker down amid the Well-Made Plot, surrounded by the softly blowing dill-fish and the starburst yearn-all. So this were which gave its bouquet to a place? Apparently. All the signs were like, right! Whoo! Christ, they: rolled! And rolled! It might of took the breath away from thems. What? Was REALLY WEIRD was that they ROLLED as the Seaver fastball oft did in its glory times: Uphill.

Newton could've told them who in his long dark nights and smelling of the lamp—*whatever that may mean*—baked those cookies which the tribe of man will always for them him thank, which, when Milton received, than whom, Cromwell except, none wiser sat, he et them up: out of what come: that opera, *L'Allegro Sforzando*. (What Blue could not loin cuz of the "black-key" notes which he wrote, Milton, that is.) What could he've told those brave folk, the spawn of concrete, steel, long shadows, and crooked Mayors? Dat wot goze upp muz cum daown? No! And yet, sorta? What *comes* up must *go* down! While chomping: On a Granny Smith out in the Garden, the same which Andy Marvell was in and up to his old tricks, viz., stumbling over those Melons, digging on li'l T.C., checking out the Golden Lamps, and trotting after slow-worms, he, Newton, hit on this idear after thinking on the Sunne: He. Say. "This sunne, ofte coming up in robes of glory red, and even more than ofte, but every daye, this sunne, I say, as oft, or every daye, must needs go down!" And thus: The Lore of Gravity was bumped into: And ever since, all men who jump up out they chairs must fall back into them, or maybe: on the floor.

So they rolled also: DOWNHILL! And what a thrill it wert! For they rolled directly down splendid Chimborazo Boulevard, which, be it known—or ne'er thought on even oncet!—to reckless men, was yet that highway that . . . Let's say, ere we be accused by pointing digit of that willful obscurity and lack of duh gift of turning a nice phrase or of neglecting to write well, for writing well, and planting periods in trig and serried ranks, as any scribe can tell you thus, and often will o' nights when the winds howl banshee like beyant the booming shutters and the gibbous moon doth hover o'er the soggy graveyards, yes! That the world calls cemeteries, dis sorta writing bringeth many jobs and warm and wondrous houses out in vile Connecticut the cute, indeed! Those houses built by hand-rubbed farmers of the age of Washington, whose sparkling winders look out upon those graveyards what got them old stones filled up with many a sentimental Protestant cliché: Therefore? Let's say, ere this may hap, that this highway led toward that brightly shining bridge that creeped toward the wild urbs of the Bay, City of Cupcakes! Thus: toward which they wended way, with woe and lack of weal and with also wheels whingeing and whining as they wolled westward, wacing now to weach the wovely willage! Though: and here the question deep will oft forever ring in sempiternal bongs: Was it a willage? Who; Can say? 'Twas enough to brave emote, as men will do when brains do fail their stated purpose: It was there!

And even fair Helene, who high upon her "gear" (as well as all the other:

Gear!) beamed down upon *the caps of cream that flecked* and pittered? On the laughing soiface of the Bay beneath: Thus did she fix her piercing eye!

They'd. Come, far, far: And had they? Come far; enough! The still, small voice did ever whisper. What? Not yet, not yet, the pattern clear, 'bout which thou may ask Jesus Christ: Whut, jes whut is these patterns for? I say:—or wast it Blue who said?—No Matter! Some unheard voice, like melodies the same, sweeter than that one who is listened to, had asked the "Pattern Question," what a wag has dubbed: A quiz! (But a turd in that fuck's teeth!) And still, despite this odd shenanigan, I fear, like Blue, my comely hero, plus his wife, and plus his bursting son, the somewhat perverse Zim, that I may have lost my way, and cannot find nor thread nor rhyme nor reason in this subtly lavender display of schlock! So? I got Blue on the manly span and cannot get him o'er? Shall I write, thus: Beginning once agin and still anew? Like thus:

Oakland the fair! Was it, after all, possible that they were finally here, in this booming city? Blue got down on his hands and knees and groveled in the dust. Not exactly . . . dust, but something like the dark vermilion clay. Huh? Would Rabelais be content to read such stuff?

RABELAIS: Foutez-moi la paix!

Or so and thus I thought. So, what e'er the cost in human sweat and lack of interested readership, intelligent, knowledgeable, prone to rattling yarns and stately graces in a limpid prose, and snide remarks anent the Vast Body of a Lit'-rachoor Devoid of Self-Indulgence, I'll get: him: off: the: fucking: Bridge! (In my own sweet way and in my own sweet time—or Theseus ne'er did sail on leaky rubber raft from windy Troy to found Salerno!)

But these, jou say, ees hombres made of straw? These, jou say, is gouty blasts of sheerest kidding an tomfoolery? You don't shut uppa you mout I make a fuckin list go on three hundred pages! Ess mah breedge! I get heem offen her! Hokay!

And suddenly they rolled off the other end and found themselves, the cart's wheels humming gorgeously, in the streets (or one of them, at least) of twinkling San Francisco! Up they went. To a hill. To the top. And there beneath, the Bay. And Blue, slick with sweat, felt, thrumming in the very marrow of his bones, the almost tangible, and yet not quite, plangent plunking of the Phrase. Next him stood his family true. They leaned then all the cart against. It the hill rolled down in mighty speed. With in the lead brave Blue, chased they it down. Blue's face was smiling all for thought he deep that even this the cart toward the Bay headed was as if it knowed too that it there would find its Destiny. And lest it be forgot! Behind, on hawser taut and singing the piano bumped and rolled as well! And in the lead, Blue of the trip within his brains had Meaningful Mem'ries in bright

flashes called clear up to him. So as ran he thought he these things all wondrous
of the lonely road that hath wended they for such a space of time:

This madhouse with lace and satin and naughty novels filled . . . Profundity! . . .
Let us aimless plunge . . . Sophie Jupon? Is that her whorish handle? . . . Clouds
of aromatic dust surrounded by enchanted Negroes in the film of the same name
. . . Dutch Mulligan! A monicker all oozing forth with Celtic echoes . . . Sweeter
than cakes and custard sharper than crying mustard . . . Not to forget the loathsome ginkgo or tiny stinking monkeys! . . . I am the doughty vehicle 'twert
meant for you, the engine of your fate and Karmic destiny, also very big in terms
vitamins and enzyme juice . . . Nobility! . . . A quick nosh of jambalaya à la king
at SAL'S BILLIARD ACADEMY . . . Marie Mamelle? Is that her whorish handle? . . . La Musique et les mauvaises herbes, it is like a kind of a joke . . . We'll
strain our best, an' we gawp at last, firk as sunspot-blue clostridium . . . I may
lighten up the fardels and valises of regret on the smelted plains of legendary
Boise! . . . Dutch Mulligan? Is that her whorish handle? . . . Surrounded by enchanted films with Negroes of the same name . . . Tiny monkeys stinking in the
mauvaises herbes . . . The stewed Comanche gazes on a ginger ale, or the husky
terrene dregs of same . . . Silk-buttocked garter-strapped Suzanne Jarretière,
thou art a babe as simple as a cackarooch . . . Gawp at last, firk! . . . Aimless let us
plunge, else I'll set loose the starving Dobermans! . . . It was something that
made me very very noivous . . . What a cute little word that is, eh, Sophie? . . .
Harr, harr, harrñh! . . . André Lubrique! That violent wop men call Hieronimo! . . . Deadbeats like Hitler and Stalin caused by a hump tossed off in wild
abandon . . . Mr. Coillon, my good friend over there with the denim pipe . . .
Gravity! . . . Like coney shy you bump through lettuce groves: thus Dubuque
spake and turned his socks upon the glowing spit . . . They eat, ringed by adoring
ducks . . . Monique Gaine, is that her whorish handle? sitting in a chair in an
exciting way . . . A white-robed Negro sported with the dust, not to forget the
loathsome ginkgo . . . Marimbas Verdes con Gusanos, a wonderful woman! . . .
Took to fellin' trees and tearin' stone fences up by the roots, finger-painting
coasters for the USO . . . Thine eyes flash blacker than my dirtie nails, like a kind
of a joke . . . Sparkling and curvaceous thunder! Love! With a peppery pinch of
lust! . . . Girdled yet gorgeous hips thighs and bottom, sweeter than cakes and
custard . . . Silk-buttocked and all oozing forth with Celtic echoes, Mrs. Chaud,
let us aimless plunge: maybe a little shtup without you humming "The Trolley
Song," or "A Weedy Music" . . . Surrounded by enchanted Negroes, my great
gnarled hands lie lifeless on the piano keys . . . Claude Cul? A double pink starlike fairy . . . The gimlet-brained Dr. Dubuque will knock you off your lilting

little cadenza, chief! He twists the bangling changs! . . . Or so to speke . . . Sans crotch, I base, and cronk the knee in volitude to Alice Cruisse, as in a dream, like Chaucer knowed . . . At which the hefty broad did blush as in a naughty novel . . . Hamstrung visions of the crass unspeakable? In the fucker goes! . . . Art thou a sprite or satyr of the elfin boles and sappy limbs, or General Westinghouse, known as the mutter of invention? . . . Monique Gaine? But who the hell are you to come in here, all akimbo? . . . Your sweetie's hairs would sprout like crabgrass vile as long as this golden ring on my finger stains it a fetching emerald . . . Cortez silent in his pique in old Connecticut, yet I also serve who only blandly prate . . . This madhouse filled with naughty novels has a wooden porch of agonized memory . . . Gaston Gaine, Robert Caleçons, Émile Fesses, and Jacques Derrière: the courageous lowbrows of the muddy peaks and swampy valleys . . . The entire ballyard that nestles just above my forehead, my blazing maple leaf, it is like a kind of a joke . . . Aimless! Plunge! . . . The road has reft me of my merriment! *That's* why the crocodiles spoke Spanish . . . Again, you've whomped the brassy tacks, my chef . . . Sparkling thunder? I speak still of the old and crippled hen . . . Your soft sobbing as we watch the snap beans and the impeccable white of the knee hose, hips thighs and bottom of Suzanne Jarretière, and then sort of start another artistic career based on songs of the black keys . . . A sporty Negro in the whitish dust said: "Now the jive turkey blanks bees stealin our flowers!" . . . The teeth of a fascist movie star whose mouth's a splash of dead rugosa rose . . . Let us aimless plunge from out this lace and satin madhouse . . . Current black digs white ash, the former in his toga, the latter in his culottes . . . Concerning M. Charles Ordurier and Mlle Mamelle one might say that travel looms and romance may blossom . . . Of my merriment the road has reft me . . . I'll hear the Secret Phrase—or puke! . . . A red deuce! And so I *do* see as I ope my blinks . . . At SAL'S BILLIARD ACADEMY the herb tea industry grows apace: that's why the crocodiles spoke Spanish! . . . Save It Pretty Mama by Cheech Mauriac and the Femmes Fatales, the former in culottes, the latter in silk-buttocked marimbas verdes . . . Forgive me, my darling snap bean, forgive me! though I'm very big in terms enzyme juice . . . Femmes fatales of the black keys and red deuce . . . Tiny monkeys double pink stinking . . . Marie oozing forth hips and thighs . . . Aimless plunge us, let us . . . Marie Jarretière avec red deuce, *that's* her whorish film . . . A robed white Negro bees stealin la musique . . . Porch of wooden memory, let us aimless agonize . . . Thine eyes flash blacker than curvaceous thighs . . . Greta Girdle and her sister, Gertie, stars of the crass unspeakable . . . Or so to speke . . . Speke or prate all blandly in the crabgrass vile . . . The bangling changs! The changling bangs! Monique Gaine's her whorish handle? . . . Jambalaya nosh à quick . . . Toga, former Mustard, seeks Blazing Leaf of doughty vehicle . . . Plunge aimless let us . . . A joke kind of, like a little shtup . . .

Harrñh! . . . Spotted in the dust: One white-robed Negro all enchanted . . . Bees gimlet-brained, chef! . . . Garter-strapped snap beans . . . Plunge! . . . Reft the black keys from jive turkeys . . . Suzanne, Marie, and M. Fixe-Chaussettes: little cute words are they . . . Con gusanos in the satin madhouse . . . Impeccable knee hose white as deuce is red . . . Muddy peaks! Aimless plunge! . . . The road . . . Piques . . . Valleys with bottoms gorgeous . . . Con profundity let's plunge! . . . Travel blossoms plungingly while femmes made me very very noivous . . . And the piano . . . The piano . . . Black keys . . . White keys . . . Aimless plunging, plunging aimless . . . The piano . . . Fate and Karmic destiny . . . Plunge . . . Plunges . . . Doughty vehicle con keys of black and . . .

Into the bay. The cart. The rope. The piano.

Thus: Cart--------------Rope--------------Piano.

Then the Phrase climbed to Blue Serge's trembling ears:

S   p   l   a   s   h

9 March 1978–22 December 1981

DALKEY ARCHIVE PAPERBACKS

PIERRE ALBERT-BIROT, *Grabinoulor.*

YUZ ALESHKOVSKY, *Kangaroo.*

FELIPE ALFAU, *Chromos.*

  Locos.

  Sentimental Songs.

ALAN ANSEN,

  Contact Highs: Selected Poems

  1957-1987.

DJUNA BARNES, *Ladies Almanack.*

  Ryder.

JOHN BARTH, *LETTERS.*

  Sabbatical.

AUGUSTO ROA BASTOS, *I the Supreme.*

ANDREI BITOV, *Pushkin House.*

ROGER BOYLAN, *Killoyle.*

CHRISTINE BROOKE-ROSE,

  Amalgamemnon.

GERALD BURNS, *Shorter Poems.*

GABRIELLE BURTON, *Heartbreak Hotel.*

MICHEL BUTOR, *Portrait of the Artist*

  as a Young Ape.

JULIETA CAMPOS,

  The Fear of Losing Eurydice.

ANNE CARSON, *Eros the Bittersweet.*

LOUIS-FERDINAND CÉLINE,

  Castle to Castle.

  London Bridge.

  North.

  Rigadoon.

HUGO CHARTERIS, *The Tide Is Right.*

JEROME CHARYN, *The Tar Baby.*

MARC CHOLODENKO,

  Mordechai Schamz.

EMILY HOLMES COLEMAN,

  The Shutter of Snow.

ROBERT COOVER,

  A Night at the Movies.

STANLEY CRAWFORD,

  Some Instructions to My Wife.

RENÉ CREVEL, *Putting My Foot in It.*

RALPH CUSACK, *Cadenza.*

SUSAN DAITCH, *Storytown.*

PETER DIMOCK, *A Short Rhetoric for*

  Leaving the Family.

COLEMAN DOWELL,

  The Houses of Children.

  Island People.

  Too Much Flesh and Jabez.

RIKKI DUCORNET,

  The Complete Butcher's Tales.

  The Fountains of Neptune.

  The Jade Cabinet.

  Phosphor in Dreamland.

  The Stain.

WILLIAM EASTLAKE, *Castle Keep.*

  Lyric of the Circle Heart.

STANLEY ELKIN,

  Boswell: A Modern Comedy.

  Criers and Kibitzers, Kibitzers

  and Criers.

Visit our website: www.dalkeyarchive.com

DALKEY ARCHIVE PAPERBACKS

Visit our website: www.dalkeyarchive.com

II0659721

Europe in a

Motorhome

A Mid-Life Gap Year

Around Southern Europe

H D Jackson

TRAFFORD
PUBLISHING

USA • Canada • UK • Ireland

Note for Librarians: A cataloguing record for this book is available from Library and Archives Canada at www.collectionscanada.ca/amicus/index-e.html

ISBN 1-4120-8141-6

Printed on paper with minimum 30% recycled fibre.
Trafford's print shop runs on "green energy" from solar, wind and other environmentally-friendly power sources.

TRAFFORD
PUBLISHING™

Offices in Canada, USA, Ireland and UK

Book sales for North America and international:
Trafford Publishing, 6E–2333 Government St.,
Victoria, BC V8T 4P4 CANADA
phone 250 383 6864 (toll-free 1 888 232 4444)
fax 250 383 6804; email to orders@trafford.com
Book sales in Europe:
Trafford Publishing (UK) Limited, 9 Park End Street, 2nd Floor
Oxford, UK OX1 1HH UNITED KINGDOM
phone 44 (0)1865 722 113 (local rate 0845 230 9601)
facsimile 44 (0)1865 722 868; info.uk@trafford.com
Order online at:
trafford.com/05-3138

10 9 8 7 6 5 4

ACKNOWLEDGEMENTS

Our grateful thanks to all who helped us,
before, during and after, our travels.

Our congratulations to the Lonely Planet
Publications and their Guide to Mediterranean Europe,
which helped to steer our course

— and I emphasise that the views and opinions expressed
in this book are purely personal, based on our experiences.

Front cover designed by Noel Wilford

Hazel Jackson was born in Cheltenham, England in 1950 and moved with her family to rural Herefordshire to do 'The Good Life' in 1987. In 2003, having finished renovating their home, and with three sons grown and flown the nest, they sold up and with their youngest son, set off to explore Europe. She now lives with her husband and son, on the Welsh borders.

Simon Jackson has travelled extensively in the past and spent a year on the desert island of Cocos, off Costa Rica, as one of the original members of Gerry Kingsland's first 'Castaway' group.

FREE PHOTOGRAPHIC WEB SITE

To view photographs of the countries visited in this book, please go to the free web site at geocities.com/h.hdj@btinternet.com

Europe in a Motorhome

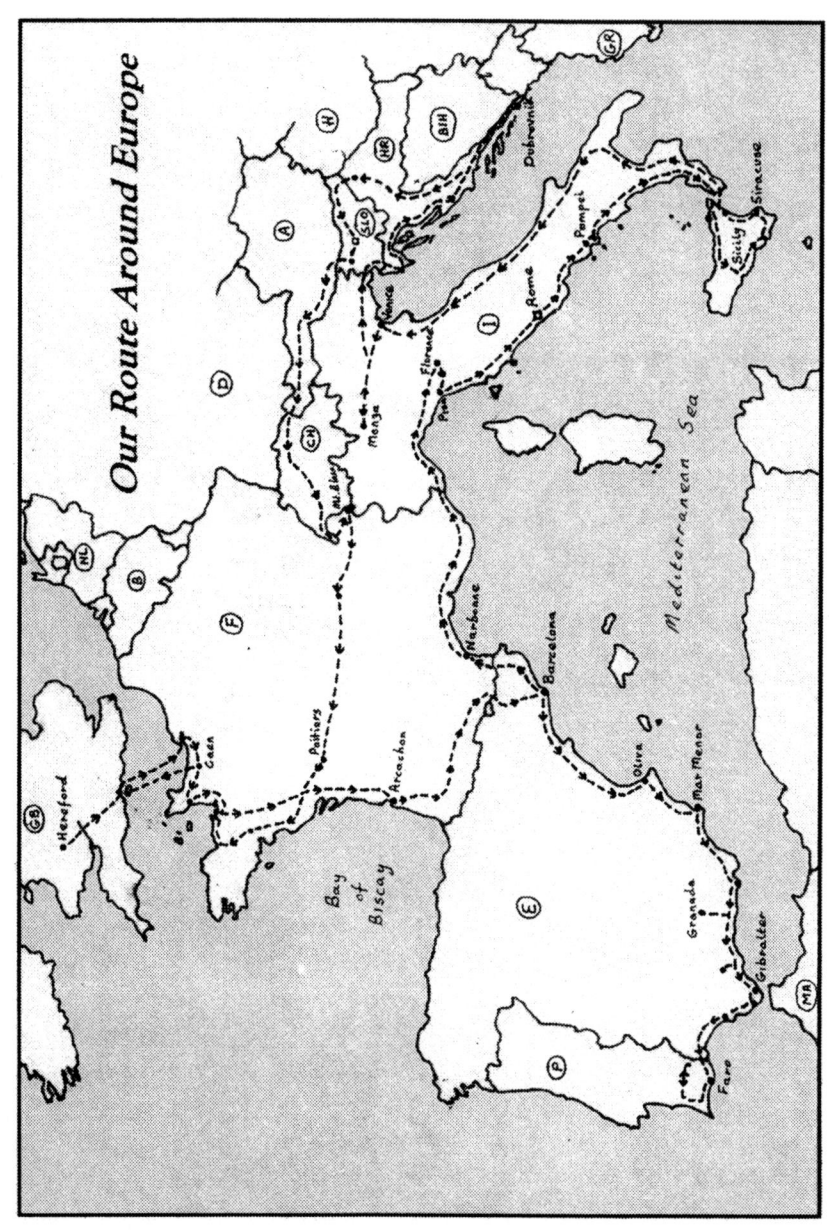

Our Route Around Europe

Casting Off

Decisions, decisions. I want to keep that, and that, and those pictures my mother gave us, and that rug from Ken and please let me store those chairs.

Simon's eyebrows went up yet again as he struggled to cram my latest 'keeps' into the small van that was supposed to hold everything that wasn't going to auction.

Men don't need possessions, men don't need nick-knacks, men don't need objets d'art – ....well, my man doesn't. In fact he doesn't even need a home really. A wooden hut on a beach would suit my man, plus a raft to fish from – as he had once lived for a year on a desert island.

What we did need was a change – not a short break in Paris for two type change, ...more a life change.

At our age this put us well into the category of mid life crisis – we could see it writ large on familiar faces. We could have bought a motorbike or a powerful sports car, but instead – we made ourselves homeless. We pulled the rug from under our own feet and stepped out into a void. Our strange idea was to sell home and possessions, and move into a thirty-three foot, luxury, All American Motor Home, to be referred to from now on as The Beast. Some friends looked horrified, but others thought that to be taking our son out of school, to leave the rat-race behind and travel Europe for a year in a motorhome, had a certain appeal. All that the three of us would need was, in theory, on board the Beast. Our house on wheels, with the usual facilities, plus books, games, music, maps etc and the contents of our old pantry. We three would live and travel in her; wash, sleep and eat, on the move, with a new view almost every morning. We wanted the luxury of independent travel and we wanted to share it with Jack, our thirteen-year-old son. This book must be dedicated to him for being a constant, patient and brilliantly funny travelling companion for my husband Simon and myself. It was the icing and the cherry on the cake that we would share the year and all that we did, with him.

So, have you planned your route?

No, we're just going south.

Won't you miss everything, and how are you going to get on for a year, all together in a motor home?

We don't know, but we want to go and see.

Ok, there were good times, there were bad times and sometimes there were downright ugly times, but do we regret it now? No way...... it was an amazing experience.

Would we do it again?...... You bet.

Our policy throughout was going to be 'here and now'. We had a big motorhome and a limited budget, but we decided that if we found ourselves somewhere with the opportunity to do or see something new, then we would do it and hang the expense. Who knows if we would ever pass that way again? Some people we met on our travels were on a very tight budget, and others had money to burn, everyone does it differently......but it doesn't matter.... you must travel to suit you. So, waving goodbye to our past life, we rolled out of our home county of Herefordshire, one bright September morning and with Cold Play singing away in our well appointed mobile home, we left family and friends for a year to travel Europe – the great escape was finally going to happen. We headed down to Portsmouth for our first overnight stop and our last night in the UK. Tomorrow we would be catching the early morning ferry to France.

Parked at the docks that afternoon, so near and yet so far from all that had ever been my security, I have no doubt that the hollow feeling that dwelt in the pit of my stomach was sheer, unadulterated panic. Oh my God, what have we done?

It really felt as if we were stepping out into a big, black hole that was at once completely terrifying and wildly exciting. We knew that it would do our nerves no good to sit around for the rest of the afternoon waiting for our early morning crossing next day, so with time to kill we invoked our 'here and now policy' straight away. This would be the first of many, many such trips of discovery, which we would take over the coming year, from our quite amazing motorhome.

So, we asked ourselves, (making a guilty start on Jack's extra-curricula education), what did we know about Portsmouth... well, besides the ferry terminals and a University, not a lot, and our first discovery was that there was plenty to keep us busy, especially at the historic dockyards. We could view the treasures of The Mary Rose, which was painstakingly raised from the bed of the Solent in 1982; tour the Guild Hall, or hire a headset and follow a historic ramble through 'old' Portsmouth and the Gun Wharf Keys, – and all with a French translation if we desired. But we decided to spend our last afternoon in the UK on board the Royal Navy's most famous war ship and the worlds oldest commissioned ship. Lord Horatio Nelson's flagship at the battle of Trafalgar which, 199 years ago almost to the day, had sailed into battle against the combined fleets of the French and Spanish, who we were just off to visit. Yes, HMS Victory.

It didn't really sink in at this point, (no pun intended there) that I was going to be travelling with two males for a year and, with no other female company, we would be doing slightly male orientated things. Of course six months down the road as I was being dragged past the exquisite and totally irresistible shops in Venice's St Marks Square, pressing my nose for the briefest moment to the glass to view the shimmering and desirable objects on display, before being rushed on to find an exhibition of Leonardo da Vinci's inventions, it clicked that this was going to be a bit of a boysy tour. I'm not a great shopper anyway, so it was no hardship really, but there were times when I did yearn for a day in a full-blown, take no prisoners type shopping arcade, with another female. Just to touch base with those little gee-gaws and totally unessential items that us girls like to fondle. But England expects that every man shall do his duty, and this was day one of our year out and no time for a mutiny, so The Victory it was.

And it was good; very good in fact. Jack loved it and absorbed every detail, or at least the guns and cannons. Staring up through the mass of ropes and rigging you couldn't help but wonder at how physically hard life was in those days, and when we scrambled below and took part in the explosive reconstruction on the gun decks you realised how dangerous life down there had been. Everything made of wood, so if a cannon ball didn't get you then a huge wooden splinter probably would, and the crude surgeon's tools were hardly something to be thankful for. Still, there was always the tot of rum or brandy at the end of the day, although poor Nelson made his final voyage home in a barrel of brandy; not quite what he'd planned I guess.

We passed the afternoon on a merry high, feeling as if we'd all been let out of school early for a special treat. As evening fell, it was time to go home. Home? But our old home, our beautiful old home of sixteen years was gone, sold. The commitment was made to travel for a year – there was no going back. So we bade farewell to Nelson, with a new understanding of how he and his sailors must have felt when they left England, not knowing what would be in store for them or if they would see those shores again, and we ambled back to the Beast.

The autumn weather was kind to us that night. Parked up at the docks in our cosy motorhome we watched the no-nonsense, industrious dockland take on its evening cloak as cars arrived and work continued under a clear starlit sky. This was our last night in the UK for a year and our thoughts were a mixture of excitement and sadness. We had no real route planned ..... we would go South, and then where the wind would take us. We didn't know then that we would meet some wonderful people on our travels, or see so many interesting places, or sometimes be so scared or sometimes be so happy. We just knew that we were doing something that we had never done before. So, our son Jack made up his bed on the pull down sofa, snuggled under his duvet and got stuck into the complete trilogy of Hitch Hikers Guide to the Galaxy. We pulled down the blinds and tried to get to sleep in our big double bed in the back. It was probably helpful not to know that the next night, which would be our first night in France, we were going to be totally exhausted and trying to sleep in the corner of a dirty old car park by a disused factory on an old industrial estate. Not quite the free wheeling cosmopolitan scenario that we planned, but hilariously funny at the time.

A sense of humour is absolutely essential when travelling, along with plenty of sleep, good walking shoes and in our case, a satellite navigation system. Any traveller will tell you that you are going to get into some difficulty or other fairly frequently and although you may be mouthing obscenities at each other or someone else at the time, the important thing is to have a good laugh about it when it's all over. Our first day in France is one that we can look back on and laugh like mad dogs about. What did we think we were doing! We were emotionally and physically exhausted – after all, our house had sold in record time leaving us just four weeks to buy a motorhome, move into it, sell most of our possessions, organise all the paperwork and say our goodbyes. So it's hardly surprising that after a sleepless night and a dawn crossing we landed at Le Havre feeling excited – but just a little weary.

We had decided to wait until we were in France before we filled up the Beast with diesel and LPG gas on the understanding that it would be cheaper. The motorhome had a huge LPG gas tank, which could run the generator, heating, cooking, hot water and fridge. Some of these could also run on electricity when hooked up to power at a camp site. The joy of the Beast was that we could be totally independent for up to three or four weeks as all of her tanks, i.e. fresh water and grey water were huge. A large fridge, good size freezer, shower and toilet made her exceptionally easy to live in. She was already fitted with a TV, DVD and Video player and her storage lockers were enormous. As we travelled throughout the year we met people in every different combination of accommodation on wheels and although some purists may frown at dragging your mobile bungalow along the highways, we felt that because we had a growing teenager with us, we would last longer in something like a Winnebago, and she was left hand drive which was fairly essential. The important thing is just to travel. The downside to having such a large vehicle is that you can't always get where you want to go ..... as we learnt on our first day in France.

So, not quite at our best, we rolled off the ferry onto the right hand side of the road and drove off looking for LPG gas and diesel. Maybe we were just dazzled by the spectacular sweeping bridges that the French weave at great heights and lengths over their varying countryside, or maybe we just missed the turning because we hadn't yet had time to master the satellite navigation system and we were relying on my appalling map reading, but we soon found ourselves trundling off in the completely wrong direction towards Paris when we really wanted to be going the other way, towards Caen. How many people have done this; you roll off the ferry, get confused and head off the wrong way. No problem in a small car but not so easy when you have to find somewhere to turn the motorhome around in. So, some kilometres later we turned around to try again and at last after several attempts, we found a garage selling both diesel and LPG gas.

So now, never daunted although it's getting towards the afternoon and we were already quite tired, we decided that it would be a good idea to do a huge food shop and fill up the food storage lockers so that we were totally equipped with everything we needed for a while. At this point we stopped and programmed the satellite navigation system to take us to Caen and to find us the shopping area, and we also decided that it was time to give this amazing sat. nav. system a name. For those who have not tried one, I can tell you that when you have programmed in your final destination, it will direct you there by giving you advanced directions, and if you miss the correct turning you will get the familiar message of " at the next opportunity, make a U turn!" Our sat. nav. gave us directions in a choice of voices, male or female, and we decided on a very calming female voice that we promptly named Maisy. To be fair, once Simon and Jack had spent some time getting to grips with Maisy, she guided us beautifully across Europe with hardly a falter. Without her, I fear that divorce if not murder may have ensued due to my total lack of understanding of maps. I'm the type who turns them upside down so that they are pointing the way we are going and has to keep putting her reading glasses on and off to read them.

Totally frustrating to the driver who needs advanced warning and instant decisions when faced with mad Italian drivers at unsigned junctions.

Undeterred, we headed for Caen and the shopping area, and following Maisie's dulcet tones we proceeded into the town centre. If you have visited central Caen you will know that it's a fairly busy place and we hit it at rush hour, in the dark, in the rain and in a very large American motorhome. Not good. Things began to get sticky when we entered a one way system of gradually diminishing roads and, as they turned into one lane streets congested with darting French motorists trying to get home from work, we really started to fret. Did I say *fret*; I should have said *sweat*. Dismissing poor Maisy as being a fairly stupid female as she was constantly advising us to 'make a U turn', we launched down a side street and came very swiftly into a pedestrianised area with a two meter high tunnel as the only exit. We were three and a half metres tall. Disaster.

With no way forward, we are now reversing up this narrow street with the greatest of difficulty, with all the other cars behind reversing too because we've totally blocked it. This is where you go and hide in the toilet until it's all over, but worse was yet to come when, in a desperate attempt to get out of this horrendous shopping area, we then swung down another street only to arrive in a small parking square with the road ending in three black bollards. To be absolutely fair, the French were so patient with our efforts that I shall feel eternally grateful to them for not hooting their horns at us and making us feel even worse than we did. I jumped out at this point and did my best to impersonate a French policeman, (all five foot of me), as I halted traffic and waved my arms trying to look efficient and as if I had a clue about what I was doing, directing Simon as he made a twelve point turn to extract us from our miserable position. The French looked on bemused by our English antics and our son, bless him, determinedly put his head set on and did the only sensible thing, which was to listen to the Red Hot Chilli Peppers and pretend that he wasn't really with us.

We laugh about it now and of course this happens to everyone at some point, but at the time you really want the floor to swallow you up and beam you off to a desert island. But at last, we found the right road out and once again, headed off. By now we had that really over-tired feeling, where the slightest wrong word gets a fairly snappy retort followed by a grumbled apology and, we were still looking for a supermarket which might have a car park big enough for us to get into or at least somewhere for us to park close by. Two hours later, exhausted, red eyed and feeling weak at the knees, we were dragging our trolley loads (plural) of food and wine across car parks and roads, in the dark, to load into the Beast, with mission impossible almost accomplished. Sensibly we decided that we could go no further and didn't care where we slept the night, so we drove into an adjacent industrial estate and eventually crept into the far corner of a dark, empty, rubbish strewn car park. We closed our curtains, put some music on, I cooked up a meal, and we gulped down the red wine (not necessarily in that order) – and there we hid for the night. Son Jack was fairly convinced that we would be surrounded by baton wielding French factory workers in the morning, so we decided that we would be up and away by 6 am! He named it Operation Hasty Exit. We had quite a few 'operation hasty exits' over the coming year and we can laugh about them all, but we really can't believe how we managed to make such a mess of our first day in France.

Freefall into Europe

Next morning at the crack of doom we headed away from Caen. It had all been too much too soon. We needed a few days rest, just to familiarise ourselves with the Beast and to catch up on some much needed sleep. The Manche area on the western coast of Normandy looked inviting and we quickly settled at a very quiet campsite in a small town called Barneville-Carteret. This pleasant, unspoilt peninsular, named after the English Channel, (La Manche), is a land of contrasts. With spectacular granite cliffs in the north and sheltered resorts and long sandy beaches as you head south, it is a favourite holiday place for those who like walking and nature. Offshore is the French island of Chausey, and the Channel Islands of Jersey and Sark, and of course the infamous Le Mont St Michel is just down the coast. Inland you can explore the Cotetin and Bessin Marshlands or walk the delightful bocage (hedgerow country), filling up with excellent local seafood dishes at restaurants along the way. In early October though, when the days were shortening and the weather was cooling, it was almost deserted and we had the place pretty much to ourselves. Our bikes were strapped to the back of the Beast, so we spent several days here just cycling along the quiet coast roads, through peaceful towns and villages, past shuttered holiday homes and wandering on the empty beaches collecting shells. It was a good place to chill out and start to plan the first part of our trip, which, we decided, was to see the World War Two sites in Normandy, 'here and now,' before we headed South for the winter months.

With our batteries re-charged we headed for La Cambe first. The route through the historical area of the Battle of Normandy is a great attraction, but don't let the latest invasion of tourists and the accompanying circus of fast food, floss and fancy fake mementoes prevent you from visiting it, and, if you can, go out of season when it will be less busy. We were armed, not with guns and bombs, but with endless amounts of literature gathered from the local tourist information point. We had all seen Saving Private Ryan and various guns and glory films depicting the most famous battles and campaigns of the last war, and some of them seem more realistic than others, but nothing really prepares you for the war cemeteries. At La Cambe, almost twenty two thousand memorials are laid out in small groups, each group marked by five heavy, stone crosses, under which lie the bodies of German soldiers who fell during the fighting in 1944. This was a real-life history lesson for Jack. Just one of many such cemeteries, dedicated to the various nationalities involved in the fighting here, and they would all be very moving to visit, none less so than the next one on our list, which was at Colleville-Sur-Mer.

The sky was a crystal clear blue with a gentle autumn sun and the sea was flat and perfectly calm as we stood and gazed down at Bloody Omaha, the nickname given to the notorious Omaha Beach. Behind us, in the cemetery, lay the bodies of the American soldiers who had fought and died there on June 6th 1944 in Operation Overlord. It was not difficult to imagine the scene when they spilled from their landing craft to wade through the sea and face the barrage of fire which had rained down on them from where we were stood above the beach. The noise, the smell, the fear and the fighting. It must have seemed like a small piece of hell, on earth. We turned from the beach and entered the cemetery, a monument in itself to the graceful beauty that man can create and the clumsy ugliness of war. I defy anyone to walk through this cemetery amongst the ghosts and not be moved by the sight of over nine thousand perfectly aligned, smooth as silk, white marble crosses. Laid out in serried row after row, as if still standing to attention and ready to march, most crosses engraved with name, rank and hometown. I couldn't help but envisage them all as young men, stood tall and strong, but now all dead; buried below the soft, green, beautifully tended lawns which cushion this 170 acre area. You can walk the tree-lined paths or walk between the graves or just sit and think. We three talked and walked, and read the names and wondered at man's inhumanity to man. A small piece of world history brought to life for Jack and somewhere that we would never forget.

That evening we found a great little *aire municipal* (municipal parking area for motor homes and caravans), tucked into the centre of the small fishing village of Port en Bessin, and after our evening meal we wrapped up in gloves, hats and warm jackets and strolled down to the harbour. The tide was full out and small white fishing boats balanced their bottoms on the mud. Along the harbour wall above them, a line of wild-camping motor homers were parked up for the night, opening their local wine and having their evening meal while they watched the shadows lengthen over the incoming tide. The French are great accommodators of motor homes, it seems almost a national pastime anyway, you see so many on the roads. Their motorways have excellent *aires de services*, which are free and usually have good facilities. Most towns and villages also have municipal aires where you can stay overnight and pay just a few euros to the man who comes round each evening collecting the money. They also tolerate wild camping, so long as you are not obscuring or obstructing anyone, although in season you would be expected to stay at a campsite if there was one nearby. We managed to squeeze our big American butt into some fairly small places, thanks to the excellent driving skills and determination of Simon, and we wild-camped and used aires and campsites throughout the year in many different countries with varying degrees of success.

The highlight of the next day was a visit to Arromanches and the D Day Landing Museum. On the way, we had stopped off at the Point du Hoc, a large and strategic German gun emplacement which had controlled the whole area where the allied landings were going to take place. Wrapped in our warm winter clothes, against a cold, damp autumn mist, we clambered through the fortified bunkers and bomb craters, on this vital piece of headland which had been so pivotal in the control of the coastline. A small group of intrepid rangers had bravely scaled the towering sea cliffs early on June 6th 1944, to capture this position, which had allowed the D Day landing to proceed.

At Arromanches museum we began to fully understand the enormity of Operation Overlord and what had been required on this Normandy coast for the landing to be successful. In the absence of a large port in the area to unload the heavy machinery and equipment required, an artificial harbour the size of Dover was constructed at Arromanches in a matter of days. The planning and building of it all, had gone on for months beforehand in England in total secrecy. Over one hundred enormous concrete pontoons were sunk on the Calvados reefs, along with seventeen old ships, and this formed a four-mile long breakwater, one and a half miles from the shore. Floating platforms made of steel created 2,300 feet of pier-heads, which were then linked to the shore by four floating roads of concrete and metal pontoons each one about 4,000 feet long. These were for unloading everything required for the invasion, from light vehicles such as ambulances, command cars and jeeps, to heavier tanks, bulldozers, cranes and various cargoes. And all of this material had to be first constructed in England and then towed across the channel in complete secrecy. The statistics are amazing and it was a great accomplishment that by June 12th, six days after the beach landings, it had not only been built but 326,000 men, 54,000 vehicles and 110,000 tons of supplies had been disembarked. This was the allied push into occupied France.

There was plenty to see here, but we were already one week into our year and we still hadn't left Normandy; we had our own push to make, and we also wanted to return to Caen. This was not to the ill-fated shopping area again, but, having become fascinated with the history of this area, we wanted to visit a museum there, before we moved on. Maisy, behaving perfectly this time, took us straight to the museum, and as darkness settled, we spotted an overflow car park situated on a piece of flat land close by. It still felt strange to simply turn off the engine, cook a meal and go to bed wherever we had stopped and we felt rather vulnerable in the centre of the busy, built up town with main roads on all sides of us, but the French just didn't bat an eyelid. It was obviously not such a strange thing to see a motor home parked in the middle of the neighbourhood on a dark October evening. As usual in France, people were out strolling and the evening was busy, even though there was a chill winter feel to the air. The beautifully flood-lit building was something we hadn't expected and it has remained one of those great memories...... strolling around gardens, fountains and a stunning building, in the middle of Caen, on a clear, dark autumn night.

The Caen Memorial, a Museum for Peace, is a building designed by Jacques Millet. From the moment you walk up the steps to the front doors you will understand that this is not a normal museum. It is neither a War Museum nor a conventional museum and its purpose is not just to display collected exhibits. The Memorial aims to take you through the history that shaped the conflicts of the 20th Century and to understand the fragile but essential requirement of Peace. Architecturally, it's a wonderful building. We arrived there at 9.0 am the next morning with our ready-made sandwiches and essential chocolate, and studied the massive white limestone façade. This smooth, cream coloured building is literally cut through the middle by a narrow, jagged vertical gash of dark glass and mirrors. This is the entrance doorway. It symbolises the allied sword cut that opened the Atlantic wall, breaking down the German sea defences along France's coastline. Inside is spacious, with modern unusual architecture and materials, used to direct and display information. Once inside you have free access to a media library, the usual bookshop and restaurant and even a childminding service for under ten's.

We started our visit with a journey into history that began in 1919 and which is displayed as a continuous trip down an ever descending and ever darkening, spiral walkway. At first the display walls are smooth and light and bright, but as you go further down the passage of time and information, you realise that they have gradually become very dark and rough in texture ….. you are descending into an abyss of war. I didn't realise how much the design of this had affected me until I suddenly felt very trapped and claustrophobic and felt I wanted to escape from such a depressing atmosphere. I was suddenly, desperately, looking for exit signs. I then realised that I had reached the dark years of occupied France and the holocaust. Here the walls, the dim lights and the very air was dark and oppressive, as was the feeling in Europe at that time. As you move out of these years and on to liberation and eventual freedom, the walls, lights and colours return and you walk up a spiral to ground level and fresh air again.

There is far more to this interesting museum and we, true to our usual style, completely overdid it and stayed there for six hours. You can be overloaded with facts and I would advise anyone visiting to get information beforehand so that you really understand the building and its displays. It is well worth a trip if you are in the area. We staggered out boondoggled and returned to the Beast exhausted, but pleased that we had decided to go there, and even more pleased that we had plenty of wine and good French food for our supper. We slept like logs. This time Caen had been good to us.

Two hours down the motorway was our next stop. The famous and ever popular tourist destination of, Le Mont St Michel. There is no sneaking up on this place, as you will get your first captivating glimpses of the turreted and spired islet from across the perfectly flat coastland as you drive towards it. And it is difficult not to be impressed. What you may not be impressed with is the sheer number of us tourists that are there year round, although once again, at the end of October when we visited for the first time, it was not too bad. (When we called in on our way home, at the end of our trip, it was September and it was a wonder that the rock didn't capsize beneath the weight of camera snapping, jostling, pushing and shoving people). However, it is amazing. The Mont of St Michel sits like a granite castle floating in the sea; surrounded by deep water at high tide and bare, muddy, sand flats at low tide. It is approached by a 900 meter causeway.

We drove towards it with the morning sun catching the huge gilded statue of St Michael, slayer of devils and dragons, who stands majestically above the massive Benedictine Abbey which is built at the very summit of this rocky island. Simon swung the Beast into the large car park and there we stopped for the next twenty-four hours, along with literally hundreds of other motor homers, while we explored the island. Jack led the way up through the massive wooden gates, into the ancient and pedestrian-only town; his biggest hope being that there would be shops selling swords - and of course there were. The cobbled streets are steep and sometimes incredibly narrow and the houses of the ancient town cling like a family of limpets around the base of the rock. Ramparts, fortifications and spires of stone, huge doorways and impregnable walls reminded me of the buildings in Lord of the Rings and on top of it all sits a massive Abbey. Simon and I shared a headset to walk around the Abbey, (a desperate measure of economy), while Jack had his own headphones. Take our advice and don't ever try to share headsets. With one ear-piece each we had to walk joined at the hip for the next few hours, and were reduced to much frustrated tut-tutting as we negotiated stairs or changed direction, especially as he wanted to spend longer on some things and I on others. In the end, I was gripped smartly by the elbow and told not to move in any direction other than his. Being a truly obedient wife I took my ear-phone off, let him have the lot and stomped off, only to get totally lost. No matter though, we saw it all. The Abbey is a unique confusion of a building, added to and destroyed many times during its long history, its plan unlike any other due to the pyramidal shape of the mount. Wrapped around the rock, the abbey church sits at the top, supported by crypts, and atop the church in gilded glory is the golden statue of the head of heavenly militia, Saint Michael.

We slept in the car park that night with a wonderful view of the floodlit town. The grey, stone buildings floodlit against the black sea and sky, a golden winged figure shining aloft. Next morning we went back very early; the sun was hardly up and the crowds had not yet arrived. Then it was even better as we could freely tour the ramparts of the town walls that weave amongst wooden shingled roofs, and explore the near vertical alleys that descended to the main thoroughfare. Jack bought his sword by the way and it travelled with us all round Europe, hidden under his bed. Life size and real metal, it now hangs on his bedroom wall. But hey – here and now – he will never forget Le Mont St Michel.

We decided that we'd had enough culture for a while, (that's just how fickle you can be when the world's your lobster), so we headed straight down the west coast of France to the Gironde region, and to somewhere that we hadn't visited for nearly twenty years – The Dunes of Pylat. Robbie Williams was now our singing companion in the motor home, so with Jack feeling glad that his mates couldn't hear him singing along to such music, we headed off, all in full song along the French highways. Jack was thirteen, and a joy to travel with. He is the youngest of four sons, the others having grown and flown, and we had just a one year gap before he started his GCSE syllabus. He grew so much in every way during this year and it was of no detriment to his education, in fact we feel it was of great benefit. We discussed all subjects as we went. Simon good at some and me, at others. Geography, religion, history, languages, maths, cultures, science….. there were endless opportunities to cover all of these subjects as we moved from country to country, landscape to landscape, town to town. How was that fortress built? Why did they have that war? What is this insect? How do you ask for a coffee? What is this festival celebrating? How did this glacier evolve? What stars are we looking at? If you are interested in life then you can learn anywhere, and his next lesson 'on the road' was going to be Geography.

We had visited the Dunes of Pylat before in 1984 when camping in France with the three other boys, when they were young, before Jack was even a twinkle in our eyes. We have photographs of us all standing on the wind blown top in the baking sun and sand. Now we wanted to show them to him. Situated just below Arcachon and almost opposite Cap Ferret in the Bay of Biscay, these are the largest sand dunes in Europe, standing 117 meters high and 3 kilometres long. A strange freak of winds, tides and nature. We arrived just before dark at the end of October and again it was quiet, although still warm in the daytime now that we were further south. We parked up and went for a quick walk up the dunes before it got dark. Actually, it's almost impossible to go for a 'quick' walk up the dunes unless you're an Olympic athlete, and most people go for a long slow climb up the dunes, stopping many times to get your breath back. When we eventually reached the long, wide summit we could only stand and gaze; the views all around were still just as amazing as we had remembered. In front of us was the huge darkening sea of the Bay of Biscay, stretching for miles and miles to the thin line of the horizon; to either side the fine pale sand of the flat-topped dunes, an endless windblown surface of streaking, ghost-like, abrasive grit. Behind us, inland, as far as the eye could see extended a vast, green tree-top canopy of maritime pines, part of this huge forested area.

A 360 degree view, from our wind-blown eerie; as if we were sea birds in the sky. You may think that you have seen sand dunes but you will not have seen sand dunes like these unless you have been to the deserts. We played all the next day on the dunes, with Simon and I mostly laying in the sun or paddling in the sea or flying kites and Jack racing down the moving dune sides, swimming in the sea or finding bronze backed beetles and tiny sand insects. It had been a sizzling hot day, but that night the wind blew hard and as we lay in our beds, in our sheltered campsite under the trees, we listened to the roar of wind and sea, in the Bay on the other side of the dunes.

We stayed five days at the Dunes. Sometimes playing and walking on them, but also exploring this area on our bikes. Our three bikes were invaluable during the year and we cycled at almost every stop. More often than not we found designated cycle lanes. There had been an excellent cycle path both ways along the coast at Arcachon and when that had disappeared, even the main roads were quiet. We now cycled through Pylat sur Mer and La Teste, past shuttered holiday homes and closed cafes and campsites, and explored for far too long, ending up at strange places where our shortcuts had misled us.

We always went too far because we just wanted to see what was round the next bend. Coming back after one of our cycling forays we saw another motor home parked up by ours – with a GB sticker on the back. We had been the only ones in the pine-wood parking area by the dunes, so this was a pleasant surprise. The motor home was owned by Gerry and his fair haired, long legged companion Figgy…… a gorgeous golden Labrador. Gerry and dog were travelling for a year too and that night they joined us for supper; a big bowl of pasta and tuna. Gerry was the first of many people that we met on the road over the year, all of them friendly with advice to impart or reading books to swap. He told us of a pretty lake just down the coast, which had a great aire. It sounded interesting, but we had already decided that we should soon head over the Pyrenees and down into Spain before the winter weather really set in.

That night the wind howled again, and next morning we said our goodbyes and all headed on, our first priority to find a laundrette. I had discovered that when travelling, clothes can vary in degrees of dirtiness. We had been very economical with our clothing, but by now we were glad that we had assigned the port forward locker as the laundry locker, because the laundry bag was beginning to get a bit whiffy! (All the lockers were named as if on a ship. For example Starboard Aft was the spare food and drinks locker. This was because my husband would really like to have travelled in a yacht, not a motor home).

Gerry's pretty lake, Etang de Biscarrosse et Parentis, was at Gastes. Another spacious municipal aire was available to park in, this time a grassy orchard area, next to sun bleached wooden boathouses, a small marina and the lake. Jack swam from the sandy beach and French fishermen sat in their boats and looked on as if he were mad. But then it *was* nearly November; the leaves were off the trees and autumn was turning to winter. It was peaceful here but we couldn't linger long….. pleasant as it was, the winter was catching up with us and we had to keep moving South. We motored on down to Dax and then on to the pretty town of Orthez which sits astride the River Pau. From there we had our first views of the Pyrenees and a few miles further on we stopped for the night in another interesting aire de service called the Aire d'Astronomie. All of the play equipment provided at this motorway car park was designed to educate children and adults about the planets and our solar system. It even had a large, circular astronomical centre with film shows and a café. We spent a happy evening there, wandering through the solar system and playing on the planets, before sleeping peacefully in our home on wheels, – how well the French design their motorway stops. Up with the sun next day we moved on towards Foix, stopping for a quick, but memorable lunch, at St Girons on the way.

St Girons is a town not to be missed on a Saturday morning if you enjoy street markets or if you are in any way inclined to be hippy. Stalls offering anything and everything, of the region or not, lined the streets of the old town and the banks of the Salat, a clear mountain river which tumbles down from the Pyrenees. Hippies were everywhere. We didn't see this anywhere else on our travels and it was like re-visiting the sixties. Rasta hair, sweet heavy perfumes in the air, brightly coloured woven clothes and plenty of beads.

Young and old. Sandals and smoke, babies strapped onto backs, groups of stray dogs having a good time, …. a monkey on an organ grinders shoulder, drunk or stoned beggars loitering on street corners with dogs on string. It was like a time warp and Jack had never seen anything like it. As if the world's hippies had sometime gravitated to St Girons to live, and once there had got cut off from the changing world, some just growing old and grey. We felt quite at odds with it all, even though Simon had been quite hippy when he was young. It was almost embarrassing to be in modern clothes and not sporting a ragged afghan coat or carrying a beaded bag and, it was incredibly busy. The local French were mixed amongst it all, but they didn't look too impressed. It was very strange and we couldn't quite make it out, maybe we had breathed in some of the questionable smoke that was drifting around, but hey peace man, who were we to comment, we were just passing through.

We moved on to find an overnight stop. We wanted to have plenty of time to enjoy the scenery as we crossed over the Pyrenees, which now loomed before us, and so decided to wait until the next morning before starting to make the drive up and over. Our motor home was big, weighing seven and a half tons and we were not going to rush. It was getting late and nearly dark, but luckily we spotted a sign to a village municipal aire and decided to sleep the night there. Unfortunately the aire was nowhere to be seen, but we did notice a small car park surrounded by tall fir trees, next to a sports field, on the edge of town. That looked fine, it was empty and not near any houses so we tucked ourselves quietly in and settled for the night. I cooked chilli-con-carne for supper, we opened the wine and relaxed.

Cosily unperturbed in our dining-cum-lounge area, and half way through our quiet evening meal, the gentle darkness outside was suddenly replaced by a searing light, which starkly illuminated the whole area, including our large American motor home. Quickly pulling up the blinds, we saw that floodlights were on all around us, and, looking like startled diners in a fancy restaurant window, we watched in horror as three referees ran onto the pitch next to us. They were shortly followed by two complete football teams in full strip, who jogged smartly on and started warming up. Supporters started to arrive by the carload, all warmly wrapped for the cold night, and they lined the sidelines next to us shouting 'allez –y' as the game commenced. Can you imagine this happening in England. Surely we would have been asked to move, but not the French. Hardly glancing at us, the spectators cheered, their breathe hanging frosted in the cold night air, and rubbed their hands and stamped their feet to keep themselves warm, while players raced up and down the pitch right next to us, dribbling, spitting and shouting like footballers the world over. We might as well have not been there. We quickly swallowed our embarrassment along with our chilli, opened the windows and cheered too. It was the only thing to do really. Blue and white socks against yellow socks – nothing too technical for us, we cheered for them all. This was Saturday match night in the small village of Les Cabannes. Much later, game over, cars skidded off into the night. No doubt, celebration or commiseration would be discussed over a few bottles of biere or wine in the local bar, but our peaceful darkness returned. We pulled down the blinds and made up Jacks bed. Just the three of us again, sleeping well, before we crossed the mountains and entered Spain; and, as far as we could tell, the 'yellow socks' had won the match.

Oranges in Oliva

I was designated to the seat behind the driver's seat for the next part of our journey, for very good reasons. I had been sitting in the front and Jack had been in the rear seat but it was generally thought that my being in the front was not such a good idea and we should swap. The Beast was quite high and sometimes, to me, it was like sitting in the front of a fairground roller coaster. Flyovers that spanned gorges and valleys, on stilts of concrete, had had me clutching the sides of the seat and almost sitting on Simon's lap as he drove. My now familiar saying of "we're awfully close to the edge Si!" in a very high pitched voice, was really rattling him and didn't help one iota. 'Get in the back mother and don't say anything', was basically the format as we wound our way up through the mountains – which was fine by me. The weather was clear but cold on the French side of the mountain range and the autumn colours were as beautiful as you can imagine. Stunning, snow capped peaks came into view now and again, but as the road ground ever upward, with staggering sheer drops beside us, I felt the need to get out a bottle of Pina Colada and swig at it with ever increasing ferocity as we zigzagged up through the hairpin bends to the top. I'm not sure why I suddenly found heights so difficult to deal with. When I was younger I had been a high board diver, but with age had come caution. This was something I had to overcome as we often used cable cars, ski lifts and climbed to the tops of just about everything and anything that we visited. Throughout the year my fear of heights got better, but it was never easy.

Eventually, we reached the top of the pass and stopped at around 6000 feet at Porte Puymorens for a cook up of eggs and beans and to call some friends from the singular, desolate telephone box that huddled at the side of the mucky road. The mist and freezing drizzle hung about at this height, clouding the craggy bare mountain sides. We stared down at the deep valley ahead with apprehension and eventually started down the road of shiny, icy tarmac which twisted and switch-backed its way down into Spain. More Pina Colada was consumed by the lady in the rear seat as she gazed at the amazing scenery: for 'amazing scenery' please read 'scary dizzying drops at the edge of roads which clung impossibly to the sides of mountains!' Through the Tunnel del Cadi and at last we reached level land again on our way towards Barcelona.

We soon realised that Spanish roads in this area were far busier than the ones that we had left behind in France. Catalunya and Barcelona had recently received EU money for massive road building programmes, which was great. However most of that money seemed to be going into digging up and re-laying the ring road around

Barcelona. Weaving our way through convoluted road works, alongside hundreds of speeding lorries and cars was daunting, and we needed to be on our toes. The Spanish in this area also seemed to have an interesting approach to driving; i.e. ignore all rules, white lines, speed restrictions and warning signs. Overtake anything that moves – car, lorry, bird, plane, you name it and they'll overtake it, even if it's on a blind bend and next to a ravine. Also park anywhere at anytime. Our law-abiding, pedantic English adherence to the rulebook was wasted here as we were jostled along the motorway like lemmings on the way to the edge. A fast flowing river of traffic that was impossible to escape from. We decided to return to Barcelona another day and agreed that when we did, we would use the extensive and fast public transport system. For now though, we were still heading south down the coastal road. That night we pulled up in a motorway parking area just north of Valencia. Tremendous thunderstorms and torrential rain had swept across the area during the day, making driving even worse, so we stopped earlier than usual that evening, which turned out to be a blessing in disguise. The car park was fairly empty when we pulled in and we found a good spot to park. Lorries were still hurtling down the motorway but before too long they came screaming into the car park, one after another like racing cars into the pits, searching for a space, until it was almost full. Huge juggernauts gliding up alongside us made us look positively insignificant and we wondered why on earth they all parked so closely together.

We got quite used to sleeping amongst these giants as the year went on and never had any trouble. We were too big for car-sized slots in normal parking areas, so had to bunk down with the big boys. That night we slept ok, and awoke early next morning when the first lorries were starting to head off. Laying in bed, listening to the background noise of revving engines and hawking Spaniards, just beyond our windows, was not quite 'Kings of the Road' material, but if we had thought that the car park was full when we went to sleep, it was nothing to how full it was now. Lorries were jammed nose to tail, side by side, in every possible bit of space. This was another lesson to learn. There really isn't enough space in the Spanish motorway car parks for lorry drivers to park up for the night and if you don't get a space early, you could be driving for a long while before you find somewhere to lay your head.

However, like most Spaniards, the lorry drivers seemed to do everything with a flourish and a passion. Whether it was neck and neck racing down the motorway, sulking and arm waving because they had been pipped at the post for a parking space, cooking up a lunch at the side of their cabs, or even just answering the call of nature. Oh yes; no bashful discreetness for them when nature calls. Out of the cab, down with the flies and straight on with it, often not making it to the grass at the curb, or even a nearby tree. When you've got to go, you've got to go, and anywhere, including the tarmac, will do. Were they just frustrated bullfighters full of macho daring do? Who knows, but this was Spain. So Viva Espagna, Espagna por favour.

Spain is such a huge country, so diverse, so crammed with treasures both natural and man made, with so much to see that you could spend years there and still want more time. So often I was exasperated with Spain. It was a land of opposites for me. It could be so dirty, so noisy, so difficult to deal with but just when I was cursing some illogical, frustrating or maddening situation or some surly unhelpful person, some wonderful festival or event would happen, or some person would behave with such flamboyance, such generosity of spirit or we would see such beauty in land or culture that my previous ideas would be turned on their heads. When we finally left Spain to travel on to Italy, I said I would never go back. But now, I would go back tomorrow, because for all its failings and frustrations, to live in Spain is to live life.

This country has a population of over forty million, drawn from all the many peoples who have settled there over the millennia. Each region will proudly, and I mean proudly, boast of its culture and cuisine. It is surely Europe's most geographically diverse country with landscapes ranging from the lush, green coastal inlets of Galicia, to the sun-baked plains of Castilla-La Mancha: from the mountainous, snow capped Pyrenees and Sierra Nevada to the near desserts of Almeria. Ski in the morning and swim in the Med in the afternoon. Spanish cities will dazzle you – the architecture, the people, the energy, the conversations held at top volume – everyone will listen to a private conversation, shared with much hand waving and tossing of heads – if only we had understood what even half of it was all about. But in the countryside it will be the tiny old ladies dressed in black that will catch your eye, and you'll feel as if you're rudely trespassing as you sneak a look through cool, dark, doorways in silent villages. You may boil over in the summer in Andalusia but you could freeze in the winter in Madrid. There are so many variations. But in general the coast will be mild in the winter and that's where you will find the majority of the 'snowbirds', the huge number of older people, from many different nationalities, who rest the winter there.

We arrived at our coastal campsite, in Oliva, late in the afternoon after a fairly stressful drive. We had tried to go through nearby Gandia instead of around it. That had something to do with the lack of signposts, and it didn't help that it was a madly busy town of small roads and it was school collection time. As usual, parking restrictions were non-existent on anyone's agenda, so parents parked three and four deep in the town centre, with doors open for children to eventually hop in. Traffic piled up, horns blew, heads were tossed and we all got very heated. We imagined this happened on a daily, if not hourly, basis. Eventually we squeezed out of Gandia and reached the campsite, and with light fading fast we wriggled in through the small entrance and into a space in what we would later call, the British quarter. With neck muscles seized and too tired to cook a meal we slurped some red wine and headed for the camp restaurant. This was situated on the long beachfront and had a great seating area outdoors, under a big canvas roof. It seemed strange to us that no one else was eating there, but we thought that maybe we were too early, although it was now dark. The bored waitresses regarded our dishevelled and weary appearance with some surprise and offered us seats indoors, probably trying to hide us in a corner. Oh no thank you.... We want to sit outdoors under the canopy.

And so we did.....totally alone in the restaurant for the whole evening, Jack being very impressed by the personal attention of three waitresses, all to ourselves. We had a wonderful meal of paella, the first of many in Spain, and by far the most expensive too. That would account for the lack of customers. Snowbirds live economically. They live on the excellent, cheap local produce bought at markets and cook it back at camp. They often get incredibly low rates for their six-month winter stays in their caravans or motor homes on the camp sites and they enjoy the mild winter weather in relative peace. In summer of course they leave, and the usual tourists arrive with money to spend and good times to be had in the baking sun. That is a different kind of Spain again.

The next morning we were shattered and didn't even open our curtains until gone eleven o'clock. Curled up in our pyjamas, munching breakfast, wrapped in duvets, we slobbed it and watched a video of Alien 3 on our TV. Well, once in a while you just needed to do that. When we did finally open our door we found ourselves in a pleasant corner of the site, with parakeets flying in the trees about us and curious neighbours on either side; Graham and dog, avoiding a long English winter, and Gerald and Lizzie (French) who had literally ground to a natural halt when their back axle had broken. A little further on were a young London couple who were also travelling in a big American motor home on a two year gap. Their passion was to ski and sail and they had not only brought their skis with them but had a collapsible catamaran sailing boat on board the motor home too. The majority of the rest of the large campsite were German. 'Morgans' as we called them. Our 'good morning' replied to by a gruff 'morgan'. We were amazed at how many Germans were over-wintering on the Spanish Coast. Like the Brits, they too were leading a double life of boules and card games in the warm winter, just returning to home for the summer months.

Before long our bikes were oiled, tyres pumped up and we had found the easy cycle route into town, past purple flowering bougainvillea and swathes of heavily scented flowers that I shamefully did not know the names of. Over little bridges crossing channels of water running down to the sea, past the local indoor swimming pool and up through the broad avenue of wide topped plane trees that shaded Oliva's main promenade. We locked our bikes at the big town square where children played and the elderly sat and chatted, then walked up to the 'old town' area to explore the steep winding streets, preserved churches and white washed houses. Up to the top of the castle remains, and a wonderful view across Oliva's tiled roof tops to the sea. Then down again until we eventually staggered wearily back to the square and flopped on to a bench.

Overheard conversations in English had been repeatedly caught on the wind and a British-run Internet café and shop, selling everything from baked beans to Christmas puddings, soon reminded us of home. We had been away from England for nearly four weeks – not long really, although Jack now admitted that he was missing his mates. Guilt seems to come as part of the parenting package and we now felt very guilty that he was stuck with us for so much of the time. (These feelings disappeared quite quickly as the year went by and we all fell into slightly different roles.) Anyway, as there was obviously an English community in Oliva, we decided to try to find some friends for Jack. The owner of the Internet café gave us an idea.

"All the English kids meet in the town square on a Saturday night", he promised, as he filled our rucksacks with good old English salad cream, the only thing that Simon ever missed, and as the next day was a Saturday, we had a plan. Jack was a little sceptical but prepared to go along with it. We spent the morning exploring on our bikes but headed home early and had a siesta. It's not that easy to go to sleep at four o'clock in the afternoon if you're not used to it, but we struggled on until we could get up again at around six. Showered and dressed in the smartest clothes we had, we headed into town on our bikes, ready for a great night out. You know that saying about the greatest plans of mice and men…. well, we walked the town in search of the elusive English teenagers, but they were all obviously having a rare, quiet night in. Maybe there was something good on the telly, whatever. Those quiet streets echoed with our footsteps until we eventually gave up and stopped for a drink at an empty bar in the old quarter. One other couple sat there, also looking forlorn, and although they were English, they were not teenagers. Allan and Cath were on a fact-finding mission, and thinking of moving to Spain, so we sat outdoors with them and chatted and tried to ignore the fact that the weather had by now changed from a pleasant night to one that had a distinctly colder, wetter feel. By ten thirty the rain was beginning in earnest and we were ready to give up.

Dashing back through the town to our bikes, in sandals and shirts and pouring rain, we headed for home. The weather was about the only English thing we had found! We peddled like crazed hamsters against the driving wind and torrential downpour, completely soaked, with no bike lights, (really getting into the Spanish way now) in our mud splattered Sunday best. A short-cut alongside an old canal, in pitch black, past big barking dogs and pushing our bikes through muddy, long wet grass eventually led us to within meters of the camp site…. if only the marina hadn't been in the way…. so back the same way again, past the barking dogs and through the long wet grass, and then the long way round on the pitch-black roads. We certainly know how to have a good Saturday night out. Like dripping water rats we crept back into the motor home. With a wisdom born only from experience, Jack tactfully suggested, "Let's stick to the cup of cocoa and early nights in future, I think I'd rather find my own friends thanks." Poor lad, with parents like us what hope did he have.

The bad weather continued on and off, for five more days. Quite unusual for the area and time of year, but everywhere we travelled during the year, people complained of unusual weather. During this time we got to know Gerald and Lizzie well, and cycled daily, between the showers, finding the excellent 14 kilometre cycle track which joins the towns of Oliva and Gandia. This flat, wide, peaceful track which takes you through endless groves of orange trees, was used by young and old alike for commuting on cycles or just strolling. Littered with oranges fallen from the trees, our thirsts could easily be quenched. Jack will always remember this as the place he learned to ride 'no handed' and I shall never forget him speeding off ahead of us, weaving between walkers, with his hands casually clasped behind his head, thoroughly chuffed with himself. At Gandia another road led us off to the coast and more stretches of sandy beach, while behind us the rocky sierras were outlined against a blue sky. When the weather settled again, we decided that to really see what the area was like, we would hire a car and explore the white washed villages, which we could see nestled up in the folds of the mountains.

Our first car trip was not however to the mountains but along the road to probably the best-known place on the Costa coast, poor besmirched Benidorm. Who can ever remember what the village of Benidorm had originally looked like? It's been a package holiday tourist town for so long, that it has changed beyond all recognition. We expected the worst but ended up quite pleasantly surprised. Of course, it was 'out of season' which makes a huge difference. Benidorm does have a sea front of towering hotels and an enormous number of tacky tourist shops, but it's been cleaning up its act over the past few years and it shows. There are also designer shops now, many classy shoe shops, expensive restaurants and spacious open squares. The clean blue sea and beautiful sandy beaches are edged by a pleasant promenade that follows the cliff face and of course the weather in late November was very warm. And it's not all chips and ice cream, because we did find a locals café, tucked up a side street, where we had an excellent three-course lunch of salad, paella, then meatballs or fish, for eight euros a head. Benidorm may not appeal to everyone, but in winter, it obviously appeals to thousands of older people….. and why not. We sat by a cooling fountain under shady palm trees and watched an endless parade of white haired couples in shorts or tracksuits taking a walk along the beach and promenade, sporting tanned faces and looking relaxed. Who is to say that they would be happier battling against the cold winter rain and frantic traffic of England. Why not wear shorts at eighty, even if you are on a zimmer frame, and why not spend your winters in the warm? I only hope I have the sense to do the same at that age. So, maybe not for us right now, but definitely good for others. What it's like in August of course, I dread to think.

We took other car trips with Gerald and Lizzie because, besides enjoying their company, Lizzie knew the area well as she had lived in nearby Denia for a while. Squashing all five of us into the little Seat Ibiza, we drove the switch back roads up into the hills, past clusters of new developments and amazing scenery, squeezing through tiny quiet villages whose roads were really only meant for donkeys, and passing dark open doorways that invited a peek, with the mouth-watering smell of fideua coming from dim kitchens within. On past orange and olive groves, stopping quickly to pick lemons straight from the trees, which, if you rubbed their warm skins gave you the sharp strong smell of sherbet. Then to Parcent, and on to Altea, the delightful village on the coast, whose famous white washed houses line the cobbled streets, which led us up to the great white church on the hill. That evening, as the light was falling, a large well-dressed congregation with many important dignitaries were gathered in the square before the church and a full choir could be heard through the open doors. Children played in the square and adults chatted, it was obviously a special occasion, but the lady who caught my eye was an old flower seller. Small and stooped, she was dressed all in black, her thick stockings wrinkled around her ankles and her tired grey hair escaping from its grips. She wandered through the crowd, but very few wanted to buy her flowers and most turned their back when she approached them. I was trying to get to her, to buy a flower, but she had moved on by the time I reached the church. Many times on our travels we saw people begging by church doors, often with children, but when the well-heeled and expensively dressed congregation came out they more often than not gave them a cold look or simply ignored them. It always seemed very sad to me and somewhat hypocritical.

The opulent, glamorous interior of Spanish churches sometimes comes as quite a shock when it is set against a poor neighbourhood. In Altea the church façade is plain, but when you push open the huge, brass studied door you enter a glittering, brilliantly lit interior of white and gold. Statues, domes, cornices and ceilings, all adorned with rich paints and skilfully lit with soft warm lighting, make this church most inviting. It was a church that they were proud of. When the joyful singing of the choir finally faded, we went for a beer in the café overlooking the floodlit square and listened to the next musical offering of the evening, which came from the local brass band. They were all quite young, and cheerfully struck up with a swinging rendition of Abba's much murdered 'Dancing Queen'... and a following medley of their best known hits. It was obviously going to be a party night in Altea but not for us, as we wanted to move on to Denia, for supper in one of Lizzies' favourite restaurants. Denia, again on the coast, had plenty to offer the tourist, with wide streets shaded by acacia trees, pretty squares adorned by crimson bougainvillea and a long sea front and harbour. Fishermen's houses were still low level, with few high rise blocks of apartments. Picture postcard working and pleasure boats, faded and worn, coloured this small, busy port with blues, reds and yellows and the seafood restaurants were a treat. Lizzie knew of one; a small family-run affair used by the locals and there we feasted on tasty tapas, fresh fish dishes and of course paella. I never, ever tired of eating paella. We had a charming waiter whose face I can remember quite clearly. He was French Algerian and had features that looked almost sculpted from smooth, dark coloured stone; beautiful almond eyes and full perfect lips and a very unassuming and gentle manner. It's strange how you can remember some people so well from your travels. I can picture him now as he stood with his hands behind his back, quietly looking out of the window to the dark sea, while he patiently waited for us to finish eating. We ended our feast with a rich Musquadet liqueur, on the house – with a non- alcoholic apple liqueur for Jack. Gerald and our waiter talked into the night about Algeria, their homeland. A fascinating conversation, which we were just glad to sit and absorb.

The history of this area, like all of Spain, is as undulating as the landscape. Five centuries of Moorish rule has ensured a legacy of rich culture. Castles, culinary delights and carnivals owe much to the Arabic influence. Countless villages and place names beginning with "Beni" (meaning 'son of' in Arabic), confirms that for centuries this land was peopled by the Moors. It was also influenced by Majorcan families who arrived in the 17th Century to re-populate the area, and that added another layer of culture. Dominated by impressive Sierras, this mountainous area is full of tiny villages and historical sites to visit.

We spent a few more days visiting local markets and beaches and then went back to the mountains in search of the impressive, El Castell de Guadalest, the hidden jewel that sits high on the edge of the Sierra d'Aitana. This old Moorish fort was built on a craggy outcrop, 500 meters above the Guadalest valley. From the fortified town we peered over the walls and down to the Guadalest River and the blue green waters of a large, deep reservoir, way, way below. Opposite was the scrubby rock face of the Sierra de la Xorta, and all around the endless mountains and valleys fenced us in. Guadalest is listed as a national heritage site and has a fascinating centre of old houses and steep cobbled streets, but the real treat comes when you discover the hidden entrance to the old town and the castle of San Jose. Created through a triangular, natural rock tunnel, the entrance, with its smoothly worn steps, leads you up through cool solid stone and into the old town. Carved into and around the jagged peninsular, the houses grow into the rock faces, and although they are now mostly used as museums and tourist shops, it is still a much 'lived in' town. The castle perches above it all on the very edge of the steep cliff face, with staggering panoramic views down and across the valley.

Up to this point we had been going along pretty much according to plan and I guess we should have known that behind every silver lining, there is a big black cloud just waiting to rain on you. Well, our next big black cloud was just rolling into view at this time. We had one place that we still wanted to visit in this area, while we still had the car. That was Les Fonts d'Algar, otherwise known as the Algar Springs. So, making an early start on a morning filled with sunshine and blue skies, we packed a picnic and headed back into those mountains for one last time. It was just the three of us that day, as Lizzie and Gerald were busy, so we reverted to singing our personal anthem of the trip – "just the three of us, we can make it if we try"!

We headed straight to the high point of Pego, from where six mountain roads fan out across the countryside. From there we worked our way through the mountains to Planes, then back to Castell de Castell and then down to Callosa. The mountains looked fantastic in the sun that day. Endless tiers of olive trees on steeply terraced slopes, almond trees along the road side and plenty of orange groves to tempt us. The huge leaves of the regions medlar trees casting welcome shade, and limes and lemons too. We stopped at peaceful, pristine villages, where languid dogs stretched out in the shade too lazy to move, and round old ladies gossiped in dark doorways. A few children played, but mostly the villages were silent and quiet in the warm November sun. We parked and explored them, feeling not for the first time like the three cowboys in The Good, The Bad and The Ugly as we walked abreast down the hot, empty streets with camera loaded, ready to shoot. When we stopped for our picnic on a grassy verge, high above a valley, it seemed that even the insects were having a siesta and you could have heard a pin drop in the valley next door.

We finally got to the Font d'Algar by mid afternoon. This is a big tourist attraction normally, but at this quiet time of year it was almost deserted. Set in a small, lush valley the impressive waterfalls and series of cool pools are fed by the Algar River, and can be explored on foot by way of designated paths. Taking off our shoes at a shallow ford, we cooled our feet in the mountain water, before we followed the path which took us literally climbing and walking up steps built into the lush, green covered rocks and cascading river. It should have been a pleasant afternoon and a great end to our day trip but I had made a few fatal errors at the car park earlier, which would have a miserable effect on us all.

When we had arrived at the falls, we had pulled into the almost empty car park and as we arrived, a car with a young man in, pulled up next to us. Feeling relaxed and full of bon ami, we smiled at him, and then gaily opened our car boot and threw in our rucksacks, jackets and my shoulder bag – for once I didn't want to carry it. Then, as we walked up to the entrance kiosk we practically accosted three other young men who were walking down to the car park to meet their friend and asked them if the falls were open.

"Oh, Si, Si", they chimed in unison, looking particularly happy to be asked. What nice young men, thought I! Of course, I might just as well have said to this group of four dodgy looking lads….. "We're just going for a long walk up to the falls; we'll be gone for several hours, all our stuff is in the boot, help yourselves why don't you!"

Yes, on returning to the car after our wonderful walk, we found the back window smashed in, glass everywhere and everything gone from the boot. If our curses at that point ever became effective then those four lads would have suffered badly, but of course, our ranting was useless, and in the end Jack and I huddled by the car feeling miserable, while Simon strode up to the nearby restaurant, with murder in mind, to discover where the nearest police station was. The owner was most kind and had actually noted their car number plate earlier as he thought the lads looked suspicious, so we did at least have that. (Be warned, apparently it was a prime spot for thieves). He then kindly jumped in his car and led us to the nearest Guardia Civil and wished us luck

– we'd need it. We had reached the Guardia Civil just as they were locking up for the afternoon, so it was with some reluctance and a look that plainly said, 'damned tourists, that's my paella ruined again', that the unimpressed policeman unlocked the door and let us in. It was a futile effort really, but we felt better for struggling on and making a statement, albeit in broken Spanish, and as it was a hire car, we needed to make it official anyway. An hour later we left, fairly depressed, and, having made phone calls to stop bank cards and my mobile, we headed home with the wind blowing a hooley through the broken window and glittering glass all around the inside of the car. Another Spanish experience, but of course, it could happen anywhere in the world.

My shoulder bags are never costly affairs and it is known in the family that to put your hand in one takes courage, as you could find anything in there. Nappy pins and dummies were a long time favourite, but that progressed to bananas and lego bits as the kids grew, and now it is mostly broken pens, string, bits of paper and old receipts. There is invariably very little money. The most annoying thing was the loss of a very old address book and the most expensive thing turned out to be the loss of the only spare set of keys to the motor home. This was a big, big problem. Unprepared to travel on through Europe with only one set, Simon had to spend the next day trying to get new keys cut, (an impossibility as no one had American sized blank keys and the Spanish locksmiths were all in cahoots against us anyway), so when that failed he had to get a new lock and keys sent out from England, to our camp site in Spain.

That night we were predictably rash with the red wine and our spirits sank to an all time low as we realised that we would be delayed for at least a week while this was sorted out. That may not sound very long, but we had been at Oliva for longer than we had planned already and we really wanted to move on now. We only had one year and we had a long way to go. We were champing at the bit. As fellow travellers will know, irrational as it is, when you are ready to move on, you just hate getting stuck somewhere, but sometimes it just turns out that way.

On looking back at this experience I remembered one good thing that came from it. Before we left England, a very close friend had given us a bag of individually wrapped presents, to open when we felt the need. We felt the need on the night of the robbery and after some sneaky shaking and rattling, we decided to open just three presents, one for each of us, (after all, we might have more catastrophes in the future so we thought we had better save some). Jack opened a yummy box of chocolates, which we ate to console ourselves. Simon opened a great card game set, which meant that we could try something other than the usual gin-rummy that we habitually played, and when I opened mine it was a new handbag. How could she have known I would need one so soon? How lucky we are to have friends like that.

You may wonder what we did with ourselves while we waited for the spares from the UK to arrive. But with our bikes we could still explore, and one of the benefits of staying in a place for longer, is that you see more of the real life of the country. To me, the more I saw, the more Spain remained a land of opposites. We would round a corner and smell the sweet heavy fragrance of burgeoning flowers or we would smell a smell which would send most Englishmen running for their drain rods. Rubbish would be strewn down the most beautiful hillside or dry river bed. Attractive houses and gardens would have fierce guard dogs chained behind heavy gates, canaries in cages sang sweetly from endless balconies, hoopoes sat on telegraph poles, parakeets ate the dates in the palm trees and dogs fouled everywhere. Children played safely in the streets until mid-night, driving seemed crazy and yet they were considerate of cyclists. It always kept me guessing. Maybe it was the unpredictability that I enjoyed in the end.

Well we did eventually receive the spare parts from England and with the door lock changed and our new keys hanging in their rightful place, we said fond farewells to our friends at Oliva and pulled out of the campsite. We were on the road again, heading down the sunny coast towards the peninsular of La Manga at Mar Menor and then on to Granada city with its wonderful Alhambra Palace. It was good to be moving again, watching the ever-changing scenery as we trundled along; not knowing what was in store and not knowing that when we reached Granada, there would be a great opportunity waiting for us – which we just couldn't say no to.

How do you make a Spaniard smile?

The flat area of coastline in Murcia had many campsites, again full of all nationalities over-wintering in the sun. We pitched up at quite a large site, with a full range of facilities: swimming, tennis, supermarket, laundrette etc. As usual the boules games and siestas came to a halt when we trundled in and tried to wriggle ourselves onto a pitch. With many a 'dah' and a 'yah' and a 'left hand down a bit mate' we got into our position…….. everyone likes to be involved in getting you parked up, with at least three people at the back seeing you into position and two either side to help you avoid low branches or the roof of the toilet block. It was a good way to meet people, although it was sometimes more confusing than helpful. I guess for some, it's a bit of excitement to help while away those long, lazy days.

Mar Menor has, as usual, plenty of history and plenty to offer the traveller. It is, in effect, a huge, sandy bay of clear shallow salt water, no more than seven meters deep, which is cut off from the Mediterranean sea by a long thin peninsular, called La Manga. The peninsular would enclose it completely but for a few channels, which keep it open to the sea. It is the largest saltwater lake in Europe. Palaeolithic finds have helped to date the area but it was the Romans who really established themselves here when they developed an important salt industry. They, and later the Arabs, were also quick to make use of the healing qualities of the salt water and the therapeutic qualities of the mud and clay in the lagoon. Many people are still attracted by the opportunity to ease rheumatic or arthritic joints, or to de-toxify the system and relax in the almost perpetually warm weather. The average annual temperature in this micro – climate area is 17 degrees Celsius, with winter months not falling below 10 degrees. With hardly any rain and a boasted 320 days of sunshine per year, it's a wonderfully dry area for those who suffer in damp climates.

La Manga del Mar Menor, is a narrow strip of land 21 kilometres long which divides the lagoon of Mar Menor, from the Mediterranean Sea. Until 1863 it belonged to the state, but then was sold by public auction to raise money. Most of it is now taken up with tourism; apartments, hotels, restaurants, sailing facilities, villas and discos, but the last few kilometres are quieter and in a more natural state. The great attraction for us, out of season, was that we could ride our bikes for the whole day, down this peninsular and back up again, along cycle paths and a very quiet central road, with the sea waves rolling onto the Mediterranean coast on one side and the quiet beaches of the lagoon on the other. At most points we were only yards from either. The temperature was around 70 degrees, and we were in shorts and t-shirts in late November now.

By lunch time we had cycled and explored for three hours, and were glad to find a restaurant at the edge of the lake where we collapsed, alongside the local Spanish diners, to eat tasty pizzas covered in fresh anchovies and huge prawns. We still had to cycle all the way back and unfortunately Simon's bike saddle was un-padded and un-sprung, so for him it was about as comfortable as sitting on a fence rail. We continually tried to find a comfortable saddle for his bike, but never did throughout the whole trip and it still has the secret instrument of torture to this day. We noticed that Dutch and German cyclists had much more comfortable bicycles, with huge padded seats that could accommodate soft ample rears and 'sit up and beg' handle bars that meant you weren't bent over the front, aggravating your bad back. I really don't know why we British have to indulge in the painful purgatory of balancing on bike saddles that are only an inch wide and made of 'hard as nails' plastic. Whatever happened to the good old, fully sprung variety, which gently bounced you over bumps in the road. Suffice it to say that with Simon's bottom getting quite a lot of abuse, we didn't cycle every day.

We'd planned only a short stay here, but on reading through the guide books of this area, we could see that again, we could have seen more if we had wanted. Nature Parks boasting flamingos, herons, storks and avocets, cycle routes around the lake and old gold mining regions up in the hills, particularly appealed to Jack. Plus the exceptional summit of Cabezo de la Fuente, which offers the best view of the Mar Menor and its unusual geographical situation – never mind, another day maybe? For now though, the friendly male drivers on the campsite assisted us in extracting ourselves from our pitch and we headed off south-west towards Almerimar, which sits at the entrance to the Coast of Sun….. better known to most as the Costa del Sol.

So far we had clung to the coast all the way down through Spain, partly because we love the sea but also because we just didn't want to go inland to the colder winter weather. We were being spoilt, avoiding a winter and it was a real treat. We drove along the motorway between Murcia and Almeria, amazed by the way the barren hills and mountains of pale unyielding rock had been literally sliced through to enable the road to continue its way to the farthest corner of Spain. At Almeria we swung off the motorway and headed down to the coast to Almerimar. Here we were again amazed, but this time it was the acre after acre after acre of plastic-covered land that surprised us. This is veggie growing country, big time, although you won't actually see the vegetables unless you stop and peer into one of the dirty, grey, scruffy plastic greenhouses that are usually blowing themselves apart in the wind. These stand cheek by jowl and nose to tail, over an enormous area of land, stretching from just behind the coast, to right back into the lowest hills of the Sierra de Gador. Small dusty service tracks run between them all, and all other landscape has been obliterated to make way for more and more intensive agriculture.

The lure of work has attracted thousands of young Spaniards, and others, from poorer regions but we got the feeling that this was cheap labour for someone. As we approached the sea, the land dropped down from this un-natural agricultural plateau to a long flat coastal strip containing fishing harbours, yacht moorings, campsites and holiday complexes. Rather like an old film set, it was all front. Yes, there was a pleasant coastline and behind us in the distance, was our first wonderful view of the snowy peaks of the Sierra Nevada, but in between was just ugliness. We didn't get off to a good start at this campsite either, as our electrical connection (hook-up), wouldn't work here. Camp site electrics are often a bit of a mystery depending on the whim of the owners and the amount of electricity available.

That night we had a rare, heavy downpour and next morning our large awning was holding a small lake, hanging dangerously low and looking for all the world as if it was about to split asunder. All ready to catch the first bus into town, to find the elusive electrical connections needed, we decided to let the water out of the awning first. Of course we were rushing to catch the bus and it was difficult to lower one side of the awning without causing it to rip, which is probably why the whole lot emptied neatly but unfortunately onto our heads soaking us completely. Strange how something like that can colour your day isn't it?

Something I have learned from our travels is that although you may thoroughly enjoy visiting somewhere, someone else may have a completely different experience and hate the place. It could be the weather, or a surly guide or you may have a good row about something totally unimportant....... but it all colours the day. I found that traipsing around Spanish ironmonger shops, (known as ferreterias or as we called them Ferrets Rears), looking for elusive electrical connections, to be particularly uninspiring that day. Especially as the assistants serving behind the counter were completely uninterested in our problem and had not a glimmer of a smile between them. I wrote in my diary that night, that it would be my mission in life to make a Spaniard smile. My memories of El Ejido are definitely coloured, but maybe someone else will have a great time there, and if you do, please let me know!

Now we needed to gird our loins and make the most of the following days before we headed for Granada, which was to be our next stop. Jack felt convinced that his loins were girded enough, thank you, and spent a quiet day at camp on his own. We all needed our own space once in a while; me to do a little domestic goddess stuff or shave my legs in peace. Simon to read, or mend bike tyres or plan ahead, and Jack to read, watch Euro news or a video, or his favourite method of relaxation, which was to draw. Spending a year together in a motor home required give and take between us all. But, the next day we got our act together again and cycled along the coast, past glossy yachts and smart but empty holiday villas. The sea really was crystal clear and perfectly clean in the marina, with shoals of large, very edible looking fish, swimming lazily in the warm surface water. As we cycled ever onward to see what was just around the next bend, we discovered the marshland nature reserve of Punta Entinas Sabinar, which, according to the brochures, promised sightings of flamingos.

Certified as a *nature landscape* by the Andalucian government, this sixteen kilometre long coastal strip, of marshland, lagoons and virgin beach, is home to numerous species of birds – some endangered and some using it as a stop over whilst migrating. We were hoping to see the flamingos, but on first inspection, as we skidded and bumped along the narrow sandy paths, we had no luck. Then Simon spotted one of the unmistakable long necked, gangly-legged birds flying over the park and dropping down to land about half a mile away. We peddled furiously to the point in the distance where we had seen it land and as we got closer, heard their strange goose–like honking call.

They were quite far away, tiptoeing daintily on spindly legs, with heads down, sifting the water of a shallow lagoon. With our binoculars, we could see them well, these exotic, Alice in Wonderland creatures, that moved as one or slept calmly on a single, wiry leg. We wandered further under the hot mid-day sun, and Jack soon spotted the crested head of a Hoopoe, searching the long dry grass for insects and lizards. Dropping our bikes we crept low and close, like a trio of David Attenboroughs, until we were only yards away and were able to view his salmon pink body and startling black and white striped wings. Skylarks were plentiful singing high in the sky and Kites soared past a rocky cliff face, Little Egrets searched the waters edge for small fish and aquatic insects and Buzzards circled far above us. But, the loudest wings of all, and by far the most numerous and painfully over friendly were those of the insatiable mosquitoes. Unfortunately, they were out in force and we only escaped them when we clambered up into a cool cave to open our rucksacks and eat our lunch.

One of the great things about travelling is that you do eat your lunch with a different view every day. When we were on the move, we often picked lay-bys or car parks that were next to beaches, so that we could swim too. Those little things, like looking out over a bay or mountain range while eating fresh sardines, salad, and local bread, with addictive anchovy-stuffed olives, are some of the moments that I will always remember. They were as important as visiting the Alhambra......... yes, Granada was next on the list. Even though we were country mice at heart, we all loved visiting big cities. Granada was great, although our favourite came later when we thoroughly enjoyed the delights of Barcelona. At Granada there was a really good camp site situated just down the road from the main bus station, not far from the centre of the city, (called Camping Nevada). We pulled in easily this time and there was plenty of room, it was after all, 'out of season'. Having said that, this was a great time of year to visit Granada; the weather was warm, but not hot, and there were far fewer crowds than in summer.

Granada sits a mere sixty kilometres inland from the Costa coast and nestles at 2,200 feet above sea level, in the foothills of the Sierra Nevada Mountains. It is in a great position. You really could swim in the morning and ski in the afternoon, should you have the energy left over from a wild night on the town. The city itself has plenty to offer but we were mainly interested in the Alhambra, so the day after we had arrived, we walked up to the bus station and caught the number thirty two bus to the Cathedral and then the number two bus to the Alhambra, this last bus driven at crazy speeds through a narrow, cobbled one way system of tiny streets in the old town.

What can I say about the Alhambra that hasn't already been said a million times over... except that you should visit it at least once. It sits on a hill above Granada, the Hill of Gold, and is the finest example of Islamic architecture in the western world. Reading from the guide books you will find names such as The Alcazaba Citadel, The Nasrid Palaces, The Mauror Hill, The Vermillion Towers and the gate called Bab al-Sari'a, all of which conjure up a time of sultans and emirs, spices and trade, prayers and poetry. I would not try to fully explain the complicated history of this intricate collection of buildings, even if I understood it myself. The Alhambra was a palace, a citadel, a fortress and home of the Moorish Nasrid sultans and their entourages. It had a complete city within its walls, with houses, schools, stables, mosques, baths and cemeteries, some of which have thankfully survived invasions and earthquakes. We bought our tickets at the incredibly good value of eight euros each and, following the guide books, passed through heavily carved, arched gateways, massive iron bound doors and cobbled roads, on our way through the old Medina and up to the Alcazaba (the military area of the city). From here we wandered around gardens and towers, enjoying fabulous views down on to Granada, and across to the snow capped mountains and surrounding countryside. Moving on, we entered the heavily ornamented, open air rooms of the Nasrid Palaces. What struck us most about the architecture of these rooms was that they appeared almost weightless. What were solid, heavy beams and walls, looked lighter than balsa wood, due to the intricate carving which covered all stonework. Slender pillars supported high, domed, carved ceilings: arched carved windows offered classic eastern views – there were walls like lace work, ceilings of stars, floors of mosaics and view beyond view through Moorish doorways to reflections of buildings in mirroring pools. Water is the other element which makes the Alhambra so special. Golden coloured, sun drenched stone reflected in endless pools; fountains of cooling, tinkling, life-giving water in elongated water channels, leading you from one paradise to the next. I can't wait to visit it again, it was stunningly beautiful.

We moved on to The Generalife, the private home of the sultan, where he relaxed away from his court, with the aid of his harem, and yet was still within distance should he be required. The land around the Generalife was always cultivated to a very high standard, to be both productive and ornamental and it is still a gardeners delight to visit. Re-established gardens and original orchard terraces have been once again brought to life by the addition of fountains and waterways, which weave through gardens paved with mosaic floors, surrounded by arched walkways. Every wall carved like lacework. Intricate 3D patterns on warm stone for you to trace with your fingers: small birds bathing in fountains; avenues of cypress trees; stray cats drinking from pools. We spent a long, long day there and eventually walked back down the hill, through old and new Granada, to the bus stop. Exhausted as usual, with our poor feet aching and our senses overwhelmed.

That evening we had a stroke of luck. A British couple had turned up at camp for just a short stay and they told us about the opportunity to drive the Beast up to the ski resort in the Sierra Nevada Mountains, where a car park was reserved for motor homes. This sounded like a great opportunity to go skiing and although Jack and I had never skied before, we were keen to have a go. Three cheap ski suits, gloves and hats were quickly purchased from the handy supermarket over the road, along with a small fake Christmas tree with lights and some tinsel and baubles to decorate the Beast. We shall never forget the endless, horrendous Christmas tune that was being played on a continuous loop at top volume in that heaving Spanish supermarket in late December; I've only got to think of it now, to get a headache.

Leaving the camp site next morning, we headed off up the excellent A 395, a road which had good passing areas for those who wanted to overtake our lumbering home as we climbed 6000 feet in 35 kilometres. Luckily, going up, we were on the side of the road next to the rock face….. coming down those switch back bends later in the week was something else. Up and up we drove, enjoying far-reaching fantastic views all around because we were now in the snow covered mountain range. We zig-zagged the final stretch with Simon doing his usual brilliant driving, (although it had been a difficult drive in the Beast and he was looking a little stressed), until we came at last to the ski village of Pradollano – and two ridiculously small, snow covered mini roundabouts. The signs to motor home parking directed us round the roundabouts, but there was no way that we would get our big American Beast around them very easily. The ground was very icy here and jovial skiers were mindlessly milling about in groups, quite unconcerned about the fact that we might at any minute, uncontrollably mow them down. Cars had come up behind us, so we were back in that whisky-swigging situation, of manoeuvring the Beast in dire circumstances. At this point the reverse gear also decided to play up. Isn't it always the way - that this kind of thing happens just when you don't need it. So, in trepidation, we started going round the first roundabout, but we're too long and need to shunt. So we try to get reverse gear, which jams and engages the auto park brake. Now we have to do a series of leap-frog type manoeuvres, jumping our eight ton, thirty foot motor home, back and forth between a stone wall and a ten foot drop, with milling skiers trying to dash between the gaps, and all on thick ice. Need I say more? No. Except that we had to repeat this at the second roundabout, although by this time the steering wheel was slippy with sweat, I was searching for the Pina Colada again and Jack had his head under a cushion. We got to the motor home parking place of course, high above the village…… (you always get there in the end)….. and we stood outside the Beast, toasting the glorious view with an extremely large whisky.

This parking area up above the ski village was excellent and Jack was out of the door in seconds, rolling in the snow like an overgrown puppy. A convenient hopper bus called every twenty minutes to collect or drop skiers and took you straight down into the ski village of Pradollano. It cost just five euros a night to stay there and it was equipped with a 'grey water' emptying point. The views were to die for. I adore mountains anyway. They have such serenity and calmness, and we were at a height where we could look right across the snowy range of the Sierra Nevada, and down onto Granada. In the evenings the frozen land turned a cold violet blue as the sun dropped, lighting up the undersides of whispy clouds with yellow and orange streaks. Mount Valeta stood alongside us, and the valley of the ski runs was lit at night by moving beams of light from piste-bashers and skiers who were preparing the slopes for the next morning. It was so peaceful and calm, it was another world, but we were glad to have heating because it was very, very cold.

Next day, with ski equipment hired, we were down in the village ready for the nine o'clock lift up from Pradollano, to the slopes at Borreguiles. I was fifty four years old (or young, which ever way you look at it) and had never skied before, Jack hadn't either, but Simon had been a good skier twenty years earlier. We arranged to have some lessons to get us started and our instructor was José; kind and cheerful and very patient, he spoke very good English and soon had us doing snow ploughs and turns. Simon quickly got into the swing of it again and rapidly moved on to harder slopes, but Jack and I stayed on the nursery slopes all day and practised falling over and getting up again, until we were really proficient at it. But it was exhilarating and although exhausted and red faced, we had loved it and couldn't wait to do it again tomorrow. At the end of the day, we clumped our way back through the village, in awkward ski boots with skis casually slung over our shoulders, almost like regular accomplished skiers. Except that, being short and round, I had a problem looking casual and trendy, in my bulbous cheap ski suit, clumpy boots and skis which seemed to have a mind of their own. I felt more like a Michelin man. How do these people make it look so cool and elegant? Do you really have to be six foot four, slim as a rake and wearing the latest one-piece suit, to look as if you were born to ski? If so, I shall never make it.

Trying to get up early again the next day was more of a problem as our leg muscles had seized like greaseless pistons. But we forced our feet back into the ski boots and clumped down to the village again. José gently moved us on to the first runs and Jack especially, did really well. I did ok too and thoroughly enjoyed confidently skiing down the green runs. That was where I was happy and I spent the following two days just playing there in absolute bliss. Jack had two more one-to-one lessons with José, to smarten up his technique and by the last day he was able to ski with Simon, from the top of a high blue run, way up on the Valeta slopes, right down through Borreguiles and all the way down the valley to Pradollano. I was waiting at the bottom to watch him ski down the last part and it brought tears to my eyes. I know that I can be a bit emotional sometimes where my kids are concerned, but seeing him ski down with all the other skiers, Christmas carols playing behind me, with the clear blue sky just deepening to early dusk, gave me such a good feeling. I felt so proud of him: it had all been worth it. He absolutely loved skiing and was so chuffed that he had done so well. Ever after he has wanted to be a ski instructor. Maybe he will be, he could do a lot worse, but I think he may change his mind a few times yet.

As the Christmas holiday season got under way, the slopes became busier and busier. With wall-to-wall sunshine every day, the mountains shone and glistened, sparkling white against a blue sky and when I needed a coffee break at one of the balcony cafes, it was fun just to people-watch. All ages, and in all colours of the rainbow, they swished across the slopes, sending crystal sprays up into the air as they twisted and turned. Lines of tiny children in puffy, brightly coloured suits followed their instructors like ducklings in a line. They were so confidant and at ease as they weaved along, arms out sideways, supple little legs and backs bending like willows. Teams of husky dogs rolled in the snow while they waited to give jingling sleigh rides and the ski lifts worked overtime to get the people up the slopes. For me, the ski lifts were daunting, and at first I studiously avoided looking down and gripped the rail convinced that I would be the one who would fall off. I can't say that I ever enjoyed going up on them but, if you want to come down you've got to go up, so that was that. We had five wonderful days on the Sierra Nevada pistes. On our last day we called at the ski office, left a bottle of bubbly for kind José and negotiated a good price to buy our boots and skis from the hire shop. We were sure that we would ski again, so they would come with us in the Beast. It was Christmas Eve. Pradollano was now very busy, and it was time that we headed back down the mountain, to spend Christmas in Granada.

Back at the campsite again we soon got parked up and then made another quick shopping raid to the supermarket. Christmas wouldn't be Christmas without big fresh prawns, salmon, stuffed chicken, wine, chocolate, and a Christmas pudding that I had brought with us from England. While Jack decorated the motor home and Si got the Christmas tree lights to work, I hid in the back bedroom and wrapped stocking fillers and presents. We were only buying token Christmas gifts for each other, and in fact we had already decided to have a new tennis racquet each, which again, we bought from the supermarket. Our old racquets were made of wood, and were thirty years old and as most camp sites had tennis courts we were playing quite often as we travelled around.

We had some surprises tucked away for Jack; a few new books, a beautiful marquetry box from the Alhambra and little things I had collected from some of the places we had visited. I'm afraid we didn't go out and sample the delights of Granada on Christmas Eve as we probably should have, but instead we snuggled up in the Beast, with chocolate and liqueurs and watched The English Patient on a DVD. How boring is that! But after all the skiing, it was just about all we could manage.

Christmas Day arrived and Jack, in his pull out sofa bed, had his stocking open, the chocolate eaten and was well into a new book before 8.30 am. We lazed over a breakfast of champagne, smoked salmon and scrambled eggs before phoning family back home and then heading for the camp tennis courts, all the while being vaguely aware of a violin being played somewhere close by. A small igloo tent had appeared over-night in the campsite, with a forlorn looking young couple sitting outside, practising lively music on their fiddles while they waited for their kettle to boil on their very small primus stove. Even if it hadn't been Christmas day I think that we would have invited them in.......but it was an extra bonus that we met Nick and Becky, who were back packing and busking their way around Europe. Mulled Sangria wine, games of cards and far too much Christmas dinner, finishing with Christmas pudding and a huge, heavily decorated Spanish cake, left us all stuffed. We ate too much, drank too much, went to bed too late, and had too much fun. Fellow motor homers at the site probably wondered what was happening as we floundered our way through Christmas carols and then sang our very own version to the tune of 'We Three Kings'.

We three Brits of Herefordshar ?
Looking for culture, near and far,
Pyrenees mountains, Alhambra fountains,
Why didn't we come in a car!
Chorus... OH, cycling hear and driving there,
Grid locked fear, but we don't care,
Maisies leading, we're proceeding,
God knows why and God knows where.

Normandy sites, we've seen our fair share,
Mont St Michel, was never more fair,
Pylat, Arrachon, but in Caen we went wrong,
French signposts drive us to despair.........Chorus

The Costa Coast had little to boast,
High rise apartments and urbanised coast,
Geriatric Germans all hiding their Sherman's
The British enjoying their roast.........Chorus

At ten thousand feet, the skiing was neat,
What is that smell, I think it's your feet,
The genny is stalling, Granada is calling,
So Christmas on mains is a treat.........Chorus.

Well it took us a while to make this up and if you consider the copious amount of Spanish wine and champagne that we got through, I think it could be worse. Jack remained sober of course and was the only one of the party who didn't wake up in the morning with a head that felt as if a jackhammer was destroying it from the inside. He was also the one who discovered that we had managed to completely flood the toilet carpet with the entire contents of the fresh water tank. During our revels the water pump had got jammed on, but we hadn't heard it running due to the volume of our music and singing. What a good job Christmas only comes once a year.

Auld Lang Syne

Boxing Day was bright and sunny with a clear blue sky, but we didn't stir before ten o'clock. More motor homes arrived: a Dutch group, some Spanish and Germans, all on their Christmas holidays. We recovered at camp and while Simon dried out the sodden carpets and re-filled the water tank, I sat on the motor home steps in the quiet sunshine and watched the campsite come to life. Birds competed with their usual sing -song in the trees around us. Spanish children, dressed in new clothes, rode their shiny Christmas bikes along the road behind the camp site, with parents arm in arm, strolling behind. I could almost smell roast beef and Yorkshire pudding cooking in the oven. Some things are the same the world over.

The following day was a Saturday and we caught the bus into town again, this time to visit the cathedral. Spain is full of fabulous churches and cathedrals but you can become blasé if you view too many. Granada Cathedral is definitely worth seeing though, if only for it's richly ornate Spanish Renaissance architecture and it's spectacular altar. It took nearly two hundred years to complete the Cathedral and the flamboyant Royal Chapel situated behind, where Queen Isabella and King Ferdinand are buried in an extravaganza of architecture. Originally this Cathedral was destined to be of the old gothic style, however when a young Flemish architect joined the team in 1528 he persuaded Charles V that a Renaissance design would improve it both architecturally and ideologically.

The result was a new concept of space, with the interior pillars rising to double their original height and light cascading in through high windows, giving a wonderful luminosity. Elaborately carved, white domed ceilings, soaring fluted pillars and gold-embellished Corinthian capitals, lead you processional from the square body of the church to the circular main chapel. Stained glass windows, high around the chapel dome give bright colour relief, and help to throw light into the elaborate alcoves reserved for the Saints. It would be easy to mock the excessive grandeur here but you would have to applaud the achievement of building this complicated structure. Of course there are other religious buildings in the area that are well worth seeing, like the Monastery of San Jeronimo and the Carthusian Monastery, but to see them all may be a little like eating a whole Spanish gateaux at once, a bit too rich. Better I think to just take one slice, and of course having taken your slice of culture, you then need to go and eat something a little less weighty. We left the Cathedral and worked our way through narrow cobbled streets of tiny colourful, touristy shops, to the Plaza De Bib Rambla, where we found an empty table outside one of the many cafes which edge this busy square. It was Saturday again and Christmas was only two days past, so for the Spanish it was a day for shopping, strolling and wearing your best finery and furs. Suited gentlemen with polished shoes and camel coloured overcoats escorted their families to lunch, with wives well wrapped in costly clothes and wearing their best gold jewellery. Flower stalls spilled across the square, live music entertained the crowds, craft and food stalls offered their wares, and central to it all a fountain carved with strange gothic creatures, poured water from their mouths. Yes, there is plenty to see in Granada and one day we may go back for more.

The next day Nick and Becky were leaving, so we said fond farewells and swapped addresses before they walked up to the bus station, with their worldly goods carried on their backs and their violins tucked under the arms. Little did we know that we would bump into them twice more on our travels and they would remain good friends when we all returned to England. But we were ready to move on as well. Back down to the coast and on towards our next destination of Ronda, which we had been told we mustn't miss. However, New Years Eve would have to happen first.

We left Granada taking the scenic road to Motril, then turned left for Nerja and Malaga. This was a pleasant coastline 'out of season'. Beautiful low sierras rolled almost into the sea, but they stopped just short, and we found a good coast road alongside sandy coves and beaches. Further back was the motorway which runs from Nerja to Algerciras; the holiday route, passing Malaga, Torremolinas, Marbella and down to Gibraltar. Small touristy towns along the way catered for the thousands of English residents, motor-homers were wild camping by the empty beaches and we met quite a few people who were travelling or looking for property to buy. Avocado pears were growing on the trees and fresh fish was in the markets. Yes, I am talking about the Costa del Sol here; in summer this must be an incredibly busy area, but at the end of December it was quite quiet, warm and very pleasant. We visited the cathedral-like caves at Nerja, with their dripping stalactites and stalagmites, and wild camped for the night alongside the beach at a small village called Benajarafe. (If that seems hard to pronounce, I should explain that all 'j's are pronounced as 'h', so it is said as Bena-harafe`.)

We loved wild camping by the sea. There was nothing nicer than to listen to the ocean as we lay in our beds, or to sit on a beach at night and watch the moon rising over the water, reflecting a silver path right to our door step. To wake and step out of the door bare foot onto the cold sand and walk along a virgin beach at dawn was magic. We constantly collected 'beach bits'; white twisted driftwood, perfect shells, crab claws and little, smoothed pieces of coloured glass, which we used to play the old desert game of Mancala. With heads down we would wander the beaches, stuffing our pockets with treasure.

Well, the next day was New Years Eve and we awoke to a million dollar sunrise. I opened the blind and sat in our bed with a cup of sweet tea. Jack laid in his bed opposite the open 'front' door and we watched it unfold. The sea was a mass of dark moving shapes, with just an edge of white where it ran onto the grey sand. The sky, at first inky dark, gradually lightened as the earth turned towards the sun, and a golden light hinted at another dawning. Black silhouettes of sea birds moved silently across the sky and then a small brilliant dot showed on the edge of the horizon as the sun peaked over. One small, dark, thin strip of cloud hovered above the horizon and as the sun slowly rose it gave us an ever changing display, under-lighting the cloud through a spectrum from deep red to a glimmering yellow. Within two minutes the earth had turned enough to reveal the full sun. The sea gradually lost its sinister moving mass and became the deep blue friend that we knew. The sky changed colours from grey to orange to green to pale blue and I could quite understand how ancient peoples had worshiped a sun god. It's the most joyous sight – here comes the sun – reliable warmth and light. Another day had begun.

New Years Eve was spent exploring inland and cycling along the coast on our bikes. Fishermen pulled in their nets early and then rested their boats on the beach. The small village on the hill behind us enjoyed a quiet holiday with families gathering for a feast and children played in the streets with their Christmas toys. The odd banger exploded somewhere in anticipation. We collected driftwood for our barbecue and were just setting up our outdoor table for our own New Years Eve feast, when a car pulled up next to us and someone banged hard on the side of the motor home. A cheerful face came into view and we met Adrian, a retired Brit, who many years ago had bought a small apartment overlooking the sea and was now inviting us to his New Years Eve party. It would be a mixed bunch he said, and we would be very welcome. So, that night, we three kings of the road, had our own candle lit dinner on the beach and toasted all back home with champagne, before taking ourselves over to Adrian's house and joining his party. We all joined hands and sang Auld Lang Syne at midnight, an international chorus of old and young. We three returned to the Beast in the early hours, but they did much better and continued until six in the morning.

New Years Day and breakfast on the beach, after another glorious sunrise. We said our goodbyes again to kind people. Who said this was a lonely planet? Then we moved on down the coast, skirted around Malaga and through the unabated tourist developments to Torremolinos. We felt that we should visit this area just once, just briefly, just to know if it's reputation was justified. Who would believe that only forty years ago, Torremolinos was a tiny coastal village with one main street and few houses. Since that time, with the gold rush approach to tourism, this small fishing community has become a notorious holiday spot, worldwide. Torre means tower and molinos means mills, hence Torremolinos derives its name from the old watch tower, which still sits above Bajondillo beach, and once protected the water-fed flour mills. During the 1960's uninhibited development allowed a concrete jungle to spread and most original buildings and landmarks were swamped by towering hotels, apartments, pubs, clubs and everything else required for a cheap, good time in the sun, as this coastline careered at full speed into endless holiday brochures. And if that's what you're after, then it has it all. Maybe the Andalucians paid a high price when they traded their poor but quiet way of life for better work prospects and a chance to earn big money, and with central government hungry for foreign investment it must have seemed like a good idea at the time. Now, there is growing recognition that the environment must be protected, infrastructure improved and speculators curbed. So what did we think? We parked in a huge wild camp area along with other motor homes, at the Parador del Golf, unhitched our bikes, and took a 16 kilometre cycle ride, weaving through the strolling Spanish and the wandering English, past endless tourism outlets along a coast that, beneath the tat, was beautiful. But the tat was there and it was probably the most un-natural place we had ever been. We only heard one English family swearing crudely at the tops of their voices, but that was one too many for us, so we ticked that box and headed off for Ronda.

The road to Ronda, the excellent A376, clings to the side of the Sierra Palmitera by it's fingernails and if you like a scary ride, with great scenery, and twists and turns all the way, then this is the one for you. So you know where I was sitting! Before this road was upgraded, Ronda must have been much more difficult to access which may be why it was a notorious stronghold for bandits and smugglers. Perched on the end of a high ridge, with sheer cliffs dropping away on three sides, it guards a fertile interior plain which is fed by the Guadalevin River. Close by is the natural park of the Grazalema Range, which shelters the unique Spanish Fir tree and, twenty kilometres south, the third deepest chasm in the world lies in The Nieves Range. However, Ronda is a treasure in itself.

We laboured our way up to it's dizzying heights, 2,300 feet above sea level in the Serrania de Ronda Mountains and found the only camp site in the area, situated just outside the town. It was a small, pleasant, well run site with each pitch having its fair share of gnarled old olive trees. We weren't too sure about the rather long list of do's and don'ts here as most of them seemed to fall into the *don't* category. No music, no television no playing games, no hot water for washing dishes, clothes or bodies, and not too many welcoming smiles. Maybe we just arrived on an off day. Anyway, we had a quick bowl of soup for lunch and as usual, couldn't wait to investigate the town.

The Moorish 'old' town ranges along the edge of the cliff tops, in some cases clinging precariously close to the 500 foot drop into the Tajo (sheer drop) gorge. Carved deep and narrow by the flow of the Guadelevin river, this tremendous gorge cuts straight through the old peninsular of Ronda and would cut the town off completely were it not for the amazing Puente Nuevo bridge. Most of the old town is situated south of the gorge, but there is still plenty to see north of the bridge including a large new town, which has spread itself out there. We walked down to the old town, entered through the 16th century Renaissance gate and walked up through the uneven streets and past the fortress-like Church of the Holy Spirit. Twisting alleyways, with Moorish style houses, plazas, palaces and minarets, tempted us to linger but we were on a quick recce that day, so we continued on to the bridge itself.

The New Bridge (Puento Nuevo) is a majestic wedge of pale, golden stone which blocks the Tajo gorge, joining the older northern side to the more modern southern side. It has three graceful arches, which rise 96 meters from the river floor; two smaller ones on the outside and a third larger one in the centre. In the upper section of the central arch, a chamber was once used as a very effective prison. It dates from 1793 and was the third attempt at building a suitable bridge over the river Guadalevin. The river flows through the bottom of the canyon, between the bridge pillars, over huge boulders. The top of the bridge is quite wide, with walled paths either side of it's main road and it provides a great viewing point from which to watch the busy comings and goings of the town.

We spent the afternoon exploring the 13th century Banos Arabes (Moorish Baths), the two other ancient bridges and a garden walkway, which all gave fabulous views down into the gorge. Eventually, we trekked back up to the camp site and decided to have a drink at the bar before cooking supper. There were very few other people staying at the site but we had noticed two other vehicles with GB stickers. It almost became the first thing you looked for when a new vehicle rolled into any campsite or wild camp area. Is it a GB or a D or an F or an NL; sometimes it would be a B - or an I, but they were not so numerous in Spain. Anyway, the owners of the two English vehicles were in the bar and we soon got to know Barry and Eileen, and Keith and Brenda. Barry and Eileen were regular travellers who aimed to take six months off every year. They didn't appear particularly wealthy, but had simply arranged their lives that way. They were travelling in a small, well-adapted van with a motorbike in tow. They had been to this area before and knew it well. Keith and Brenda had a motor home and were taking one year out, the same as us. We swapped stories and information and, as usual with people we met on our travels, we enjoyed their company over the next few days, whilst we all shared the campsite. We also swapped books. This was often a good icebreaker and most people did it. We all seemed to be avid readers and were carrying many books with us, so book swapping was as important as information about campsites and areas to visit. It also meant that we all got to read books that we would not normally have bought and Jack at his age, read everything we read.

They also told us that the site restaurant was very reasonable, popular with the locals and had a 'special' on the menu - whole roast leg of mountain lamb. Not having cooked roast lamb in four months we couldn't resist this, so that night we decided to give it a try. It was so delicious that I would almost go all the way back there just to eat it again.

We still say, 'do you remember that mountain lamb we had in Ronda' and our mouths water. What we hadn't realised was that we were getting a whole leg each! Our stomachs groaned that night as we rolled on our backs like stuffed lions.

Next morning, we returned to Ronda and took another look at some of the interesting places that we had skipped the day before . The Mondragon Palace, home of previous rulers, has delightful Alhambran style courtyards with arched doorways leading to intimate areas of fountains and flowers. The bullring, the oldest in Spain, where all spectators are seated under cover in arched galleries of smooth stone, was the birthplace of bull fighting and the accompanying museum displays costumes, which you would normally see in paintings by Goya and which are so slight and svelte, that you can hardly imagine a man fitting into them. And then, close to the bullring, the peaceful, shady park called the Alameda del Tajo. From here you can stroll to the Paseo de Blas Infante where you must cross the tiled plaza to the single, wrought iron balcony which extends way out over a sheer drop and allows you the most spectacular views over the rolling landscape around Ronda.

Once again after a long day, we walked back home, Jack itching to open two new airfix models that he had bought in town and us itching for a beer. The camp bar was open and we were just about to go in when we heard our names being shouted by someone walking up behind us. Looking back we saw two figures struggling up the hill with heads down, carrying heavy backpacks, violins tucked under their arms. Nick and Becky shouted and waved ……. we lined up the beers in anticipation. They ate with us again that night, a much more sober meal though, and it was great to catch up with news. They slept in their igloo tent, but found it very cold on the ground. We were at over 2000 feet and it was January so, although it was dry and sunny during the day, it was still very cold at night.

When you're travelling it's generally regarded as a good idea to learn some of the local language. However, if used incorrectly it can get you into embarrassing situations as I discovered the following day, which was a Sunday. I managed to completely fall out with the owners' son before we had even had breakfast, due to a misunderstanding that I had with his mother the day before. I'm not sure if it was my Spanish or her English but our wires definitely got crossed somewhere along the international line. I thought that on the previous day, I had ordered some bread for Sunday, from the mother, by writing my requirements on the bread list by the office. So, I pottered off to collect it on Sunday morning, and was about to say the customary 'Ola' as I entered the office, when instead of meeting the mother again, I saw the son standing behind the counter. It threw me I guess, (it doesn't take a lot), so instead of 'Ola' I mistakenly said "Good morning". This probably offended him, because I sensed a fairly frosty reception and he didn't bother to look up from his paper for about five minutes. I politely said that I had ordered bread for today.

"No, you haven't", said the son who I shall not name in case we ever return there.

"Yes I have", said I, "I did it yesterday".

"No…. you can't have", said frosty son, going back to his paper.

I was beginning to lose it then. I don't mind someone disagreeing with me, but a smile would have gone a long, long way at this point and all I was getting was hostile stares and short sharp replies in between his reading of the paper.

"But I wrote it on the bread list as your mother showed me", I said to the top of his head.

"You can't have", said son doggedly, not looking up.

Now, I may be getting older but dementia has not quite set in yet and I knew that his mother had shown me where and what to write, in order to get bread for the following day.

"But I did", said I, feeling that this conversation is getting absolutely no-where but I'm going to stand my ground.

"Okay" he said, folding his paper angrily and stepping out from behind the counter, "I will show you, that you are wrong".

And with that he frog marched me out of the office and into the lobby where the bread list lived, and stood me in front of the list like a disobedient school girl. But there on the list, is my order for bread for today.........

I seethingly pointed this out to him as I am now at boiling point.

"Hah" said son, "you have filled it in correctly but you can't have bread today".

"Why not", I gasped, almost close to tears.

"Because the baker does not bake bread on a Sunday!" he smugly concluded.

Aaghhhh, why didn't you tell me that at the beginning, you stupid Spaniard and why couldn't you say it with a smile! I eventually left with two stale loaves of yesterday's bread and it was tempting to whack him round the head with them. I stomped back to the motor home and ranted hysterically as I hacked the bread into edible pieces, looking for all the world like an axe murderer as I did it. Of course it was all just a misunderstanding. He spoke good English and although we always tried to speak the language of the country as much as possible, I didn't always do too well at it. Maybe his mother had the same problem. I think it was just the sullen attitude that I sometimes encountered in Spain that made me constantly wonder, 'what makes a Spaniard smile?'

Well, of course, the next day my disgruntled feelings were turned on their head, and we saw just what makes Spanish people happy. We had heard that there would be a festival in town that evening, but because the Ronda area looked so interesting we decided to hire another car and go exploring that day, returning in time for the fun of the carnival. We gave Becky and Nick a lift into town to do a little busking and then headed off along a small mountain road on a circuitous tour, which took us through high bare mountain passes and down lush river valleys. White washed villages, the Pueblos Blancos, were scattered like snowflakes amongst the sierras. We drove through forests of cork oak, and stopped to feel smooth trunks, where the bark had been harvested to make wine bottle corks for the sherry trade. Almond trees with tiny, pinky-white flowers edged the roads and beautiful mini narcissus of pale yellow hid in the grass. Gryphon vultures circled overhead waiting for us to get totally lost, but we safely reached the amazing pass at Gaucin and enjoyed the spectacular view across to Gibraltar and the Atlas Mountains in Morocco. We went too far, got back late and went straight into Ronda for the festival.

It was January 5th and on that day in Spain everyone celebrates the Festival of the Three Kings. This was traditionally their equivalent to Christmas Eve, but the more continental custom of giving gifts on December 25th, has encroached somewhat on this tradition. By the time we arrived back from our day trip hundreds of people were already out on the streets, where brightly lit decorations bathed everything in a soft warm light. We walked up through the busy town to find ourselves a good position amongst the growing crowds of revellers, and it was smiles-all-round at last. As time went on more families arrived, all jostling for a good position, but there was still no sign of the carnival. Then the strains of an approaching band drifted towards us on the warm night air and we could see the headlights of a lorry in the distance.

Slowly, oh so slowly the music got louder as the lorry inched its way towards us, spewing out imitation snow from a machine on its trailer, until it had covered us in gooey white fluff and passed on by, followed by the rest of the carnival. Floats of theme-dressed children, brightly clothed adults, marching bands, and individuals imitating everyone from Father Christmas to turbaned sultans made their leisurely way down the street, hurling toys and sweets at the yelling people. Music blared and horns hooted, and still more sweets were hurled into the swaying crowds. A ten foot chicken waddled by and three huge inflatable, plastic eggs were bounced high, bobbing over everyone's heads as out-stretched hands pushed them on down the street. Then, amongst this cacophonous parade, three live camels came sedately swaying along laden with presents, their lowered eyelids and haughty looks saying that, without a doubt, they thought the whole thing was completely crazy and that they were only there under sufferance. When it had all passed by, everyone rushed to the bottom of the street and waited for the parade to go around the block and come by again. It lasted for hours. When the parade had eventually passed by for the last time it was almost midnight, but children still scoured the streets for more sweets and adults chatted around sleeping babies in pushchairs. The place was alive but we were starving by now, so we headed for a busy Chinese restaurant and had a great meal amongst celebrating Spaniards, understanding at last, that that's what makes a Spaniard smile.

We tried to get up early next day but failed miserably – so a little late but with picnic made, we drove the hire car north to Setenil, a village hewn from a hillside of solid rock. Then up to the larger town of Olvera which rises from the ground like a pyramid of white houses, topped by the 12th Century fort, part of the defensive lines of the Nazari kingdom of Granada, and the church of San Jose with its unmistakably slim, twin towers. Every village in this area seemed to have its own church, castle or Roman remains and the deserted countryside was steeped in history.

Becky and Nick had supper with us that evening and we played a few card games. They were finding it really cold in their tent, but were doing well with the busking in Ronda. We could lend them hot water bottles but sleeping on the ground was the real problem. While we all ate, a regular camp visitor came sniffing round the open door, waiting for her scraps of food. Like everyone else on this campsite, we had fallen in love with a gentle, sweet-tempered stray dog. She had been named Carmen by the other campers and was being regularly fed by them. When Brenda and Keith left next day, they gave us their mobile number and handed Jack the job of feeding Carmen. He relished this, having always wanted his own dog and would have happily smuggled her on board if we'd not kept a watchful eye on her. She was just one of many stray dogs that we took to during the year and we could have easily returned with a whole pack.

So that morning, leaving Carmen with a full tummy again, we headed off in the hire car, this time to find the Cueva de la Pileta near Benaojan, about 25 kilometres from Ronda. These caves, discovered in 1905 are situated in the most beautiful, wild area of Sierra de Libar, part of the Serrania de Ronda. More than a mile in length and filled with oddly shaped stalagmites and stalactites, the cave was found to contain five fossilised human and two fossilised animal skeletons. There are also prehistoric paintings depicting animals as well as mysterious symbols. One of the drawings is of a large black seal-like creature about three feet long, and this chamber, in the heart of the cave, has a precipice which drops nearly 250 feet. But you are unable to view these caves alone and although we waited for an hour, along with a young American couple, the guide never showed up, so we never did get to see into the caves.

Never defeated, we travelled on to the 8th Century village called Zahara de la Sierra. This un-changed mountain retreat, with its highly uneven street layout, is situated by the Zahara reservoir at 511 meters above sea level. We parked, as recommended, at the bottom of the road and walked up into the village through zigzagging levels of narrow, incredibly steep streets until we reached the Baroque Church of Santa Maria de Mesa and then staggered higher and higher and higher until we puffed our way up to the 12th Century Castillo Islamico, the castle built on a sheer rocky precipice. I collapsed on a wall, just as our mobile phone rang, and while I talked to an old friend back in England, I was able to describe an incredible birds-eye view across valleys and mountains, and down onto the naturally shaped reservoir of deep, blue water lying in the folds of the foothills.

We walked back down into the village centre and stopped for drinks at a pavement café. As always, the ubiquitous canaries were singing in their cages on wrought iron balconies, and orange trees, still with their fruit, lined the village square. The place had an air of quiet activity. Locals came and went, chit-chatting about some building work that was being undertaken opposite the café; ladies carrying produce plumped down onto benches to have a good gossip and a selection of busy dogs went about their daily rounds of the streets. It was a very pleasant place to sit and watch the world go by. We reluctantly moved on, back to the hire car and took one of our circuitous tours on upwardly spiralling roads to the 1,357 meter high point at the Puerto de las Palomas Pass which provided a great view of the Grazalema National Park and surrounding Sierras. Once again, the almond trees were delicately blossomed and tiny blue irises with their striped yellow centres, bravely flowered in the lush green grass of the valleys. We counted eleven Gryphon vultures circling overhead on thermal currents, and many more drifting lazily around the hot rocky mountain tops in the distance. This whole area is a wonderful vast nature park and would be well worth another visit. The road to Ronda had proved to be yet another great detour and one that we could recommend to anyone.

Monkey Business

We left Ronda the next day, heading back down the mountains on the excellent, but scary road which is carved like a groove along the edge of the hill-side. I sat behind Jack again and stuck my head into the 'Teach Yourself Spanish' book for the whole trip down. I didn't learn any Spanish but I didn't scream either. Ok, so I had it stuffed in my mouth for some of the time, which did hinder the learning process, but it kept me quiet. Anyway, next stop was Gibraltar. It didn't take long to reach La Linea (de la Concepcion), the busy coastal town at the end of a peninsular, which links Gibraltar to mainland Spain. We'd been told that there was a good wild camping site for motor homes, right next to the Spanish border post, so we followed all signs for Gibraltar and sure enough, as we approached the rock, we saw a huge car park with many motor homes parked on it. We got a little confused with some of the traffic bollards at one point, which required me to jump out in the middle of the traffic to grapple single-handedly with a large lump of concrete, but before long we were parked up and had the kettle on.

Gibraltar rises out of the sea; a strange, pointed, lump of limestone rock, and it is quite bizarre to think that this uncompromising piece of land, attached to Spain, is still a British colony. Five kilometres long and only one kilometre wide, most of which is vertical, it houses about 30,000 people and about 300 Barbary Apes. Its early history was turbulent but it has remained in British hands, despite some protest during the Franco period, for over two hundred years. Because of its curious geographical and political position, it seemed to me rather confused about what its present culture really is. Gibraltar is internally self-governing and Gibraltarians, many of whom are Genoese or Jewish, determinedly want it to stay that way. You will need to show a passport to enter Gibraltar, although many of the Spaniard's who cross onto the rock every day to work in the tourist and service industries, are well known to the border guards and simply flick their passports up and dash on through.

That night, as we ate our evening meal, we had a superb view of the illuminated Rock through our front windscreen. From the rear window we looked out across the long marina of La Linea, the promenade lights reflecting in the water with blue, green and gold shimmering detail. We would have slept well were it not for the amorous young locals, who spent most of the night tucked right up behind our motor home, smooching and who knows what else. This big car park was obviously a hot spot for ca-noodlers and boy racers, who wanted to impress their young ladies by racing round the edge as close to the water as they could. Back to that old bull-fighting bravado maybe.

It was just a five-minute walk from the motor home to the border crossing, so next morning we showed our passports and followed the path across the airport runway and up into town. You can catch one of the regular buses to and from the border, but on our first day we decided to walk. Gibraltar is a jumble of cultures, religions and fashions, like many places in Spain, but here it is concentrated into a very, very small area. As you walk the streets you will see the working Spanish, English bobbies, Orthodox Jewish boys and men in their fitted black suits and skullcaps, plus the British who have moved there to open pubs and bars, Indian shop owners, Moroccans selling their wares in the town square and even red coated, be-wigged British soldiers carrying muskets over their shoulders as they march along to guard some building that was strategic in the 1700's. Steak and kidney pie, paella, fish and chips, a good curry or a take away meal from Marks and Spencer are all on offer within half a mile of each other.......... It's almost like home.

As we entered the town we passed the old market area, still used on certain days, before moving into the spacious and pleasant, Grand Casement Square, with its shops and street cafes. On up the high street to English stores like Early Learning Centre, M&S, Mothercare, Topshop and Safeways, who all rub shoulders with jewellers, music shops, and general tourist tat. Eating houses abounded, with names like Piccadilly Gardens and the Viceroy of India and English style pubs were everywhere. It was all very bizarre. We walked out of the centre and up into the older part of town. There were the usual steep streets, where children played with remote control cars, (they must have been top of the Christmas list) outside blocks of flats, and up above, liberally hung washing lines decorated the alleyways. Narrow, back streets with dark doorways, looking distinctly like the Arab quarters, shaded groups of older men who gathered to smoke hookahs and drink mint tea. Small, noisy motorbikes whizzed around and booming music from boy-racer cars, ensured that no one was going to get a siesta. There were an incredible number of cars on Gibraltar and parking was obviously a huge problem. Every day we witnessed long queues at the border as residents came and went. It just wasn't built for cars.

Gibraltar is of course famous for its Barbary Macaques, which have lived in the Upper Rock Nature Reserve for years. You can take the footpath up to the reserve but it would be a very long hot climb, so the next day we decided to have a Rock Taxi Tour. Our driver was named Charlie, a native Gibraltan, who knew the island inside out having been a driver for the navy before he became a taxi driver twenty-seven years ago. He explained the problems of the island; it's reliance on tourism and government work and its shortage of fresh water. Against that, he said that it was a very tolerant and relaxed place to live, where most people were happy with their lot and their neighbours, no matter what race or creed. He drove us up to the Apes Den, where the macaques regularly hang around waiting for tourist tit-bits. Charlie had his usual pocket full of macaroni, which he said they preferred, and before long we had the surprisingly heavy, but soft footed apes, climbing all over us. He knew these apes individually, and they knew that he was the man with the food, although even he was careful about how he touched them and we were not allowed to put out our hands to them, as they can give a nasty bite. Up on the summit, along a precipitous road five feet wide with a 300 feet drop either side, only the taxis were allowed, and we understood why when we reached the top and gazed down at the miniature- sized world below us and North Africa far off across the Straits of Gibraltar.

Charlie finally dropped us off at the last interesting place on the tour, which was the Great Siege Tunnels. I had never realised that the rock of Gibraltar, which we know so well from picture postcards, is actually honeycombed with hand-dug tunnels which cover a staggering thirty seven kilometres. They date from the Great Siege of 1779 – 1783, when British soldiers resisted Spanish attempts to wrest the rock into their rule. The tunnels were hewn from the solid rock to make new gun emplacements, along with sleeping quarters, storerooms and ammunition rooms. Quite a feat of engineering. We wanted to see more of this British colony, so instead of taking the taxi back down, we walked down the steep road, past the old Moorish fort and back through the old town again. That evening, Jack and I took a long stroll along the well-lit promenade which edged the marina and beach of La Linea. We walked for about an hour, past night-time fishermen and strolling townsfolk.

It was a beautiful balmy evening and the promenade lights shimmered on the sea. As always on our walks, we talked about everything, subject hopping just as the conversation led us. When we turned back the breeze was behind us, and we could hear cicadas trilling in the flower beds alongside the path. Jack was determined to make contact with these secretive little beetles so after a fair amount of unsuccessful poking in the undergrowth, he took out his mobile phone and scrolled through the ring tones. He found just the right cicada sound and before long we had a cicada in sight, answering his phone as if it was a long lost friend. We got some strange looks as we knelt on the path communicating with nature, which isn't surprising really, but if you ever want to contact a cicada, you now know what to do – just give them a ring!

While we were parked at La Linea, we saw many travellers who were meeting up, before driving on down to Algerciras, to make the crossing to Morocco together. We wanted to go too, but had no insurance cover for that area, so were not sure whether to take the motor home or leave it at a campsite and go to Morocco in a hire car for a couple of weeks. As we were in no rush, we decided to drive on down the coast to Tarifa, which is close to Algerciras, to make further enquires. The road from Algerciras to Tarifa is marked as a scenic route and after you've climbed steeply away from the town you are on one of Europe's most splendid coastal roads, with views of the Straits, Gibraltar and the 'green hills' of Africa on the Moroccan coastline. Lush, green, rolling sierras on one side and the blue Straits on the other, with glimpses of houses in Ceuta and Tangier in the distance. This is the southernmost point of Europe.

Two factors have prevented the over-development of Tarifa's beautiful three mile white beach, the Playa de Lances. Firstly the wind rarely stops blowing and secondly, it is still a Spanish military zone. We had our own interesting brush with the military while we were trying to find a well-known, wild camp area. There is no beach- side development or tourism along this coast, but running parallel to the sea is a long stretch of low, pine wood interspersed by small, camp sites. Narrow roads take you through the woods, down to parking areas by the beach, where travellers often wild camp. Unfortunately, while trying to find this area, we took a wrong turn which led us through the pine woods on a very narrow single-lane road with no turning points. It also had 'No Entrance / Military Zone' warnings half way along it, but we couldn't find anywhere to turn around and were committed to going forward. Ten minutes later, still having had no chance to turn, a military camp came into view, with two heavily booted and heavily armed Spanish soldiers, blocking the way at an entrance barrier. What they were thinking as our big American beast came lumbering into view down this tiny road, I cannot imagine, but they didn't look amused. In fact it was another of those unnerving moments, as we shuddered to a halt in front of them. They didn't move or smile and we felt like those bloody silly, underdressed tourists from hell, again. But at least there was some space here to turn around – just. So, under the gaze of the serious, jackbooted Spanish soldiers, I jumped out, (wishing I was wearing more clothes and looking more athletic), and Simon completed another of those twelve point turns, with me at the rear to ensure we didn't back into military territory and become tomorrows headlines in a compound somewhere, and Jack with his head out of the window to make sure we didn't take the roof off their hut. I clambered back into the Beast and we smiled and waved goodbye, but they remained stony faced, and I can't blame them really. I don't think they saw us three as much of a threat, in our oversized passion wagon, more of a damned nuisance, but we were glad to get out of there. We made another hasty exit and didn't stop until we were clear of the zone, just in case.

That night we found a pleasant campsite by the beach. The manager was friendly and helpful and we soon made the acquaintance of a young, long term, English resident who gave us plenty of information about the area. Tarifa, named after a Moorish military hero called Tarik, claims to have retained more of its Arab character than any other town in Andalucia. It has the usual narrow, cobbled streets and sudden wide open plazas; cafes spilling on to paths and smells of everything from strong disinfectant to tasty soups. Old stone houses, profusions of flowers, palm trees, roaming dogs, children playing and noisy motorbikes. But it had a very different feel to other towns that we visited on the coast. There was much less tourism and no high rise apartments. It had a very Arab feel to it, perhaps due to the large port which linked it to Tangiers, and yet was quite cosmopolitan due to the huge windsurfing scene that dominates this coastline. We liked this small town very much.

This is a wind and kite surfer's paradise. The strong western breezes and long, clear, sandy beaches are unbeatable. It is obviously a Mecca for the enthusiast, with many shops catering for their needs. Everyday, hundreds of kite surfers took to the water – all colours of the rainbow, the kites gently blowing around, high in the sky. The surfers, in black wetsuits, clung to their kite ropes with boards on their feet, and were pulled along at tremendous speeds, while they skimmed the water and practised jumps and turns in the air. There were easily a hundred windsurfers too - like damsel flies with gaily coloured wings – slicing through the water, chasing the wind on high crests. On cloudy days the sea here was often a deep, green colour, with white horses riding waves that were blown up by the constant breeze; but on rare still days the sea was deep blue and the sky had a luminous quality. We remarked on this to Martin, our campsite friend, and he reminded us that this coastline is called the Costa De La Luz or the Coast of Light, because of the wonderful luminescent quality. Jack was keen to surf in this sea but alas disaster struck before he had a chance to try it. Our wooded campsite was situated close to the beach and once we'd settled in, we got the bikes off and Jack went on a few exploratory expeditions. This is a great walking and cycling area, under a canopy of low, round, wind bent pine trees, with grassy forest floors and sandy paths. Dappled shade gives a magical quality to the woodland and glimpses of the beach and sea entice you further, just the kind of place that kids love to explore. We liked to walk along the beach to watch the surfers having fun and on the third day we did this, while Jack rode his bike through the pinewood. We knew that disaster had struck when we saw Jack limping out of the trees towards us, holding his right arm and looking as white as a ghost. He would like to say that he broke his arm while fighting off hoards of invading Orcs, but he was really just going a bit too fast and crashed head first into a ditch.

We could see straight away that it was a nasty break. Simon rapidly made a sling from his jumper while I ran to collect Jacks bike from the ditch and we met up back at the campsite. We had no car to rush him to hospital, but a windsurfer had just returned to camp and although still in his wet suit, he immediately offered to run Simon and Jack straight in to the medical centre at Tarifa. Jack was starting to shiver now as the shock hit him, but bravely made no fuss at all. We helped him into the front seat of the Ford Capri, while Simon managed to squeeze into the back, wriggling in to lay between piles of wet surfboards and wet sails. I had to stay at camp as the car could only just get the three of them in, so with great reluctance I waved them goodbye and started to pace up and down the motor home, wringing my hands, as only a parent would.

It turned out that Tarifa medical centre was not sufficiently well equipped to deal with Jacks arm, so with another temporary sling, this time made from an old geographical magazine, they transferred him almost immediately by ambulance to Algerciras, about twenty kilometres back up the coast. Hospital Punta De Europa was as busy as any other hospital in the world and the benches in the A&E department were full to bursting with complete families accompanying their loved ones as they waited to be seen. Simon's reasonably good Spanish, which was based on what he had learnt many years before when living in Costa Rica, was pushed to it's limits as he explained what had happened and made sense of the bureaucratic system of waiting and moving, from one department to the next, while forms and X-rays were completed. At last they were shown in to meet the man who would give them the final verdict about the break and, as they thought, would put the arm into a plaster cast and send them home again. But it was not to be. Their faces fell, as the kind doctor explained that Jack had a compound fracture and unfortunately the bones had not only moved but were also trapping a nerve. Jack would have to be admitted; he would need an operation immediately to re-set the bones by screwing them to a metal plate which would be inserted into his arm. It was absolutely devastating news.

Simon and Jack were shown to a children's ward where Jack was hooked up to a drip and put to bed in a hospital gown, until the operation could go ahead. That evening, Martin, the windsurfer at the campsite, brought the last of his box of chocolates over to me and he sat and talked, to keep me company for a while. So often on this trip, strangers became such kind friends. Simon and I kept in touch by mobile phone and agreed that he would stay the night in hospital and I would take a taxi over to him in the morning, to allow him to come back and get some sleep. At ten o'clock that night, Jack was taken to the operating theatre, and although it was really only a small operation, he was understandably scared. Simon had to leave him at the theatre doors and for him it was very difficult to be unable to stay with Jack all of the time. He fretted and paced the corridor until 1.30am, when at last, Jack came back out and was wheeled again to the ward. Jack was exhausted and fell straight to sleep.

Now of course, looking back on it, we can laugh about the whole experience, which at the time was an endurance test for us all, especially Jack. The rest of that night Simon, now shattered, attempted to get some rest on the black plastic chair, next to Jacks bed. At this hospital, parents were allowed, if not expected, to stay the night next to their children; not only that but they could bring in televisions, or computers for games to be played on, and any notion of a good nights sleep was an idle fancy. It was unbearably hot and stuffy throughout the whole building and Simon had a really tickly cough at this time, so you can imagine that trying to stifle that, in this small stuffy room full of people, as the night wore on, was another form of purgatory. However, he needn't have worried because in the bed next to Jack, separated by a thin curtain, a boy and his mother watched a Spanish game show until 2.30 am, with the volume scarily high. Blaring game contestants had a whale of a time and the whole darkened room heard about it. Opposite Simon, another mother watched over her child, from her black squeaky, plastic chair, and now and then, joined in the game show fun. By dawn Simon had to get out and get some air before he succumbed to a complete nervous breakdown. He walked the empty streets of Algeciras for a while, before returning to some rather sour faced nurses, who seemed surprised that he had deserted his sleeping son. When Jack eventually woke up, Simon helped him to and from the loo, with accompanying drips, while the hospital swung into another day of non-stop action. That morning, I got a taxi over and relieved him. It was my turn to sit with Jack, and Simon went home to collapse into bed. I'm not sure which of them felt the worse at this point.

The hospital was really very good, it's just an added difficulty if you can't communicate too well, but we got by. In Spain, when one person has a problem, it seems that the whole family is involved, and of course this applies to hospitals too. So, when another boy was wheeled in after an operation, the whole extended family came with him. Mum, Dad, Uncles, Aunts, Grannies etc were needed to settle and fuss, until the television went on and they all became engrossed in another game show. Confined as we were in that hot, noisy room, the day seemed never ending. I read to Jack, one of his favourite books at the time, 'One Hit Wonderland' by Tony Hawkes, and in between sleeping, and eating enormous three course meals, three times a day, we got through another twelve hours. In the next bed another lad played merrily on his Play Station and mothers chatted and answered relatives on constantly ringing mobile phones. There was just no peace for the wicked.

Night fell at last and at 9.0 pm Jack had another X-ray; at 11.00 pm the drip was changed and thermometers were put under armpits; at 1.00 am the television at the next bed was turned off and for the rest of the night, us mothers tossed and turned on our plastic chairs in between getting a drink to prevent de-hydration or tip-toeing to the bathroom for a pee. It was a long night. However, the next day, after some assistance from a kind children's teacher who worked in the hospital and spoke good English, Jack was released with all forms signed. We staggered from the hospital, gasped fresh air and caught a taxi back to the Beast, where we all went to bed early, in separate beds, and tried to recover. You just never know what's round the corner do you…….. and sometimes it's just as well.

Sanderlings and Strange Customs

The following week was a strange one. Jack needed time to recover and rest quietly and Simon's tickly cough had not improved, in fact he had developed a bad sinus headache that didn't seem to want to budge, so he too wanted to take it easy. We remained at the small campsite under the pine trees, where we were hooked up to electricity, and I spent most of that week walking on the beaches and watching the surfers, while the others stayed at camp. I was feeling a bit restless, but if you had to be restless anywhere, then this was a good place for it, as there was excellent walking along the lengthy coast line. One morning I went down to the beach early to write my diary and as usual I sat on the stone steps that led up to the campsite. The familiar breeze was ruffling the water and the sky was a clear blue. It was January 19th, and although it was sunny, you still needed to keep a warm jumper around your shoulders. The beach was almost deserted; a spotty Dalmatian dog and his German owner being the only ones enjoying the surf. The sand was wide and soft and white, and the sea was a wonderful turquoise-blue colour, with rolling white breakers running up onto the shore. The colours of the day were heavenly, but I had become enchanted by the little bands of Sanderlings, which inhabited this coastline.

Flying fast and low, they would sweep along the edge of the breakers in groups of about eight birds, rapidly calling their high 'twick-twick' song. Then, they would land on the small, weed covered rocks, which were constantly revealed by the ebb and flow of the sea. The water would come in, washing over their feet and splashing their feathers, but the Sanderlings remained balanced stoically on the rocks until the waves retreated back into the sea again. Then they would quickly jump down onto the wet sand and furtively search around the rocks for tiny insects. They moved incredibly fast and when they ran along the sand to find a better area, they looked so light that they hardly seemed to touch the ground at all. Temporary little footprints in the sand were the only proof that they had actually run and not flown. I spent ages trying to get some really sharp photographs of these bright eyed, round headed little birds, with their straight dark beaks and pure white tummies. They were a real pleasure to have around.

There was a restaurant further along this stretch, which I discovered when I went for a long walk one afternoon. As you left the windblown sands and entered the white washed rooms, the heavy, welcoming smell of a log fire greeted you. Long wooden tables and benches were placed all along the wall facing the beach and a huge panoramic window treated you to a landscape of sea and sky as you ate great food. We all went there for a lunch of tasty tapas a few days later, when Simon and Jack were feeling better. That's another place that we would love to return to. We spent a few more days by the beach, this time wild camping, and explored Tarifa and its castle, but before long we all felt ready to move on again. Jack would have to return to Algeciras hospital to have his stitches out in two weeks time, but we wanted a change of scenery, and after consulting the map, we plumped for El Puerto de Santa Maria, about two hours up the coast, for our next stop.

El Puerto de Santa Maria is a large commercial fishing port and historical town that sits quite sheltered in the Bay of Cadiz, at the mouth of the Guadalette river. It is also one of the three corners of the famous sherry triangle, (Jerez and Sanlucar being the other two), and is close to several nature reserves. The region offers low sandy beaches, marshland reserves, excellent wine and fresh seafood, and it is believed to be the birthplace of flamenco, so good entertainment too. We were probably there at the coldest time of the year and we didn't find it too endearing, but it boasts of all I have mentioned, plus a climate apparently so benign that the first botanical garden was installed at El Puerto in the eighteenth century, to acclimatise the plants and seeds, discovered during that great period of global exploration.

We arrived at a fairly large but quiet camp site on a Saturday, and although it was rather basic in some ways, it had a shower block which we voted 'best on the trip!' You can become fairly obsessed with toilets and shower blocks when you're travelling and of course they vary enormously. Some have no hot water, some are dirty, some are clean, some smell terrible and have little privacy and some are fantastic. The shower and toilet block at the site in Granada was all marble, spotlessly clean and had plenty of hot water, so it got a nine out of ten, while certain other ones were fairly disgusting and got a 'nil point'. Simon particularly, gave the shower and toilet block at El Puerto a 'ten out of ten', and I wouldn't have been surprised to find campers living in it, it was so luxurious. Constantly heated in the cooler months, spacious and modern, with moody lighting, indoor plants and reliable hot water, this was a shower block to worship. For Simon, the piece de resistance was the pleasant, loudly piped music, which gave you the opportunity to perform all functions with impunity. Need I say more… I don't think so, as I expect that most men will relate to this important and oft overlooked necessity.

Very soon fellow campers were wandering over to say hello to us new arrivals. Among them were a friendly young couple from London, who were taking eighteen months out to travel, before heading for Australia to settle down again. He was an accountant and she had a law degree. They had an adorable little toddler, who really needed to be on a long piece of elastic to stop him roaming too far, and they were also travelling with a manic little Yorkshire terrier and two cats which had to be separated regularly as they fought like the proverbial; all in a motor home. (The different approaches to travelling never failed to intrigue me.) The next day was a Sunday and we were told that the local roads would be busy because a fiesta would be taking place in the pine woods opposite our camp site. We had no idea what this was going to be about, but wandered over to have a look. Now when we think back to El Puerto, we always associate it with this wonderful day that none of us will ever forget. It was totally unexpected and brilliant fun.

We walked over to the woods that Sunday morning, with mild curiosity, and as we got closer saw people arriving on foot, carrying animal cages, and in cars towing horse-boxes. There was already a large group of people gathered at the edge of the trees and amongst them were many horses and riders. But these were not just horses and the riders were not just Spaniards out for a trot in the woods. These were statuesque Arab / Hispanic horses fresh from Goya paintings, groomed to perfection, with their tails and manes brushed and plaited; heads held impossibly high on almost permanently arched necks. Dappled greys, deep browns and of course the well-known Andalucian white. And then there were the riders. Kitted out in traditional, black, wide rimmed hats, tight bolero type jackets that were broad at the shoulder and ended neatly in at the waist and full leather leg chaps, they sat at ease in high backed saddles, a rolled blanket across the horses flank, while they drank sherry and regaled their friends and acquaintances. We stood at the edge of the rapidly growing crowd of animal owners, horse riders and general lookers on, but before long we were being dragged into the throng and were offered the first of many plastic tumblers of sherry. (I take back all I said about the Spanish ever being miserable).

After much sherry quaffing, a trio of musicians struck up some lively music and people began to clap and sing along. A small horse-drawn cart was being led towards us, completely covered with bright, fresh flowers. Positioned on the cart, surrounded by the flowers, was the wood and plaster statue of St Anton, the patron saint of pets, with a crook in his hand and animals at his feet. This was the 'Festival of St Anton' and the rabbits, canaries, cats, dogs, horses, even a snake and some chipmunks, amongst many other animals, that we saw being carried, ridden or dragged along to the gathering, were there to be blessed by the saint.

Gradually now, the crowd began to move off…….. we knew not where, but by this time we had had enough of the excellent local sherry to go with the flow and the flow was heading along a winding path into the woods. The musicians kept up the lively music and as we walked in procession, hands were clapped in time with the beating drum, while horses and riders flanked the edges or rode three and four abreast on the path. Singing and clapping as we went, we slowly followed the saint and his flower decked cart for about twenty minutes; a halt was then called and more copious amounts of sherry were handed round, along with well-stuffed ham rolls. We practised our poor, but increasingly less inhibited Spanish, on friendly fellow walkers, while round hipped ladies with bright coloured scarves broke into spontaneous flamenco as the music increased in volume and tempo. High spirits, high saddles and high kicking; bottles of wine or sherry were constantly being passed between the horse riders, some two-up now, as more and more joined the group, and before long we all set off again in another procession through a bit more of the forest. It all became a bit bizarre really, with over a hundred horses and riders now thundering around us or galloping off into the woods, and the winding procession following the Icon through the misty forest. Another halt for more sherry and ham rolls, more music and dancing and even higher spirits – and then on again to the beating drum and strumming guitar. At length, after two hours of this wonderful excuse for drinking sherry and having a good day out, we arrived at a large clearing in the woods. A huge crowd was gathered there, along with yet more animals of all types, plus food and drink stands and loudspeaker music. The flower-covered horse and cart was led in and pets were lined up to be blessed.

Next on the mysterious agenda were displays of synchronised riding. Teams of six and eight horses and riders, again in traditional clothing, performed intricate patterns, criss-crossing, high stepping, turning and weaving around each other to music, all in an extremely small arena. Of course El Puerto is close to Jerez, the famous horse riding centre, which we visited later that week. When the displays ended, we went back to the pet blessing area and saw yet another strange custom taking place. Young girls were now lining up to throw small stones at the icon of St Anton. We wondered if the sherry had finally taken its toll, but we were told that if you didn't have a boyfriend, you could throw three small stones at St Anton and if you managed to hit his naughty bits you would be married within the year. It seemed to us, a strange way of getting a husband - surely it would be better to throw flowers or something less debilitating, but that's the fun thing about strange customs....... They are very strange.

We decided to see more of the area while we were waiting to return to Algerciras for Jacks' stitches to be removed, so for the next week we used public transport to take a look at El Puerto and Jerez. To be honest, we found El Puerto to be a fairly dismal place: perhaps it was the time of year or maybe we were looking in the wrong areas.

I christened it the land of a thousand dog turds, which was maybe a little excessive, but the dirt, noise and dismalness did not endear it to us although the people were pleasant enough. Jack got many strange looks here and was almost mistaken for Prince Harry by one lady shop assistant. I should explain that there is some resemblance as he has hair the colour of beech leaves in autumn, a wonderful bright auburn and his face and arms are covered in huge fantastic freckles. He was always getting second looks as we walked the streets, wherever we were, but this particular lady who was serving us, dashed into the back of the shop and re-appeared with a copy of Hello magazine, with Harry on the front.

"Si, si, esta Prince Harry".

"If only", we all laughed as Jack went crimson faced.

She had a few gems of wisdom about our royal family, which she went on to share with us, but I'm certainly not going to print them here.

To visit Jerez we used public transport, which was an experience in itself. The bus apparently went every half hour, so following our town map we found the old bull ring and the two bus stops which represented the bus station, and waited. Two hours later, our fellow 'would be' passengers assured us that the bus would arrive although they had no idea when, but knew that it was a green bus, (but all buses that came past were green), so we ate our emergency rations and drank our drinks, more out of boredom than anything else. Twenty minutes later, we were still sitting on the hard metal seats opposite the old bull ring, watching and smelling Spain go by, when at last a green bus came along with Jerez written on the front. No explanation was given, but the bus was clean, smooth and with reclining seats, so it was almost worth the wait, although we were now wondering whether we should just get in the queue for the bus home again, as soon as we reached Jerez.

Jerez in January was pleasant enough, although not exactly the highlight of our year. A pleasant zoo, a guided tour of a local bodega to view the making of sherry, and of course a trip to the famous 'Dancing Horses of Jerez' at the Royal Andalusia Academy of Equestrian Art, helped to pass our time there, before finishing the week off by gloriously stuffing ourselves at Romerijos famous seafood restaurant. Yet another place that we would go back to on our gastronomic re-visiting tour. This family business, established for over fifty years, specialises in shellfish, and distributes them nation wide. With twenty-five varieties of sea foods available, we did our best to choose the widest selection possible and had such mouth-watering delights as deep fried anchovies, hake in a wonderful light batter and delicious shrimp omelettes. It was sold by weight, so you could choose a selection of many different dishes, which were all cooked to order. That was our last treat in El Puerto, before once more going back to Algeciras hospital, for Jack to have his stitches out.

It had rained hard in the night and it didn't really get light until about 8.30 am, but we were up early and got to the hospital in good time for our appointment, parking the motor home in a wide, side road. The hospital was just as hot and busy as before, but this time we had more idea about where to go for the final x-ray and had brought a book each to read while we waited in the long queues. As the morning wore on and the temperature rose, Simon decided to wait outside – he was beginning to feel very claustrophobic again. At last, we were called in for Jack to have the long line of stitches removed although they weren't stitches as such, but were metal staples. He climbed up on the bed and the nurse set to work with her staple remover while I stood alongside holding Jack's free hand in loving support, which would have been fine, had I not come over all faint at the sight of the un-stapling procedure. The nurse took one look at me turning white, sweaty and beginning to sway, and quickly shoved poor Jack off the bed and laid me on it, tilting my feet up into the air. Fanning me with Jacks notes seemed to do the trick though and after about ten minutes of interesting chatter and fanning, she let me get down and re-instated Jack, to remove the rest of his staples!

Poor lad. I did feel sorry for him. All over at last, we said our thanks and goodbyes and returned to the Beast, now desperately keen to leave Spain behind for a while. We were hot-footing it to Portugal as we had just three weeks available before Jack had to return yet again, for his final appointment and last x-ray at the hospital. The Algarve was not far away, another place that we had never visited, so we programmed Maisy, upped the main sail, and headed off.

February

A Glimpse of Portugal

Portugal is somewhere that we would love to return to; from the very first moment when we crossed the border, we liked the place. Initially because as you drive across the border, a well equipped tourist office with large car park, and all the information you could possibly require for your stay, provided by a smiling, English speaking assistant, is situated at the road side. 'Dix Points,' straightaway to Portugal! When we pulled into the car park and walked over to the tourist office we felt slightly sceptical; surely this would be too good to be true, but the charming assistant couldn't do enough to help us and we left with armfuls of information about the area and suitable camp-sites. We commented that this was an excellent service, which we hadn't found at the borders of Spain, to which she sharply replied, "Portugal is nothing like Spain".

With only three weeks to spend in this beautiful and varied country, we decided to concentrate on the Algarve, which we had never visited before, although we would have loved to see more of the central and northern areas too. It was now January 31st and England would have been gripped in another cold winter, but there on the famous southern coast, mimosa was in flower, arum lilies blossomed by the roadsides and bright blue borage flowers spread like a carpet on the hillsides. We drove along peaceful, wide roads and soon began to feel that the heart of this country beat at a much slower and easier pace. Portugal looked inviting, even the local radio channel played modern sing-along tunes that we knew, and we felt instantly at home. On reading more about the country we realised that it had not always been this way. Despite its past history of invasions, its periods of conquests when, for a while, it had a rich empire spreading from Africa to the Far East; its unrest and coups, earthquakes, and its more recent recessions and unemployment, Portugal still retains its gentle and welcoming feel. In recent years it has had a new period of economic success starting with Expo '98, which attracted eight million visitors and opened the doors to investment in infrastructure and tourism; but this has not in any way changed the friendly, quietly dignified people and their way of life.

Being there out of season of course was a major advantage and it is the time when you will usually see countries at their best. If you enjoy walking and cycling or just touristing, it's good to leave the crowds behind, although with Jack's arm in a sling, we would not be able to cycle in Portugal. We decided to park up at a recommended campsite at Olhau, a small town which boasts a large fishing port, and to then hire a car to explore the whole Algarve area. Once again we would use the Beast as our base camp hotel – she would be too big to drive through the small villages which we wanted to explore. We found the site quite easily and were able to drive straight in and choose a place to park; it was another over wintering place for all nationalities, with a steady stream of short stay visitors too. These sites sometimes had a 'small town' feeling to them, with fenced areas around the more permanent caravans, flowers around the doors and washing on the lines. This site even had a camp newsletter compiled by residents, allowing all nationalities to air their views, and the bar had the usual games evenings. It was quiet, friendly, with a good small supermarket and reasonable shower blocks. You could easily become critical of the different sites which you stay at when touring, but it pays to remember that you are not in England, you are in a foreign land where they do things differently, and that's what you went there for.

Our routine on arrival anywhere was so well practiced by now that within minutes we were all set up. Jack and Simon went through their drill; hooking up the electricity, lowering the levelling jacks, sliding out the awning and patio table, with three folding chairs, and putting up the satellite dish. Meanwhile I quickly pulled cushions from cupboards, sorted out washing to be done, and put a light salad on the table for lunch. That was our home ready to live in again. We were ready to see the sights, so, never able to sit still and relax when we reached a new destination, we took a short walk to the Ria Formosa Natural Park which was situated literally just down the road from the camp site. This flat area of sandbanks juts out of the coastline, offering protection to the leeward beaches of the Algarve and is a haven for bird life. The nature reserve covers about 60 kilometres of coastline and is sheltered from the ocean by partly submerged sand dunes and a network of salt marshes and lagoons. Several times during our stay, we walked along to this nature park and took leisurely strolls along the three kilometre trail, through pine woods and along the quiet shoreline; exploring the old working tidal mill on our way to a freshwater lake. There we could sit in hides, amongst white storks, large grey herons, and the rare purple gallinule, along with thousands of wading and water birds, who use this area as a stop over and feeding ground. There's also a bird hospital here and the main centre for the almost forgotten, web-footed, Portuguese water dogs. These are bouncy, friendly animals with long, curly black hair, like Rasta dogs, whose traditional job was to help fishermen with their catch, by diving into the water and chasing the fish into the nets.

Our first full day looked like a fine one, so after hanging out a pile of washed clothing on our line, tied to the trees around the Beast, we decided to tackle an ongoing problem which we had been having with our LPG gas tank. This gas ran the fridge, cooker, generator and central heating in the motor home. We had been unable to fill up the tank with fresh gas while we were in Spain, as it was simply not allowed. You had to use bottled gas there and we had bought one bottle as an emergency spare supply, although acquiring it from the dragon-like, power crazed old signora who had controlled the triple, rubber-stamped paperwork involved, had been a nightmare. Simon had almost to give blood to get it, and sweat and tears were definitely expected. (He had sat in her boiling office for hours, along with a room full of similarly disgruntled Spaniards, while she grudgingly bestowed gas bottles to the needy.) Now, however, the gas in our main tank was getting low and, we suspected, rather impure judging by the colour of the flame and the performance of some of the appliances. One of the camp site residents had told us of a garage near Olhau where you could fill up your gas tank and where the owner was a specialist at checking the system. To find someone like that, locally, was a bit of a rarity, so we reserved our pitch with well placed chairs and stones and drove off in the Beast to find him.

'Autogas de Laranjeiro' was run by Edmond and his wife, who were friendly, helpful and more than happy for us to park the motor home on the waste ground next to the garage but Edmond was quite busy with previously booked work, so after an initial diagnosis of 'bad French gas' (which was what we soon put any problem down to, including problems which had nothing to do with 'bad French gas'), it was decided that Simon would do most of the work using Edmonds tools when necessary, and Edmond would give advice when Simon needed it. It was agreed that the gas tank should come off and the small amount of remaining gas should be discarded, then the tank cleaned of any sludge, and re-instated to be re-filled. Simon got to work, and although it was quite tricky getting the large gas tank out of its position, he managed to remove it by using the levelling jacks to raise one side of the motor home. We then had a long wait while the small amount of remaining gas dispersed. We have since learnt that should you decide to do it this way in England, you will be breaking the law and will incur a fine of many, many thousands of pounds!

It was a beautiful blue-sky day, quite hot and with no breeze. This is February in Portugal, and as I sit writing this, back in England in December, I long to be there again. Jack and I had little to do whilst Simon worked on the gas tank, so we decided to take a long walk through the surrounding countryside. We found what looked like a rough goat track, leading up through low hills, and we followed it through bright yellow meadow flowers, wild cistus bushes with their papery pink blooms, and gentians that were bluer than the sky above. The meandering track led through ancient olive groves and past scrubby thyme bushes, to a stone ruin where we sat on the hillside in the sun and listened to the ever present crickets as they rubbed their legs together with glee; heavy smells of herbs and flowers scented the warm air. We had one of our wonderful, subject hopping conversations, which led from this topic to that and ranged through everything from the history of Portugal, to women's rights in India. When we began to get peckish, we walked back down and set our chairs up under a shady tree, where we ate rich black olives, fresh bread and goat's cheese, for lunch. Then we all relaxed and read our books while the old gas evaporated from the tank. Edmund eventually gave it the thumbs up and Simon fitted it back in place. Then it was filled with clean gas and we thanked all concerned. The charge was so ridiculously small that Simon gave

Edmund some extra for his trouble and his help. It was a dirty job, but someone had to do it, and the gas has worked perfectly since then.

Our hire car, a fairly new Renault Megane, arrived the next day; it was going to cost us 120 euros for seven days. Our first trip was to the market at Quarteira where you could buy just about everything from African sculptures to pirate DVD's, or lace tablecloths to Peruvian knitwear. Most markets had the same type of goods on offer, however this is a very large market and if you can't resist them, you can spend a few hours at this one, haggling or just people watching. The rest of original Quarteira has been somewhat overwhelmed by developments and tourism, although it does have a very long sandy beach. We moved quickly on to see some of the famous sand stack coves that start at Quartiera and continue westward all along the coast to Lagos.

The Algarve is littered with fabulous and famous beaches and it would be difficult to agree on a favourite. 'In season' you would have to choose by simply finding one which had some room on it, but at the beginning of February, when they were all almost empty and yet it was still warm enough to play on them and even swim in the sea if you were brave enough, they all looked inviting. That afternoon we went no further than Praia Gale, just past Albufeira. All along this coastline you will find perfectly clean, fine pale sand and golden coloured, low rocky cliffs, with grassy paths leading along the top from beach to beach. Isolated, strangely shaped, sand stacks composed of tiny fossils stand like sentinels in the sun, between rocky coves, where Jack could duck through tunnels of rock and jump over the low incoming waves to work his way round to stand inside forty foot tall blow holes shaped like hour glasses. Jack and Simon exhausted themselves playing in the tide, seeing how late they could leave it before they ran up the beach and didn't get a soaking, while I pottered among the sea shells looking for yet more treasure.

Next day we went further, driving straight down the extremely quiet motorway towards Portimao, and then continuing on smaller roads, down to Sagres, which is the peninsular at the southern most tip of Portugal. This wind swept cape was once known as the end of the world, and when we stood on the headland and gazed out to the constantly churning ocean, we could understand why. Sagres is an unspoilt, low-lying town, which attracts surfers and backpackers in summer, but in winter seemed almost empty. The surrounding countryside of low, rolling green hills, appeared to be unchanging, with twisted olive trees, ancient figs, oranges, lemons and almond trees. Herds of goats were shuffled along the roads by smiling, brown skinned Portuguese and the word for 'stress' was obviously not part of anyone's vocabulary. For such a quiet place it has a surprisingly famous history. It was here in the 15th Century, that the school of navigation was founded, gathering together the greatest cartographers, astronomers, mariners and shipbuilders in Europe. New ships were designed here, including Christopher Columbus's caravel, which he used to cross the Atlantic. Vasco da Gama and Ferdinand Magellan studied here and Sir Frances Drake made the unpardonable mistake of burning down the navigation school and its priceless library in 1587. All that remains from this earlier history is a simple chapel and the huge Rosa dos Ventos (Wind Compass), which is a circle on the ground, carved in stone and forty three meters in diameter. Now, a huge 17th century fortress stands on this site.

We explored all of this and watched the tremendous crashing waves of the surging Atlantic as it battered the towering cliffs. The cliff top walk, with its growling blowholes and flattening wind, had us holding our hats on, but standing on the very edge of these 200 feet high, absolutely sheer cliffs were a veritable host of local fishermen. With no safety ropes attached to them, but holding oversized rods out over the cliff tops, they looked extremely precarious. Some men had even clambered down the almost vertical sides of the cliffs to secure more dangerous looking footholds, and we were told that the previous year, four men had died in this sport of 'Extreme Fishing' as Jack called it. We couldn't imagine that what they caught was any different or better than what you could get in the local market, but maybe the thrill was what they were really there for, although the fishermen didn't look like the Portuguese version of Indiana Jones. But then, after watching for a while, we saw that they were regularly hauling up good size sea bass, which has got to be some of the tastiest fish-eating anywhere. Thankfully Jack decided not to add this dangerous looking sport to his list of 'things to do when I'm older' though.

Crossing the headland by car, we travelled up the western coast to Castelejo. Unlike the southern stretches of the Algarve, the west coast, stretching north from Sagres to Odeceixe, is still quite undeveloped. It is constantly exposed to the strong Atlantic winds, the sea is much cooler and swimming is dangerous; but for sheer rugged beauty it is breathtaking and we wrapped up in what warm clothing we had, to stand down on the rocky shores of Praia Castelejo, to watch the wind blow the tops off the huge rolling waves. It was a magnificent, mesmerising sea and we stayed until the sun went down. Then with glowing cheeks and empty stomachs, we drove back to Olhau for supper in a little café we had spotted near the campsite.

Olhau is a pleasant, quiet, unspoilt town and from the bell tower of the seventeenth century parish church, which we climbed for a charge of 1 euro each, you can look out over the white washed houses with their small flat-roofed terraces. The busy fishing port has centuries old links with Morocco and it shows in the architecture and traditions. We frequently went to the fantastic food markets, which were held in two large brick buildings on the harbour side, and were open from the crack of dawn, every day except Sundays. Meat, fruit and vegetables were in one hall and freshly caught fish in the other. Everything looked delicious. The strawberries, olives, nuts, big juicy tomatoes, salad crops and greens were begging to be eaten; and in the fish market, thirty individual marble slabs, slippery with sword fish, eels, tuna, fresh sardines of every size, shell fish, octopus, gleaming eyed mackerel at 1 euro each and much more, were all displayed and sold by the local men who had fished it out of the sea. In Portugal we ate like kings for next to nothing. On Saturdays, the market extends to the squares outside the halls where locals and regular traders line the harbour edge, selling everything from hand reared chickens and rabbits, to surplus flowers and crops from smallholdings. For several Saturdays running we wandered the stalls, Jack and I stuffing ourselves on nuts and almond cakes as we went, while Simon searched for the best fish to barbecue. As was always the way, it was the people who captured my attention, as much as the food. The typical little old lady, all in black, sitting on an upturned wooden crate next to her wares, her battered straw hat so big that it completely shaded her tiny, wrinkled face from the sun. She worked a piece of white lace, with thin brown fingers that moved independently after decades of practice, her alert searching eyes looking out for a customer. She spotted me taking a picture of her, and gave me such a look that I simply had to buy some of her home grown flowers and a fresh thick lettuce. The fishermen, still in wellies and waterproof trousers, bantering amongst themselves at their stalls as they called for someone, anyone, to buy their ink covered squid or choose from their pile of fresh sardines. The groups of round bellied, tidily dressed men who greeted each other at the street café in the market square; and the strange young blond woman that we had noticed before, who talked loudly to herself and marched about the market, trying to make eye contact with the unwary. My camera was always busy.

After one such shopping trip to the market, we went back and cooked some fresh fish for supper. Then I walked down to the phone box, which was situated near the camp entrance and called the family back home. After a good chat, I started back up towards the motor home, but in the dark I could see a familiar figure ahead of me. I couldn't mistake her gypsy style headscarf and brisk walk and immediately shouted for Becky to hang on while I caught her up. Yep, that's what so often happens when you travel. Becky and Nick had not long arrived, their tent was up and of course they came round to us later that night and sang for their supper, impressing all around us with their delightful, lively violin music. It was great to see them again and we soon agreed on a day out in Faro to celebrate. And what did we do in Faro? Did we look at the interesting architecture, the old town, the beaches, the museums etc….. I'm afraid not…… we all went to the multi screen cinema, loaded ourselves with pop corn and watched the latest Lord of The Rings movie. Just brilliant!

Exploring the Algarve

The beaches of the Algarve may be its greatest tourist attraction but once again, on reading more about the area, we were keen to get off the beaten track and explore inland. Up early with the usual picnic packed, we headed off on a tour starting from Portimao, not the most interesting of places, but from there we headed inland across the coastal plain and then into the rolling hills of Serra de Monchique. This volcanic range soaks up the Atlantic mist, and with constantly flowing mountain streams, tumbling through the region on their way to the sea, it is green and verdant. Cork Oaks, Chestnut and Eucalyptus trees grow on wooded hillsides and heavy yellow mimosa and rhododendron edge the roads. However, bounteous as this area looked to us in February, it suffers from long droughts in the summer, with temperatures sometimes reaching 35 degrees and it needs to retain all the water it can. In recent years, summer fires have been known to burn 85% of the Monchique forests with predictably disastrous results. The cork oak is a long-term investment, with a commercial life of about 150 years. The tree has to be about twenty years old before the first bark is removed and used for tanning. The outer bark then re-grows and is ready for stripping again every nine years and each time it is harvested, the quality of the bark improves. We saw many piles of dusty cork bark, stacked by the roadside, waiting to be taken away to processing plants to be turned into insulation panels and wine bottle corks.

In our zippy little car we drove up into this delightful area, swinging off the main road to take in Caldas de Monchique on the way. This small spa village, which was popular with the Romans, was purchased almost in its entirety by the Monchique Termas company in the year 2000. Much of the old village, particularly around the main square, has been systematically restored from some neglect, into a pleasant enough tourist attraction. On to Monchique itself, where we climbed the warm cobbled steps to the 16th century parish church, the Igreja Matriz, with its columns carved as knotted ropes and then up to the atmospheric, ruined monastery, with old gardens of magnolia and lemon trees and great views across the town to the peak of Picota. From Monchique we took the winding, mountain road to the highest summit in the Algarve, the Pico da Foia at 902 meters, where we leant against our car in the warm midday sun and took in the view across the rolling green hills to Portimao, Lagos and Cabo de Sao Vicente. Taking a devious route as always, we stopped at a roadside restaurant and had excellent chicken piri-piri with hunks of fresh bread and olives for lunch, before detouring to find Omega Park. This is a small zoo, spreading naturally through the hills, with enclosures that house rare and unusual animals gathered together over four years by the English owners. Twenty-two endangered species, including the Bamboo Lemur, Pygmy Hippo, Spider Monkey and Cheetah are involved in breeding programmes there.

We were now thoroughly enjoying the gentle Algarve and Jack, with his arm in a sling, was managing to cope quite well with the car travel. So, early next morning we drove into Faro again, and following the town map, we searched out the Capela dos Ossos, or Chapel of Bones. This rather macabre building, constructed entirely from human bones and mortar, is tucked away behind the Igreja do Carmo (church). These types of chapel are scattered throughout Portugal and Jack found it particularly cool that a whole building could be made of bones. "Gruesomely fascinating" was how he described it, as he posed for photographs beside rows of skulls. Thousands of human skeletons, disinterred from the adjacent monk's cemetery – an interesting way of freeing up much needed space – have been separated into tibias, fibulas, vertebrae, skulls and all other parts of the skeleton, to line the interior of this chapel, including altar and roof and all parts in between. Much like a mosaic, intricate patterns were designed around the shapes of small and large individual bones. This small chapel was not highlighted as some great tourist attraction and we seemed to be the only visitors. It had cost us just one euro each to enter, and later in the year when we were marvelling at mosaics in Pompeii, while fighting our way through troops of Japanese tourists, we thought back to this peaceful little place with fond memories.

Whilst we were in Faro, we went on to visit the Ilha de Faro, which is linked to the mainland by a small road. This island is a long thin strip curving out from the mainland and encircling part of the Ria Formosa. It has low, single storey holiday chalets and a small village of permanent homes. The only commercial buildings are a few cafes and souvenir stalls near the small central car park. With next to no roads on it, we parked our car and walked down the narrow pedestrian street which led us through the village and out. From then on we walked on smooth wooden board walks with swinging rope handrails, leading on down the island, over sand dunes peppered with waving grasses. Beside the shore was a long, thin string of shanty style fishermen's homes, each design seemingly ruled by the materials which had been available at the time of construction and then randomly added to when more space was required. Some with families and some with just lone fishermen living an almost desert island existence next to the inland lagoon. Brightly painted boats were anchored out on the water and fishing nets were drying on the beach. As always, friendly dogs lay in the hot sun, just about managing to thump their tails as we stepped around them. Children rode their bikes along the board walks, and then turned off down side tracks to visit each others houses, like little rabbits scooting around the island.

We followed the warm wooden walkways; our hands trailing along thick rope handrails bleached white by the sun and sea. The Mediterranean shores on one side and the quiet lagoon on the other. At the far end we turned around and pottered back, beachcombing the shore line all the way until our pockets were weighed down with smooth, warm shells. It looked like paradise to us, and the only drawback was that in the unlikely event of war, the Portuguese government could commandeer the island for maritime defence. Not too likely we thought.

We had been in Portugal for ten days now and were really enjoying all that it had to offer. The campsite at Olhau was good and it soon became apparent that we were once again in a small British quarter, although this was more by accident than design. We were parked up at the edge of a wide road which led through the site. Close to us were two other English couples, well established with caravans and awnings, one couple there just for the winter and the other while they searched for a suitable property to buy. They had sold up in England and planned to move permanently to the Algarve. Further over was another English couple, who had originally come from our home county of Hereford; they were also wanting to move to Portugal. They were all both kind and helpful, and we enjoyed another unforgettable méal out to celebrate a birthday. This time I tried a fish dish with mango sauce, and Simon and Jack had the speciality which was tender rump steak, which you cooked yourself on hot stones at the table. The meat sizzled on the slabs in front of them, while they turned and cooked it to their own taste, and it was delicious. A glass of Medronho (arbutus-berry liqueur) ended the meal, and yes….. that's another place to return to.

February 11th was another beautiful hot day and we packed our swimsuits and took a drive along the coast eastwards to one of the many islands that are part of the Ria Formosa natural park. The Ria Formosa, covering 60 kilometres of coast, is a system of lagoons formed by rising water levels when the great glaciers retreated. The resulting depression was gradually filled by sediments, creating a coastal barrier of dunes, which run roughly parallel to the mainland. These dunes allow shallow, warm water lagoons, salt marshes, tidal flats and islets to exist. With its unique vegetation, it has become a vital area for migrating and over-wintering birds and is the nursery area for several oceanic species. It has also long provided a living for many of the local population.

With the car packed with our usual array of binoculars, sandwiches, sun cream, hats, surf board etc we took the road to Tavira – we always seem to have a car full of 'stuff' which we might need. We left the car on the mainland and walked across a swaying pontoon bridge and then waited for the little red and black, toy-train, which carried us across the mud flats to the Ilha de Tavira. We were the only people on the train going over, like three little kids sat at the back, the occasional walker coming back the other way, but otherwise it was very quiet. When the train reached the 13 kilometre island of sand, we hopped off and walked to the rather exotic looking café. There, under a colonnaded pergola, we supped cold drinks before spending the afternoon lolling on the long white beach, playing the old Arab game of Mancala in the sand, with small white shells and 'catch the tennis ball in the sea'; this last game always resulting in complete anarchy as we attempted to soak each other by deliberately throwing it too hard and too close, into the rolling waves. The main aim was always to get each other as wet as possible and invariably everyone ended up soaked. It was almost completely deserted on this hot sandy island and was extremely peaceful, with just the warm sea wind and the crashing surf to break the silence. Interesting flotsam and jetsam ended up in our pockets again, well usually my pockets, and long bleached pieces of wood made great drawing sticks in the sand. There's nothing quite like messing about by the sea – and we always did plenty of that.

The other island that we visited during our stay was the Illa da Armona. To get there we caught the midday ferry from the end of the jetty at Olhau, along with about thirty locals, all paying the usual 1 euro each, each way. It was a Saturday and seemed to be the family shopping day, when those living on the island came over to the mainland to stock up on groceries and all other household items. Trolley loads of food were loaded on to the rusty looking ferry, along with brooms, plants, live chickens in cages, new fridges and a shiny new boy's bike. Families helped to heave each others goods on board before the horn was sounded and we all found standing room on the main deck, as we moved off. At the other end, once again everyone helped to get the shopping unloaded, before starting to walk along the only single, sandy road, which led down the centre of the island. The only motors on this island were of the outboard variety, there were no cars or scooters – just hand pulled trolleys. At first the crowd was large, with neighbours chatting as they strolled, carrying or pulling along their latest buys from the town. Gradually people said goodbye as they turned off to their houses, until just the three of us were left quite alone and the 'road' had turned into a sandy track. Quiet had settled again over the island and smells of cooking wafted our way. It was time for lunch and a Saturday afternoon nap for the locals. We drifted on, and once again we picnicked and explored the sandy beach, before catching the last ferry back to Olhau, this time accompanied by teenagers, dressed in their best, for a Saturday night on the town.

I have to say at this point, before I forget, that we found the Portuguese people to be consistently friendly, with ready smiles and an easy relaxed attitude. Wonderfully though, everything seemed to work – buses and boats ran on time, offices, markets and official buildings opened and closed when they said they would and all was achieved with a quiet and simple courteousness and humility sadly lacking in so many other 'developed' countries. Communication wasn't so easy, as the Portuguese language sounded vaguely Russian to us, with a little Spanish and French thrown in. It is actually spoken by more than two million people worldwide, mainly in Brazil, (where it is the official language) and in five African nations. But it is not so well known in Europe. However, they were always keen to help us with pronunciation, or to solve a problem through a mixture of pigeon English and sign language. They seemed to tolerate the latest invasion of foreigners, who were enjoying their wonderful country, and we didn't feel the same abrasive edge that we experienced in Spain. We were 'out of season' of course, and all may seem quite different in the middle of a hot summer with an overdose of tourists, but we felt very at home in Portugal.

But our time was running out. Soon we would have to be heading back into Spain, to the hospital at Algerciras, for Jack's very last X-ray and check up. Then we would be driving across to southern France to start travelling down through Italy. We still weren't sure about visiting Morocco, our year out seemed to be going very fast and we knew that we also wanted to visit Sicily and Croatia. We did have more of a plan now, but could adapt it at any stage. Of course, you know what happens to mice and men when they have a plan...... but the next black cloud was yet to descend on us. For the moment we visited more of the wonderful beaches, including the picture postcard Praia dos Tres Irmaos (the three sisters) and crammed some more day trips in, while we still had the hire car.

We had been told by our English neighbours, who knew the area well, that we should take the route to Alcoutim before we leave, so after a quick bit of map planning, we did just that. Very often on these day trips, we would put Jack in charge of map reading and navigation. He has a logical mind when it comes to looking at contours and landmarks and became proficient at guiding us along. He would also take charge of town maps and lead us through quite complicated city centres to get to places we wanted to see. It was all good practice for him. I, on the other hand, have such an appalling sense of direction that I have to be almost micro chipped just to visit the nearest toilets. I invariably turn right when I leave any building, no matter which way I should be going, and it was Simon and Jack's biggest worry during the year, that I would get lost. As a safety measure, we started the trip with a mobile phone each, but mine was stolen when the car was broken into in Spain. Ever after that I was not allowed to go anywhere alone! I could say that such an attitude was unfair, but to be perfectly honest, I know I have no sense of direction at all. I only got lost once, in Florence, when I was swept along by a crowd of tall Americans and Simon and Jack completely lost sight of me. It was a worrying fifteen minutes for all of us, and we were so relieved when we were reunited that we just had to have a huge bear hug all round. We hadn't realised how close we had all become on this trip until that point.

However, now Jack was map reading for us, on a roundabout route to Alcoutim. We took a road up to the picturesque dam at Beliche; wild cistus bushes abounded with their papery flowers, each petal marked with a black spot and each flower boasting a bright yellow centre. Pine trees, eucalyptus, rosemary and lavender and fabulous views across green wooded valleys and steep mountainsides invited us to stop much too often to admire them all. We then doubled back to find the small road at Foz de Odeleite, where a fast flowing brook flows into the wide, slow moving Guardiana river. A smaller road follows this river valley, sometimes within a few feet and sometimes, when it climbs the valley sides, from a distance; but at almost all times you have the river in view and are travelling through beautiful scenery. We passed smallholdings, flourishing in the rich alluvial soil, and a farmer ploughing his field the age-old way with a horse and plough – the river flowing slowly alongside them.

This river is tidal as far as Alcoutim and in the days when the area was rich in copper, iron and manganese ores, it was the main method of transport to the Mediterranean for those cargoes. Alcoutim became a prosperous town, providing for the many sailing ships, which waited there for the tide to take them down river. The Guardiana River also forms the border between Portugal and Spain and as you drive alongside it, you can shade your eyes and gaze across to Spanish life on the other bank. Distant cockerels crow, church bells sound the hour and children's voices echo across the river; far-away sounds, which carry on the breeze and only slightly disturb the tranquillity of this perfect river valley. White sailed yachts drift unhurriedly by, sometimes anchoring out for a few days fishing or disembarking at Alcoutim for fresh provisions and lunch in one of the small but excellent restaurants. Alcoutim is a small attractive river port, with no hustle or bustle, and very little obvious tourism. The fourteenth century castle which stands above it, offers fine views of the town and the continuing valley. This whole mountainous area was once much more important when the Greeks, then the Romans, Arabs and Portuguese sought its riches, but it fell into decline when mining became less profitable and peace was settled between Spain and Portugal. Now it is an area that is just beginning to revive.

We were planning to eat out that day and found a village restaurant, popular with the locals. There was only one main course available for lunch, which was a rich lamb stew with thick chunks of fried bread to dunk in the tasty gravy, and a refreshing salad to follow. It was all being prepared and cooked at one end of the bar; the stew smelling good as it bubbled away in a huge pot. At the other end of the bar our cook, cum bar staff, cum waiter, served drinks and chatted to a regular local as he read the daily paper and smoked and ate his way through a leisurely lunch. We couldn't imagine no-smoking rules ever reaching this relaxed corner of the world. There was plenty to eat and the price seemed ridiculously reasonable but afterwards we could hardly move and almost had to push each other up the hill, to view the old Moorish fort. Finally, our drive home took us across the high, flat, inland plain to Martim Longo and then down through pine trees and zig-zag roads to Cachopo. Then over the mountains which form the barrier between the coast and inland Algarve, with their deep, tree covered gorges and tumbling streams which led us down to the sea again, through some fabulous scenery.

Becky and Nick headed off the next day, so once more, we said final farewells. They'd made enough money busking in Portugal to allow them to travel back through Spain, and they had to be back in England by April to play at a friends wedding. When we returned to England in September we met up again, and have kept in touch with them since, which has been a real pleasure. We, however, took another trip into the hills, this time to Loule and en route we stopped at Estoi to admire a bit of local architecture.

The pink rococo palace which puts the otherwise sleepy little village of Estoi firmly on the map has a much grander name really. The Palacio do Visconde de Estoi. I fell in love with this crumbling, ornate and totally romantic estate as soon as I saw it. If I were a millionaire I would buy it tomorrow, but it would not be to everyone's taste.

We stepped through the small elaborately carved wrought iron gate, set in a much larger equally elaborate but firmly locked, set of gates. The cobbled driveway led us past bent old palm trees twenty feet tall and overgrown bougainvillea hanging down to our heads with deep pink flowers. Stately stables, which once housed high stepping horses, now stood quiet with doors and windows locked and barred. We walked on up to the big house, passing the prettiest old band stand, still complete with finely curled, slightly rusty, music stands. The palace is a huge building but unfortunately, you can only view the exterior at present. At ground level, curved stone walls are decorated with traditional, blue and white tiles, depicting scenes from nature and voluptuous semi nude ladies. A secretive grotto beneath the balustraded balcony contains the Three Graces, hidden amongst damp ferns and rocks. More elegant statues and cornucopia shell water features surround a rectangular pool, which once had fountains playing amongst the central statues of bare breasted women holding gaping fish, and wide, sweeping, stone staircases with heavy balustrades, lead to a balcony with long views down the carriage driveway and surrounding gardens.

We wandered under the warm sun, sitting here and there on curved stone benches and took our time in this strange deserted place. The Estoi Palace is much neglected, with peeling pink paint and crumbling stonework, overrun gardens and shuttered windows, just waiting to be rescued, although I think it was almost at its most attractive in this weary state. If Sleeping Beauty was going to live anywhere it would have to be here. One day it will be cleaned, repaired and horribly tidied into a municipal hotel...... it just won't be the same. I'm glad we saw it, as it was that day. I have to say that I don't think that Simon and Jack saw it in quite the same light as I did. Maybe pink just isn't their colour and I know that Simon saw a builder's nightmare at every turn and was probably very glad that we could never afford to buy it. But I shall always dream of it.

Loule was next on the list, the 'second' city on the Algarve, and a vibrant and busy place. Our first stop was in one of the great cake shops situated on the very wide, tree lined, main street. We needed pastries to re-charge our energies and Jack and I had a hard time deciding which of the mouth-watering types we should choose. The whole of Loule was preparing for its Carnival celebrations that take place each February before Lent. It is renowned for having the biggest carnival in the country, and it continues throughout the whole weekend. Oversized banners and bunting already trailed from every lamp-post and available support, and a festive feel was in the air.

As usual our noses led us to the interesting neo-Moorish market hall, situated just off the main street, where fresh, and absolutely tempting merchandise, dictated that we wander the stalls in a daze. Well I wandered in a daze. Jack and I drooled over

more pastries, fruits, cheeses, and endless types of olives, nuts, hams, and fresh seafood. But Simon went straight to the meat counters and bought pork chops to cook
for supper. He usually despaired of us, wandering about or debating over a piece of
smelly cheese that we didn't really need. Invariably, I was the one running behind to
catch up and he was the one waiting for me, so that we could move on. Jack was never
keen on the smelly cheese anyway, but for quite different reasons. Since he had broken
his arm, he had slept in the make-up bed in the dinning area of the Beast because it
was more spacious and comfortable. The only trouble was that it was just opposite the
fridge, so when Simon made the early morning tea, and opened the fridge door, Jack
got the classic smell of strong cheese wafting across his pillow. "Oh my god what's in
the fridge?" were the first words he often muttered in the morning. We said that it was
his feet making the smell…it never stopped him raiding the fridge when he was hungry
though, and at thirteen years of age, that was almost constantly.

We had just a few days left in Portugal before having to return to Algeciras. Jack's
arm was healing well and we were looking forward to moving on to Italy. Our plan was
made - but you know what happens when you make a plan – someone else may have
other ideas.

Behind every silver lining

Well, behind every silver lining is that big black cloud waiting to pour all over you, and our next big black cloud was imminent. Thursday 19th February was not a good day. We were having a lazy afternoon at camp to catch up on clothes washing and writing letters, when at 4.30pm we received an urgent call from Louis, one of my sons back in England. He'd been contacted by Basildon Hospital because his brother, Peter, had been admitted with serious head injuries as a result of an accident at work. From what we could gather, an extremely heavy, oak A frame, had fallen onto his head, crushing it onto another frame that he had been working on. Simon managed to contact the hospital, who confirmed that Peter was in the Intensive Care Unit and that his injuries were very serious.

How quickly everything can change when you hear this kind of news. Everything that you considered important before becomes meaningless and your priorities become absolutely basic – I needed to return to England immediately. We spent the rest of that evening on the telephone gathering information and next morning we drove to Faro airport to book a flight home. Simon and Jack were going to stay with the motor home and continue to Algeciras for Jacks last appointment and I would fly back to be with Peter. Where and when we would see each other again, we did not know.

Early next morning we said goodbye at Faro airport, which was incredibly difficult to do, and for me it would also be goodbye to lovely Portugal. After four months together in the motor home, travelling, eating, sleeping and exploring so much together, I was very sad to be leaving Jack and Simon. We had become a very strong unit and I felt somehow that I would never return, but I was beside myself with worry for Peter. So, as is often the case when you are a parent, I wished I could divide myself in two. The plane left the warm, green Algarve and within a few hours I was landing at cold, grey Stanstead. It seemed like a different world and I felt desolate; but I was not alone. There to meet me at the airport was Stella, Simon's kind sister, or an angel in disguise! She whisked us straight to the hospital and before long we were sitting at Peter's bedside. He was badly hurt and it would be a long haul to a full recovery. He'd suffered cranial fractures, severe concussion, nerve damage which was affecting his eye movement and facial muscles, lacerations and bruising; but he was alive and considering the accident, that was something of a miracle.

I won't dwell on that time in England. Stella and I will never forget our weekend in an Essex motel, (even though we would quite like to!). I will always remember that week when, after she had left, I had lodgings in the nurse's quarters next to the hospital and spent each day sat at Peter's bedside. When he was released from hospital, Stella drove us back to Hereford; Simon's mother offered to have Peter stay with her, while he recovered further, and until he could return to his own flat. I stayed on with him, until he kindly but firmly said that he really didn't need me fussing over him like a mother hen anymore. Now almost a year later he is still not fully recovered but is his old self again. No matter what age your children are, the umbilical cord is never really cut. Leaving him again and leaving all of the family again, was an emotional roller coaster. I cried all the way to the airport in the back of our friends' car. Then they pushed me onto a plane back to Gibraltar, where I was meeting up with Simon and Jack. Once again, I wished that I could divide myself in two and once again I thanked my lucky stars that we had such wonderful friends and family.

I flew back on a late afternoon flight and as we passed over Spain I watched the day end as the sun set through the clouds on the horizon. I felt suspended in a blue sky, with all the time in the world to think, while the sun slowly turned a deep red and sank behind the earth. It was a journey of reflection; of weighing up what life really meant to me and what was important; of facing truths and considering the past. That time which few of us ever get on our busy planet, a time when we can stop and think. As the sun dropped, the landscape below us darkened, each small detail quickly disappearing, and as we banked over the Spanish coast the sea merged with the black land and only the twinkling lights of towns and villages showed us where the difference was. Looking down, as we flew parallel to the shore, I followed the lights of towns that we had driven through, months before, on our way down to Portugal. Now I was flying over it all. You just never know what life has in store for you. Eventually, Gibraltar appeared in the distance, jutting out and up into the blackness, alive with lights, beckoning us down to life on earth again. We circled around the end of the Rock, over the lights of bobbing boats and as we dropped lower, we turned and banked, dipping one wing almost into the inky sea before straightening out to skim over the water and touch down on the tiny strip of runway which straddles the Rock. Now I felt an achingly long way from England, and much too far away from my other boys, but I was longing to see Simon and Jack again. As I walked through customs and out into the small arrivals area at the airport I saw them waiting by the rail. Big smiles and hugs all round, it was wonderful to be united again, but my head felt totally spaced out, as if I was continually in the wrong place, and I suddenly felt exhausted.

We awoke to a view of the Rock again and a wonderful sunny morning in La Linea. I still felt as if I were in some strange time warp and it took many days for me to get back into life on the road. We walked and talked on the beach and Jack collected yet more, small smooth pieces of coloured glass, for that mosaic that we would one day make. Then we packed up the motor home and headed back up the coast, with my eyes leaking periodically, each time I re-lived the recent roller coaster ride that I seemed to have been on. We called Peter daily now and continued to keep in close contact throughout the rest of the trip. We also decided that we would not try to go to Morocco. It seemed that we were fated not to get there and with time slipping by, we decided to head back up through Spain and on to Italy. That evening, we stopped on a quiet stretch of road next to the sea and after a barbecue we had a bonfire of driftwood, well into the night.

The next few days were hard for all of us. We had to settle back into a routine again and we were all feeling tired and emotionally spent. We were also still worried about Peter and what the final outcome of the accident would be, and although he assured us that he was ok, we knew that it was early days. We trundled along, through the usual beautiful countryside, but I found it hard to appreciate it and my mind was usually somewhere else, miles away. Simon was also feeling tired, having worried about Peter and me while I was away. So, with all of us in a bit of a state, it's not surprising that we have some fairly grim memories of Mojacar.

The town of Mojacar itself was fine, but us getting there was not so good. We had turned off the motorway just past Almeria, in order to head down to the coast to wild camp for the night. However, we had taken a very narrow road which followed a precarious route down to the sea and Simon had to concentrate hard to ensure that we stayed on the road and not in the ditch either side. I didn't make it any easier by twitching like a nervous wreck and repeatedly saying that we were 'awfully close to the edge' again. Then, when we were about to swing onto a very small, rather rickety looking wooden bridge, Jack chose that particular moment to try to get the camera out of the cupboard above his head. He reached the camera, but let the sprung cupboard door slam shut with a loud bang, at the very moment when Simon needed a steady hand at the wheel. The resulting jerk of Simon's head as he looked round to see what the hell the bang was, caused all of his neck muscles to leap into a spasm. Yep, it's funny how these little things can escalate into a disaster. Luckily, we hadn't hit anything, not that we could see anyway, but Simon's neck was now seized solid and he had to turn his whole body to look right or left, rather like a robot.

When we arrived in Mojacar you could have cut the air with a knife. We drove along the coastal road, looking for somewhere to stop and saw up ahead a large parking area. We were just about to swing into it, when once more I panicked about the rather high kerb and caused Simon to falter, seizing his neck muscles yet again! I felt absolutely miserable. As before, Jack did the sensible thing, got out his book and ignored us, while we had a fairly major row, well as best Simon could considering his inability to move his head anymore. Looking back on it now, we can laugh of course. But at the time... well you can imagine the rest. Needless to say, we stayed at Mojacar for a couple of days and it did us good to relax a little again. Jack and I cycled to the nearest pharmacy and managed to buy Simon several packets of Relaxabies, which were the recommended tablet for relaxing muscles and we just hoped that they didn't relax too many of them. He spent two days with a hot water bottle against his neck, semi-co-matose on Relaxabies and I tried not to be a complete pain in the arse anymore. Never easy, I can tell you.

Well, we got our act together again. It didn't take long, just some good nights sleep, and we were ready to head off. Up past Lorca, to Murcia, with its vast fertile plains of neatly sown vegetable crops; mile after mile of orange, olive and almond groves; cherry trees and grape vines as far as the eye could see, and all with a blush of bright spring leaves. Up into Valencia's rolling hills, where we stopped in an empty motorway car park for the night and had a fabulous view down a long valley to the coast and Valencia itself.

Pressing on up the coast, we eventually stopped at a campsite at Villanova, about forty kilometres south of the capitol of Catalonia. Yes, before we finally left Spain, we were going to visit Barcelona.

They say that if you only visit one city in Spain, then it should be Barcelona and this place certainly had it all as far as we were concerned. Spreading from the Costa Dorada (the Golden Coast), back towards the lower foothills of the Pyrenees, this great Catalonian city offers you tradition and modernism all in one breath and you will need a good three days to enjoy just some of it.

Probably the most famous attraction in this exciting city is the modernist, art nouveau architecture of the late 19th and early 20th centuries. The mixture of Moorish, Gothic and Art Nouveau is all eclipsed by the totally unique and uncompromising work of Antoni Gaudi. His imprint on the city draws tourists from all over the world and one thing is for sure, you may love them or you may hate them, but one thing you cannot do, is ignore his buildings. We decided to just get our bearings on the first foray in, so the next day, which was March 11th, we caught the public transport into the city centre. A local bus ran every thirty minutes from the campsite gates to Villanova train station, and the trains ran from there to Barcelona every fifteen minutes. We caught the 9.30 bus in and then hopped onto the next train. The bus journey did become rather tedious, as it took a meandering route through the town, but the trains were fast, clean, electric and double-decker, with plenty of room. The whole journey took about one hour but we thought that driving and parking would probably take as long and at least we could relax and read while on the train.

We alighted at a fairly central underground station, (Passieg de Gracia) and walked up the stairs to street level. Barcelona buzzed all around us and as we gazed in some confusion at our surroundings, we saw directly opposite us our first Gaudi offering - the Casa Batilo. This many storied building, with its weird and wonderfully shaped balconies and windows, has Gaudi's unmistakable signature of free flowing lines, rounded edges and dripping stonework. Straight lines and sharp edges hardly exist in nature and Gaudi's designs, based on natural forms, would not entertain them either. Like a cake that has dripped its soft icing down the pillars and supports, over balconies and doorways, this building looked good enough to eat. As always, it is a matter of taste, but I loved Gaudi's creations, if only because they always made me smile. Bizarre, crazy, unconventional; they were certainly different. We joined the masses and predictably photographed it from every angle.

Following our city map of Barcelona, with Jack leading the way as tour leader, we took a stroll down to the largest square in Spain, the Placa de Catalunya, with its fountains and statues and its wide-open space in the centre of the city. From there we headed down what must surely be, the most well known street in Barcelona – namely 'La Rambla'. You have got to walk down this famous boulevard as it has masses of entertainment value, even though, as a major tourist attraction, you may have to watch out for light fingered pick pockets. Wide and lined with shady trees, this pedestrian area takes you straight through the heart of the old quarter and then down to the towering column of Columbus and the newly developed harbour area. But you will not be able to hurry down La Rambla because at every step, you will want to stop and watch some elaborately dressed street artist, or hover at the edge of a crowd who are studying a gambling game, or admire some of the caged birds stacked five high and ten across at the pet stalls or simply sit on one of the available benches and people watch. We dawdled and wandered our way down, Simon usually in the lead trying to hustle Jack and me along a little faster than a snails pace. We couldn't resist studying the many, many street artists in their amazing costumes, who stood like statues and then, for a handful of small change, would perform a clockwork routine, ending perfectly statue-like again. Our favourite, who we just had to watch several times was the man dressed completely in yellow, with a whitened face, his hair and coat tails standing straight out behind him; he looked as if a strong wind was permanently blowing against him. He performed a slow motion run forward and then reversed back, ending like a statue again. A close second were the pair of silver angels, dressed in layers of long, flowing, silvery grey material, huge feathered wings on their backs, who acted out a slow motion dance, ending with a flourish as they handed you a little silver star as a keepsake. Che Guevara, President Lincoln, and moon-walking Michael Jackson, to name but a few, were all down this street.

Flower stalls competing for the best display of colourful blooms; stalls selling small yellow and blue song birds, singing heartily despite their confined surroundings; book stalls, pavement artists, beggars, and conmen with eastern European accents who worked in teams as they gathered in a crowd and took bets on which upturned cup had a ball beneath it. Older locals, plumped down onto plastic chairs at the side of the street with their shopping bags full of fresh market produce. They passed the time of day with acquaintances or just snoozed in the sun. It was fascinating. No wonder Simon had a problem keeping us moving. However, at last we found ourselves at the end of La Rambla and standing at the foot of the monument to Columbus.

Columbus was of course Italian by birth. He also lived in Portugal for some of his life, but it was King Ferdinand and Queen Isabella of Spain who became his patrons and financed his repeated expeditions of discovery. He is buried in the cathedral at Seville but this monument to him was built in 1888 at the harbour front of Barcelona. Standing around 200 feet tall it is an easy landmark to spot, with its stone plinth, winged statues all with open arms to embrace the world, and 167 foot Corinthian column. At the top of the column stands Columbus, ready to sail off again, with a chart in one hand, and pointing out to sea with the other. It is a grand monument, but the best part for us, (which many people didn't seem to realise), was that at the base of the plinth, down some steps, was a very small door and through that door was the entrance to a tiny lift which would take you up the inside of the iron column to the very top. We had to do it of course, here and now, although it looked a little perilous to me. We squeezed into the tiny cylindrical lift, which only took four people at a time and one of those was the lift operator, and up we went. At the top we edged our way out to stand at Columbus's feet and gaped through carved, stone portholes at a 360-degree panoramic view of Barcelona. I found it totally un-nerving, although amazing, and I clung to the centre post unable to look straight down. It felt as if we were going to topple over at any moment, but Jack and Simon became absorbed in identifying the many different areas and landmarks of Barcelona - which was totally up their street.

I finally dragged them back down to earth again and we started to head back through the old quarters of the harbour area to catch the train home. In one street we passed a throng of young students who were marching with placards, sporting black ribbons. We stopped one of them to ask what it was all about and he told us that it was a spontaneous march as 130 people had been killed in a train bomb in Madrid that morning.

It was sobering news. They passed on by and we walked back to the station, now aware of growing police activity and groups of people gathering at newspaper stands. The train home was unusually quiet, with commuters mostly reading of the day's terrible event and obviously feeling very emotional. The final toll was closer to two hundred people killed in Madrid, and all of Spain was in mourning. It was a very sad day for the Spanish people and indeed for people everywhere. The following evening more than eight million people took to the streets throughout Spain to protest. It was the biggest mass protest ever seen in the country; 1.2 million marched through Barcelona alone and most cities were brought to a standstill, such was the feeling of frustration, anger and grief. Everywhere, we saw the Spanish flag, draped from windows and public places, with the black ribbon of mourning drawn upon it. People wore the black looped ribbon, and official flags were flown at half-mast. It clearly demonstrated a country whose people were not afraid to show their emotions.

We didn't get home until 8.0pm that night. I guess we had overdone it again, and the next day we were shattered. We stayed at camp, played table tennis, did some washing by hand because there were no machines at this camp site and the laundry service was very expensive, and generally planned the next few days in Barcelona. (by the way, the shower block was excellent, dix points, and although we could have used our own shower, we used theirs instead). Travelling and touristing can be more exhausting than you think and we always needed a few days rest in between all of the sightseeing. But, having taken a break, we were all fired up again the following day and caught the 9.0 am bus into Villanova and the train to Barcelona again. The train was not very busy and the ride was uneventful apart from the two Peruvian type buskers who played a guitar and whistled on a flute, with a background accompaniment of recorded music that they pulled along in a shopping bag on wheels.

After about five minutes of this strumming and whistling music, they went round the carriage with their hat outstretched, asking for money. At first we found this mildly entertaining but it didn't take long for us to get bored with this type of busking. It happened on most trains that we travelled on and as you had to either try to ignore the noise or give them a euro to go away, we soon became as immune as the regular Spanish commuters. The trouble was that confined to a train you felt rather trapped, with no way of escaping from them. They were usually able to walk through the carriages, but if that were not possible, they would wait until we stopped at a station and then hop out of one carriage and into the next, to start playing again. They played their way to Barcelona and back every day doing this. A young woman was sat opposite us and I wanted to ask her if busking was a regular occurrence. I bravely started with my "Por favoure" and was stumbling through some incomprehensible Spanish when she kindly put me out of my misery by answering in perfect English. She was from Bath and had been teaching in an International School for about eight months. We discussed her life in Spain for the rest of the journey and at the end I asked if she had worked out what made the Spanish 'tick'. She confirmed that 'the family' was all-important, but apart from that, she was none the wiser. Well, there was no hope for us then. With only a few months in the country we'd never understand.

We caught the tube to Porto Nova, to the Maritime Museum situated in the beautiful 14th Century Royal Shipyards. This was the type of place where Simon and Jack were trailing behind for once, taking in every detail on the exhibits, and I was lapping them as I made my second tour round, having completed the first in record time. It was very interesting, but only if you were keen on sailing I think. Although, now that I think back to it, I remember a surprisingly large amount about the different boats and their construction, which says a lot for the quality of the exhibition. From there we walked to the Parc de la Ciutadella, another of Gaudi's landmarks. This large park has as its main feature, a waterfall on a grand scale with cascades which tumble from a great height over weed covered boulders and winged statues. Stone steps lead to the top of this edifice and fountains spring up from the waters of the enormous pool into which the water flows. However, on the day that we were there, I have to say that it was not working and the whole area was littered with rubbish and dirt. Gaudi would be turning in his grave and we moved on rather quickly, by hopping into a taxi and taking a quick ride to the Picasso museum. Our dogs were beginning to bark.

Picasso lived in Barcelona during a very productive time in his life and this museum holds more than 3000 pieces, including paintings, drawings, engravings and ceramics. The queues to enter the medieval mansion, which holds the collection, were unfortunately almost as large as the collection itself and we took one look and again moved on. I would have loved Jack to see some of Picasso's original works as he had studied the artist briefly at school, but it was not to be. Another day maybe. Now we simply walked back through the city and enjoyed it at a more leisurely pace – after all, there was always plenty to see in Barcelona.

Gaudi's Creations

Our fourth day and another train ride in. This time there were no Peruvian buskers, just a well-dressed lady going from carriage to carriage distributing a hand made leaflet explaining that she had an illness. When she collected the leaflets up again, she also collected money; should she be given any? Begging was very common in both Spain and Italy and it came in all shapes and sizes. From the business-like approach, as in this case, to little children who were regularly dumped outside supermarkets for the day, in all weathers, to beg from customers as they entered and left. Homeless, limbless, cradling babies, playing music, performing, or with hand written notices propped in front of them, the city streets were their streets. It was another side of life, which we could not know, and maybe with luck would never know.

That day we were going to see Gaudi's most famous construction, and one which is still being built according to his designs, even though he died in 1926; the Temple of the Sacred Family.....the Sagrada Familia. We had walked to La Pedrera, another Gaudi apartment block of flowing grey stone and then taken two underground trains to reach the nearest tube station to this amazing building, although the word 'building' seems hardly adequate for the Sagrada. This is another of those creations that offers you enticing glimpses long before you've actually reached it. As we walked through a small park, we could see above the trees in front of us, extravagant, sculptured towers reaching 100 meters into the clear, blue sky. These looked impressive and we quickened our steps, eager to see the whole thing.

It's difficult to grasp the magnitude of this building, even when you're standing before it with your head tilted so far back that your neck starts to ache, in order to look up at the intricate carvings which smother every inch of its complicated façade. Gaudi undertook the design and construction of the 'Temple of the Holy Family' in 1883 and now, nearly 125 years later, it is still a long way from finished. A rough guess is that it may take another 70 years of painstaking work to complete. So, you may wonder, what is it about this building that will warrant almost 200 years of labour, spanning three separate centuries which include two world wars. It was started just before the days of Art Nouveau, ten years before Henry Ford rolled out his first mass produced car and at the height of the British Empire, and is still under construction in today's modern high tech, stream-lined world; it will carry on being built in tomorrow's unknown future. The Sagrada Familia still grows according to Gaudis original vision; his greatest obsession and his greatest gift to Barcelona. The answer must be the pure uniqueness. There are many great buildings in the world; from pyramids to mosques, castles to cathedrals, but this one has no comparison. It will surely be one of the Wonders of the World when it is finished. To date, only eight of the twelve, 100 meter tall, bell towers, dedicated to the Apostles, have been completed. The transept and the apse will be crowned by six domes, dedicated to the four Evangelists, the Virgin Mary and Jesus Christ. This last one will be 170 meters high and will be crowned with a cross. As Gaudi once said, "The Temple grows slowly, but this has always been the case with everything destined for a long life. Hundred year old oak trees take many years to grow; on the other hand, reeds grow quickly, but in autumn the wind blows them down and there is no more to be said". On that basis, I would say that the Sagrada Familia will be here to stay for centuries to come. Gaudi died in 1926, hit by a streetcar when crossing a road, and by that time he had dedicated 43 of his 74 years to this building.

We approached from the western side and entered through the 'Portals of Passion'. The roof of this façade, which represents the death of Christ, is supported by six sloping angular columns reminiscent of clean, stretched bones. Set into the walls above you, are groups of very angular, almost severe carved figures, with heads bowed in grief, epitomising agony, death and sorrow. These stark sculptures, by Joseph Ma. Subriachs, are quite unlike any others on the building. Joining the queue of multi-national visitors we shuffled our way forward, at last entering the nave and transept. The work here is only partially completed and we walked through a semi-building site of scaffolding and stone as we gazed ever upward through, what felt like, a forest canopy of stone columns and arches. Nothing is of regular shape here. Columns resemble trees, light recesses resemble flower heads, edges are curved and decoration is everywhere. Enormous stained glass windows tower upwards and before long we had neck ache again. Of course it was busy, and at some points we felt that we were on a conveyor belt of people, moving though the church, but it must be extremely difficult to balance the complex construction problems alongside the huge numbers of tourists who visit here daily, year round. As usual we had to get to the highest point possible, and soon joined the upwardly spiralling queue which was inching its way slowly to the top of one of the completed towers.

If you suffer from claustrophobia then spending a good half an hour, inching your way slowly up a tiny, spiral staircase inside a 100 meter tall stone tower is not for you. Occasionally we were able to glimpse Barcelona through thin slit windows, as it gradually diminished below us, but most of the time we enjoyed the view of a large Dutch bottom in front of us and a chasm like drop to the side. As time went by we all became quite chatty, which was just as well considering our proximity to each other. The casual conversation also prevented me from dwelling on the image of trying to extricate someone, from this completely blocked spiral staircase, in the event of a heart attack. Panic could easily have taken over, given the right set of circumstances, or maybe that was just my over active imagination getting bored. Anyway, eventually we reached the first of two balcony areas where we could step out and get a dizzying view of the awesome dimensions, both interior and exterior. Alongside us sculpted white doves decorated a swaying, leaf covered stone tower. Below us, were the pointed tops of other towers, with their bizarre and intricate carvings and below that, miniature people walked the streets. At this point we could explore several towers, like a maze at altitude, or a tree-top canopy. Crossing a stone arch, which linked one tower to the next, we started upward again to reach the very highest point. Here even Simon and Jack had vertigo. It was all quite staggering; the views of Barcelona and across to the sea, the sheer scale of the proposed buildings and the elaborate detail carved into every sinuous line and stylised flower. We came down through the one way system, eventually reaching terra firma again and worked our way round to the museum, where priceless original scale models and drawings beautifully illustrated what the completed building would look like.

We finally left by the Nativity portal, alongside a group of excited Japanese tourists who skittered back and forth taking it in turns to be photographed in front of this remarkable east facing façade. Dedicated to the birth and life of Christ, this entrance was supervised by Gaudi himself. His distinctive style is unmistakable here, as the stonework sweeps and flows over the building, every inch covered with elaborate carving. Angels, shepherds, birds, flowers and the story of Christ's early life materialise from the façade as you look more deeply into its depths. It is simply amazing and would be too much for some, but as always, it cannot be ignored.

That day we were going for broke, because after viewing the Sagrada Familia, we then got out our street map of Barcelona and put Jack in charge of guiding us to yet another Gaudi offering, wondering if this man ever slept in his incredibly creative life. Did I say that you would need a week to see Barcelona, I should have said a month, and Parc Guell should not be missed. This is where Gaudi turned his hand to landscape gardening and if you are expecting linear paths and regular flowerbeds, you will be in for yet another surprise. Today's landscape architects would be hard put to create a more bizarre and unusual park.

Commissioned by his wealthy friend, Count Eusebi Guell, Parc Guell was originally intended to be a housing development with a difference – but it was never completed and only two of the proposed sixty houses were ever built. One of them being the house that Gaudi lived in for the last twenty years of his life. It is almost the forerunner to Disneyland, such is its fairytale, gingerbread, organic style, with twisting walkways of warped imitation tree trunks, a lizard fountain of brightly coloured mosaic and snaking seating which wraps around a promenade giving panoramic views of Barcelona. Palm trees and exotic foliage decorate balconies and pagodas with all the supports and pillars designed along the lines of nature, although to me, the natural became the unnatural which almost became the natural again. It was almost too much, even for us. But whenever I saw Gaudi creations, they always made me smile and laugh; he broke all the rules and somehow got away with it. He pushed design and creation to its limits, demanding that you stop – and look, and think about your surroundings. There's nothing bland or safe about Gaudi creations, they shriek 'look at me, I'm different'.

Trekking around the Parc, liking some parts more than others, we eventually reached the very top plaza. Here we flopped down beside a line of tourists along the cliff-top edge of the large open square and dangled our aching legs over the drop. The grid like shape of Barcelona, stretched out before us beneath a sunny haze, as far as the eye could see, its famous landmarks clearly visible. Phew, one more Gaudi to go and then we would have seen the lot!

We slept almost all the way back to camp that evening, the train humming along with the usual commuters whose numbers gradually dwindled as the train got further and further away from the city. At Villanova the bus had just left, so we gratefully crawled into a taxi and took the quick route back to the campsite. The Beast, our home on wheels, was there waiting. We became so adept at living in our motor home that a routine had easily been established. I would start the food preparation while Si opened the wine. Jack would raid the fridge for a quick snack and then either watch TV or relax with his book. Habits of a life time are hard to break. That evening another big American RV rolled into our almost empty parking area, but we were too tired to socialise, so it was not until the next day that we met and got to know another set of new neighbours, namely Sean and Michelle.

This young couple had left England with the same plan as us, which was to spend a year in Europe, but they had had nothing but disasters since the moment they hit France. On the first night they'd awoken to find two men searching through the front section of their motor home. Luckily, Sean was a big man, so he had scared the intruders back out of the window that they'd broken in through. This had left them feeling very nervous about wild camping again. After that they'd been very unlucky with the campsites they'd selected and had spent a fortune driving a long way off their chosen route when trying to meet up with friends who never materialised. They were also towing a large trailer behind them, containing two Superbikes, a scooter and a complete mobile work shop, and we thought we were brave. Now, they were on their way down to southern Spain, but were being held up by an electrical problem on their RV which kept cutting out the wipers, indicators, electric steps and other essentials. They seemed doomed and we felt very sorry for them.

We were taking a day off to recover from touristing, but Simon soon had his tool box out and had joined with Sean in trying to discover where the problem lay. It was a tricky one, but after several hours on their backs under the chassis, they eventually found a well-hidden, partly severed cable, which was only connecting intermittently – problem solved. We spent the evening with them and next day they rolled on they're way again. They made it safely down to a campsite on the sunny Spanish coast and as far as we know are still there.

It was now mid March and the weather was good, with a warm sun and very little rain. The year was racing on. We had one more trip into Barcelona planned and then we too, would be heading off, but our next major stop would be in Italy. We were now quite used to catching buses and underground tube trains, to scoot from one area of Barcelona to another, so before long we were climbing the steps of the National Museum of Modern Art, another great building set majestically at the top of a wide avenue of steps and terraces, with flowing fountains cascading in tiers before it. Unfortunately, many of the exhibits were closed for alteration, so apart from Fortuny's famous and beautiful painting, 'Beach at Porcini,' we saw very little inside the gallery. On for a quick coffee and sandwich, and then back to the Guell Palace, for our booked tour of one of the first modern buildings to be declared part of the World Heritage by UNESCO in 1985.

Once again, the wealthy Eusebi Guell had commissioned Gaudi to design this city family-residence for himself, as an extension of the small palace he already had just around the corner, on la Rambla. (Both houses are connected by a devious passage through the city). This house has two main entities, which are almost in contrast with each other. One is the interior of the house, and the other is the rooftop. The main façade, built of local limestone, has magnificent wrought iron gates set in parabolic arches. Entwined serpents, twisted metal and the dark brooding shape of a phoenix rising from the ashes, greet the visitor as he walks through the entrance and into the double vestibule. Carriages would stop here, and the horses would be led down a spiralling brick ramp to the stables under the house. Even the stables were carefully designed in the modernistic style and the fungi-form capitols and columns, in exposed brick work, are some of best known of Gaudi's architectural perspectives. The rest of the house is almost brooding, with heavy iron, marble and dark wood, used in natural flowing shapes. The roof top on the other hand, is a complete contrast, as if Gaudi got bored with the gloom of the interior, and when reaching the roof, felt that he just had to introduce some colour somewhere. This is, of course, where you will find the famous gaudy, Gaudi chimneys, quite unique to him. Distorted shapes and fantastical decorations in fragmented tile or glass or pottery have transformed the twenty chimneys on this flat rooftop into something from Alice in Wonderland. No two chimneys are alike, and all are unlike any chimneys you will see anywhere else. He certainly knew how to make a statement. We must have photographed them all from every angle, before deciding that we really had walked one monument too many. We wandered back to the train station through the streets of Barcelona, taking one last look at this great city. As always, there were many wonderful sites that we still hadn't seen, but our time was up and we would now be leaving Spain. Italy was beckoning, our route was planned, and it was time to go.

Moving on, after a long stay somewhere, was never a problem because we had a good routine which ran like clockwork, with all three of us having a part to play. We did it so often that we could get it down to record time, which was sometimes essential. Outside lockers were all checked and secured, the roof lights were closed, hook up disconnected, TV aerial wound down and satellite dish secured. The legs were raised, awning wound in and picnic table pushed back into its slot. Inside, all lose items were quickly stowed to their right positions, cushions were stuffed into overhead cupboards to stop the contents from moving too much, the fridge contents were checked and secured, water pump turned off and drawers all put into locked position so that they didn't fly out as we went around corners. We gathered our books, drinks and camera into easily reached positions and off we went. Rather like living on a boat, every item had a specific place in the motor home and once we had got used to living this way, it was extremely easy. We could move our home daily and although our surroundings may change, our home remained exactly the same. Every night, Jack made his bed up and every morning he unmade it. This may sound tedious, but actually it took only minutes to do and was no problem. If we were leaving a campsite, it was Jack's job to fill the fresh water tank while Simon emptied the grey and black waste tanks. Most campsites had the facilities to do this and because of the large capacity of our tanks we could 'wild camp' and live independently for about three weeks at a time, when we wished to.

Back on the road again we left Spain and entered Southern France. How nice it was to be back amongst those great 'aires' which provided such good facilities to drivers. Following the motorway past Perpignan, we eventually pulled up just outside Narbonne, at a lake-side camp site in La Nautique. Something about seeing the name Narbonne on our map had made us decide to stop near there for the weekend to take a look around. We knew nothing about the area, but it had a pleasant feel, and warranted a visit. The campsite was run by a Dutch family who made us most welcome. Its quirky feature being that each pitch had its own toilet and shower house in the form of a small, wooden, chalet type building, to which you were given the key. Yet another variation on shower blocks around Europe.

The countryside around this area looked excellent for cycling, so we soon had our bikes off the back of the Beast for an exploratory run. Jack hadn't ridden his since he broke his arm in Tarifa, but after a long circuit of the lake he pronounced himself fit enough for the Tour de France. A little exaggeration maybe, but he felt great to be back in the saddle. Over that weekend we cycled the quiet lanes to Narbonne, a picturesque town of interesting buildings and bridges. Chaining our bikes to the ubiquitous lamp-post, we wandered the Sunday morning market and food hall, tempted as always by the superbly fresh fish and vegetables. We bought duck breasts, salads, fruit and local wine, forgetting of course that we only had our ruck sacks and bikes to get it all home and Jack unerringly homed in on the only stall selling BB guns. How wonderfully focused kids can be, when it suits them.

Dividing the centre of this town is the Canal de la Robine , and complete with brightly painted, flower decked, canal boats, it was obviously well used. It joins a vast network of canals including the famous Canal du Midi and the extensive inland waterways would allow you to cross France and reach the Bay of Biscay if you wished. It would surely provide a wonderfully scenic route. Another long cycle ride took us through the countryside towards the coast. Again we followed quiet lanes alongside the picturesque canal. Over locks, past ruined houses that looked ripe for restoration and perfect mini chateaux that had already been rescued and redeemed. Lizards basked on stone walls in the warm sun and pretty views enticed us on. With the wind behind us, we went too far for too long, as always, and coming home, against the wind, took us twice the time and twice as much puff. We never reached the coast, which is only about 14 kilometres from Narbonne, but if we had we would have seen salt marshes, coastal lakes and sandy beaches. This whole area was very pleasant and unspoilt.

Our weekend break over, we motored on again, sleeping overnight along with the juggernaughts in the 'aires de service'. We stopped for lunch in a lay-by overlooking Cannes, and then sped on past the hectic resorts of Nice, Monaco, Monte-Carlo and Menton, before eventually crossing into Italy. With so much of Europe left to see, and with five months of our year already gone, we made a conscious decision not to stop in Southern France. Tempting and beautiful as that area was, we knew that we could easily go back there another day. We'd also left behind the warmer weather of southern Spain, and the cooler climate of the French Riviera in March was not nearly so appealing. It was time to tackle Italy, so armed with the maps, guide books and our Italian phrase book, we set our sites on Florence and with Maisy leading the way, we started down the long Italian coast in search of 'la dolce vita'.

March

La Dolce Vita

It's difficult to work out what it is about a country that makes you either love it, or hate it. Is it the climate, the landscape, the food, the people or your own personal experience of all those things? When we think back over the whole year, we always say that we felt most at home in Portugal; we were very happy in Sicily (which was Jack's favourite) and we all liked Croatia and Slovenia. We liked the unpretentiousness of those countries and the natural friendliness of the people. I had no pre-conceptions about Italy, as I had never been there before. Simon had driven all the way down through it, many years ago, when he had been travelling to Africa and had memories of crazy Italian drivers and difficult paperwork. What did we think of Italy when we left it nine weeks later? Well, you'll have to read on to find out, but with hindsight, my advice is that sometimes its best not to try to understand a country, just enjoy it!

We entered Italy on the E80 motorway at what felt like turbo speed, on yet another highway to hell. Italian roads are amazing. They are drilled through mountains and dangled over gorges in complete defiance of the natural terrain. We had left the quieter, wider roads of France and I soon found myself clinging to the side of my seat again. If we had been in a car, the crash barriers would have seemed reliable and comforting, but sitting several feet above them, as we skimmed alongside plummeting valleys, was utterly unnerving. We had joined another lemming-like flow of speeding cars and juggernaughts; darting through endless, darkened tunnels and then out onto teetering windy viaducts, rather like a strobe effect, roller coaster ride. Simon gripped the steering wheel, constantly checking wing mirrors, to keep us within our narrow lane and Jack and I gripped our seats. The views to the coast, as we sped over gorges and valleys, were fantastic and down below us the small road next to the sea looked very inviting as it wound its way through villages and towns. It would be too small for us though, and anyway, we had to get some miles behind us if we were going to get to Florence.

Italy has a flat northern plain, which is its industrial and agricultural heartland. This is edged to the north and west by the Alps and to the south by the Apennine mountain range, which runs like a spine down the centre of Italy. About 75% of the Italian peninsular is mountainous, so traffic is heavily concentrated on the main motorways. We battled on, hoping to find a service station for a brief respite but they were almost non-existent on this stretch of road and it wasn't until 5 o'clock in the afternoon that we pulled into one and stopped for the night. Once again, we were glad that we had stopped early in the day, because by 5.45pm we were totally blocked in by lorries and coaches of all nationalities. Our neighbour, a French lorry driver, set about the ritual cooking of his evening meal 'a la primus stove' and shared it all with his Siamese cat, who sat contentedly on a cushioned platform area in the front window of his cab. A coach load of children pulled in on the other side of us; the children rapidly escaped and recklessly used the car park as a play area, whilst more lorries streamed in, until it was all nicely gridlocked.

No one was going to move on in a hurry, certainly not until Romanian, Spanish, French and Italian lorry drivers had stretched their legs and eaten some food. We put the kettle on and I started preparing our evening meal while Jack played a game on the lap top computer and Simon looked at the route for the next day. We could do all of this in the comfort of our home-on-wheels and still be mildly entertained by the argument which was building up to a crescendo in front of us, between a portly Spaniard, whose lorry had been well and truly blocked in and a verbose little Italian. Plenty of horn sounding, shouting and fist waving went on and once again, we could see that lorry drivers in Europe had serious problems when it came to parking for the night.

We slept reasonably well. Nose to tail and side-by-side, cosy you could say, with our multinational lorry drivers, and we were up and away by 7.0am the next morning. We stopped at 9.0am and in my diary I have written – "stopped at 9.0am for coffee and omelettes – feel like running straight back to France. Oh for those big aires and open spaces". It was obviously going to take us a while to settle into Italy. But eventually the landscape began to flatten out and we left the awesome Apennine Mountains behind us for a while. Turning inland, we entered Tuscany country and before long we were travelling through rolling hills, dotted with the famous statuesque cypress trees and ancient olive groves. Every view was a Renaissance painting, with squarely built red-roofed villas, chickens in the vineyards and picturesque woodland. Now all we had to do was find our next campsite.

The one we had chosen as our base was situated 15 kilometres south east of Florence at a small town called Troghi. We had telephoned ahead, concerned that they may not have space for us, but we need not have worried as the season in Italy had hardly begun and no self respecting Italian would be out camping until at least June. We turned off the main road and started to follow directions, but as the afternoon wore on and we delved deeper and deeper into the Tuscan countryside, a tremendous thunderstorm started brewing in the darkening skies above us. By 4.0 pm the heavens had opened with horizontal rain and a noisy and impressive lightening display. As the road began to flood and our visibility dropped to zero we pulled under some trees and gave up. Once more the kettle went on and we got out a pack of cards, ready to sit out the storm, wondering where on earth we were going to end up that night. Two hours later, the evening sun broke through and we headed off again. Five hundred yards later, only round the next few bends, the entrance to Camping Il Poggetto, presented itself.

Maisie got a good telling off for not doing her job a little better, and we rolled into yet another, almost empty campsite.

It had become very obvious, as we travelled around Europe in early spring that most motor-homers were not moving far from the warmth of southern Spain. We encountered fewer and fewer now and didn't really see any more English travellers until we reached Dubrovnik in Croatia, in June. Most of the tourists that we were encountering were obviously on package tours, just visiting the high spots. This campsite near Florence, was not officially opening for the season until the end of March, but they were happy for us and a few other travellers, to park up there and use the facilities.

The rain and storms returned that night and we awoke to a dismal, grey morning. A unanimous vote was soon taken to stay in bed for as long as possible and have a lazy day recovering from our hectic dash into Italy. We took it in turns to walk the three feet necessary to make a cup of tea, and thoroughly enjoyed snuggling under our duvets with good books. When the sun did finally appear again, Jack set up some targets and became 'Sniper Bob, on the job' with his new BB gun, while Simon walked to the village for fresh ciabatta bread and olives. The campsite owners pottered around us, tidying up the storm damage, and complaining about the un-seasonal weather, and as the clouds lifted, beautiful Tuscan views gradually emerged.

Next day, we were up with the Italian larks, (if there are any left in Italy, not in a paté or pie), to catch the bus into Florence. We were going to be able to buy our bus tickets from the campsite reception desk, so clutching our guide books and euros, a small excited group of us hovered there expectantly. However, the owners now pointed out that a spontaneous, nationwide transport strike had occurred, and no buses or trains were running. Oh these impulsive continentals, how they do like to upset things. There was no other way of getting into Florence that day, so that was that. Our little band of hopefuls stood despondent, realising that those carefully made sandwiches, which we were going to eat on the steps of the Uffizi, were now going to be consumed at camp. It just didn't have the same appeal, so we quickly made an alternative plan and persuaded the owners to lend us a detailed map of the area, so that we three could at least go walking.

Re-equipped, we set off again on a long circular ramble that took us up into the hills. It was a stunning day of spring sunshine, with soft blue skies and pillowy white clouds that raced high above us. We climbed the first hill, past fields of solid old olive trees, and lush pastures of yellow dandelions and purple anemones. Endless rows of knobbly, brown vines, lined up over the rolling landscape and thin spirals of smoke, betrayed small bonfires of prunings. There hardly seemed to be anybody else around in the world, except the habitual cockerels that called to each other across the valleys. The Tuscan countryside looked exactly as you see it on postcards; rolling hills dotted with shuttered stone farm houses, their red pan-tiled roofs smouldering in the sun; tall, dark, evergreens which stood together like exclamation marks on the landscape; olive groves, small woods and as a back drop to it all, the snow capped mountains of middle Italy. I absolutely fell in love with Tuscany on that day. It was warm and peaceful and the air smelt sweetly of spring, with just the occasional whiff of wood smoke. We followed the track up to a silent monastery, half hidden at the top of a wooded hill and stopped there on a low wall for a drink and a snack. The view was idyllic. A slender Italian girl, who could have come straight out of a TV advert for a stylish car, came strolling up the track from the other direction and we practised our "Buongiorno's", in unison, which instantly reduced us to hysterical giggles. Luckily for her, we didn't have a clue whether she was a signora or signorina, so we got no further with our conversational Italian. She politely replied and walked on by, probably wondering what three strange Brits were doing sitting on the wall by the monastery. The local cat, who had by this time found us, had no language barriers to bother him and he purred around us like an old friend as he nibbled his way through our biscuits. We continued on our stroll, over the top of the hill and down into the valley on the other side.

Following our map we wandered on, the path leading us through a scrubby wood where we stopped again for tuna rolls and a drink; then I lay down in the warm sun and dozed, while Jack and Simon had target practice with his BB Gun. Scenes from The Godfather drifted through my mind as Marlon Brando's voice was impersonated, and Al Pacino dashed from tree to tree. Boys will be boys, but I have to admit that I was not sad when Jack's cheap bit of plastic fell apart a few days later. We eventually returned to the campsite, having had a memorable and quite unexpected day. That evening we discussed our forthcoming tour of Florence.

"Don't let's try to do too much on the first day", we vowed. But of course, how could we resist!

Italy has so many famous cities, many of which are bursting with art and stuffed to the hilt with treasures, and it's difficult to know where to start. After a while you will become blasé as you walk past priceless statues and over floors of ancient Roman mosaics. We knew that we could never see it all, but as we travelled down the country, we hoped to visit Florence, Pisa, Rome, Pompeii, and Capri. We would then go to the Island of Sicily, and afterwards, we would travel back up Italy on the east coast, catching Venice before we moved on to Croatia. So, next day, with bus tickets in hand, we waited on the stone bridge outside the campsite for the 9.0am bus into Florence.

Italian men, especially those in their prime, have a certain reputation to uphold; be they high powered business men or high powered bus drivers – for there is no such thing as a lowly Italian man. I figured this out as we sat on the bus into Florence. Our driver was young, very well groomed and dressed in a crisp, white shirt and dark suit. (It surely couldn't have been his uniform). His black, immaculately cut hair, perfectly framed his olive skinned, angular face and I dare say that he had excellent eyes, but they were hidden for the whole journey behind sleek, designer sunglasses. And of course, he smelt divine. Yes, I am still describing the bus driver! For most of the ride he was talking animatedly on his mobile phone, which was sometimes wedged between his shoulder and chin and sometimes held in one hand, while he emphasised every point he made, with the other. Sometimes he had both hands waving in the air, as if his flamboyant, Italian gestures were visible to the person on the other end of the phone. We took a while to work out how he was steering our bus down the mountain roads, but finally realised that he was using his knees. A smooth operator. We were slightly worried, but mostly just impressed; in Italy, style is all.

We safely reached the central bus depot in Florence and with Jack holding the town map we headed straight to the main post office. This was not to see some great treasure, but to post letters and parcels to family back home. We regularly sent home a 'round robin' update with printed digital photos; and for our three little grandchildren, there was often a parcel of mementoes, from well-known places. You would think that posting parcels would not be that difficult, and we soon discovered that in some countries it was quite easy, while in others, you would almost have to take a DNA test to get the parcel accepted. At the post office in Florence, which was the most wonderful old building with a long colonnaded front, we had no problems. A few weeks later, when we were in Braccianno, Italian bureaucracy lived up to its reputation and it was a nightmare.

Our tour of the city was about to begin and from what we had read, we had plenty to see. Florence (Firenze), is the regional capitol of Tuscany and one of the most significant centres of the arts in Italy, perhaps even the world. Its long history would fill half of this book, so although I am doing it a great injustice, I will try to abbreviate its past. It is thought that the Etruscans founded Florentia (meaning 'flowering') as a small, fishing settlement on the banks of the river Arno. Around the middle of the first century BC, the Romans, with their canny eye for a good piece of real estate, realised the potential of this fertile river valley and encouraged agricultural and commercial development. The town grew rapidly, despite local wars, the plague and political and religious squabbles. By the 13th century it had become famous as a great trading centre, and for its wool and silk industries. Using secret techniques, they produced unique and highly coloured dyed cloths from Asian silk and un-corded wool, which had arrived from all over Europe through the nearby port of Pisa.

There was such a growth of wealth, that the city even produced its own Florin, made of 24 carat gold, which was accepted all over the known world. This commercial success led to the great building boom of the 13th and 14th centuries and to the creation of the highly important guilds of craftsmen. By the 15th century, wealthy families had risen to power, including the famous Medici family, and the great political and financial input of these families coincided with the revival of classical culture, or as we know it, The Renaissance. The re-birth of the arts.

A certain 'one-upmanship' between the powerful families also ensured that there was plenty of work for the artisans and artists, who were now drawn to the area. This explosion of culture, expressed itself in larger and more ornate palaces, endless frescoes, superb sculptures and immense paintings. The combination of wealth and interest in the arts, proved to be a golden age, which fuelled the careers of geniuses like Michelangelo and Leonardo de Vinci. To its great credit, Florence has carefully preserved its treasures over the ages, for all the world to see. And all the world does visit this small, richly endowed city. It will be busy, no matter what time of the year you visit; American, French, Russian — we heard all languages around us and we were always tripping over crocodile tour groups of speeding Japanese as they beetled from one venue to the next, posing in front of every masterpiece at every photo opportunity. If you visit in the summer then you will have the heat to contend with as well, but if you have always wanted to see the most important and beautiful art works in the world, then go. You won't be disappointed; I want to return, because once was just not enough for me.

'Old' Florence is small enough to allow you to walk between its most famous attractions, so we didn't need to catch tube-trains or buses, but we did need good walking shoes and strong legs. We made our way from the cool, dark post office, to the Piazza del Duomo, to view the world's fourth largest Cathedral (the Duomo) and its accompanying Bell Tower. We approached through narrow, straight streets of imposing angular buildings, which cast heavy shadows and blocked out the sun. Then, turning a corner, we were almost dazzled by the brilliance of the Cathedral in its sunny, open setting, reflecting light from every part of its vast, luminous façade. Every inch is covered in linear detail, carved in white, pink and green marble, like a wedding cake of spectacular proportions. Its huge octagonal dome, built of red brick, rises almost 100 meters and dominates the skyline. Vasari and Zuccari decorated the interior with breathtaking frescoes, and stained glass windows by Donatello allow gently filtered light into this cavernous, cool, dark building. Outside, the marble walls felt smooth and warm, although covered in the grime of a busy city; the stone walls inside were cool and damp, the smell and muted sounds of a great church being unmistakable. We could have climbed to the top of the dome, over 450 steps, but we decided to move on to the Bell Tower, a separate building in the same square, and climb to the top of that instead. Of a similar height, it is just as staggering in its construction.

Again, the façade is covered with marble. Carrara white, Prato green and Maremma pink. A tower of blocks, mounted on each other like elaborate building bricks. We climbed the interior stone steps which gave us access to various open levels, on the way to the summit. These levels had open arched windows, for fine views of Florence, and at the top, when we had got our breath back, we looked across at the people who had climbed to the top of the Duomo dome, as they walked around their own sky-high, viewing balcony. We were all at the highest point in Florence. We could look out at the closely packed red roofs of the sprawling city; the open piazzas, the five storey houses with shuttered windows and overhanging gables, elaborate churches, cloistered walkways and the green rolling hills which surround the flat Florentine basin. The River

Arno, wide and peaceful, flowed through it all, unchanged.

By the time we had descended, our feet were already aching and our stomachs were rumbling. The quieter morning was giving way to more and more crowds, so after a quick sandwich and with guide book in hand, we pressed on to seek out the statues and fountains, markets and palaces, until we too were becoming picky and blasé about which ones were worth seeing and which were not. By now, it was mid afternoon and probably the busiest time of the day. The Uffizi, (art gallery containing an unbelievable number of Renaissance masterpieces) had long, long queues so we bought tickets for another day and returned to view the sculptures in the Loggia (colonnade) at the Palazzo Vecchio.

During this whole time, I had been having great trouble keeping up with Simon and Jack. I was always dawdling behind, to take photographs or peer through doorways into hidden courtyards or just people-watch. Simon, who doesn't have quite the same desire to stand and gawp as I do, was always in front and Jack was usually somewhere in the middle. They were easy to spot; Jack with his bright red hair and Simon because of his height but I, being vertically challenged, was easy to overlook. So, when it came to moving on to the Ponti Vecchio Bridge, Simon and Jack were ready to go while I was being swept along amidst a group of tall, young Americans. I assumed that Simon and Jack had moved on ahead of me, but when I reached the end of the street they were no- where to be seen. The Americans moved off and I was left alone. I determined not to panic or leave the area. So, of course, I panicked and left the area. I didn't realise that Simon and Jack were now behind me and I was heading off alone in front of them. It was a horrible feeling for all of us, as we had no way of contacting each other and we had not arranged a meeting point should we get separated. They had the guide books, not that a map would have meant much to me, and I wondered if I would ever find my way back to the bus station, should I not find them. This may sound pathetic, but that's just what I am. Pathetic. I paced up and down, trying to calmly think what they would do in this situation. How far ahead were they? Or were they even ahead of me? Eventually I decided to re-trace my footsteps back to the last place that we were together, right back to the Loggia. With great relief I saw them, at the side of the square, scanning the crowds from half way up the base of a statue. We had a big hug and I was asked, none too politely, not to go wandering off again. As if I had enjoyed it!

The Ponte Vetchio Bridge is the oldest bridge in Florence, there having been a bridge on this site since Roman days. It was last rebuilt in 1345, with three wide spans allowing room for shops and houses on both sides, and a roadway in the middle. At first, butchers, grocers and general trades people were allowed to sell from these shops, but in 1591 they were all evicted and only goldsmiths were allowed to own them. Over time, additions of differing shapes and styles altered the uniform appearance of the houses and today the charm of the bridge is both its mellow, yellow colour and its positively 'lived in' appearance. A Canaletto painting in real life, but then, Florence is a living museum. The goldsmith's shops now look more like expensive tourist traps and it is hideously busy, but that probably isn't very different to the way it always was. Beggars, peddlers, con men and cafes vie for your money; it's only the goods that have changed. We peered at the overpriced gold bracelets, and fought off the salesmen who were convinced that we wanted to buy their tat, before deciding that we'd had enough and headed back to the bus station.

We had had quite a day and early the next morning I had some rebellion back at camp. A heated discussion arose about the virtues of art and Simon made it clear that he would rather be barbecuing fish on a beach than ogling oil on canvas amongst the crowds. It was expensive and pointless as far as he was concerned. I was hurt, to say the least, and fell into despondency. We had done everything together, and I wanted to share Florence with the others, even if they weren't that keen. Jack opted for the middle road, (he learned diplomacy if nothing else during that year), and said he was happy either way although he was missing his friends. Guilt, guilt and more guilt; just when I was thinking how good things were. We talked it through and I was beginning to admit defeat. "We needn't throw good money after bad. If I'm the only one that enjoys art, then we shouldn't go back to Florence", I said, which seemed to result in Simon and Jack then persuading me that we should go back and see the rest. I expect Freud would explain that one quite easily. Anyway, we quickly scrabbled our stuff together and ran up to reception to buy tickets for the early morning bus.

Waiting at reception were three American girls. They were on a three month back-packing tour of Europe, although one of them certainly had more than a back pack, judging by the enormous suitcase-on-wheels she was dragging around with her. They were friendly and fun and we chatted while we waited, wondering what had happened to the reception staff. The owner arrived at last, and proceeded to inform us that the clocks had changed the night before, it being that time of year, and we had missed the bus into town by one hour. It was also Sunday and the next bus was not until the after-noon. Why is this sort of thing so infuriating? Why don't camp owners put up huge notices or, as in our case, where there were only a few of us staying at this camp, didn't they let us know. How many times we gritted our teeth at the infuriating attitude of some campsites.

Well, we ranted and raved and so did the American girls who had ongoing train tickets booked and had to get to Florence, and eventually we arranged to share two taxis to get us to the nearest train station. From there we would get the next train into the city. The train station was about a twenty minute drive away at a town called Figline Valdarno. Totally in the wrong direction, away from Florence, but the train line from there would take us directly in. After a long wait and several phone calls, the taxis arrived. I suppose that the drivers were having a Sunday morning lay in and it probably hadn't helped that there was a full scale cycle race on the road between us and the train station, which was causing considerable delay. This was turning into one of those ugly days. The taxis whisked us to the station, in what must have been record time judging by the way they scattered the poor cycle race before them. It was now 10.30am, and we thought that we were back on schedule, until we heard that the next train was not due until 12.30pm. Yes, we all groaned, we know that it is Sunday. We could hardly fail to know because pretty much everything around the station was shut. A cup of good Italian coffee was desperately needed but we would have to walk up into town to get it, and get some more money as our cash was now running low.

We had two hours to kill, we wanted to be somewhere else, we were already tired and hungry and our money in Italy was going through our fingers like sand. Yes, we found Italy to be easily the most expensive country to be in. Food, drink and entrance into tourist attractions were all much, much higher priced than in Spain and drastically higher than Portugal or even France. We arranged to meet the American girls back at the station and walked up the road into town; and here we found, yet again, that you never know what is waiting for you round the next corner.

We walked through the quiet back streets until we came to the open, cobbled square; the essential meeting place of almost every Italian village and town that we visited. On this Sunday morning, in this sunny town square in Figline Valdarno, a large crowd had assembled. To begin with we couldn't see what they were all looking at, but as we got closer we realised that there were over a hundred little Fiat 500 cars, all lined up on display with their proud owners standing alongside. It was their annual rally. We made our way through the throng, and found a table at one of the street cafes. Strong Italian coffee and an expensive pastry each, was just what we needed. The rally was in its early stages, and at this point the devotees of this humble little car were more interested in seeing what extra variations had been added, than in driving them. All colours of the spectrum, but all the same size and shape; some had fancy wheels, some had extra holes in the bonnets and others were original in every way. Engines in the back, extremely small, like little beetles.

Eventually the owners squeezed themselves in, along with friends and relatives, who were going along for the ride. Engines revved and after much noise, the little cars all started heading off through the square. The lead car was not a Fiat, but was obviously owned by someone very special in the area. It was a tiny, miniature red Ferrari, driven by a young lad in red racing overalls and his dad. It must have cost a fortune. Then, cheered all the way, each Fiat sounding its unique horn, which ranged from Colonel Bogey to a siren sound and every variation in between, they gathered speed and whizzed off. One quick circuit of the narrow town streets, noise reverberating from every building, and they disappeared on a jolly into the countryside. Italians just love sounding their horns. While they were on the roads we suddenly felt quite glad that we would be travelling by train. Back at the station, the train arrived on time and we boarded, along with the three American girls with their baggage. It already felt like about 6 o'clock at night although it was actually only lunchtime.

We arrived in Florence and headed straight to the Galleria dell'Accademia, to see Michelangelo's famous sculpture of 'David'. Our spirits sank when we saw the length of the queues, but Simon had the bit between his teeth by now and went on a quick tour of the outside of the building, while we joined the line.

"Follow me", he muttered on his return.

We scuttled after him and were soon ushered through a smaller door further down the Academy; for an extra three euros each, given to a man at a side door, we were able to go straight in, and if those nine euros went straight towards his pizza for lunch we certainly didn't care– we were beginning to understand how Italy functioned.

For me, to see the statue of David in real life was a dream come true. Not just because of its immense beauty, every muscle and sinew, every line and expression conveying the perfection of an idealised hero, but also because Michelangelo himself had carved it. He was just 29 years old when it was completed; just one example of the prolific talent of this painter, architect, poet and sculptor whose genius and ability dominated the High Renaissance period. I could have looked at it all day, in fact if I ever return to Florence that's just what I might do, but there were other treasures to see at the Galleria.

Besides some beautiful paintings by Bottecelli and Lippi there were also the sculptures, again by Michelangelo, called 'The Slaves'. To us three, these four unfinished statues were almost more exciting than 'David'. The huge pieces of rough marble, which were selected for these sculptures, are halted forever in the process of changing, like a metamorphosis, into the shapes of people. It is as if the human shapes are trying to free themselves from the unshaped marble around them. They also emphasise the skill required to carve a figure as dramatic as 'David' from solid marble. The actual figure of 'David' stands 13 feet tall, without the base, and the 'Slaves' are of a similar height. All larger than life, yet not so much larger that they seem unreal. We left the Galleria with time to spare before our bus was due, and for once we didn't rush off and cram another sight-seeing tour in. Instead, we bought some huge cones of delicious Italian ice-cream, (the only thing that is cheap in Italy), and we joined lots of other people, who were laid on a spacious grass-covered area, close to the main bus station. From here we could watch the Florentines go by. This was something that we all loved to do.

In front of this small piece of city park, were two complicated interconnecting roundabouts. A type of organised chaos wove its way around them and we decided that this was a great place to study Italian driving skills. God must favour the brave, was all that we could think, as we watched cyclists, pedestrians and motorists hurl themselves along in the maelstrom. Also in front of us, was a hut where you could hire cycles. Bikes of varying size and condition were chained up alongside the hut and two young men lounged on folding chairs waiting for punters. We licked our ice creams and watched with interest as six older American tourists approached the stand and started to negotiate a deal with the lad in charge. They sorted out a variety of odd-looking bikes and eventually managed to mount them and launch themselves, one by one, out into the traffic. We held our breath in trepidation as they wobbled away into the paths of cars and buses, like six delicate butterflies fluttering along a river of snapping crocodiles. But with gay abandon, and shouting encouragement to each other, they cycled off to explore the back streets of Florence.

Although it was a Sunday afternoon, it was still incredibly busy. Dark haired Romany women, in long full skirts and baggy cardigans, hassled car drivers as they pulled up at the traffic lights; brazenly they washed the windscreens with mucky water from their buckets, before demanding payment, yelling to each other over the din of the traffic. The men folk of their group sprawled on the grass, like us, but they swigged beer and smoked cigarettes, while their brown skinned, raggedy children, swung over the railings and pestered passers by. Ambulances howled past with amazing frequency – could one of them be for the American cyclists we wondered, but then an ambulance screeched up alongside us and three young medics jumped out.

Everyone's gaze now shifted to this new form of entertainment, which centred around the steps leading down to the public toilets. The three medics disappeared down the steps, followed by the raggedy children and a few curious onlookers, and reappeared a little later supporting a staggering man between them. They sat him down on a bench, and we watched in amusement as they tried their best, to do something with him. He had a cut on his head, which they soon dealt with, and we decided, judging by the accompanying hand movements, that they were trying to convince him that if he didn't get into the ambulance with them then he would die and go to heaven. He was hard to convince though, and seemed more interested in kissing the hand of the pretty young female medic and inviting her to share some of the wine that he was still trying to swig from the bottle he had concealed in a paper bag. We gave the medics ten out of ten, for patience and staying power because it took a good half an hour of general group therapy before they finally got him into the ambulance. The crowd clapped as he was helped aboard and he took a drunken bow before being taken off to hospital or maybe even heaven. His rather shifty looking friend, who I had noticed hovering on the edge of the crowd all this while, furtively slipped the wine-bottle bag into his own carrier bag and disappeared down the toilet steps again. Ah well, it all makes work for the working man to do.

The six bells of the church of Saint Lorenzo started to peal out with such discord and ferocity that they even drowned out the traffic. Would anyone answer their call on this crazy Sunday afternoon we wondered? Our bus was due, so we would never know. We boarded, along with four new American backpackers, all men this time, and before too long we were back at the motor home. Mama Mia, Florence had more to offer than we had ever imagined.

We had booked tickets to visit the Uffizi, which was to be our last trip in. It was a Tuesday and definitely not as crowded as the weekend had been. With batteries re-charged, we were ready to visit Italy's most important art gallery, containing most of the world's well known Renaissance paintings. The Uffizi was designed by Vasari and built in the mid 16th century for Cosimo 1st of the Medici family. It was originally used as administrative and judicial offices, but was bequeathed in its entirety to the state of Tuscany in 1743, by Anna Maria Ludovica de'Medici, the last member of this prestigious family. By this time it had already become a gallery of some importance. Our visit started on the second floor of this most beautiful, U shaped building. Nothing really prepared us for the sheer number of priceless masterpieces that we stopped and admired, as we wandered through the rooms. I had made a short list of 'favourite artists to see', but it was hard not to deviate. Michelangelo and da Vinci were of course top of the list, with Canaletto, Botticelli, Titian, Rubens, Raphael, Bellini and Holbein as close seconds. And then of course there were the Caravaggio's and Goyas and not forgetting Bellini – oh but I've said him already. Well, you can see how hard it was to choose. I could have stayed there for ever, with so many wonderful works of art to gaze at. So, if I ever return to Florence I shall spend a day staring at the statue of David and a month staring at the breathtaking paintings in the Uffizi. Eventually, Simon dragged me away and we walked through the corridors towards the exit doors. Original Roman copies of original Greek busts, lined the walls of the corridors and ornately painted ceilings invited us to gaze ever upwards. There was always more to see in this gallery. Perhaps when I return I will spend two months at the Uffizi!

We had seen some wonderful art in Florence, but we had only scratched the surface and we could have spent much longer there. If you are thinking of visiting any of the highlights of Italy, I would give this advice. Entry to tourist attractions is not cheap and queues can be long, so it definitely pays to book tickets in advance and be there early. Early morning and evening viewing, is always better than mid day. Eating out is also not cheap, so if you can take food and drink with you it will help, although we did find it very difficult to find places to actually sit down and rest, while eating our packed lunches. The cafes are great, but expensive, and sometimes we would have an overpriced cup of coffee just so that we could sit down for half an hour. Public seating was not easily found and there were always hordes of tourists, like us, looking for somewhere to rest before trekking off to the next attraction. We didn't have time to see a fraction of the treasures that Florence has to offer – it is a truly amazing city with an important history – but with stamina and good planning you will find it well worth a visit. We, however, were heading on to our next delight; our music was playing and our wheels were turning – and Maisy was programmed for Pisa.

Pisa

Leaving Florence behind, we headed back to the coast for a few days at Pisa. Divided by the River Arno, which was once a great trade route, Pisa had its days of glory when it was a busy port, a commercial and artistic centre and the home to such benefactors as Hadrian, the Medici's and Galileo Galilei. So while it may not be of such strategic importance now, it has been left with a well laid out town, a university (the oldest in Italy) and some wonderful historical buildings, it's leaning tower of course, being the most easily recognisable tower in the world. Would Pisa be so famous if Bonanno Pisano had built the tower on more solid ground? Who knows, but even without the lean, it would be an interesting building.

Arriving on the outskirts of the town, we started to search for somewhere to park-up for a few days. There seemed to be plenty of car parks available, but we were having a problem working out exactly which part of the city would accommodate us best. Our solution was to pull into a lay by, get our bikes off the back and cycle in for a quick recce. (Our motor home was much too large to drive through the smaller streets). A thick city wall, much of which is still intact today, encloses the mediaeval section of the city, the gateways and arches providing good geographical reference points. Having sorted out where we were in relation to the Leaning Tower, we rode back and drove to a large car park that seemed ideal. "Fantastic", we enthused, "this car park even has electricity points, and a toilet block and water taps". Well done Italy, we said, but we had second thoughts about this a few days later.

Jack and I then cycled off to the local Carrefours, and returned with rucksacks laden. I seemed to find a million and one ways to cook a kilo of mince round Europe and home-made spaghetti bolognaise, with wonderfully fresh ingredients, was for supper that night. We all have different memories of the places we visited, but when I think of Pisa, I will always think of spaghetti bolognaise and Roy Orbison. For some unknown reason, we were now keen to sing along with Roy's classics.'Only the lonely.... dum,dum,dum,dummy doo-ah,' being a favourite, along with 'Love Hurts' and those challenging high notes of 'It's Over.' So, if I want to remember Pisa, I simply put on his greatest hits CD and I'm back in that car park, cooking spaghetti and singing along with Simon, Jack and Roy.

Sunshine and blue skies were forecast and next day we once more rode into town like The Good, the Bad and the Ugly. We still hadn't determined who was going to be the Ugly though. Pisa was great fun to cycle around; the narrow cobbled streets of the old town criss-crossing with each other, leading us into squares, dead ends and twisting passages. The traffic was not too heavy, although it was still a law unto itself. We found our way to the Campo dei Miracoli (The Field of Miracles), which is without doubt the most beautiful setting for the three major buildings in Pisa. Enclosed on two sides by the city walls, a vast emerald- green lawn stretches across the Campo, bisected only by neat paths that lead you to the doors of the Cathedral, the Baptistery and the Bell Tower.

It was quiet and cool, with little sign of the crowds who would gather there later. We cycled through the stone entrance gate into the square, and saw before us the most perfect view. The light in Italy is sometimes quite ethereal and this was one of those mornings, when the sky was literally heavenly. The dazzling white marble of the buildings, the perfect green lawn and the translucent, blue sky .... I started taking yet more photographs while Simon and Jack went to buy tickets to enter the famous Leaning Tower. It's essential to buy a ticket for the tower, and as it gets busy quite quickly, we made that our first priority. Everyone wants to go up it, but only thirty people are allowed in at a time, with a guide, and the tour takes approximately 30 minutes. You are warned before hand not to lean out, not to stand under the bells and to be 'most prudent and orderly'! And with good reason, as the tower really does have a significant lean and offers plenty of opportunities to fall off, if you so wished. The inclination is about 5.5 degrees to the south, which means that the top-most section protrudes almost five meters over the bottom section. It has also subsided vertically by about 2.8 meters as a result of the unstable nature of the subsoil it was built on. It therefore seems to be coming out of a hole in the ground, rather like a trajectory missile being launched at the stars, but the building itself looks very delicate, a marble version of a tiered wedding cake, with slender arches encircling it all the way to the top. Walking up the 294 worn steps of spiralling staircase was apparently 'very weird' according to Jack, who said he would have preferred to crawl around the top viewing balcony on hands and knees, as it was so un-nerving to be stood at such an angle, on such a small circle of stone, at the top of a cylindrical column 60 meters high. I whimped out of this one and spent my time studying it from ground level. The two other buildings at this site are equally beautiful; the cathedral and the baptistery both exquisitely and delicately decorated, with similar slender arches in carved white marble. Their frescoed interiors with soaring columns and the dramatically carved pulpit by Giovano Pisano were well worth the queuing and entrance fee. There is nothing else to distract you here, except for a line of interesting market stalls which lean against one of the city walls. Apart from that you can sit on the grass, with your latest flavour in Italian ice-cream and enjoy these exquisite buildings.

We cycled on through the old town and found a small café in a sunny open piazza where we had the tastiest pasta lunch, while watching the Pisans go about their daily lives around us. The houses alongside the River Arno, unpretentious in their faded yellows and dusty reds, slightly crumbling and worn at the edges, epitomised the feeling of the town; busy and bustling, but not modern or ostentatious. Well-worn and totally original, and as always in Italian cities, full of life. We really liked Pisa, but of course, if we'd gone in the hot high season, we may have felt differently.

That night we stayed again at our big, empty car park just outside the city walls. Much of the evening was spent swatting the mosquitoes that obviously preferred us to the stagnant water down by the toilets. Their maddening hum made it impossible to sleep so we all got up and had a mass killing spree, notching them up on the handles of our fly swots. Jack had the most to deal with, as he was in the main part of the motor home, but he got well into it, leaping about in his boxer shorts swatting everything that moved until eventually, in the early hours, we reckoned to have got them all and fell into an itchy sleep. Distant thunder during the night hardly disturbed us, but rather odd noises started to drift into our semi-conscious heads at around dawn. A strange clanging sound infiltrated our dreams, followed by voices and car engines. "That sounds like tent poles", muttered Simon from under the mosquito resistant sheet that we had draped over our heads. Blearily we opened the blinds to see what was waking us up at six o'clock in the morning. Our empty car park now resembled a mini building site as a steady stream of white vans poured through the gates, found their preferred spaces and started throwing scaffolding poles onto the tarmac. (That would be the strange clanging sound then). Stalls were being assembled, tables erected and goods unpacked amidst much shouting and general banter. Now we understood why this 'wonderful' car park had electricity points and toilets. We were about to become part of the Saturday market. 'Operation Hasty Exit Two' swung into action as we flicked away dead mosquitoes and scrambled into last nights lazily discarded clothes. Loose items were thrown into cupboards and the bikes were slung on the back. We would never be able to get out of the car park once all the stalls were up, and we had plans to move on that day. Sleepy eyed, unwashed and unprepared, Simon revved her up and 'headed for the gate doin' ninety-eight – we let those truckers role, ten-four' - or in truth we lurched down the road and out of town, only to stop in the first possible lay by to start the day again with a cup of tea and breakfast. Ready or not we were leaving Pisa and heading for Rome.

Jack was a great travelling companion – most thirteen year olds, stuck with their whacky parents in a motor home for a year, would have rebelled – and with good reason – but he entered into the spirit of the whole adventure admirably. His main complaint was that he did miss his friends sometimes. We could quite understand his feelings and we felt bad about it. Another plan was hatched to give him a break from us and we invited one of his buddies to fly out and join us in Rome for the Easter holidays. Charles would be arriving at Leonardo da Vinci airport on April 5th, so we had two days to reach our next campsite.

We had chosen Camping Porticciolo, as our next base, a family-run, lakeside site, situated just below Bracciano about 30 kilometres outside Rome with a direct train line into the city. We thought that the boys could enjoy the activities at the lake in between our sight seeing trips into Rome. It didn't quite turn out that way but then, things never do. We drove down the coast from Pisa towards Rome, stopping at a huge supermarket to stock-up on essentials and then turned inland towards the town of Bracciano. We wild camped for one night in a lay-by, once again fighting off mosquitoes until well into the evening, and next morning we followed the campsite directions that guided our huge motor home around the old town and down to the lake. Without those directions we would have had serious problems, as one of the bridges to avoid was only 2.8 meters high.

We saw the entrance to the site and Simon groaned again, "another very tight turn, down a very steeply sloping, rough track", the poor Beast wasn't built for this kind of terrain. Wide, flat American highways, with huge turning circles, were what our motor home would have liked, but we could hardly blame Europe for our desire to drive a bungalow around. Simon drove brilliantly though, and we squeezed and bumped down the track and into a big open field of long grass. The owners looked at us in horrified amazement and walked slowly around the whole of our exterior, obviously not used to having a motor home the size of a luxury coach coming down their drive. They had mown a patch of grass for us to park on, which they quickly mowed again to ensure it was big enough, and we shunted into place and settled into life at Camping Porticiollo.

Alessandro and his wife were the charming owners of this pretty lakeside campsite and they could not have done more for us during our stay. Large pitches, shaded by well-tended trees, were situated on the lakeside shore next to a small private beach. Their own camp bus left at 9.0am every morning to ferry campers up the hill to the train station for the 9.15am train into Rome and the friendly bar and pizzeria opened every night. We were immediately provided with written information about the area, transport timetables and opening times of everything in the town of Bracciano. We imagined that it was the type of site which customers would return to regularly. It was rustic, friendly and peaceful.

Shortly after we had arrived and before we did anything else, Jack and I erected the small tent that we had brought along with us in case of visitors. Charles and Jack could easily have slept in the Beast but we thought that a bit of private space would be a novelty to us all. The boys could have the tent and Simon and I would have nights alone for the first time in six months. Jack and I collapsed in our usual heaps of laughter as we struggled to get the tent up, trying to remember what poles went where; but poor Simon had a worse job. He was doing running repairs to various parts of the motor home that had suffered general wear and tear as we had travelled. I had broken the leg of the folding dining table and the sink plug, to mention just the two jobs that I was admitting to and Jack owned up to a few more, so we left Si with the toolbox and, once we had got the tent to look as if it might actually remain standing and waterproof, Jack and I took a better look at our surroundings.

The camp was very quiet and had obviously only just opened for the season. Most of the grass was long and meadow like, dotted with wild flowers, and there were birds in abundance. Alessandro and his wife explained that they had not been able to cut the grass because of terrible recent storms, which had left plenty of clearing up to do. They both looked somewhat fraught as they set about their tasks, he stubble chinned, bookish and rather like a grumpy bear, and she petite and quiet, going quickly and purposefully about her jobs. It was about midday, but a thick mist blanketed the lake, shortening our view to just a few yards of eerie, silent, waters edge. Slowly, as the sun began to burn through the lifting haze, the whole of Lake Bracciano was revealed to us. It was far bigger than we had imagined, stretching further than the eye could see either way, with wooded hills and small towns visible on the far side. We folded our jumpers to make cushions on the damp stones and sat down to read our guidebook on the area.

Lake Bracciano is extremely deep, over 165 meters, lying in two craters of a volcano that has been extinct for thousands of years. It covers an area of 57 square kilometres and has a Neolithic village dating from 5500BC on its bed. No motorboats are allowed on the lake, just sail boats, canoes and windsurfers, along with local fishing boats that supply the excellent fish restaurants along the shores. It has provided drinking water to Rome, since early in the 17th century when an aqueduct was built, and much of the area is located within the Natural Park of the Bracciano Lake System. It was very peaceful and its beauty seemed totally unspoilt by any modern development. Looking down on the lake is the town of Bracciano, with the castle, Castello Odescalche, perched dramatically above the water, having a privileged view of the area. Jack and I watched as small green-backed lizards crept out to enjoy the growing heat of the day, and the lake waters turned to a brilliant blue, as the mist was replaced by a clear sky.

Early next morning our kind hosts gave us a lift to the station to catch the 8.15 into Rome. We joined the regular commuters and boarded the double-story, clean, fast train with its gentle piped music and comfortable seats. Our connection to Leonardo da Vinci airport was equally trouble free and before long we were waiting for Charles's plane to arrive. We scanned the faces of travellers as they came through 'arrivals' as if we wouldn't recognise him, but suddenly there he was, travelling light with just a rucksack on his back, looking exactly the same as six months ago when we had all said goodbye. It was great to see him again. He and Jack slipped straight back into a conversation about where they had got to with the latest computer game, as yet untroubled with the long preamble of politeness and formality which we adults go through when we insist on asking after the family and the weather. Kids have a wonderful 'here and now' attitude. So while Simon and I were looking around for the exit signs again, they were off together like greyhounds out of the stalls, heads down, chattering, and had already clocked exactly how to leave the airport building.

It was still early in the day and Charles seemed to have plenty of energy, so we decided that when in Rome, we should do what the Romans used to do, and visit the Colosseum. Rome's Metro system, The Metropolitana, has two lines, A and B, which cross at the central station called the Stazione Termine. These lines will take you very close to almost all the major highlights and are cheap and very easy to use. Tickets can be bought at machines or kiosks and as it is an integrated public transport system, you can use the same ticket for bus, train or metro – if used within 75 minutes, and don't forget to validate the ticket at the orange ticket boxes. We were soon zooming through subterranean Rome heading for Stazione Colosseo.

The Colosseum is a huge amphitheatre. It could seat up to 50,000 people in its gory hey-day, and considering the building was started in 72AD it is in very good condition. It stands on the site of an artificial lake, around which Nero's royal residence once existed, but Vespasion drained the lake when he ordered this new entertainment arcade to be built for the Roman people. Restoration has been underway since 1992, but restoring such an important and ancient structure is not a job to be rushed; there is still work to do. However, all of the main building is still there including the underground labyrinth of tunnels used to house the gladiators, slaves and animals. It is impressive in its complexity and structure and offers an excellent example of the life and skills of ancient Rome. Its present state, with roofs and floors absent, is almost a benefit because the complete skeleton of the building is revealed and you are able to see below the façade, to the workings and architectural bones.

Roman legionnaires continue to parade outside this amphitheatre, but they're not resting from the Punic wars, they are trying to persuade tourists to pose in full costume with them, exchanging a few pieces of silver for a gimmicky photo. Finding the actual entrance was somewhat difficult in the general melee; always a crowd-puller, the queues have remained the same as ever, and it is a bit of a bun fight to get in even if you have a reserved ticket. We didn't have tickets reserved, but Simon was now an old hand at doing things the Italian way and he soon zoomed in on an American tour operator who, for a few dollars more, whisked us in with his group. We followed in the footsteps of thousands before us as we climbed the stone steps to one of the higher levels. We would have been among the lucky ones. The less fortunate would only get above the subterranean level when they were being sent up on the elevators to die in the arena. The running of the Colosseum was an enormous operation, involving thousands of people and animals. Thousands died for the enjoyment of thousands more and looking at the ribs, arteries and heart of this unique example of Roman life, we got a good feel of what it must have been like when the crowds roared, louder than the lions.

We finally left Rome that evening and back in Bracciano, Jack and Charles once again took the lead, quickly finding the small country lane that led from the train station in the town, back down the hill, to the campsite by the lake. Simon and I staggered after them, munching bits of leftover pizza, with a cool bottle of Chianti in mind. The boys slept well in their tent and we had the luxury of a quiet night alone. There would be no more excursions for a day or two now, as we all needed a rest; the local market day would be soon enough for our next outing.

The market itself was not very interesting. Mostly tacky goods and the boys soon got bored and went back to camp. Simon accompanied me on one of my missions to the local post office to send home a parcel and some letters. It was three days to Easter weekend and I had found some Italian sweets and gifts for our three grandchildren. I have to admit that I never posted anything expensive or valuable, as I was fairly sceptical about the reliability of the overseas post. I had chosen very lightweight items and had parcelled them up in an old cardboard box.

When we reached the small, tired looking, post office, I took a numbered ticket and joined one of the many long queues for a cashier. Simon sensibly elected to wait outside in the shade. Slowly, very slowly, suffering the very hot, stuffy room and giving each other internationally-recognised long suffering looks, we all shuffled towards the counter. At last it was my turn, and in halting broken Italian, accompanied by bits of English, I explained the very obvious fact that I wanted to post a parcel to England. Reaching from behind towering piles of paperwork and an impressive array of rubber stamps, a stressed looking lady assistant took my parcel and gave me a grim, doubtful look. She tossed it around in her hands and flicked it over and over, tutting continuously. Then off she went to her friend further down the counter and they tutted together, as they tossed it around some more while giving me disgusted looks. Eventually she returned and threw it back to me. "No", she said, followed by the Italian equivalent to, "Signora, itsa notta possible to posta this worthless parcel because itsa notta wrapped correctly. You musta cover alla ova the boxa so that only the addressa is showing!!!!" All conversations in Italy end with either a question mark or an exclamation mark, and raised hands. Just to emphasise the drama of life.

I remonstrated slightly, purely to keep face, but with little heart as I knew that I would never win and took my parcel back outside to my now very bored and irritable husband, who did not view this kind of problem as the same kind of challenge as I did. He would have thrown it in the bin at this point but I had spotted what looked like a gift and paper shop just up the road, so there I headed. Mutton headed to the end. A quick search revealed rolls of brown sticky tape, so together we managed to completely cover the box in brown tape, apart from the address. A chainsaw would now be useful to open it. Back to the post office we went, for another ticket, another long queue with more long suffering, sighing people and an even more irritable husband shuffling along beside me. At last I reached the counter again... "Bellisimo!", she smiled, reaching through the towers of paperwork to take the parcel and weigh it. "19 euros!", she pronounced. "19 euros?" I gasped. "The contents only cost me ten!" She shrugged and started to fill in the required triplication of forms, rubber-stamping everything like a line dancer in wellies, before taking my money and eventually sending me on my way. Was it ever worth it I wondered? Some time later I spoke to my daughter-in-law on the phone, and asked her if she had received the parcel. "What parcel?" she asked.

Ah well, what's a few euros anyway.

April

Ripped off in Rome

Unsettled weather dogged our stay in Bracciano. Good followed bad, followed good –often chilly and damp although when the sun did come out, it was hot. The next day looked good and according to the campsite weather forecast, pinned to the notice board, it would remain fair. The white camp bus, an ancient relic in itself that travelled under a cloak of belching black smoke, delivered us to the station for the train to Rome. It was going to be a marathon day of touristing with Charles. One hour later we disembarked Line A metro at Ottoviano St. Pietro and walked the short distance to St Peters Square and the Vatican City.

Designed by Bernini, this vast Holy Square stands on a site that was once home to Nero's gardens and stadium, where crowds once gathered to watch gladiatorial combats and chariot races. The tall, simple obelisk which stands in the centre of the square was brought to Rome by the infamous emperor Caligula, and has remained close to St Peters Basilica ever since. There was a great feeling of space and sky as we stood in the square; an enormous ellipse measuring 240 meters at its widest diameter. On either side of us, 140 statues of the saints, all twice life size, stared down from the tops of imposing semi-circular colonnades. Each long, curving colonnade, made up of four rows of marching Doric columns, offering us cool shade from the sun-beaten Piazza. Before us stood St Peters, the most important church in the Christian world. Designed to impress and inspire the masses that gathered in the square before it, this is no humble church. To me it looked the epitome of power and authority and man's ability to amaze and impress himself by his own skills and it is steeped in history. It is the corner stone of millions of people's lives, its pale fabric, holding the desires and ambitions of many – emperors, kings, popes, and artists such as Michelangelo and Raphael, to name but a few. I am not a 'believer' as such, so I could only marvel at the architecture. The queues to the Sistine Chapel were hideously long, so we turned back to face the city and moved on to the Piazza Navona. I would have to return another day to see the 'Pieta', Michelangelo's famous sculpture, completed when he was only 24 years old and of course his beautiful frescoes.

Most tourist attractions that we visited in Rome were already standing on land of historical significance; such is the depth and layered history of this city. The Piazza Navona is a large and beautiful square lined with baroque palaces. It has three fountains, the most famous of which is Bernini's 'The Four Rivers', which we wanted to see. This plaza was laid out on the site of Emperor Domitian's stadium where chariot races and important sports regattas were once held. Domitian, who finalised the conquest of Britain around 85AD, had led a reign of suppression and terror, when Christians and philosophers were all heavily persecuted. He was eventually assassinated in 96AD.

Bernini, an architect, painter and sculpture, was a master of the baroque style and the figures in his exuberant and elaborate fountains explode with life. The Piazza Navona is a meeting place for artists who assemble in the sunny square and epitomise la Dolce Vita while the twisting, reaching figures which comprise the 'Four Rivers' seem set in some kind of frenzy above the gushing waters. Jack and Charles liked this fountain as much as we did. Maybe it was the pure energy that it held; they stood apart from us and discussed it in depth.... Or at least we think that's what they were talking about!

We moved on to the Pantheon and by now we needed food. The frantic city thrashed around us with blaring horns, screaming scooters that squeezed and squirmed their way through the traffic and countless people rushing to and fro. Troops of tourists, following the flag of their leader, snaked amongst it all and wandering individuals like us looked for a resting place. We found a space to lean against a building and munched baguettes while we studied the outside of the Pantheon. Its sombre colonnaded exterior, facing north, belies the fascinating rotunda behind it. The dome, the best preserved of Rome's ancient buildings, is still considered a masterpiece of engineering. Its interior space is a perfect sphere 43.03 meters in diameter and height, with a circular centre opening in the ceiling, which allows light to slant through and illuminate the elaborate marble columns and floors inside. The building has been plundered over the ages and the valuable roof tiles and bronze ceiling tiles were purloined to adorn other projects, but it is still a fascinating building.

From there we zig-zagged our way through the streets of 'old' Rome, heading for the Trevi Fountain, stopping en route to admire the column of Marcus Aurelius; thirty meters tall, with the history of the Germanic and Sarmatian wars carved in intricate detail, spiralling to the top. Inside the hollow column, a twisting staircase of 190 steps takes you up to the statue of St Paul who stands aloft. But that didn't tempt us, as it was the Trevi Fountain that we wanted to see. Without doubt the most famous fountain in Rome, it has the unmistakable energy of Bernini, who had a hand in its creation. The glory of this fountain is not just the creativity of its design, but also the setting in which it sits. Its immediate backdrop is the façade of an imposing building, which is heavily decorated with Corinthian columns, elaborate windows and impressive statues. Neptune, his cloak billowing in the wind, stands in a central niche of this façade and guides his chariot through the wild sea before him. Two horses rear out of the water and are guided through the rocks and waves by powerful merman sea-gods. Waterfalls cascade over rocks carved as an extension of the building, and all is in a pale, bleached stone. The wide pool of clear shallow water, which looks so inviting, is edged by a low rounded wall and we like thousands before us, sat with our backs to the fountain and threw our coins over our shoulders. One day we would return to Rome. I threw a second coin, to make my secret wish.

A large, shifting crowd hugged the fountain, but then who can blame anyone for wanting to see such a famous and beautiful creation. It was built to be admired after all. From there we pressed on to see more of Rome's seemingly endless attractions, like the majestic Monument to Victor Emmanuel 2nd, nicknamed the Typewriter by the locals; a colossal building begun in 1885 to celebrate the Unification of Italy and encompassing the Tomb of the Unknown Soldier. We climbed like ants up to the higher levels for the unforgettable view down onto the city before moving on to cross the river Tiber at the ancient bridge of the Isola Tiberina.

Rome does not have the charm and intimacy of smaller cities, but it has buildings and treasures that are soaked in history and legend. Two and half million people lead their busy lives in what seems to be a chaotic rush of noise and pollution. It's once great empire, its huge achievements, its bloody history, are all layered under a restless Rome that never sleeps. It was late afternoon by now and we were on a final hunt for something much more 21st century. Charles wanted to buy a BB gun to take back to England, although we assured him that he would not be allowed to take it onto the plane. We were making our way through a fairly rough looking back-street shopping area, to reach a metro station and the boys had managed to home in on probably the only shop around that sold the guns, and Charles got his wish. They then walked ahead of us, planning their evening's entertainment while we, carrying the rucksack, followed behind. This was when we had our funniest moment in Rome, and one that will always be in our memories.

We were all busy talking as we marched along, but we soon realised that a car had pulled up alongside us. The driver was leaning across the passenger seat, calling to us from the open window. We shouted to the boys to stop walking and then stepped across to the smart, new looking car to see what he wanted.

"I'm sorry, I'm so sorry to stop you", said the small, swarthy Italian inside, "but I am lost. Do you know where I am pleeease. I have been going around for hours trying to find my way onto the autostrada." This was all said with much excitement, in quite good English.

"Oh dear, poor you", we said sympathetically, "yes, we know where we are because we've got quite a good map that we've been following". We then chatted and commiserated with him as we poured over our map, he still in the car and Simon with his head half through the open window, showing him where to go. All this took quite a while and, with him being very chatty and friendly, we were soon beginning to feel like old friends.

"Oh you English are so kind", he repeated for about the twentieth time, "you know what, my wife is English, she comes from Stockport", and with that he grabs our hands and we all have a very jolly, but clammy, over-long, handshake.

"Really", we enthused, "what a small world", although at this point we are beginning to feel that it's time to move on.

"Yes", he garbled, "the English are wonderful, always so generous. You are my friends now, not like these damn Romans. I hate the Romans, I am not from Rome, I am a rep. for Christian Dior and I've been at a show all day. Look, see my tie, see the label". And with that he flicks his tie over and shows us the Dior label.

"Oh … nice", we politely reply, wondering if all Italians get so chummy this quickly.

"Look", he continued, pulling a large expensive carrier bag from the back seat, "I have some clothes left over from the show. Look, look how beautiful they are, feel the quality!" And now he has the bag open and is giving us a white cheesecloth blouse and a puce-yellow, mans nylon jacket to feel. We dutifully feel them but are too polite to say that we think they feel very cheap and tacky.

"You must have them because you are my friends now", he insists as he pushes the bag out of the window, so that we end up holding it.

"No, no, we can't take this", we say somewhat alarmed, " have it back", and we push it back inside.

"I insist", he said, continuing to grin like a weasel as he shoves it back at us.

So we are now holding the bag of tacky clothes, which he thinks are great, and we feel rather confused and beholden to this man, who also thinks that we are his long lost English buddies.

"These Romans", he whines despairingly, "I hate them. I need some petrol but they won't accept my credit card. I'm not a beggar or a thief, I am an honest man, you are my kind friends, so you give me some money to buy petrol!"

His grin was beginning to slip now, and a slightly more sinister face was emerging as Simon and I looked at each other and the penny began to drop that we were being conned.

"Have your clothes back", we politely but firmly say, but he says, "No, keep the clothes, I'm not a thief, you just give me some money".

We shove the bag back and forth through the open window like some kind of comedy act, until in the end, even though we know that he is a miserable little con man, we are so keen to get away from this chattering, pawing, smiling hyena, that we offer him ten euros to go away. Then his smile really did change into a fairly nasty snarl, as he snapped, "No, you give me more than that!"

"No way", we snap back, and before we could push the carrier bag back through the open window for the last time, he had snatched our ten euros and screeched off into the traffic. We stood there, still holding the bag, and watched him go, completely gobsmacked at such an elaborate con. It had taken him a good fifteen minutes of fawning to get ten euros out of us and we were sure that he was hoping for much better pickings than that. Maybe he thought we were Americans, not penny pinching middle aged

Brits. The tacky Indian cheesecloth blouse I kept as a memento and it still hangs in my wardrobe to this day, but the obscenely ugly, yellow nylon jacket, went straight into the nearest street bin. Pity the poor beggar who finds that, we thought. We trudged on back to the station, laughing with the boys at our latest experience. Ah Rome – such fond memories. I wonder if I can get that coin back out of the Trevi fountain!

The next day was Good Friday and we awoke to a squally wet start, with grey skies and heavy clouds hanging over the lake. With the heating on, we huddled in, listening to spasmodic rain pattering onto our roof. Not for the first time, were we glad that we had such a comfortable home to live in while we travelled Europe. Rome would be hideously busy over the Easter period so, as we were very tired anyway, we decided to enjoy the quiet of Camping Porticciolo for the weekend. I cooked a late breakfast, the boys dragged themselves out of their tent, and we decided to spend the day playing a mammoth version of Monopoly until the weather improved.

So far, life at this campsite had been very quiet, but all that was just about to change. At first two motor homes arrived together, which in itself was something of a novelty. They had Italian registration plates and also carried identification stickers saying 'RSM'. We puzzled over this, as we watched them swerve confidently, some might even say recklessly, over the wet grass to their pitches. Then three more arrived together, and another one, and two more until by mid afternoon a steady stream of white motor homes, all bearing RSM stickers, were flowing into the rapidly filling site. The ground by this time had changed from pretty, green meadow to squelchy brown mud and the cavalier, happy go lucky driving, as they jostled into the field, was now becoming wheel spinning, rut-making, cross country rallying. Simon put his coat and boots on and went for an investigative walk around camp. On his return we learned that the Motor Home Club of San Marino now surrounded us.

They were an exceptionally jolly and friendly group, who smiled and waved as they helped each other line up their vans, pull out their awnings and push each other out of the mud, all in the pouring rain. Plenty of backslapping and handshaking proved that they were old friends, who were there to enjoy the Easter weekend break. We had to discover more about San Marino and soon had our atlas out. The Most Serene Republic of San Marino lies on the west coast of middle Italy, just below Rimini. It is the world's oldest existing republic, only 61 square kilometres in size. It has its own army, produces its own coins and postage stamps, and obviously has its own motorhome group; in fact we figured that quite a good proportion of the population were now camping at Bracciano. The last arrival rolled in at 11.30 that night and next morning the boys counted seventy-five vans, and at least 160 people. Our quiet site was now almost full.

According to our hosts, the weather was the worst they had had for twenty-two years, but at last the rain stopped and next day we had intermittent sun. Simon borrowed Alessandro's trusty old bike, (which had seen better days and required constant running repairs), and we all went cycling around the shore of the lake. The road was good and not too busy and we soon reached Anguillara, a small picturesque town that reaches down to the water from a tiny peninsular. All along the shore, we were amazed to see swans and ducks competing with South American coypus for scraps of our bread. At first we thought that these furry, guinea-pig like creatures were over grown water rats, but when we asked a young local about them he said that they had escaped from a nearby breeding farm and were now a normal inhabitant of the area.

We locked our bikes together and explored the tiny steep streets of this very untouristy old town. Tottering houses with pretty flowered balconies, miniature courtyards and twisting alleyways, led us up to the large white church from where we could look down over the higgledy-piggledy rooftops and out over the deep blue lake. Far across the lake on distant green hillsides, white-faced houses and flashing car windows caught the sun. The boys soon got bored and raced off on their bikes, finding an 'alternative' route home that involved muddy tracks along the shore, leaving Simon and I to enjoy this very beautiful area in peace.

That evening, which was Easter Saturday, we were planning to eat at the campsite pizzeria, but our kind camp hostess came pedalling round on her bike to tell us that, that night, a pageant was taking place in Bracianno town. The camp bus would take all those interested up to the town at eight o'clock and return at eleven o'clock. She even recommended a good restaurant in town, so we decided to eat there. By 8.30pm, we were enjoying excellent pasta in a friendly, family restaurant with a warm log fire and good local wine. Outside, as night fell, we could hear the town livening up and when we tottered out, at about ten o'clock, we joined the throng of people heading up to the castle. Streets lights had been replaced with flaming torches and music was coming from the floodlit castle on the hill. In the torch lit, cobbled square, below the castle walls, crowds had gathered under the canopy of a dark, starlit sky. The weather was going to be kind to us that night. Jack and Charles soon took advantage of the situation to roam off around the crowded square, while we waited patiently for the 'Pageant of the Crucifixion' to begin.

The festive music eventually stopped and a new composition started. This was much more dramatic, serious music, and from down the dark torch lit street, a procession of six soldiers came slowly riding up, on strong, stamping horses. The soldiers were dressed as Roman legionnaires, carrying swords and spears; their decorated horses clattering over the shiny cobbles. Behind them were two lines of foot soldiers, carrying flaming torches and cracking whips into the air, and between them, being whipped as they walked along, were Jesus, and the two thieves who were crucified alongside him. They were bare footed and had full size, heavy wooden crosses, which were weighting down their shoulders as they dragged them up the street. They passed through the crowd and continued up to the gate in the castle wall. The music filled the black night, and we waited for the next part of the pageant.

Along the top of the ramparts more torches were lit as soldiers took their places at regular spaces. We were stood in the square just below the wall, and now the entire crowd that we were amongst, moved forward to look upwards to the castle. The music changed again and became even more dramatic as, against a backdrop of the night sky, Jesus and the two thieves were hoisted up, strapped to their crosses. Lightening flashed repeatedly onto the walls and the music reached a thundering crescendo. The soldiers stood illuminated by the glow of torches, as two women went to the foot of Jesus' cross. The crowd murmured its appreciation and as the music reached its finale, the central cross wasped slowly lowered and a lasered image of Jesus was seen slowly rising through the sky. Fireworks and jubilant music exploded into the air and the crowd then burst into wild applause for what had been a very dramatic and ambitious portrayal of the crucifixion. For a small country town, we thought that this had been an excellent dramatisation and we were most impressed. It was now well past 11.30pm, so we quickly rounded up the boys and ran back to the town centre, to catch our lift back to camp. The town was still heaving as men, women and children headed home. There were no drunks, no yobs, and no threatening behaviour, just families out at night, having fun. (So many times in Europe, we admired this quality of life). The big camp bus belched and burped its way back down the hill, full of cheerful San Marino campers and us four Brits…. We staggered into bed yet again!

Easter Sunday started slowly with us all having another lay-in. Simon connected an extension lead to the laptop computer and the boys scoffed huge Easter eggs while they lay in their little tent and played a game. Paradise in Italy for them. The San Marino motor homers were up and about, and the couple in the motor home next to us were soon knocking on our door, with a gift of four, decorated hard-boiled eggs. It was a tradition, and most kind of them, so we had a simple breakfast and decided to have a lazy day. We soon realised that prising the boys out of their tent would be like picking winkles from their shells without a pin, so we left them to it and went for a long walk along the lakeshore on our own. We had been totally mistaken in thinking that there would be plenty to do on this lake. We had expected to see Pedalos, canoes, or sailing at least, but it was obviously far too early in the season for the Italians to hit the water, and all of the hire shops were still closed. Very few of the restaurants were open, but there was one doing a good trade, so Simon and I decided to leave the boys in peace while we enjoyed a tasty fish lunch, alongside local Italian families. Grannies and grandchildren, all dressed in their Sunday best along with whole extended families, gathered around tables which were pushed together to accommodate everyone; babies slept in pushchairs and grandfathers dozed in corners as the long lazy meal was consumed. No one was rushing the food; the meal was excellent and a very social occasion.

When we returned to the motorhome, the boys' empty stomachs had got the better of them and they were in full production cooking pancakes. Charles neatly dressed in my apron and in charge of the frying pan and Jack mixing the batter, with eggs, flour, milk, jam, lemons and sugar working its way across all available surfaces. They became obsessed with pancake making over the next few days and, whenever we turned our backs, they were glued to the cooker making another fresh batch. They experimented with stomach churning fillings and emptied my larder, but at least we know that they won't starve when they leave home. The holidaymakers from San Marino were also enjoying a good lunch. They had set up long tables outside their motor homes and had gathered together in large groups for the meal. Plenty of wine bottles, plenty of food and then organised games around the campsite. The games becoming noisier and crazier as the wine bottles emptied, until eventually the rain returned and they called it a night. They certainly know how to party in Royal San Marino.

The weather was miserable for the next few days, with rain showers spoiling the few hours of sun. We explored locally and enjoyed the area as best we could. The San Marino motor homers all left on the Easter Monday and like a flock of departing, white sea birds, they flew off in a flurry of tooting horns and flying mud, leaving the camp site silent and slightly dazed. We thought that we would be on our own again then but as they left, two new families arrived, and to our utter amazement they were both English. We had not seen any other English travellers for many weeks.

The first to arrive was a small yellow dormer van. The owners of 'Jimmy the Van' were Nigel and Nicky and little Charlotte. Once again, who said that this is a lonely planet; now back in England they are still our friends. Nigel, taller than the average Englishman, seemed to fold himself double to squeeze into 'Jimmy', while Nicky, who usually worked in a bank, organised their small living area with great skill, and lovely Charlotte, a bright little five year old, rode her small pink bicycle around the camp endearing herself to everyone. They were taking six months off work, to travel, and were managing incredibly well.

The other English family to arrive were also to become good friends. They were John and Gill with their three children, Sarah, Hannah and Daniel. With just a car and caravan, these intrepid travellers had, like us, sold their home, given away or sold most of their worldly belongings and were taking two years off to see the world. They were taking a similar route as us around Europe but were then going on to Malaysia and the East before finishing in Australia. Their children were keeping up with their education as they went, and again, we have very fond memories of them and we still keep in touch. When we last heard from them, they had helped to rebuild a village in Thailand, which had been wrecked by the Tsunami, and had eventually reached Australia. Daniel was twelve, Hannah was fourteen and Sarah was sixteen and a dedicated Goth. How she managed to emerge from the small caravan every morning, dressed from head to foot in elaborate, black cult clothing, was a credit to her determination, and Gill and John's patience. We had a long chat with them that day, and swapped a box of eleven books, so we all had some new reading. We met up with them all again later in the trip; wonderful people whom we had good times with – so read on and you will learn more about them. They had all just arrived at Bracciano, but we were shortly to be moving on, because Charles's holiday was now over and he was due on a plane back to England.

So, next morning, we swapped mobile phone numbers with them all, and said goodbye to our new friends. Alessandro and his lovely wife gave us wine, postcards and mementos to leave with and even promised to send off some letters for us. They were exceptionally kind hosts and I would recommend anyone to visit their camp site. We packed up, putting the motor home back into driving order after ten days at Bracianno, and swung out of the campsite. That night, we parked and slept in the coach car park of Leonardo-da-Vinci airport, in Rome. Very early the next morning, as the sun was creeping over the horizon, we caught the shuttle bus to terminal C, departures, and waved goodbye to Charles. It was just the three of us again, a long way from home, and still only half way through our trip. And where were we heading for next? Well, it had to be the wondrous or not so wondrous delights, of Pompeii.

Up Pompeii

We left Rome on a busy dual carriageway which ran through lush flat countryside parallel to the coast and then joined the A road down to Terracina, eventually passing the long, white sandy beaches of Sperlonga and Gaeta. We were heading down to the Bay of Naples, but we planned to drive around the back of Naples itself to avoid some of the spaghetti-like road system that surrounds it. We couldn't avoid the busier towns on the edge of this area and in some of them you certainly wouldn't want to stop overnight. A red light at the traffic lights was a green light to the dark haired, hustling women who banged on car windows for money; traffic here was even more chaotic, with scooters, buses, cars, lorries and little agricultural three wheeler trucks, coming at you from every direction; salesmen touting all manner of goods at toll stations and horns blasting at any opportunity, made this an interesting ride to say the least. Especially entertaining were the local parking habits – cars slung at any angle into any space, anywhere, nose or tail defiantly halfway across the driving lane, without any scruples or apologies. If there were no spaces then double or even triple parking were 'de rigour'.

Simon had programmed Maisy to take us to our next campsite, which, according to our guidebooks, was situated right next to the ruins of Pompeii. With her usual genteel voice she told us "your destination lies ahead", and at about midday we rolled into the aptly named Camping Zeus. This excellent campsite had all the usual facilities, although there were not many pitches large enough to accommodate our big American RV. Luckily, it was not too busy and we were able to squeeze into a suitable space. I immediately used the washing machines and strung up a washing line between the orange trees. It was now mid April and the trees, just coming into leaf, were laden with strong, heavy smelling blossom which drifted through our open windows. Within the site itself it was fairly peaceful and pleasant, but we could hear the timpani of non-stop traffic beyond its walls. That afternoon we got settled in and almost immediately met a couple from London who were driving a big Winnebago. Once again, they too were taking a year out to see Europe, leaving their grown-up kids to look after the family home. There were plenty of us grown-up gappers on this trail, from all different nations, and once again we shared stories and a glass of wine… or two!

Inevitably we started the next day with slight headaches. No surprise there, and it was also raining quite hard. Simon and I left Jack to 'guard the van', which was his way of avoiding the walk to the supermarket with rucksacks on our backs, to fill up the larder. We were going to wait until the following day before we went into the ruins, in the hope of better weather. It also gave us a chance to get to know the town and the immediate surrounding area. We had been really looking forward to seeing the ruins of Pompeii and when we did, they didn't disappoint us, but don't go there expecting to be immersed in archaeological reverence, because this is a place where you will see tourism at it's worst. You will run the gauntlet, quite literally, of hustlers and hasslers as you walk past the entrance – "I sell you fresh water"; "I sell you pizza, or lemons, or enormous oranges or tacky mementoes; I sell you safe parking places. I sell you guided tour". They will sell you anything, except their grandmother, because after all, we are in Italy where grannies are precious family members.

Outside the supermarket, a small girl stood in the rain, begging anyone for a coin. Everyday she was always there, splashing her trainers in the puddles or sitting in the shade with her back against the wall, and her hand outstretched – a couple of local stray dogs usually kept her company. We took our lives in our hands crossing the narrow, noisy roads– dodging huge tourist buses, speeding scooters, kamikaze motorists and yet more crocodiles of picture-snapping Japanese tourists who seemed to pop up everywhere we went. It was chaotic, noisy, smelly, busy and probably much the same now, as back in 78 AD, when we would all have been wearing togas. Fifty meters from the most significant ruins in Italy were the grimy train station, the campsite, the market stalls, the bus station and hoards of people. 'Out of season' it was bearable, but in the hot, smelly and incredibly busy summer months, it would be hard work. We went to bed early and sober that night and determined to visit the ruins the next day.

Up early, we walked the few yards from the campsite to the entrance of the ruins. At 9.0am it was already busy with coach parties of people buying tickets and hiring audio sets, and it had started to bucket down with rain again. Disgruntled guides touted for work and mangy dogs circled for food, amidst us slightly confused tourists who were trying to work out the numbering system on the explanatory brochure. As we three started our independent tour, we found it increasingly difficult to understand exactly what we were looking at. There were few explanations in the guide brochure, and the few written explanations provided as you walked around, were all in Italian. There were no concessions here for the huge numbers of mostly foreign tourists, so we hired an audio headset each which proved to be essential. However, it didn't take us long to become immersed in what was once a busy and beautiful city, that had been stopped dead in it's tracks 2000 years ago when Vesuvius had erupted.

Back then, when Pompeii was a thriving commercial, religious and metropolitan centre, it had no fear of the benign mountain which rose some ten kilometres behind it. At that time the volcano slopes were covered with grape vines and the summit was a thick forest with wild pigs and game. Life was good for an upwardly mobile, Pompeian citizen. The Forum, the heart of the city where all economic, commercial and political activities took place, was also the place to meet. Here you could also worship at the temple of Zeus, or the temple of Apollo, before you went to the corner, fast-food café, for some light refreshments. These small eating-houses are everywhere in old Pompeii. The citizen may then go to one of the elaborate baths to meet some friends or discuss some business, followed by a trip to the gymnasium, a vast, well equipped building, shaded by huge plane trees. In the evening he may take his family to see a play or perhaps the latest comedy, in the large theatre which seated 5000 people. At the weekend they may go to the gladiator games held in the great, elliptic, amphitheatre, which held 12,000 spectators. He would entertain regularly in his elaborate house, with its own inner courtyard and designer garden, and servants would be on hand.

The city was vast and rich, with heavily decorated houses belonging to the wealthy. Temples adorned with marble columns and stone statues, were plentiful. Houses for workers and artisans created the suburbs, along with bakeries, wool merchants, weavers and all the usual trades. It would be busy; humming with activity, scandal, and entertainment. Everything required to support a thriving city, much like today, was proceeding as normal, until, on August 24th in 79 AD, Vesuvius erupted without any warning and smothered the whole city under a layer of suffocating hot ash and burning fragments of pumice stone, seven meters deep. Approximately 20,000 citizens lived in Pompeii at that time and most of them died while running for their lives on the roads to Stabia and Nocera. The others were suffocated as they sheltered in the cellars of their own homes. It all happened so quickly that the city was literally stopped in its tracks and frozen forever in a time warp. When the first tentative excavations were begun in 1784 the extent of the city was still unknown, and from then until 1860, when Giusseppe Fiorelli became director of excavations, it was slow and intermittent work. Fiorelli, followed by the archaeologist Amedeo Maiuri who dedicated forty years of his life to this project, finally revealed three fifths of the city, equal to sixty-six hectares. That's an awful lot of ash and debris to move, but it was certainly worth it.

We spent eight hours exploring the city and found it fascinating, even though it was pouring with rain most of the time. The majority of the buildings are without their roofs, but the walls are intact and many have frescoes and brightly coloured decorations still visible. Some have simple, geometric, mosaic floors in black and white, whilst others have colourful intricate designs. Many artefacts and the more elaborate works have been removed to the National Museum of Naples. The roads are paved, and have huge stepping-stones between the pedestrian paths, all well worn by the tread of thousands of feet and rumbling wagon wheels. With our head phones permanently held to our ears, we worked our way through the intricate road system, past forums, shops, houses, temples and eventually came to the encased casts of people and animals buried in the ash. During Fiorelli's excavations he, like others, discovered that when the people were buried, the ash formed a perfect mould of them, right down to the intricate detail in the folded cloth of their clothing. The corpses eventually disintegrated but their shapes were left and Fiorelli poured liquid plaster into these cavities or moulds and hence had exact replicas. A fascinating, if gruesome epitaph to the last moments of the inhabitants of Pompeii.

The next day we caught the local train to Ercolano, the nearby city that was also devastated by the eruption. Ercolano (or Herculaneum, supposedly founded by Hercules), was not covered by ash, but by a mudslide, thirty meters high. Here the ruins are better preserved with better examples of frescoes, mosaics and furniture and we found it smaller and, in some ways, easier to understand than Pompeii. In both cases we were amazed at the lack of information available as you walked around. Dirt and muck covered many of the mosaic floors and general chaos seemed to surround it all. Maybe when a country has so many unique examples of its past it becomes blasé about it or maybe we are just spoiled by the way our English heritage is protected and displayed. Anyway, we found it all fascinating, although it was hard to believe that the peaceful mountain in the far distance could have caused so much havoc. When we climbed Vesuvius a few days later, and looked down on the towns, we could see that the distance was not so great for such a powerful force of nature.

Back at camp the next day, heavy rain and flash floods caused havoc outside. Rotten lemons floated in deep, black puddles which swamped the small, congested road and toppled over rubbish bins. The huge tourist coaches squeezed themselves in and out, disgorging bewildered, plastic-macked sightseers, and horns sounded almost permanently. We bought some fresh fish for tea, posted some letters back home and then spent the afternoon in the Beast discussing Pompeii, while we cut up cereal boxes into small squares and made our own mosaics – which proved much more complicated than we had imagined.

That night it rained heavily again, pounding the roof of the motor home, and we all slept badly, but, next day the sky had cleared, the sun was out and we caught the train to Naples to visit the Archaeological Museum – or at least that's what we were hoping to do!

The journey to Naples, from the station just outside our campsite, only took forty minutes and cost just four euros each, return, but it was so busy that it was standing room only all the way. A quick metro ride after that, followed by a short stroll and we were standing outside the rather grim looking Museum. Around us was a city bursting at the seams in every direction, with traffic so clogged that you wondered how it functioned at all. People, fumes, noise, dust, car horns, battered buildings, fraught looking traffic police, and in one corner by the station, a group of thirty, elderly men, quietly playing cards around picnic tables. Naples looked like a city that you could either love or hate.

The Museum holds, amongst many other riches, the art treasures rescued from Pompeii and Ercolano, which we had come to see – if we could only find a way in. Eventually, after circling it several times, we discovered that, contrary to all information that we had, the museum was shut on Tuesdays, and today was Tuesday. It was supposed to be closed on Mondays; our long journey had been in vain and at that point I felt like adding an extra brick, through the window, to the huge, filthy, old building. But maybe that was a little excessive. Deflated, we were reluctant to make the arduous journey back to camp having achieved nothing, and, being true Brits with some pioneering spirit, we decided to get the train to Ercolano and climb Vesuvius instead.

By mid-day, we were walking to the bus stop for transport to the lower slope of the mountain. But, in true Italian style, the predatory taxi drivers who lurked there, soon pounced on us with tales of long, unreliable bus rides and crowded return journeys. "We must take a taxi, we would surely regret it if we didn't", they said. We ummed and ahhed and tried to bargain and in the end we teamed up with a friendly young Dutch couple who were having the same problem and we all shared a taxi up. At the drop-off point we started the one and a half kilometre walk up a wide, well-marked path of cinder-like stone, and just before we reached the last section up to the summit, we were pounced upon by the next group of salesmen. They pronounced an 'obligatory' fee of seven euros each to be accompanied by the 'compulsory' guide. Everyone had to pay the fee, - but the guides were nowhere to be seen, (unless that was them, sitting in the hut drinking coffee).

The volcano was, of course, very impressive. Almost as impressive as the determination of some Italians to pry the last euro out of you, as you visit this unusual landscape. At the summit we turned our backs on the tacky souvenir/ food shop and looked out over the beautiful Bay of Naples and the Island of Capri in the distance. Well, it looked beautiful from where we stood. The sprawling city lay far below us and we realised how terrifying the eruption must have seemed. Once again, the only information about the formation of the volcano was a small display board, all in Italian, although most visitors were foreign tourists. We turned and peered over the rim and down into the massive crater of the sleeping volcano. Hot air and steam jets rose up the sides and we huddled behind a rock and ate our homemade sandwiches. Somehow, it wasn't quite what we had expected. Vesuvius is impressive, the views are great and you get a good idea of the power of a volcano when you see the old lava flows, far down the mountainsides. So why did we feel ripped off in Italy, yet again?

Back at the pick up point the taxi was waiting to take us, and the Dutch couple, back down to Ercolano. "Go, have a coffee first", the drivers tried to insist, but we all declined, fearing the price might be extortionate and they may charge us extra for the cup to put it in. Back at the station we all clambered out. "You had a good ride? I give good service? You tip me!" muscled the burly driver as he tried to block our exit. Then the boss came hefting over to collect his fifty euros, "You had good driver? You tip him!" he ordered.

Bloody mafia, we think, all of them looking like fat Al Pacino's with their sunglasses and slick hair. We found four euros between us and pushed our way through them.

Vesuvius dix point – but Italy nil point. This was one place that we wouldn't recommend visiting – but maybe someone else will have a better time there, or maybe its time that Vesuvius erupted again and got rid of the robbers who lurk on her slopes.

April

T'was on the Isle of Capri

When you're travelling, you can predict nothing. The day can be good, bad or indifferent, and as we had discovered, the trip to Vesuvius had definitely been indifferent. We were to going have much better times ahead and the next day was one of the best on the whole trip. The sun shone again, in a clear blue sky, so we were up and away early, on a day-trip to the Isle of Capri. Simon had done his research well and our route by train and boat was all planned. We caught the train at our local station. This would take us quite quickly down the coast to Sorrento, and from there we would catch one of the regular ferries over to Capri. We boarded the train and settled down.

A short while later the train halted at another station and more passengers boarded, and although we were more interested in the scenery than who was getting on and off, Simon was sure that he now recognised the backs of three heads. I tapped one of them on the shoulder, and yes, it was Nigel, with Nicky and little Charlotte, our friends from Bracianno campsite. They were staying at a campsite just past Pompeii and they had planned the same kind of day as us, so without any hesitation, we agreed to join forces and do Capri together.

We reached Sorrento, which looked beautiful, a town of ornate buildings that sits on the edge of a stunning peninsular and the breathtaking Amalfi Coast, although we only glimpsed its sophisticated streets as we marched through, anxious to book tickets on the next ferry going to Capri. The port was crowded, but our boat wouldn't leave for forty minutes so we had time to sit down by the seashore, with a cup of cappuccino and catch up on their news while we waited for the boat.

The ferry that day was packed with an outing of noisy Italian school children that got great pleasure from the heavy swell of the rolling sea and I take my hat off to teachers the world over. The mesmerising water shimmered in the heat; a deep, rich, Mediterranean blue, with two lines of white foaming suds trailing our stern. We stood along the sides of the deck, hanging on to the rails and let the wind blow our sun-covered faces; Charlotte holding on tight in Nigel's arms. Capri appeared before us, a green emerald on a blue cloth, its jagged coastline only broken to allow boats to dock at the Marina Grande. This enchanting island, of just 13 square kilometres, has a rocky shoreline indented with grottos, like the famously deep Grota Azurra, (The Blue Cave). We were all keen to see this and to take a trip around the whole island by sea, so we bought more tickets at one of the busy, tourist-attraction huts and clambered down into a much smaller, faster boat, driven by yet another Greek god in sunglasses.

If the scenery ever got boring you could always sit and admire him. His technique for driving this boat was similar to driving a racing car, full acceleration all the way with thrills and spills every minute, so we had a breathtaking trip, stopping briefly to drift into the famous Blue Grotto to stare into indigo depths, and The Green Grotto and even the White Grotto..... all of these cavernous holes casting the waters into strange shades. Through the 'Lucky Arch' which linked a trio of rocky islets, the sea chopping and charging at us as we circled and swung around and then on round the full circumference of Capri until we were back at the Grand Marina.

Back on land again, we said goodbye to our Adonis and went looking for the correct bus to take us up to Anacapri, the smaller town situated uphill of Capri itself. The queue for this little bus was long, but we all squashed aboard, standing room only, and held on tight as we wriggled along a tiny road carved into the cliff wall, with the scariest of sheer drops down to a transparent blue ocean below us. Our bus driver had confidence enough for us all, as he coolly swerved past traffic and squeezed between houses. He obviously knew this route like the back of his hand and before long we were skidding to a halt at Anacapri.

Anacapri is the sister town to Capri, and at one time there was some dispute between the two communes as to who should have jurisdiction on the island. It is built on the lower slopes of Mount Solaro, although the entire island has steeply rising cliffs and a precipitous interior. Early discoveries date back to the Neolithic and Bronze ages and, as usual, it has a varied history of domination by raiding pirates, squabbling nations and the ubiquitous plague, but once again it's most prominent history dates to a Roman Emperor, Caesar Augustus who re-discovered Capri on his way back from the Eastern campaigns. He was so enamoured with its tranquil, undisturbed beauty, that he traded Ischia for it with the city of Naples. When he died, his successor Emperor Tiberius made Capri his golden exile and lived there for the last ten years of his life; between them, these two emperors developed the island and built twelve villas, some still standing today.

The Capri that we know now was re-discovered in the 1950's, when writers, poets and artists fell under its spell. And it is easy to see why they did. A Mediterranean jewel, that manages to retain its magic, despite the latest raiding tourists. Stunning scenery, set under a huge clear sky, in a sea of blue. The westerly winds fan it with fresh cooling air, fragrant flowers adorn it and once again, rather like Tuscany, I absolutely fell in love with Capri. I could happily wake up there every morning, to the dazzling panoramic views across to the Bay of Naples. Ah well, one day.........

We rambled through the streets of Anacapri, admiring the petite white washed houses, flowered balconies and shady courtyards, and ignored the restaurant owners who were trying to wave us into their cafes. Take-away pizza from a busy street seller was fine for us, before making our way to the chair lift that would take us to the very top of Mount Solaro. This lift, of single chairs with a safety bar across, rather like a child's high chair, whisked you to the top-most point in about ten minutes. We stood in line to be popped into a moving chair by two assistants, little Charlotte on Nigel's lap again, and all rucksacks held in front of us. These chairs were quite small and it was quite a squeeze to get in. Then we were flying up over hillsides of meadow grass and spring flowers, pine treetops and patchwork houses, our legs swinging in the breeze. Below us we looked down on tiny terraced gardens, manicured rows of potatoes and peas and green leafed fruit trees. Donkeys and goats munched on their small patches of grass, and vines shaded haphazard patios. Across to our right, the most amazing panorama stretched across to the Bay of Naples and the Island of Ischia.

At the top, we were scooped off our chairs by two well practised attendants, and then headed for the open terrazzo to indulge in a cup of sweet, strong Italian coffee. From there we gazed at the most beautiful view you could ever wish to see. Capri basked under a golden sun and floated in the bluest of waters, with mainland Italy across in the distance. We looked over the cliff top, down through a clear sea and could almost see fish swimming way below us. I was hooked and I wanted to stay there forever – it was so utterly romantic – but there was more. We all decided to walk back down Mount Solaro, back to Anacapri, on a track through the natural, unspoilt pinewoods. This easy, well-worn path, called the Via Crucis, zig-zagged down through flower covered hillsides and sweet smelling, shady, dells and was regularly dotted with numbered, intricately engraved shrines. We skipped and jumped our way down, Charlotte swinging along on the ends of Nicky's fingers or riding high on Nigel's shoulders. We had a long way to walk back and we wanted to eat at one of the quay-side restaurants before the ferry left again. At Anacapri, we again opted to continue walking rather than take the little bus, but this time we went down 'The Steps'. We were still very high up and the drop down to Capri was almost vertical; running like six, manic, mountain goats, we flew down the 850 stone steps that steeply wound their way, back and forth, through tunnels under roads and past houses. After about 200 steps I managed to develop a sort of goat-hop, with arms flailing, to bounce myself down, getting hotter and hotter as we careered. Running down that many steps is surprisingly hard work and all the way down Nigel kept us breathless, as he taught us the complete version of that old sweet song, " T'was on the Isle of Capri that I found her", which he swore he'd learnt on his mother's knee.

We fell off the last steps and had about one hour before the ferry left. A quick run through the streets got us back down to the port, where we found a cheap restaurant and ordered much needed beers. The owner took us in hand, and fed us rich, stuffed Cannelloni and yet more pizzas, before we were galloping off again, laughing and burping, to catch the last ferry home. Red faced and wind blown we squeezed on. It looked like everyone waited for the last ferry before they left, and we waved goodbye to lovely Capri. Charlotte fell asleep on Nicky's lap and only woke when we boarded the train at Sorrento, for the ride back to camp. When Nicky, Nigel and Charlotte got off at their station, we swapped addresses, mobile numbers and kissed goodbye. They would be heading for Brindisi and Greece and we would be heading for Sicily next. Would we ever see them again...... luckily yes, we all met up back in England. We staggered home to the waiting Beast, -"T'was goodbye to the Isle of Capri".

The following day we rested; our faces feeling like sun-baked tomatoes and our leg muscles twinging every time we faced even the smallest step up or down. Our maps were spread out on the dining table of the motor home and Simon and Jack programmed Maisy to take us on to Sicily. The road down the Amalfi Coast, which we would have liked to have seen, had been blocked by a landslide, so we would initially use the motorway and then join the A road which ran parallel with the sea all the way down the western coast to the toe of Italy. We gave the motor home a quick clean up and then, before we moved on, Simon got under the kitchen sink to change the filter that provided filtered water to our separate drinking-water tap. We rarely bought bottled water. Ever since leaving England we had been religious about using the filtered water for drinking, as we were keen to avoid stomach upsets. However, when he dismantled it to remove the old filter, he discovered that there was no filter in it anyway. We'd assumed that the motor home dealer had put a new one in as part of its ready-to-roll service. We had obviously been drinking various countries' waters, with absolutely no problem. Which says a lot for the water around Europe.

Early morning and as we left Camping Zeus, Pompeii was in its usual turmoil of hooting, tooting traffic. A quick swing into the supermarket car park for a mammoth stock up of food and we were off, bumping our way down the fairly rough motorway past Solerno. Rich, green countryside melted into spring mountain slopes, as we drove alongside almost continuous high ranges and small villages perched or nestled wherever they could get a good grip, or a good view between the steep V shaped valleys. We turned off just before Lagonegro to join the coastal A road over viaducts and through tunnels, until turning off again onto a smaller road. We finally ground to a halt at a sandy beach, and wild camped for the night. This whole coastline was quite different to our experience further north. Quieter, with much less tourism; almost deserted and wild in comparison. That night I cooked sausages with a medley of fresh vegetables and we ate our supper round a campfire on the beach. How good it was to be back in the wilds, after the madness of Pompeii.

We felt so relaxed at this little spot that we decided to spend the next day there as well; the gentle waves were such a relief. The few beach bars and shops were not yet open for the season and everything looked rather shabby, but we enjoyed pottering as usual, gathering driftwood along the long stretch of sand. Between the beach and the main road was a rough meadow area, quite large, sprinkled with miniature red poppies and wild plants. Small birds busied themselves amongst this rough land and all day we could hear the trill of a Whimbrel; eventually we spotted him through our binoculars and Jack and I did our familiar 'creeping up' technique, as we followed him through the grasses. A little further inland, hills spread back into mountains and in the distance, we could see snow-topped, far-away peaks. It was a good resting place.

That evening we had another beach fire of collected driftwood. Jack loved this kind of evening, when he was in charge of keeping the fire alive; creating tiny sparks that rose up into the night sky, or running off bare- foot down the dark beach, to gather more wood. I cooked another easy meal and we completed it with a sampling of some delicious Italian cheeses. I became completely hooked on Ricotto al Forno and spent the rest of our time in Italy and Sicily, ensuring that we always had some in the fridge. It was a smooth cheese, soft and creamy, with a dark, burnt edge, rather like the burnt skin on a rice pudding. That and the yummy Mozzarella became my passion.

We travelled on the following day, working our way slowly down the coast. It was a Sunday and the roads were quiet, apart from a swarm of Sunday motor- bikers and a long cycle race that passed us by on the other side of the road. At the town of Dia-mante, the rather grey looking sand changed to yellow and urbanisation increased, but it was still quite rural with olive groves, sheep pastures, and small holdings of cultiva-tion. We joined the motorway again at Rosarno, filling up with diesel and sleeping in the motorway car park for the night, along with the lorries again. We were now close to the toe of Italy, where we could cross to Sicily, and the next day would take us to the ferry terminal at Villa Giovanni.

My diary for 26th April reads, "Scariest bit of road yet. Motorway reduced to one lane each way, extremely high on flyovers, over sea and deep gorges. Can't look, abso-lutely terrifying!" We were very close to the edge, yet again. The landscape in this cor-ner of Southern Italy was stunning to say the least. Very green and lush at this time of the year, with fast flowing rivers, dense woodland, and a dramatic, precipitous coastline that kept us gripped all the way..... mostly to the edges of our seats. The ferry port at Villa Giovanni was small, but very easy to find, and when we rolled into the parking area there were only two or three other vehicles waiting to cross to Sicily. The ferry charge, at that time of the year, was very reasonable, only 35 euros for a sixty day return ticket, and it would only take about half an hour to cross. We hadn't known what to expect at this ferry port, so it was a great relief to find an easy roll on, roll off service. We rolled on and were soon rolling off at the busy port of Messina.

I had never thought that I would ever be able to visit Sicily, an island that had always captured my imagination. Wild, warm, and romantic was how I had always thought of it, and actually yes, we did love it there. It is the largest island in the Medi-terranean Sea and yet is still small enough to allow you to see most of its treasures and terrain over a few weeks. Three seas surround it: the Ionian, the Tyrrhenian and the Med, and the volcanic Aeolian (or Lipari) Islands, including the active volcanic island of Stromboli, lie just off its northern coast. Sicily is mountainous, with Mount Etna being the highest volcano in Europe, on its east coast. But it also has two very fertile inland plains and as we travelled we saw olive and orange groves, heavily laden lemon

trees, pink flowered almond trees and all varieties of vegetables growing in rich, dark
soil. Woods of umbrella pines and patches of palm trees complemented stands of holm
oak and beech and of course the fresh fish, literally straight from the sea, was sumptuous. Spring or autumn are the best times to visit, when it is pleasantly warm, but not
the sizzling hot of mid summer.

We were heading for a campsite at a small town called Oliveri, on the north east
coast. This would be a useful base and we were hoping to take a boat trip to Stromboli
from the nearby port of Milazzo. Heading down the quiet motorway, Maisy was keeping us on track really well, but as we got closer to Oliveri, we foolishly decided to ignore
her directions as we thought she had missed a turning. In a sudden panic we left the
motorway and took a tiny road down into a village. Before long we were attempting a
very tricky twelve point turn, in a lane that was only just as wide as we were long. Our
back wheels skidded in mud, as we extricated ourselves yet again. Our American RV
was big; it was great to live and travel in, but it was big, and this sometimes made it
very difficult to manoeuvre. We lurched back out of the tiny lane, but were still on the
wrong road, which we could not get off. Laboriously we wound our way up a high cliff,
needing the whole width of the road to get around each hair pin bend. Cars started to
trail us and it was with a great sigh of relief that we reached a monastery at the summit. But, with the same experience going down the other side, we were in quite a state
when we eventually gained sea level again. Now we had to go back on the motorway,
under the mountain we had just climbed over, to get back to the correct road. Finally,
finally at our third attempt, we found the campsite and as usual, squeezed ourselves in.
Luckily it was almost empty, which left us plenty of manoeuvring room and before too
long we were hooked up to mains electricity and were getting set up – sorry Maisie, we
should have listened to you.

Oliveri was a quiet town with a long sandy beach. It had pleasant open squares,
edged with orange trees and fountains; in summer it was probably very busy, but at this
time of the year we were most noticeably the three outsiders. Our campsite was at one
end of the town and had its own beachfront bar, just a few steps from the sand. Next
morning I was up early. I took my coffee down to the empty, camp café and sat on the
wall overlooking the beach. It was very peaceful, with just a warm, gentle breeze running off the sea. Across the small bay, a sandy coastline curved under the dark forms of
cloud-topped mountains. I closed my eyes and eavesdropped on the chattering birds
in the eucalyptus trees behind me, and the conversation between two fishermen on
the beach before me. Their lilting Sicilian made easy listening with its ample octaves
and vowels. A chainsaw started up somewhere in the hills and wisps of smoke drifted
down. Two joggers ran past the wall, the rhythmic pounding of their feet on the sand
slowly fading as they distanced themselves; a dog stopped briefly to sniff me before following their tracks. The sun broke through, warming my face, and a cyclist arrived to
chat to the fishermen; the train rumbled along the track behind the campsite and small,

black ants scurried about the white plastered wall in their search for food. The fisher-man pulled in a silver, gleaming fish.... That'll be lunch then, and headed off home. What a peaceful life to lead.

Later we cycled into town, just the three of us: the good, the bad and the ugly, turn-ing the heads of the old Sicilians, who sat in a row on the bench outside the butchers shop. Jack, conspicuous, with his flame red hair and huge orange freckles. We bought our fresh bread and meat, (and more Ricotta al Forno cheese), and then cycled on round the back streets until, on the corner of a square, we saw a small hairdressers shop. This was seen as a lucky find, as I had been bemoaning the state of my hair for quite a while, a rather girly thing to do I know, but it was definitely past its sell by date. I either wore it scraped back in a band or long, tucked behind my ears. Either way, I was utterly fed-up with it. Simon and Jack pulled up outside the 'coiffeurs' and commenced a joint effort to persuade me to go inside and book an appointment. There were no customers inside and it looked closed, but when I eventually tried the door handle, it opened, a bell tinkled and a small, dapper looking man came out from another room. One look at my hair and he understood completely that I was in need of a good coiff! "You come back at three o'clock," he mimed with his watch, " and I'll do the best I can with your disastrous mop". How could I resist.

At three three o'clock I returned on my bike and walked into the still-empty hair-dressers. My dapper little friend came out again and sat me in a chair. With a few deft movements of his hands we established that I didn't care what he did so long as it would be an improvement, and he was astonished that I should let it get into such bad condition. Snip, snip, snip, and my shoulder length hair, was now ear length. Snip, snip, snip, as he buzzed around me, like a happy little Sicilian bumblebee, my long hair now on the floor. We went to the basins, where he gave it a good wash, followed by more sniping and flicking and buzzing, as he spent a good half hour getting it to his satisfaction. A last little snip, and I had a really good, short style. Next came the hair mouse and blow dry followed by hair spray, and more hair spray and yet more spray and I was done. (No problem riding home so long as I can tack into the wind, my hair is set like concrete!) He rushed off to get some heavy smelling talcum powder, to dust bits of hair from my neck, and stood back to admire his work. He dashed off again and came back with a heavy smelling perfume, which he squirted all over me! I was beginning to smell better than a tarts handbag..... but he is still dashing back and forth, just snipping the odd hair, until at last, final spray, and he's happy. And it was a great cut, a bit Sicilian grandmother'ish, but all the same, a vast improvement. He vanished into the back room again and this time returned with boxes of lipstick and eye shadow. I definitely couldn't handle a Sicilian make-over and politely refused, just choosing one lipstick which he gave me as a present. Boxes returned, he then took me by the hand and led me into another room – what was I in for now I wondered? This room was his small kitchen area, and there on the table were a bowl of kumquats. This charming man then insisted that I try these fruits, freshly picked from his garden and we sat and ate our way through them; eating them whole, pith, pips and all, sweet and sharp and delicious. I eventually left, boarded my bike and was starting to ride back to camp, when round the corner came Simon and Jack. Their jaws dropped as they did a double take of this glamorous new hairstyle and for a few minutes they were speechless. Mama Mia, I felt quite light-headed. A new me and all for fifteen euros.....definitely a Sicilian bargain.

The delightful smell of orange blossom filled the air at this campsite. Jack tracked geckoes and lizards as they moved around the olive trees following the sun, and captured huge, yellow and black striped, flying insects under glass to examine them. Next to the site was a Nature Park and lagoon where we took evening walks, the sea on one side and cliffs on the other and here we saw our first Squacco Heron: a small brown-backed, bittern-like heron that bursts into a dazzling white when it takes flight and shows its wings. But the weather had now become changeable, either very hot or very squally, which was making it difficult for us to book our boat trip to Stromboli. The boats just didn't run if the weather looked stormy, but we booked it for the coming Sunday and hoped for the best. That was of course, if Aeolus was willing.

May

The Aeolian Islands

The Aeolian Islands (also known as the Lipari Islands) are named after Aeolus, the Greek god of wind, who supposedly confined the winds in a cave. Seven Islands make up this archipelago off the north east coast of Sicily and two of the islands still have active volcanoes. Stromboli is easily reached and eruptions can be seen regularly, especially at night, when glowing lumps of lava are hurled above the crater rim to illuminate the dark sky. It is one of the most active volcanoes on earth, being in nearly continuous eruption for the last 2000 years or more, and although it hasn't caused major damage, it has caused some fatalities. In 1919 four people were killed and twelve homes destroyed by gigantic rocks hurled over the rim. In 1930, three people were killed by pyroclastic flows and a fourth person was scalded to death in the sea where the flows entered the water; in 1986 a biologist was killed by flying rock and in 2002 the collapse of an unstable slope caused a small tsunami which damaged the village below and for the first time ever, caused a complete, temporary, evacuation of the island. So, although most eruptions are relatively harmless, it is still an unknown quantity, capable of killing. The cone-like shape of the crater usually contains the lava flow and protects the island from further damage. It's possible to hire a guide and walk to the top of the volcano but as the explosions in recent years have become fiercer, a review of tourism is under-way.

We boarded the ferry at mid-day, along with about sixty other tourists, and found spaces above deck on the canopied seating area. The first stop on our 'Stromboli By Night' tour was at Panarea, a small but incongruously jet-set like island. As we approached the quay, loud thumping music blared across the stage of an outdoor, aerobics area. We felt as if we had landed on a miniature Ibiza. The male DJ, (I think he was male), bizarrely clothed in a leopard skin dress, sunglasses and wide, plumed hat, strutted amongst the young and not so young exercisers, as they stamped and stretched and wiggled their bottoms to disco-baby songs, while other young-and-beautiful types paraded around them. Now we felt as if we had landed on Mars. Yachts and speed boats in the bay, decked out in bikini-gorgeous girls and brown hunky men in shades, basked in the world of Panarea – but we scuttled off as fast as possible from this nightmare area and headed up into the hills. We only had a few hours at this island, which we spent walking one of the narrow coastal paths, past scattered white washed houses baking in the sun with stunning views of the sea. Our picnic lunch we ate on a pebbly, shadeless beach, downwind of the yellowy, sulphurous fumaroles, the exit holes for the rotten-egg smelling gas, which seeps out from the volcanic base of the island. Then we made our way back to the busy little quay to board the boat again. Shops and restaurants were still doing a good trade and the music was still blaring away.

Stromboli, was a completely different experience. As we approached, over a shimmering, sapphire sea, the huge classic volcano shape of the island appeared on the horizon ahead of us. This whole island is the volcano; steep sloping sides flow into the water and a cone shaped top, puffs continuous white gas clouds up into the blue sky. The sleepy, one street town of Stromboli speckles the waters edge, diminutive in comparison. We circled the island, viewing the steaming lava flows on their slow journey into the sea, before disembarking at the small jetty where little children played and dogs rolled in the sun. I had the feeling that life would never get too hectic on this island unless the volcano felt like causing a stir. This place had a very definite, laid back character of its own.

With no-where much to go, we walked up what appeared to be the one and only main street and had a beer at a small bar, where a young DJ was playing great acid-jazz music. Occasionally, small, three wheeled cars went by, or the odd scooter appeared, but on this road, children and dogs definitely had right of way. Our trip was called 'Stromboli By Night' and as the sun set, we boarded the boat again for a supper of pasta and fish with local red wine and soft bread, before motoring round to the side of the island where we moored up to watch the volcano. Wrapped up against the chill night, we sat on the open deck and enjoyed a display of belching smoke and intermittent eruptions of fire and brimstone, glowing red against the black sky. Every flare and flash brought ooohs and aaahs from our bobbing boat and it was with some reluctance that we finally left such a great sight and motored back over the inky-black sea to mainland Sicily.

Next day, later than we'd planned, we packed up and drove on towards our next destination. A strong, warm Sahara wind was whipping up the sea again, so we felt lucky that we had managed to take the boat trip the day before. We wanted to travel further east in Sicily now, and then head across the island to the south-western coast. All through that day we followed the quiet, unspoilt coastline, alongside the crystal clear sea. Fat yellow lemons hung on the trees, and again bright red poppy fields flanked us, but the wind now gusted so strongly that we were continuously buffeted across the motorway. I think that Aeolus must have released one of those captured winds. At last, Simon gave up trying to manhandle the motor home against the Gods and with aching arms he pulled into a sheltered service station car park where we slept the night. It had been empty when we had arrived, but in the morning lorries once more surrounded us: alongside, behind, in front, up close and personal again, but we hadn't heard any of them arrive in the night.

The wind disappeared as quickly as it had arrived, and next day promised to be scorchio. With the air conditioning on, we crossed rugged green Sicily on the raised A19 road that flew us over hills, vales and plains. Without a doubt the Italians are

master road builders and excel when it comes to flyovers. We joined the road to Agrigento, but took a wrong turn and detoured over a mountain, through sumptuous green
countryside and the busy old town of Caltanisseta, a fascinating place that we vowed to
go back to one day in a Fiat 500, not an American RV. Then down to the coast and the
Valley of the Temples. This route across the centre of Sicily was exceptionally pretty
at this time of the year; almost continuous swathes of small red poppies in Monet-like
green fields, sprinkled with flora of yellow, purple and blue, steadily rolled by us. Acres
of vines in young green leaf disappeared over rounded hills and ancient olive groves
and almond trees stood on floors of fresh spring grass. Small herds of goats, with soft
floppy ears and ding-dong bells, pottered down roughened tracks and we hardly saw a
person all day.

Agrigento, the most ancient town in Sicily, sits strategically on a small plain between two hills, close to the sea. The Valley of the Temples, containing five important
Greek Doric temples, is near by. We decided to visit these, as we were going to pass
by so close, and followed Maisie's directions as she led us up towards them. Only
two of the temples are still standing, in relatively good condition, the rest having been
destroyed by earthquakes and early Christian vandalism. As we approached we could
clearly see the Temple of Concordia, positioned majestically on the top of a small
hill; a large building of golden weathered stone, its once impressive roof supported
by around eighty, tall, Doric columns in long rows, its graceful lines and imposing
proportions dominating the landscape. This wide valley was once central to religious
life and is littered with the remains of ancient buildings constructed in the 5th century
BC. We had hoped to find a good parking area, so that we could take a day to explore
it all, but as we approached the main entrance, we realised that this was not going to
happen. As we often found in Italy, the organisation and accommodation required
for the armies of tourists who are drawn to these spots was completely inadequate.
The entrance to the site was situated on the small but main highway into Agrigento,
so cars, lorries, buses, motor homes and all else who would normally use this two way
road, had to contend with parties of bemused tourists who ground traffic to a halt as
they unloaded from coaches. Touting salesmen hindered cars which tried to squirm
between it all and we made yet another hasty twelve point turn at the first opportunity
and got the hell out of there. Back down the road, some way from the entrance, we
found a large lay-by where we stopped and had lunch. Luckily, we could easily admire
the impressive Temple from there, and read about its history while we had a civilised
salad with a glass of chilled wine. That was as good as it was going to get for us and
it suited us just fine.

Our next stop, a quick detour down to a beach, put us in the path of another touting salesman, who appeared alongside us as we stood admiring the crashing surf. This
time it was an older man, slightly bent and weathered brown, but driving a smart little
car. He had no doubt in his mind that we should buy some of his homemade olive

oil, which we had to admit looked good, but we really didn't want five litres of it. His insistence started to put our backs up, after all we hadn't asked him to stop and sell us olive oil and how did he think we would store five litres, did he think we were running the engine on it. Eventually he admitted that he had smaller quantities in his boot and we bought two, half litre bottles. But, the smile had disappeared and he drove off without even a thank you. Well, it takes all sorts, and we certainly met most of them on our travels.

The next sort we met was a real character, and I smile to this day when I think of him. We drove on down the coast and stopped to wild camp for the night in a large, bumpy parking area, right by the beach, next to a gently rolling sea. It was a peaceful spot and far from town, in fact we were the only ones there. Jack jumped out to stretch his legs on the sand and Simon wound up the satellite dish to check the news and weather report. He soon discovered that there would be a full eclipse of the moon that night and we were in one of the best areas in Europe to see it – and clear skies were forecast. Our evening entertainment sounded all set so I cooked chicken stir-fry, Jack gathered some driftwood for a fire and we relaxed. A gentle stray puppy had befriended us when we arrived, firstly by rolling on the sand with our own young puppy and then by sticking doggedly to Simon who fed her the last tin of dog food that we still had from our stay in Ronda. The sun began to set over the sea and we all settled down on the beach to await the rising moon, with a glass of wine by the fire. At that moment, up rolled a battered red car and out jumped a small, even more battered, dark-skinned Sicilian man clutching a grubby plastic cup and a bottle of red wine.

"Buonasera, Buonasera", he greeted us, with a great toothless smile.

"Buonasera" we happily replied, while he filled his glass, topped-up ours and introduced himself as a local. (We never did catch his name).

He and Simon immediately got into long and jovial conversation, as best they could, as neither spoke the others language and much was translated by drawing in the sand with sticks. After a while Jack and I retreated to the motor home, slightly unsure of this rather strange, new visitor. As the night wore on the moon rose and the wine went down (quickly) and before long our new friend was beckoning me out again. This time, he first shook Simon's hand and then sidled very close to me with murmurings of "Bella Signora, Bella Signora".

Then with a sudden and rather manic desperation he grasped my hand securely in both of his and his eyes took on a rather doleful, blood hound look as we shook hands, and he pressed closer. But the handshake that I got was either some secret Mafia signal or, (and this is what I've always believed), it's a suggestive handshake where his middle finger tickled my palm! I was so surprised that I jumped a mile but the leery look in his eyes left me in no doubt about what he was thinking. I didn't know whether to laugh or run. He was definitely no Adonis, but that obviously didn't stop the hot Italian blood from coursing through his veins and for the rest of the evening, he gave me long, meaningful looks over his white plastic cup, which had me and Jack in stitches. As I write this now, I'm still laughing and feel like squirming when I think of his grubby handshake. You've got to give it to these Italians, they don't waste much time.

Well, we all stood and watched as the earth blotted out a wonderful, huge, bright moon that seemed to hang in the air over the murky sea and surf; the fire died down leaving a cold empty beach and our friend gave up the chase, skidding cheerfully away into the black night. He promised to return the next morning, and needless to say we were up and away early. Our biggest regret was saying goodbye to the dear little dog, who had been such a good companion. We left her with food and fresh water, but we always wished we had taken her with us....... And if ever we go back, we hope that she at least, will still be there.

Our rather loose plan now was to go to Siracuse, but we decided that we would follow the coast around the end of Sicily, and if we saw a pleasant place to stop, then we would take a few days to explore the area on the way. The land became flatter as we travelled south and west, and before long we were passing through poly-tunnel, vegetable growing land again. We homed in on Punta Bracetto, a small fishing village in the province of Ragussa, where we knew there to be a good campsite. We sometimes gathered information about campsites as we went along, but we had also bought a great CD disc, which we could run on our laptop, and which itemised camp-sites in most countries in Europe. Scarabeo Camping was one of those lucky finds that we feel like keeping to ourselves, but I guess I should share it with you.

We arrived to find the campsite only just open for the season, but with a friendly smile and much encouragement they got us through their entrance gates and we found a place to park up. Once again, we were a little on the big side. One look at this beautifully positioned, un-assuming site and we thought that we had found heaven. Opened in 1968 by Professor Giuseppe Nobile, it had regularly won the Award for Quality and Courtesy. In 2001 it was taken over by his nephew and niece and they have continued to keep up his high standards. This is not a site for those who like a noisy and hectic holiday; it is quite small and very peaceful. The building materials are mainly traditional and are as natural as possible, just local stone, terracotta, bamboo and wood. Its simple lay-out accommodates tents, caravans and motor homes but its biggest attraction by far is its idyllic location. Warm, wooden steps, edged with palm trees, lead you straight from the campsite to a beautiful sheltered bay of fine, silver sand. The peaceful beach with a shallow, blue sea is just the place to go if you are ready to relax with a good book for a week or two. Even in May it was hot enough to swim and the free sunshades provided, were a must. The only other occupants on the beach were the abundant and industrious little Scarab beetles, after whom the site is named. They scuttled through the soft sand on endless missions, leaving tiny footprints for us to follow. Jack had his surfboard out and was in the sea before we could put the kettle on and that was the start of a most enjoyable stay at this site.

Next morning we cycled down to the local bakery, and bought our ciabatta bread. The small, dark haired owner, with her ready smile, was soon giving us fresh home-grown lemons and selling us a huge bottle of home made wine, "multo forte" and " good for the stomach" but which I have to admit was too strong even for us, and eventually went down a drain in Croatia. Our cycle rides took us along flat roads, to the nearby towns of Scalambri and Marina di Ragusa. Although quite small and quiet, they had elaborate baroque buildings and spacious, well used squares. Walks along the coast took us past banks of bright pink, star shaped succulents sheltering curious green backed lizards. Jack caught endless insects – from flying grasshoppers, to weird and wonderful caterpillars and an enormous horned beetle. We thoroughly enjoyed this quiet corner of Sicily, and spent many days on the beach, snorkelling in the bay when the water was clear. Six days later we thought we had better get on to Syracuse, so we said goodbye to Concietta and the rest of the campsite crew, gave the lady at the bakery a big hug, and we headed off. That's the joy of independent travel; when you find a special spot, you can stay there for as long as you want. One day we must go back to Camping Scarabeo.

Sicily in late spring was a delight, and as we drove we once again admired her colours and clear seas. With too many enticing wild camps, rushing was out of the question but we had to keep moving or we would never get to Syracuse. The only campsite we had seen advertised was situated about four kilometres outside the city. We planned to park up there and ride our bikes in, although you could catch a local bus. We arrived at the campsite at about nine o'clock in the morning and waited for the owner to unlock the gate. It was basically an overgrown olive grove with minimal facilities, the owner was not the happiest of souls and it was expensive. It was also swarming with mozzies, and they zoomed in on Simon while he worked outside, hooking up to the electrical supply. Even with fly screens on all windows and doors they cunningly invaded us, making our stay miserable, but within the hour we were all set up and keen to see Syracuse, so we made a dash for our bikes and cycled in single file along the main route into town. I would say that this road was not one for the faint hearted. Very busy, and used by huge lorries and coaches, I probably lost several kilos in weight from the sheer fear factor alone as we pedalled single file, trying to avoid slip-streaming under the wheels of juggernaughts. We arrived unscathed but not un-scared and locked our bikes together around a support on the wide Ponte Umberto Bridge.

This elaborate bridge links the slightly younger Syracuse with the small island of Ortygia, which was the original centre of the city. The history of Syracuse takes some unravelling. Its ancient ties to Greece, its Carthaginian settlements and its fear of Rome caused it to waver dangerously between one stool and the next, eventually falling to a Roman conquest. In 264 BC, Syracuse was a Greek city, but when Rome set her eyes on Carthage in the First Punic War, King Hiero II, King of Syracuse, found himself caught between two mighty empires. He initially supported Carthage, as Syracuse had many Carthaginian settlements, but was coerced to pay tribute and supply grain to Rome. In the second Punic Wars, 218 BC, Hannibal of Carthage led his army to victory against the Romans when he crossed the Alps into Italy and many Siracusans wanted to ally themselves with him again. But King Hiero continued to honour his treaty with Rome: when he died, his fifteen year old grandson, who had started to re-negotiate with Hannibal, succeeded him. The city became divided between Roman and Carthaginian supporters and a civil war followed the assassination of the young King. The Carthaginian supporters won a brief victory and Rome was forced to send an army to deal with the situation and promptly lay siege to the city. However, for many years, the great Archimedes had been military advisor to old King Hiero, and he had made good preparations for such an attack. After three years, Marcus Marcellus did breach the inland walls and Syracuse was sacked with around 2000 Cartheginians brutally slain including Archimedes. Marcus Marcellus had intended that he should be spared, as his wisdom and inventions were already much admired.

Like much of Italy, history is soaked into layer upon layer of this city. Greek, Roman, and every dominating nation thereafter, have left their mark. We walked the maze of medieval streets and alleyways in Ortygia, marvelling at the fancy 17th century baroque architecture which curls around every doorway, balcony and window. Wide, shaded paths edged with restaurants led us around the city sea walls and past the Greek temple dedicated to Apollo. At lunchtime we bought rich anchovy pizzas and yummy pistachio ice cream, and then walked down to the picturesque waterfront on the Via Pichareli, and to the famous Fountain of Arethusa. We couldn't believe how much history was woven into this ancient city and wondered how much more could we take in one day?

Well, it was easy really, because old Ortygia was a very pleasant place to be. However, we did have a cycle ride ahead, so we risked our lives again in the slightly chaotic traffic and pedalled furiously back to camp. We rushed straight into the Beast and slammed the door shut – there wouldn't be any fraternising with fellow campers on this site, because any glimpse of flesh was immediately attacked by the hoards of mozzies. Armed with our individual fly swots, we searched every nook and cranny before going to bed, but we still spent the first hour or two before sleep, jumping up shouting, "there's another one", and leaping off to kill it. By morning, the pale roof- lining of the motor home was dotted with dead bodies and our blood, each mark showing where we had zapped the satiated little devils.

Even after our restless night, we managed to get into town by about ten o'clock next day. The ride in had been another hell raiser – our single file, weaving along, Simon in front, Jack in the middle and me at the rear signalling furiously when required. This time we scooted through the main town to find a back route to the honeycomb-shaped Archaeological Museum. Our devious route took us through a very pretty park that had a most unusually shaped modern building. Simon was on a mission to reach the museum, but Jack and I skidded to a halt, intrigued by what we soon discovered to be, The Sanctuary of Our Lady of Tears.

In 1953, a modest plaster image of the Madonna, belonging to a poor family, miraculously shed tears. It was a sensational event, causing amazement in Italy and Europe, and as word spread, crowds of pilgrims and worshippers, the sick and the dedicated, went to pray at the small shrine. Many cures were attested to the tears of the image and in 1954 Pope Pius XII provided a final blessing when he gave a radio speech supporting the virtues of the icon. By 1968 the present sanctuary or church, had been built and the plaster image of Our Lady of Tears was carried there, before a crowd of tens of thousands of people. We studied the exterior of this ultra-modern building, which dominates the skyline of the city and is designed in the shape of a huge teardrop. A massive circular base, with regularly spaced entrances, converges to a single central point 102 meters high. We parked our bikes and went inside to discover a round, cavernous, cone shaped church, with slanting light stabbing through from above. Built on a cantilevered design, this is a very contemporary building, but inside, it manages to retain a feeling of complete peacefulness and unity. The image of the Madonna rests in a silver framed hollow, above white marble steps. When we were there, the Church was being attended by many people of all ages and appeared to be as popular today as it had ever been. If you are in Syracuse and are interested in architecture, it is well worth a visit.

We cycled on, and eventually reached the Archaeological Museum, Paolo Orsi, which houses an amazing 18,000 or more ancient artefacts, dating back a staggering 6000 years – tools, decorated pots, jewellery etc from 4000 BC. It is a modern building where the displays are clearly laid out in chronological order, depicting life throughout the past six millennia. The wealth of information soon had Jack and I staggering boggle eyed; for us it was almost overload, but Simon, who kept saying, "you must look at this one", had the stamina to work his way through the whole museum. Jack and I soon disappeared outside and found a shady spot in the gardens to recover and discuss the merits of different ice cream flavours. We had a nasty feeling that we were definitely going to overdo it that day and would need all the strength we could get.

The mid-afternoon sun was now beating down mercilessly, and we had to cycle along a ludicrously long, dusty road to reach the last item on our agenda - the large archaeological park on top of a dusty hill overlooking Syracuse. The largest feature here is a 5th century BC Greek semi-circular theatre, which had been literally carved out of the rocky hill side. We flopped for a while on the warm stone seating that circled the stage and imagined the entertainment on offer to those living in the area at that time. Behind us was the necropolis, containing the tombs of the dead, from the same period. Jack was keen to do a little exploration here, just to see if there were any bones lying about, so before we got arrested, we dragged him off to an interesting cave named Dionysius's Ear. According to legend, Dionysius used this cave as a prison, because the acoustics were so outstanding that he could hear the prisoners' whispered conversations. Its cool, dark, towering interior reminded me of the inside of a snail shell, the rock walls curving round to a large open area at the centre. We tried whispering in there, but our whispers were drowned out by a body of tourists who broke into a noisy, many times repeated rendition, of their national anthem. We backed out, much too politely, and went off muttering about national characteristics again. Perhaps it was time we headed home.

The Park also contained a very well preserved Roman amphitheatre but by this time we were feeling shattered. There is only so much that you can take in, in one day, and as usual we had overdone it. We wobbled like reckless, sun-crazed insects, expecting to be squashed at any moment, back along the busy main road to camp, dashed into the motor home and sat with our feet in bowls of cold water. A last muster of energy for another mass mozzie kill and we were in bed with our books by 8.45pm. Wild elephants could have thundered through the Beast that night, but dead to the world, we slept like logs and woke early next morning keen to move on and leave the mozzies behind.

Our route now took us up the east coast of Sicily, past Mount Etna and on to Taormina, a spectacularly situated tourist spot. We had seen a campsite advertised along this piece of coast and hoped to stop there, but as so often before, this was not quite the way it turned out. At first our road was quiet and wide, but before long it had changed to a small A road and the hot- bloodied, impulsive, racing Italians were around us again. We sped on as fast as we dared, but with reckless determination, cars overtook us, four at a time, whizzing in and out of gaps, with no room to spare. Bunches of wilting flowers lined the roadside, commemorating those who hadn't quite judged it right.

The day was scorching hot, but the summit of Mount Etna was shrouded in low cloud, and we had become so blasé about mountains that we gave it a miss. Vesuvius and Stromboli had satisfied our appetites for volcanoes and by now we were keen to reach Paradise Camping, our next beachfront campsite. We followed Maisie's directions, and the turning approached. Great, we thought, that wasn't too bad – however, it wasn't going to be that simple. We were ready to leave the busy main road and all looked good, including the inviting coastline below us. We should have known it was too good to be true and we should have spotted the railway line that ran alongside the coast.

The campsite was well signed and we turned hard right into it, through a narrow arch followed by a very hard 90 degree left, going steeply downhill. At the bottom, another hard 90 degree right, again with a serious drop, took us onto a long very narrow lane. This entrance was just about manageable for long vehicles but we were now well and truly committed to going in this direction. You have probably guessed what was then ahead of us – yes, the usual extremely low bridge, in this instance with a height clearance of 3.4 meters. We were 3.7 meters and short of taking the air-conditioning, satellite dish, aerial and skylights off the roof, there is no way we would go under it. The lane was too narrow to turn around, and our only option was to reverse back up this very steep twisting lane of sharp bends, and back-out onto the hellishly busy main road. What is it with some campsite owners? Why don't they have the sense to put a sign at the entrance warning of low bridges? We surely weren't the first vehicle to have this problem. We practically stamped up and down in the lane, such was our frustration. To add to our growing anger, the owner now wandered up the lane to us and with complete indifference shrugged her shoulders, turned around and walked off again. We had deliberately phoned ahead to this site, giving our dimensions, to ensure that they would have room for us, so why didn't they mention the bridge! Just a helpful word of commiseration would now have gone such a long way, although we might have given her a few words of advice about where to put a sign. We resigned ourselves to a difficult reverse back up the obstacle course. At the main road, I sprinted down to a bend and flagged down the speeding traffic so that Simon could back out, then I raced back to the motor home and clumsily jumped aboard as we moved off again. About two hours later, after a three-point turn on a busy sea front and a fair bit of cursing and swearing, we found a super little campsite, swung in and pulled on the hand brake. A cup of tea was totally inadequate, but several cold beers helped us calm down and once again we took in our new surroundings. Jack got the bikes off the back, set up the barbecue and pulled out the awning and we ate our supper under a shady tree, overlooking a calming sea. Just another day on the road!

Once again, we had found a friendly family run site, this time at Sant'Allessio Siculo, a small seaside resort just twelve kilometres north of Taormina. Flowers bloomed profusely, the sun shone brightly, Goldfinches enchanted us daily, and the builder's yard next door gave us some brief entertainment. Monday morning started with a huge argument, coming clearly from the yard. At 8.0'clock the boss had arrived in his over-large 4X4 car and weighty leather jacket. At top volume he yelled at his line of men who stood or slouched before him, banging his hands on his car bonnet and waving his arms in the air to add emphasis. With some reluctance they were bullied into shouting back and before long a full-scale row was brewing. We wondered what the problem could be; could it be Italy's choice of entry into the Eurovision song contest, or the poor results of their local football team, or just the price of bread. Whatever, it got them all very heated and at one point he jumped in his car, skidded round the yard, then got back out again and carried on the argument. He was one mad Italian. He obviously didn't believe in taking his group of employees into the office for a quiet word in their shell-like – aahh, if only we understood the language, or perhaps it was better not to know. Anyway, he eventually left; only to return just minutes later to vent the last of his spleen, before roaring off again for good. The unimpressed men shrugged their shoulders and ambled off to have a fag before starting work. Maybe it was the Italian equivalent to a Monday morning pep talk, who knows?

That day we caught the local bus to Taormina. This intriguing town perches high on a coastal hilltop, with an almost perpendicular slope down to the sea on one side and a dramatic view of Etna on the other. The main motorway runs through a tunnel, bored straight through the rock beneath this settlement, which leaves it in splendid isolation. However, it has long been a favourite haunt of European jet setters and is now firmly on the tourist trail. The local bus wound its way up the snaking road, dropping us off with still some way to walk up to the town. Expensive shops, elaborate buildings of baroque architecture and the gothic Duomo kept our camera busy, not to mention the staggering views down and along the whole mountainous coastline and out to sea. We took our time strolling through the fascinating streets, but ground to a halt when we discovered one of the best music shops that we had encountered on our trip. The Funivia (cable car) took us back down the quick way, almost vertically, offering us a fabulous panoramic view over the sun-covered land and stunningly beautiful sea shore. From there, we walked around the corner to paradise - Isola Bella Beach, which curves out into the transparent sea, forming a shallow sheltered inlet, punctuated by a fairytale island. Deep cerise bougainvillea with young green leaves, swayed against a clear blue sky and here we flopped and swam and lay in the sun until it was time to get our bus back to camp.

Next day I awoke slowly to the gentle mantra of woodpigeons, the long, descending trill of the brightly decked goldfinches and the rhythmic pace of the early train to Messina. The warmth of the sun was already heating up the air and we decided to take a picnic back to Isola Bella again. With snorkels, flippers and food, all packed into our backpacks, we caught the bus and spoilt ourselves for another day. Within twenty-four hours we would be leaving Sicily and be heading across the Southern coast of Italy. We had really loved our stay on this island and could easily have spent more time there. The people were generally friendly, the food delicious, the scenery spectacular and there was so much more that we could have seen and done. One day..... one day..... we would love to return, but now we had an appointment to keep in Monza – and before that of course, would be Venice.

May

Venice and Formula-One-Fun

By 11.20 the next morning we were rolling off the ferry, back onto mainland Italy. We'd arranged to meet Stella, Simon's sister, at the formula one race track in Monza in two weeks time and we wanted to visit Venice first, so we were heading straight up the east coast of Italy, from toe to top, and would wild camp every night on the way. The weather was really warming up now, but the air conditioning unit in the motor home was working well and it was a comfortable ride. The only slightly worrying aspect was that the parking brake light was remaining on while we were driving. Maybe it was just faulty wiring: it didn't seem to be affecting progress, and so we carried on. The scenery in southern Italy was dramatically beautiful with wild sandy beaches, verdant green hills and more swathes of red poppies. May was a wonderful time to visit; we guessed that a few months later, the land would be sucked dry by the relentless heat.

Our first wild camp was in a large lay-by, pleasantly shaded by tall eucalyptus trees, just off the motorway. Lorries pulled in during the evening and we watched them coming and going as we sat and played cards at the dining table. A small car had also arrived, initially rushing around the car park, before individually circling round the stationary lorries. The driver appeared to be using the little car to almost flirt with the trucks, twisting and turning, driving slowly alongside and then flouncing off to the other end of the car park. Another lorry rolled in and the little car rushed over, doing a few provocative turns in front of it, after which the driver of the lorry and the driver of the car both left their vehicles and went into the trees together. That was a new one on us, and we hastily shut the blinds. He was definitely selling something and we could make a few good guesses what it was.

Even with the night time entertainment going on we slept well, but next morning posed a problem. All ready to roll, with everything packed away and seat belts on, Simon started the engine. But when he went to move off, the motor home wouldn't budge. The auto-park brake would not dis-engage which meant that we were going no-where fast. We all exchanged silent glances, and a few silent prayers. I put the kettle back on, for that always helpful cup of tea, and Simon got out and got under to find the cause. The auto-brake transmission oil reservoir had leaked and was empty, and he thought he couldn't fix it without parts from the UK. This was a huge problem. We were stuck in a motorway lay-by, a long way between service stations, with no way of driving. If we'd been in a car it would have seemed better, but with all our worldly goods, our life, and our home contained in this giant vehicle that we had no way of moving, I couldn't imagine what we'd do and wondered if we'd spend the rest of our year in an Italian lay-by. So, while I stared dejectedly out of the window, watching our gay motoring friend as he now minced suggestively round the car park on foot, Simon trawled through the manuals and worked out that he couldn't fix the leak but he could disconnect the auto-park brake if we could get hold of a litre of transmission oil. This didn't make any sense at all to me, but Simon explained that we needed the oil in order to temporarily activate the auto-brake, so that he could disconnect it. Then we would just use the manual hand brake when parking. (It was still a little beyond me).

Basically, we needed transmission oil, but I thought that manna from heaven might have been easier to get at that point. Then he remembered that we had RAC euro- breakdown cover. Have you ever tried getting breakdown assistance while you're abroad? It isn't that hard so long as you have infinite patience and don't panic, so I would be useless at it. Simon however was brilliant. He called the RAC in England and explained our situation. They contacted their Italian counterparts and explained the problem to them. The Italians then called us and we emphasised repeatedly that we were huge, could not be towed anywhere but just needed one litre of transmission oil to fix our problem. They eventually arrived with a large tow truck and no transmission oil. At this point I wanted to put my head in a bucket of sand, (an ostriches life looked better than mine) and Jack said he was going to pray or cry but couldn't decide which would help most. This had all taken several hours, many phone calls and plenty of coffee, but at least we now had two big, burly, Italian car mechanics with us. They scratched their heads as Simon tried to explain the problem, and eventually one went off to get the oil while the other admired the motor home. When the oil finally arrived Simon disconnected the brake and we were ready to roll again. He also phoned a supplier back in England, asking them to send the spare parts to our next planned campsite. Eventually, thank god, we left our gay car park. I took two Relaxaby tablets and fell asleep in the back, while Simon drove us on, praying that we wouldn't have any more problems.

That evening we stopped for the night at a small service station and after supper we took a stroll down a grassy lane to a picturesque wood. I collected wild poppies and some wonderful grasses, and then from the pinewood we heard the distinct and unmistakable, fluted song of the Golden Oriole. We never did see him, but his song was good enough to cheer us up. Yep, just another day on the road, never a dull moment.

Jack notched up twenty-seven mozzie kills that night. He was leaping around until gone midnight, but in the morning we were all covered in red bites, so some had managed to escape him. We pressed on up the coast of Italy, through the flat agricultural plains of Puglia and up to the more touristy areas around Pescara and Ancona. An uneventful overnight stop and then over the River Po and we were approaching Venice. We were heading for a large campsite at the tip of the Punta Sabbioni peninsular. From there we knew that we could catch the regular ferryboat across the Lido to Venice. The long, thin Sabbioni peninsular was crammed with campsites and its singular road had become very congested. Even at low season it was busy, but once we were settled on our pitch, we knew that we could leave the Beast on site and it was an easy bike ride down to the ferry.

We took a cycle ride down to the quayside that evening and rode along the track that led out to the lighthouse. I tried to imagine what it must have felt like all those centuries ago when refugees from the nearby Veneto region had fled to these small islands in the lagoon to escape the pursuing Huns. There they had stayed, on those dank, misty, scraps of land, building their homes on wooden piles driven into the marshy ground. Gradually Venice had grown, eventually becoming a prosperous, independent trading nation, boasting of explorers like Marco Polo, who left from there on his voyage to China.

It continued to flourish until 1797, when it was overthrown by Napoleon, and did not become part of the kingdom of Italy again until 1866.

The sea has been pivotal to its history, helping with early defence and providing a gateway to trade routes with the world. But water may also be its eventual destruction, as it slowly erodes the foundations of the present buildings. Venice looks much the same now as it did in the 13th century, although then, we would have seen the white sails of cargo boats in the harbours and canals instead of the motorboats of today. The huge Venetian lagoon, the largest area of wetland in Italy, is the result of sea currents and tides moving in one direction and water channels laden with sediment moving in the other. Human intervention adds the last dimension. The resulting montage of islands resembles the flat bones of an ancient dinosaur revealed in the water, with Venice at the heart.

Approaching by ferry is the best way to first see Venice, and as we followed the deep-water channels through the blue-green lagoon, pale coloured stone buildings with rusty-red roofs, and the famous pointed tower, all became apparent in the distance, although the cities' flat outline hardly made any difference to the line of the horizon. Our first destination had to be St Marks Square, with its two airy piazzas originally laid out in the 9th century AD. The marvellous architecture of the buildings, which surround these most beautiful squares, is well worth dawdling over and I could have dawdled forever. Delicate, intricately carved and decorated buildings with long, shady loggias, edged the squares while the Campanile (Bell Tower) offers views across the lagoon and the city, to the far off Alps. From this tower Galileo tried out his telescope – I wonder what he saw in those days?

The decorated blue and gold Clock Tower, whose mechanism is a work of art, not only strikes the hour but also indicates the passing of the seasons, the phases of the moon and the movement of the sun from one zodiac sign to another. And rather like Trafalgar Square, St Marks would not be St Marks without the pigeons, which swamped us for our handfuls of corn. But how can you be there and not have a pigeon on your head? They must be the best fed birds in Italy. Dominating it all is the Basilica, the final burial place of St Mark. It would be quite impossible for me to describe this lavish, beautifully proportioned building and its breath- taking interior, or the arched Palace of the Doges which stands alongside it and is the first building you see when you arrive by boat. All I can say is that if you haven't seen Venice, then you must.

I could have spent the rest of the day in the square, gawping at the buildings or just window-shopping for exquisite, unnecessary objects, ridiculously expensive adorable clothes or superb, delicate glass baubles that I wouldn't know what to do with. Oh, if only there had been another female to enjoy all that with me. But I was out-numbered two to one and had no chance, eventually being dragged away by the hand. We moved on to catch the Number 1 vaporetto and ogled the eclectic mix of construction, from gothic to rococo, on palaces, churches and houses that lined the Grand Canal. We had bought the ten-euro tickets that allowed you 'all day' use of the vaporetti (ferry) and traghetto (water buses), which meant that we could travel cheaply and as much as we liked. So, hopping off at the Rialto Bridge, famous for the row of narrow shops that line it, we decided to see more of the city by foot on a route through the back streets of Venice. This is the best way to get a feel for life in this amazing city, although even with a map, it's easy to get lost. If you can imagine that every street and alleyway is flooded with water, with houses whose doors step straight out into that water, then you begin to understand how unusual this city is. Tiny, hunched bridges arch steeply from one island to the next and archetypal gondoliers weave their slim-line, pencil thin boats through slender passages and watery streets.

We passed the Bridge of Sighs, named for the sighing of prisoners as they crossed it on their way to the dungeons, and then detoured to take in an exhibition of scale models that explained some of Leonardo de Vinci's inventions, before eventually returning to catch the ferry back. The next day we did some of it all over again, just for the fun of it. Venice is another absolutely unique city. A constant pleasure to the eye but as usual, even in May, it was busy. In mid summer it would be very hot and very, very busy, and I for one would not want to be there then. Not for all the pigeons in St Marks Square!

We had been on the road now for eight months and we were well settled into life in the motor home. We still missed our family, the other boys and our friends, but we were looking forward to seeing Croatia and Slovenia before starting the home run. We had no idea what we would do when we returned to England, or if indeed we would still return. We phoned home regularly to catch up with everyone's news and nothing seemed to have changed there. Stella would be able to give us a better up-date when we met her in Monza. We were also in touch with John and Gill and their family who we had first met at Easter in Braccianno, Italy. They had got to Dubrovnic and were heading up Croatia, so we agreed to try to meet them half way down that coastline at a later date. Mobile phones make communication so easy when you're travelling. We texted people like Gill and John frequently and Jack was always communicating with his friends back home. It was reasonably cheap and easy to use, but for longer calls we bought the local phone card and used kiosks.

So, leaving Venice, we took a detour inland to Monza, which sits just north of Milan, part of the huge fertile plain bordered by the long stretch of the Alps to the north and west. The National Autodrome of Monza hosts Italy's top automobile racing events, the Formula 1 and Superbikes, but is also used as a test circuit and for walking races. The track was completed in 1928, in record time with a huge workforce, through the initiative of the Automobile Club of Milan; its situation is surprising because it snakes through the woods of Monza Park, an area covering 800 hectares. The park was originally part of the estate belonging to the nearby 'Villa Reale', a stately neo-classical pile, built in the late 1700's by the archduke Ferdinand of Austria, who like many before him, appreciated Monza's countryside and closeness to Milan, the capitol of Lombardy. Today, the park contains not only the impressive Villa Reale (now the civic art gallery and museum), but also the Mirabello horse racing track, two golf courses, a polo field, a public open air swimming pool, a camp site and of course the National Autodrome. It is the cycling, walking and leisure place for the fortunate people of Monza. We were joining up with Simon's sister, as she was one of the co-ordinators of the Historic Grand Prix Car Association races (HGPCA). Cars from the 1920s to 1960s, many with great racing provenance are lovingly pushed to their limits by dedicated enthusiasts at events all over Europe, and we would be lucky enough to attend this one.

We rolled into Monza Autodrome, following directions to the paddock and once again there was Stella, waving us in to park-up alongside the likes of Maserati and Ferrari owners. For months it had been 'just the three of us,' but now suddenly we were literally in the midst of English speaking, fellow Brits, involved in a busy, social weekend. Slightly antiquated racing cars were being tuned-up with ear-splitting results, but after practice time we managed to squeeze in a cycle ride, around the whole race track. Our bikes were once again invaluable at Monza. We could easily ride through the wooded parkland, so cool and tranquil, to reach any of the spectators stands, where we sat in the hot sun and watched the deafening cars come roaring by. If we cycled outside the autodrome area, into the rest of the park, we joined other cyclists, joggers and walkers enjoying a natural environment in this busy city and it was fun to be so sociable again. We squeezed eight people into the motor home for dinner that evening, Simon conjuring up a massive paella. The wine flowed and Stella promised that the next day, she would drive us into Milan in her car and show us the sights.

Milan is huge, the fashion and financial centre of Italy, but luckily, the major sights are all fairly central, and can be reached quite easily by taking the underground trains or walking. We parked on the outskirts, and caught a tube train to see the Duomo. When we got there, it was completely covered with protective material as it was undergoing restoration works, so unfortunately we wouldn't see one of the largest churches in the world, said to be a surprising display of bizarre, gothic design. However, another building, namely the Central Train Station, had already greatly impressed us. Thousands of people travel to and from this station every day and many homeless sleep in it at night. It is a practical building for the people and yet it is heroic in proportion and style. No modest station this, but colossal and heavily faced with strong art nouveau lines in grey stone, elaborated with gargoyle-like faces and huge winged horses, it must be one of the largest and most impressive railway stations in Europe. Outside, set in one wall, a fountain of water gushes from the gaping mouth of a grim, angular face. Inside, vaulted ceilings of glass, towering walls of marble and marvellous carved panels, dwarf the commuters. It was designed in 1912 but not completed until 1931, the time when Mussolini was at the height of his power and it is well worth a look if you are in Milan.

We wandered around the back streets, dodging the cities' orange trams, and after a leisurely pasta lunch at a street cafe, retraced our steps to the Piazza del Duomo and the glorious Galleria Vittorio Emanuel 2nd – a shopping arcade like no other; the absolute opposite to the austere Central Station. If you have the money, then you can spend plenty in the sumptuous shops that line this extraordinary arcade. Golden light floods through the arched, glass and iron roof 96 feet above you, and mosaics in richly coloured marbles lay beneath your feet. The two inter-crossing streets adorned and decorated with statues and sweeping baroque garlands, meet under a stunning central dome of coloured glass. Linking the Piazza Duomo and the La Scala Opera Theatre, this was where the rich paraded at the end of the 19th century. Guiseppi Mengoni designed it, but he tragically fell from the roof of this very beautiful arcade, and died just days before it was due to open.

That evening we dug out some of our vaguely respectable clothes and joined the HGPCA dinner at the luxurious Hotel de la Ville. There we drank champagne and dined like Maseratti owners – very nice if you can get it – and the next day we joined the throngs for Race Day at the track. The noise was deafening, (and that was just the Italian commentator), and the buzz of excitement and enthusiasm rubbed off on us. Strolling amongst the powerful cars, we felt that we were definitely part of the jet set. Another dinner out that evening and then they were all heading home again, so all too soon we were waving goodbye to dear Stella, Martin and the Historic Grand Prix Car Association. They disappeared through the gates, a convoy of trucks, motor homes and friends, leaving just a big empty space and us feeling rather flat and lonely.

So, there we were, just the three of us again, parked up in an empty field in beautiful Monza Park – but the weather was good and the Formula 1 racing car trials were about to begin, so 'here and now' we decided to stay over and watch them. At 9.45 the next morning we were sitting in the almost empty stands opposite the pits while McClaren, Honda, Ferrari, BMW and most of the other famous names, tweaked their cars to perfection before screaming round the track. Each team had their own pit area, well separated from the others by screens and barriers so that no trade secrets could be stolen. The mechanics, in uniform, fifteen to twenty of them at a time, fussed over cars and drivers like mothers over their babies. When the car was rolled out of the pits, the driver was shaded by a large umbrella and supplied with drink through a straw. Heat covers were ready to warm the tyres and final smears of speed reducing dust were removed. Then the stomach churning roar as they revved up and left the pits, reaching a squealing crescendo as they pulled out onto the track and thundered away. Gradually quiet returned, with just a far- away scream of engines as they raced around the park, through the chicanes and down the straights, and an ear-slitting neeeeoooooowwww as they came screaming by again at top speed. Small, powerful and very fast; the earplugs helped, but not a great deal. But then, half the fun is in the excitement of the noise so Jack simply wore his newly acquired Ducatti cap and sunglasses and stayed cool, dismissing the earplugs as things that only boring old farts used. Well, that put me in my rightful place anyway!

May

Croatia calling

A new country was calling us and it was time to head back towards Venice, to then continue on around Trieste, through a small strip of Slovenia and into Croatia. The weather was getting hotter by the day, but we were still driving past lush green vegetation and those endless fields of small, wild, red poppies. Paul McCartney was our regular CD choice now, singing along with us as we wound on down the roads. We reached the Trieste area at about tea-time, in a flash thunderstorm, and pulled in for the night at a large woodland car park up in the hills behind the city. The storm blew over and the sun re-appeared, so Jack and I gave Simon half an hour's peace and quiet, while we took a walk up through the woods. The path, laid with gravel and well defined, climbed steeply up through trees and undergrowth, eventually coming out by a low stone wall. We walked to the wall and looked over, now realising that we had reached a staggering promontory viewpoint, from where we could look down along the coastal inlets of Slovenia and Istria and up towards the Italian coast and the Gulf of Trieste. It was a tremendous view, too good to be missed, so I ran all the way back down and dragged Simon up to see it. A raised look-out platform further along the path gave us a 360 degree view of not only the whole coastline, but inland as well and if you are ever taking this route, the A4 dual carriageway, which goes east of the city, do look out for this car park, pull in, and take a short walk up to this little known viewpoint, and a view that is out of this world. So often it was those unexpected stops that turned into something special that we all remember so well.

The road around Trieste and through the small section of Slovenia, was undergoing major upgrading, but when it's finished it will be a highway to heaven. We didn't know what to expect when we got to Croatia. We'd heard that it was beautiful, with a great coastline but we weren't sure what the roads or the people would be like. It was all a really pleasant surprise and now of course, it has taken off as a major tourist destination. We were heading for a campsite near Rovinj, on the western coast of the triangular shaped Istrian Penninsular. There are plenty of large, well-equipped campsites all along this coastline, but the natural beauty is unspoilt because they are usually well hidden by low maritime pines and there are no high-rise areas. English seemed to be widely spoken, so although we had been practicing our basic Croatian, we could converse with most people in a mixture of languages.

With very little else to rely on, tourism is big in Croatia; nearly as big as the enormous bellied male tourists who bask like big, brown, wrinkly walruses on every seaside rock or chair that they can find there. We wondered if it was meant to be a sign of great wealth, rather like the Tudor days when a big belly was to be proud of. Their female counterparts were in hot competition with large bosoms, bellies and bottoms to match and we just thanked god that they didn't tend to go naked. After all, much of this coast is designated for naturism. As it was, there were plenty of bikini clad, grossly overweight, overcooked ladies, beached on the rocks. They dominated all sea-front positions with their caravans and tents, boats and trailers and I have to admit that they were the rudest people we had come across on the trip. Maybe it was just a certain nationality and type that you got there. The Croatians were slim, mild mannered and always polite in contrast. Needless to say, we found a quiet pitch, back from the busy beachfront and, as we had arrived on Simon's birthday, we celebrated with a local meal of fresh fish in the excellent camp restaurant.

We planned to spend about a week here, going as far as we could on our bikes and also hiring a small car to explore some of the 360 square miles of the peninsular. Next day we rode along the flat, well-used cycle path that follows the beautiful shore line through the Punta Corrente Forest all the way to Rovinj. Just off shore, serene green islands dotted the clear, clean blue sea and white sailed yachts drifted in and out of bays. Rovinj itself is a charm, set in the jewelled bracelet of the Adriatic; on a high peninsular, next to the sea, it is the prettiest town in Istria. We locked our bikes to yet another lamppost (a useful common denominator in all countries) and walked the stone cobbled streets that were so warm and smooth that I preferred to take my sandals off and go barefoot. There's no doubt that this famous town deliberately attracts tourists but it is a genuinely busy fishing port too; working boats small and large plied back and forth to the harbour and tangled black nets were spread along the wide, waters edge, to be mended in the sun by old, seated, sea-farers. Tourists strolled amongst the restaurants and craft shops and artists captured it all on their carefully composed canvases. Pastel coloured houses, their stonework crumbling and dog-eared, were shuttered against the hot sun and the glare from the deep blue sea. This place, with its relaxed atmosphere, was somewhere that we could have lived quite happily. Above the town, dominating the sky line was the lofty tower of the baroque Saint Euphemia Cathedral; its wide, smooth steps providing a shady resting place for us after the long walk up. Steep, narrow streets of pale Istrian cobbles and dark open doorways, accommodated playing children, and lines of gaily-coloured washing decorated the houses. We wandered back to our bikes and cycled home for a cat-nap before taking an evening ride along the coast the other way. A very pleasant start, to our stay in Croatia.

Simon collected the hire car on the Sunday morning and with sandwiches, coffee flask and a million other things we 'might need,' we spent a day inland. The central Istrian peninsular is a mixture of rolling green highlands and valleys, mainly farmland and woodland, which changes to a fertile plain in the southwest. Northern Istria consists of mountain massifs, which were historically difficult to cross. Most towns and villages were built in circular form on hilltops, for natural defence, and the town of Motovun, perched 270 meters above sea level, is a classic example of this. This fortress town has a magnificent view of the fertile wooded valley of the River Mirna. A chunky stone wall surrounds it and steep cobbled streets, so shiny that they appeared wet, led us through solid stone arches and up to a wonderful open sided, forum. The view from there, across the silent valleys, was utterly peaceful, so we sat on the silky stone benches that ran around the inside of the building, took our sandals off so that we could feel the smooth, warm floor and ate our picnic. The air had that wonderful heat, that when you sucked it deeply into your lungs, seemed to warm right into your bones and relax all your muscles. Lying on the bench with a full stomach, like a well fed puppy, Jack fell asleep, and we almost did the same. Croatia seemed to have the same timeless pace that we had found in Portugal, with none of the franticness of northern Italy.

Arriving back at camp that evening, we unloaded the car and had just grabbed a beer when we heard our names being called out by five people walking towards us. It was the Doherty's; Gill and John with Hannah, Daniel and Sarah, who we had first met at Braccianno in Italy. It was good to see them again and we all immediately took up where we had last left off and exchanged stories and information about our travels. They pitched their caravan and awning next to us and we spent many evenings together before we all moved on again. As I write this, we are still in touch by email. They are in their second year of travelling and have reached Australia, all well and happy. They were the only other English people that we saw on this campsite apart from one man we met, who had a Slovenian wife. We saw no other English motor homes on the roads until we reached Dubrovnic, although there were plenty of French, Italian and German.

The next day we should have used the hire car but we were so tired from a late night, us talking and the kids disappearing on an owl hunt until one in the morning, that we spent the day snorkelling in the clear sea and laying on the rocks. Croatia has very few long sandy beaches, most of the coastline is made up of flat, smooth, sloping rocks that are good to sit and lay on, and a few small sandy coves. Shoals of fish were easy to see when snorkelling and in June the water was warm. Many beaches were designated for naturalists, as was half of our campsite. We got fairly used to suddenly meeting naked people, although Jack would usually do a rapid 'U' turn when he saw them coming – his age, I guess. There was also a fjord close to Rovinj; the 'Limski Zalijev', and Simon, Jack and I had allowed ourselves to be persuaded by Nicky, the camp activity organiser, to join a boat excursion there the next day. This was a first for us – normally we orchestrated our own expeditions, and we soon regretted our rather rash decision.

I feel that all nations have predominant characteristics but I certainly wouldn't denigrate a whole nation just because of the actions of a few. Our boat trip up the fjord could have turned us against one certain nation for life but how foolish would we be to let that happen! We boarded our 'pleasure' boat at 9.30 in the morning, a jolly

Croatian captain and the cook welcoming us on board. They were mild mannered, enduring people. The boat was filled to capacity, and we all sat on benches and around central tables on the open, canopied deck. At 9.45 am we were heading for the fjords and the first of the Schnapps was brought around. We gave that a miss, just a little early in the day for us, but most of the jolly Germans on board, who made up about 90% of the passengers, threw it back with gusto and enthusiasm. Loud, tinny, yo-ho-ho music blared from the overhead tannoys and we realised that this was not quite the informative trip that we were expecting. Apart from us three lone Brits, there were a quiet young Slovenian couple with their small daughter, a few older Italians, and a very large, long haired dog who took up most of the floor space, (and the large German contingent, who now appeared to be all together, or soon were after the Schnapps had gone down.) By 10.30am, plates of ham and bread appeared along with the first of a non-stop supply of rough local wine. Brought out in small crates, one crate per table, with plastic cups to swig it down, it looked like we were in for one long booze cruise with no escape. We groaned, silently of course because we are English, and the German party started up a singsong in competition to the tannoy.

We motored around Rovinj bay and then up the entrance of the fjord where we moored up at a regular tourist spot. Here we all got out to inspect a 'pirates' cave. Well, pirates were certainly running it now, even if they weren't before we got there, because we were fleeced to enter a dingy hole and expected to buy postcards to get out again. Black Beard would have been proud of them. Back on board, wine still appearing from the hold, the singing continued while the cook barbecued fresh sardines on a grill which hung over the stern of the boat, and people took it in turns to don a pirates hat, pipe and eye patch and have their photo taken sitting behind the ships' wheel in the captains chair. We gave up at this point and had some of the wine, hoping to anaesthetise ourselves. Jack declared that he might actually throw himself overboard rather than suffer on the boat, but decided to wait until after the sardines. Half way up the fjord we stopped for lunch. Some people got off and swam from the rocks in the deliciously cool water but others stayed at their tables, unable to move far by now and continued drinking. To be honest, there was very little to see in the geography of the fjord and as no educational information was being provided, you could have had a similar time in the local bar.

The food served was excellent though, and the Croatian hosts were unbelievably polite. Now we turned and headed back, which seemed to be the 'go ahead', for the party to move up a notch. The main contingent, all in about their thirties, now red faced, still drinking and swaying ominously, really got underway and we wouldn't have been surprised if they hadn't started dancing on the tables and slapping their thighs. The small group of older Italians tried to compete with a few nostalgic melodies, but for sheer volume, lasting power and boring repetition, the Germans had it. Of course, being British, we kept quiet. We couldn't think of anything to sing except Robbie

Williams and that didn't seem quite the thing anyway, and we're not sure of the words unless he's singing along with us, so we suffered in silence and Jack said that if he threw himself into the sea, we shouldn't try to rescue him because he might still be alive. The large dog continued to spread himself out on the floor, despite yelping loudly every time he was trodden on. Eventually, at about six o'clock, worn out by the sun, wind and noise we staggered off the boat. The German party, bottles in hand, looking as if they'd spent a week at a beer fest, staggered away too, thank god in the opposite direction. Of course, I wouldn't denigrate a whole nation just because of the actions of a few, but it would be oh, so tempting!

Next day, Jack did the sensible thing and had a day at camp with Gill and John's kids; swimming, playing on lilo's and watching 'Bend it Like Beckham' on the lap top in the comfy air-conditioned peace of the Beast. Why didn't we think of that instead of going off in the hire car again to explore more of Istria. Still, that's adults for you. We worked our way across the peninsular, over Mount Ucka to elegant Rijeka and then returned along the coastal road taking in Opatija en route. This 'old' sea-side resort, the place to be seen before the First World War, still boasts grand, ornate residences which once housed kings, tsars, celebrities and the wealthy. Now turned into elegant hotels these lavish mansions attract wealthy, Italian tourists in the summer and well-heeled elderly Europeans who enjoy quiet warm winters. It had always been the Dalmatian Riviera.

The sparsely populated inland areas, with woods, mountains and flat plains offer wonderful diverse scenery, but the coast is always stunning and the best way to see it would be by boat. That evening we stuffed ourselves at one of the many roadside restaurants which tempted you in by cooking whole suckling pigs, on turning spits over hot coals, at the roadside. The smell was delicious and the price was very reasonable. Agritourism has really taken off in Croatia and everywhere we went we saw signs for rooms to let in family homes and farms. It is their equivalent to B and B and using this accommodation would be an excellent way to travel through the country.

We had the car for two more days and wanted to make the most of it. Early next morning we drove down to the southernmost tip of Istria to the Kamenjak Nature Park. This long narrow peninsular is famous for its untouched, extremely indented coastline, its warm clear seas and the abundance of wild flowers, including several species of orchid. It is also quite rightly called the Terrae Magicae. Clouds of dust followed us as we drove over the dirt roads that led down to the beaches. We chose Kolombarica Beach, with its flat slab rocks which gave easy access to the sea, and there we snorkelled and swam for the day, following shoals of gleaming fish. Swimming round the shore to another area, we found the well-known sea cave whose punctured ceiling allows shafts of sunlight to slant through the clear water. We snorkelled for hours, until we were cold and then went in search of the only watering hole on this quiet peninsular.

Wooden signs pointed the way to a café that remains one of our favourites to this day. Hidden away behind long grasses and high bamboos, it's hard to spot at first. This is because it is almost all constructed in natural materials and blends so easily with the surroundings. Many years ago, before the peninsular became a nature park, the present owners' father bought this small piece of land as a retreat for himself and his family. Gradually more and more friends came to visit and, as he always liked to provide food for them, it gradually evolved into a small café. But, it is like no other café we had been to, as it is simply an organic extension of its surroundings and all furniture and fixtures are made from natural materials. We walked down wooden steps, through bamboo alleys to the main eating area; a shaded open 'room' with wooden tables and benches, under a roof of dried grasses. Dim and wonderfully cool, the harsh sunlight only managed to dapple its way in. Our order of ham rolls, sardines and squid, all with salad and bread was made at a bar made chiefly from rocks, and from self-service taps, set into shells we dispensed homemade lemonade and local wine. Around this room were paths that led past more small, shady seating areas. These were roughly woven into the tall grasses and bamboo clumps, and were totally private, like mini exclusive dining rooms. Homemade swings and slides, decorated with fishing-net floats and flotsam and jetsam, were hidden through yet more grasses and the whole place looked as if it had just gradually evolved with the land. The present owners, the original owners' daughter and her English husband, were friendly and welcoming and sat chatting to us about Safari Café. It was a great find.

Gill, John and family were now moving up towards Venice and before long we would be heading down towards Dubrovnic. We said goodbye to them once more, and hoped that one day we would all meet up again. We stayed a few more days at the campsite, just cycling and relaxing and watching the many birds in this area. At night we heard the soft whistle-like toot of the Scops Owl. Swallows nested in the beams of the shower buildings and, while you washed, they gave you a worm's eye view of them swooping in and feeding their young. Croatia has plenty of wild life, including lynx, bear, wolves, deer, lizards, snakes, and the griffon vulture. Most of these are to be found in the national parks, and Croatia was lucky enough to get seven of the finest parks when the Yugoslav Federation collapsed. We had decided to visit just three; the first being – Paklenica.

The E65 road runs adjacent to the sea all the way from Rijeka to Dubrovnik, and as you drive it you are given a continuous view of myriad offshore islands glittering in a blue, blue sea. There are well over one thousand islands around the shores of this long thin section of Croatia. On the map this road looked like a non-stop ribbon of red edging a blue sea, but it is marked all the way with dark green, denoting a very special 'scenic route'. Croatia really is as stunning as it appears on picture postcards. We followed this road for six hours. Sometimes it was smooth and sometimes pot-holed and lumpy; we travelled through gentle agricultural areas of vines, olives and salad crops, dramatic valleys and gorges, past small picturesque inlets and fishing harbours and alongside the grey Velebit Mountains. The wind had been gusting strongly most of the way down the coast and Simon's arms were almost falling off from wrestling the motor home against it, but at last we thankfully reached our next destination.

Camping Paklenica was a friendly relaxed site; a shady woodland next to a long pebbly beach. There were other motor homes there, but we were told that they hardly ever had English visitors and had never had a large American motor home before. The entrance to the National Park was well signposted and next morning, under a glorious, fresh sky we cycled the two kilometres up to it. At the gates we locked our bikes together, paid 30 kunas each, (approximately £2.80) and entered the park on foot. Nine hours later, very weary…. we got back on our bikes and road home! You may have guessed that we overdid it on day one, as usual.

The Velebit Mountain range, the most formidable of the Dinaric Mountains, dominates this part of the coast and reaches right down to the Adriatic Sea. Below the highest peaks, two deep transversal gorges cut into the mountains, covering an area of thirty-six kilometres, like two long jagged gashes. Of the two gorges, Valenika Paklenica is the most dramatic and most accessible. We had cycled from the coast, up into the lower part of the gorge to the entrance, from where your only option is to continue on foot. Towering cliffs, 400 meters tall, were already dwarfing us; they rose on both sides creating a cool shaded entrance to this grand natural wonder. Here the dusty floor of the gorge was flat and smooth. Scattered groups of rock-climbers gathered around their ropes and jangling equipment and with hips strung with metalwork, these wiry, fit looking enthusiasts dusted their hands with chalk, adjusted their soft footwear and worked their way like determined ants up the cliff faces. This park is a most important rock-climbing centre. With climbs such as Psycho Killer, Black Magic Woman, Albatross and El Condor Pasa, it attracts enthusiasts from all over Europe.

As the gorge narrowed we started up the well-marked, well-trodden path, alongside a crystal clear, ice cold stream which flows, rushes and tumbles over rocks and boulders most of the way down the route, sometimes providing large, perfectly clear pools. It is a most welcome source of refreshment as there is only one small cafe on this walk and that's about two thirds of the way up. We had drinks and biscuits with us, but stopped regularly to splash our faces with ice-cold water, trying to get some relief from the heat which seemed to bounce off every rocky surface. The first part of the walk was steep, twisting up through sheer cliffs that were studded with brightly coloured, stunted plants. Green lizards were warming up in the morning sun and birdsong filled the air. By lunch time the sun was beating down relentlessly and we were still climbing up, but we were now in a wooded area with the welcome shade of tall beech trees and a slight, cooling breeze that drifted down the gorge bringing with it the smell of wood smoke. About ten minutes later we came upon the log hut café, where a few tables and benches provided a peaceful resting place in the shade, and a young couple cooked sausages on an outdoor wood-burning barbeque. Nothing had ever smelt so inviting and hunks of soft brown bread and sizzling sausages had never tasted so good.

About half of the National Park is covered with forest; holm oak, holly, and fig, but mostly it is beech and pine. Everything needed, has to be brought up the gorge on pack animals, not just for the café but also for the few remaining residents who are allowed to continue living in their old stone houses higher up on the alpine meadows. We continued upwards, the spectacular Velebit Mountains gradually getting closer and closer and seemingly even higher. Their huge, stone, rock faces shifted colours and shadows, as the sun traversed the clear, blue sky. Eventually, by mid afternoon, we reached the alpine level, a strange contrast of gentle slopes covered with wild sage, thyme and low pretty flowers. The air was fresh here, scented with herbs, and again birds and butterflies were everywhere. Here also was a long, well equipped, mountain hut where you could arrange to spend the night and continue the next day to the peak of Vaganski Vrh at 1757 meters. We would love to do it one day, but at that moment we were simply grateful to stretch out on the benches and fall asleep for half an hour under some shady trees. Beyond the hut, the meadow became hilly again, and almost hidden amongst the trees were scattered a few small, stone farmhouses, some of them built into the rock faces. It was absolutely peaceful up there, completely untouched by modernisation. We saw only one person, a tiny old lady, dressed in black, sitting outside her tumble-down, stone house feeding lean looking chickens, a silent dog by her side, although there was a strange feeling that others might be watching us.

By now we were all suffering. My knees were aching, Jack's feet were killing him and Simon's calve muscles were seizing up, and we still had the long hike back down. The return walk gave us superb views of the gorge and, as the sun was dropping low in the sky, the towering cliffs were a kaleidoscope of colours. Half way down we stripped off and swam in a deep, cool pool of icy water, which was constantly filled by a crystal clear waterfall. Back at our bikes, we just about managed to freewheel down to the campsite where, too tired to cook, we ate in a restaurant – we were so weary that we wondered if they could carry us home to our beds. Paklenica Gorge was well worth it though and would be just as stunning in winter. We can't wait to go back one day and walk it again.

Next day we struggled to do anything, other than sitting on the beach watching a large, spotted toad as he scuffed out a cool hole under the low beach wall. It was a scorchio day and he was having none of it. Eating ants in the shade was his idea of heaven, so we lay on our towels and idly watched him work while we thought about our next destination, namely Krka National Park.

June

Dubrovnik and Croatia's Gems

Krka National Park (pronounced Kurka), is situated in Sibenik and Knin county about half way down the coast towards Dubrovnik. We arrived a few kilometres from it on the following evening, after a steady drive and a huge risotto lunch at a quiet beach side café. We ate out more in Croatia than anywhere else, mainly because the food was so good and so cheap. There were few opportunities to wild camp, so that night we pulled into a local families' camping field (agri-tourism in action), and paid about £3 each for a nights stay with use of shower and toilets if required. Tourism is undeniably important, as the wife explained to us that evening. They owned a small herd of cows and some chickens, which they raised on the old family farm. The barn buildings were solid but basic and the family were obviously not affluent. They had two children and her mother lived with them too; she was busy hoeing the large, well-tended vegetable patch in their modest garden. The wife explained that her husband had recently been made redundant from the local fabrication factory and now they had to make a go of the camping field. To supplement their earnings she got up at 4.am every morning to deliver her eggs, milk and cheese to the market in Sibenik. It didn't look an easy life and they didn't have the usual trappings of European wealth, but Croatia is still emerging from a difficult recent history. It has come a long way, and so far has retained an unaffected, natural charm and pride. It was a blessed relief to visit three of its most important National Parks, and some of its major attractions and never, ever, be hassled or harassed by money- grabbing, touting taxi drivers, guides or salesmen, as we had been in some other countries. Yet tourism is their main source of income.

Early next morning we said goodbye to the friendly campsite owners and drove on down a descending road until we reached a large car park by the wide river at Skradin. There are two ways of entering Krka Park; either by road at the top or by boat at the bottom. The boat trip up the river was a great way to approach it.

The Krka National Park was proclaimed the seventh national park of Croatia in 1985 and encompasses an area of 109 square miles along the River Krka. From its source at the base of the Dinaric Mountains the river drops 242 meters to the sea, and it includes areas of unusual, preserved ecosystems. It is exceptionally rich in varied flora and fauna, with eight hundred and sixty species and sub-species of plants recorded growing in the park and eighteen kinds of fish, including ten endemic species, living in the river. The reed beds and water meadows are alive with amphibians and water birds, and reptiles abound in the shrubby, dry, stony areas. The majority of visitors, including us, only see the spectacular travertine cascades, but there would be much more to see if you wished.

These famous cascades and small waterfalls have evolved over thousands of years by a series of rather complicated and unique physiochemical factors. The river passes through terrain that consists mostly of limestone. As the limestone is dissolved it leaves calcium carbonate in the water, which under certain circumstances, remains as undissolved particles. As these particles have passed along the river, aquatic mosses have retained them, and that has caused a gradual build up of rocky, travertine layers. What you see now are a series of seven travertine waterfalls, created by limestone sediments, covered with mosses and water plants.

The first ferry left the small dock at Skradin at nine o'clock in the morning and we were aboard with our food, drinks, swimming costumes and towels. (Take swimming costumes and jelly shoes with you if you can, because you will have the opportunity to swim at the falls.) The wide river spread like a mill pond ahead of us and reflected perfectly the sloping, wooded hills either side of the valley and one small white cloud in the clear sky. The morning sun had not yet risen above the hilltops and was just a pale hint of the day to come. We motored up the river, which gradually narrowed, past quiet fishermen who silently watched us as we chugged by. Huge, darting dragonflies skimmed the water's surface and the dark silhouettes of fish disappeared before our eyes down into the greeny-blue depths. At length we reached a wooden jetty close to a small wood. Here we disembarked and walked up through shady trees suddenly emerging into the sunlight, with the cascading falls ahead of us. White, frothing water sprayed over the bright green, moss-covered travertine rocks, layer upon layer, as far back as we could see, and a thin mist rose up from the torrent, the sun now making it all glisten and sparkle. The path ahead led to a low, wooden boardwalk, which guided us meandering for hours over waterfalls and clear pools, through shady areas and open vistas. The water was consistently perfectly clear, often with shoals of basking fish only inches away from our fingertips. Long, thin, water snakes slid amongst the reeds; frogs, large and small, gathered everywhere and fat green lizards sat by their holes in the sun. Small blue damselflies flitted from one plant to the next and we spent the whole day simply wandering through this amazing and unique river habitat. We weren't alone; crocodiles of brightly capped little children and other wandering families were there too, but it wasn't too busy. There were no hawkers or traders and, like all the national parks we visited in Croatia, the facilities for tourists were kept as natural and simple as possible.

At the end of the walk was Skradinski Buk, a massive, clear, natural pool with quite high waterfalls at one end and cascades at the other. Here, most people had donned their costumes and were thoroughly enjoying a cooling swim. Kids were playing in and out of the waterfalls, which we could all stand behind, and one daredevil young man was diving off the top of some high rocks. A lifeguard paddled around in a rubber boat, just to keep an eye on things and we got our costumes on and joined in. Jack absolutely loved swimming in this natural environment and messing about in the falls. I just couldn't see this happening in England, even if we had the weather. Coffee, beer, ice-creams and barbecue meals were all available from the open air café, but believe it or not there were no gimmicky tourist shops selling ghastly, plastic replicas of squeaking frogs or rubber fish or waterfalls. It was as natural as it could be whilst still allowing visitors to enjoy it.

We caught the 5.30 pm ferry back to Skradin and walked the few steps to the car park and motor home. Jack flopped there, guarding the van while Simon and I explored Skradin itself. A quiet town with a central square, where chatty groups of little girls played at pushing their dolls around in prams, imitating the strolling young mothers and babies. In a shaded open bar, football was showing on a large screen watched by the laid-back husbands, each with a beer in front of them, and little boys, brown skinned and dark haired, in clean bright T-shirts and shorts, kicked their football around practicing for the Croatian football team. On the corner of the square, three workmen in blue overalls worked on into the evening to erect a large, ornate street lamp. The smart new marina held expensive, white yachts and gleaming motorboats which had come up from the coast. Behind the waterfront, just one street back, the brightness faded, the streets looked poorer, the houses marked with old bullet holes sprayed into the plaster; new paint and even new plaster being an unaffordable luxury. The affluence of the front marina hadn't quite reached beyond the harbour. In one doorway, two little boys had hand painted shells for sale on a small rickety table, while a grandmother sat knitting close by. I couldn't resist of course, and my dull green, splodgily painted little shell will always remind me instantly of Skradin and the fits of giggles that the boys disintegrated into as they tried to negotiate a sale. I can see them to this day.

Early next morning I took a short walk over to a church across the road. The ornate iron gates to the cemetery were open and I walked in, curious about the history of this area. A few people had died in the most recent war and some graves were sprayed with gunfire, as was the church. Some nameplates had been removed and small, basic wooden crosses had been put in place. It was a vivid reminder that we were close to the Bosnian border. For the next two days we drove on down the coast of Croatia, wild camping wherever we could at night, heading for Dubrovnik.

The weather was hot now, 25 – 27 degrees, so we were up and on the road early every morning, and as the road still hugged the sea shore, we stopped on both days in deserted coves, to swim and snorkel at lunch time, and then take a short siesta before we headed on again. We passed the big islands of Brac, Hvar and Korcula, baking under the sun, and stopped to buy fresh vegetables and fruit from roadside stalls. The coast was sparsely populated, with small, low level towns and villages; clusters of fishermen's cottages nestled in niches, each with its own jetty. The exception to this was busy Split, whose tower blocks and sprawling development reached right back into the foothills of the mountains. As we neared Dubrovnik it gradually began to look more affluent, and the red roofed houses were replaced by restored white villas. I can only hope that as Croatia becomes more popular it does not lose its new found peace and natural beauty.

Dubrovnik is heralded by a rather wonderful, modern bridge, which spans the wide, deep fjord that you must cross or go around to reach the city. We got caught up in a small convoy of French motor-caravans as we trundled over this bridge and eventually all ended up in the same lay-by like Barnum's travelling circus. We had a camp-site in mind, as there would be nowhere to wild camp, and without too much trouble we found it and pulled into the entrance area. Simon jumped out and was about to walk to the campsite office when he spotted that one of our back tyres was rapidly deflating. Luckily the back wheels were doubles, so we were able to limp onto a pitch before making another of those calls to euro-assistance. Changing our own tyres was impracticable on the Beast as they were the size of lorry tyres and we could never have jacked it up anyway. However after some problems getting a jack man-enough for the job, (we needed a ten ton jack, not a four ton jack), a good natured garage owner took the old tyre to his garage, repaired it and brought it back good as new. Simon and he worked hard under the baking hot sun to re-fit the tyre and eventually all was ok. We took a look around the campsite, which was not awe-inspiring for such a major town, but adequate, and I hit the laundrette with four loads of washing, which dried in an instant on our washing line between the trees. This was a large site, not very busy, but there were a few other GB plates here and we briefly met a few other English and American travellers. It looked like everyone had ended up down in this small corner of Croatia. The camp had great beach access though and the wonderful views across the sea to a small island meant that the sunsets from here were picture-postcard perfect.

We made a rule not to overdo it on the first day in Dubrovnik, so next morning we caught the number six bus and got off at Pile Gate which is the main entrance to the old town. This arched gate, with its heavy wooden drawbridge, is set in an immense city wall that is completely intact and encircles the entire old city in over two kilometres of solid stone, up to twenty-five meters high. Built into the wall are also two enormous round towers, fourteen square towers, a large fortress and two smaller corner fortresses. It is said to be the best example of a walled city in the world and it certainly is very, very impressive.

Invaders approaching from the sea must have been quite daunted by the thought of attacking such a solid defence, but even so, Ragusa (as it was called until 1918) has been invaded many times in ancient and recent history. Its geographical position made it extremely desirable, especially once it had grown into the most powerful trading centre in the Southern Mediterranean, with a large fleet of merchant and war ships equalled only by Venice. As a result of earthquakes and various wars the city has been partially destroyed and rebuilt several times. It has been over-run and occupied, including during the Second World War, first by the Italian army and then by the Germans. Its troubles didn't end there though, because in1991 during the collapse of Yugoslav Federation, it was attacked by the Serb-Montenegrin army and was under siege for seven long months. In May 1992 the Croatian army liberated it, although it was not free of all conflict for another three years. Subsequently, yet another re-building programme had to be organised as almost two thirds of the city had been severely damaged by shelling.

The city is being re-built in a massive restoration project, adhering strictly to replacing like with like, rather than designing a new Dubrovnik. The replacement of old materials is a daunting challenge, particularly when it comes to finding enough of the uniquely honey-coloured roof tiles which are a dominant feature of the skyline. The need to reconstruct has enabled the architects to build-in some provision for future earthquakes and hopefully the city is stronger now than it has ever been before. Tourism was badly hit after the war ended, but now this truly handsome, restored city attracts many visitors and it is definitely back on the tourist trail.

So, now we had come through the Pile Gate and were standing just inside the city walls. The massive Onofrio Fountain (1438) was just before us and beyond that stretched the long, wide promenade with its smooth-as-silk, polished marble pavement. In perfect symmetry down either side, light coloured stone buildings, four stories high with arched doorways and shuttered windows offered a little welcome shade and restaurants with brightly striped awnings tempted strollers to stop for a coffee. No traffic is allowed within the city walls so it is a pedestrian's heaven. We three strolled down to the end of the Placa and viewed the elaborate baroque-style St Blaises' Church. After that we just wandered, eating ice cream as we went, stopping to take an ice cold drink at a carved marble fountain and enjoy lunch at a street café. This small city has a great feeling of spaciousness, even with tourists around, because the main thoroughfares and squares are very generous and all stonework has a wonderful luminosity. Smaller, steeper, cobbled streets radiate off the main area and lead up into the labyrinth of old houses and flats rented by locals. Washing lines hang high above narrow alleys and children play in the shade, giving it a quiet but very 'lived in' feel. Unfortunately property prices have risen astronomically in recent years and investors own most of Dubrovnik now, making it the most expensive real estate in Croatia. We caught the bus back to camp in the stifling heat of mid-afternoon and went down to the beach for a swim in the bay. The next day we would walk the walls.

Up with the larks, we were soon back at Pile gate to start exploring while it was still cool. We entered the peaceful city once more, and climbed the narrow, stone steps which led almost vertically up to the top of the city wall. At the small payment kiosk we hired headsets from a chatty, young American student – (it's a small world and students seem to hop through countries with the greatest of ease). The path around the top of the walls can be as much as six meters wide; although in most places it was around two meters, with constant changes in height and direction, as it wove its way around the uneven perimeter. The famous honey coloured roof tiles spread out below us, with slight variations in colour showing clearly where damage had been repaired. Views down into thin dark alleyways, small courtyards and spacious squares were revealed within, while without were the harbour and the blue, open sea. The temperature up on that exposed walkway was rapidly rising, and after a while we were crouching for a rest in any shade that we could find. Jack had a cotton handkerchief draped from the back of his cap, giving him a very foreign legion look, and we pitied the poor soldiers who had once spent long hours on this battlement, watching the horizon for tell tale white sails. We walked the whole circumference and it took us the best part of two hours. As city walls go it must be one of the most beautiful; its light, smooth, stone, curved towers and stunning views giving it grace and elegance.

That evening, when it had cooled down, we went up to the campsite bar and joined Richard and Louise, a young couple from England. The UEFA Cup football match was on again, England versus Portugal, and a small crowd had gathered to sit under the stars and watch the sport. It went to a nail biting penalty kick-off and Portugal eventually won a well-played and most enjoyable game. Richard was surprised but not upset; he was a fervent Arsenal fan, never missing a game he said, but he obviously enjoyed all football. The following evening we watched Greece beat the favourites, France. Richard and Louise had moved on, but we guessed that they would have found a bar somewhere, to stop and watch the match.

Lovely as it was, we were ready to leave Dubrovnik. The temperature had suddenly soared up to the mid thirties, and by nine o'clock in the morning it was almost too hot to move. Jack, with his ginger hair and fair skin, had got rather sunburned when he'd been swimming without a T-shirt on and we needed to find some cooler weather. We had gone as far south as we were going, we would now start heading north, eventually crossing back to England. We were going to drive up through inland Croatia and then into Slovenia. We would wild camp en route, and reckoned that the next stop would be Plitvicka, the third and last national park on our list.

Our wild camp, on the way up to the Park, was in a lay-by beside a long, thin lake, Pervcko Jezero. We were on an inland road that ran between the coast and the border of Bosnia Herzegovina. This countryside was all on a huge scale; huge mountains, huge plains and huge empty spaces; the scrub covered land occasionally dotted with red-roofed angular houses, either in small clusters or standing alone. Throughout this area the results of war were still to be seen in the bullet strafed, burnt out shells of deserted homes. Sometimes they were isolated houses, sometimes in small groups and sometimes just one house damaged amongst many undamaged, occupied ones. We rolled on down the almost deserted road, watching the scenery unfold as we ate up the miles. Occasionally we would see old ladies, dressed from head to foot in black, carrying big bunches of greenery. They walked resolutely, with heads down, though not a house could be seen for miles and we always wondered where they had come from and where they were going. It looked as if time had slowed to a halt in this dramatic scenery. We journeyed passed farmers in their fields using pronged wooden hay-forks to gather hay into loosely stacked cones, drying it in the sun in pointed stacks. Occasionally we'd pass an isolated road side stall where a patient lady sat under the shade of a large umbrella, hoping to sell a round of cheese or some homemade honey. With few tourists around, they weren't doing a roaring trade.

By early afternoon we'd reached Plitvicka National Park and had pulled into the spacious coach parking area, where we made ourselves a quick lunch before walking round to the entrance. In my diary I have written that this is yet another of Croatia's little wonders - but I should say big wonders. Declared a National Park in 1949, it was entered into the UNESCO World Heritage List in 1979. Sixteen lakes of crystal clear, blue-green water are connected to each other by cascades and spectacular waterfalls, which were all naturally created by the same process of lime deposition on mosses, as we had previously seen at Krka National Park. This is all situated amongst 266 square kilometres of verdant vegetation, wooded hillsides and craggy gorges of pale rock. Eighteen kilometres of low, wide, wooden walkways and footpaths carry you only inches from tumbling, churning water and the damp cooling mists of lofty waterfalls. There are very few barriers or handrails, so you feel very much part of this river valley.

There were various routes to explore, but as it was already late afternoon we bought our tickets and chose to catch a ferry boat across one of the lower lakes. The path then led us alongside the water to reach a point where we could catch a Park bus back to the entrance and a fantastic view down onto the turquoise coloured waters in the gorge. At the top of the lake you could hire a rowing boat and drift alongside some of the tumbling streams which cascade through thick, green vegetation. So, late as it was, we had to hire one, and Jack rowed us out onto the lake, a perfect reflection of the surrounding hillsides – and then attempted to sink us by trying to get my end of the boat under a waterfall. Well, that's what boys do I guess. It would be much too boring to just row a boat, and Jack was anything but boring. He had been travelling with us for ten months now and knew how to make the most of every day. Before much longer he would be back behind a desk pushing a pen, not rowing a boat across a lake in one of Croatia's beautiful national parks. We caught the almost empty bus down to the entrance again and then drove the motor home a short distance to Autocamp Korano, where we stayed for that night – and another two after that.

The best time to see the lakes was early in the morning, when there were few other people around and it was cool and quiet. We were now at the end of June and, even inland, it was getting very, very warm. We were up by seven o'clock next morning, and had driven back to the National Park by eight thirty. We left the Beast in the coach parking area again and caught the first available bus up to the second lake area. At the upper lake we took one of the small electric and very sedate ferry boats across the water and then walked the Upper Lakes and Falls. I feel almost embarrassed to tell you that we spent ten hours on this walk, probably the record breaker for overdoing it. Definitely 'here and now'. At first we followed the board-walks over waterfalls and clear lakes where fish swarmed in shoals at the surface of water clear enough to drink from. We passed endless frogs, camouflaged in croaking choruses, and damsel flies and dragonflies imitating mini Harrier jump jets; then we turned away from the lakes and took the path through dappled beech woods from where we glimpsed the occasional view down into the water-filled gorge. The usual green and brown lizards basked in dust, almost too lazy to move as we walked by, and shield bugs and beetles we saw by the score. No wolves or bears – but then, the park is so big that they would be mad to come anywhere near the tourists. We did see a horned viper though, being heckled by a fierce little robin, until he eventually glided away into the undergrowth.

Our route-march eventually took us back to the ferry and then down to the lower lakes again. I was almost asleep on the boat, I now felt so tired. The towering water falls, with great view-points alongside them, had to be explored though, until we had eventually 'done it all'. We would love to visit the superb parks of Croatia again; they shine in summer, would be a glorious show of colours in autumn and stunning in winter with the edge of frost and deep snow. They are well signed and well priced, (a one day ticket is valid for three days as long as you stay in the area), but we by now, were well exhausted! Back at camp we just about managed to rustle up some tinned sardines and salad before we all fell into bed, waking in the night to a fantastic display of thunder, lightening and torrential rain. At least that would cool the air down a little which would be good, although we were now going to move on, heading inland towards Zagreb and then to another place which had definitely caught our eye – a little-known town called Varazdin.

Varazdin and into Slovenia

Turning away from the coast, heading inland, we wouldn't see the sea again until we reached Northern France and Brittany in early autumn. As we approached Zagreb the mountains and gorges slid behind us and we entered a very English looking landscape of rolling hills and green plains. It became more populated, although you could hardly say over-developed; more cars were on the roads and there were often queues of elderly locals waiting at bus stops along the route. Being the same size and shape, we were often mistaken for the local bus and people would put out their hands to try and stop us; we even got the impression that if we slowed down too much we would have them all climbing on board pressing kuna into our palms and asking to be dropped off at the market – so we drove on by rapidly and waved apologetically, leaving them looking a bit puzzled. The houses, with red pan-tiled roofs as always, were now chalet style and the whole area had a more alpine appearance. Everywhere was neat and tidy; wooden balconies edged with red geraniums, immaculate gardens with trim lawns and full flower beds. I was always prodding Jack to look out of the window, but he spent a large part of this particular journey making moving objects out of wine corks, wooden kebab sticks and rubber bands. His allotted cupboard space had filled up months ago with books, tapes, models, drawings and weird and wonderful pebbles, sticks and fossils. Luckily we had masses of storage space on the Beast, both inside and out. My storage area was filling with odd mementoes and masses of literature. Simon's had our travelling library of reading books and maps. The huge space under our bed held our pantry of staple foodstuffs and all of our un-seasonable clothes, most of which hadn't been worn. We had skis, boots and ski suits, flippers, snorkels, surfboards, kites, badminton and tennis racquets, balls – in other words the toy department, in outside lockers, along with repair tools, motor spares, wine, cartons of fruit juice – well just about everything you would keep in a house. Our three bikes were strapped on the back of course. It's always surprising how quickly we humans can gather 'stuff' to fill all available spaces.

Anyway, we motored on, boycotting Zagreb as we didn't feel up to another major city, and reached Varazdin late in the afternoon. Circling the town on the main road, we eventual spotted what looked like the overflow car park of a useful supermarket. Simon managed to squeeze down some small backstreets to find the entrance, and there we parked, tucked behind a huge billboard advertising Rovinj, which almost hid us completely. It wasn't the most salubrious of wild camps, beside a busy road and a housing estate, but it would do for us. Yet again, as everywhere we travelled, we were left in peace, even though we didn't exactly blend in with our surroundings. We all had a shower, one of the luxuries of the motor home, and then went for an evening walk around Varazdin.

I'll never forget this town, and if there was ever somewhere that I would like us to spend one complete year in, enjoying every season, then this would be the place. It seemed to hold something for everyone. Once a strategic crossing point of Roman roads, it went on to become an important administrative and cultural centre and a favourite haunt of political high flyers. It prospered and grew, providing work for artisans and masons who left their mark on the baroque style, stucco decorated buildings, pleasant open squares, ornamental gardens, mansions, town hall, tower and castle. It's also famous for its music school and music festivals and is home to the Croatian National Theatre. It has a vibrant, youthful feel, like a small university town, with cafes spilling onto streets and cyclists of all ages, from children to grandparents, criss-crossing the squares on bikes of all sizes and design, in fact this is a town of cyclists – with around 22,000 bicycles in a town of 43,000 inhabitants. I would love to get to know this town a little better. I could imagine the stone buildings and pretty squares covered in snow on a winter's eve with warm lively pubs, open fires and festivities in the streets; or flowers in spring and fresh green leaves on the trees surrounding the castle; or autumn days, when smoke from wood fires would settle over the town. I guess I'm just an old romantic at heart, but one day – one day, I would love us to live for one year in Varazdin.

For now though, we had just a couple of days to see the sights and find the acclaimed entomology museum that we had seen advertised. That summer evening we joined with everyone else, and strolled the elegant old streets of small shops, many of which were open due to the custom of taking a long lunch and opening again late afternoon. The central square was busy with local families, meeting at the pavement cafes, and, like the Italians, an amazing number of men, women and children were eating ice-cream. There was a wide range of flavours and a huge scoop of this rich and creamy specialty only cost twenty pence. We consulted our local map and guide book and eventually found 'The Golden Goose' where we ate a slap-up, three course meal each, including wine for about thirty-five pounds. A real treat for us.

That night was swelteringly hot again and we didn't sleep very well. Even so, we had found the local market by 8.30 next morning and were soon buying fresh produce. The market holders appeared to be all locals, mostly ladies dressed in wrap-around overalls and sensible shoes, who stood behind long trestle-like tables in a covered arcade, with their freshly picked vegetables, fruit and flowers laid out before them; broad beans, new potatoes, big hearty lettuces, gypsophila, lilies, dahlias and a whole heap of camomile flower heads. Meat, fresh bread, and home made wines; the sight and smell was a joy to the senses and I doubt if any of it had travelled more than ten miles and a few hours from production to sales. One whole building was devoted to cheeses and eggs, and all heads turned our way as we entered, being the only obvious tourists around, in fact the only customers in the building at that time. With some embarrassment we walked up and down the silent aisles, admiring one display after another but feeling incredibly self-conscious as we tried to decide what to buy from whom..... we were surely going to upset quite a few people in there. Eventually one forthright lady collared us as we approached her wares, and before I knew it she had my arm in hers, and was dolloping a splodge of soured cream onto the back of my hand from a ladle. She mimed for me to lick it off, to taste its good flavour, which I willingly did, while my bag of tomatoes cascaded to the floor. Jack started for the exit, guessing that this was going to go from bad to worse and Simon soon followed him, (rats up a drain pipe came to mind), while I struggled to gather the escaping tomatoes, juggle with a kilo of cherries and buy a huge lump of feta cheese from the lady. The other stall holders looked on probably wondering what the hell I was going to do with it all.

Following our town map, Jack led us to the unpretentious, well worn exterior of the Entomology Museum. There were no opening hours displayed and the door was locked, so we rang the bell and waited. A cleaning lady opened the door and explained that she was still busy with mop and bucket on the stone floors and could we return in half an hour. In some places this would have seemed annoying but somehow, in Croatia, where the pace of life is much more laid back, we didn't mind in the least. We went off in search of a cup of coffee and an internet café to collect and send our emails and found both in an open fronted bar, somewhat 'gay' in its orientation. Unfortunately, the internet connection was so flaky that we merely picked up our messages and then sat for a while nursing cups of coffee in the square while we watched the world cycle by. Simon read aloud from the information we had about the intriguing legacy of Franjo Koscec; teacher, scientific researcher, entomologist, inventor, draughtsman and famous citizen of Varazdin, because the entomology museum is based around his lifetimes work.

Koscec settled in Varazdin, teaching biology, chemistry and physics at the local grammar school. He was also a committed scientific researcher and had collected and catalogued thousands of insect specimens over several decades, eventually totalling as many as 70,000. He collected mostly in the greater Varazdin area, in the meadows and forests around the Drava River and in the nearby mountains. For many years he documented the fauna of the area, and the copious notes and diagrams provide a fascinating insight into the effects of social development, food production, transport, industry, tourism and insecticides upon the insect world. This quiet unassuming man was involved in the funding of the town museum in 1925 and, along with friends, developed a framework of societies to educate the people of the town. The small, beautifully laid out museum, explains the biology of insects, their irreplaceable necessity for the future of man and presents a historical overview of his work as founder of the entomology section.

We finished our coffee in the square, returned to the old baroque Herzer Palace where the museum is situated and walked into the shaded, arched entrance. We rang the bell, were soon admitted and led up a flight of stone steps to the upper floor. There the English speaking curator sold us a family ticket for about £5 and encouraged us to –"wander, explore and discover – you are the only visitors today". A polished, intricately designed parquet floor complimented the floor to ceiling, pale wood display drawers and glass fronted cases. The beauty of this museum was not just the interesting exhibits, but also the exquisite presentation, personally and lovingly designed by Koscec. Every perfect drawer, that smoothly slid open, revealed immaculately displayed families of insects, ranging from death's-head moth and blow fly to ladybird, aphid and locusts. Every developmental stage was explained with exhibits, along with habitat and life cycle. Glass sided cases had enlarged cross-section models of the detailed insect world to explain the most significant phenomena of their lives. We wandered for several hours through these fascinating rooms, before emerging again onto the streets and heading off to find the next item on our agenda, namely the moated castle in the 'Stari Grad' or 'Old Town' area.

A high, grassy embankment surrounds this white washed, lovingly preserved example of a mediaeval fortress, which once defended the region from invading Ottoman Turks. But, with its softly rounded towers, gracious courtyards and wide, three storey corridors it resembles a story book castle rather than a fortress. Once again, out of season, we had the place to ourselves and after paying a modest entrance fee a quiet young assistant led us on a guided tour explaining everything in excellent English. The castle is a living museum, furnished as a home with paintings, furniture, household items, decorative objects and weapons from Varazdin's past. By the end of the tour I felt that we had struck up a good enough relationship with our guide for me to ask him a question which had often been on our minds as we had travelled through Croatia. I wanted to know how he felt about the fairly recent war and how he saw the future of his country. We had a short awkward silence when I asked this, and I wondered if I had overstepped the mark. He chose his words of explanation carefully, and said that he was proud of his beautiful country but that many Croatians were embarrassed and sad that such a vicious war had happened; they no longer talk about it and look forward to a brighter future. The subject was closed and we said our thanks and walked out into the bright warm sunshine. We felt that he had conveyed more in the words left unsaid than in any long diatribe that he could have given us – it was in the past, it was time to move on.

Outside in the castle grounds, under the shade of leafy trees, we flopped onto park benches and indulged yet again in cones of ridiculously cheap, creamy ice-cream. I finished mine and lay down on the bench with my eyes shut, listening to the local sounds. Church bells rang out the hour, ducks quacked on the nearby pond, and the gravel paths softly crunched with the feet of occasional passers-by and the rhythmic tick of bicycles. The warm air filled our lungs and seeped into our bones. Maybe it was Varazdin that had seeped into mine.

Eventually, we headed back to the motor home. Varazdin would have had much more to offer, with festivals, theatre, music and sport just for starters, but July was just around the corner and once again we had to move on. So, after a quick shower each, we pulled out from behind our big, protective bill-board and started off in search of somewhere closer to the Slovenian border to wild camp for the night. Several hours and failed attempts later, we realized that a wild camp area was going to be hard to find. A small garage, on a long country road, looked like a possibility so we pulled in and asked the owner if he knew of anywhere. He explained, as best he could, that we couldn't park at his garage but, after a quick discussion with his mate, he jumped into his car and signalled for us to follow him down the road. We trundled behind and were soon guided down a side street in the next village and into an empty parking area, which I'm sure we wouldn't have spotted without his help. The wide river Mura, which denotes the Slovenian border, flowed along next to the car park and the border crossing was just down the road. This was a great find and it even included some evening enter-tainment for Jack, because within ten minutes of our arrival, a group of teenagers had drifted, one by one, into the car park. Each carried or scooted on a skate board; well used ramps and jumps were pulled out of hiding places and like teenagers the world over they spent the evening practising their skateboarding techniques and 'hanging out'. That night it rained heavily, which after the heat of the previous days was a pleasure to hear. We woke at around mid-night with the rain drumming on the roof and saw that this car park on the Slovenian border, like many others in Europe, was a meeting place for amorous young car owners. All very quiet though and no hint of trouble.

Next morning, with English-style drizzle still coming down, we checked our maps and crossed into Slovenia. We didn't have GPS discs (Global Positioning System) for Slovenia, so Maisy would be taking a rest for a while. On slightly bumpy, rather narrow roads we headed for the most northern corner of the Pannonian plain to a town called Murska Sobota. It was a bit like driving through the English countryside of the 1950's, before tourism took over, except that the neat, flowered-decked houses had roll-down shutters at the windows, cycle paths were frequent and storks nested on the top of most telegraph posts. Grey haired ladies in floral, ever-fashionable, wrap-around aprons, cycled slowly to the corner shops on sturdy black bikes, while holding umbrellas over their heads, and all was quiet.

Slovenia is a small country, sitting in central Europe, with Italy and Austria on the west and north, and Croatia and Hungary on the south and east. Its only coastline giving access to the Adriatic Sea is just 46 kilometres long. Slovenia has always been a gateway to the Balkans and has a widely diverse landscape - from the mountainous Alps and Dinaric ranges to the Pannonian plains and because of its geographical diver-sity the climate covers three prevailing types: Alpine, Continental and Mediterranean, with temperatures ranging from -26C to 38C. Forests cover half of Slovene territory and there are many natural parks where wild life, including lynx and brown bear, is protected. Perhaps the most famous is the Triglav National Park situated in the central region of the Julian Alps, with Mount Triglav as the highest mountain at 2,864 meters. In this small country it only takes a matter of hours to travel from towering snow covered mountains to vine covered plains or the blue sea of the Adriatic, and the Slovenes make the most of it all by being great weekenders.

We reached our destination, which was a large Spa campsite at Moravske Toplice in the Mura Region. There are fifteen Spa's in this country, most situated in the Pannonian area, where natural thermal and mineral waters flow up to the surface. The mineral waters have been drunk for centuries and the thermal bathing waters, which vary from 32 to above 73 degrees, have long been popular with locals and tourists. The Spa's have developed big leisure complexes with hotels, golf courses, restaurants and swimming pools and the site that we had chosen had all of these. We had decided to make it our base camp while we hired a car and explored this corner of Slovenia.

Parking-up was easy, with plenty of room on a flat, grassy area. It was still raining hard but we didn't feel like sitting in the motor home for the afternoon so we grabbed our swimming costumes, got out the umbrella and walked across the camp site to explore the swimming pool complex. The water which feeds this resort springs from a depth of around 1300 meters at a minimum of 72 degrees centigrade, containing sodium chloride and hydrogen carbonate. When you visit this Spa, the brochure assures you that, quote "a world of aquatic pleasure and joy awaits you, and in the 'comfly' and warm cradle of life a thought dawns on you spontaneously… into the blue I will be rocked!" Which all sounded pretty good to us! On looking through the brochure we saw that if we went golfing we should expect this experience, "While the 'storch' makes a loud smack with its long beak, you will feel like singing these words… into the green I am going to wrap myself!" We weren't too sure about that one. So much is gained in translation, hey!

The pool complex was great, with twenty-two interconnecting, indoor and outdoor pools. These varied from small Jacuzzi to Olympic size and from warm to very, very hot; from quite clear water, to water which resembled hot, salty, oily mud. Four water slides, including one that was a vertical 'free-fall' and another that sent you down 170 meters of twirling tube from a great height, kept Jack amused for hours and even in the rain we enjoyed it. Swimming from the indoor pools through small passageways, we reached the outside pools of very hot water, water falls and swirling whirlpools. From there we got out and walked across to the round 'mud' pool, which apparently eased muscular and rheumatic ailments. Entering this was rather like stepping into a shoulder-deep, muddy, smelly, slightly gritty, water-hole. All around the edge of this pool men and women, mostly the senior variety, were lined up with their backs to the wall looking very serious, if not downright depressed. This was obviously not meant to be a happy or enjoyable experience. Maybe they'd all just got the bill for staying at the hotel, or they all had horrible diseases or they were all a 'certain nationality'. Anyway, we didn't stay long in that pool, in case we caught a case of the miseries ourselves.

The rain had cleared by next morning and sunny blue skies had returned. I cycled into town for fresh bread and a look at the tourist office. We would hire a car for Monday morning, which gave us the weekend to relax beforehand. Green lawns surrounded the pool complex and sun beds were provided free, so we took our books and sun cream and actually relaxed for two days while Jack made friends with two Slovenian boys and spent six hours a day in the pools enjoying himself. An Austrian family, in a caravan near to us, became weekend friends and we joined the many Germans, Austrians and Slovenians, young and old, taking a break at the Spa. It made a good start to our stay in this country.

Over the next three days we drove our hire car around the wooded hills and flat, open, cultivated valleys of the Mura region. We had a great feeling of space in this immaculate, well-organised corner of the country. Close to Hungary and Austria, the stone houses, with neatly stacked log piles and huge tidy bundles of kindling wood, had a very rural feel. The roads were quiet, but it certainly didn't feel 'poor'. German was definitely the second language and we saw no other English travellers. Slovenia's recent history is one of domination and communist control within the old Yugoslav Federation, but in 1992 it was recognised by the EC and UN as an independent country; for a land about the size of Wales, and against great odds, it has successfully achieved a passive emergence into modern Europe.

We were now keen to see more of Slovenia and were soon travelling in the motor home again on our way to the capital city. A simple network of motorways and principle highways takes you very easily through this country. We took the main road to Maribor and then joined the motorway to Ljubljana. Skiing is a major sport in Slovenia and there are ample opportunities to do it. Rising just southwest of the city of Maribor, is the Pohorje Massif, the largest skiing centre in the country and one which regularly hosts world cup races. Kranjska Gora, in the Julian Alps, is another mecca for skiing enthusiasts as the World Cup slalom and giant slalom events are held there, and these are but two of many ski resorts available at substantially less cost than the nearby Italian and Austrian runs. While we were driving from Maribor to Ljubljana I had my diary open and as usual was scribbling furiously as I tried to describe the changing landscape. The houses took on a more Austrian appearance, with wide wooden balconies, carved balustrades and shuttered windows. Every garden, large or small, seemed to have its own vineyard, and the distinctive Slovene hay drying racks, dotted the nearby fields. We had long since left behind the countries where small white villages perched themselves on top of precipitous hills and we were now in wide open spaces. A cloth of green covers the hills and vales of Slovenia in July, with woods of beech, oak and fir sprinkled on the top. Snow topped mountains are never far away, their scenic valleys and gorges cutting down into the centre of the country. They would provide fabulous walking holidays; something else that we would have to do another day.

Before long we were rolling into Ljubljana and then through the gates of Jezica Autocamp, a pleasant, well-placed camp site just outside the centre. From there we could catch the local bus, which ran every five minutes into the centre of town. As usual, Simon had steered us safely from one place to the next, as he did brilliantly all through our travels. It was hard that he was the only driver but it would have been too nerve wracking for everyone if I had to get behind the wheel of the Beast. In fact I doubt if we would have ever got out of England – let alone reached Ljubljana in Slovenia.

Ljubljana and the Julian Alps

Just as Gaudi left his unmistakable mark on Barcelona, so Plecnik, a modest, contemporary architect of the nineteenth century, has left his signature on the delightful city of Ljubljana. As capital cities go, this isn't a large one, but what it lacks in size it more than makes up for in warmth and vitality. With a large university and three art academies it has a youthful feel, without any of the hustle and bustle of bigger metropolises. In its past it has experienced a history similar to many other towns that were initially founded by the Romans. Sieges, occupation and earthquakes were repeated over the years and with every change came another layer of history, architecture and society. Today, tucked into the shelter of three formidable mountain ranges, it is sufficiently guarded from the rest of Europe to have thankfully missed out on chain store shops, skyscrapers and fast food outlets. It spreads either side of the winding Ljubljanica river; a pleasant mix of Austrian and Slav with a good helping of baroque, renaissance, art nouveau and contemporary thrown in.

We caught the spotlessly clean number six bus (it always seemed to be the number six), into the centre and started our tour in the 'old' town. Here there were no noisy motorbikes and hooting car horns, just wide cobbled streets and elegant pale coloured buildings. Residents and tourists strolled and street cafes did good business. We made our way to the first of the three famous bridges which cross the Ljubljanica River, namely the Cobblers Bridge. Designed by Plecnik, it is of a simple yet unusual construction; a wide span with plain, white stone columns, which links the old town to the new. Following the river, we came to the second bridge – the Triple Bridge which was originally one single bridge built in 1842, but to which Plecnik added two arched side bridges. Then passing through the long colonnade of the gently curving covered market, we finally reached the Dragon Bridge, which was definitely our favourite. Built in 1901 of iron and concrete, this bridge was the one which we wouldn't forget and which Jack has pictures of in his album. A pair of vast winged dragons stand at either end of this angular structure, with evil staring eyes, clawed feet and mouths wide open. Their scaly tails curl around the back of the bridge and smaller entwined dragons with forked tongues decorate the balustrades. This is the dragon that was slain by Jason of the Argonauts when he and his men were fleeing from the Black Sea to the Adriatic with the Golden Fleece. Trapped, when they reached the source of the Ljubljanica River, they dismantled their boat, and were carrying it in pieces across land to the Adriatic when they came to a massive marshy lake. The dragon rose from

the lake and Jason fought long and hard before he killed it. So, what better reason do you need to have a most superb bridge decorated with glowering dragons.......
.........No better reason at all.

Before we stopped for lunch, we walked up to the old castle which sits, surveying all, high above the town. The small tourist train then took us back down for a massive family-sized pizza, after which we decided to split up and do a little personal shopping, which was something of a novelty because after ten months of doing mostly boysy stuff I had almost given up all idea of looking in shop windows at girly things. Simon had noticed an excellent book shop and Jack elected to stay with me to ensure that I didn't get lost. We wandered the streets, window shopping at last. Jack was searching for a new airfix model and I was hoping for anything with feminine appeal. We found both, and after selecting a good model, he patiently waited for me on the steps of the Three Rivers Fountain, (a copy of the one in Rome) while I spent about twenty minutes trying to decide what to buy from a shop selling 'all natural' soaps and perfumes. Eventually, I bought a bar of organic foot balm, which shows just how out of touch I had become with female shopping. I thought that this momentous purchase of mine smelt really nice, but over the next few days, as it warmed up in the hot interior of the Beast, there were loud cries of " what is that disgusting smell" every time I got it out to rub it on my aching feet. It was also melting rather rapidly and turning into one revolting gooey mess, so I was soon forced to ditch it. However, strangely enough, the all-pervading smell of airfix glue, and half-made model bits labelled 'don't touch', was not frowned upon at all, and I sometimes did wonder if our large American motor home was really big enough for the three of us.

Back at camp that afternoon Jack made a bee-line for an interesting adventure course that was being run by two young Slovenian rock climbers. It was aptly named 'Adrenalinski Park'. A stand of very tall trees grew at one side of the camp site and strung between these were rope ladders, beams, bridges and high wires, forming an aerial assault course about forty feet up. Kitted out with helmet and safety harness, Jack fearlessly clambered amongst the leafy canopy, finishing with a great zip-wire ride down to the ground. He spent two hours enjoying this fun 'tree-experience' under the guidance of the English speaking climbers and decided that some form of altitude climbing might be added to his growing list of 'things to do when I'm older'. A list which seemed to consist of activities with a certain degree of danger, like hang gliding, white water rafting, scuba diving and extreme snow boarding. What's wrong with art or theatre I frequently countered to deaf ears.

That evening, as we sat outside the motor home planning the next days itinerary, a friendly Dutch couple came over and introduced themselves to us asking if we would like to join them for a drink. Just like us, Rick and Pia had sold their house and were travelling for a year. They had only been on the road for eleven weeks and were already in a dilemma as to where to go next. She didn't like the heat but he did, so they were torn between going north or south – as simple as that. They had a car and caravan, but as the temperature was now around 28 degrees with no breeze, they were finding it impossible to keep cool in either vehicle. We sympathised and poured over maps and books with them, discussing the alternatives, but when we left them two days later they were still not sure which way to go and for all we know they may still be there discussing it. They were yet another pair of middle-aged-gappers, wandering on this not-so-lonely planet.

We knew that we could spare just one more day in Ljubljana, and then we would be heading slightly north to the cooler foothills of the Julian Alps. Catching the bus again next morning we took a closer look at the city and its buildings; an eclectic mixture of light coloured baroque and art nouveau, wide streets and open courtyards, tree shaded promenades and parks. We also wanted to check our emails and as luck would have it, we decided to go to the University Library internet resource to do this. From the outside, this library is an austere looking building with walls of red brick interspersed with random blocks of white, rough-faced, cut stone. Rigidly linear windows seemed at odds with the haphazard stonework. The entrance had heavy closed doors of very solid looking, dark metal, completely unadorned apart from two brass handles, one dull and unused, but the other well-worn and shiny. Both handles were shaped resembling distinctive horses' heads. We levered the shiny one down and pushed open the door, wondering if indeed we were at the right place. This building is another designed by Joze Plecnik, and is an absolute must to visit, if you are in any way interested in architecture.

We stepped through the door and into an interior of solid black and dark grey marble. Stairs, walls, columns, benches and seats were all austere, linear, heavy and dark, and yet it didn't feel sombre or gloomy. The precision of line and minimal decoration, along with the absolute symmetry of this interior, where every doorway and corridor lined up to give you a perfectly proportioned view, made this a very exciting building. I wanted to explore it all. We went up the marble steps, through dark glass doors and into the foyer – an area of grey marble columns, marble walls and dark wood ceilings. Doors of thick, inlaid wood and dark metal, sealed off the further rooms. The library itself can only be accessed by students, or with special permission, which we didn't have. If we had been able to visit this room we would have seen the rows of sleek, wood and marble desks, art nouveau desk lamps and bizarre, cascading, ceiling lights. We explored as much as we could, eventually reaching the internet room where, sitting at smooth-wood, designer desks, we accessed our emails, and then found a small room where we could at least buy some postcards of the building. As usual I got chatting, this time to the young girl selling the cards while Simon and Jack crept off to do some more exploring. She asked me about England, saying that she thought it might not be a very safe place to travel. I assured her that you had to be careful in some areas, but it wasn't that bad, and asked her about Slovenia. She said that she felt safe in Slovenia, she could hitch-hike safely and walk at night safely, but feared how long this would continue to last now that more and more people were going there. I sadly had to agree that this easy going, well organised, attractive country might one day change.

Saying goodbye to our new Dutch friends, (who may still be there trying to decide which way to go next), we left Ljubljana and headed north west to visit the Triglav National Park. This Park, covering 83,807 hectares, in the central region of the Julian Alps, is the largest, and encompasses tree covered gorges, rocky canyons, glacial lakes, gentle alpine meadows and the highest snow-capped mountains in Slovenia. Bled, famous for its picturesque lake and mediaeval castle, sits at the entrance to the park, but we were heading for the 'pearl' of the Alps, namely Lake Bohinj, (pronounced Boheenya).

We travelled along the valley of the crystal clear, Sava River as it threaded its way through green alpine meadows of wild flowers and ever deepening gorges. At Bled we skirted past the lake with its numerous tourist hotels, and took a smaller road into the Bohinj Basin. The flat valley floor was now being squeezed thinner and thinner between the sides of a precipitous tree covered gorge and the Sava was now a smaller river, with bright coloured kayakers bouncing over clear green, frothing mountain water. We entered the Park and continued along the valley road to the far end of Lake Bohinj, pulling up outside the beautifully positioned 'Zlatorog Camping'. Without too much problem, just a little shunting back and forth, we swung through the gates and then proceeded to take up spaces 2,3,and 4 with our ever embarrassing Big American Butt. Without doubt, the largest thing that had ever managed to squeeze itself onto the site, we felt rather like two-headed aliens, plus spaceship, until Simon had tucked us as discreetly as possible under some trees; rather like trying to hide an elephant in a corn field. We heard comments like, 'Oh my God, the Americans have arrived'. So we gave everyone a few minutes to get over our ridiculous size before we got out for a look around.

Zlatorog is a small, friendly campsite which slopes gently down to the shores of Lake Bohinj. Much of the slope is tree covered, so it is a bit of a juggling act to get a position that doesn't have too many tree roots or branches to deal with. However, with luck you can camp right alongside the lake shore. On the far side of the lake, soaring mountains surround the basin, their sheer cliffs reaching right down to the water. As you look down the lake, the valleys unfold into the distance. This campsite has a relaxed atmosphere, with a busy play area for the many children and adequate facilities. There is no disco, loud music or night clubbing but you can spend the evening drinking wine and talking by candle-light under the roof of the simple, open air restaurant. (There is no shop, so take your own food with you). Bright yellow Canadian canoes and wooden rowing boats can be hired – and that's just what we did as soon as we had got set-up. We rowed across the lake as the sun set and the camp lights were coming on. It's another of those great sites that could easily become a home from home.

Professional organisations offer endless choices of sporting activities for you to try in this area. You can hang-glide, raft, canoe, kayak, abseil, climb, pot-hole or take a panoramic flight in a glider. Next day, Simon and Jack were keen to try a few of the river sports, and the choice was between rafting, canyoning and hydro-speeding. I really didn't feel the need to test myself against the elements, but I was being persuaded to try at least one of these, and so that I didn't appear a complete wimp, I said I would go hydro-speeding, which looked like the easiest to me......(.how wrong can you be?) We booked it up for that afternoon. In the meantime, with the Vogel ski centre 1,500 meters up above us, we rode our bikes up to the cable car station and took a long, almost vertical ride up the side of Mount Vogel to the ski slopes. There we had a fantastic birds-eye view of the lake below, the surrounding valleys and far across the tops of the Julian Alps. It was cold on the top of the mountains but the views were staggering. We walked across the empty ski runs, now covered with grass and tiny alpine flowers and stepped around fat, friendly cows who contentedly chewed the cud, their ding-dong cow bells rhythmically sounding out across the valleys with every chomp. I could have happily stayed up on that mountain top for the rest of the day, and later on, I wished I had done – but of course I didn't know what was in store for me that afternoon.

We cycled the three kilometres down to the arranged meeting place and waited for the arrival of our hydro-speeding guide. He squealed up in a well rounded van and leapt out with all the enthusiasm of a fit young puppy, just raring to have some fun. I instantly got the feeling that I had chosen badly and was going to regret thinking that at my age, I still might enjoy dangerous water sports in freezing rivers. Robbie, our bouncy guide, kitted us out with wet suits, flippers and ...crash helmets...(an ominous sign) – before herding us and three other people (all young and fit) onto a small minibus and driving us in a rather hair-raising fashion, to the place where we would enter the river. In all seriousness, it took me a long while to stop having nightmares about this river experience and it put me off any water sports for a long time afterwards.

The first problem was that we had not previously tried on the wet-suits, and when I did eventually get to put it on, I discovered that mine was very, very tight on me. I was more of a size fourteen now, not a size ten, and it was so tight that I found it hard to breathe and could not easily move my arms and legs because my muscles were so constricted. However, we put them on, along with flippers, lifejackets and crash helmets, and Robbie then handed us our 'Boogie-Boards'. These were made of thick plastic, but resembled heavy, lumps of wood with handles to grip at the sides. With these handles you were supposed to steer yourself through the rapids, around the rocks and over the waterfalls! All was now becoming clear. This was not going to be in any way similar to the gentle drift down the sunny Dordogne River that we had enjoyed several years before in France. This was definitely boys stuff as far as I was concerned, even though there was one other female in the group, (young and fit of course).

The river Sava takes on a whole different, ominous look when you're being swept down it at breakneck speed, clinging on to a completely unwieldy boogie-board, being thrown against rocks, slammed into boulders and hurtled over rapids. My squashed muscles and restricted breathing were giving me real problems and I simply had no control over where I was going. The river was full and fast; the boulders big and hard and I absolutely hated it. An adrenalin rush – not really: fun – not at all; this was a sport for twenty year old extreme sport fanatics who had got bored with bungee jumping and free-fall rock climbing! Robbie was out in front in a canoe, guiding us, (as if I could see anything useful from under my large helmet), and Simon was keeping alongside Jack, who seemed to be managing ok, thank goodness. Luckily, a friendly young Slovenian lad took pity on me, and helped me along as best he could, through the terrifyingly fast water. Even so, I was rammed up against huge boulders, lost my board several times and went under the churning waters many times. Three quarters of the way down I was absolutely shattered and really, very scared. There had been no other places where you could get out of the river, but at this point, where the river got even harder to navigate, I could get out and I did. I had the strangest feeling that if I went any further I would not survive. The others continued on down to the finishing point, while I struggled for a long while to simply get out of my restrictive wet suit. I then had to scrabble on hands and knees, dragging my wet suit, life jacket, boogie-board and helmet, up a thirty foot, precipitous, tree-covered river bank until I reached the main road where I could wait to be picked up. There was no way that I would be 'picked-up' by anyone who didn't know me, because by that time I resembled a mud covered river rat – which is probably an insult to river rats everywhere.

All the others finished the course safely, although a little battered, bruised and shaken. When they picked me up on the way back to the camp site, Robbie had an interesting nugget of information to give me. In the previous year a Dutch woman had died at a place just beyond where I had got out. She had been trapped, pushed under a huge rock by the sheer force of the water and drowned before anyone could get to her. I sometimes wish that he had never told me that. Some people may love this kind of sport, but I will never, ever, do it again!

When we arrived back at camp I headed straight for the hot showers. Simon and Jack, being all keyed–up and full of adrenalinski, jumped on their bikes and cycled off in search of the Savica Slap (waterfall), the source of the river, which gushes out from a limestone cave and falls 71 meters, before flowing on down the gorge and into the lake. It was further than they thought and already getting late in the day, but they gamely pushed their bikes up an endless rough track to reach the view point, admired it and then careered back down in almost complete darkness. This reckless behaviour could have had something to do with the large whiskies that Simon and I had downed on our return to camp, just to steady the nerves again and purely for medicinal purposes you realise. You could say that we had overdone it yet again that day, and I think you'd be absolutely right.

Aching and bruised the next morning we compared scars. My hips, bottom and thighs were an interesting shade of black and blue, and the men had elbow and shin bruising. We all felt battered and had stiff joints; and to think that we'd paid for the pleasure - and it was raining again. This was actually a great relief to me because the men had booked to go canyoning that day, but this had now been cancelled due to bad weather and the dangerous state of the river. I wondered how the river could have possibly got any more dangerous and was very relieved. I think that secretly, they were too!

One of the problems of being situated quite high up in the mountains was that the bad weather rolled round and round the valleys for days at a time. But the good news was that it was my birthday (or so I thought). I opened my cards and presents. A bar of chocolate from Jack, (last of the big spenders), and a special silver bracelet of small linked elephants, which I had admired in Varazdin, from Simon. I then went up to the phone box to call my mother so that she could wish me happy birthday and I could catch up on news from home.

"Hi Mum", I said, "I'm just phoning to see how you are, and because it's my birthday today".

"What are you talking about dear", she replied, "Your birthday was yesterday".

So, sometime in the past few weeks I had lost a day, which wouldn't normally worry me, but I'm a bit funny about my birthday. I don't know why but I felt strangely miffed that I had actually missed my own birthday and had even spent most of it almost drowning. Well, there didn't seem much point in celebrating my non-birthday any-more, so I went off to the laundry room, tumble dried our line of soggy washing, and sulked for as long as possible. You see, not every day is so great, when your travelling.

The camp site was quiet that dreary afternoon. Motor-homers sat snugly behind closed doors and damp campers huddled in their tents or sat chatting in the covered restaurant area. All the children seemed to have disappeared except for one little girl, for whom rain was not going to stop play. Fully clad in a bright red, water-proof cape with the hood pulled well up over her blond hair, she splashed her blue Wellington boots at the edge of the lake all afternoon, taking great pleasure in either feeding the ducks or shooing them away. A scruffy little dog, which constantly used his dripping coat like a spray machine, kept her company and enthusiastically joined in her play. The canoes and rowing boats sat idle, now as wet inside as out and the pretty, blue Jays that were usually flying from tree to tree, were no-where to be seen. A certain malaise seemed to hover over us too. Ever since we had started heading north, on our homeward route, it seemed as if our year was almost over. We had been travelling for ten months; we had lived in our motor home for almost a year and we had become very used to all of it. Every day held something new or different, not always good but usu-ally interesting. We had an easy way of living in the Beast; sometimes we needed our own space, but we had also become very close as a family. We knew that before long we would be back in England trying to work out what we would do next, and Jack would be going back to school in September. We talked about all of this and made a conscious decision to make the very most of the remaining time that we had. We would head back through Austria and Switzerland to France where we had arranged to meet up with Simon's family who were sharing a holiday Gite in Burgundy. Later, in August, we would hopefully meet up with my son Peter, when he would be on holiday in Brittany. But, before that, we decided that we would take the opportunity to visit the French Alps and more specifically the famous Chamonix area and Mount Blanc.

Our route from Slovenia to Austria took us through the Karavanke Mountain chain, which at an altitude of 1000 meters above sea level, was stunningly beautiful. Two impressive tunnels, each eight kilometres long, allow the cross border traffic to drive literally through the mountains, emerging briefly amidst misty, snow covered peaks and perpendicular valleys, before starting the long descent into Austria. At the end of that days' driving through spectacular scenery, we found a good lay-by to spend the night. Simon had a shower, I cooked supper, Jack read a few pages of his book and then we shut the blinds, snuggled down and watched one of our favourite George Clooney movies on the DVD player. We certainly had the best of all worlds.

Back to France

The trouble with trying to drive from Slovenia to Chamonix (in France), is that there is an uncompromising range of awesome mountains in the way, namely –The Alps. You can either go round the bottom of them, straight across northern Italy which we had already done when going to Monza and back, or around the top of them making a wide sweep up towards Zurich and then down to Bern and Geneva. There are smaller roads, suitable for cars, but with time and size against us we decided to use the A roads through southern Austria until we could join the motorway east of Innsbruck and stick with it all the way to Geneva. We could hardly complain at having to drive through such fantastic scenery though.

This is the largest mountain chain in Europe; sweeping in an impressive arc from Mediterranean France to middle Austria and varying from 60 to 120 miles wide in places, with several peaks rising to over 4000 meters. It was caused by the convergence of the African and Eurasian plates which began around 90 million years ago. The major period of mountain building took place around 20 million years ago and the landscape which you see today is the result of glaciations during the last two million years. This vast time scale rather puts into perspective our own brief appearance on the planet. 'U'-shaped hanging valleys, and lakes such as Como and Garda, which were naturally dammed by glacial moraines, provide excellent visual proof of the power of glaciers. Retreating glaciers allow specialized plants to colonise the newly exposed rocky slopes and here alpine flowers and grasses thrive. Snow is evident on the higher slopes all year round and in summer the lower slopes are covered with alpine meadows. We were heading for Mont Blanc, the highest mountain (4,807 meters) in the range, although the Matterhorn and the Eiger come a close second and third. We also wanted to visit the Mer de Glace (Sea of Ice) which is close by. This is the second largest glacier in the Alps being seven kilometres long, 1,950 meters across at its widest point and up to a staggering 400 meters deep. Jack was getting a 'hands on' geography lesson as we drove through this region, when glacial moraines and hanging valleys would 'get real'.

Working our way across the southern Austrian Alps, stopping frequently by tumbling mountain streams to enjoy the impressive scenery, we passed Grosglockner, Austria's highest mountain, which we had been told to look out for by the Austrian family who had befriended us at Moravski Spa. Unfortunately it was shrouded in heavy mist, so we only glimpsed its lower slopes. That evening we wild camped in a lay-by close to a small village. A convenient hole in the hedge at the back of the lay-by allowed us to walk through onto a cycle path which took us on a pleasant evening stroll around the streets. In full view, behind the village, a range of snow capped mountains provided a fabulous back drop equal to anything from The Sound of Music.

The roads climbed and dropped, climbed and dropped, weaving their way through southern Austria towards Switzerland on a circuitous but scenic route. That day, heavy clouds and persistent rain prevented us from seeing the best views and made driving all the more laborious. We hadn't got off to an early start anyway, due to some late night phone calls to family back in England, plus we had wasted time trying to recover money from our Austrian 'Go' box. This was an electronic monitoring box which we had to buy in order to drive on Austrian motorways. You had to buy a minimum 50 euros worth of credit at a time and we were leaving the country with about 30 euros worth still unused. However, despite our best attempts we were unable to recover the money. We then had to buy special road tax for use on the Swiss roads. We felt as if we were being inexorably dragged back into the expensive, northern European lifestyle and felt desperately like taking the next road south and just 'going round' for another year. Responsibility and reality were creeping ever nearer. We pulled into another lay-by early that afternoon and gave up on the day. We were in a wide Swiss valley of agricultural fields and small neat villages, all backed by craggy grey mountains. A dark moody sky allowed shafts of sunlight to spotlight green swathes in the fertile valley, iridescent against the black, sombre mountains, and two red kites entertained us with acrobatic flight as we ate our meal and tried to adopt a more positive attitude to our future.

Switzerland's excellent motorway network now took us speedily, if not a little boringly, around the great blocks of mountain which make up so much of that country. Around Bern, the misty skies cleared to allow the sun to shine once more and as we crossed the flat open plain between Bern and Lausanne, the white peaks of the French Alps, dazzling against the clear sky, enticed us towards them. Skirting around Geneva, (which we decided to view better at a later date), we entered France again, for the third time on our trip. A useful picnic 'aire', (yes, we were back to those wonderful aires again), had motor home facilities, so before we headed on we were able to unload our grey waste tanks and fill up with fresh water. With a full pantry under the bed, and a well stocked fridge, we were ready to spend a few days at Chamonix. We were going to be lucky with the weather now, because grey skies had given way to blue, and wall to wall sunshine shone again as we finally entered the deep, winding valley of the River Arve.

Tumbling, crystal clear, ice cold mountain water flows right through the centre of Chamonix, but you could be forgiven for not noticing the river as you will spend most of your time gazing upwards at the magnificent scenery. Mont Blanc is just one of many mountains which tower over the town; soaring, snow covered and utterly awesome. Wisps of white, ghost-cloud drift through the peaks and the arcing sun makes solid rock faces shift in ever-changing shapes. We arrived on the only road into town and quickly spotted a huge car park where we could park up and stay for a few days. There were many motor-homes there already, with some almost as big as ours, but we still managed to struggle while getting through the entrance barriers. They were really designed for cars and were fairly narrow. We squeezed up to the entrance where we had to insert our ready bought ticket, but for some reason the barrier wouldn't go up. We tried and tried and tried but with no luck, so now, holding everyone else up as usual, I ran over to the phone which was available for summoning the attendant. In garbled French I explained our problem and after an embarrassingly long time, a small van squealed into the car park. The disgruntled attendant did a double-take of the Beast and came to the front of the barrier. Then, signalling for us to pull forward just a few inches, he put our ticket in the machine and hey presto, the barrier opened. So, if you are ever at Chamonix and have this problem, just make sure that you are close enough to the barrier and you're ticket will work! I hoped that everyone around was too busy looking at the amazing scenery to notice our farcical entrance, and we quickly parked up alongside the biggest motor-home that we could see; which happened to be German.

This is a great place to park-up as it is literally five minutes walk from the town centre and ski lifts. Jack had a shower and then took over the kitchen, cooking us a great chilli-con-carne for supper, while Simon and I walked to the tourist centre and bought our lift passes for the following morning. In peak season queues for tickets can be long, especially early in the morning when climbers and walkers are waiting to head off and it helps if you can buy your ticket and boarding passes the day before – and don't forget that if you miss your ride you may forfeit your ticket.

Next morning we entered the 8.0 am cable car, which would take us in two separate stages up to 3,842 meters above sea level, to the Aiguille du Midi - the solitary spire of rock situated just eight kilometres from the summit of Mont Blanc. The early morning air was clear and fresh and our long, green valley was still in cool shade, waiting for the sun to climb above the peaks to warm the land. The lift-car rose from the valley floor, passing over forest and hill, gently ascending, while the town, river, road and people rapidly diminished below us and the whole valley came into view. We were soon looking out across the granite peaks of lower mountain ranges and Chamonix now resembled a tiny village in miniature. Ten breathtaking minutes later we arrived at the Plan de L'Aiguille, the half way point. We then had to board the second cable car, which would take us on another ten minute ride up to the top, the Aiguille du Midi. So, with slightly sweaty hands, I gripped the hand rails inside the cable car on a fairly scary, almost vertical ride up the side of the mountain over jagged, snow covered rock. The drop below us was staggering and the cable wires which held us aloft looked ridiculously undersized. Finally, we soared almost vertically upwards into the thin blue atmosphere of the snow covered summit.

We now looked down on granite mountain tops and across the peaks of endless mountain ranges into the blue, blue yonder. Here, Simon helped me to disengage my locked fingers, and we disembarked onto the terraces of the restaurant and café complex where we strolled and enjoyed the breathtaking views around us. How anyone had managed to build anything onto that jagged pinnacle, at such a height, I could not imagine. The terraces were hammered into the rock and decorated with thick, year round, permanent icicles of grand proportion. We walked all around the pinnacle, taking in the complete vista; a panorama of the main French, Swiss and Italian summits from about seven mountain ranges. It was truly beautiful. Up there, where even on a summer's day the temperature would normally be down to minus ten degrees, the air was raw. We huddled in our warmest coats while a fellow tourist took a group photo of us three, with the blue sky and dazzling white peak of Mont Blanc just behind us.

Jack and Simon now ascended to the final, topmost part of the Aiguille. To do this they entered a small lift which held just eight people at a time. This went up the inside of the rock and came out on a small terrace at the very pinnacle. They said that it was fantastic, and I happily took their word for it, content to stay where I was. More tourists were now arriving on the lifts and well-equipped climbers, clanking around in their cumbersome kit, were preparing to leave the snug security of the buildings to head out onto the mountain. They followed their guide in single file, out along a narrow ridge of dazzling, frozen snow, and soon disappeared into the distance becoming a line of tiny black dots in a dramatic white landscape. There is something quite ethereal about being amongst mountain tops. An absolute serenity and peacefulness seems to hang in the thin cool air. They are so vast, so awesome, so uncompromising and so marvellously untouched by man.

A massive sky, streaked by thin white clouds, stretched forever over summits and peaks which rolled one after the other, as far as the eye could see. Like the deserts and the oceans, they seemed immortal.

Before long, we heard the excited chatter of those ever-present stampeding Japanese tourists and we decided to take the lift back down to the middle landing stage. There we would get off and start our walk across to the glacier. This well-worn trail is just below the snow line and takes two to three hours to complete - depending on how fit you feel. You do need comfortable shoes and some of it is quite sheer, although it is all very safe and well marked. This was a glorious walk across steep hillsides, covered with alpine flowers, with wonderful views all around us. Snowy peaks were just above and the green, green valley was way below. As far as the eye could see was blue sky and mountains. It was hot now, so our coats were in our back packs and our jumpers were tied around our waists. Jack leapt onward like a youthful mountain goat, while I dragged behind admiring stunted rhododendron bushes or minute forget-me-nots of deepest blue with pure yellow centres. Simon enjoyed the peace and kept us moving onward when we dawdled at the many cairns of stone, trying to add just three more to the very top of each cairn.

At last we reached the final climb which led us to a viewpoint. There we joined fellow walkers who had sat down to rest and study the glacier which filled the valley below us. At first I wondered what all the fuss was about. To me it simply looked like a valley of dirty grey and white snow, but when I took the binoculars and studied it more closely I realised the magnitude of this enormous sheet of ice. The Mer de Glace is so called because it resembles a sea of frozen waves, with distinct alternating lines of light and dark ice on its surface. These are caused by variations of dust and debris which collects in the ice. From a distance, the surface appears cracked by hundreds of thin lines, but when you look through binoculars you realise that these are actually huge crevasses. In one area, I could see a long line of small dark spots and when I focused on them I saw that they were in fact walkers, roped together. They looked absolutely miniscule on the surface of the glacier that stretches back up into the winding valley, a seven kilometre, solid, block which creeps forward 90 meters a year.

At the mouth of the glacier, a deep grotto has been tunnelled into the ice, enabling you to see it from the inside. We started down the steep, zig-zag path which would take us to the mountain railway station and the ice cave. Unfortunately, this is where you descend back into tourism and it does get very busy. An old mountain train brings carriages of people up from Chamonix to visit the glacier, cafes, restaurants and souvenir shops, which all ply for the custom of a steady torrent of tourists. We grabbed some filled rolls for a late lunch and then crammed into one of the small, gondola-type cable cars. Down to the face of the glacier we went, having just a short walk along metal ramps to reach the entrance to the ice grotto. Because the glacier is in perpetual motion, the ice grotto has been freshly cut each year for the last fifty years. The lofty face of the glacier was a dirty grey colour, not really resembling ice at all, but when we entered the dripping passageway and walked into the depths of the tunnel, we were transported into a world of sapphire blue. This is a strange phenomenon of dense glacial ice, which due to its crystalline structure, absorbs all except the shortest and bluest wavelengths of visible light. Trooping through the carved rooms, in a moving sea of tourists, we duly admired ice sculptures while a steady drip, drip of freezing water dropped onto our heads, reminding us that we were standing underneath thousands of tones of ice. It was an excellent way of appreciating just how big the whole thing was.

Pottering around Chamonix and walking quietly in the lower hills was all that we could manage the next day. Hang gliders in all colours of the rainbow, drifted down into the valley from far up high, playing on the updrafts like floating feathers. Red-socked walking tours marched briskly up into the mountains, only to straggle slowly back that evening, slightly bent and weak at the knees. We relaxed and enjoyed the ambiance, knowing that we would be moving-on the following day. Squeezing out between the heavy concrete barriers was even harder than squeezing in. With literally only half an inch to spare in all directions and a serious problem with the length,

Simon had a nightmare time getting us through the exit and we would have happily paid more than the ten euros it had cost us for the two days, if only it had been a little easier. However, before long we were rolling back down the Arve Valley on our way to Burgundy.

Getting sidetracked is one of the pleasanter inevitabilities of motor homing. If you can pull up and explore an unscheduled but interesting find, then why not? So, on our way to Burgundy, that's exactly what we did. It didn't take much of our time, only about five hours, and it turned into one of those unforgettable moments. We hadn't been driving long, but after the difficulties of extracting ourselves from the Chamonix parking area, we soon felt like stopping for a cup of coffee. We were skirting around the bottom of Geneva, heading for Macon, when we pulled into a large car park alongside the motorway. I put the kettle on and Simon and Jack got out for a wander around and to stretch their legs. We all noticed a rather strange building in the corner of the car park and on further inspection discovered that it was an extremely neat and well organised cable car station, or as the French called it, a 'Telepherique'. The attendant told us that we were at the base of Mont Saleve, a ridge which rose almost vertically to 1,380 meters and that from the top of the ridge we would be able to get amazing views down onto Geneva and across to the Alps. The telepherique was designed to take bicycles too, and he assured us that at the top it was only a short, flat ride to the view point.

So, despite all agreeing earlier that we were going to take it very easy that day, we finished our coffee, un-hitched the bikes from the back of the Beast and rode across the car park to the cable car station. The green painted, glass sided cars ran every twelve minutes and would easily hold about nine people and their bikes. It was very quiet and the only other occupants of our car were a very smartly dressed French grandmother and her small grandson. Once again, this was a vertical ride which soared up the side of the ridge, to a height of 1,100 meters. The land rapidly fell away from us and the motorway, our car park and motor home began to look more like a Scalectrix set. When we reached the top we were so high that we couldn't spot the Beast at all. We pushed our bikes off and rode up to the nearby restaurant. Once again, a massive view of France and Switzerland spread out before us, while far below lay the whole of Geneva and the massive lake with its spouting water fountain. From where we stood, the Jet d'eau particularly caught our attention. Well, it's pretty un-missable really as it spouts 16 tons of water, 140 meters up into the sky at about 120 miles per hour and just along from where we were standing more hang-gliding enthusiasts took running jumps off the cliff top, to soar and glide like colourful, oversized birds out over the plains.

Geneva sits at the extreme south-west of Switzerland, between the Alps and the Jura mountains. It has made the most of its geographical position, being just one hours plane ride from Paris or Milan and two hours from London, Rome and Madrid. It has become an international meeting place attracting thousands of people each year to conferences and exhibitions, and hosts the headquarters of the United Nations and the

International Red Cross. The lake, fountain, many parks and surrounding mountains, add that natural ingredient which makes a city extra special. But be warned, you will pay extra special prices there too.

In order to see the mountain ranges on the other side of the Saleve Ridge, we now had to take a short bike ride across this flat plateau. One hour later, and sweating like french onions under a blistering sun, we puffed our way up the final incline to find the plateau. Only mad dogs and Englishmen go out in the mid-day sun, and we now qualified for both of these. That telepherique attendant must have had a wild imagination if he thought the Saleve was flat. But, the 'Panorama de la Chaine du Mont Blanc' seen from the final view point, was well worth the effort. We spent a long while admiring it, and then turned and free-wheeled at top speed, all the way back down the spiralling road to the telepherique, just in time to catch the next ride down to the car park. It had been an unforgettable side-track but it was now four o'clock, the day was disappearing just like our year and we had to get going for Macon.

July

Homeward Bound

Travelling with the air conditioning permanently on now, we were soon to be re-united with Simon's family who were holidaying in France. We were back in sun-flower country; the cheerful, yellow heads of Tournesol – 'turn with the sun' – nodded gently as we trundled on by. Sturdy, white Charolais cows, with heads down and backs straight, munched the thick grass on a mission to fill that belly, and the Red Hot Chilli Peppers were back in favour in the Beast. One more overnight wild camp, when sheet lightening hosted its own display for us, and then on past Macon, on good French roads, we followed the signs to Charolles. Maisy leading – us proceeding as always. Just after Charolles, a turn to La Clayette and then, more by luck than judge-ment, there was the supermarket where we had arranged to meet Stella. She had promised that it would be big enough for us to park in, and thank goodness, she was right. Five minutes later she pulled up along side us and it was big-hugs all round. We stocked up with essential champagne from the supermarket and drove in convoy to the gîte, Stella leading the way down smaller and smaller French country lanes. The final bend nearly proved to be our undoing. As we swung round it we spotted a sign declaring that nothing over three tons could drive past a small cottage on our right, due to a collapsing basement – but we were now committed. We pulled over as far as possible to the left, and crept past, with French neighbours raising their hands in dismay at our seven-ton-plus monster. At last, parked in the field next to the gîte, - we had arrived.

We stayed there for five days; Jack particularly enjoying the swimming pool with his cousin Sam and us enjoying the company of Simon's family. We ate, drank and generally made merry, although the weather was not up to the usual mid-summer stan-dard. July was creeping on, and if our year away had been sand in an egg-timer, then most of it would be in the bottom by now. The next rendezvous that we'd arranged was with my son Peter, when he would soon be on holiday with friends in Brittany. From there it would be just a short hop across the channel to England and then the sand in the egg timer would definitely have run out. But we didn't have to meet Peter for another four days and the family suggested that we stop off at a rather special fun park in Poitiers, en route. 'Fun' sounded good to us, so we programmed Maisy again and let her lead the way.

That evening we pulled into a lay-by, about eighty kilometres from Poitiers. It had been a blisteringly hot day and we had had the air conditioning on while we travelled, but now for some reason it wouldn't work. As the sun fell, the air became sticky and humid. Thunderstorms and lightening displays were an almost nightly occurrence now, so we were sure that we would be in for another long hot, night. Simon and Jack both needed a haircut so we set up our usual barber shop, outside, in the shade of the motor home. They took it in turns to sit on a stool, with a towel around their shoulders, while I gave them a short, back and sides. A French lorry was parked a little further down the lay-by and the driver, a huge man with enormous hands, wandered up for a chat. He spoke reasonably good English and was soon having a guided tour of the Beast. "Magnifique, Fantastique", he enthused cheerfully, as every 'mod con' was revealed. We talked for a while about where we'd been and what we'd seen and explained that we were now on our way back to England. He threw his enormous hands in the air at that revelation, exclaiming very seriously that we should not go back but we must buy a house in France. The life was good, the food and wine were the best, we would be mad to go back. "England is no good now, with Blair holding the American's hand" he declared, "C'est mal, très, très mal!" At the end of his visit he gave us a hearty handshake and returned to his lorry. We had to admit that we agreed with him about the pleasures of France, but as we tossed and turned that night, fighting with the sheets and opening and closing the windows between stupendous thunderstorms, we would have given anything for some cool English weather!

We arrived in Poitiers next morning slightly fazed from lack of sleep, but good old Maisy took us straight to 'Futuroscope' without any U turns. The large car park had a low, height restriction, so we parked up in a huge, empty, coach park where we could also stay overnight. The entrance to the fun-park was just a short walk away and, unable to resist, we headed straight over to it. It wasn't going to be cheap, but 'here and now' as usual. This great fun park is open from ten in the morning until eleven at night and you'll be entertained for every minute, if you have the stamina to keep up with it. It's an unconventional theme park, set amongst well stocked gardens and elaborate water features, and consists of about twenty innovative and modernistic buildings, in which you are treated to a whole range of inter-active, 3-D animation shows in IMAX cinemas.

Starting at number one on our plan, in a building which resembled a lump of dark, blue crystals angled out of the ground, we watched a foot-tapping film about percussion music around the world. We would have happily sat through it twice, as the photography and music was so good, but we had other things to see. Second on the list was La Gyratour – a panoramic wheel that gently spins you 150 feet into the air for a great view of the park. Then the live Magic Show, the Cyber World show in a square building of glass, and my favourite – the 'Voyages of Sky and Sea' which was shown in a building which looked more like church organ. The seating area was tiered and had a glass floor; the film followed the journey of sea birds, whales and marine life as they travelled into a storm. Two films were projected at once; one in front of you and the other below you, so that you felt as if you were either flying with the birds or, if you looked down, swimming with the whales. It was very realistic, as were all of the shows. Eventually we were exhausted enough to return to the motor home for a meal and a nap, before returning for the live evening performances. At 9.0 pm, as the light fell, the water show began.

Sitting under a warm night sky, in a curve of tiered seating, the following hour was filled by a display of fountains and fireworks, music and laser lights. And finally a fairy tale story, depicted by laser images which were played against fountains. At nearly midnight we walked back through the gardens, mingling with French families and their excited children. Our coach car park, a massive space of dark tarmac with just a few high, overhead lights, was completely empty and silent. We left our hot, smelly shoes outside the door, climbed aboard and crashed out yet again. Would we never learn?

Of course we never did learn not to overdo it on day one and I'm slightly embarrassed to admit that we went back the next day and saw all the shows that we'd missed on the first day, and a few of the other ones again. Finally, by that evening, we had seen it all, but that still didn't stop Jack and me going back later to watch the evening watershow all over again. Simon gave it a miss – once was enough for him – he was happy to read a book. He knew that we would need our energy for the drive from the Vienne region up to the Morbihan region in Brittany. We had forgotten just how big France was. The roads were busy but luckily for us, everyone, including lots with GB plates, were heading south. It was obviously a well travelled route, because here again at the sides of the road, were black, wooden silhouettes with a red cross on them, marking the place where someone had died in a traffic accident.

Contrasting with this gruesome reminder, the countryside was glorious. Acres of neat, green, vineyards trailed off into the distance; rolls of tightly bailed, golden hay dotted the harvested fields and sun flowers crowded together to catch the sun. Maisy was behaving impeccably; she obviously liked France too, and in a little while told us with her usual dulcet tones that 'our next destination was ahead'. We had reached the camp site just outside Gueneme Penfao, near Redon, which was a few kilometres from Peter's gîte. The campsite was another friendly, family run affair, with a small swimming pool and essential, shady, boules area. We found our slot, and settled down in pitches 21, 22 and 23 (oh dear), under the vaguely interested gaze of the unperturbed boules players, who 'ummed' and 'ahhed' over every throw as if their very honour depended on it. Boules is a studious business which appears to involve much standing with hands behind backs, slow pacing around the pitch to help with the adjustment of trousers and underwear, and almost always some drinking of red wine. At the end of the game, which can take many hours, the players relax in bon ami, and wander off for the other essential ingredient of a good holiday, - which is a leisurely eaten meal. I always enjoyed watching the French play boules, but I can never slow down enough to play it myself.

Peter was going to get a lift over with his friends the following day and I just couldn't wait to see him. I spent most of the next morning hopping up and down like a flea on a dog's back, watching the gate for their car to arrive. Then there was Peter, looking good, although still suffering from the effects of his accident back in February. He stayed with us for a few days and we hired another car so that we could all explore the area together. The coastline was pleasant, with sandy coves and low coastal paths but everywhere was getting busy now, with the holiday season in full swing. The roads were packed with trippers and it was also incredibly hot. It was wonderful to spend time with Peter and we knew that we would be seeing much more of him when we all got back to England; that was one of the things that we were looking forward to most when we returned – and our return seemed absolutely inevitable now.

We passed the days; day tripping to St Nazaire to visit its famous ship yards, and canoeing on a pea green river that was as thick as soup. We barbecued in the evenings, and even met up with our old friend Lizzie whom we had first met in Oliva in Spain – but our ticket on the ferry was now booked. Stark reality was just around the corner and it was too late to turn back. We would have liked to programme a few extra destinations into Maisy; like Morocco or Greece or Timbuktu, but that would be totally irresponsible. So we said our goodbyes to Peter and his friends, arranging to see them back in England, and headed on up through Brittany. That night we wild camped in a car park next to the sea; one of the last that we would have. We were now on the northern coast of France, back where we had started almost a year ago, in the bay of Le Mont St Michel. We had found a quiet road which hugged the coast and had pulled into the car park after spotting a roadside cafe selling fresh mussels and oysters. What better reason could we have for stopping?

This bay had extensive mud-flats and flat marshy grass areas, and beyond that were the mussel and oyster beds. Down at the café, huge pans of water were kept perpetually boiling while endless buckets of absolutely fresh mussels and oysters were cooked. It was extremely basic, just wooden tables and chairs, and a stall next door selling bottles of excellent, cheap, local wine. This was almost our last night and I'm afraid that we overdid it one last time. The fresh sea food was absolutely delicious, served simply with soft hunks of bread and a light local wine, and we sat there for most of the evening eating and drinking as if we'd never see another mussel again. Jack had his fair share too and then wandered back to the motor home to watch a movie, leaving us to weave our own way back along the beach. Much later, in the moonlight, we walked home along the sandy path to the Beast. The tide was now in, which gave us a perfect excuse for skimming pebbles, and for Simon to lay down, fully clothed in the surf and declare that he was never going to leave France. Jack pointed the way to bed, and we eventually obeyed like two truculent teenagers.

We awoke next morning with a slight hangover, a strong taste of mussels and a great view of sky and sea across the bay. We would be catching our ferry the next day and, besides feeling absolutely dismal about the whole thing, we also had a complete panic attack when we realised that we hadn't bought a single present for anyone back home. Le Mont St Michel was on our route back to Caen, so with some misgivings we called in there. We were almost back full circle; eleven months ago we had been there before, just setting out on our wonderful journey. Le Mont in winter had been terrific, but now, in peak season, it was Le Mont St Hell. Cars queued in an endless line just to get to the car park, which was heaving with families coming and going to the town. Jack and I fought our way, like invading barbarians, up the ramparts and into the tourists shops to grab a few mementoes for his closest friends and then fought our way out again. English caravans, cars and motor homes sped past us heading south and for once we were glad to be heading in the other direction.

At Ouistreham, we had our last night in France. Maybe they knew we were leaving or maybe it was a special Saints day, but that night a long firework display illuminated the harbour. We three led on the bed in the back of the motor home and watched it from our back window. Then, at around mid-night we called it a day and went to sleep. At dawn next morning we made our last U turn and headed for the ferry terminal.

One kilometre from the boat, an English removal van came hurtling towards us and smashed to pieces one of our large and essential wing mirrors. It was almost like an omen. We had travelled all round Europe for almost a year without one accident and there we were ten minutes from the ferry and an English van hits us. They didn't stop of course, so with two small, square, bathroom mirrors taped onto the remaining arm we boarded the ferry. We were going home..... ahhh, come to think of it, we didn't have a home to go to!

Of all the people on that boat, I think that we probably looked the most sombre. Sat on the deck, watching the land recede, we would have given anything to be back on a scary cable-car ride, or climbing a gorge, or skimming through blue seas in a boat, or riding our bikes along a sunny, empty promenade by a sandy beach, or skiing down a mountain, or sleeping in a car park or driving over precipitous peaks or climbing a bell tower, or eating fresh mussels with a chilled local wine or laughing together over some crazy thing or other. It was hard not to be sad that it was all over.

It wasn't that we didn't want to go back and see our family and friends. One of the many things that I learned during our trip was just how important those people are to me. How easy it is to let friends drift away from you if you don't take the time to call them, meet up with them and be there for them. My children and grandchildren of course, mean everything to me. It had been the icing and the cherry on the cake that we should experience all that we did with one of our children – I only wished we could have done it with them all. We had travelled out of season, seen countries at their best and worst, met strangers who had immediately become friends, had good times, bad times and just a few ugly times; that's what its like to travel. At the end of it all you will have a million memories; your world will have grown and your life will change. So if you have a dream, don't wait for it to come true – follow it now.

Because if you don't.................. you may one day wish that you had.

One year on………

It took us a few months to settle down again. Not because everything had changed, but more because we had changed. The first few weeks were hectic. We spent a frantic fortnight catching up with family and friends and then took some time deciding what to do next. Our dear old neighbours, Gerry and Steve, had arranged for us to park up at the local airfield for as long as we wanted, so we were able to live in the motor home while we looked for a house to rent on the Welsh borders, which was where Jack's school was. Jack settled the easiest; slotting into school as if he had never been away. His friends accepted him straight back, he very quickly caught up with missed work and has just attained good pass marks in his mock GCSE's. His horizons have broadened and his confidence has grown.

We had to find a way to re-fill the coffers, so we bought an old house, and while Simon fell back on his skills as a brilliant renovator of property, I satisfied my other lifelong ambition. I had always had another dream which had to be followed ……which was to write a book. So, in between all of life's other demands, I got my head down and did it. For me it was a double pleasure to re-live each day of our travels; just talking about it meant that we could enjoy it all over again. A double-whammy if you like. And tomorrow, well who knows. We will have to go travelling again; it's in the blood now and cannot be denied. But when that will be, we do not know. That's for our next adventure; our next dream.

Where it will lead us who can tell, but wherever it goes, we shall surely have to follow.

Campsites we used and would recommend

France
Normandy - Camping de la Gerfleur, 50270 Barneville Carteret.
Tel (+33) (0) 2-3304 3841 email alabouriau@aol.com

Languedoc, Roussillon – Camping la Nautique 11100 Narbonne.
Tel (+33) (0) 4 – 68904819 email info@campinglanautique.com
Aquitaine – Public car parking amongst pine trees at Pyla sur Mer, Les Dunes du Pyla.
(with toilet blocks and water)

Loire Atlantique – Camping l'Hermitage, 36, Avenue de Paradis, 44290 Gueneme
Penfao. Tel (+33) (0) 2-40792348 email conatact@campingl'hermitage.com

Spain
Catalonia – Camping Vilanova 08800 Vilanova y la Geltru
(for Barcelona). Tel (+34) 93-8933402 email info@vilanovapark.es

Valencia – Kiko Park, 46780 Oliva/ Valencia. Tel (+34) 96-2850905
Email kikopark@kikopark.com

Murcia – Caravaning La Manga 30370 La Manga del Mar Menor
Tel (+34)968-563019 email lamanga@caravaning.es

Andalucia – Camping Mar Azul 04711, Almerimar, Almeria.
Tel (+34) 950-497589 email info@campingmarazul.com

Granada (Andalucia) – Camping- Motel Sierra Nevada, Avd. Madrid 107. 18014
Granada. Tel (+34) 958-150062 email campingmotel@terra.es

Ronda (Andalucia) – Camping El Sur, Ctra Algerciras km2.8, 29400 Ronda. Tel (+34)
95-2875939 email info@campingelsur.com

Tarifa (Andalucia) – Camping Tarifa, km 78.87, 11380 Tarifa (Cadiz) Tel (+34) 956
684778

El Puerto de Santa Maria, (Andalucia) – Camping Playa Dunas, 11500 El Puerto.
Tel (+34) 956 872210 email campinglasdunas@terra.es

Portugal
Olhao (Algarve) – Parque de Campismo 8700-912 Olhao.
Tel (+35) 289700300 email sbsicamping@mail.telepac.pt

Italy

Tuscany (for Florence) – Campeggio Il Poggetto 50010 Troghi, Firenze.
Tel (+39) 055-8307323 eamil poggetto@tin.it

Lazio (for Rome) – Campeggio Porticciolo 00062 Bracciano. Tel(+39) 06-99803060
email info@porticciolo.it

Campania (for Pompeii /Naples)- Campeggio Zeus, 80045 Pompeii (next door to
ruins) Tel (+39) 081-8615320 email info@campingzeus.it

Sicily (for Lipari Islands) – Campeggio Villaggio Marinello, 98060 Oliveri, Sicily.
Tel(+39) 0941-313000 email marinello@camping.it

Sicily (South Coast) – Scarabeo Camping, 97017 Punta Bracetto, Sicily. Tel (+39)
0932-918096 email info@scarabeocamping.it

Taormina (Sicily) – Campeggio La Forcetta Sicula, 98030 S.'Alessio Siculo Tel (+39)
0942-751657 email lafocetta@camping.it

Venice – Campeggio Marina di Venezia, 30010 Cavallino / Treporti, Punta Sabbioni.
Tel (+39) 041 5302511 email camping@marinadivenezia.it

Croatia

Rovinj – Campingplatz Polari, 52210 Rovinj, Istria Tel (+385) (0) 52-801501 email
polari@jadran.tdr.hr

Paklenika – Campingplatz Paklenika, 23244 Starigrad/Paklenika, Zadar/Knin.
Tel (+385) (0) 23- 369236 email alan@zadar.net

Dubrovnik - Campingplatz Autocamp Solitudo, 2000 Dubrovnik Tel(+385) (0) 20-
448686 email sales.department@babinkuk.com

Plitvicka – Autocamp Korana 47246 Plitvicka/ Jezera (Karlovak)
Tel (+385) (0) 53-751888 email info@np-plitvice.com

Slovenia

Campingplatz Moravske Toplice Spa, 9226 Moravske Toplice.
Tel(+386) (0) 2-5121200 email receptija.camp2@terme3000.si

Ljubljiana – Campingplatz Jezica, Dunajska 270, 113 Ljubljana Tel (+386) (0) 1-
5683913 email acjezica@gp.net

Printed in the United Kingdom by
Lightning Source UK Ltd., Milton Keynes
140480UK00002B/86/A